DOG TROUBLE

Kristin Varner

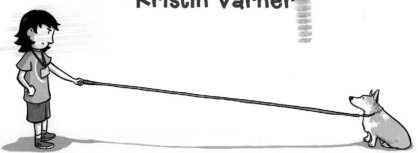

:01

First Second

NEW YORK

First Second

Published by First Second
First Second is an imprint of Roaring Brook Press,
a division of Holtzbrinck Publishing Holdings Limited Partnership
120 Broadway, New York, NY 10271
firstsecondbooks.com
mackids.com

Library of Congress Control Number: 2023948978

Our books may be purchased in bulk for promotional, educational, or business use.
Please contact your local bookseller or the Macmillan Corporate and Premium
Sales Department at (800) 221-7945 ext. 5442 or by email at
MacmillanSpecialMarkets@macmillan.com.

First edition, 2024
Edited by Robyn Chapman and Michael Moccio
Cover design and interior book design by Yan L. Moy and Molly Johanson
Production editing by Helen Seachrist and Kelly Markus
Veterinary consultant: Dr. Catherine Parks

Sketched by hand using Staedtler non-photo blue pencils. Digitally inked and
colored in Adobe Photoshop using a Wacom Cintiq. Digitally lettered with the Billy the
Flying Robot font from Blambot.

Printed in China by RR Donnelley Asia Printing Solutions Ltd.,
Dongguan City, Guangdong Province

ISBN 978-1-250-22591-7   (paperback)
10 9 8 7 6 5 4 3 2 1

ISBN 978-1-250-22590-0   (hardcover)
10 9 8 7 6 5 4 3 2 1

Don't miss your next favorite book from First Second! For the latest updates go to
firstsecondnewsletter.com and sign up for our enewsletter.

FOR MICHAEL AND SHEPHERD

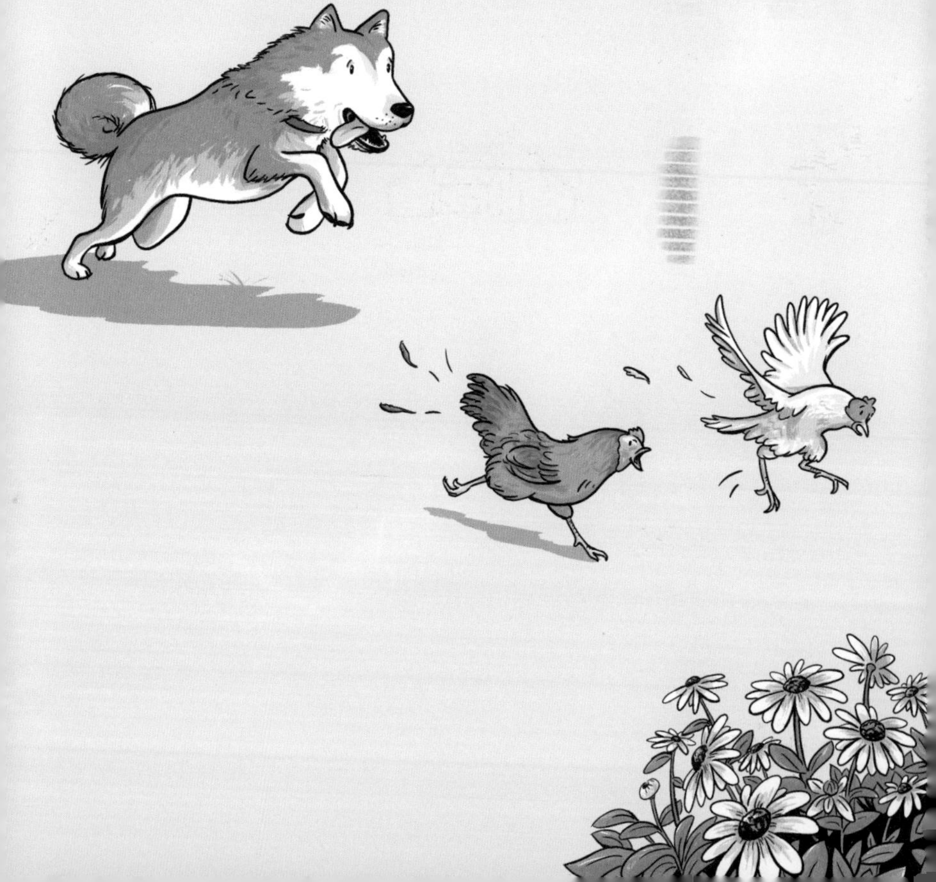

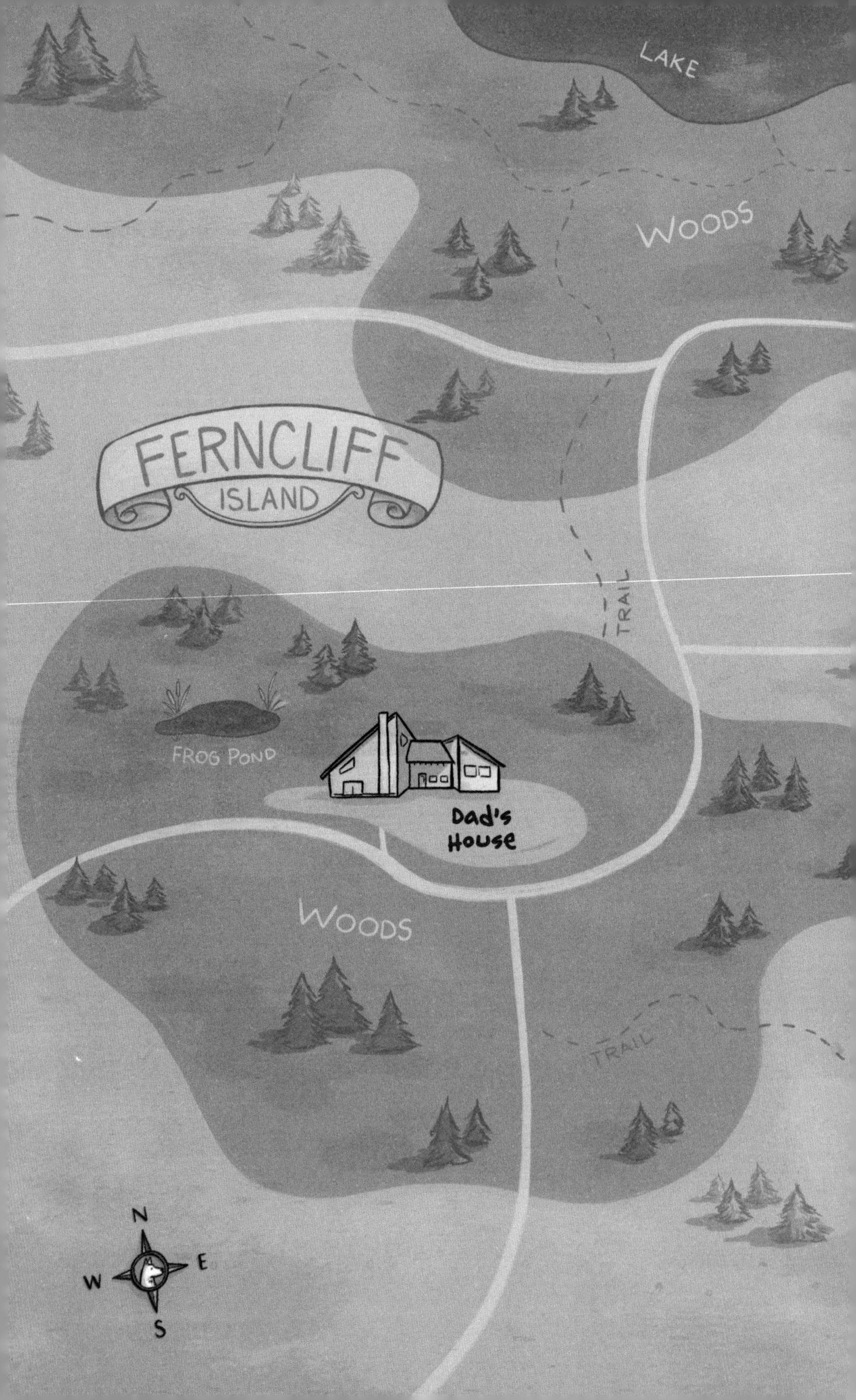
LAKE
WOODS
FERNCLIFF
ISLAND
TRAIL
FROG POND
Dad's
House
WOODS
TRAIL
N
E
W
S

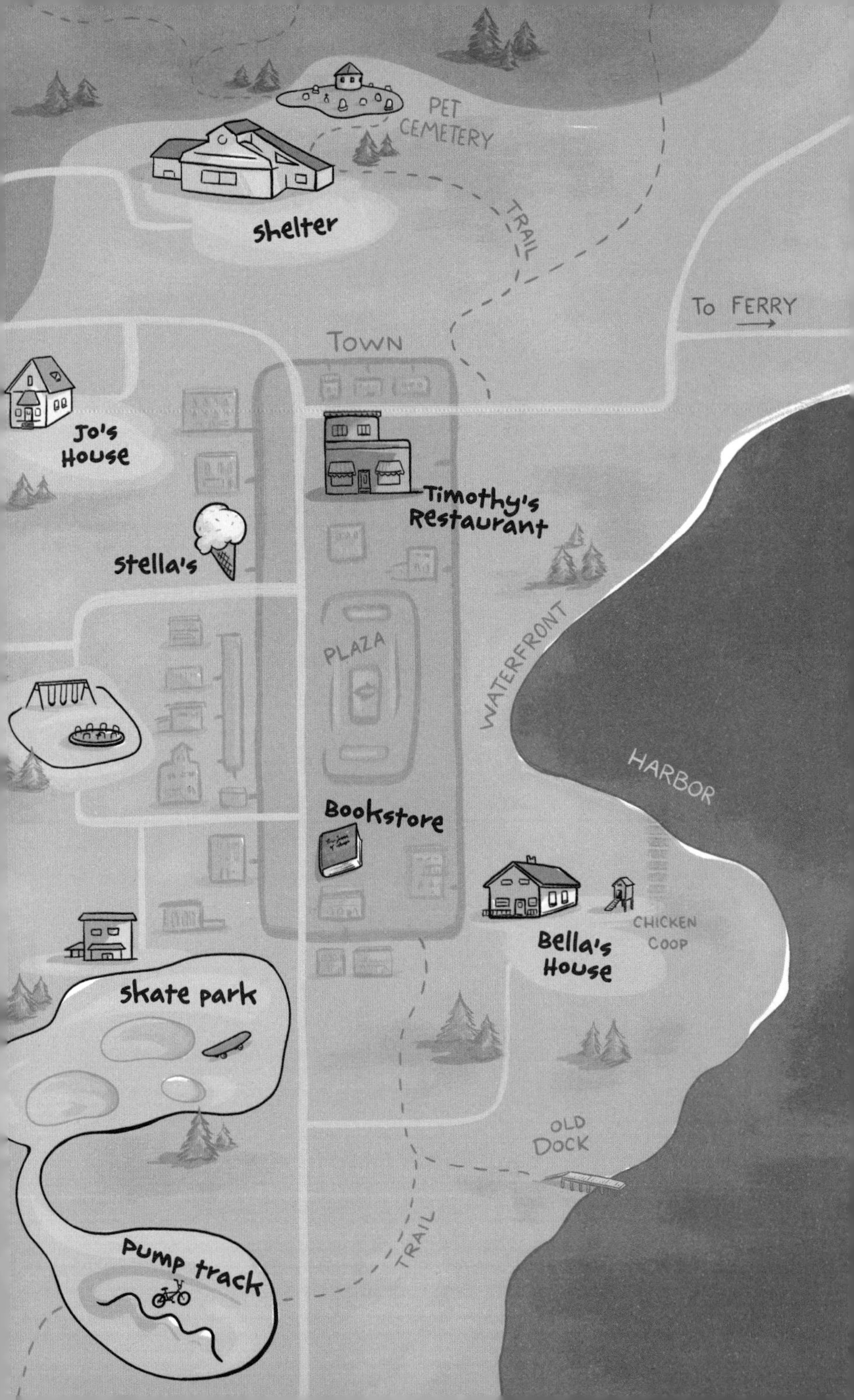
PET CEMETERY
shelter
TRAIL
To FERRY
TOWN
Jo's House
Timothy's Restaurant
Stella's
PLAZA
WATERFRONT
HARBOR
Bookstore
Bella's House
CHICKEN COOP
skate park
OLD DOCK
TRAIL
Pump track

CHAPTER 1

• Rosie •

A sweet English mastiff who snores loudly and is the couch potato champion of the house. Mastiffs are one of the oldest and the *largest* dog breed in the world. Despite their gigantic size, "masties" are gentle giants with good-natured and docile personalities.

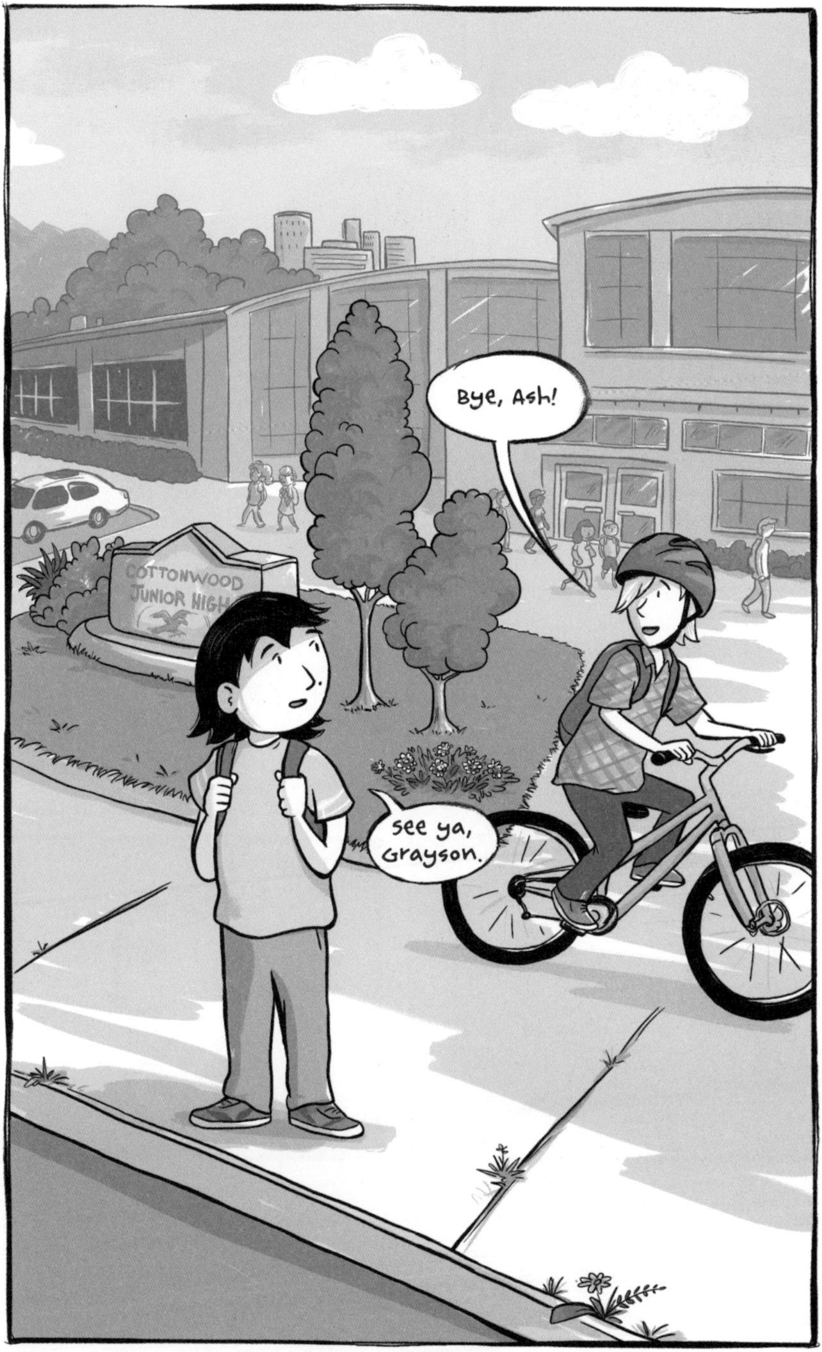
COTTONWOOD
JUNIOR HIGH
Bye, Ash!
See ya,
Grayson.

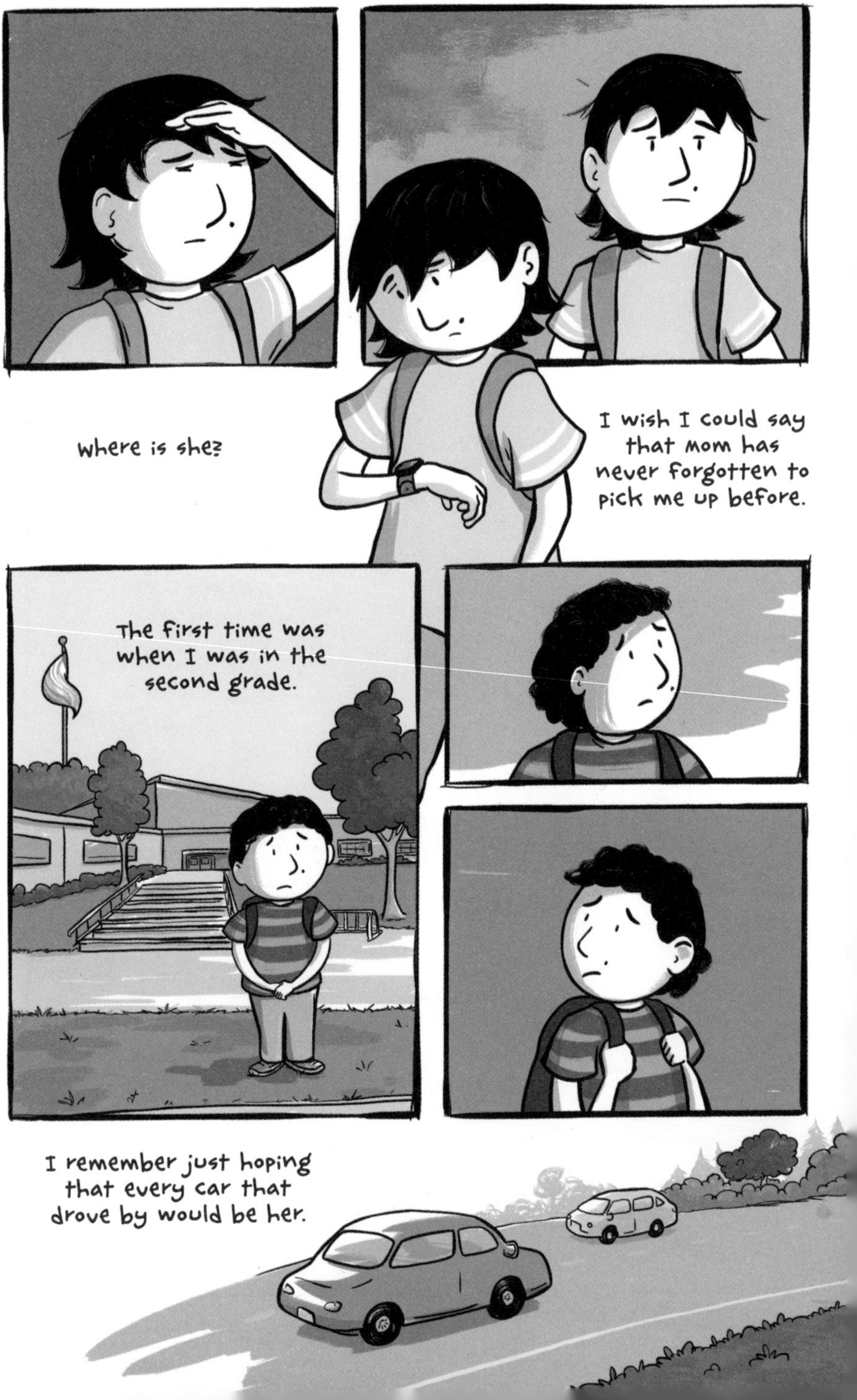
Where is she?
I wish I could say that mom has never forgotten to pick me up before.
The first time was when I was in the second grade.
I remember just hoping that every car that drove by would be her.

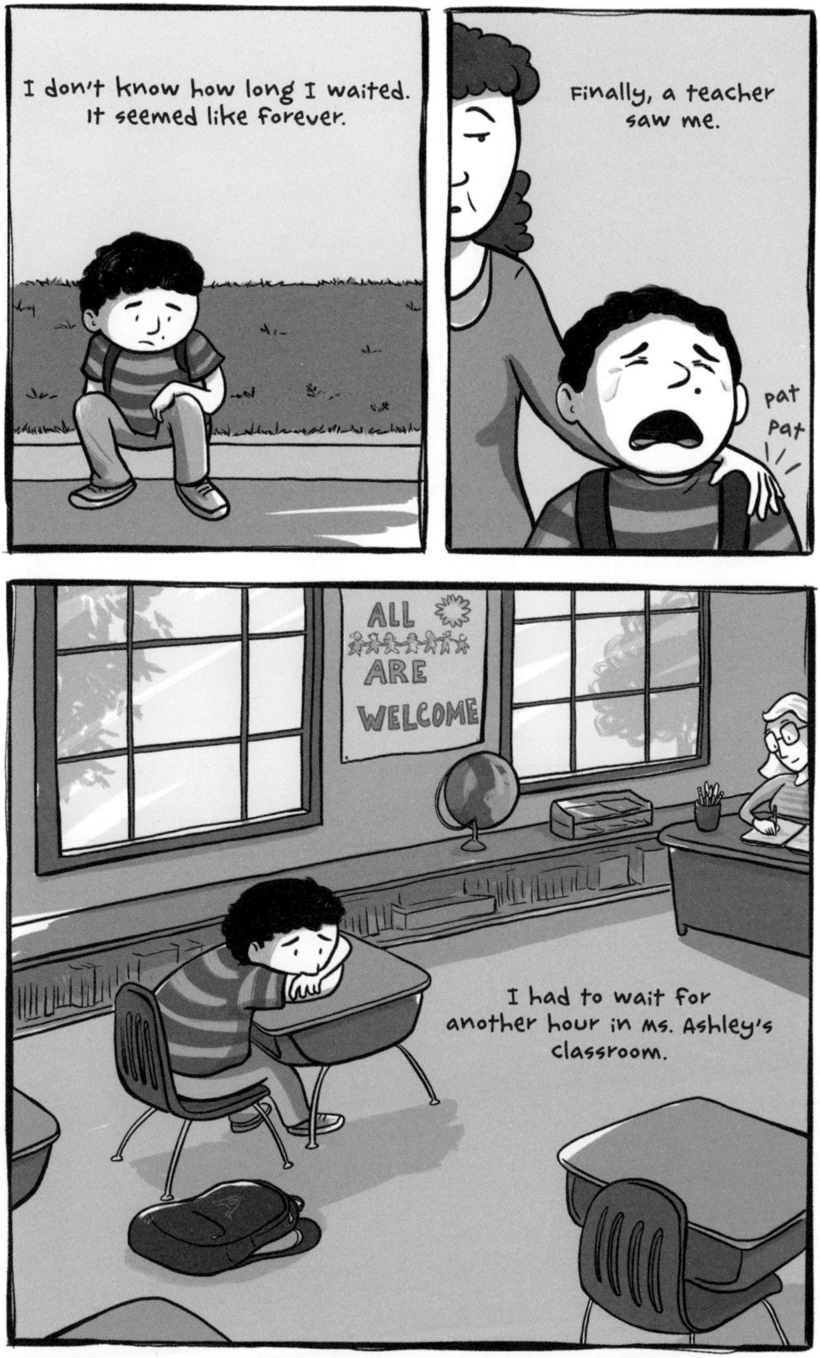
I don't know how long I waited. It seemed like forever.
Finally, a teacher saw me.
pat
pat
ALL
ARE
WELCOME
I had to wait for another hour in Ms. Ashley's classroom.

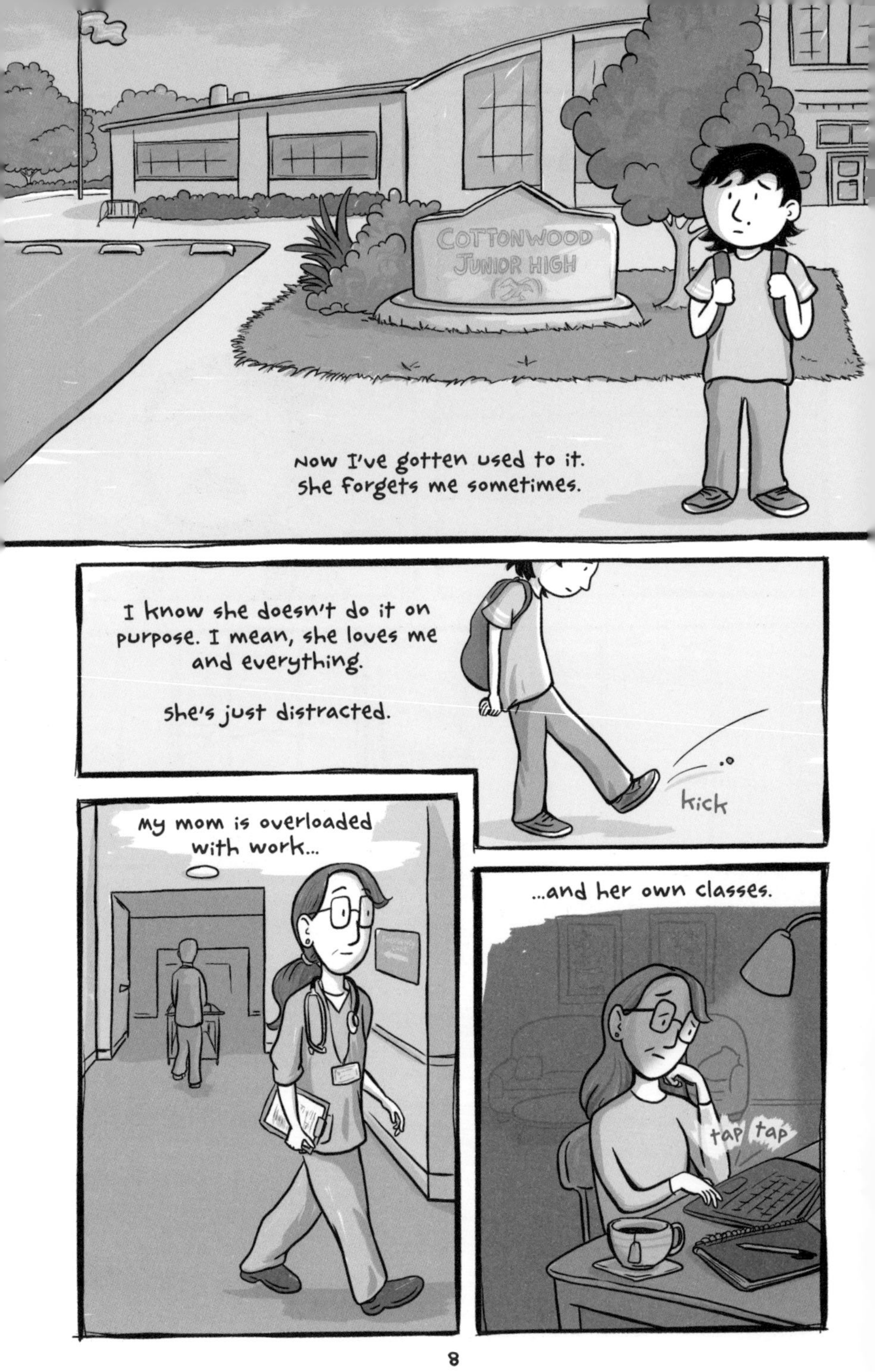
COTTONWOOD
JUNIOR HIGH
Now I've gotten used to it. She forgets me sometimes.
I know she doesn't do it on purpose. I mean, she loves me and everything.
She's just distracted.
kick
My mom is overloaded with work...
...and her own classes.
tap tap

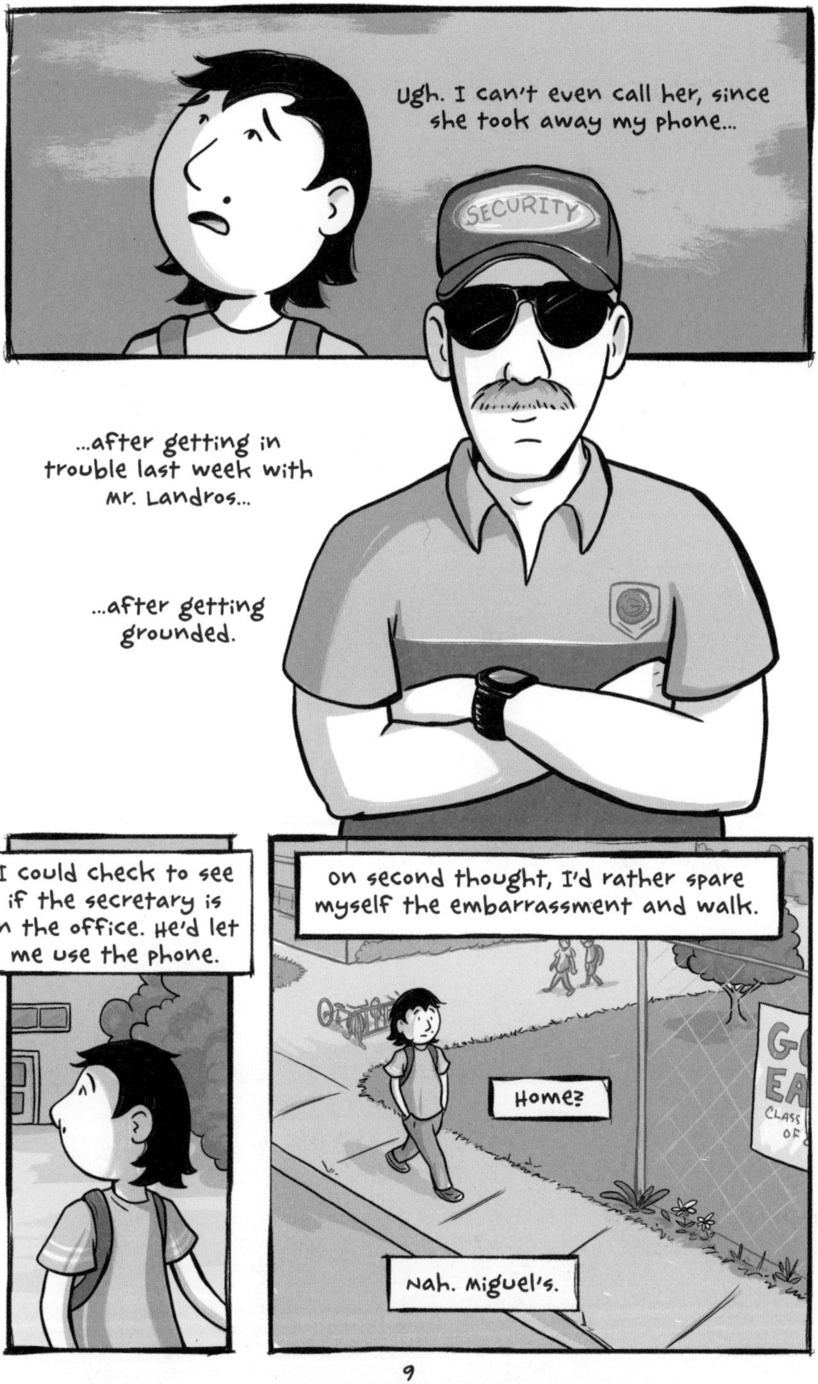
Ugh. I can't even call her, since she took away my phone...
SECURITY
...after getting in trouble last week with Mr. Landros...
...after getting grounded.
I could check to see if the secretary is in the office. He'd let me use the phone.
On second thought, I'd rather spare myself the embarrassment and walk.
Home?
Nah. Miguel's.

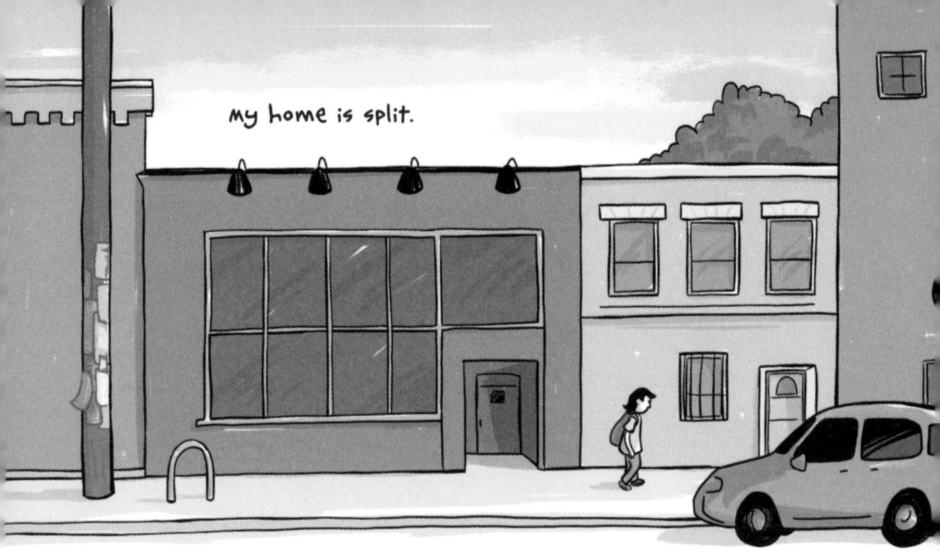
my home is split.

Home feels either vacant (mom's) or awkward (Dad's).

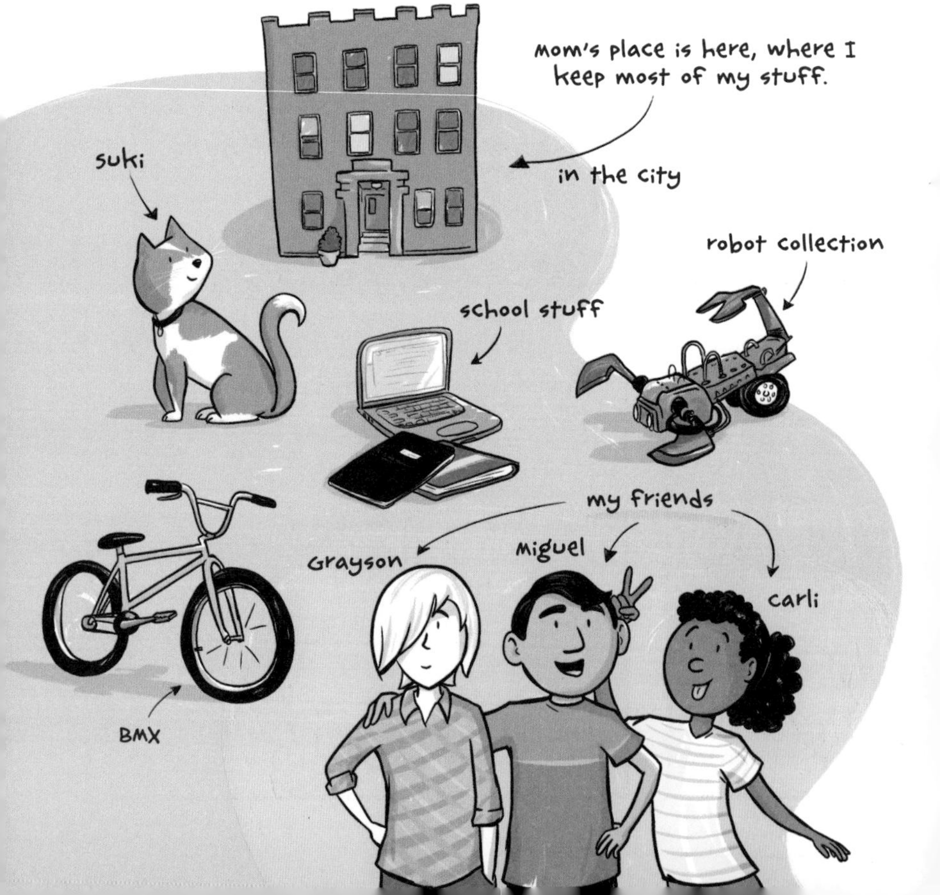
mom's place is here, where I keep most of my stuff.
in the city
suki
robot collection
school stuff
my friends
Grayson
miguel
carli
BMX

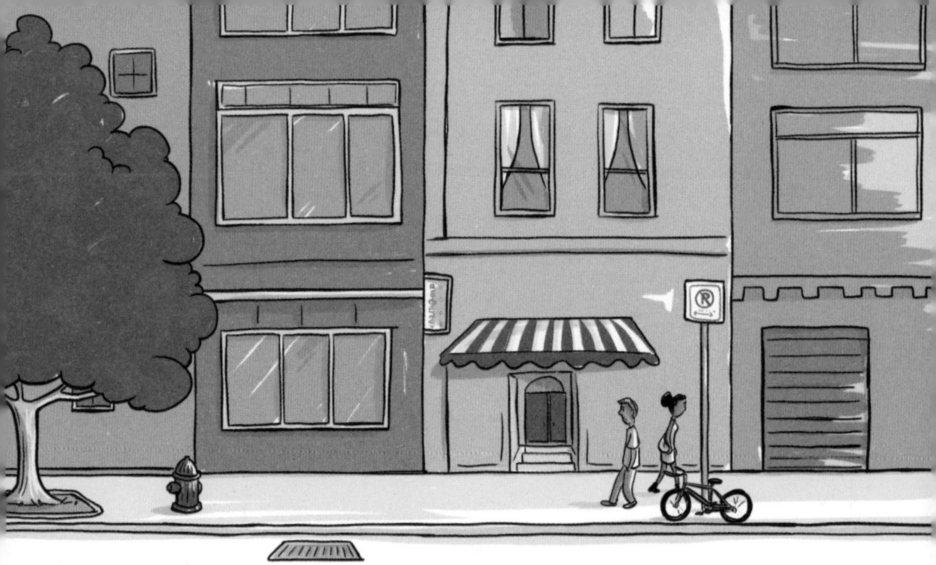

And Dad's house is here, where I keep just a little of my stuff.

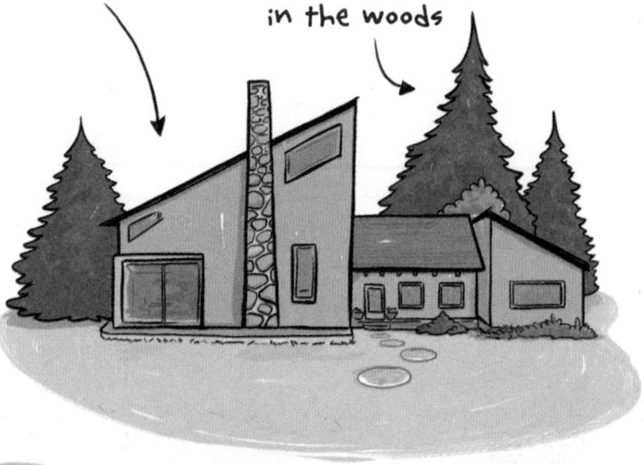
in the woods
zero friends

Luckily, I can easily bring my skateboard back and forth.

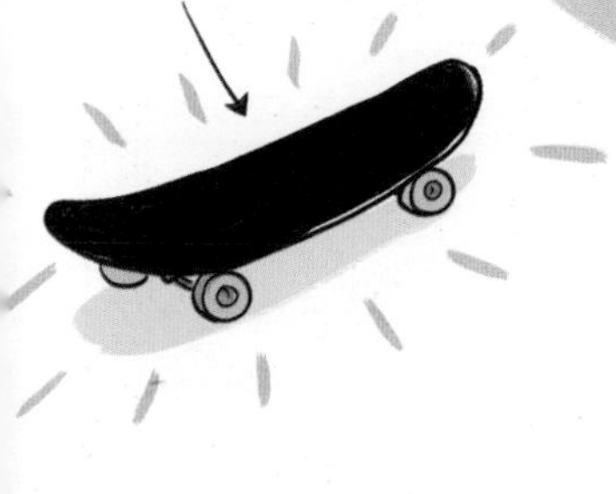

Most of the time I'm at Mom's. I usually only visit's Dad's house one weekend or so a month.

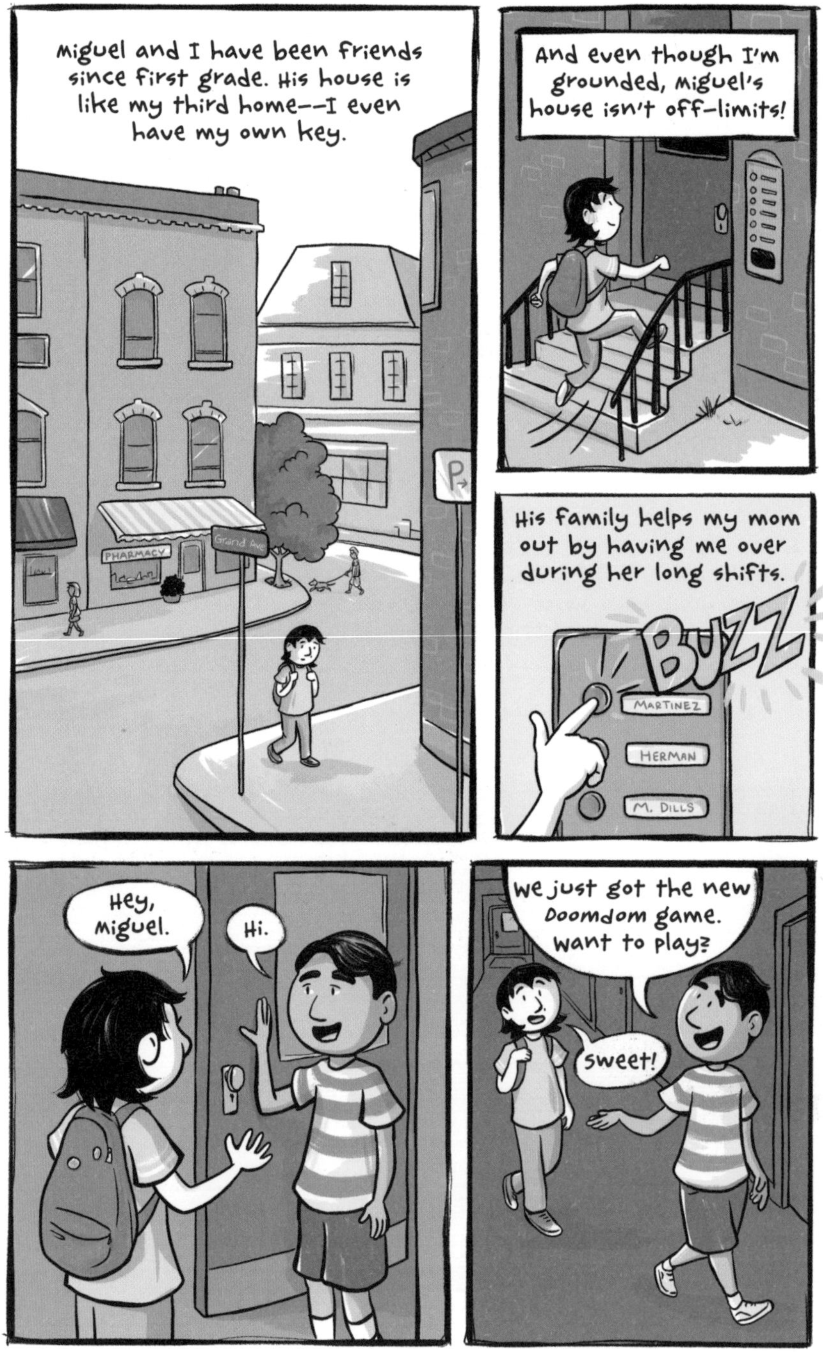
Miguel and I have been friends since first grade. His house is like my third home--I even have my own key.
PHARMACY
Grand Ave
P
And even though I'm grounded, Miguel's house isn't off-limits!
His family helps my mom out by having me over during her long shifts.
BUZZ
MARTINEZ
HERMAN
M. DILLS
Hey, Miguel.
Hi.
We just got the new Doomdom game. Want to play?
Sweet!

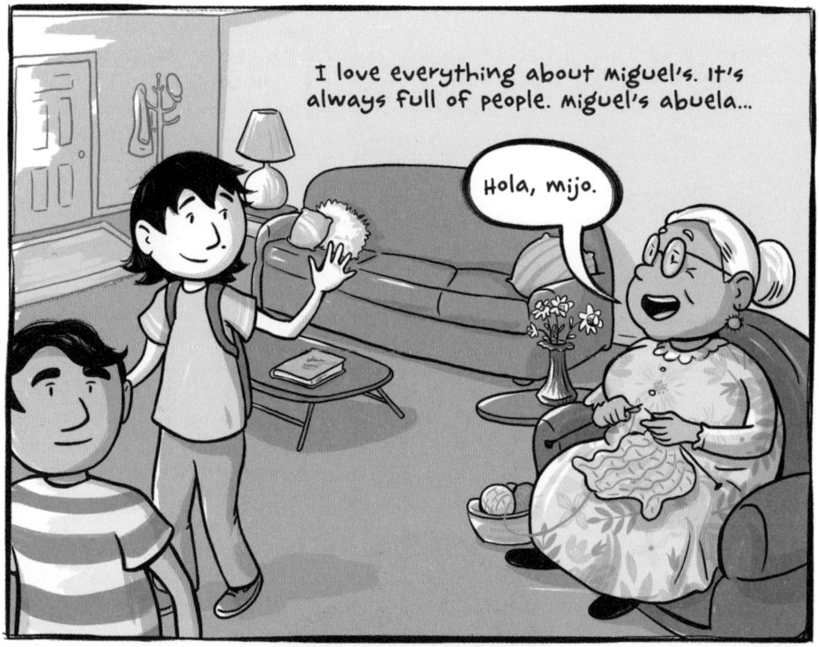
I love everything about Miguel's. It's always full of people. Miguel's abuela...
Hola, mijo.

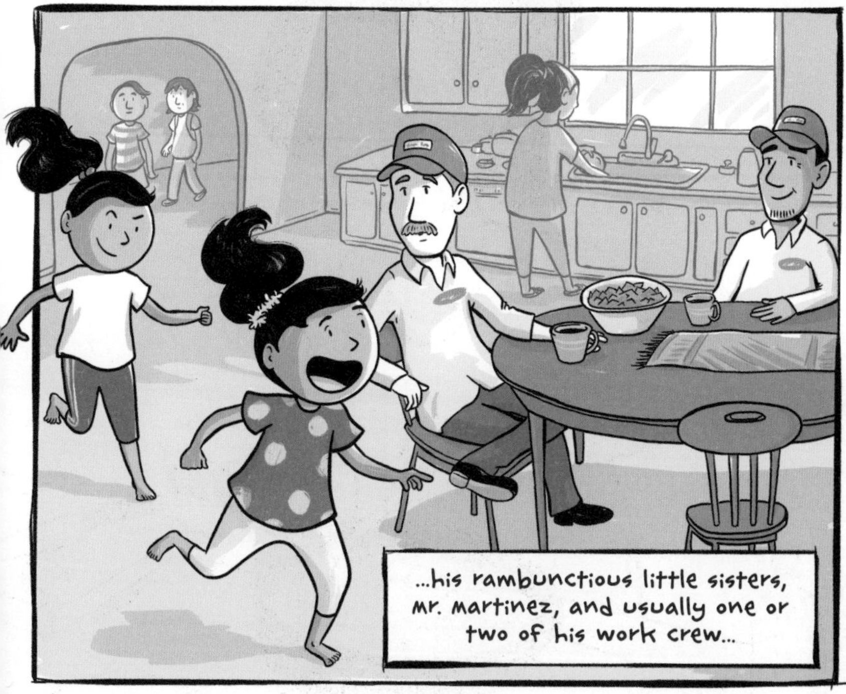
...his rambunctious little sisters, Mr. Martinez, and usually one or two of his work crew...

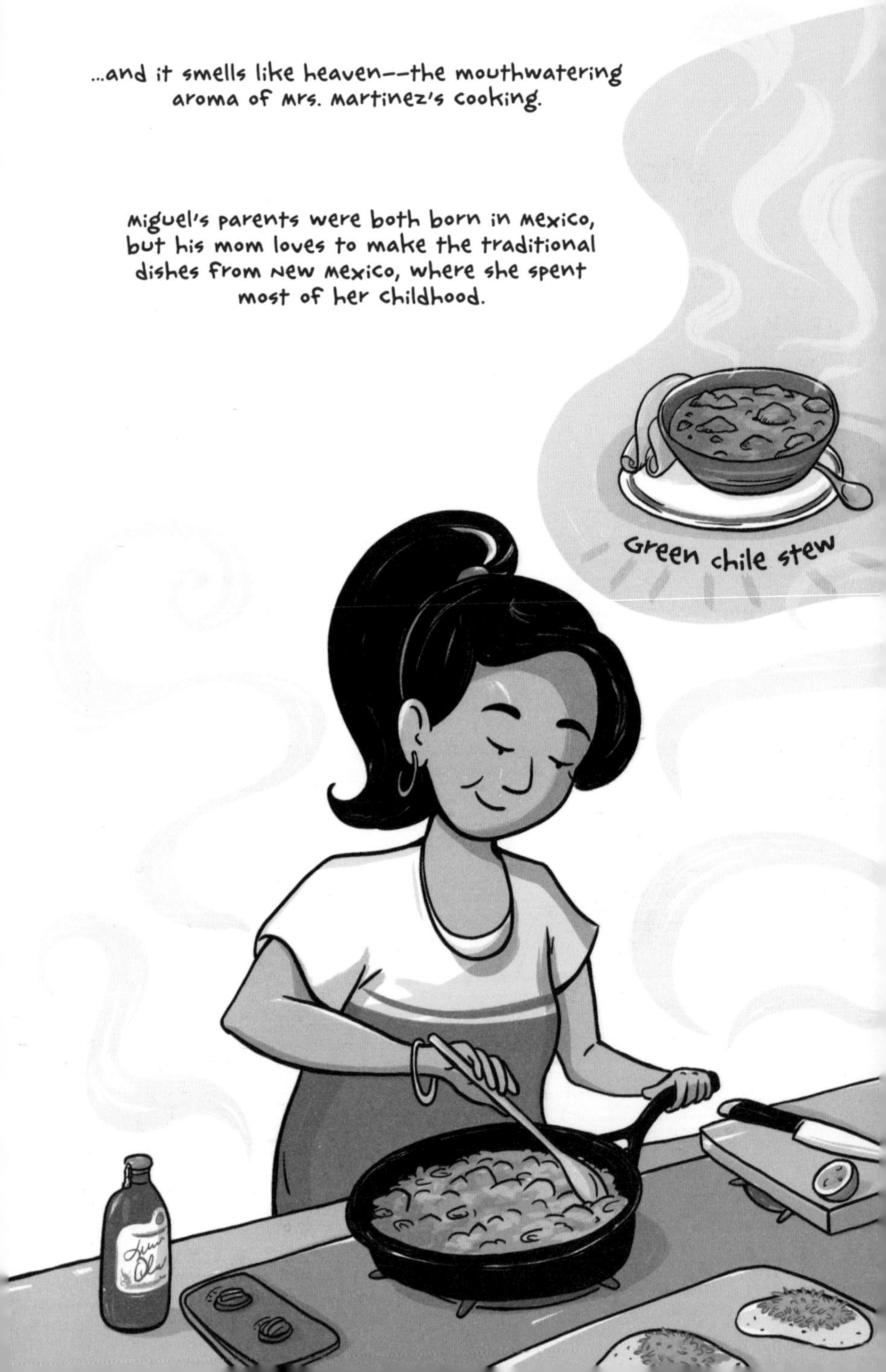
...and it smells like heaven--the mouthwatering aroma of Mrs. Martinez's cooking.
Miguel's parents were both born in Mexico, but his mom loves to make the traditional dishes from New Mexico, where she spent most of her childhood.
Green chile stew

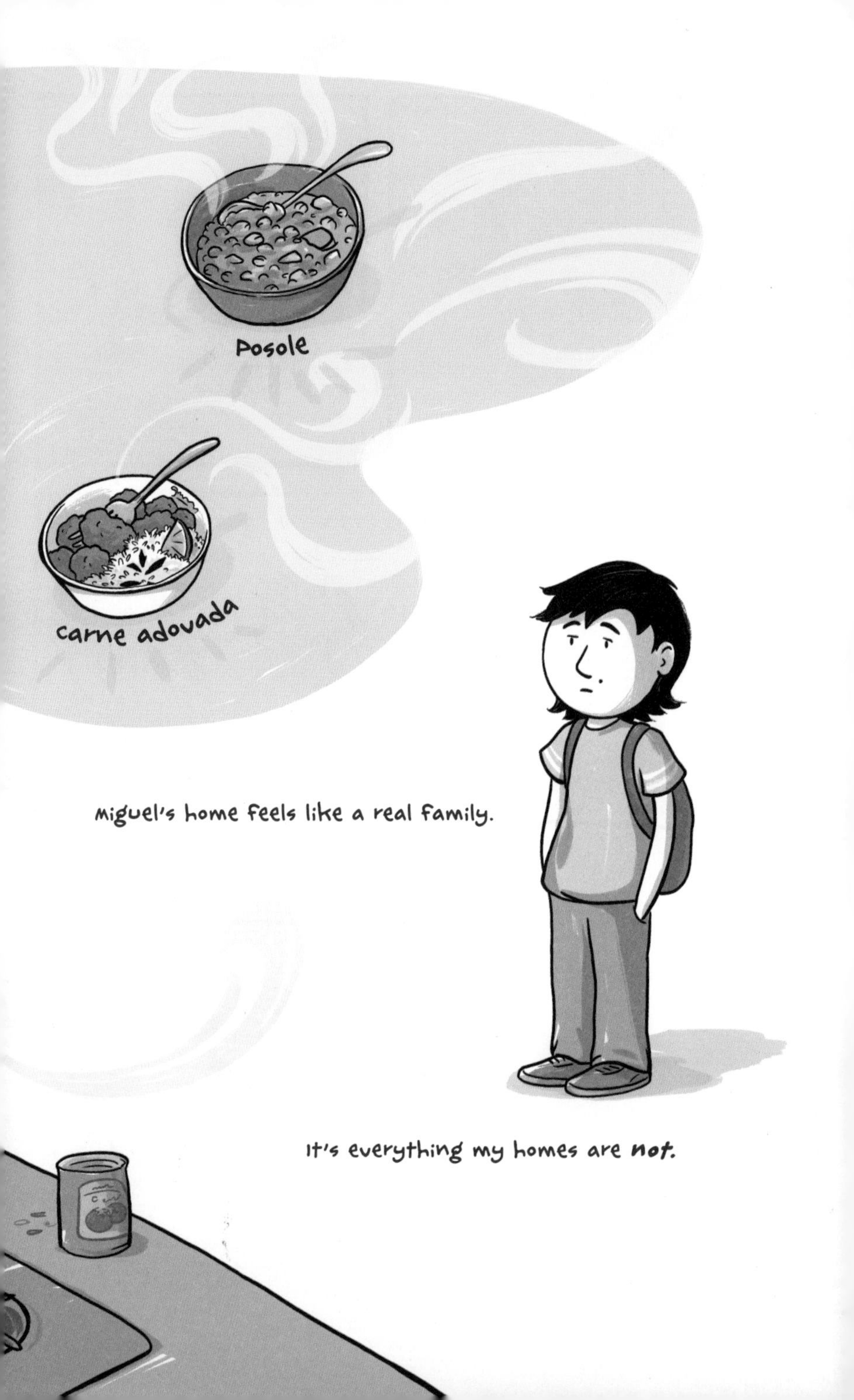
Posole
carne adovada
Miguel's home feels like a real family.
It's everything my homes are *not*.

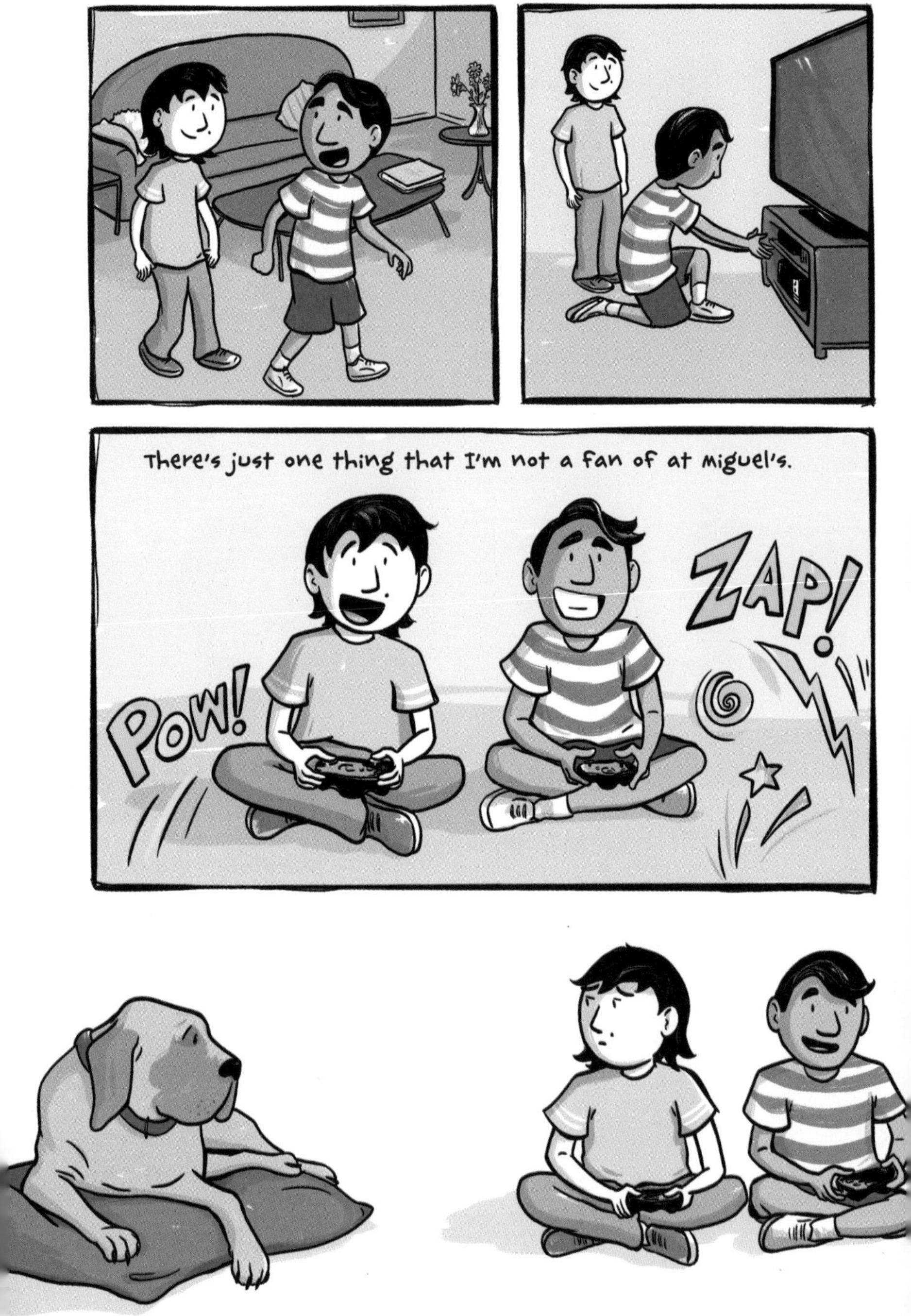
There's just one thing that I'm not a fan of at Miguel's.
POW!
ZAP!

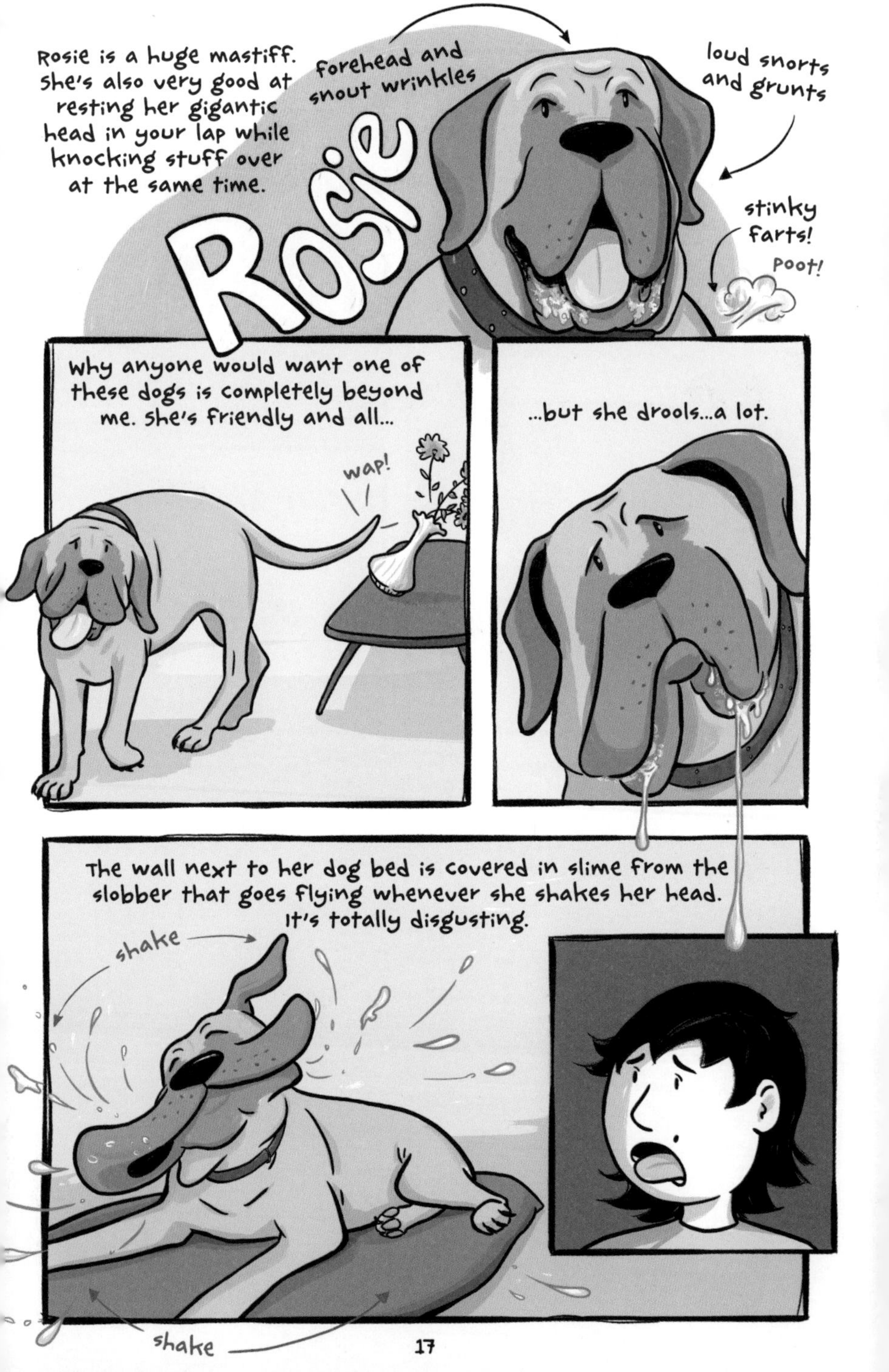
Rosie
Rosie is a huge mastiff. She's also very good at resting her gigantic head in your lap while knocking stuff over at the same time.
forehead and snout wrinkles
loud snorts and grunts
stinky farts!
Poot!
Why anyone would want one of these dogs is completely beyond me. She's friendly and all...
wap!
...but she drools...a lot.
The wall next to her dog bed is covered in slime from the slobber that goes flying whenever she shakes her head. It's totally disgusting.
shake
shake

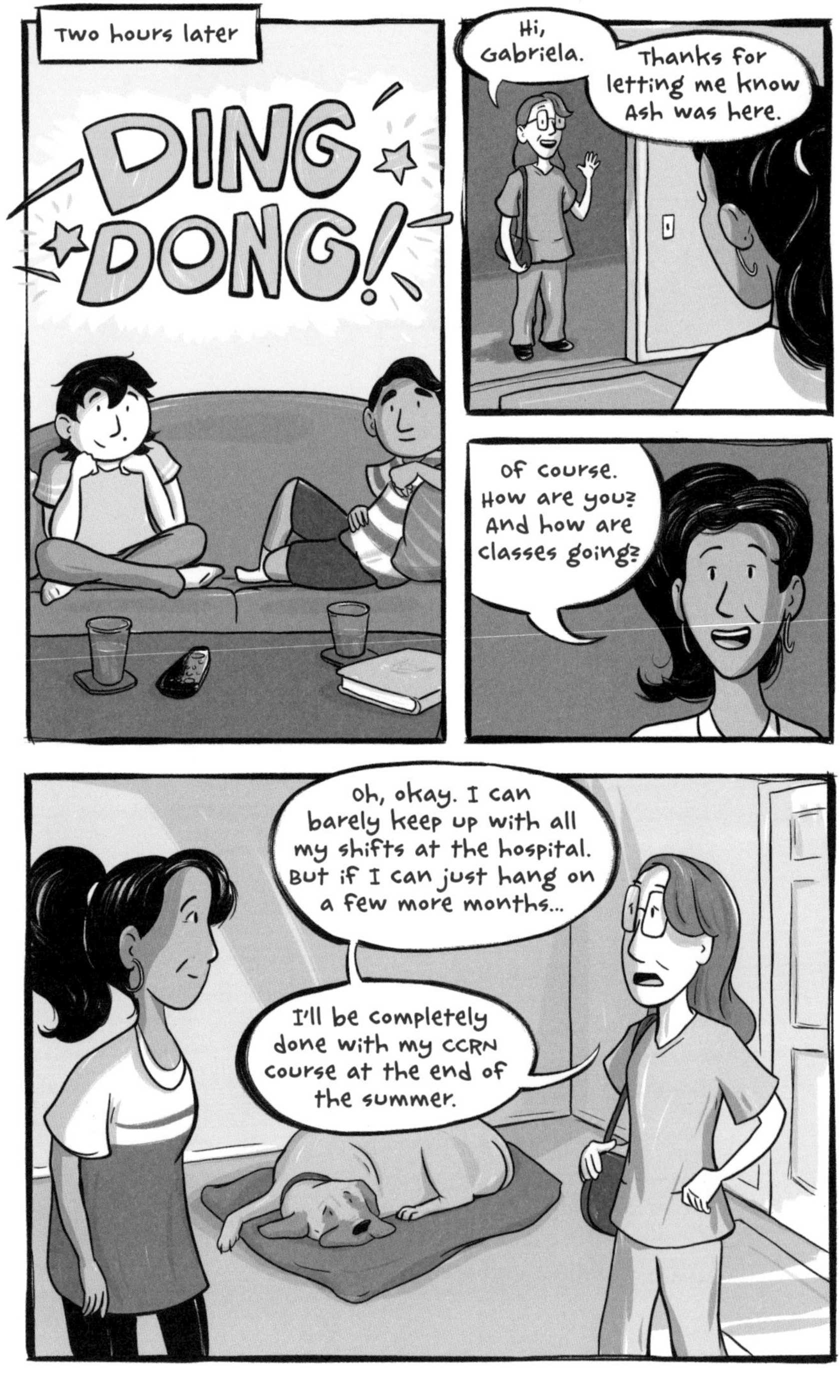
Two hours later
DING DONG!
Hi, Gabriela.
Thanks for letting me know Ash was here.
Of course. How are you? And how are classes going?
Oh, okay. I can barely keep up with all my shifts at the hospital. But if I can just hang on a few more months...
I'll be completely done with my CCRN course at the end of the summer.

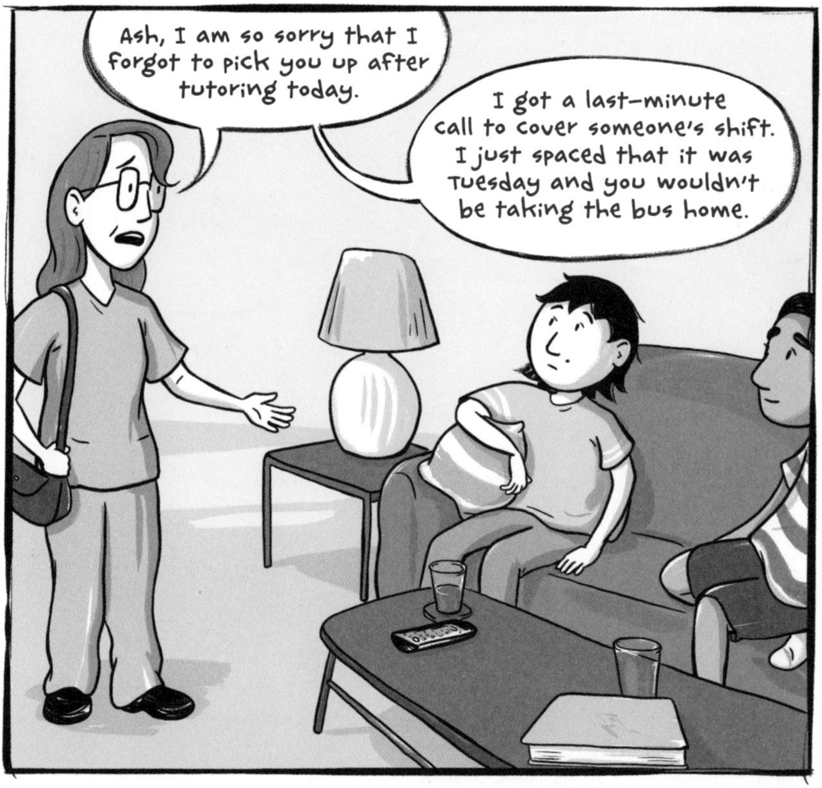
Ash, I am so sorry that I forgot to pick you up after tutoring today.
I got a last-minute call to cover someone's shift. I just spaced that it was Tuesday and you wouldn't be taking the bus home.

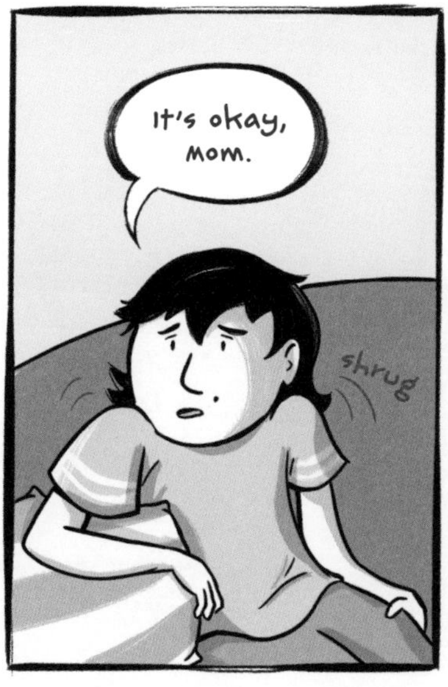
It's okay, mom.
shrug

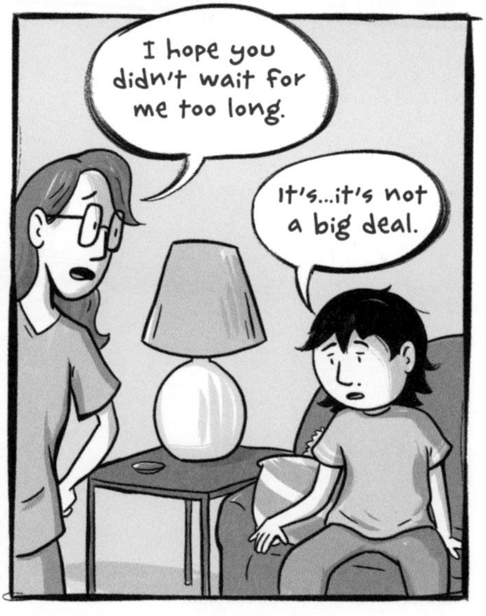
I hope you didn't wait for me too long.
It's...it's not a big deal.

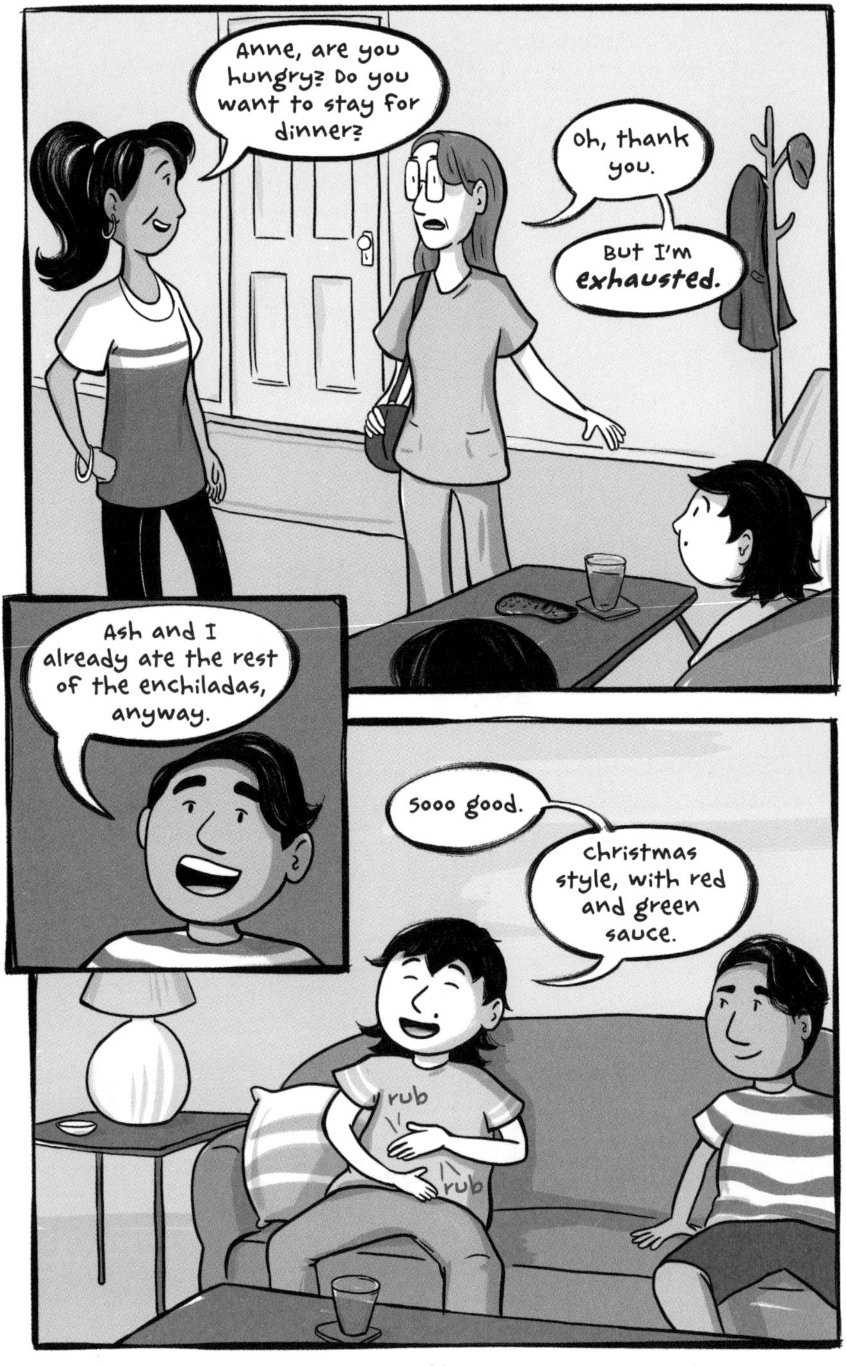
Anne, are you hungry? Do you want to stay for dinner?
Oh, thank you.
But I'm **exhausted.**
Ash and I already ate the rest of the enchiladas, anyway.
Sooo good.
Christmas style, with red and green sauce.
rub
rub

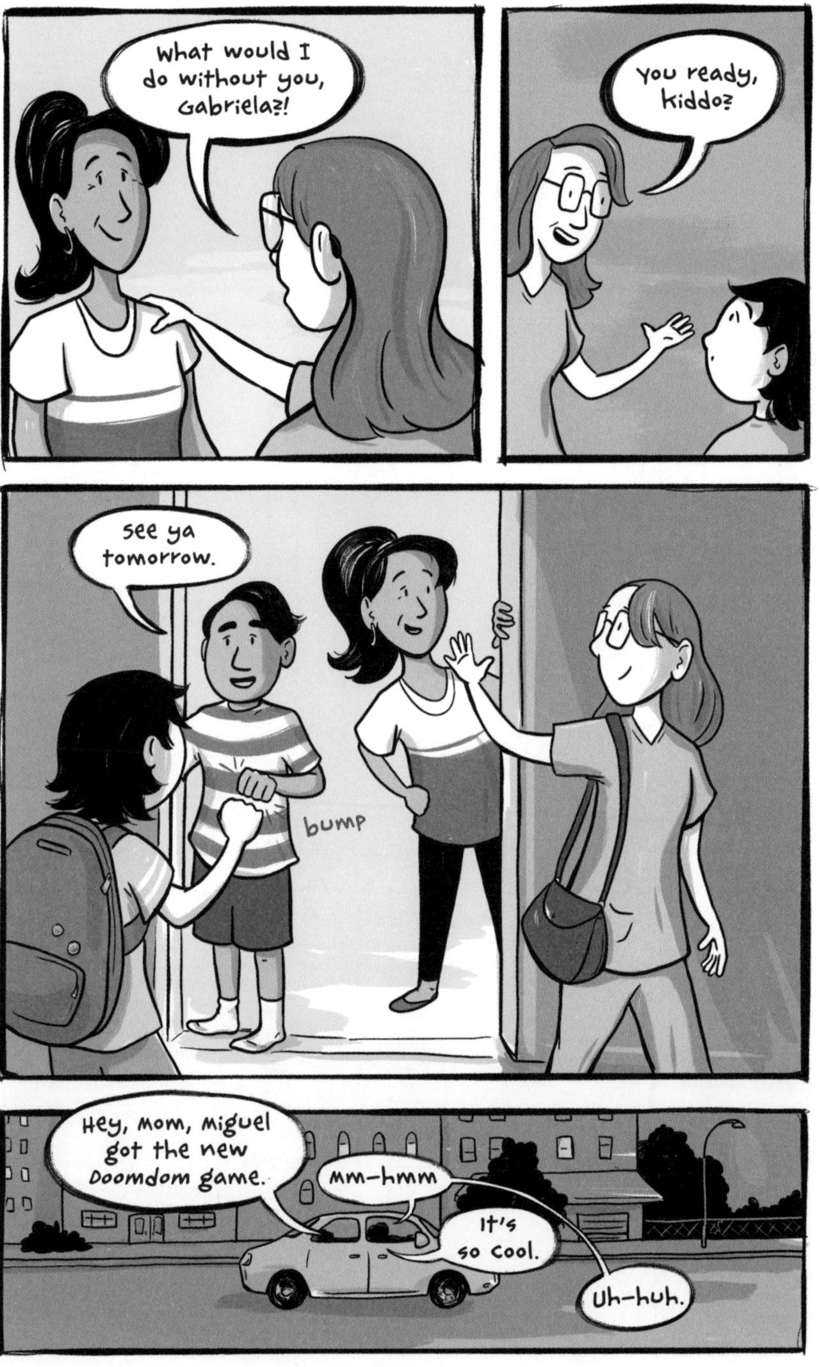
What would I do without you, Gabriela?!
You ready, kiddo?
See ya tomorrow.
bump
Hey, Mom, Miguel got the new Doomdom game.
Mm-hmm
It's so cool.
Uh-huh.

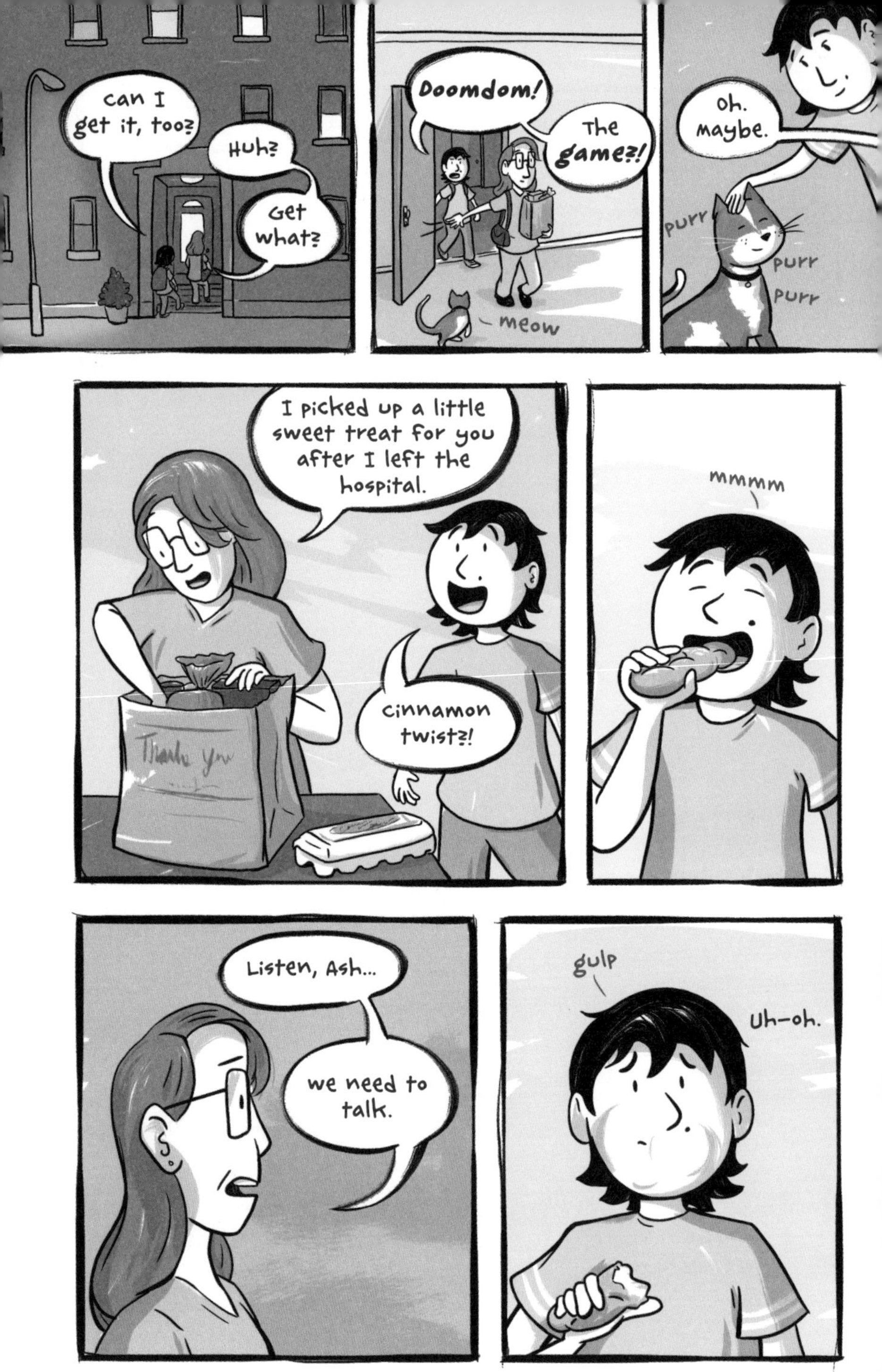
can I get it, too?
Huh?
Get what?
Doomdom!
The game?!
meow
Oh. maybe.
purr
purr
purr
I picked up a little sweet treat for you after I left the hospital.
cinnamon twist?!
Thank you
mmmm
Listen, Ash...
we need to talk.
gulp
Uh-oh.

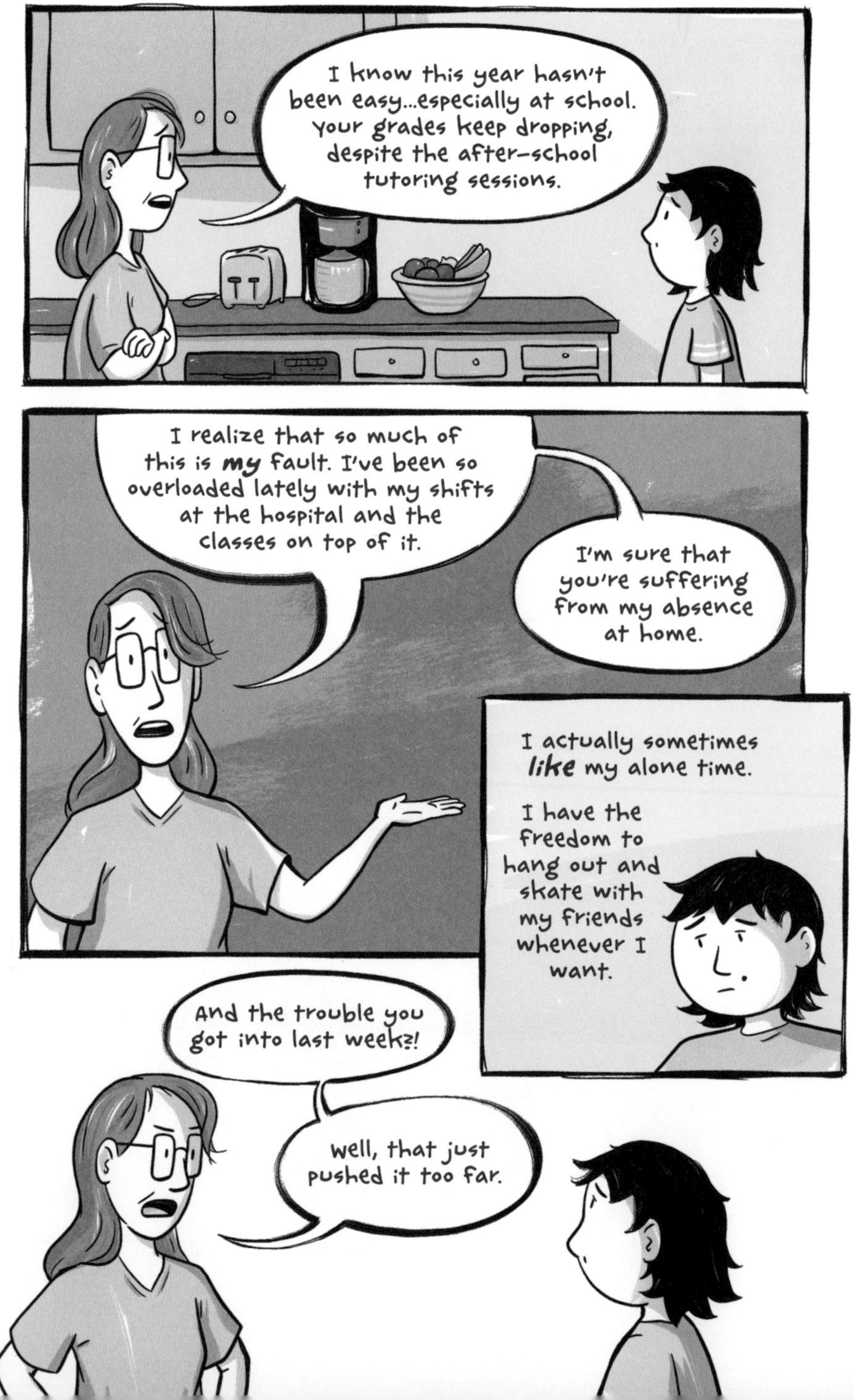
I know this year hasn't been easy...especially at school. Your grades keep dropping, despite the after-school tutoring sessions.
I realize that so much of this is *my* fault. I've been so overloaded lately with my shifts at the hospital and the classes on top of it.
I'm sure that you're suffering from my absence at home.
I actually sometimes *like* my alone time.
I have the freedom to hang out and skate with my friends whenever I want.
And the trouble you got into last week?!
Well, that just pushed it too far.

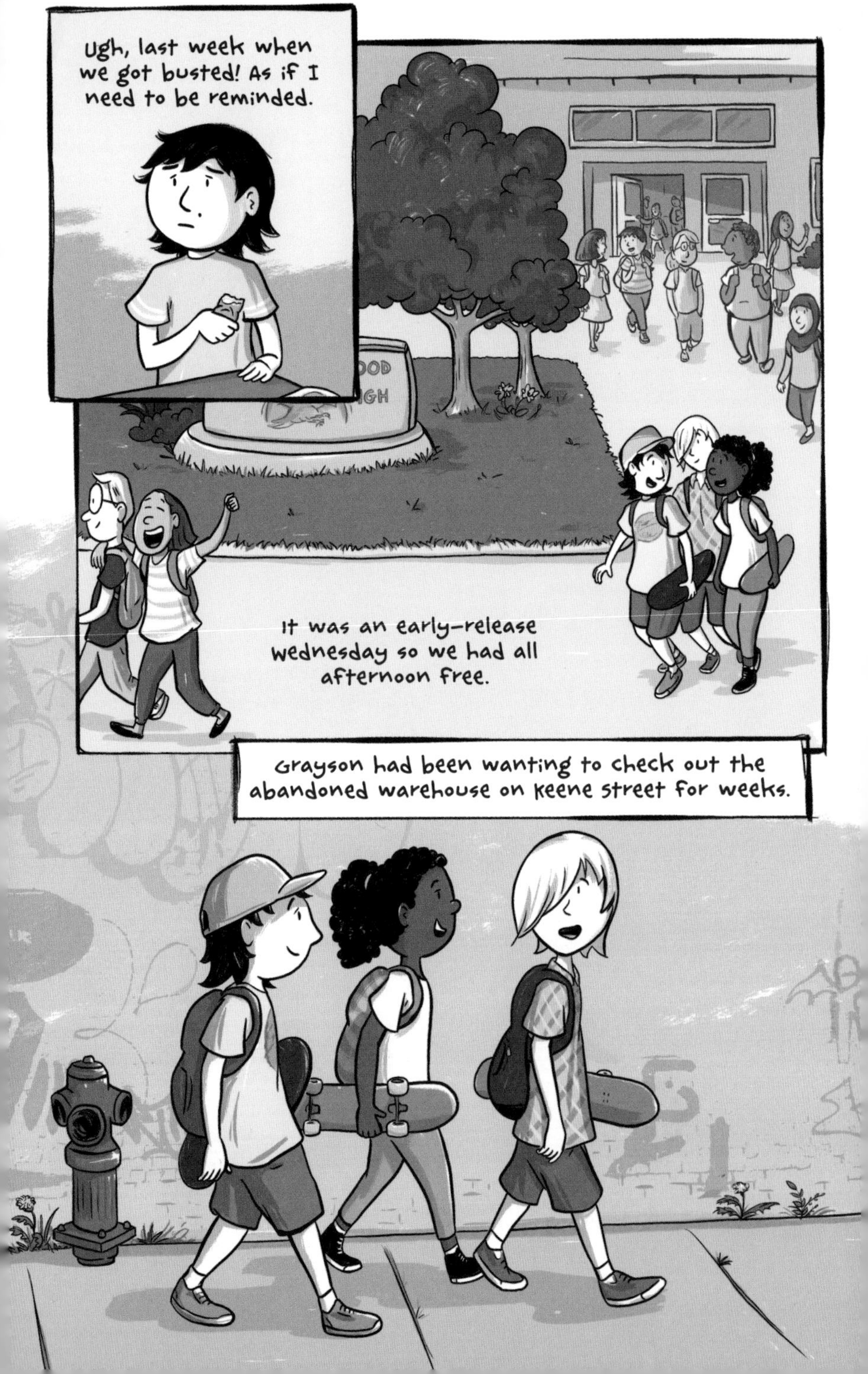
Ugh, last week when we got busted! As if I need to be reminded.
OOD
IGH
It was an early-release Wednesday so we had all afternoon free.
Grayson had been wanting to check out the abandoned warehouse on Keene Street for weeks.

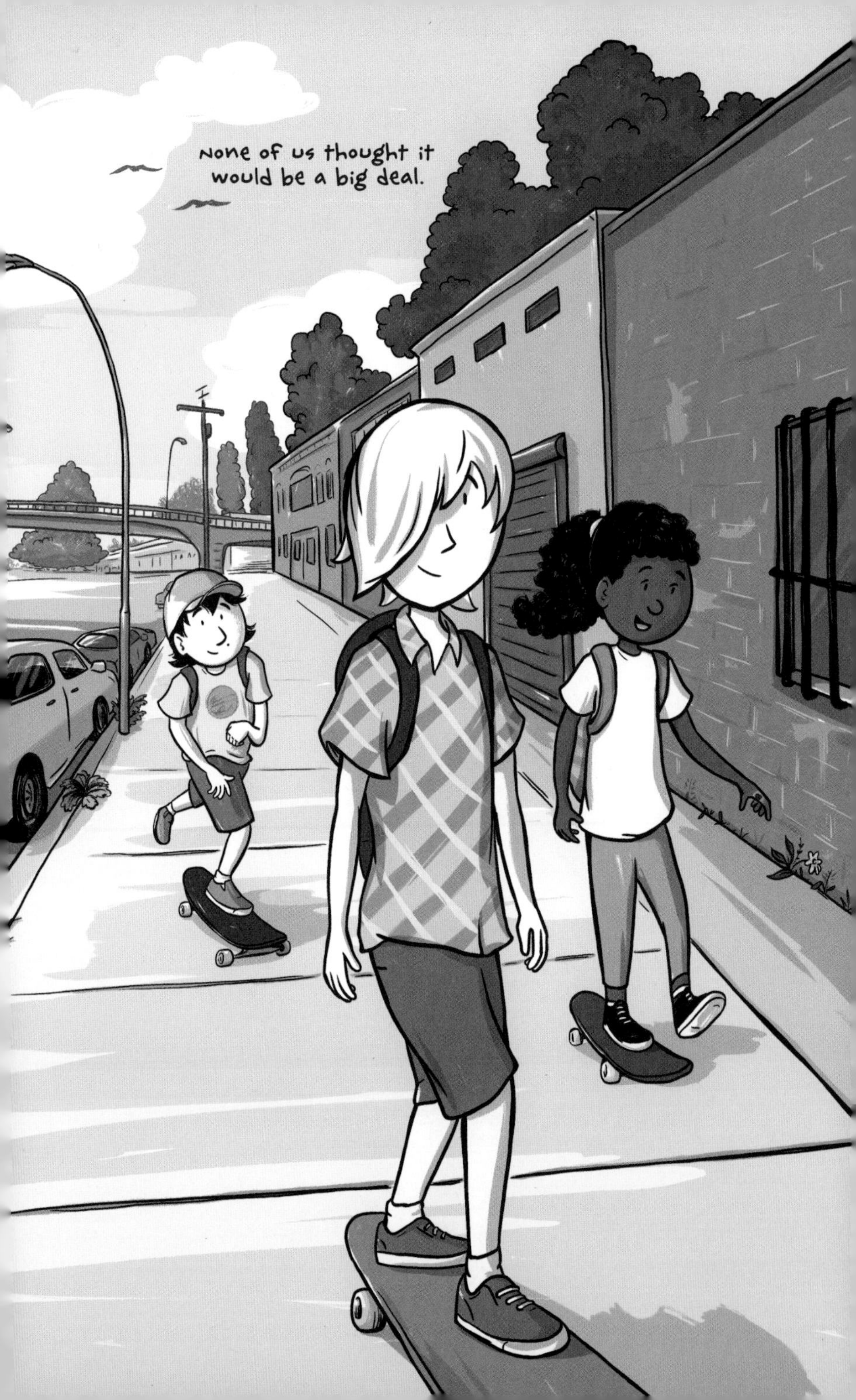
None of us thought it would be a big deal.

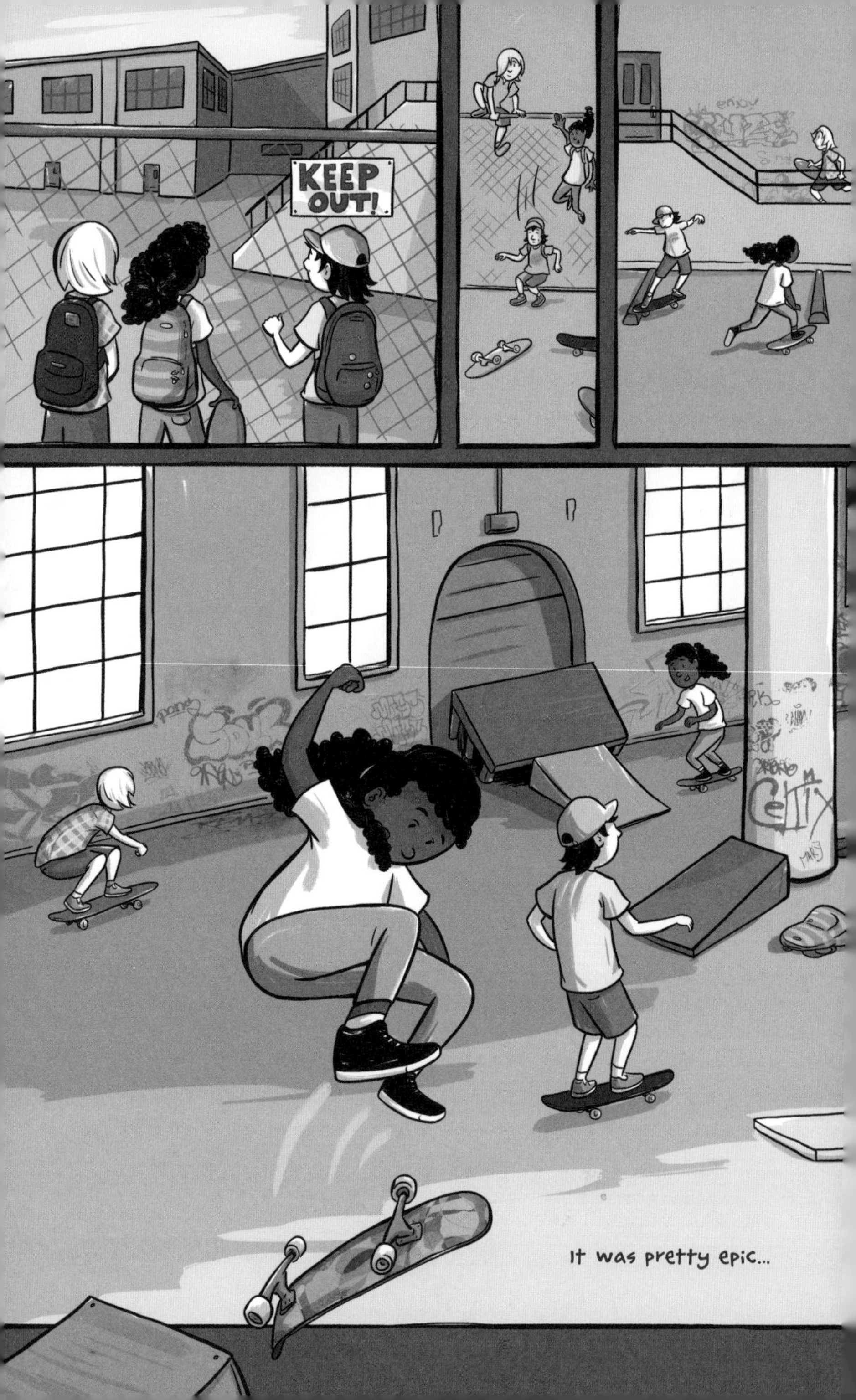
KEEP OUT!
It was pretty epic...

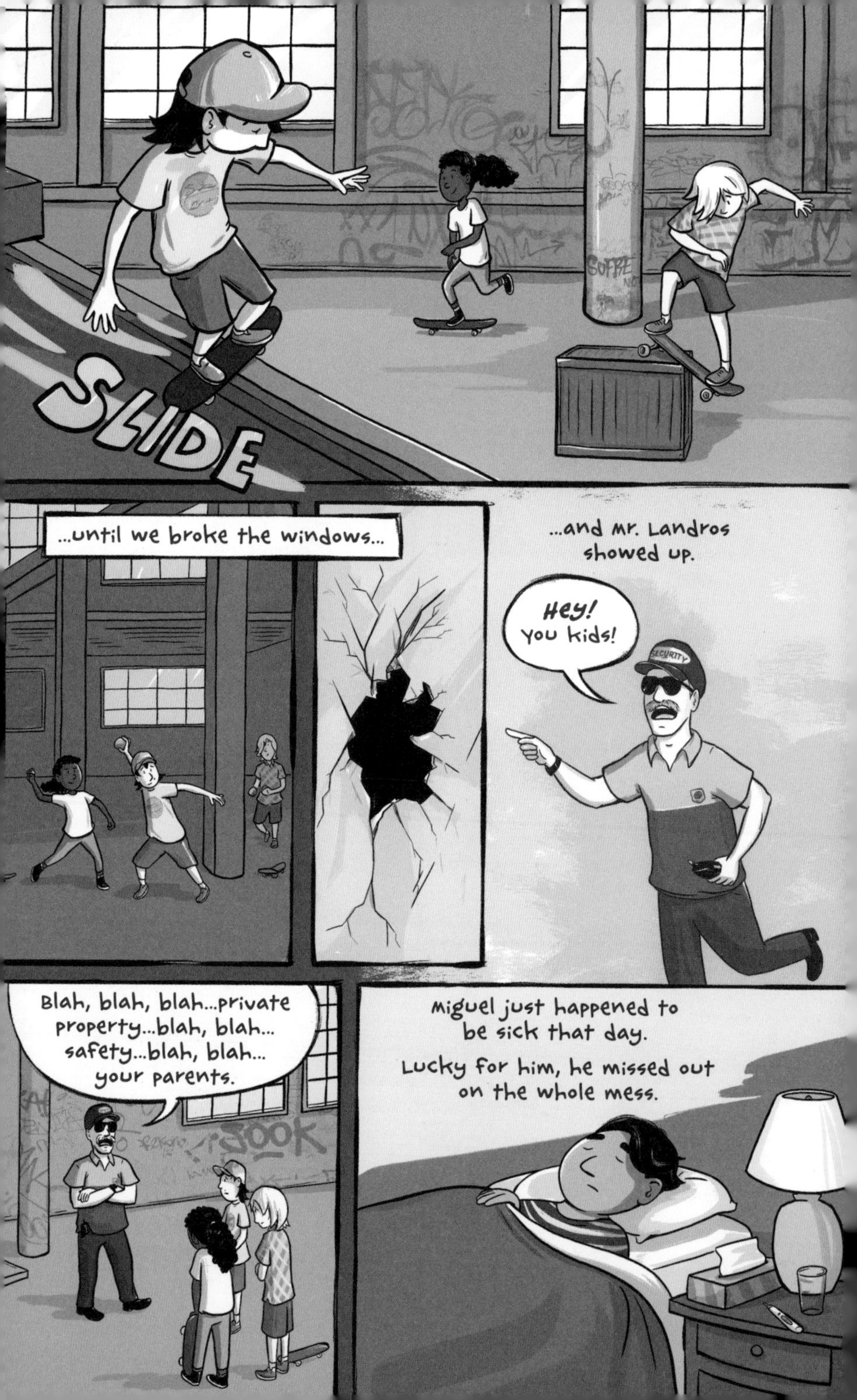
SLIDE
...until we broke the windows...
...and Mr. Landros showed up.
Hey! You kids!
Blah, blah, blah...private property...blah, blah... safety...blah, blah... your parents.
Miguel just happened to be sick that day.
Lucky for him, he missed out on the whole mess.

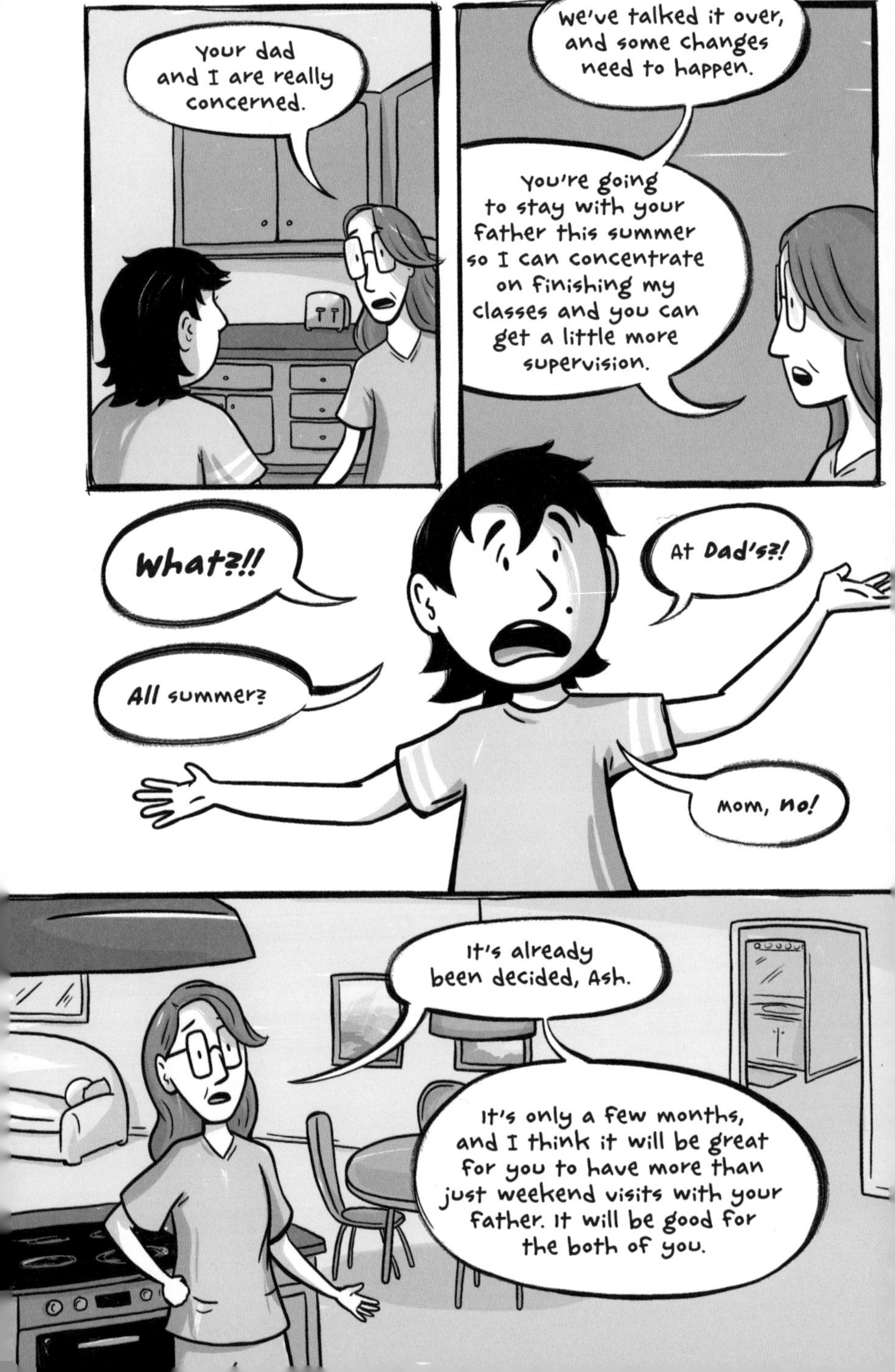
Your dad and I are really concerned.
We've talked it over, and some changes need to happen.
You're going to stay with your father this summer so I can concentrate on finishing my classes and you can get a little more supervision.
What?!!
At Dad's?!
All summer?
Mom, no!
It's already been decided, Ash.
It's only a few months, and I think it will be great for you to have more than just weekend visits with your father. It will be good for the both of you.

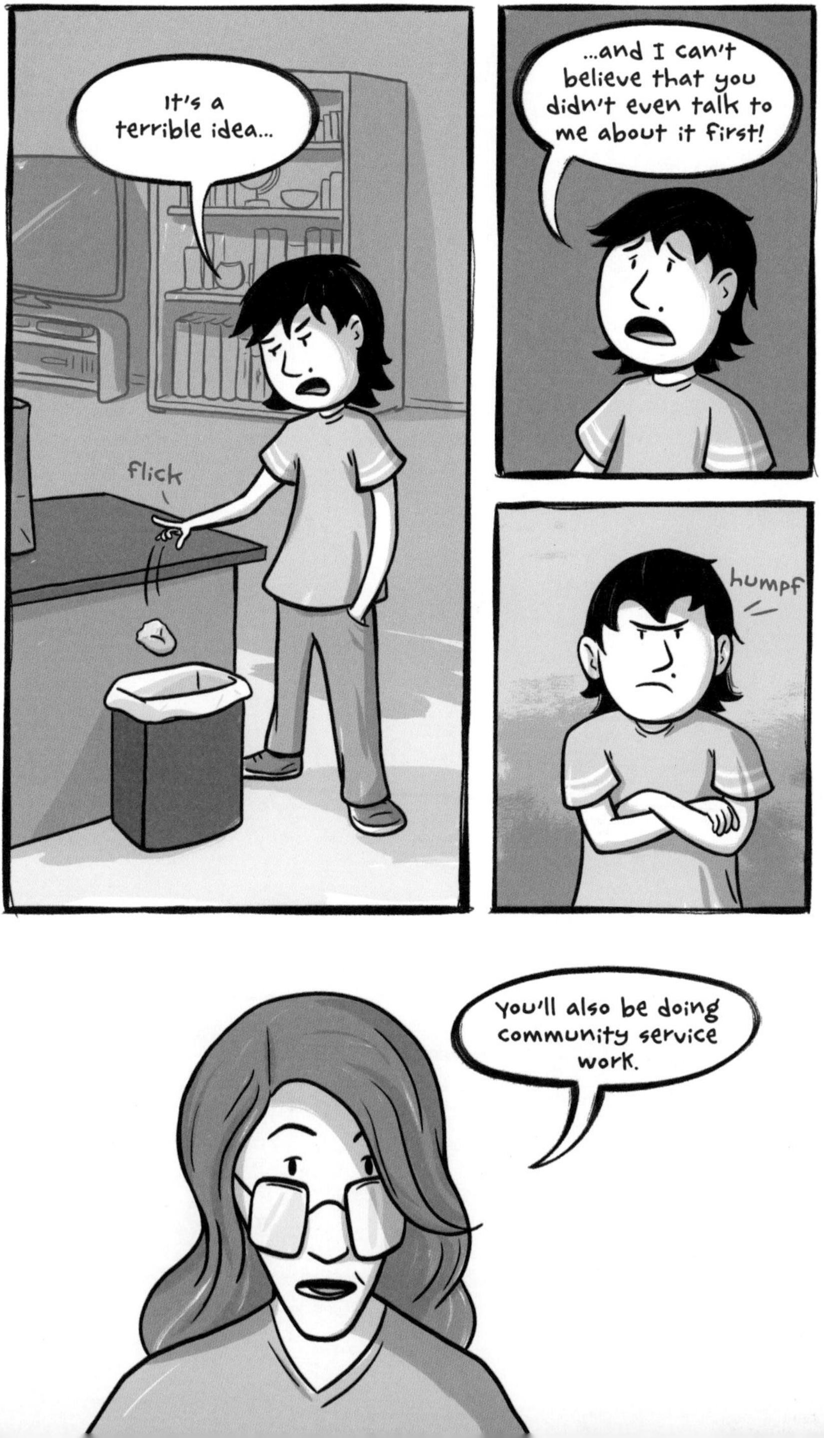
It's a terrible idea...
flick
...and I can't believe that you didn't even talk to me about it first!
humpf
You'll also be doing community service work.

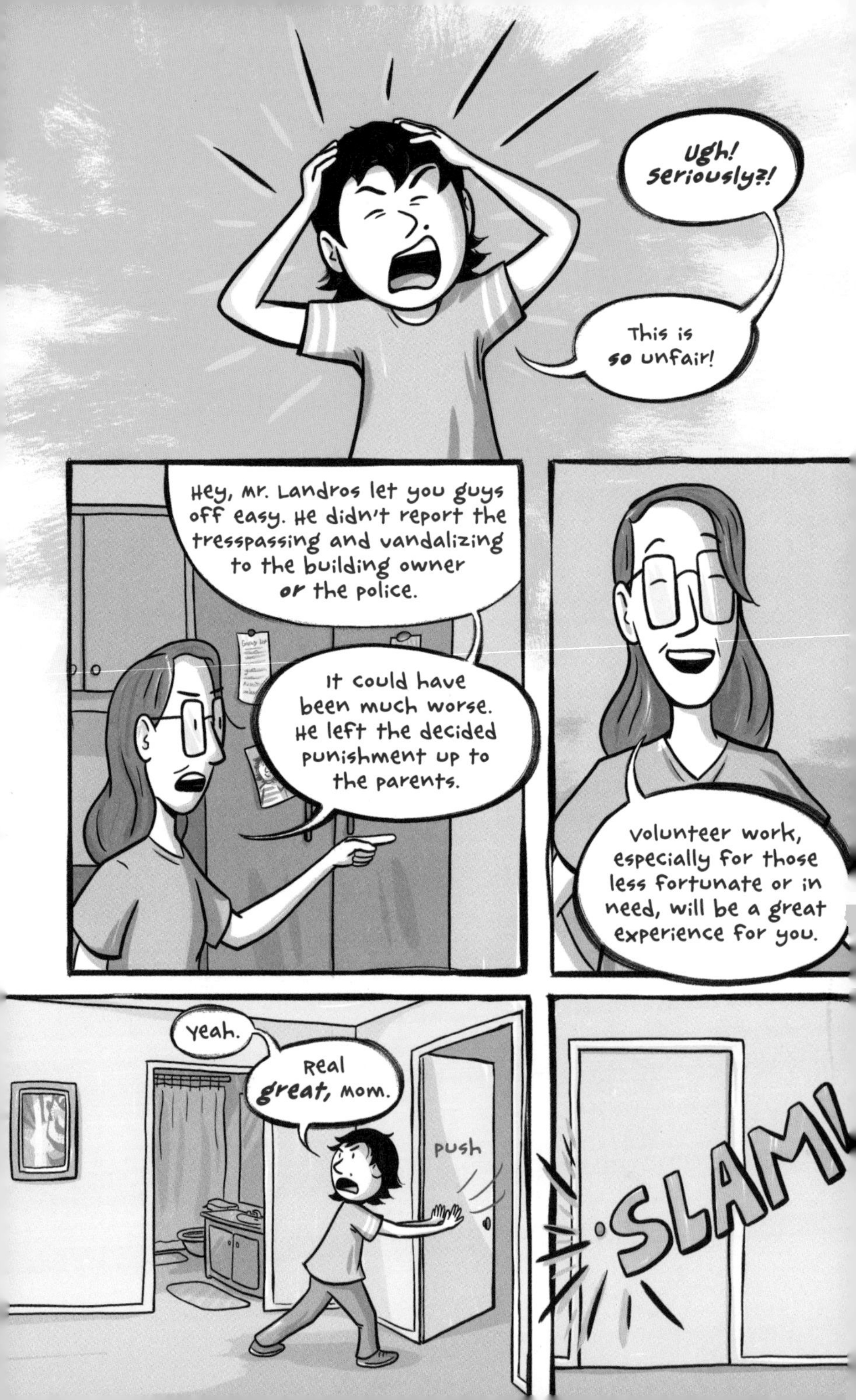
Ugh! Seriously?!
This is so unfair!
Hey, Mr. Landros let you guys off easy. He didn't report the tresspassing and vandalizing to the building owner or the police.
It could have been much worse. He left the decided punishment up to the parents.
Volunteer work, especially for those less fortunate or in need, will be a great experience for you.
Yeah.
Real great, Mom.
push
SLAM!

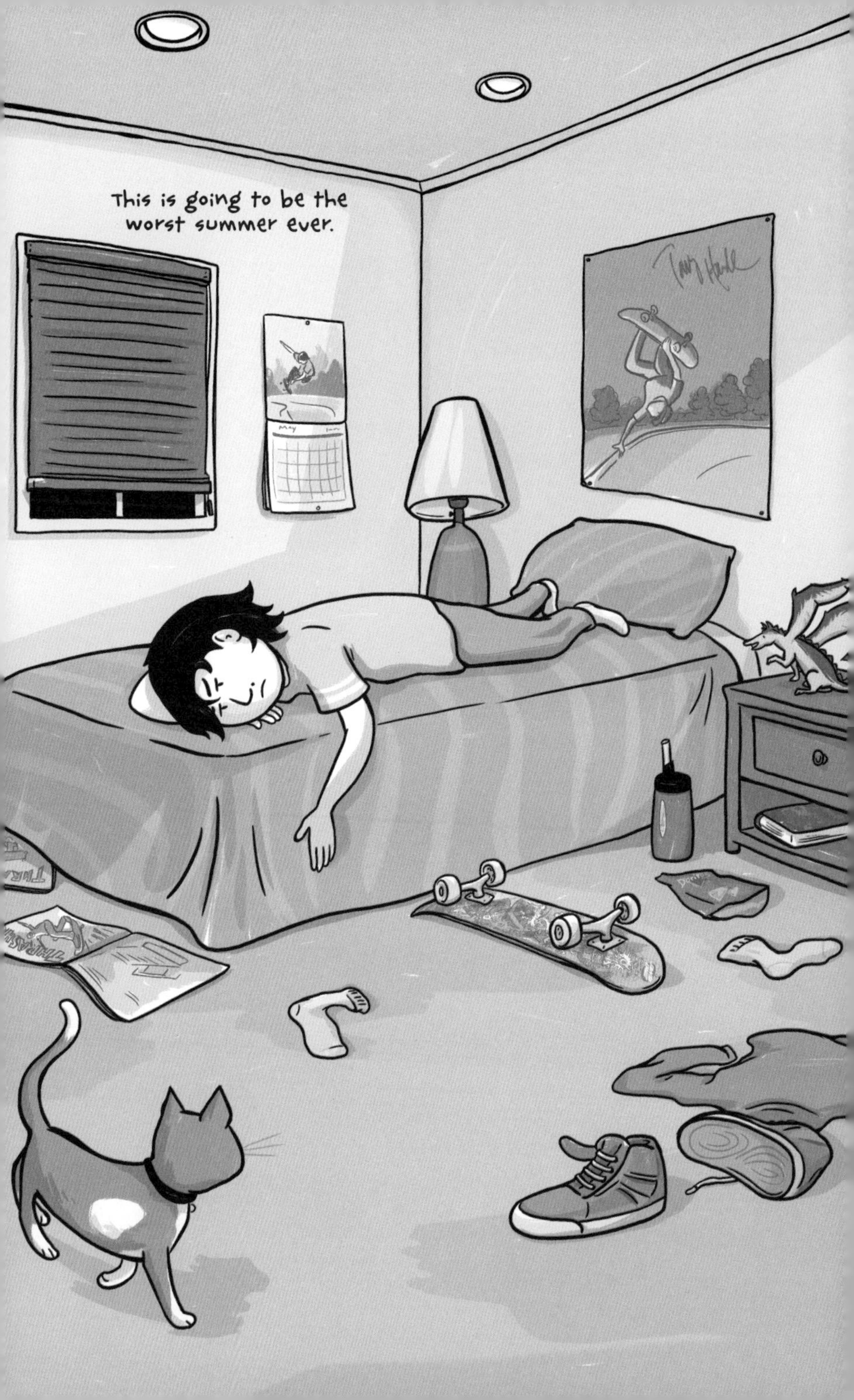
This is going to be the worst summer ever.

CHAPTER 2

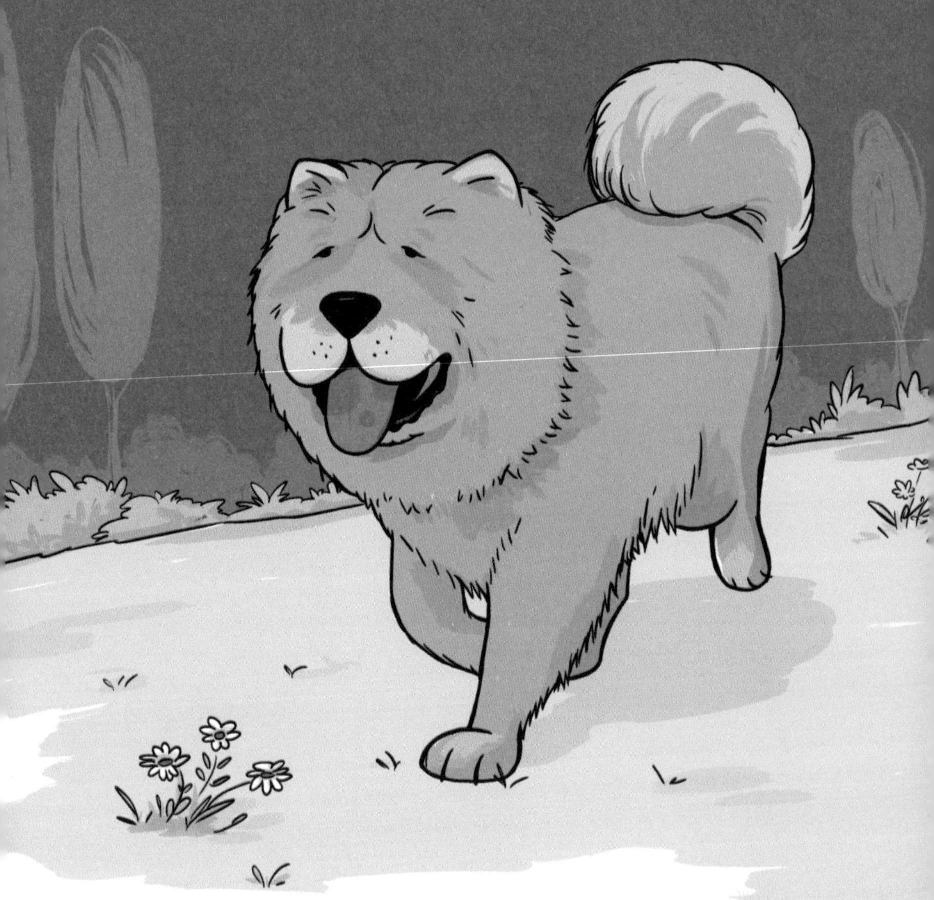

• Teddy •

An exceptionally loyal and mellow chow chow. Chows are smart, independent, and dignified dogs. They are often reserved and would rather spend time with their favorite person than do just about anything else.

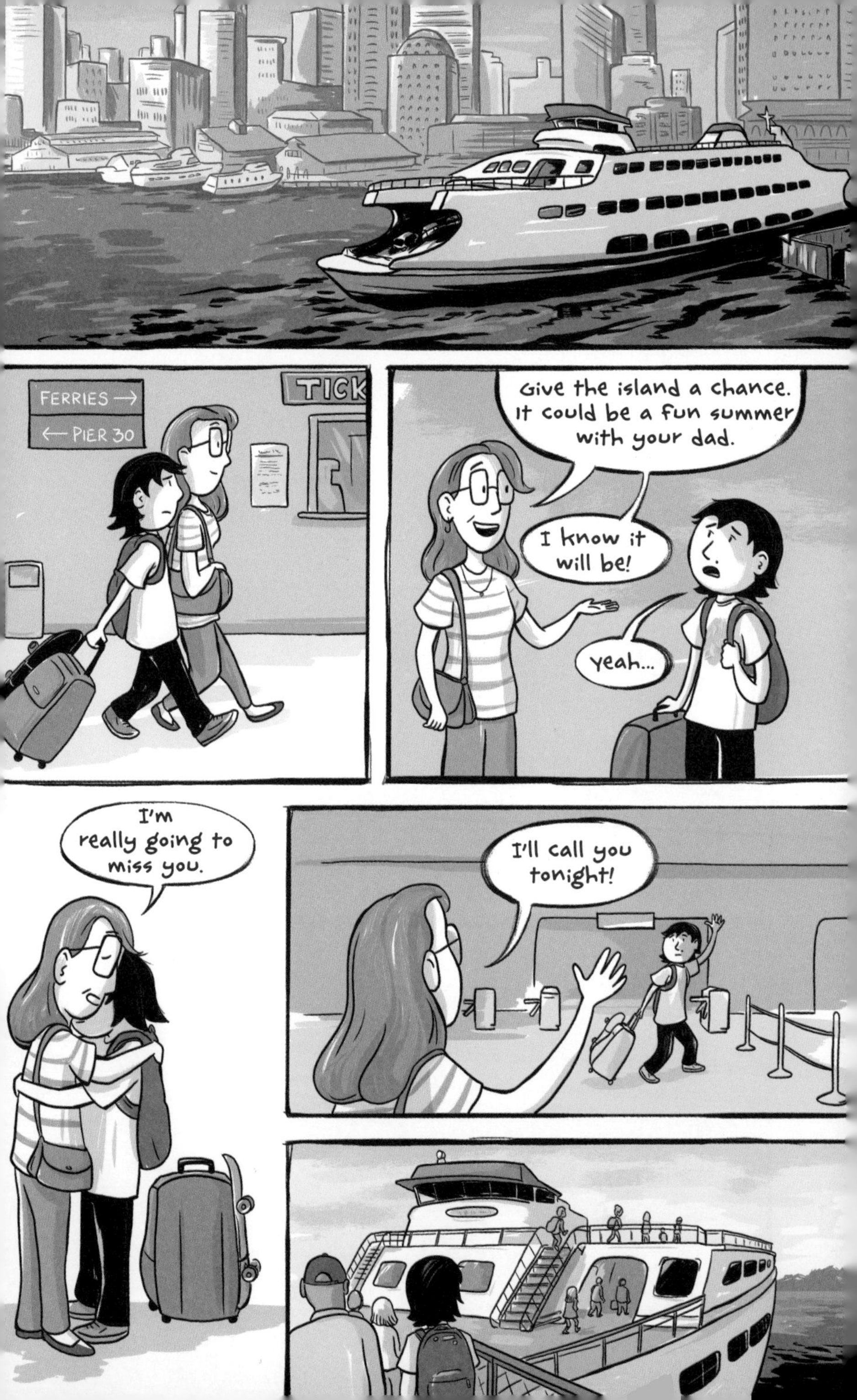
FERRIES →
← PIER 30
TICK
Give the island a chance. It could be a fun summer with your dad.
I know it will be!
Yeah...
I'm really going to miss you.
I'll call you tonight!

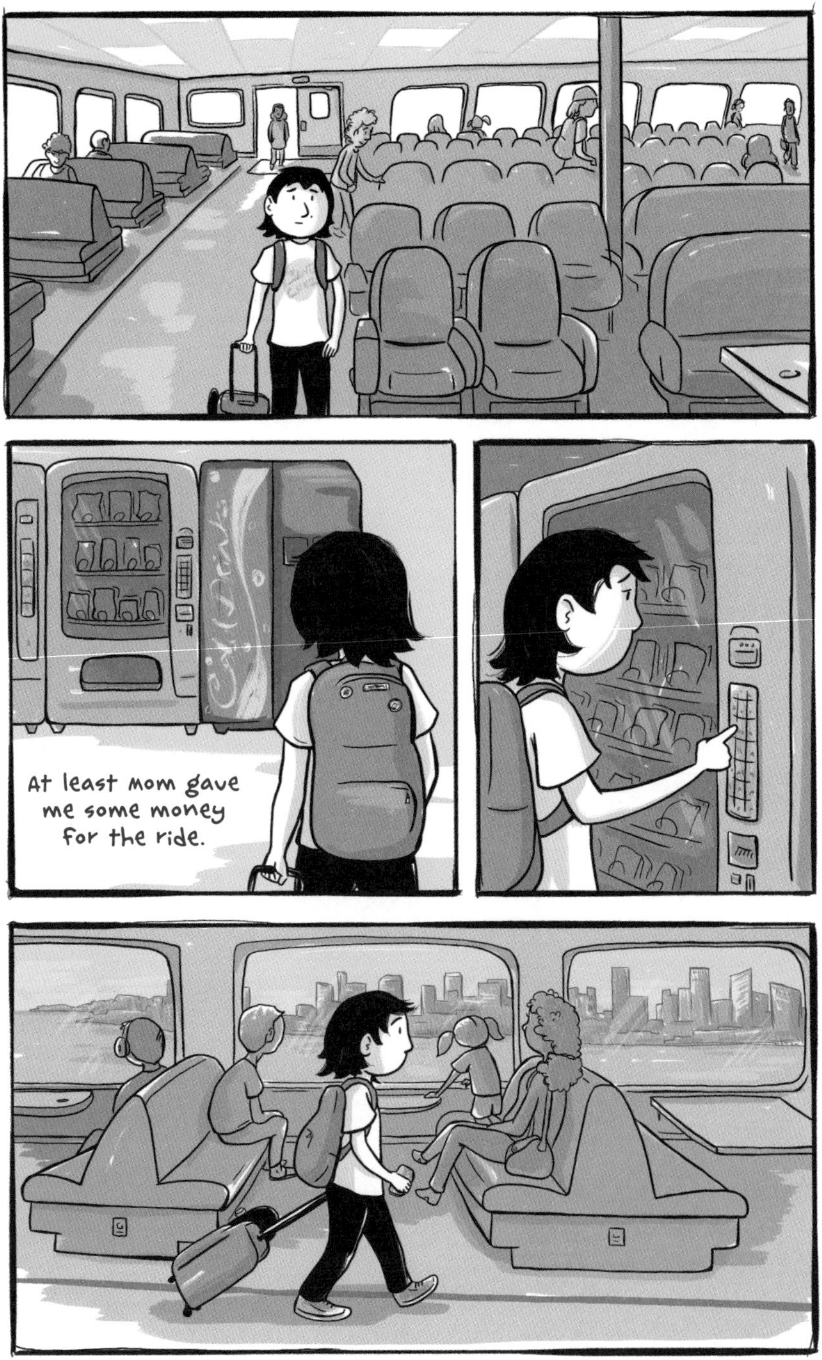
At least mom gave me some money for the ride.

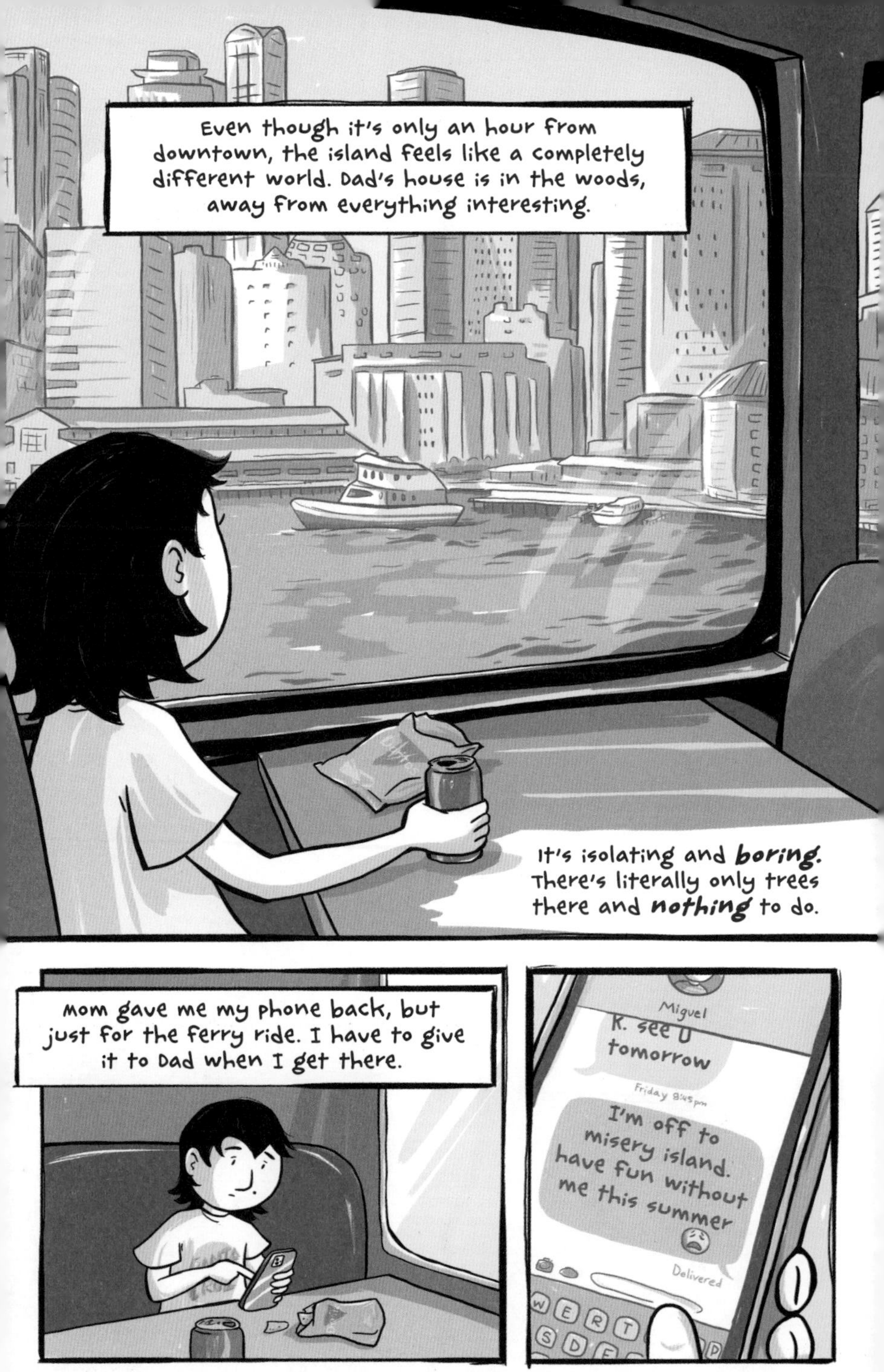
Even though it's only an hour from downtown, the island feels like a completely different world. Dad's house is in the woods, away from everything interesting.
It's isolating and *boring.* There's literally only trees there and *nothing* to do.
Mom gave me my phone back, but just for the ferry ride. I have to give it to Dad when I get there.
Miguel
K. see U tomorrow
Friday 8:45pm
I'm off to misery island. have fun without me this summer
Delivered

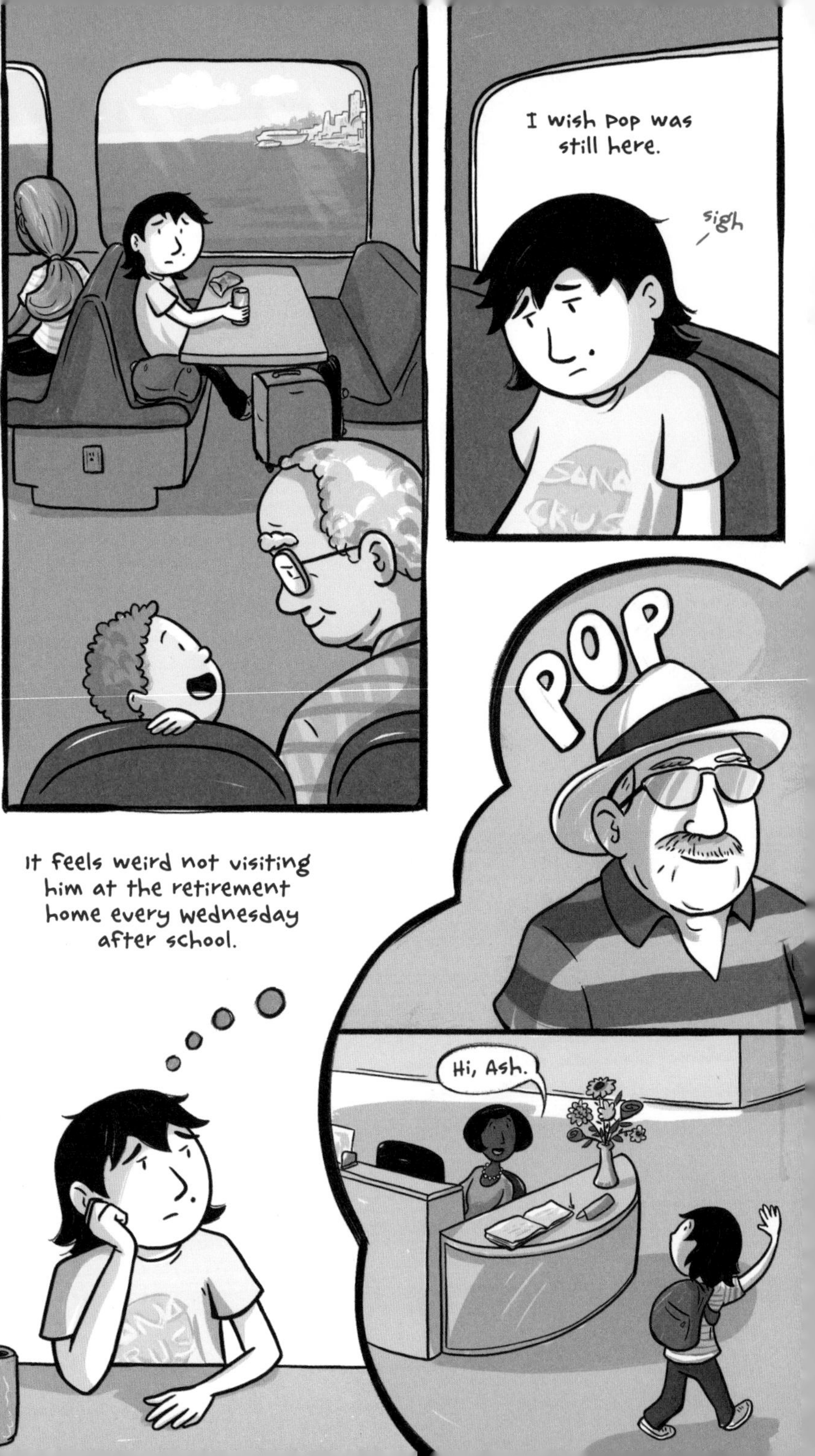

I wish Pop was still here.
sigh
It feels weird not visiting him at the retirement home every Wednesday after school.
POP
Hi, Ash.

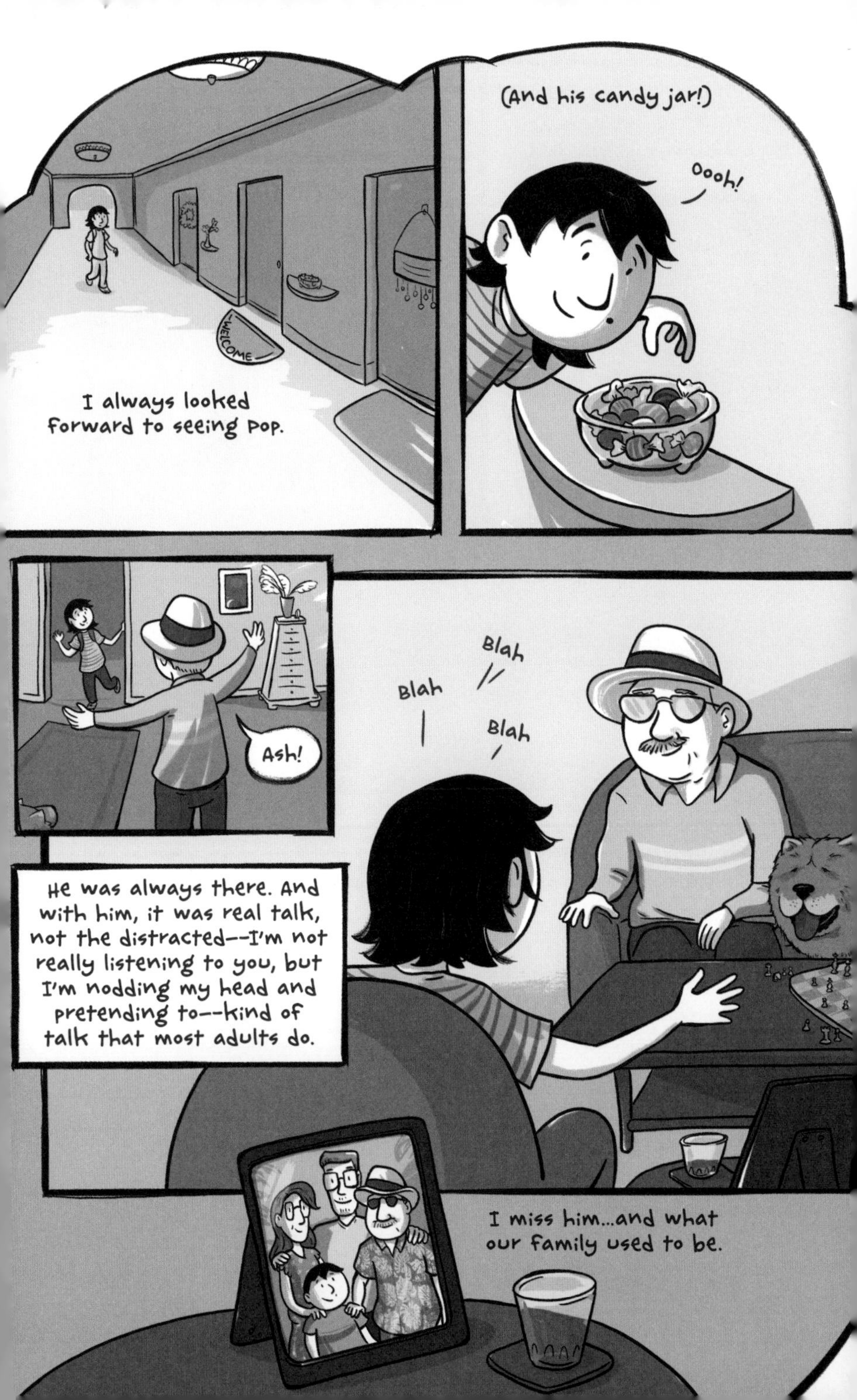
I always looked forward to seeing Pop.
(And his candy jar!)
Oooh!
WELCOME
Ash!
Blah
Blah
Blah
He was always there. And with him, it was real talk, not the distracted--I'm not really listening to you, but I'm nodding my head and pretending to--kind of talk that most adults do.
I miss him...and what our family used to be.

In all my memories of Pop, Teddy was always by his side.

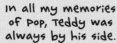

Teddy

lionlike mane

cinnamon-colored coat

purple-spotted tongue

Teddy was a big, fluffy chow who loved head rubs. He was patient and docile, and would spend hours roaming about the neighborhood until Pop called him home.

likes to sit on your feet

I remember seeing pictures of my toddler self crawling all over him.

stir

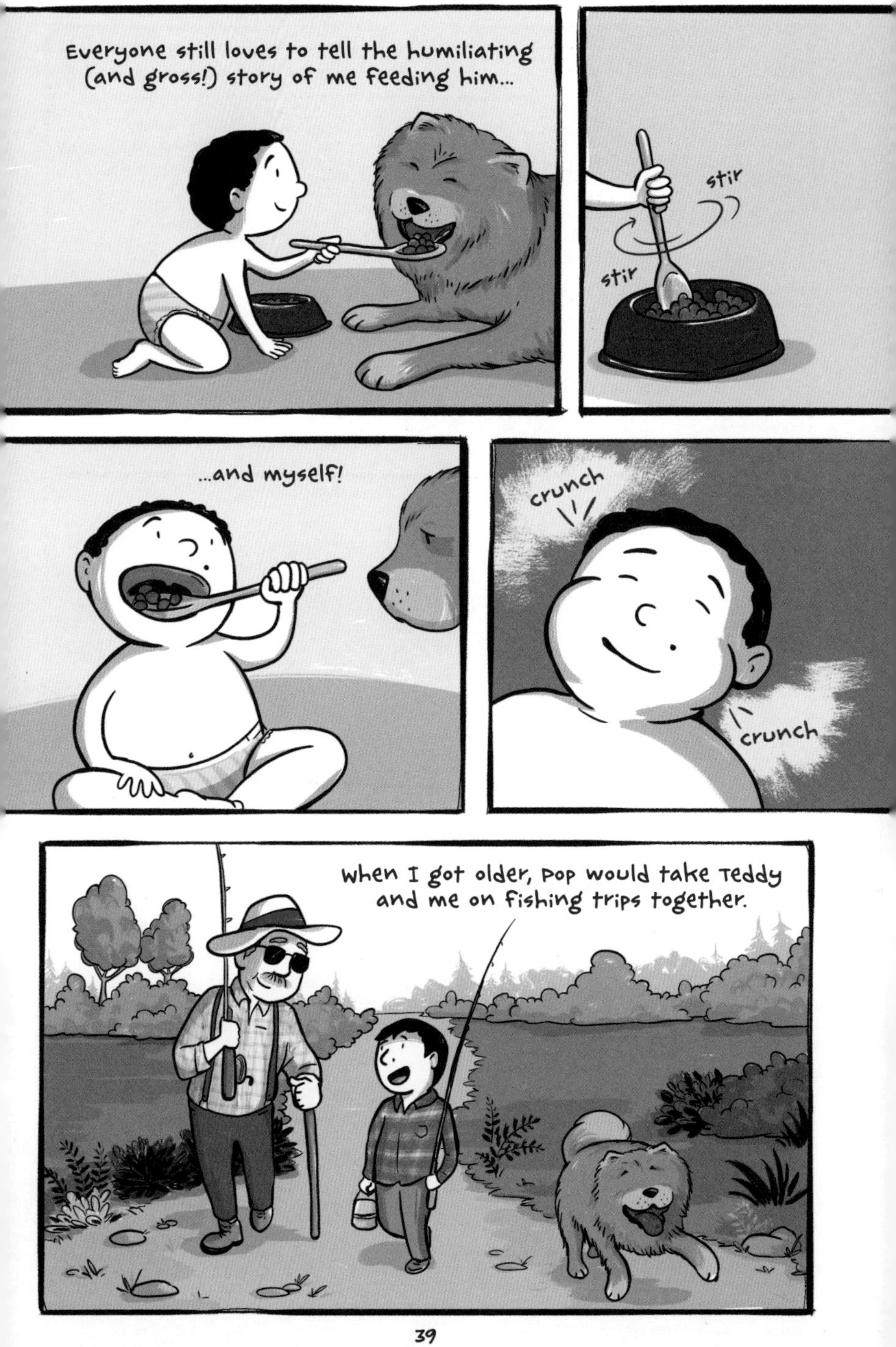
Everyone still loves to tell the humiliating (and gross!) story of me feeding him...
stir
stir
...and myself!
crunch
crunch
When I got older, Pop would take Teddy and me on fishing trips together.

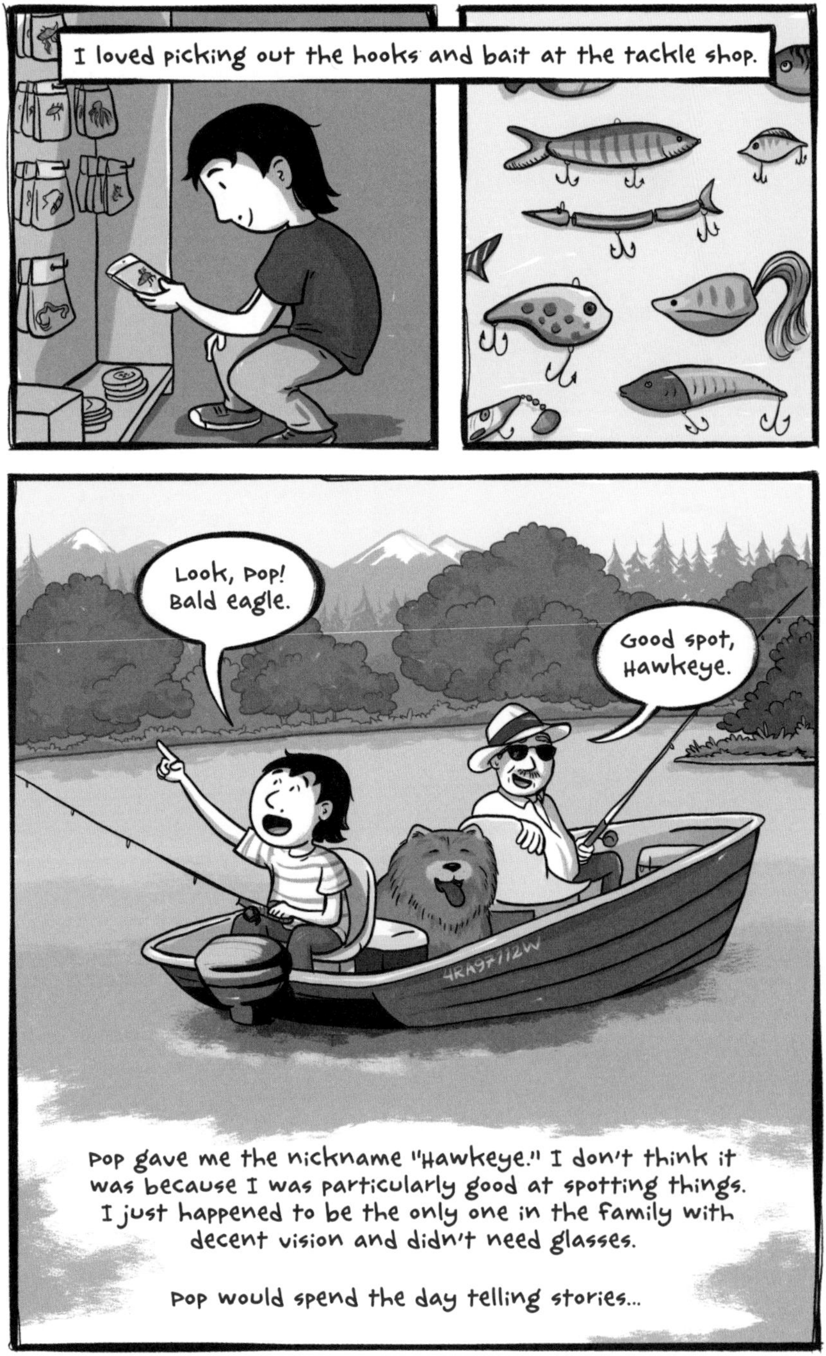
I loved picking out the hooks and bait at the tackle shop.
Look, Pop! Bald eagle.
Good spot, Hawkeye.
Pop gave me the nickname "Hawkeye." I don't think it was because I was particularly good at spotting things. I just happened to be the only one in the family with decent vision and didn't need glasses.
Pop would spend the day telling stories...

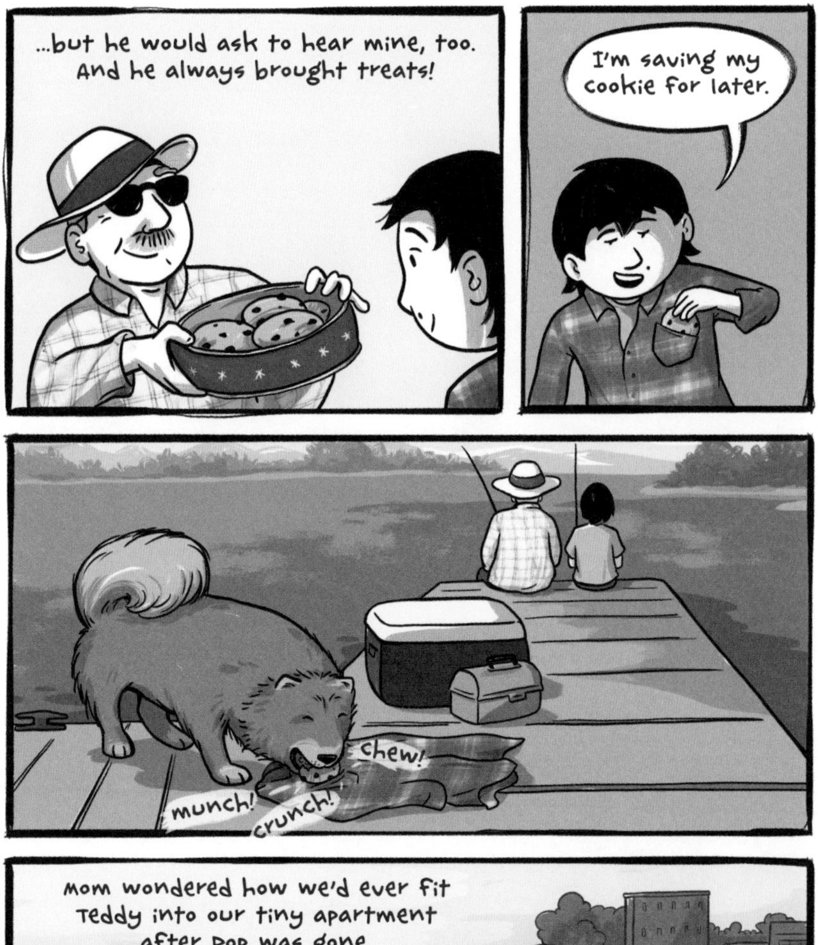
...but he would ask to hear mine, too. And he always brought treats!
I'm saving my cookie for later.
chew!
munch!
crunch!
Mom wondered how we'd ever fit Teddy into our tiny apartment after Pop was gone.

But Teddy died two days later. Mom said it was probably due to a broken heart.

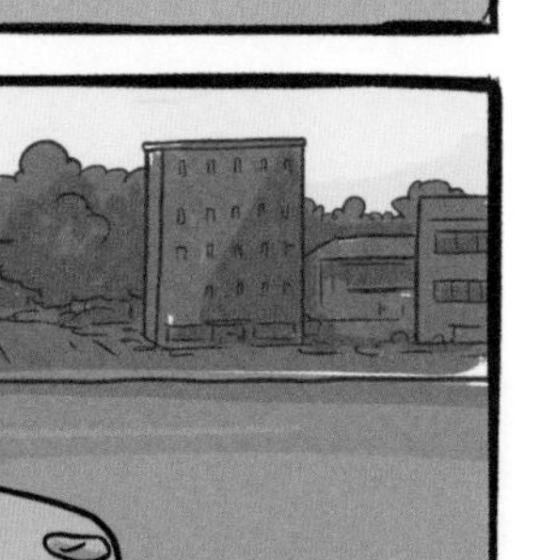
TEDDY

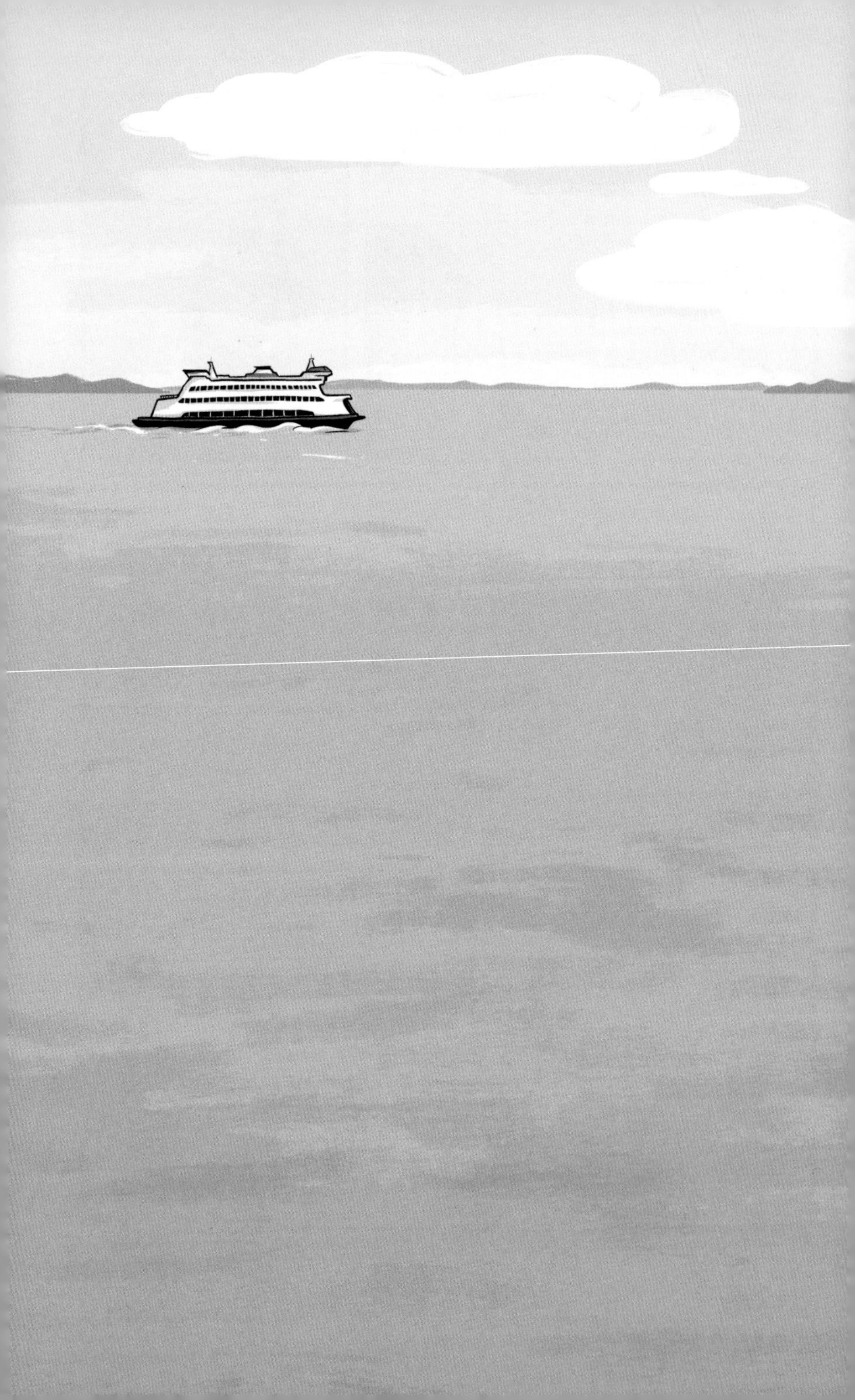

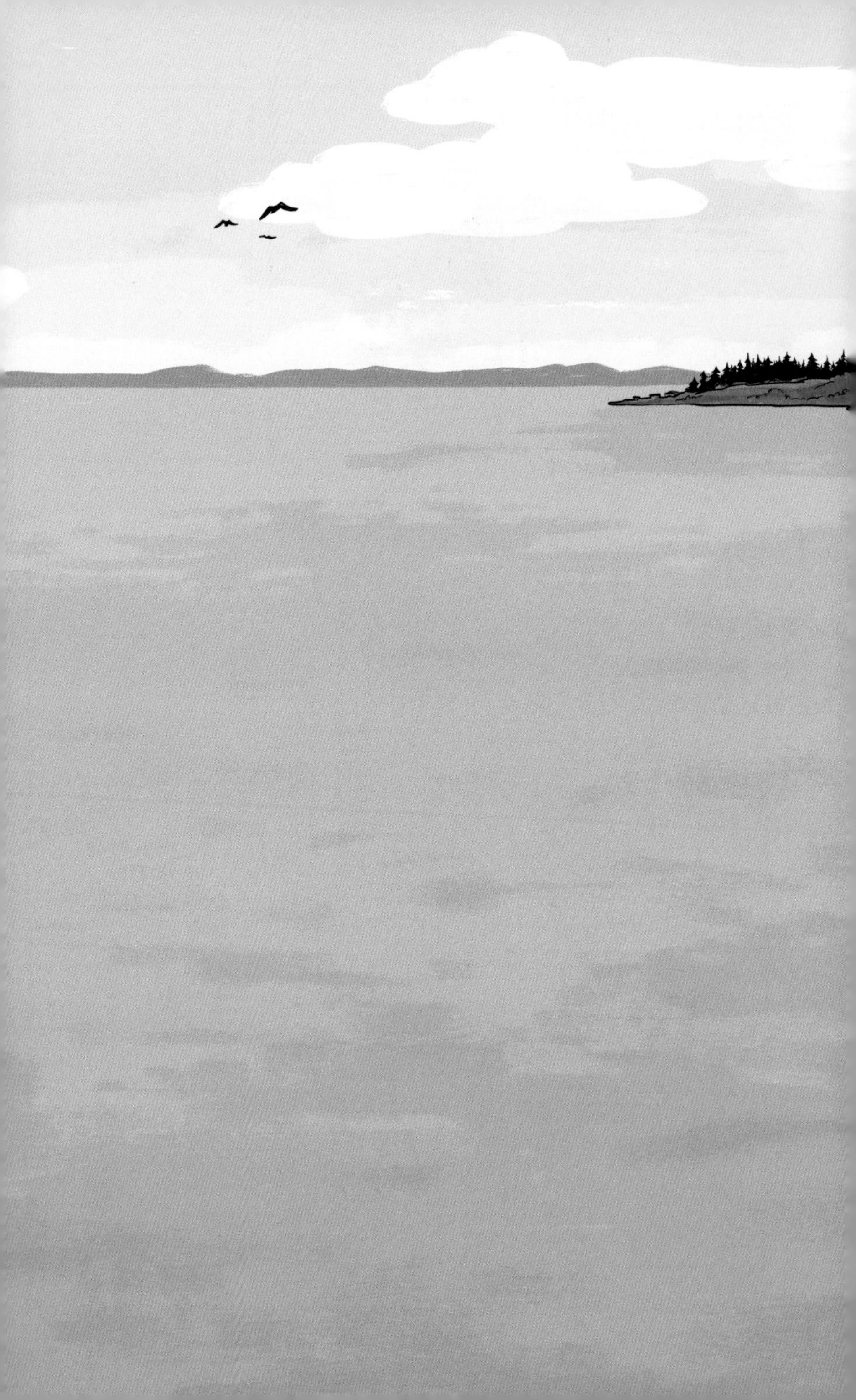

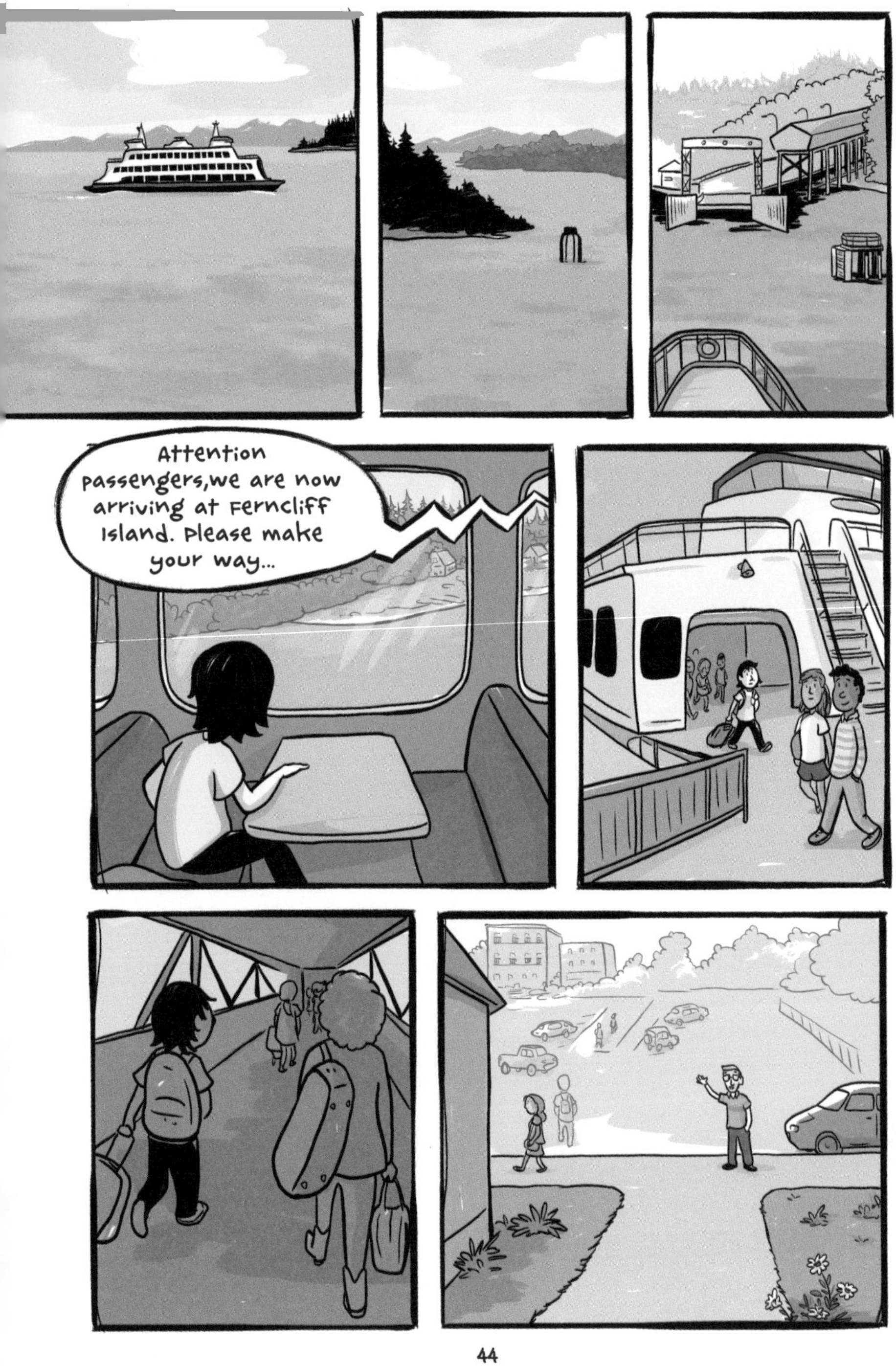
Attention passengers, we are now arriving at Ferncliff Island. Please make your way...

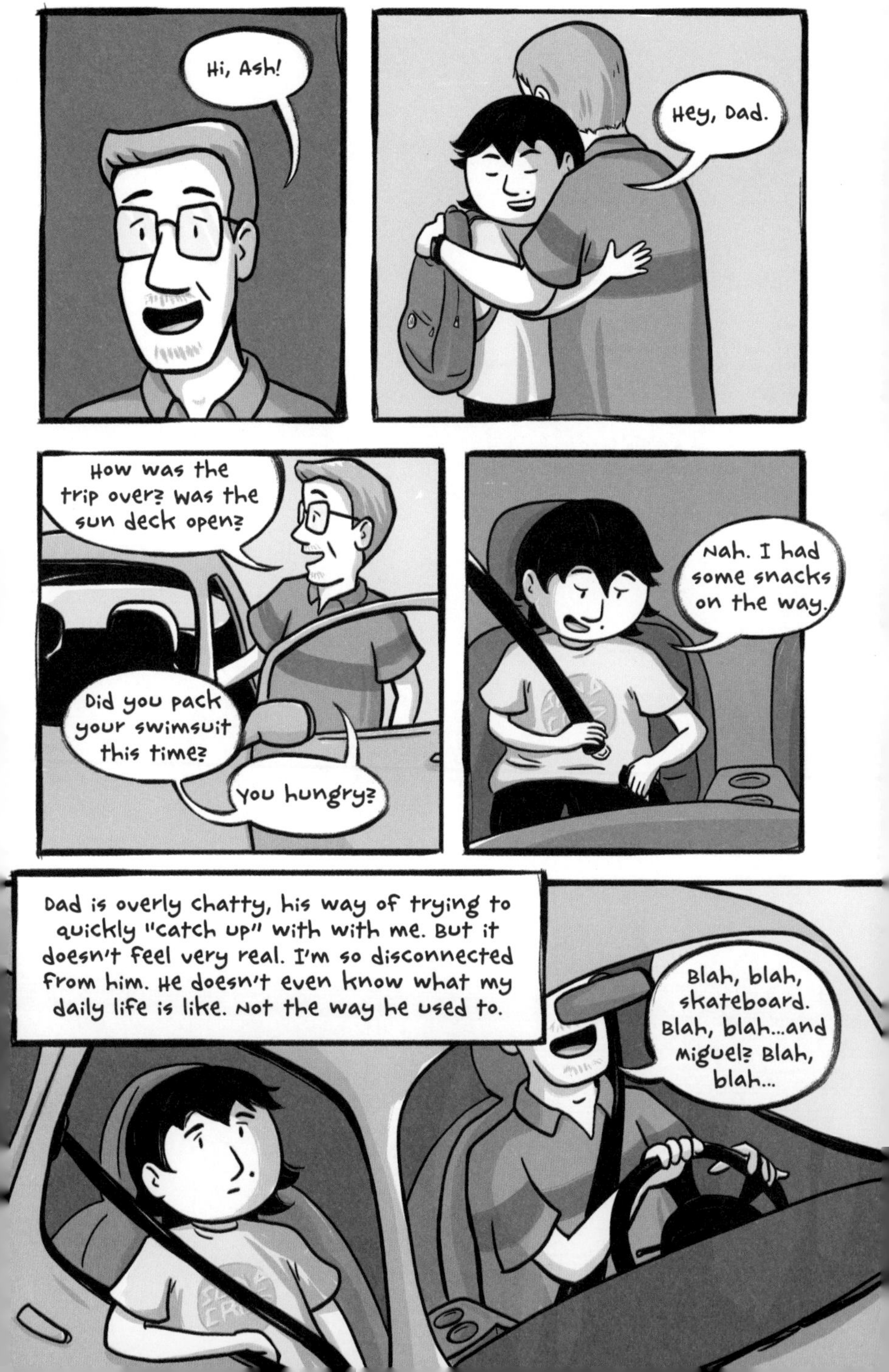
Hi, Ash!
Hey, Dad.
How was the trip over? Was the sun deck open?
Did you pack your swimsuit this time?
You hungry?
Nah. I had some snacks on the way.
Dad is overly chatty, his way of trying to quickly "catch up" with with me. But it doesn't feel very real. I'm so disconnected from him. He doesn't even know what my daily life is like. Not the way he used to.
Blah, blah, skateboard. Blah, blah...and Miguel? Blah, blah...

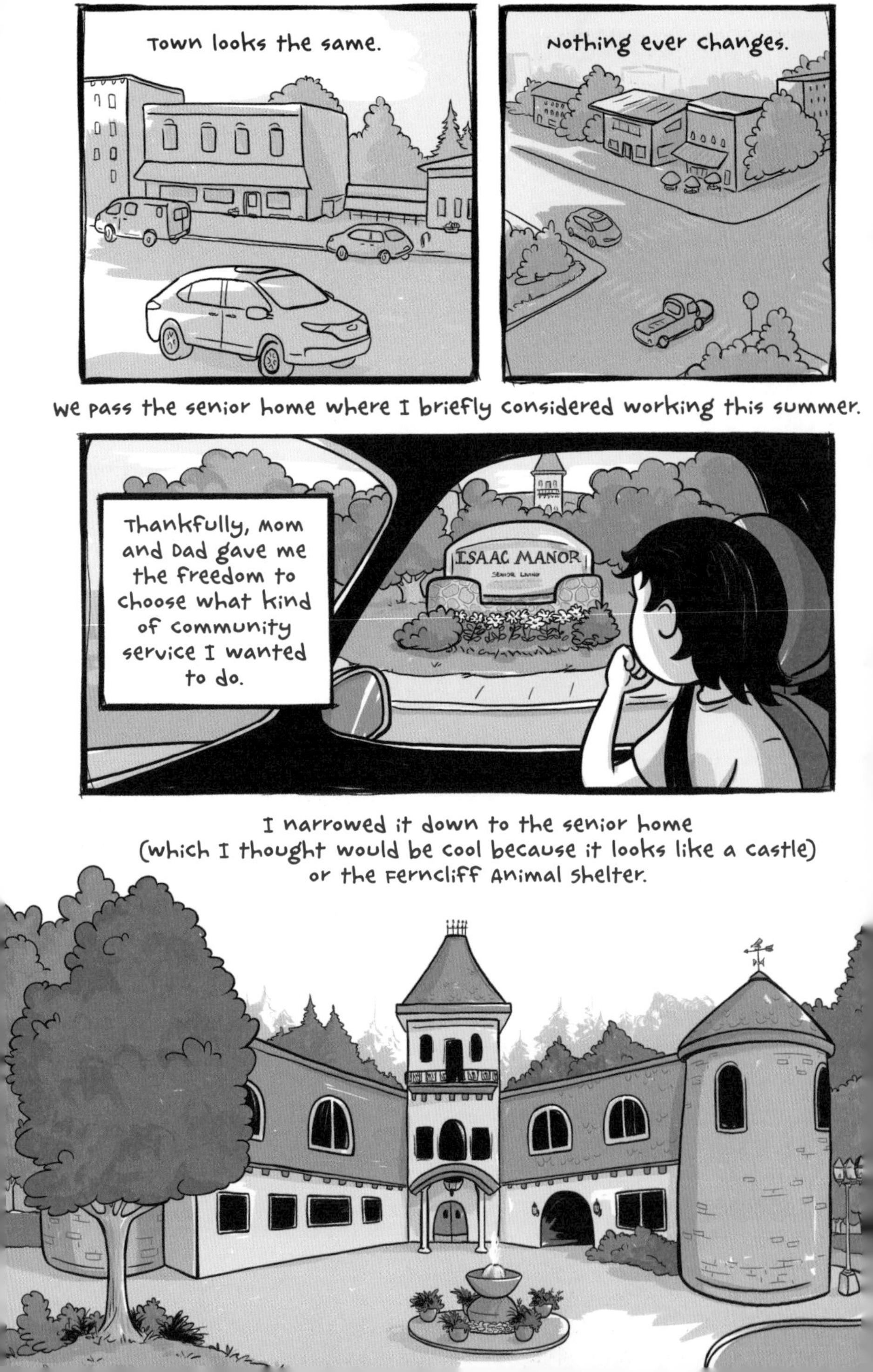

Town looks the same.
Nothing ever changes.
We pass the senior home where I briefly considered working this summer.
Thankfully, Mom and Dad gave me the freedom to choose what kind of community service I wanted to do.
ISAAC MANOR
I narrowed it down to the senior home (which I thought would be cool because it looks like a castle) or the Ferncliff Animal Shelter.

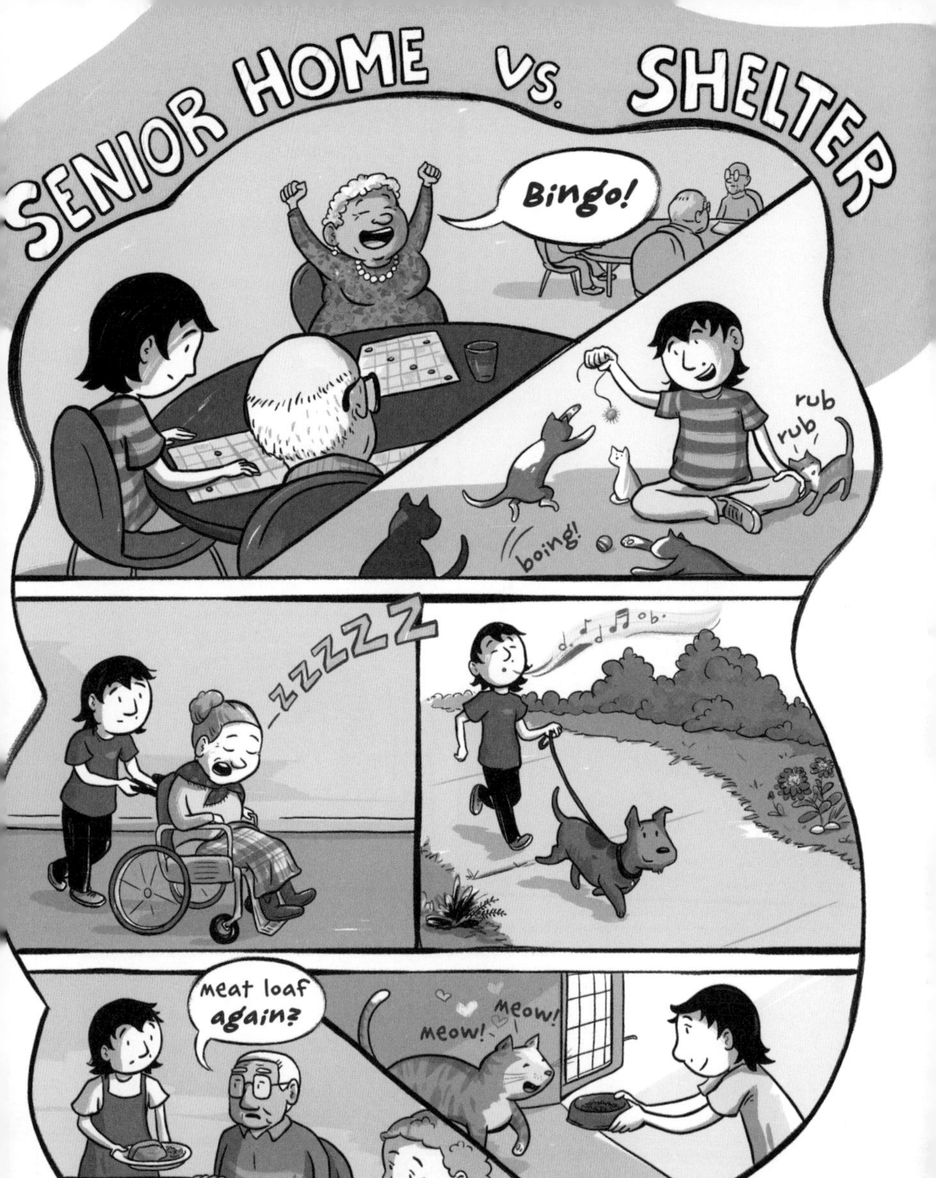
SENIOR HOME vs. SHELTER
Bingo!
rub
rub
boing!
ZZZZZZ
meat loaf again?
meow!
meow!

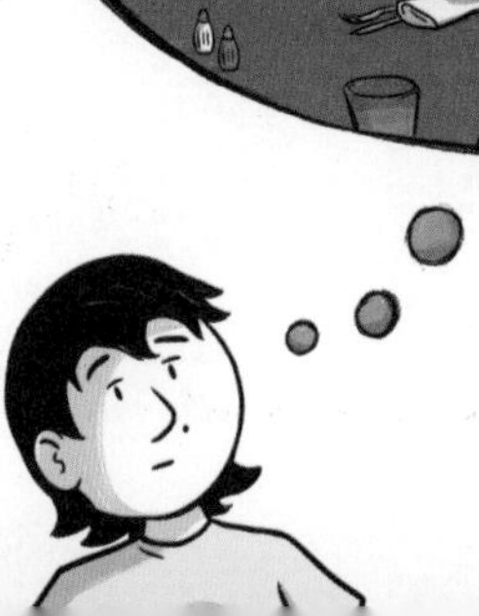

It's not that I'm a ***huge*** animal lover or anything. I like cuddling with my cat, Suki, but honestly, the shelter just seemed way more fun…and the retirement home reminded me too much of Pop.

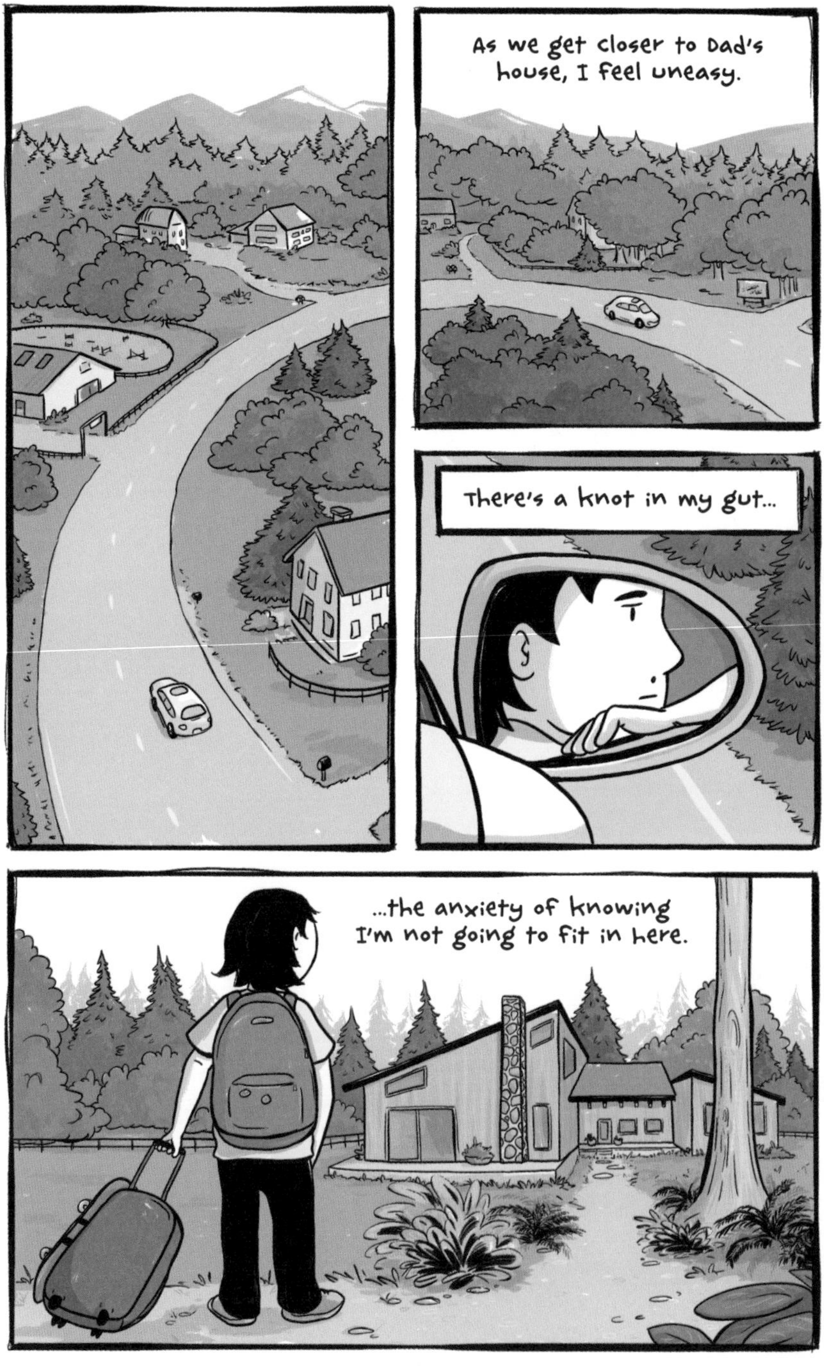
As we get closer to Dad's house, I feel uneasy.
There's a knot in my gut...
...the anxiety of knowing I'm not going to fit in here.

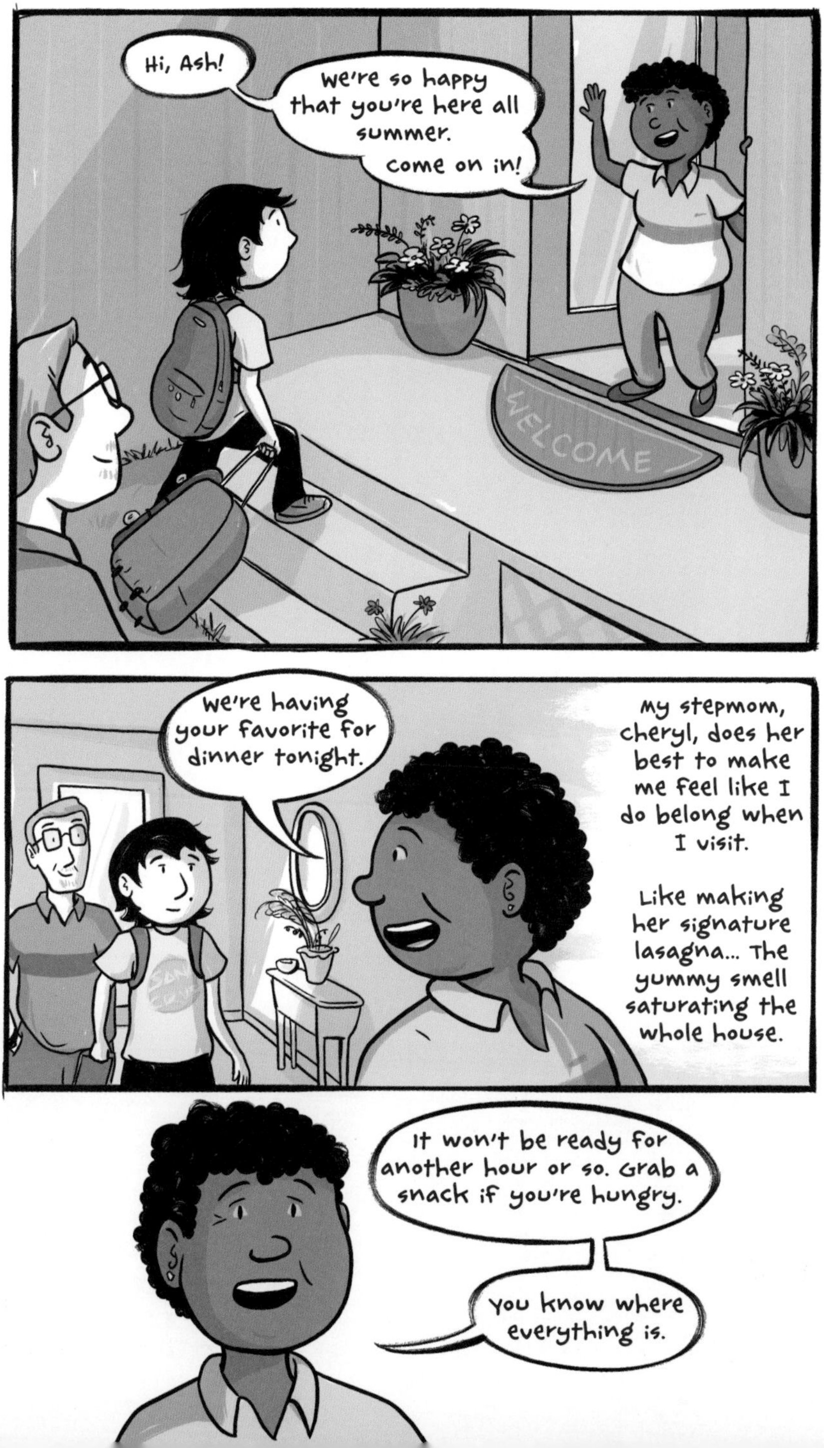
Hi, Ash!
We're so happy that you're here all summer.
Come on in!
We're having your favorite for dinner tonight.
My stepmom, Cheryl, does her best to make me feel like I do belong when I visit.
Like making her signature lasagna... The yummy smell saturating the whole house.
It won't be ready for another hour or so. Grab a snack if you're hungry.
You know where everything is.

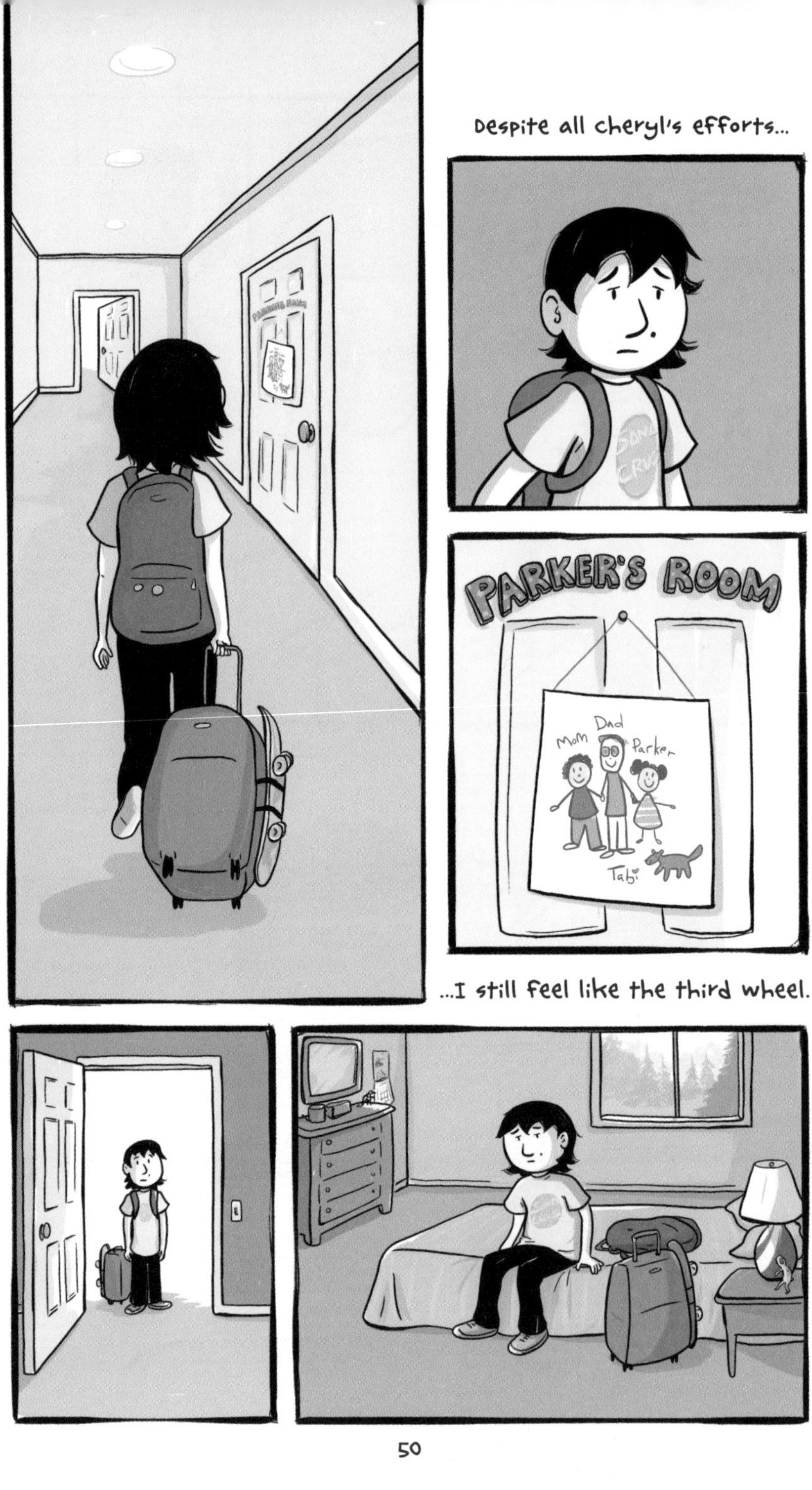
Despite all cheryl's efforts...
PARKER'S ROOM
Dad
Mom
Parker
Tabi
...I still feel like the third wheel.

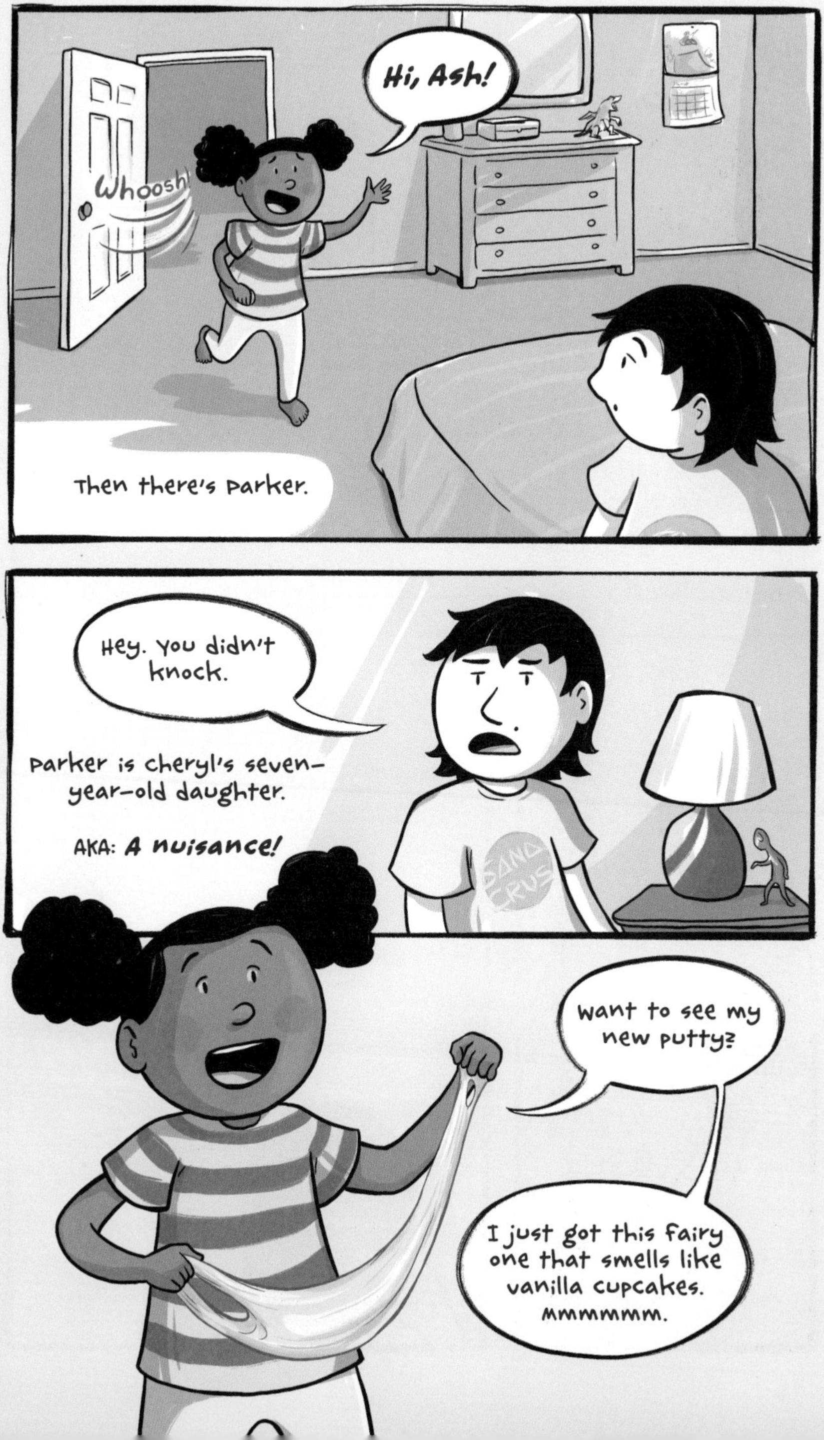
Hi, Ash!
Whoosh!
Then there's Parker.
Hey. You didn't knock.
Parker is Cheryl's seven-year-old daughter.
AKA: A nuisance!
Want to see my new putty?
I just got this fairy one that smells like vanilla cupcakes. Mmmmmm.

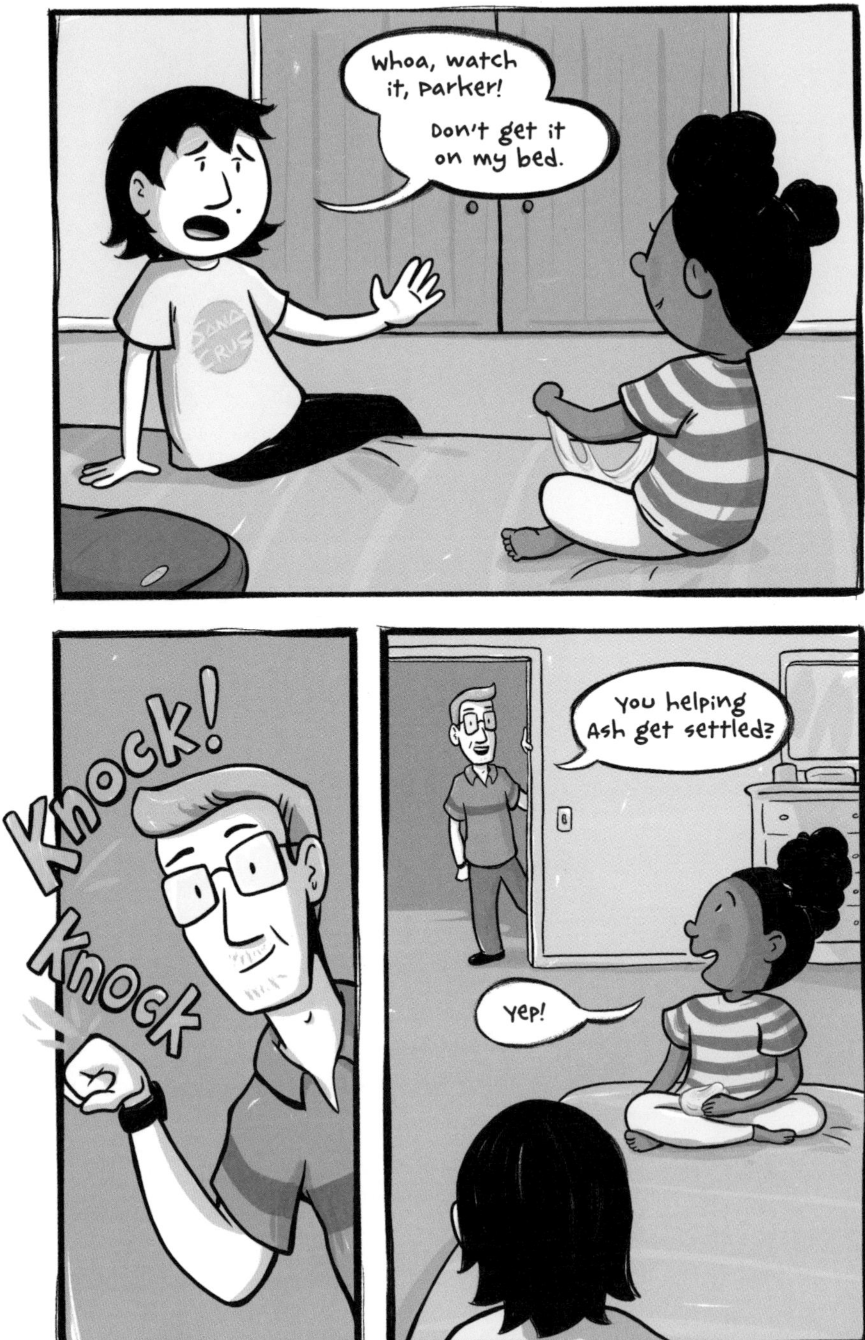
Whoa, watch it, Parker!
Don't get it on my bed.
Knock!
Knock
You helping Ash get settled?
Yep!

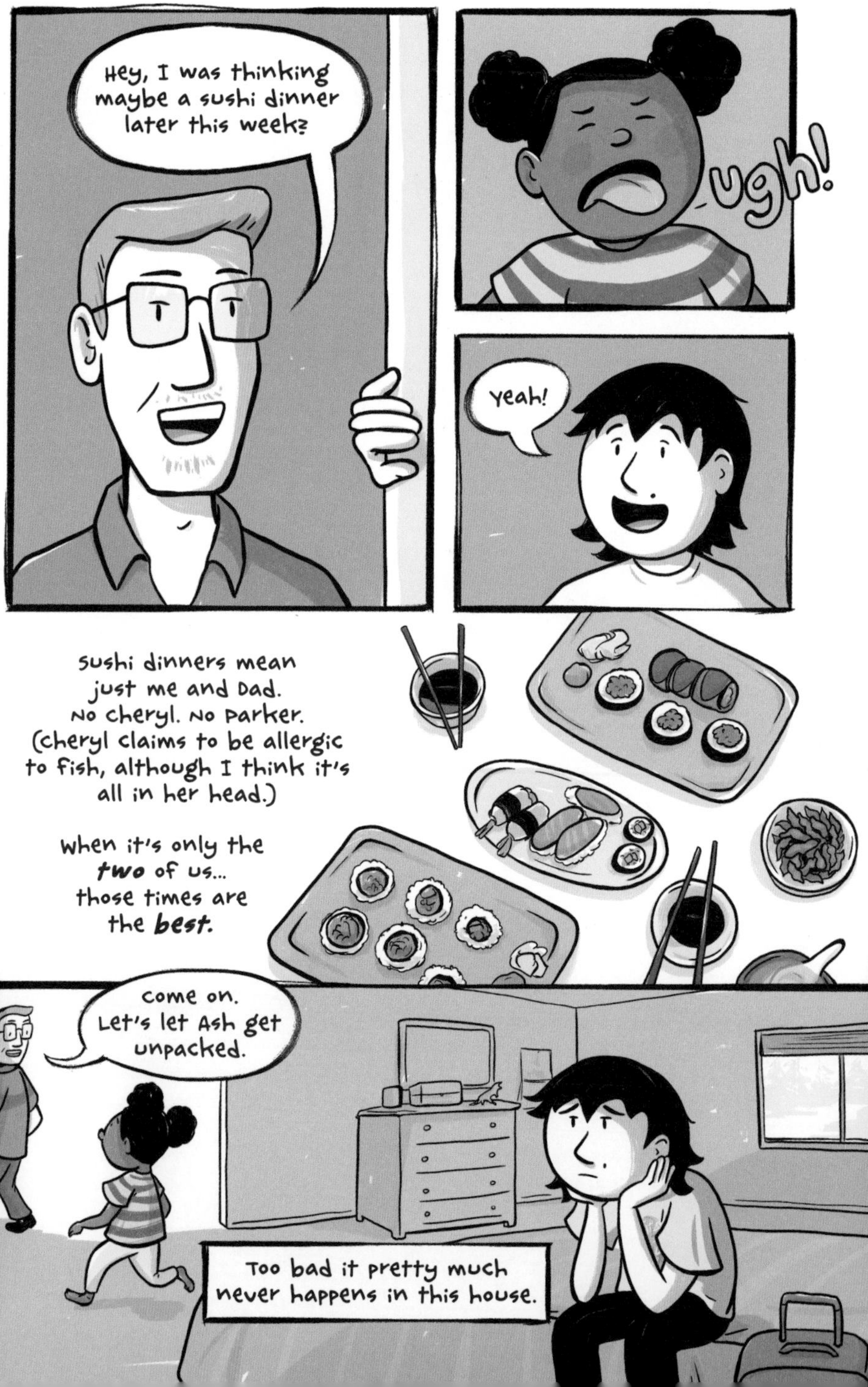
Hey, I was thinking maybe a sushi dinner later this week?
ugh!
Yeah!
Sushi dinners mean just me and Dad.
No Cheryl. No Parker.
(Cheryl claims to be allergic to fish, although I think it's all in her head.)
When it's only the *two* of us... those times are the *best*.
Come on. Let's let Ash get unpacked.
Too bad it pretty much never happens in this house.

CHAPTER 3

• Tabitha •

A vocal and sassy standard schnauzer who likes to talk back and is the "sock monster" of the house. Schnauzers are snappy-looking dogs with arched brows and whiskered faces. Originally used as a ratter, herder, and watchdog, they are vivacious, playful, and lovable with their families. However, they can be a bit stubborn and are quick to bark at any disturbance.

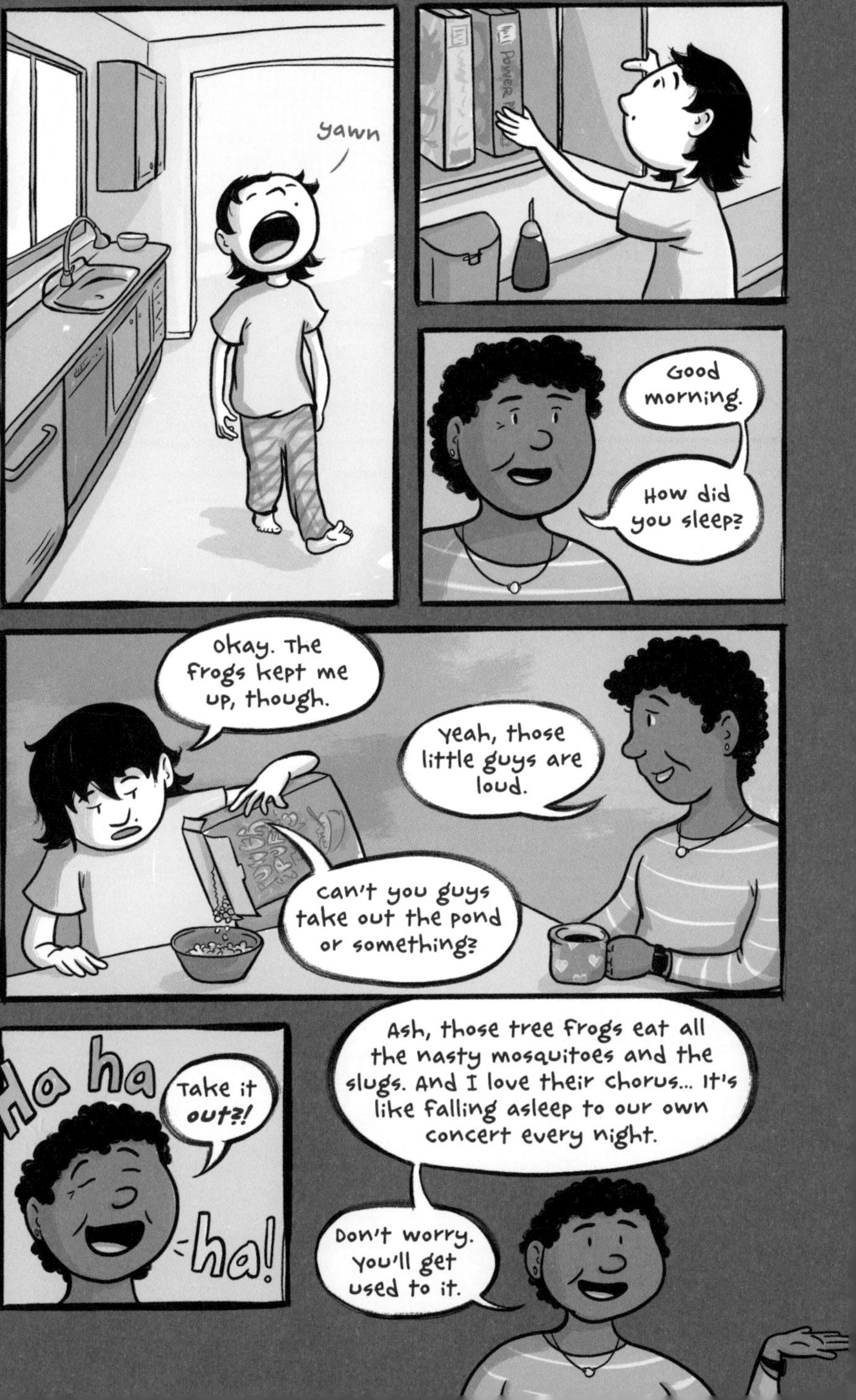
yawn
POWER P
Good morning.
How did you sleep?
Okay. The frogs kept me up, though.
Yeah, those little guys are loud.
Can't you guys take out the pond or something?
Ha ha
Take it *out?!*
ha!
Ash, those tree frogs eat all the nasty mosquitoes and the slugs. And I love their chorus... It's like falling asleep to our own concert every night.
Don't worry. You'll get used to it.

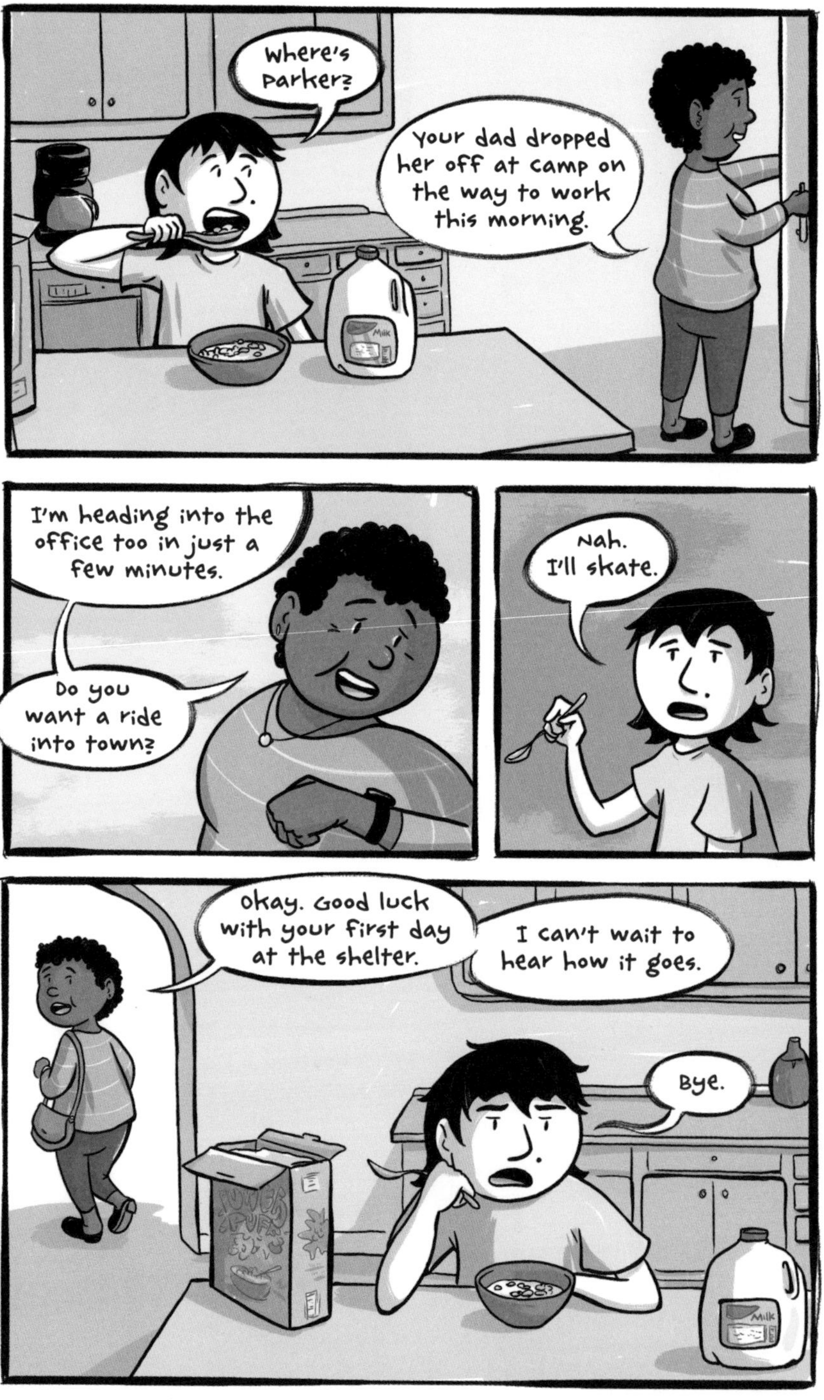
Where's Parker?
Your dad dropped her off at camp on the way to work this morning.
I'm heading into the office too in just a few minutes.
Do you want a ride into town?
Nah. I'll skate.
Okay. Good luck with your first day at the shelter.
I can't wait to hear how it goes.
Bye.
MILK

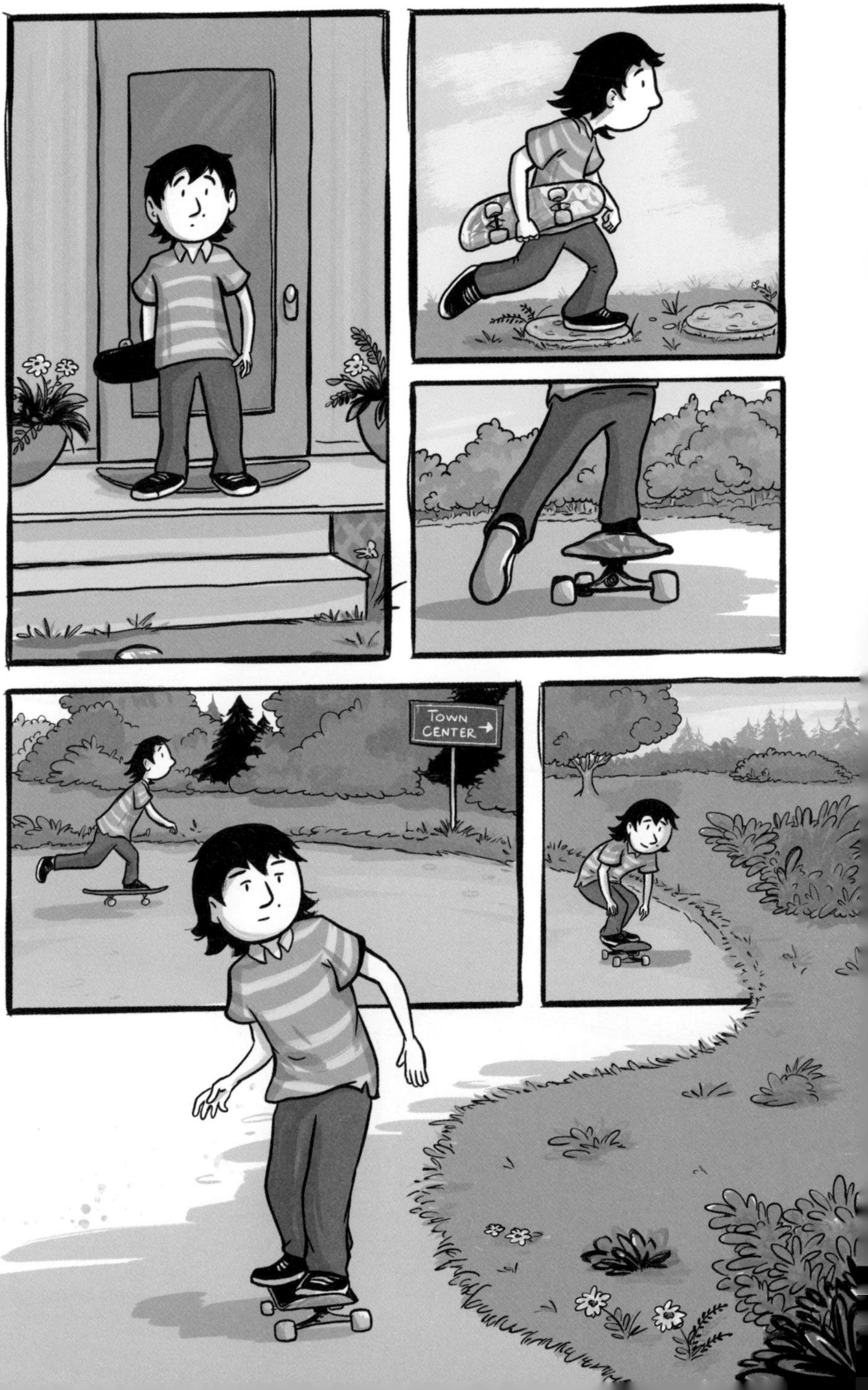
TOWN CENTER →

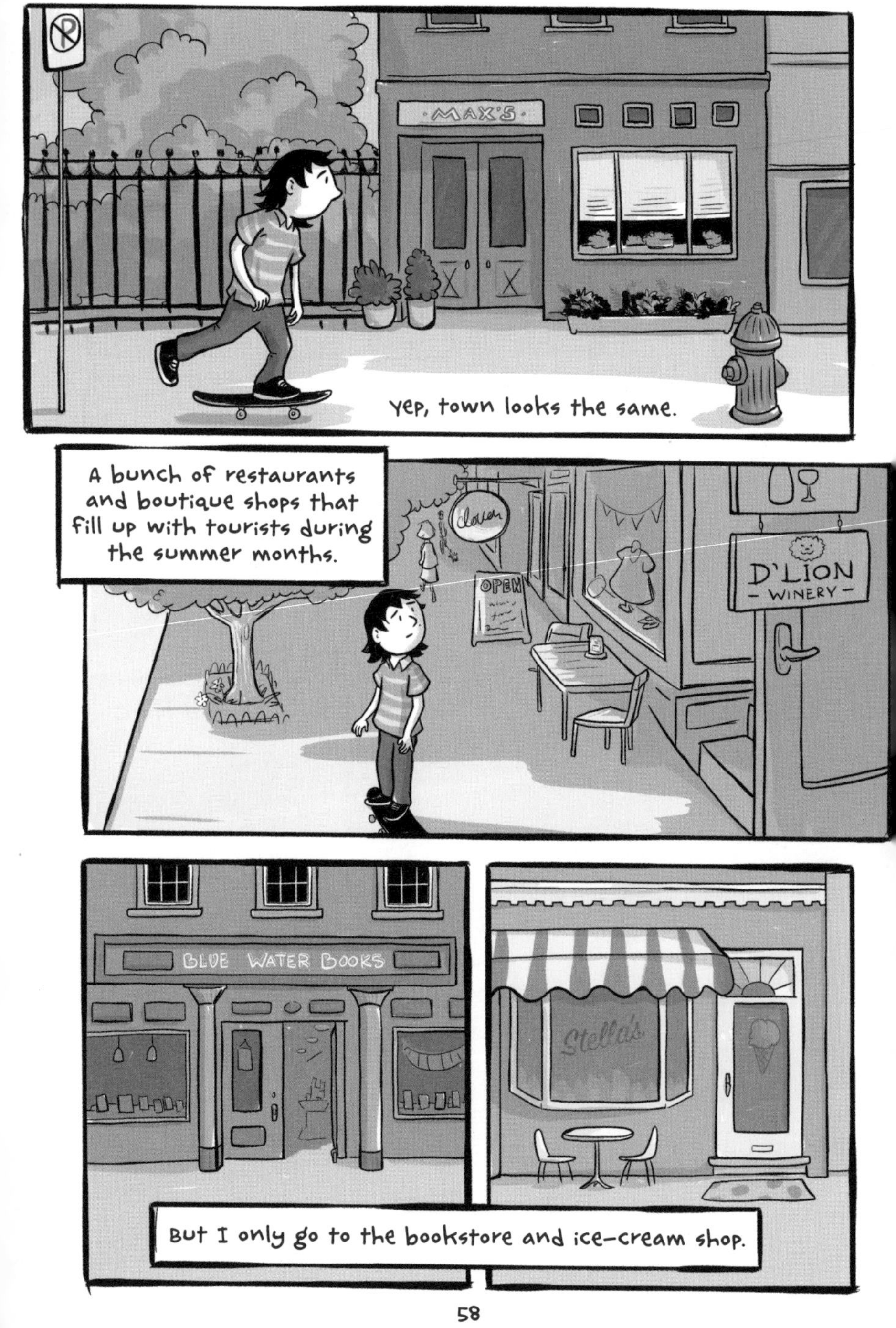
MAX'S
Yep, town looks the same.
A bunch of restaurants and boutique shops that fill up with tourists during the summer months.
clover
OPEN
D'LION
- WINERY -
BLUE WATER BOOKS
Stella's
But I only go to the bookstore and ice-cream shop.

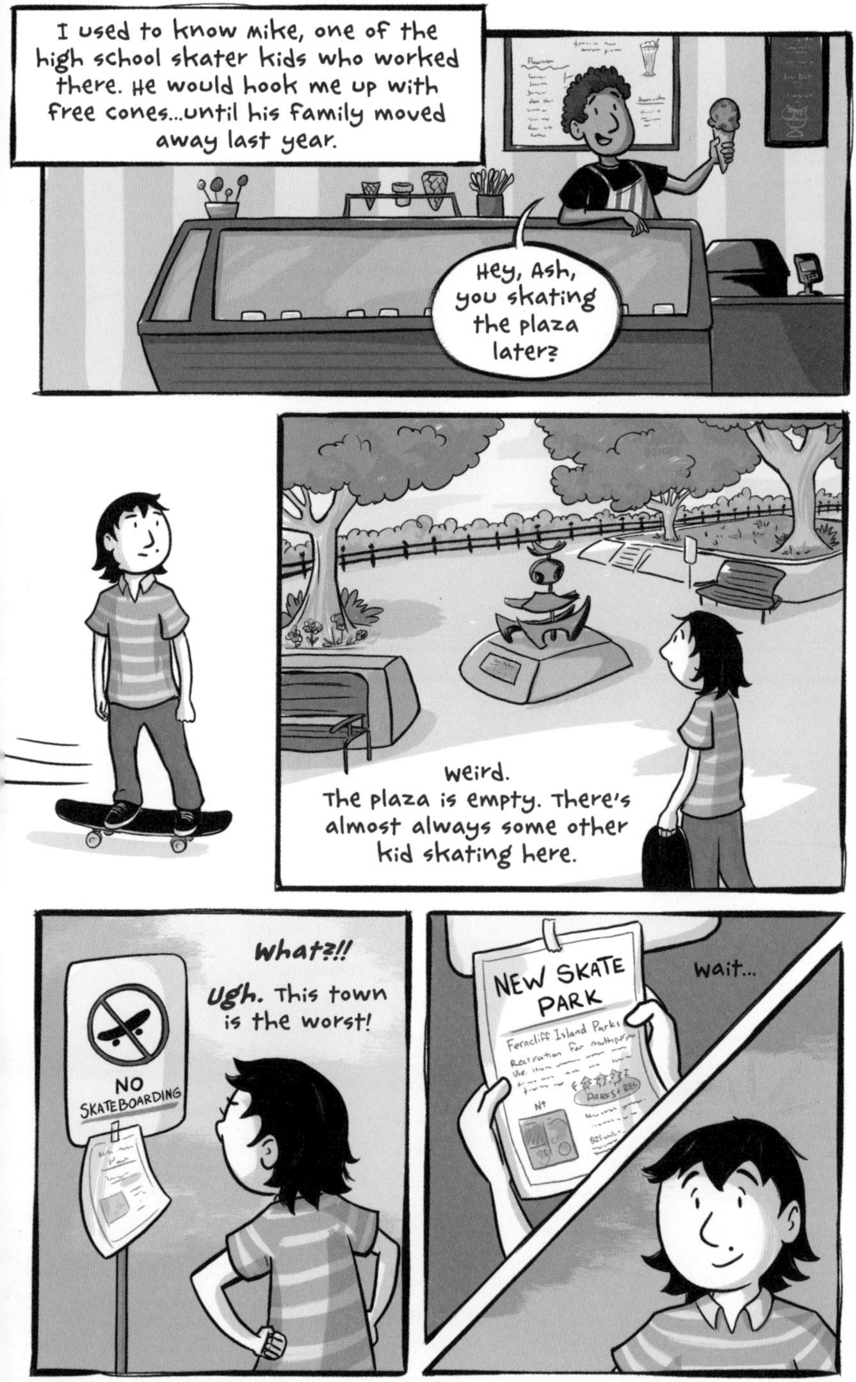

I used to know Mike, one of the high school skater kids who worked there. He would hook me up with free cones...until his family moved away last year.
Hey, Ash, you skating the plaza later?
Weird. The plaza is empty. There's almost always some other kid skating here.
What?!!
Ugh. This town is the worst!
NO SKATEBOARDING
NEW SKATE PARK
Wait...

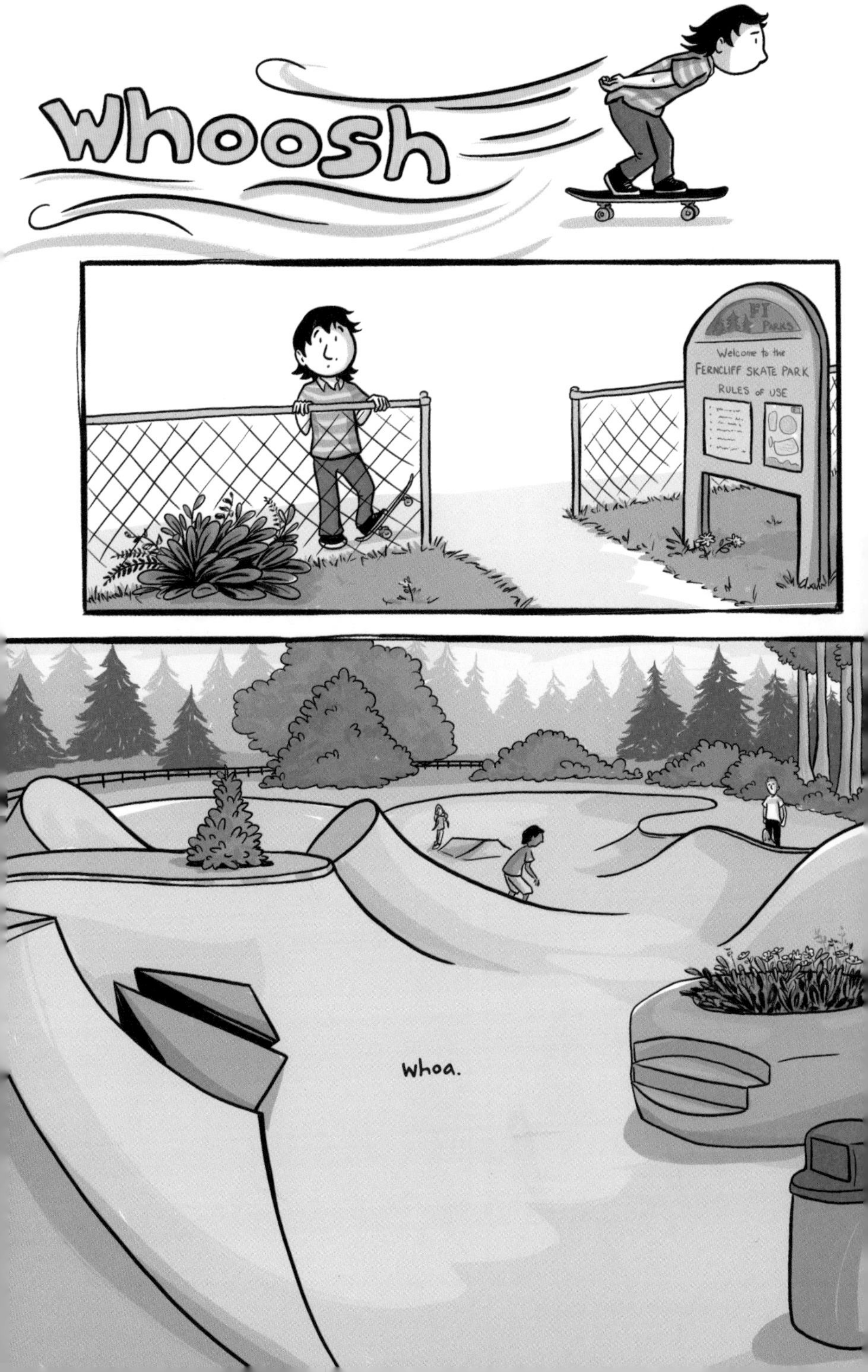
Whoosh
PARKS
Welcome to the
FERNCLIFF SKATE PARK
RULES of USE
Whoa.

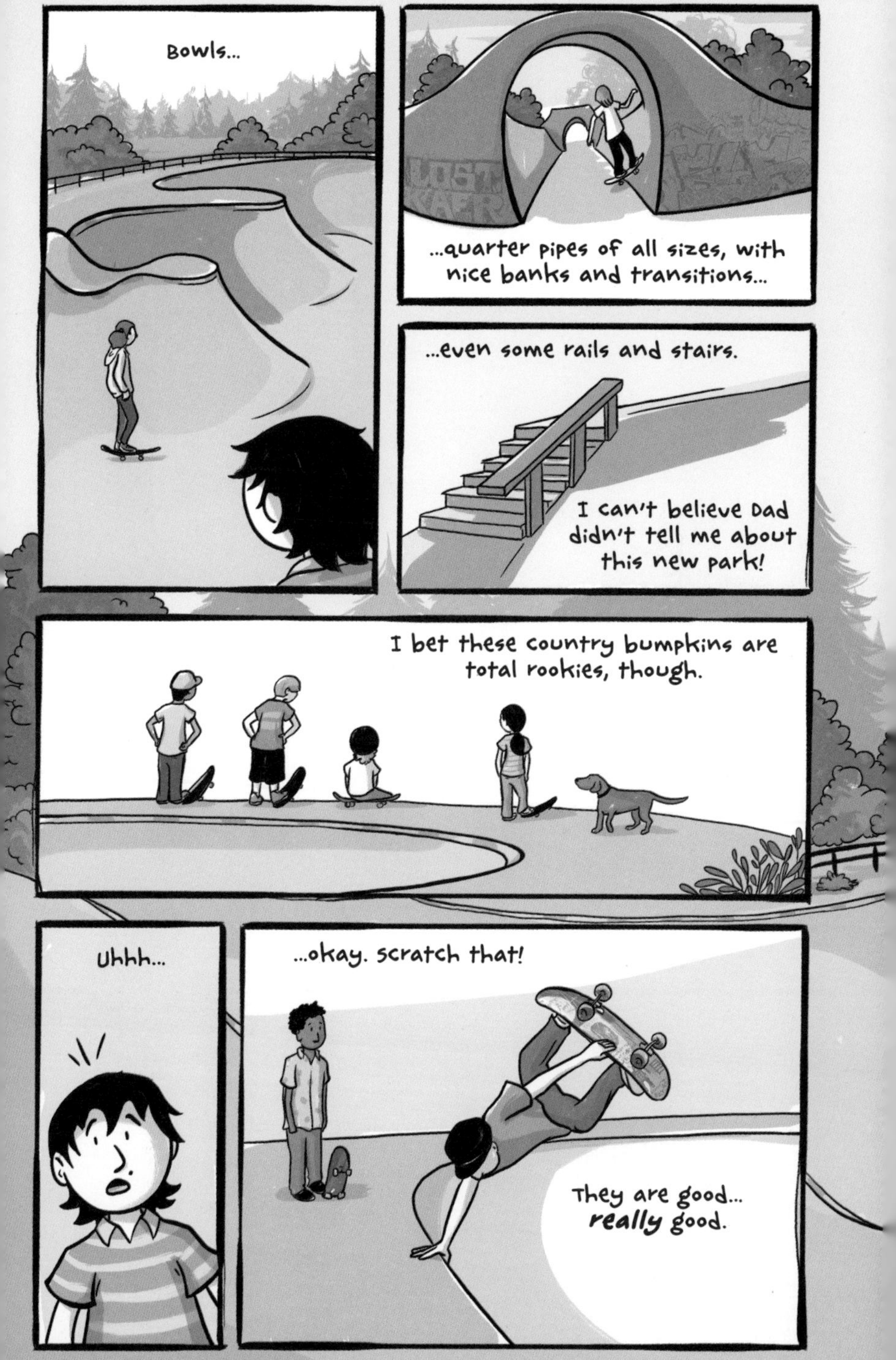
Bowls...
...quarter pipes of all sizes, with nice banks and transitions...
...even some rails and stairs.
I can't believe Dad didn't tell me about this new park!
I bet these country bumpkins are total rookies, though.
Uhhh...
...okay. Scratch that!
They are good... *really* good.

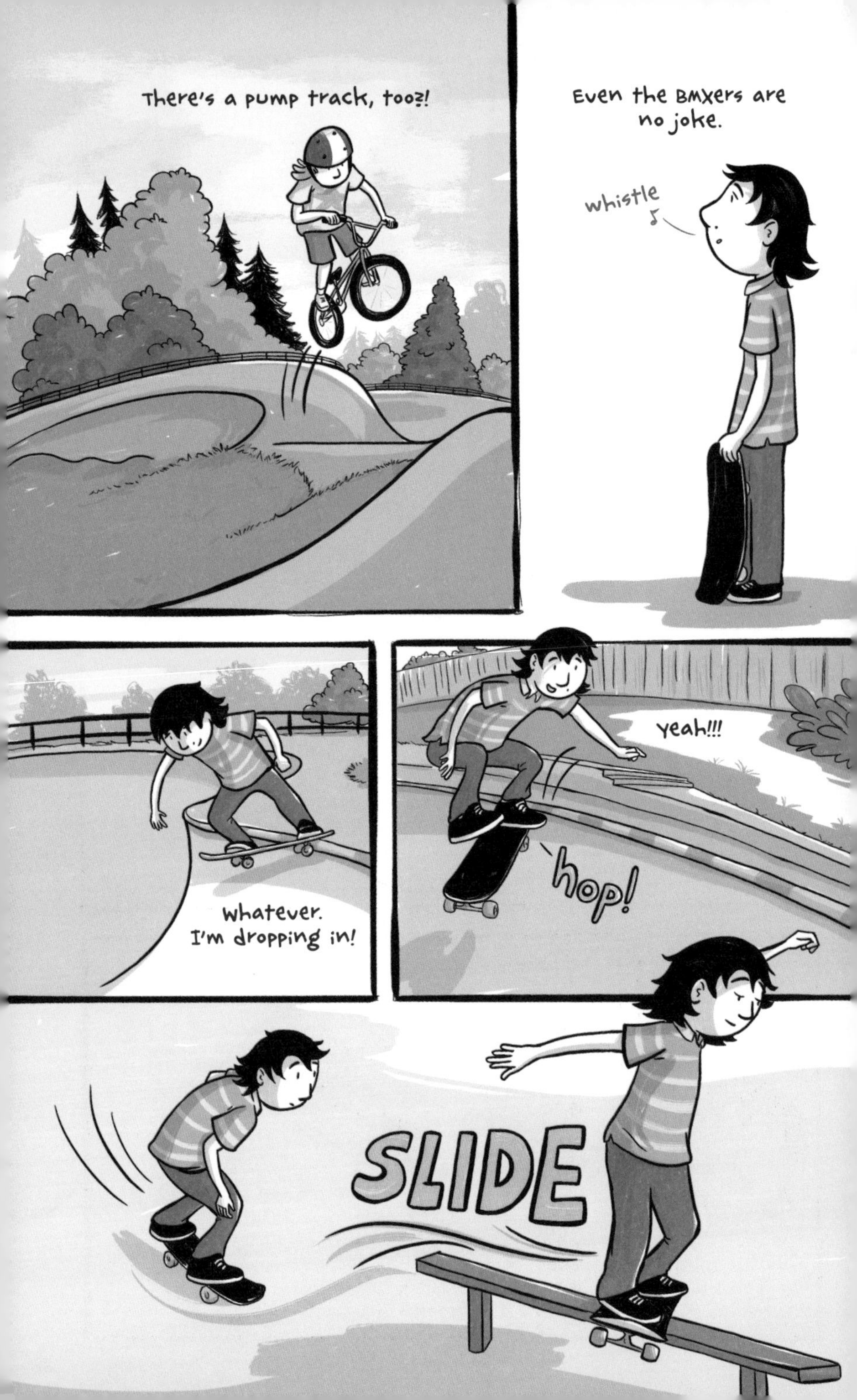
There's a pump track, too?!
Even the BMXers are no joke.
whistle
Whatever. I'm dropping in!
Yeah!!!
hop!
SLIDE

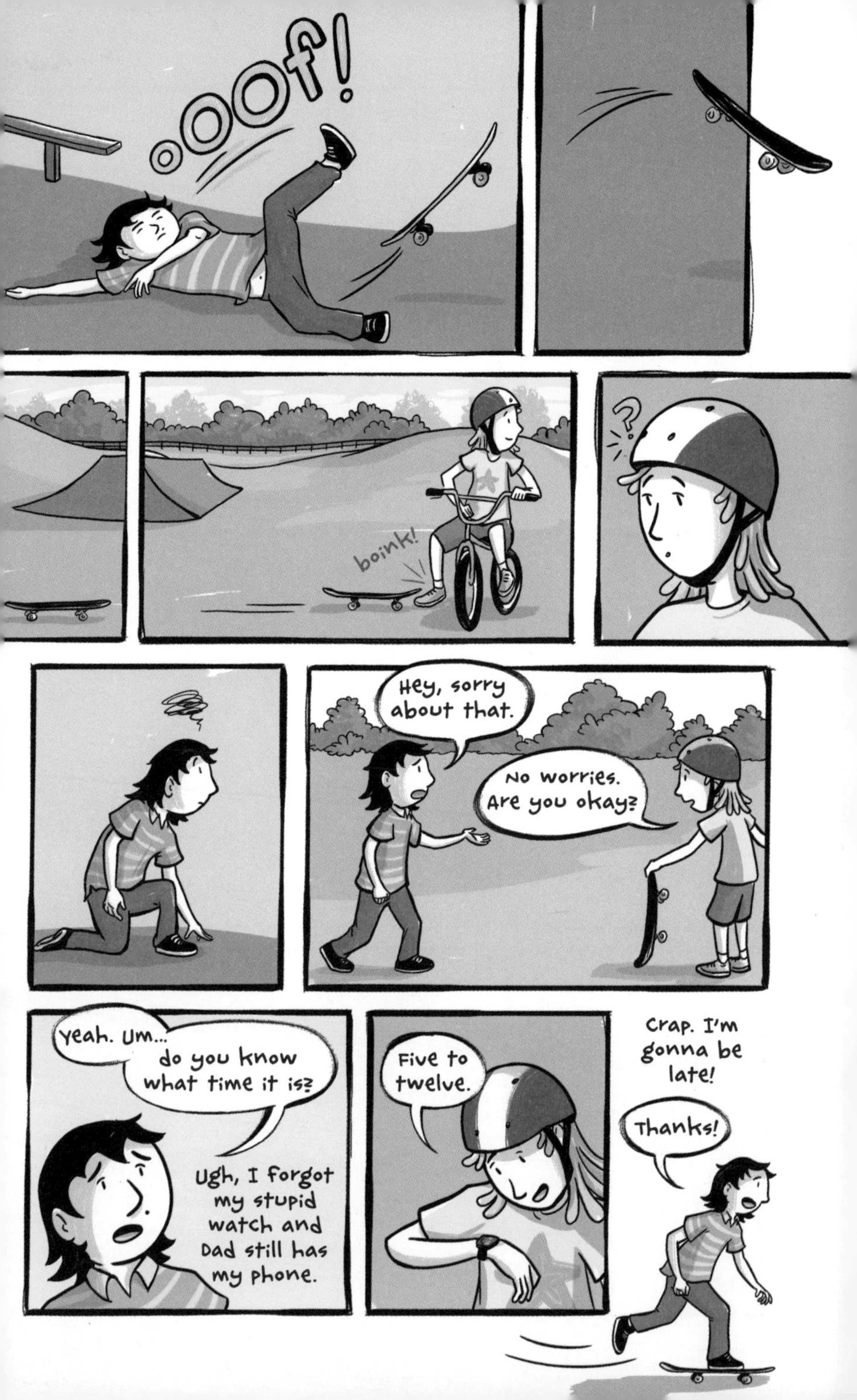
.oOOf!
boink!
Hey, sorry about that.
No worries. Are you okay?
Yeah. Um...
do you know what time it is?
Ugh, I forgot my stupid watch and Dad still has my phone.
Five to twelve.
Crap. I'm gonna be late!
Thanks!

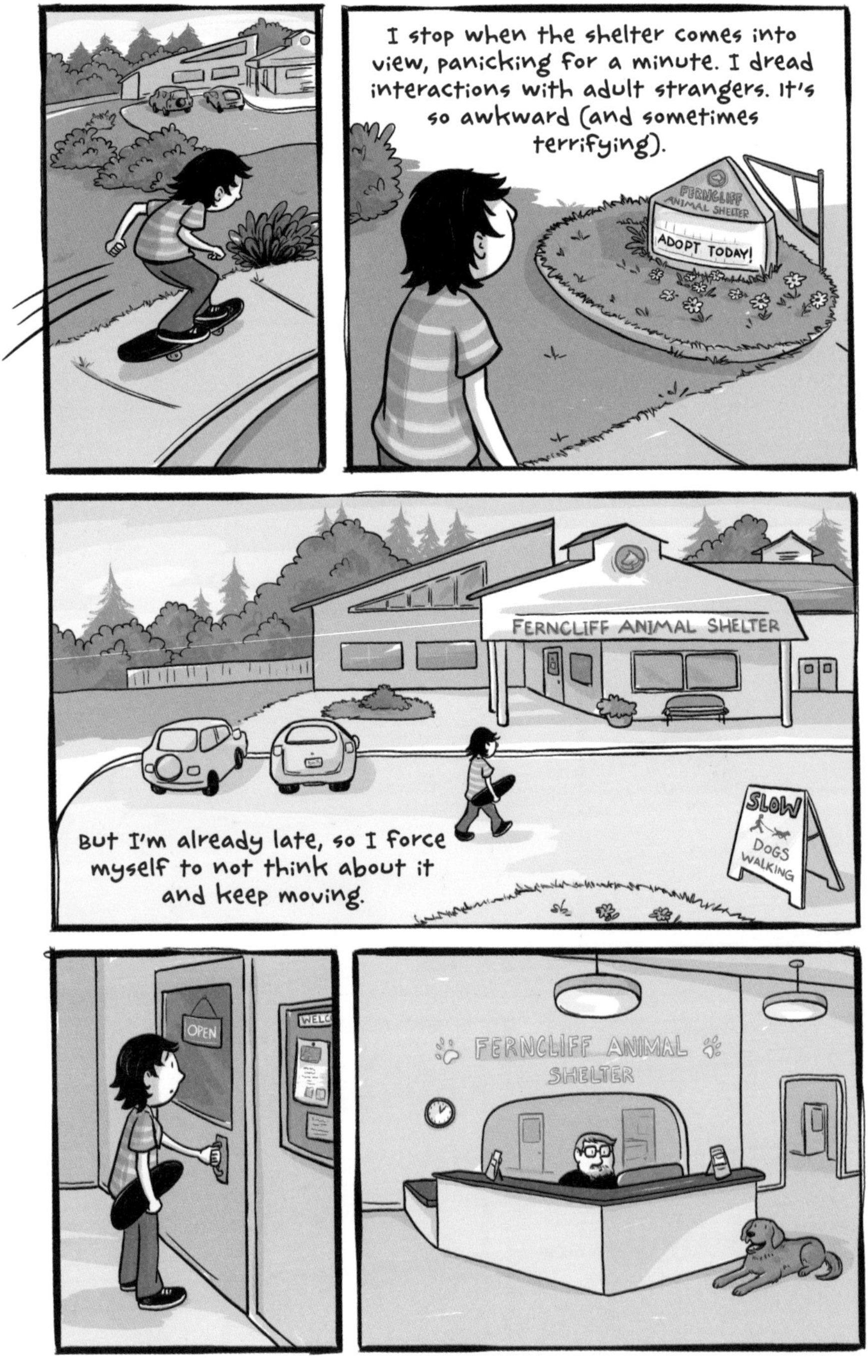
I stop when the shelter comes into view, panicking for a minute. I dread interactions with adult strangers. It's so awkward (and sometimes terrifying).
FERNCLIFF ANIMAL SHELTER
ADOPT TODAY!
FERNCLIFF ANIMAL SHELTER
SLOW
DOGS WALKING
But I'm already late, so I force myself to not think about it and keep moving.
OPEN
FERNCLIFF ANIMAL SHELTER

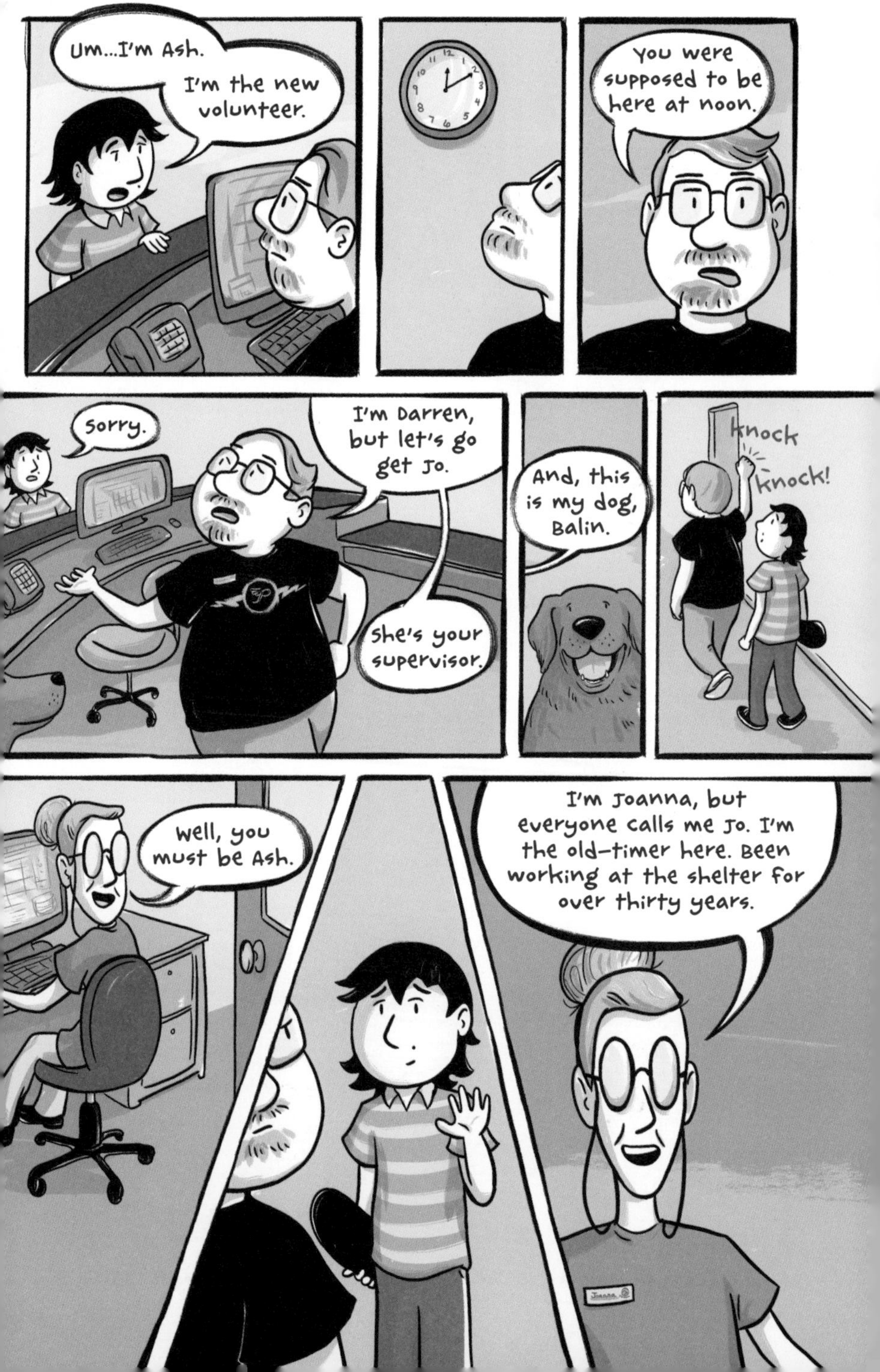
Um...I'm Ash.
I'm the new volunteer.
You were supposed to be here at noon.
Sorry.
I'm Darren, but let's go get Jo.
She's your supervisor.
And, this is my dog, Balin.
knock
knock!
Well, you must be Ash.
I'm Joanna, but everyone calls me Jo. I'm the old-timer here. Been working at the shelter for over thirty years.

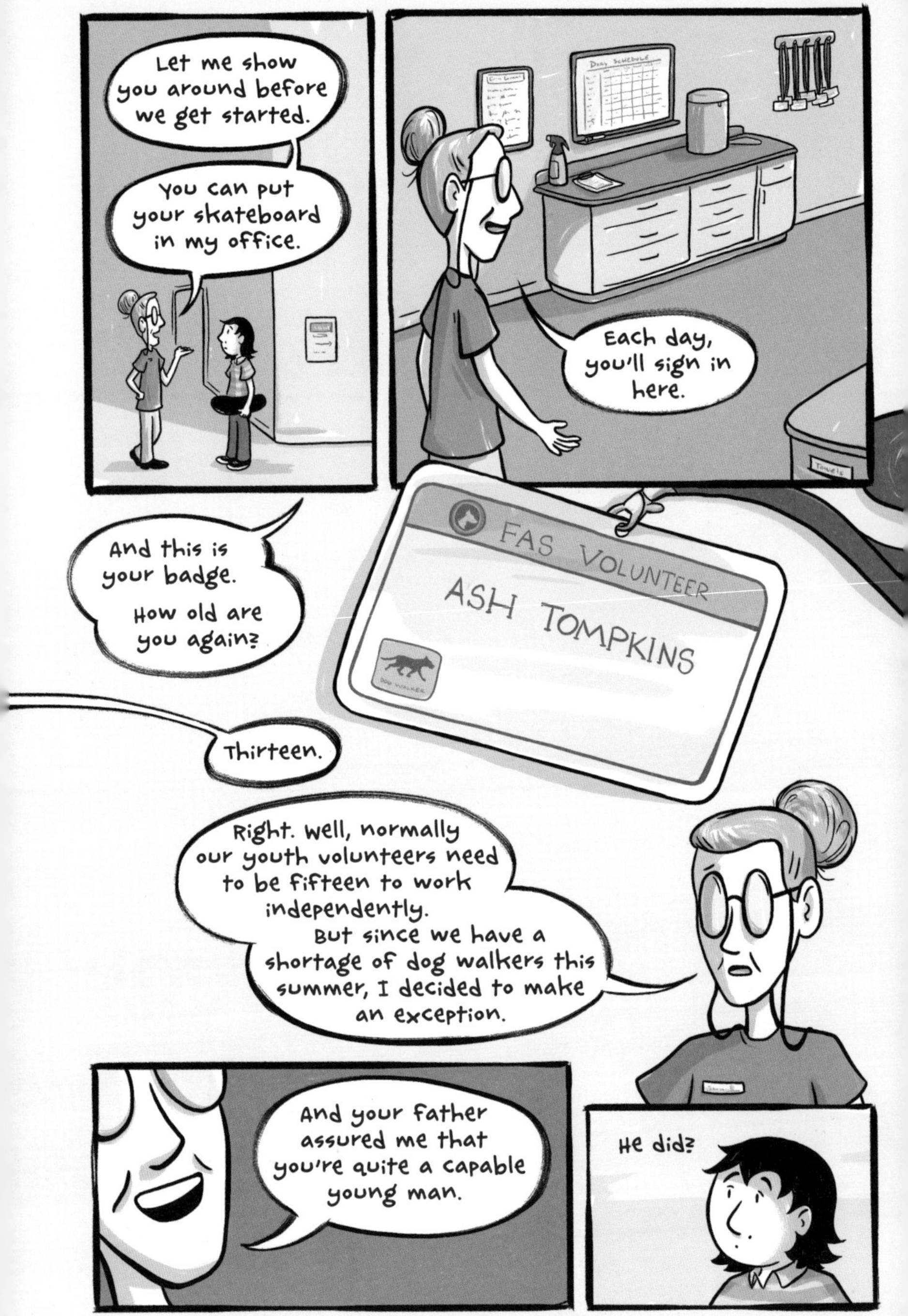
Let me show you around before we get started.
You can put your skateboard in my office.
Each day, you'll sign in here.
Towels
And this is your badge.
How old are you again?
FAS Volunteer
ASH TOMPKINS
Thirteen.
Right. Well, normally our youth volunteers need to be fifteen to work independently.
But since we have a shortage of dog walkers this summer, I decided to make an exception.
And your father assured me that you're quite a capable young man.
He did?

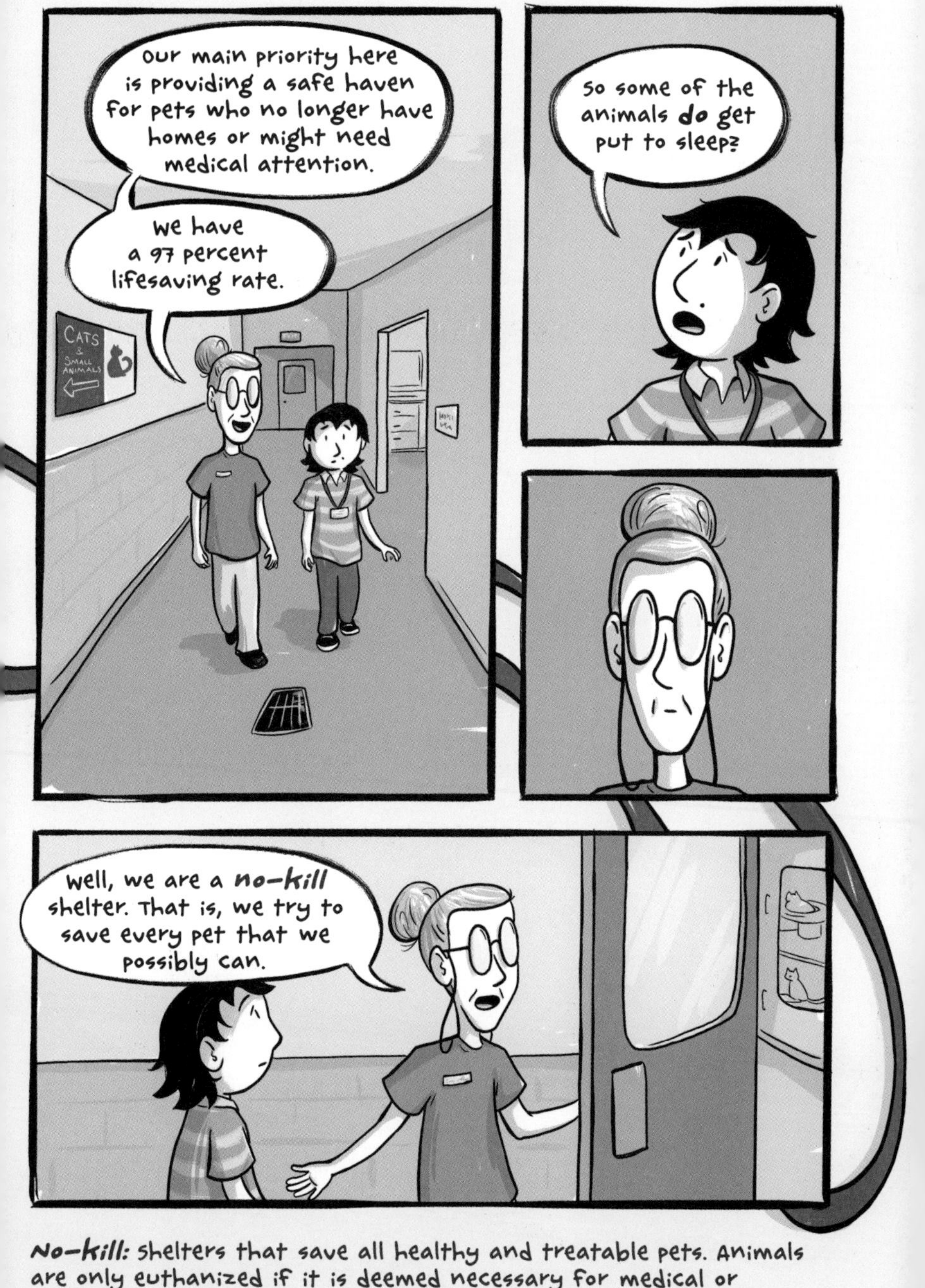
CATS & SMALL ANIMALS
Our main priority here is providing a safe haven for pets who no longer have homes or might need medical attention.
We have a 97 percent lifesaving rate.
So some of the animals **do** get put to sleep?
Well, we are a ***no-kill*** shelter. That is, we try to save every pet that we possibly can.

No-kill: shelters that save all healthy and treatable pets. Animals are only euthanized if it is deemed necessary for medical or behavioral issues--never due to lack of space or length of stay.

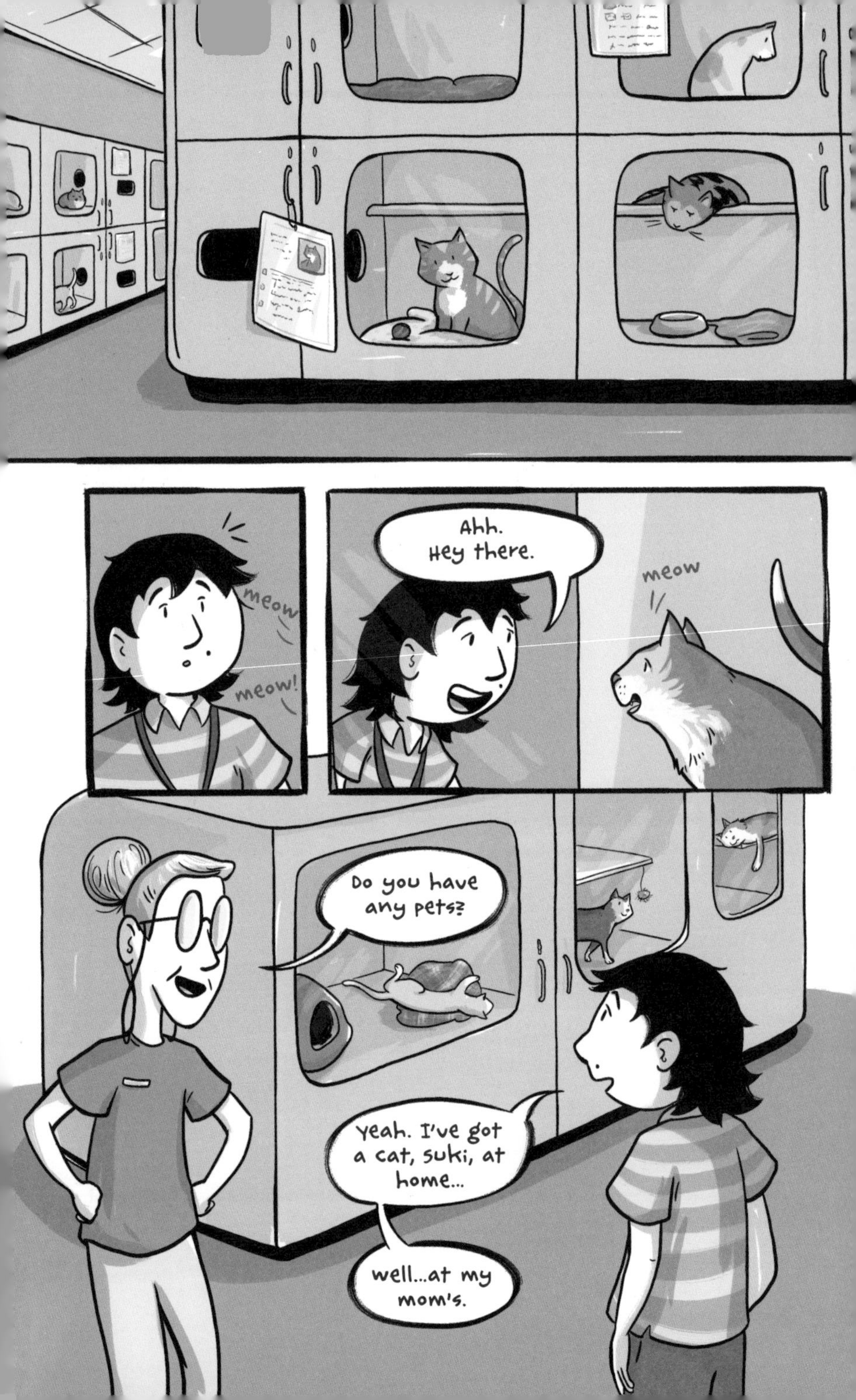
meow
meow!
Ahh.
Hey there.
meow
Do you have any pets?
Yeah. I've got a cat, Suki, at home...
Well...at my mom's.

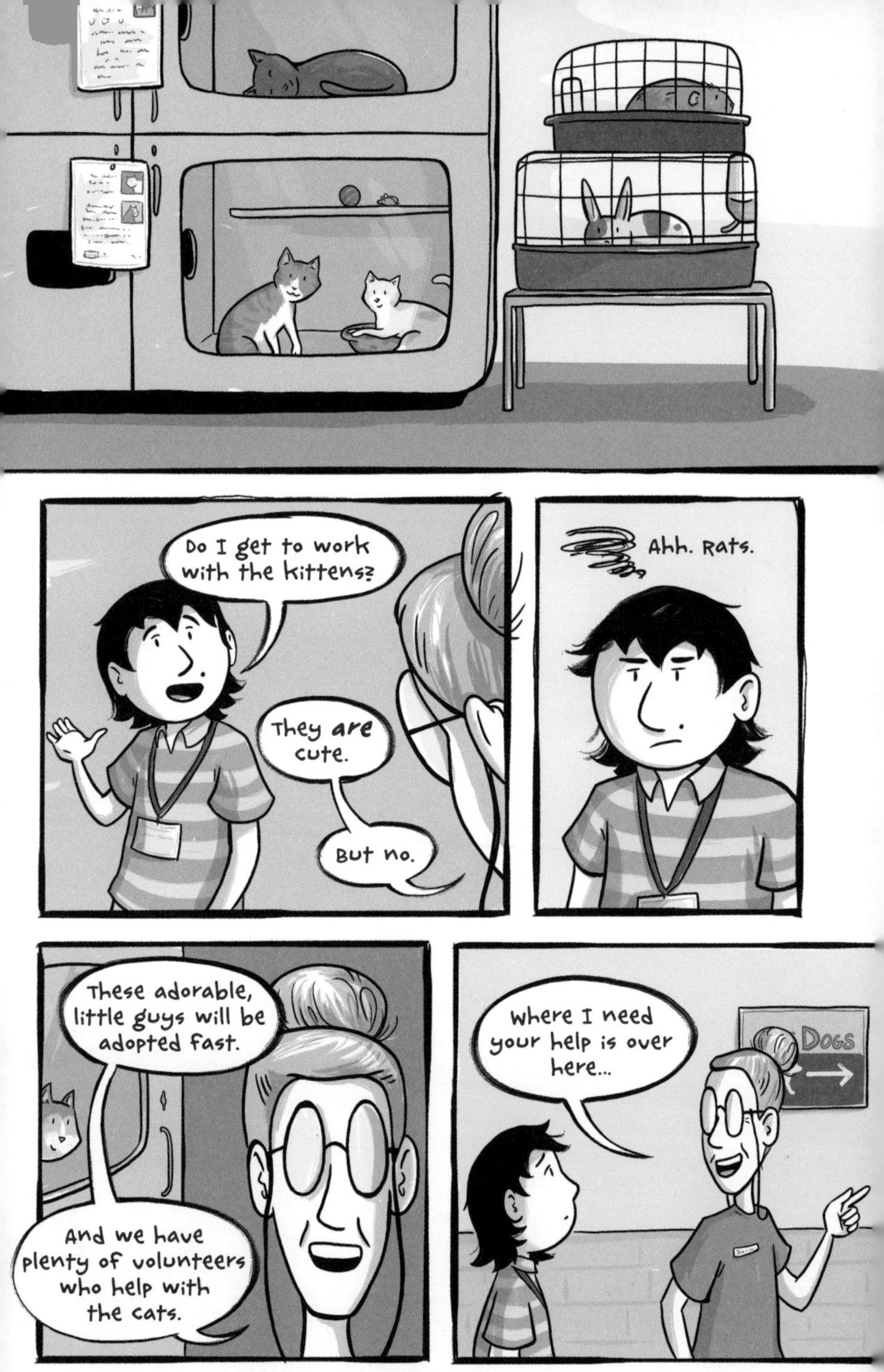
Do I get to work with the kittens?
They are cute.
But no.
Ahh. Rats.
These adorable, little guys will be adopted fast.
And we have plenty of volunteers who help with the cats.
Where I need your help is over here...
DOGS

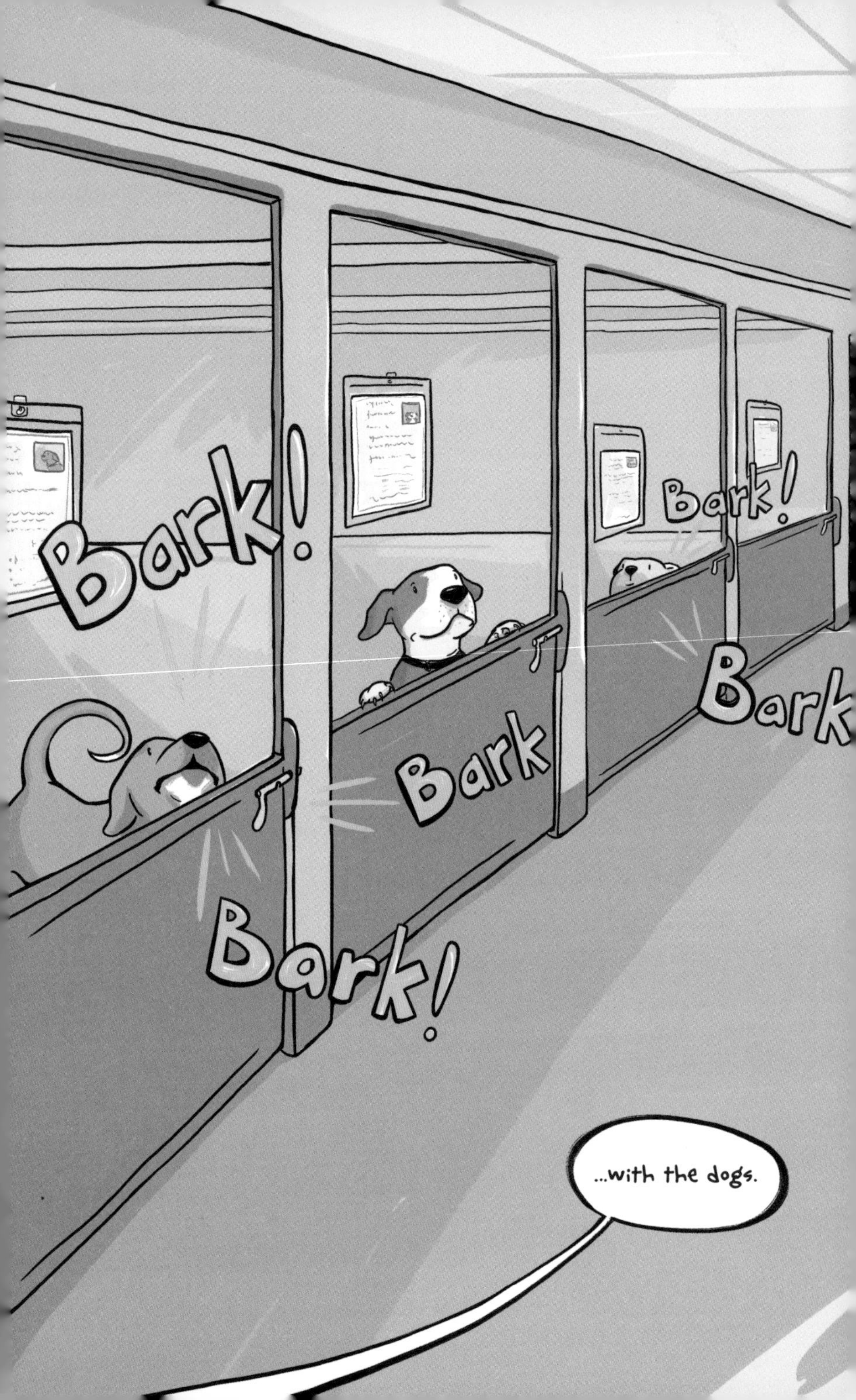
Bark!
Bark!
Bark
Bark
Bark!
...with the dogs.

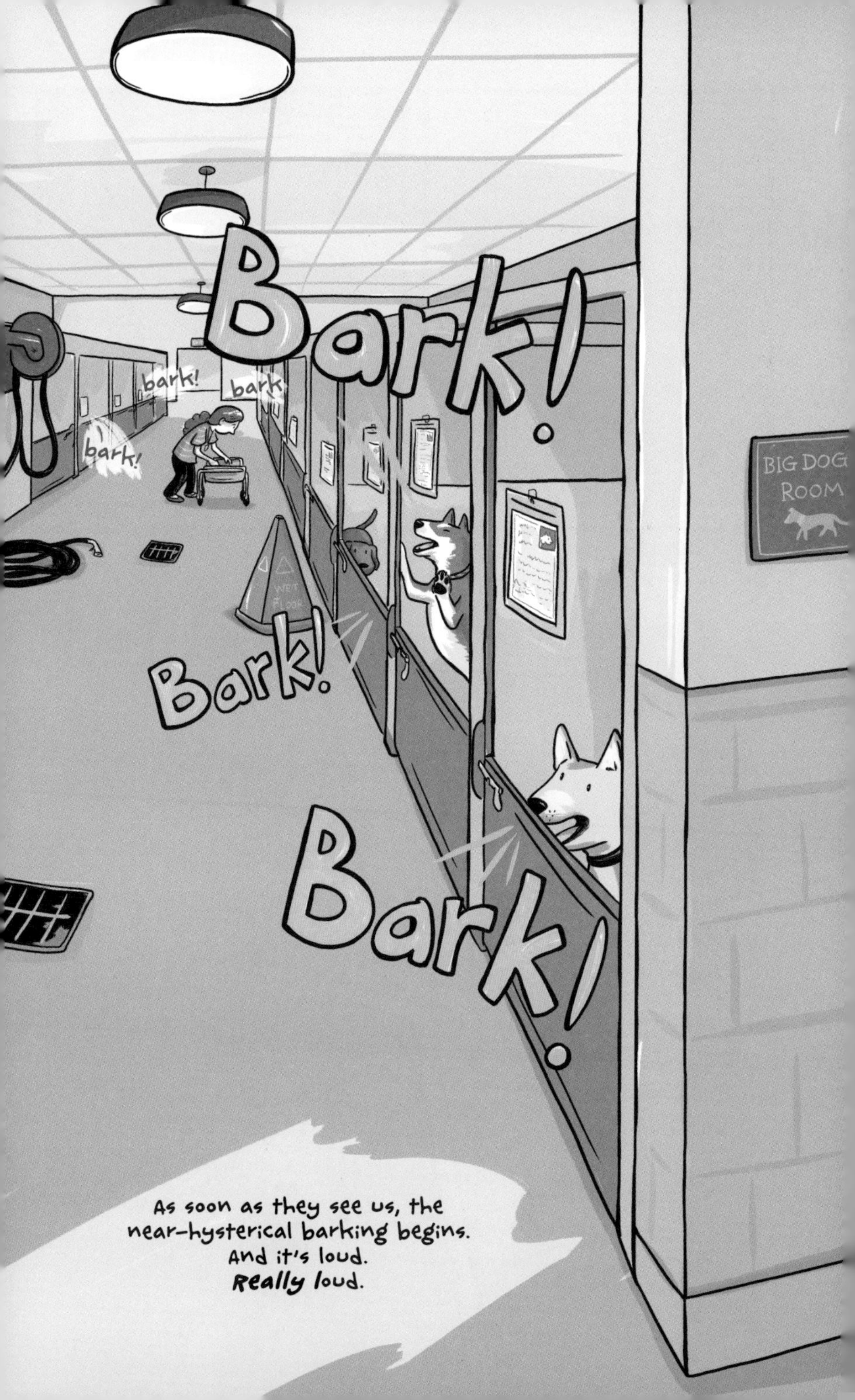

bark!
bark
bark!
Bark!
BIG DOG ROOM
WET FLOOR
Bark!
Bark!
As soon as they see us, the
near-hysterical barking begins.
And it's loud.
Really loud.

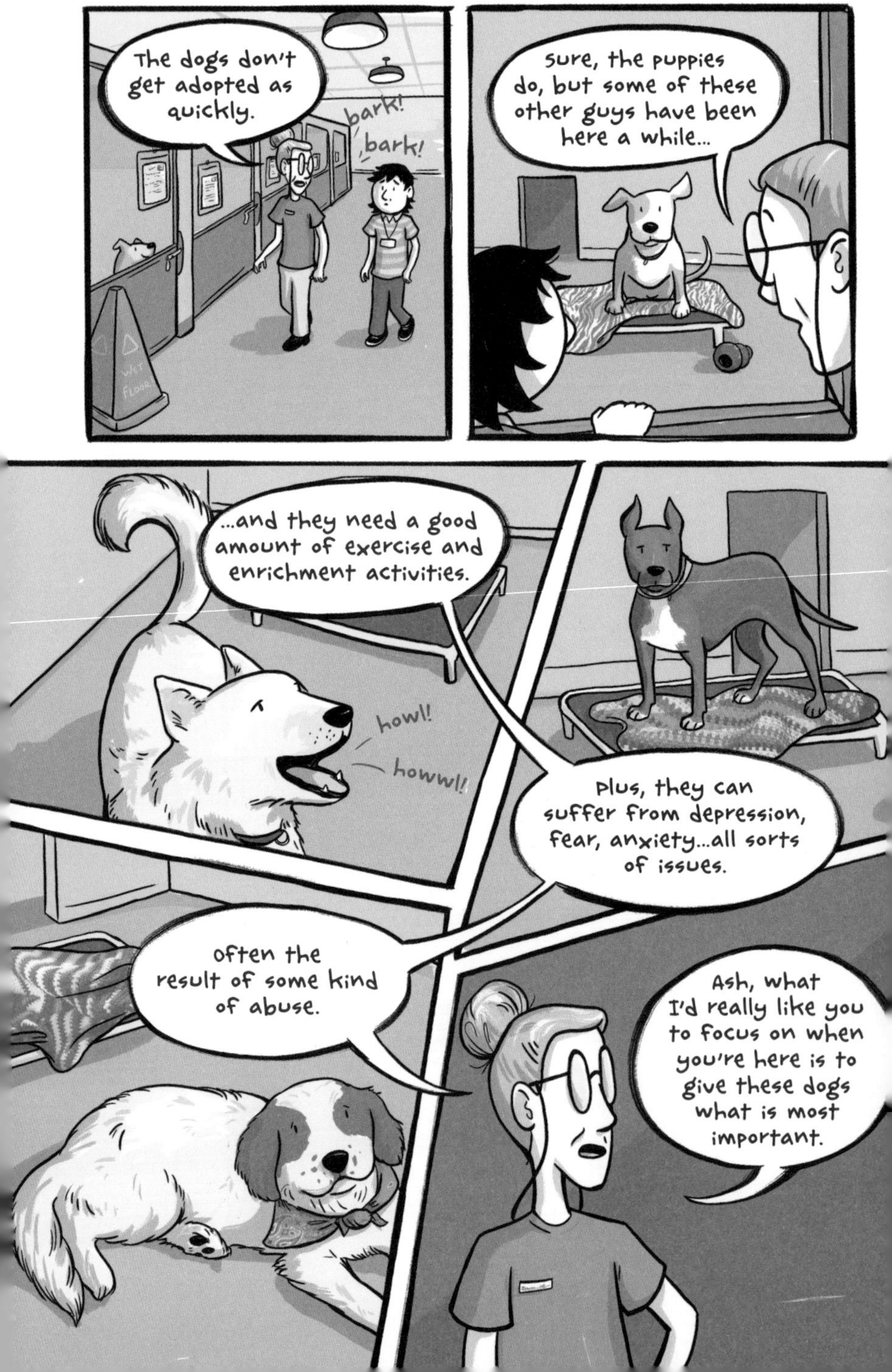
The dogs don't get adopted as quickly.
bark!
bark!
Sure, the puppies do, but some of these other guys have been here a while...
...and they need a good amount of exercise and enrichment activities.
howl!
howwl!
Plus, they can suffer from depression, fear, anxiety...all sorts of issues.
Often the result of some kind of abuse.
Ash, what I'd really like you to focus on when you're here is to give these dogs what is most important.

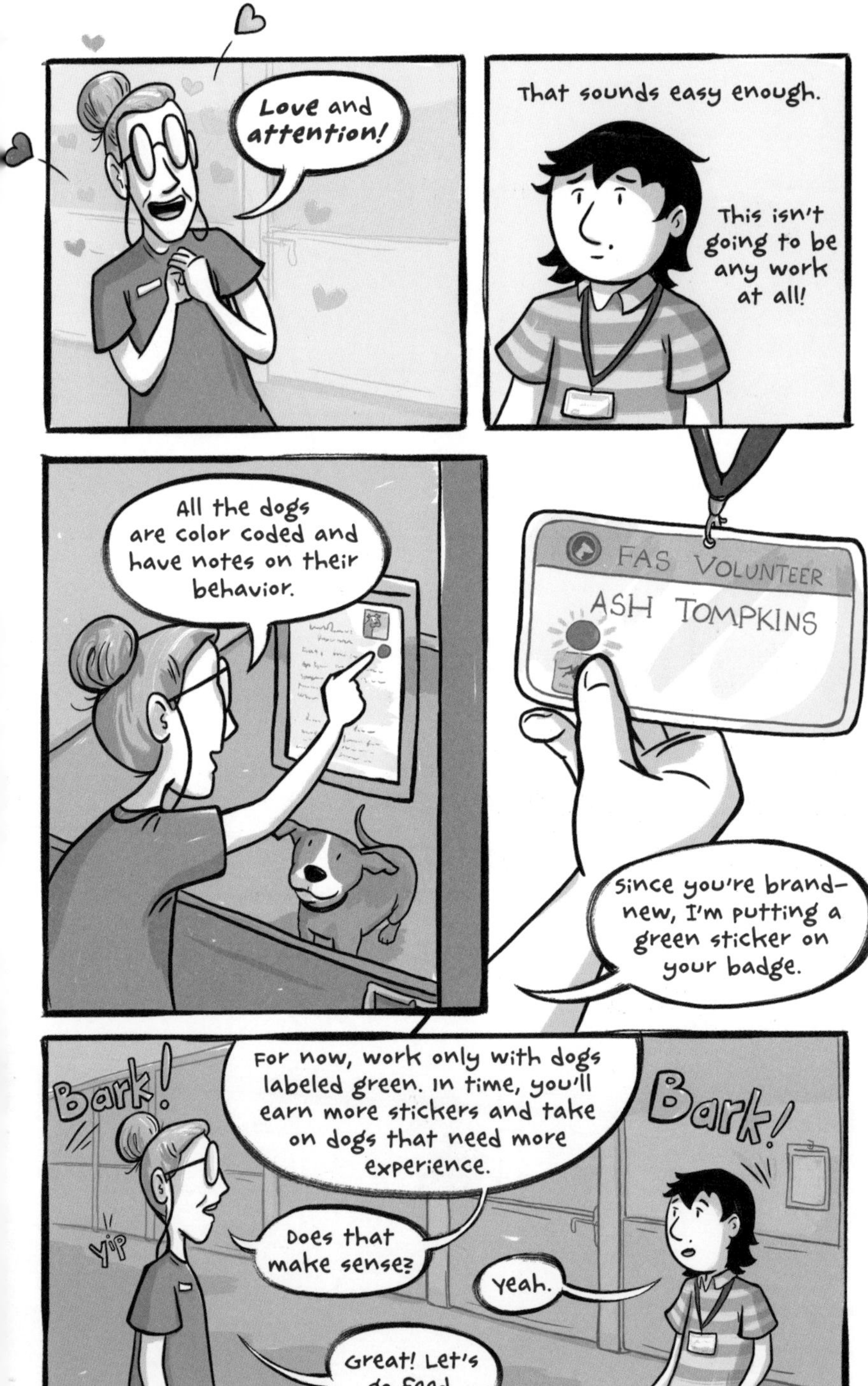
Love and attention!
That sounds easy enough.
This isn't going to be any work at all!
All the dogs are color coded and have notes on their behavior.
FAS VOLUNTEER
ASH TOMPKINS
Since you're brand-new, I'm putting a green sticker on your badge.
Bark!
For now, work only with dogs labeled green. In time, you'll earn more stickers and take on dogs that need more experience.
Bark!
yip
Does that make sense?
Yeah.
Great! Let's go feed.

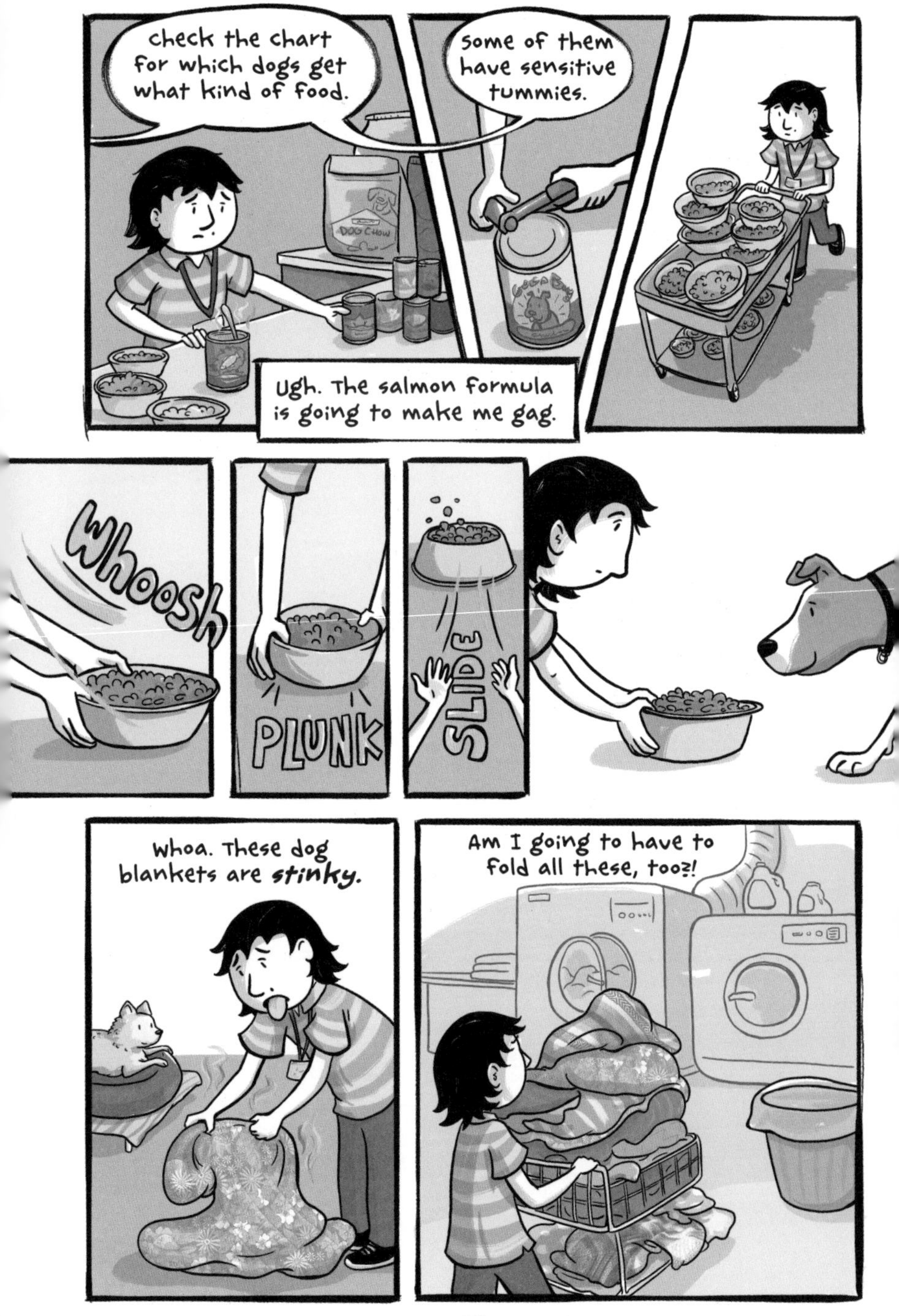
check the chart for which dogs get what kind of food.
Some of them have sensitive tummies.
Ugh. The salmon formula is going to make me gag.
WHOOSH
PLUNK
SLIDE
Whoa. These dog blankets are *stinky.*
Am I going to have to fold all these, too?!

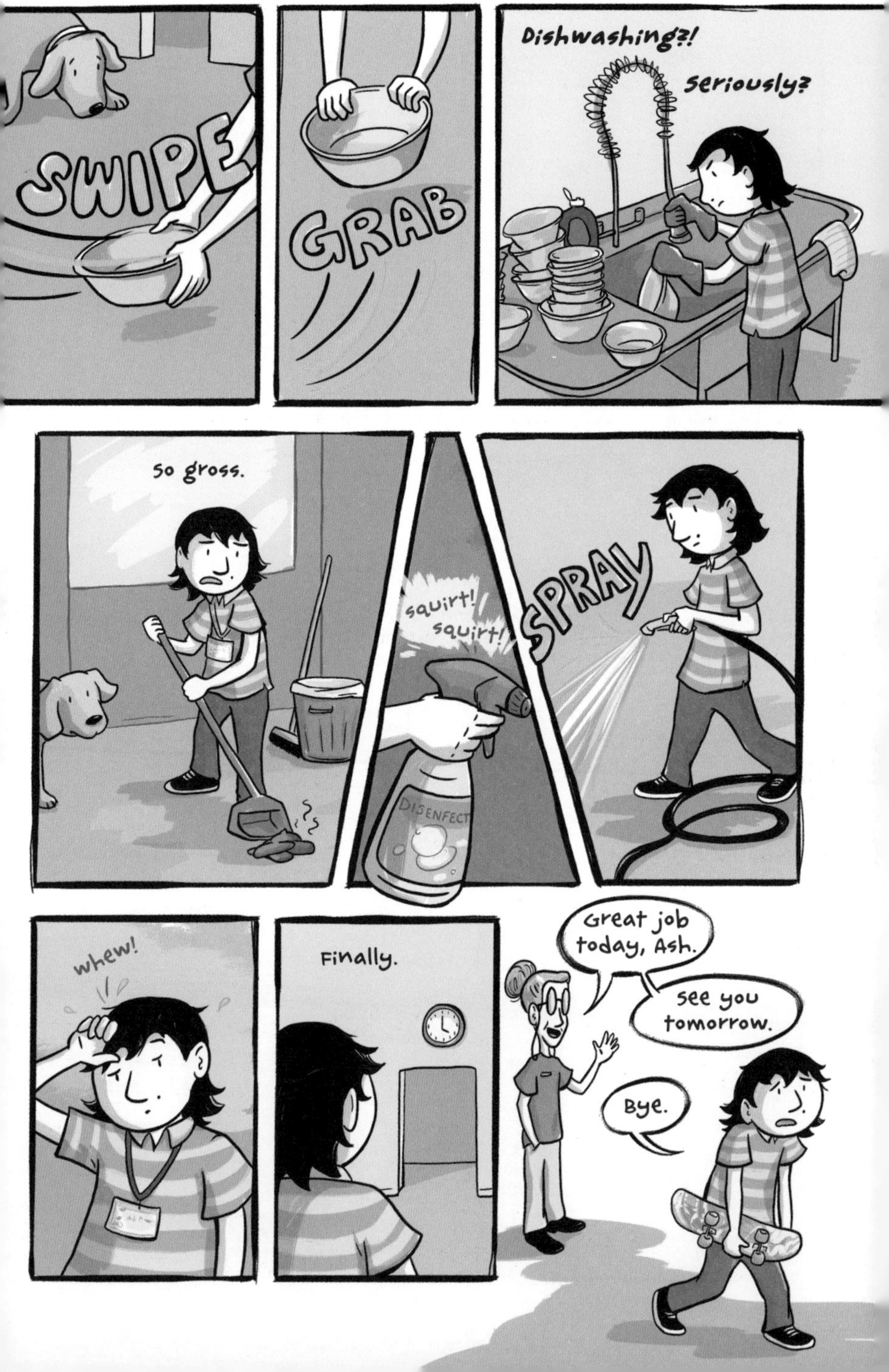
SWIPE
GRAB
Dishwashing?!
Seriously?
so gross.
squirt!
squirt!
DISENFECT
SPRAY
whew!
Finally.
Great job today, Ash.
See you tomorrow.
Bye.

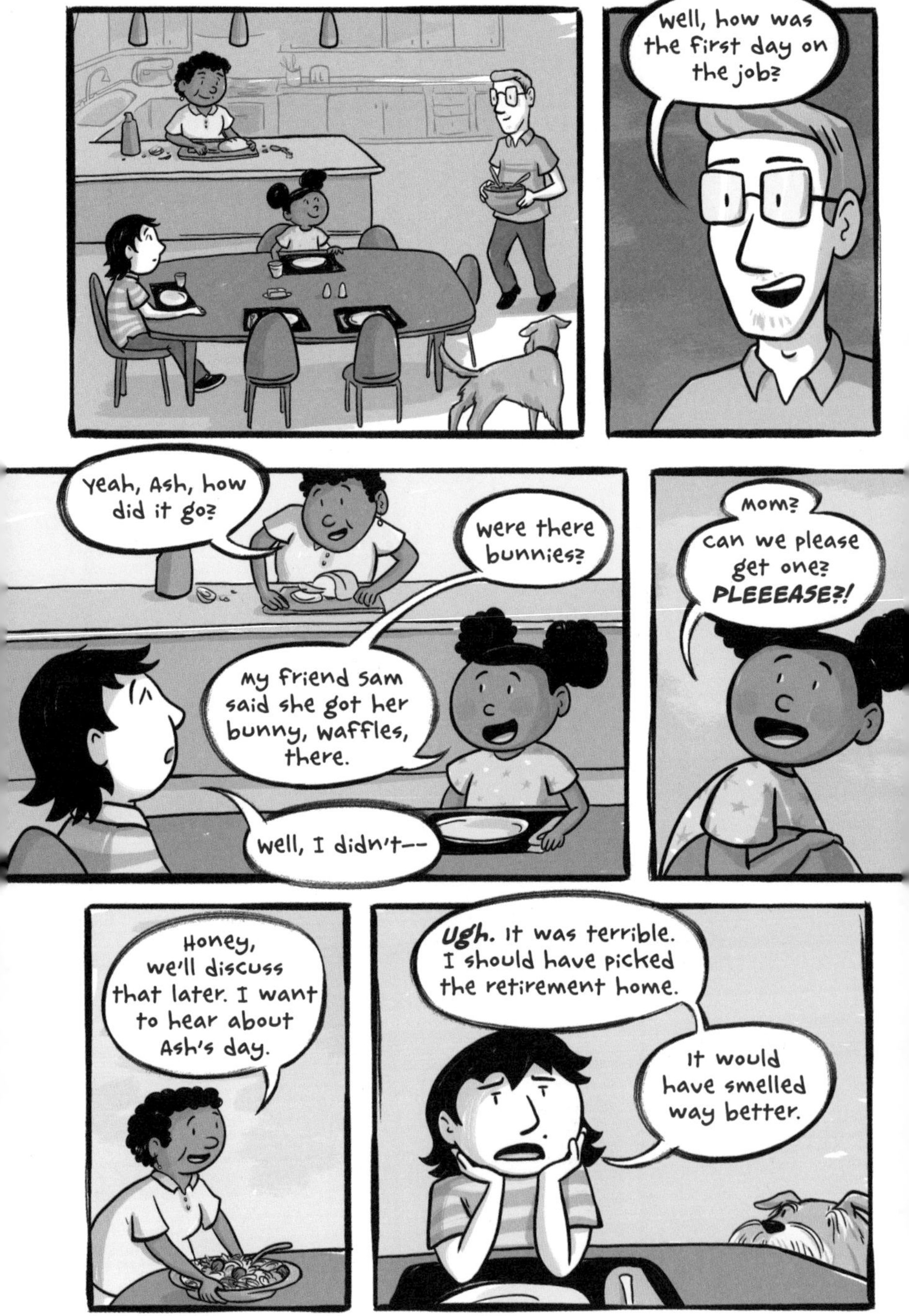
Well, how was the first day on the job?
Yeah, Ash, how did it go?
Were there bunnies?
My friend Sam said she got her bunny, Waffles, there.
Well, I didn't--
Mom? Can we please get one? PLEEEASE?!
Honey, we'll discuss that later. I want to hear about Ash's day.
Ugh. It was terrible. I should have picked the retirement home.
It would have smelled way better.

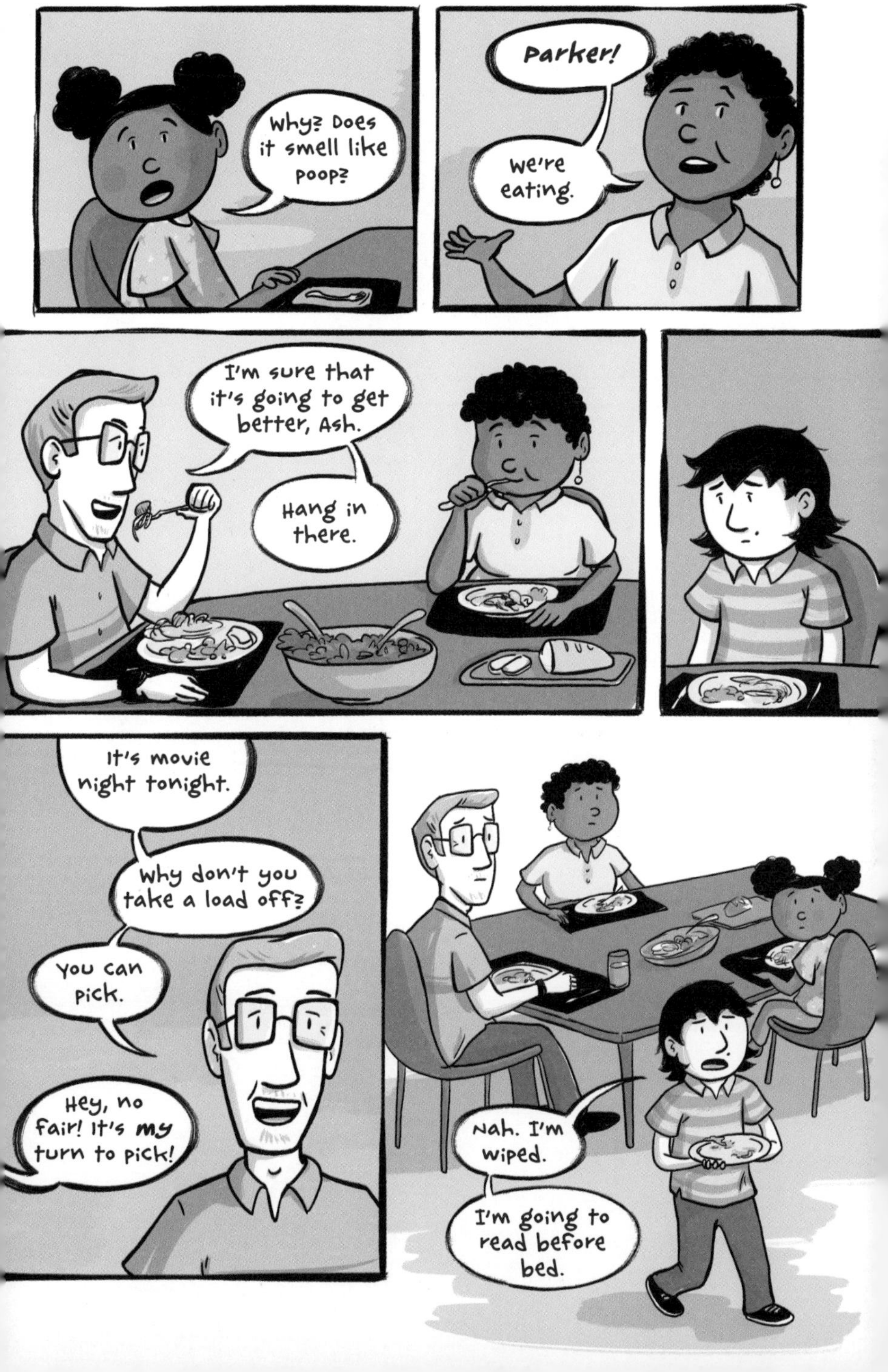
Why? Does it smell like poop?
Parker!
We're eating.
I'm sure that it's going to get better, Ash.
Hang in there.
It's movie night tonight.
Why don't you take a load off?
You can pick.
Hey, no fair! It's my turn to pick!
Nah. I'm wiped.
I'm going to read before bed.

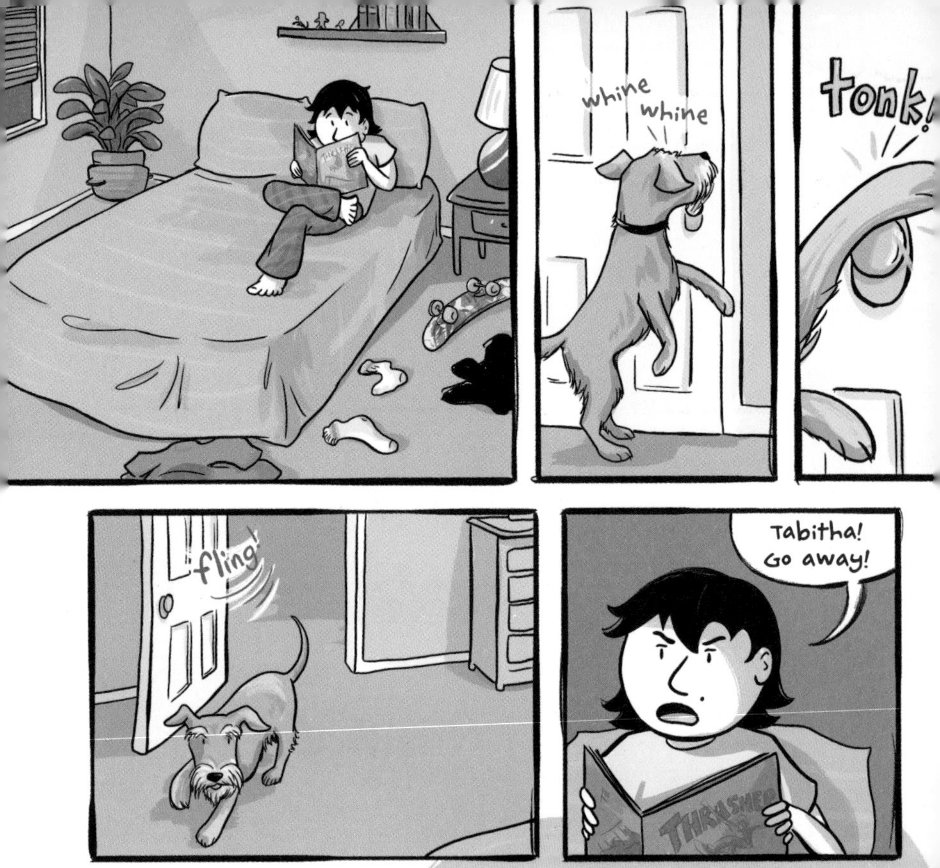
whine
whine
tonk!
fling!
Tabitha! Go away!

Tabitha

Tabitha is Dad and Cheryl's nutty schnauzer. She likes looking out the window all day and then barks her head off whenever a squirrel runs by.

And for some weird reason, she loves sneaking into my room and stealing my socks or underwear. So gross!

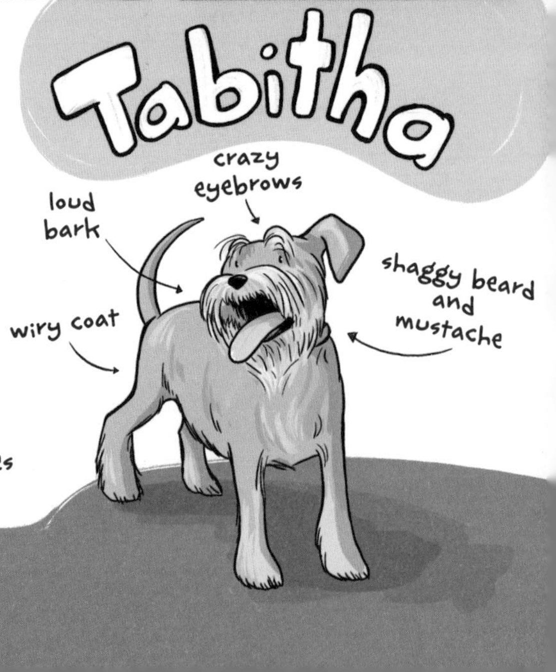
crazy eyebrows
loud bark
shaggy beard and mustache
wiry coat

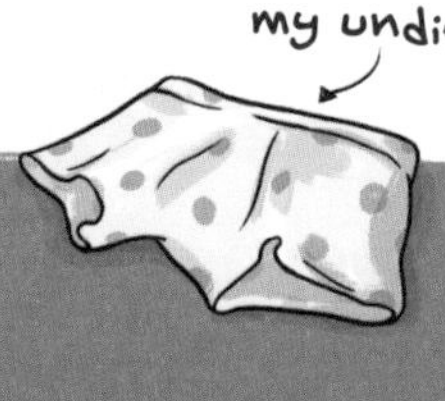
my undies

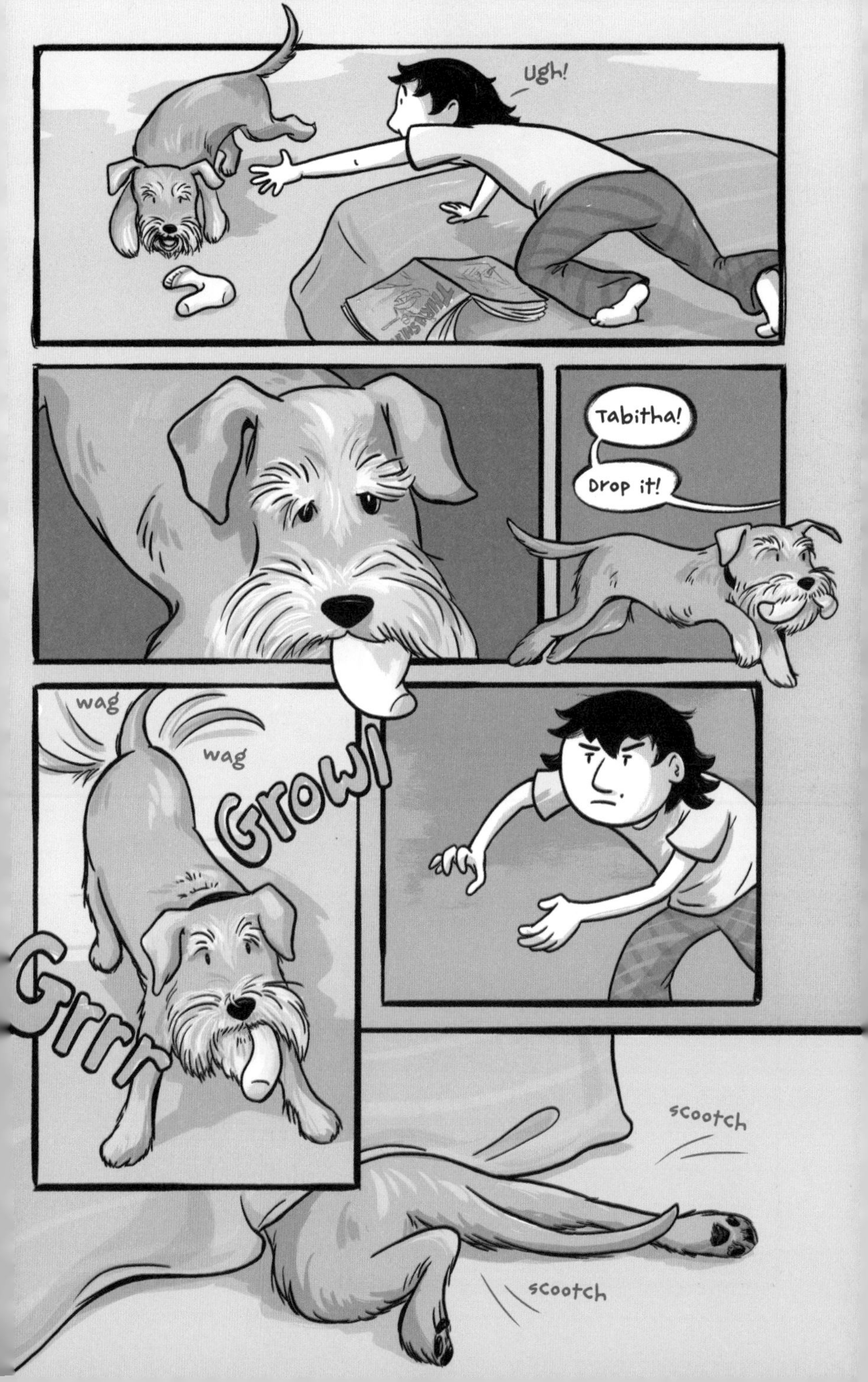
Ugh!
Tabitha!
Drop it!
wag
wag
Growl
Grrrr
scootch
scootch

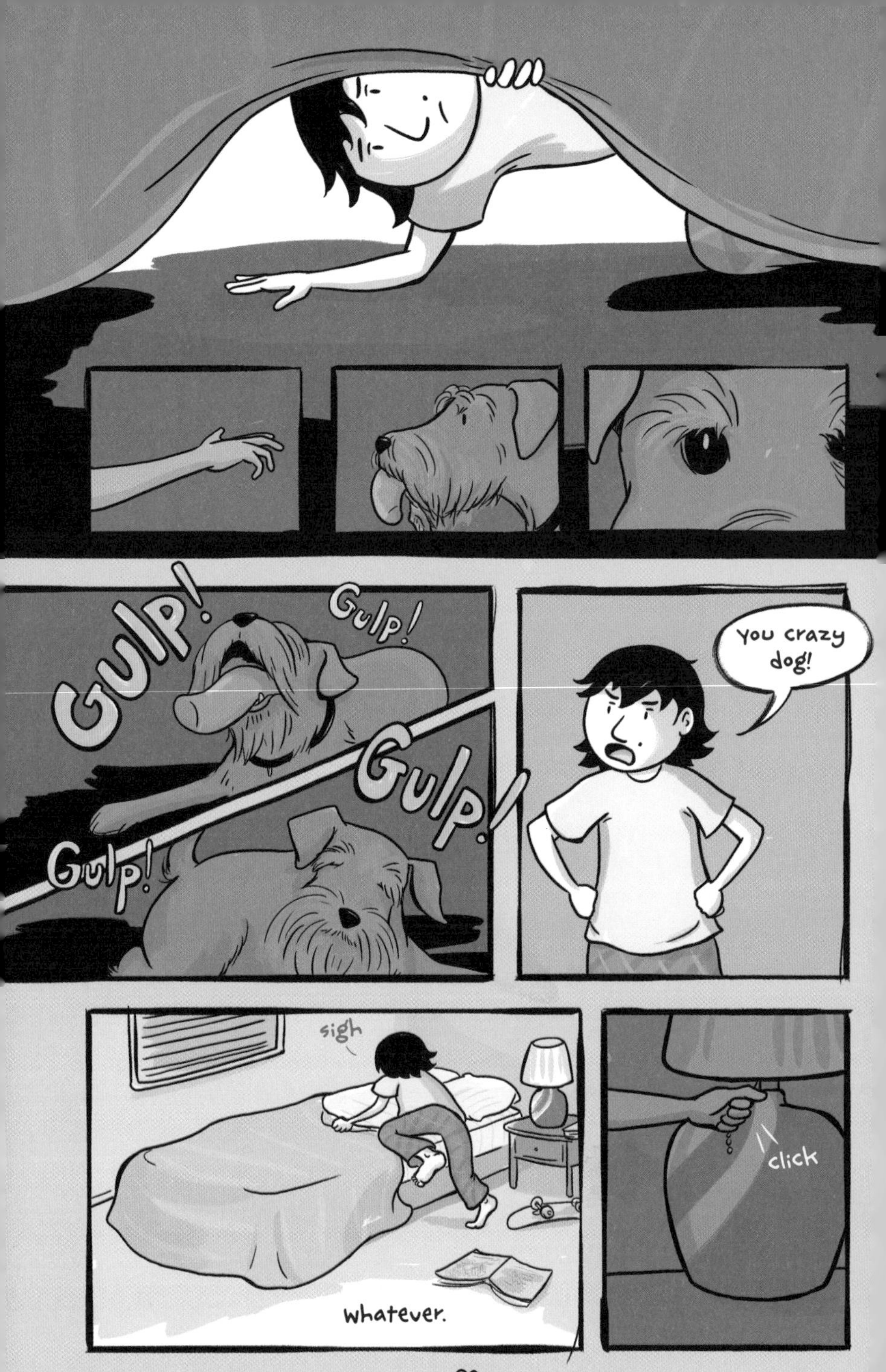
GULP!
Gulp!
Gulp!
Gulp!
You crazy dog!
sigh
whatever.
click

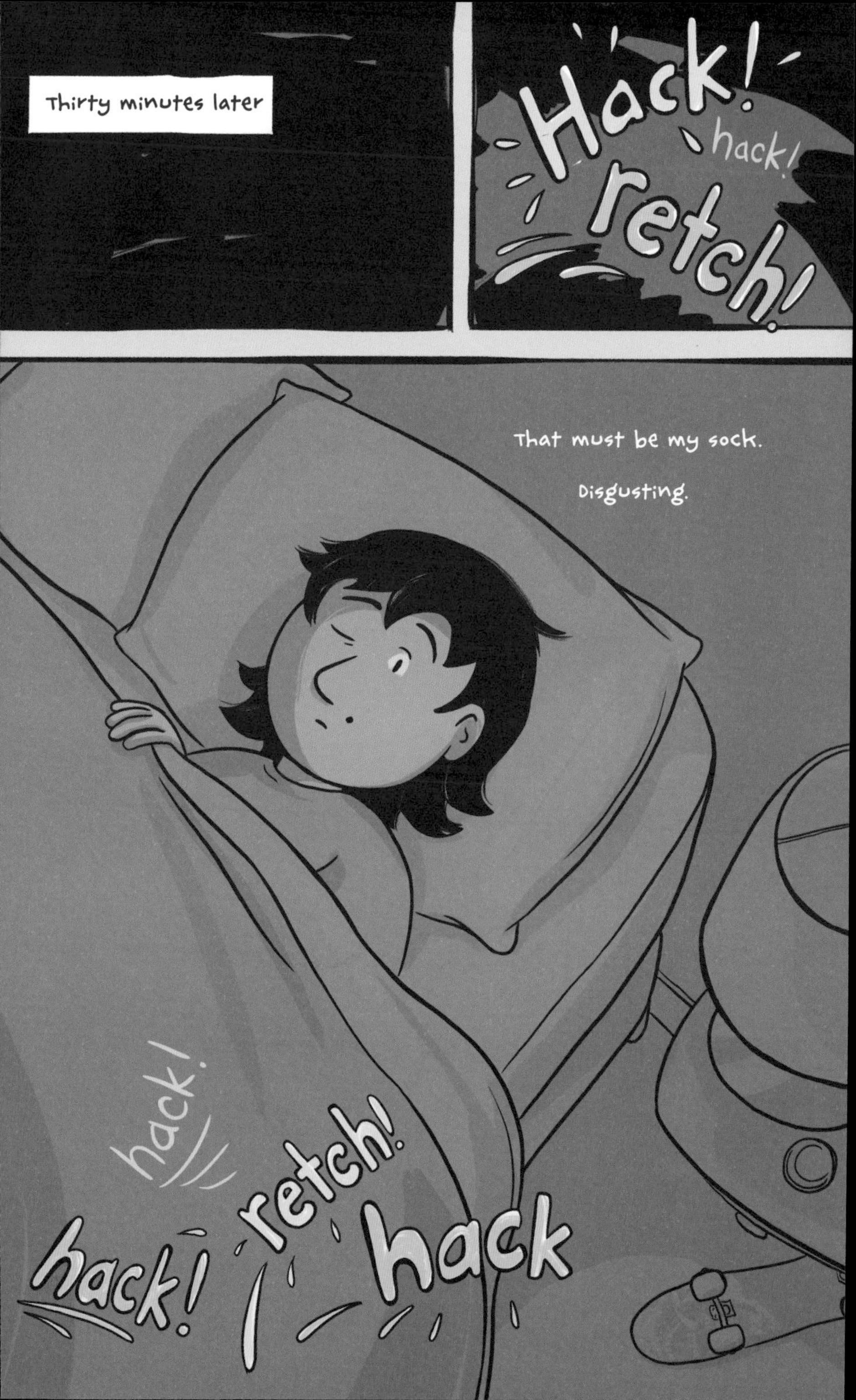
Thirty minutes later
Hack!
hack!
retch!
That must be my sock.
Disgusting.
hack!
hack!
retch!
hack

CHAPTER 4

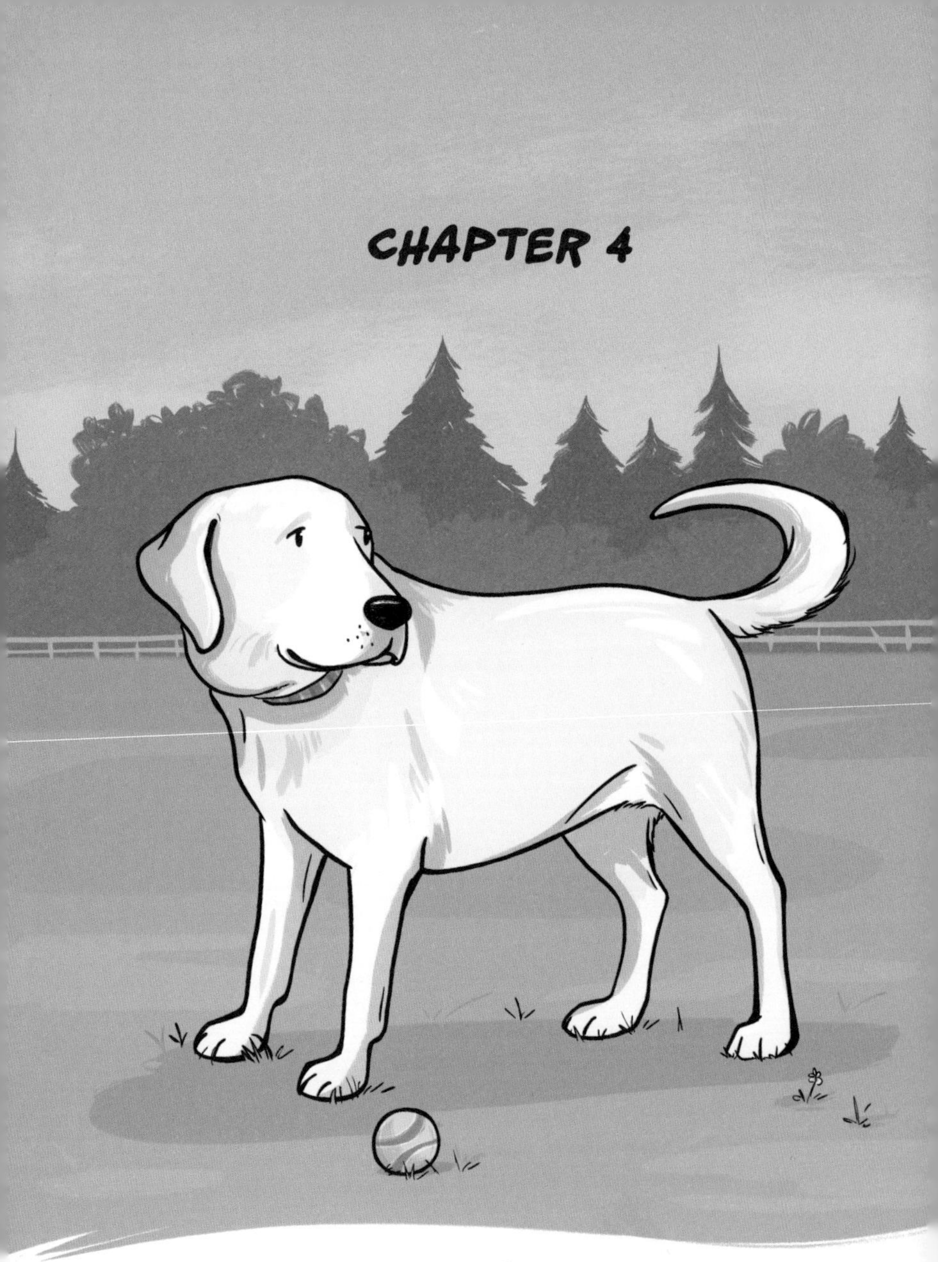

• Cody •

A yellow Labrador retriever mix who loves to chase and play fetch. Lab mixes are one of the most popular mixed breeds available from shelters and rescues. Friendly, sociable, and easygoing, Labs are well loved and have a reputation as the ultimate family pet.

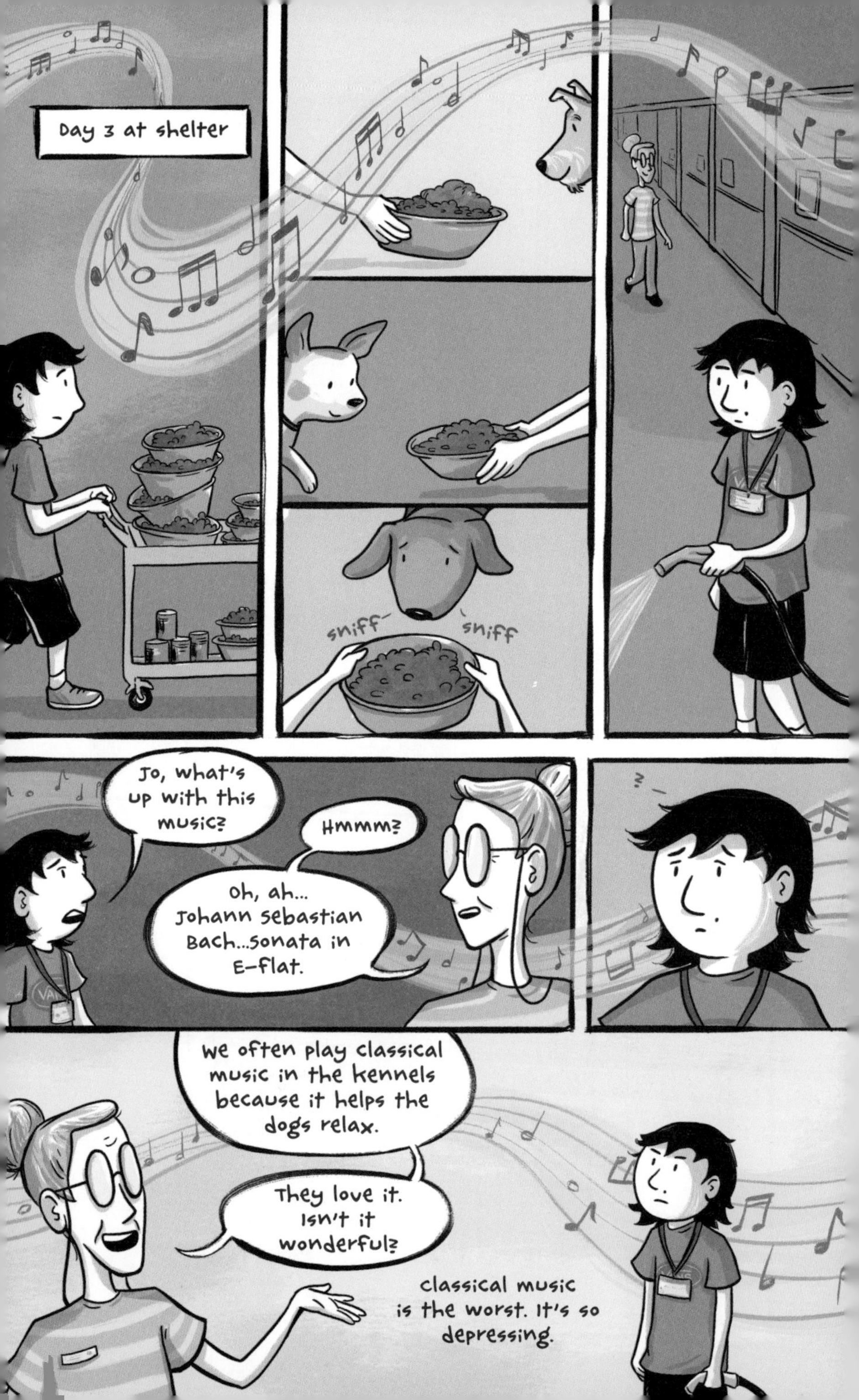
Day 3 at shelter
sniff
sniff
Jo, what's up with this music?
Hmmm?
Oh, ah... Johann Sebastian Bach...Sonata in E-flat.
We often play classical music in the kennels because it helps the dogs relax.
They love it. Isn't it wonderful?
Classical music is the worst. It's so depressing.

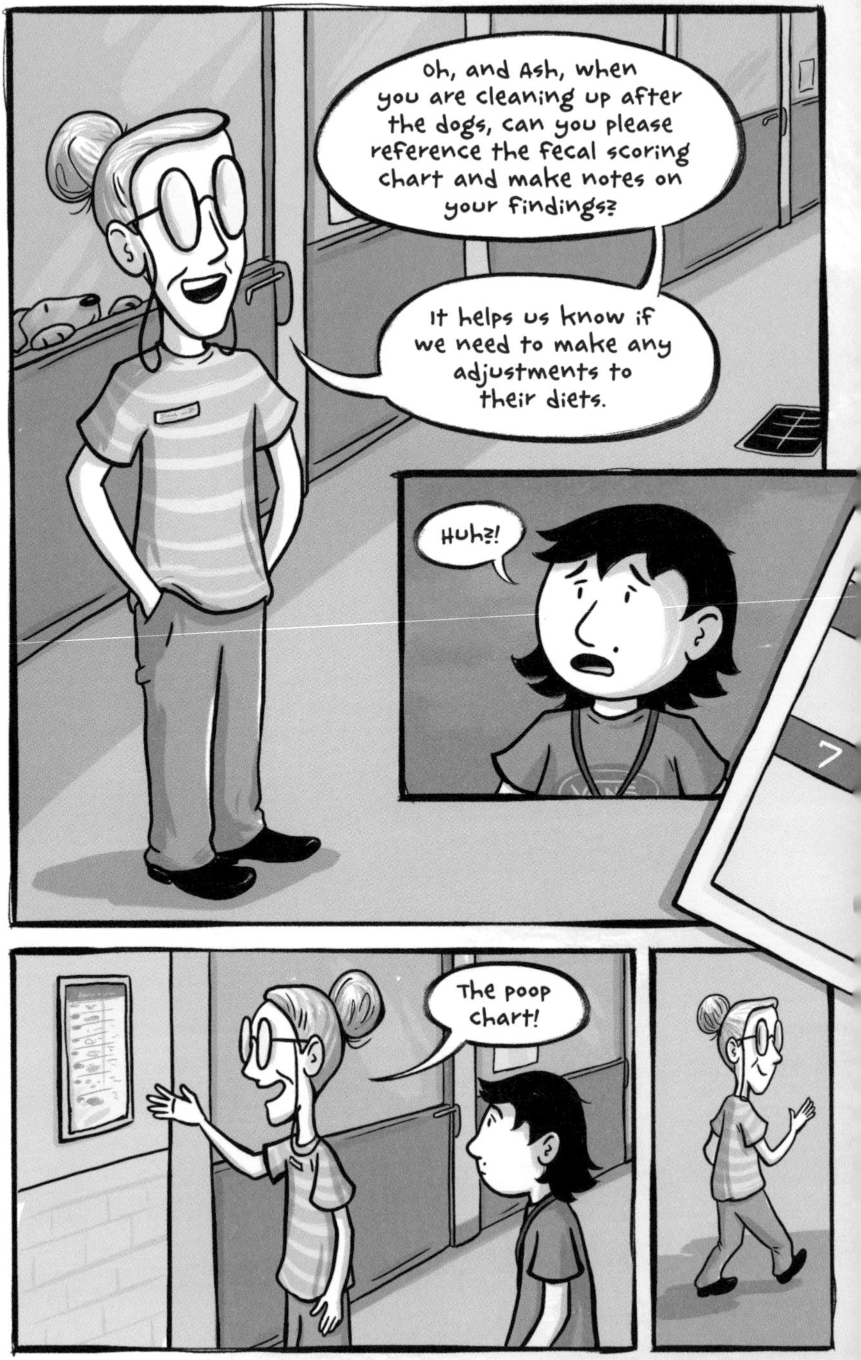
Oh, and Ash, when you are cleaning up after the dogs, can you please reference the fecal scoring chart and make notes on your findings?
It helps us know if we need to make any adjustments to their diets.
Huh?!
7
The poop chart!

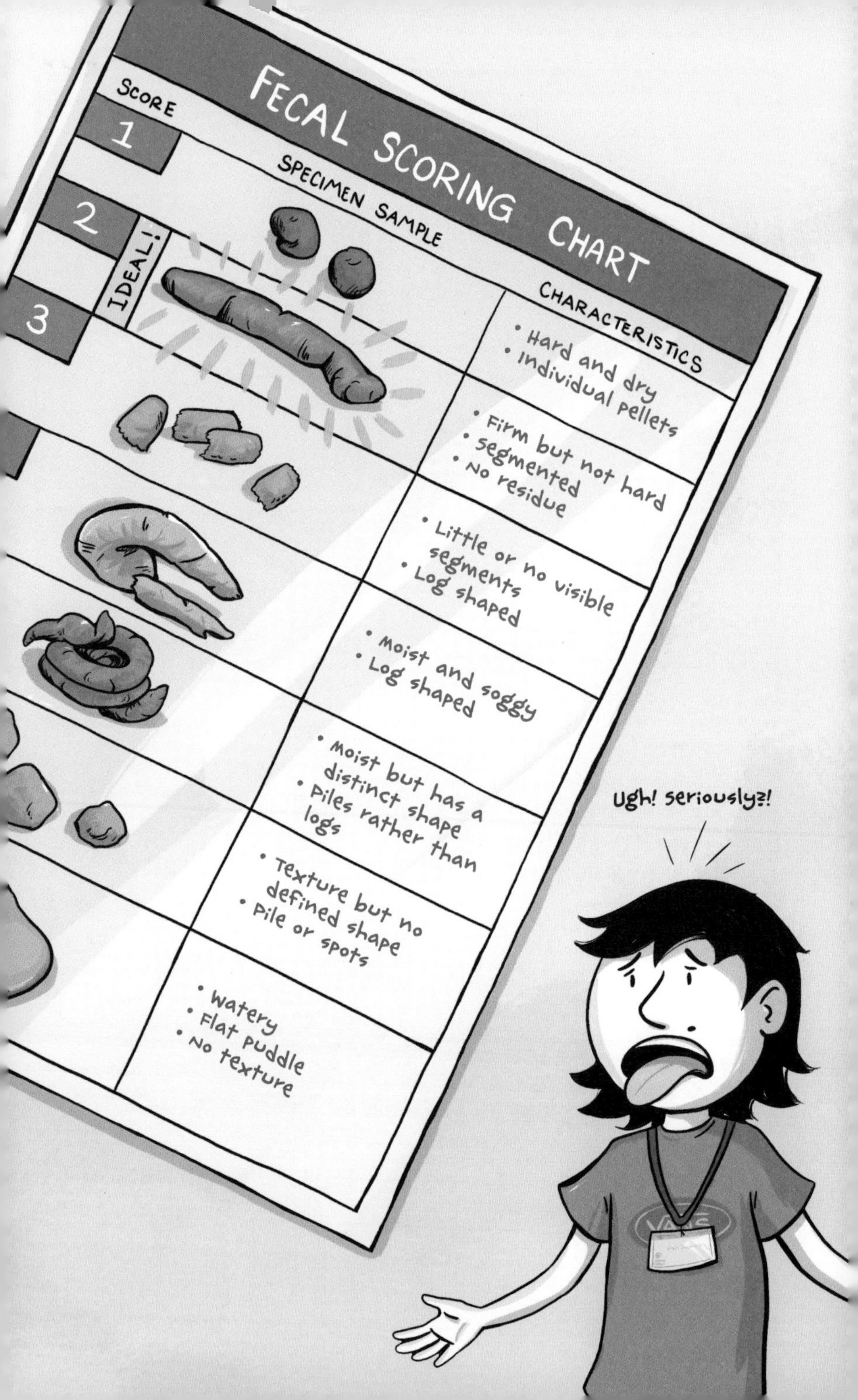
FECAL SCORING CHART
SCORE
SPECIMEN SAMPLE
CHARACTERISTICS
1
2
3
IDEAL!
• Hard and dry
• Individual pellets
• Firm but not hard
• Segmented
• No residue
• Little or no visible segments
• Log shaped
• Moist and soggy
• Log shaped
• Moist but has a distinct shape
• Piles rather than logs
• Texture but no defined shape
• Pile or spots
• Watery
• Flat puddle
• No texture
Ugh! Seriously?!

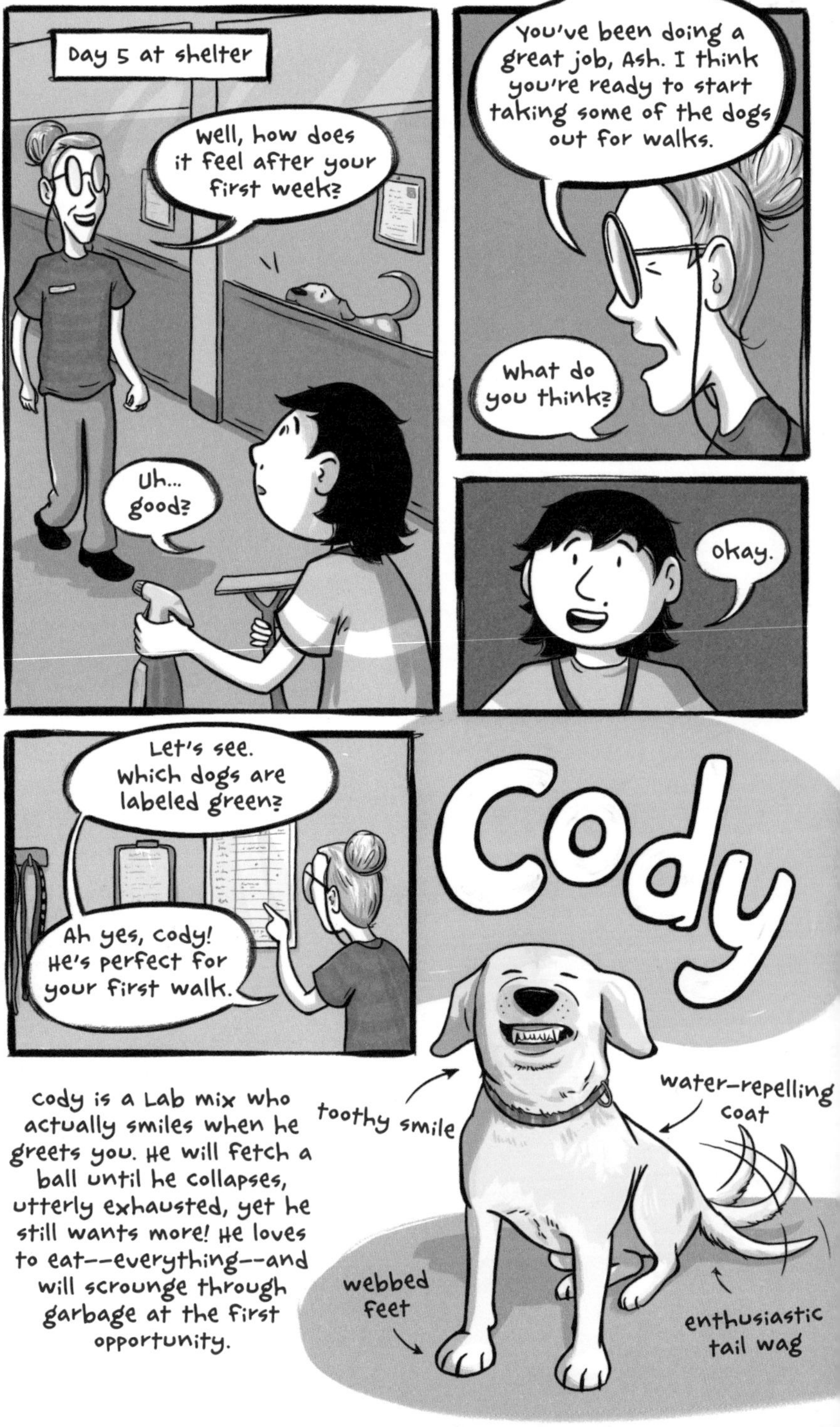
Day 5 at shelter
Well, how does it feel after your first week?
Uh... good?
You've been doing a great job, Ash. I think you're ready to start taking some of the dogs out for walks.
What do you think?
Okay.
Let's see. Which dogs are labeled green?
Ah yes, Cody! He's perfect for your first walk.
Cody
Cody is a Lab mix who actually smiles when he greets you. He will fetch a ball until he collapses, utterly exhausted, yet he still wants more! He loves to eat--everything--and will scrounge through garbage at the first opportunity.
toothy smile
water-repelling coat
webbed feet
enthusiastic tail wag

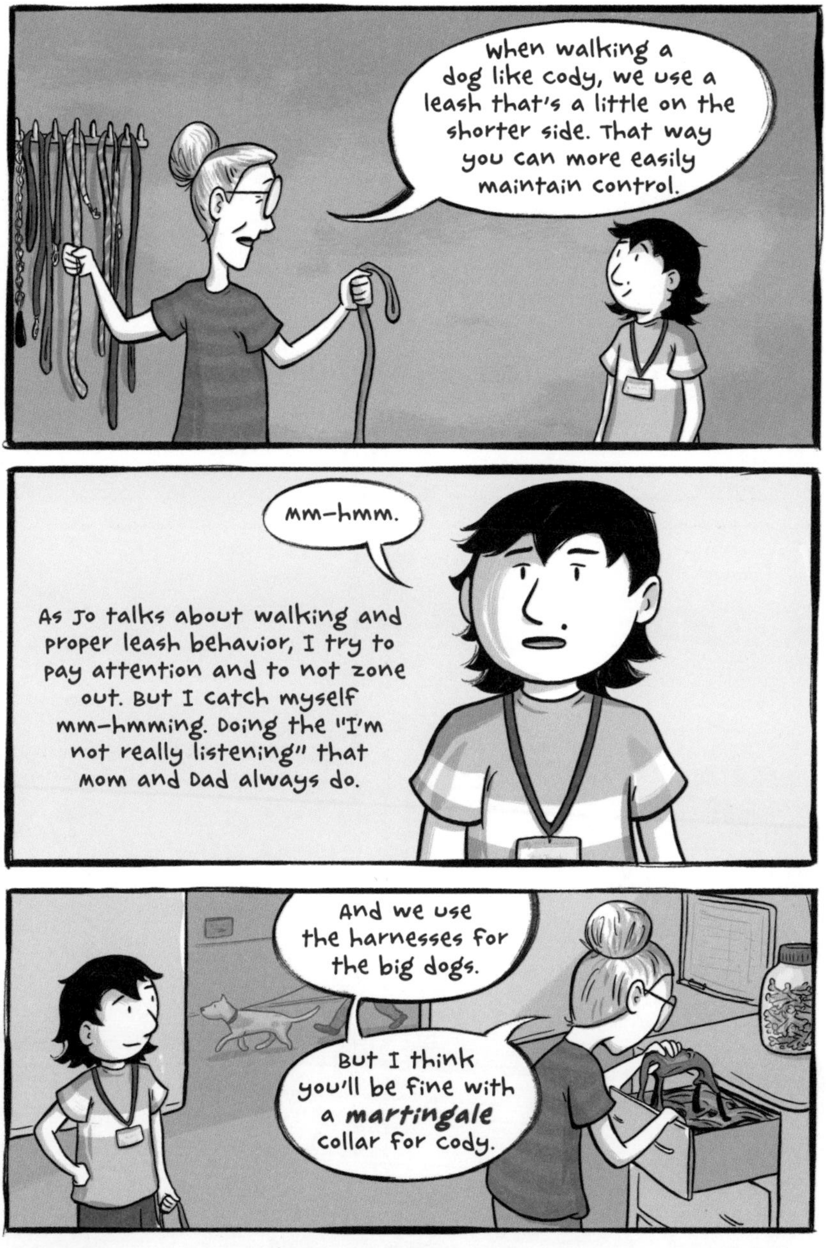
When walking a dog like cody, we use a leash that's a little on the shorter side. That way you can more easily maintain control.
mm-hmm.
As Jo talks about walking and proper leash behavior, I try to pay attention and to not zone out. But I catch myself mm-hmming. Doing the "I'm not really listening" that Mom and Dad always do.
And we use the harnesses for the big dogs.
But I think you'll be fine with a *martingale* collar for cody.

martingale: A safety collar composed of two sections, a fixed neck loop and a control loop. The leash is attached to a ring on the control loop, which adjusts. The control loop allows enough tightening to keep the dog from escaping, but ensures that the tightening will not injure the dog.

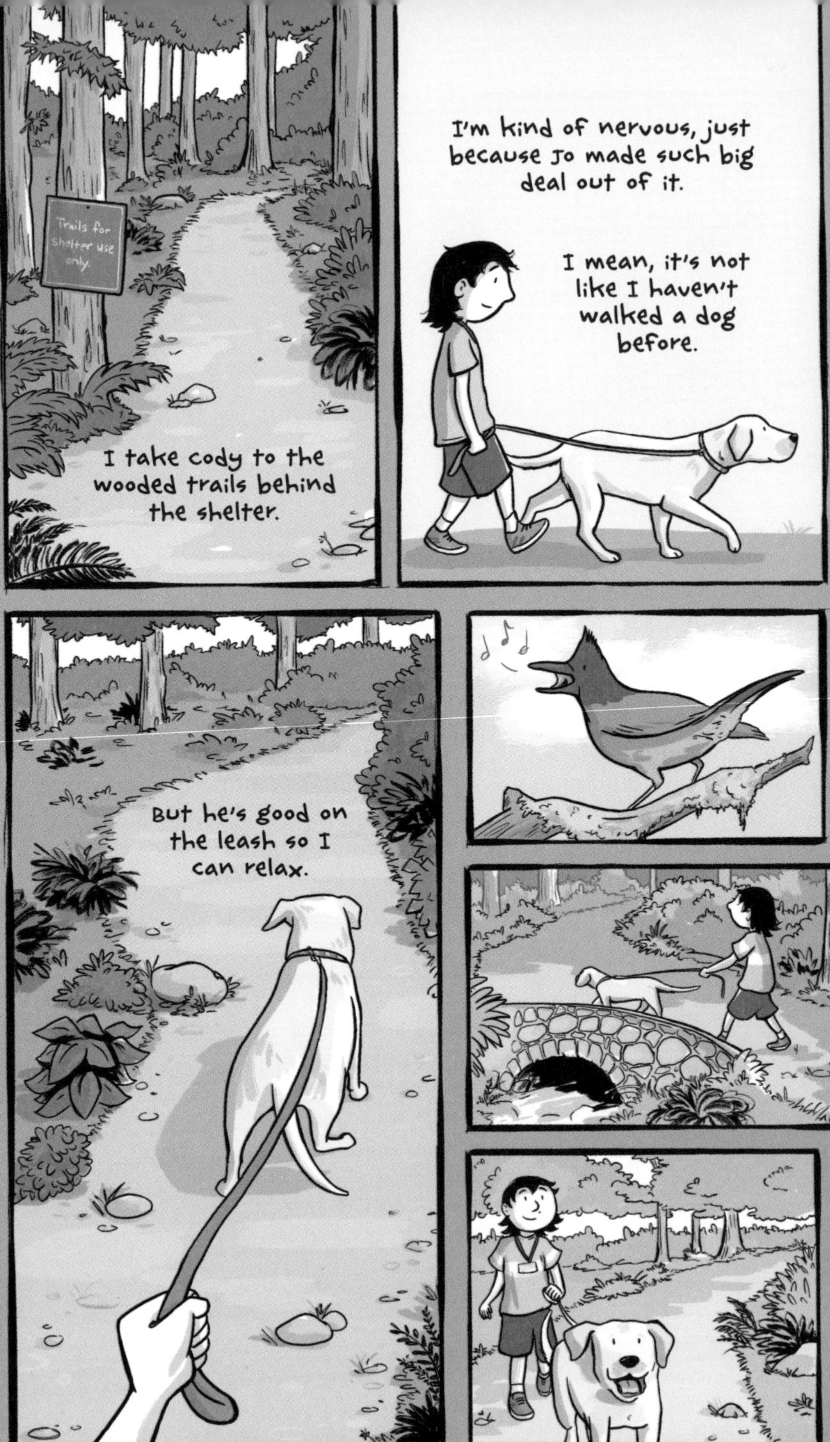
Trails for shelter use only.
I take cody to the wooded trails behind the shelter.
I'm kind of nervous, just because Jo made such big deal out of it.
I mean, it's not like I haven't walked a dog before.
But he's good on the leash so I can relax.

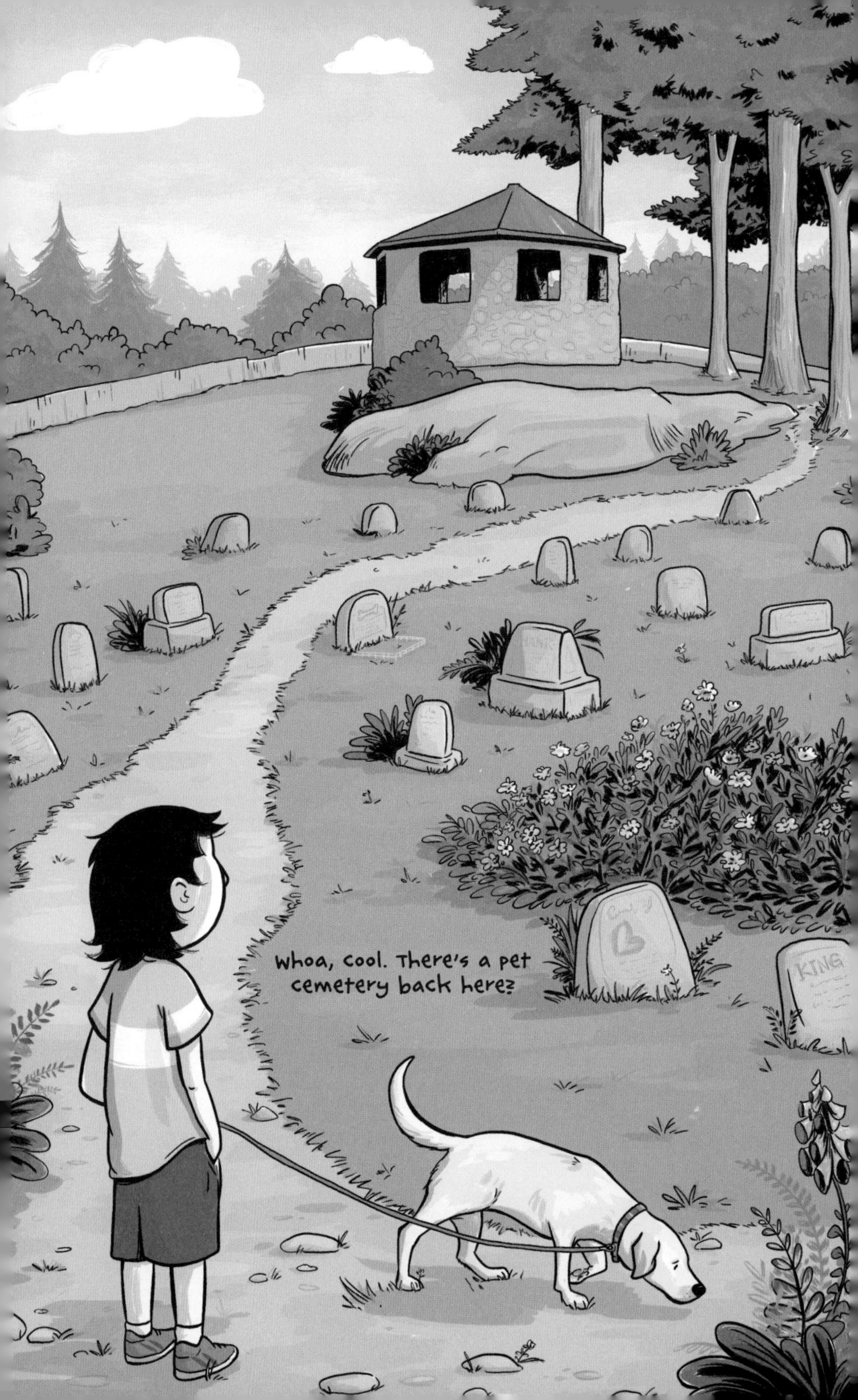
Whoa, cool. There's a pet cemetery back here?
KING

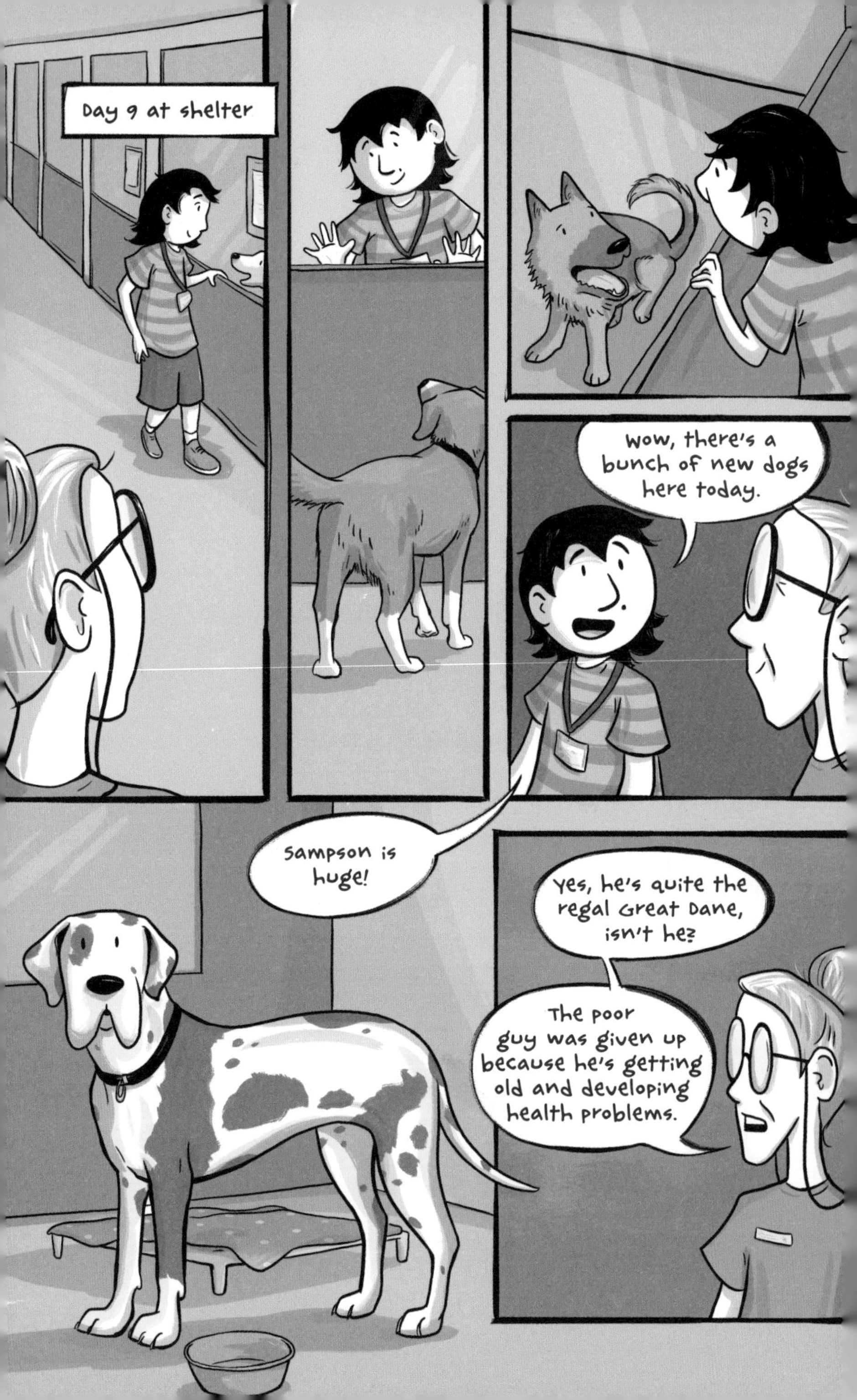
Day 9 at shelter
Wow, there's a bunch of new dogs here today.
Sampson is huge!
Yes, he's quite the regal Great Dane, isn't he?
The poor guy was given up because he's getting old and developing health problems.

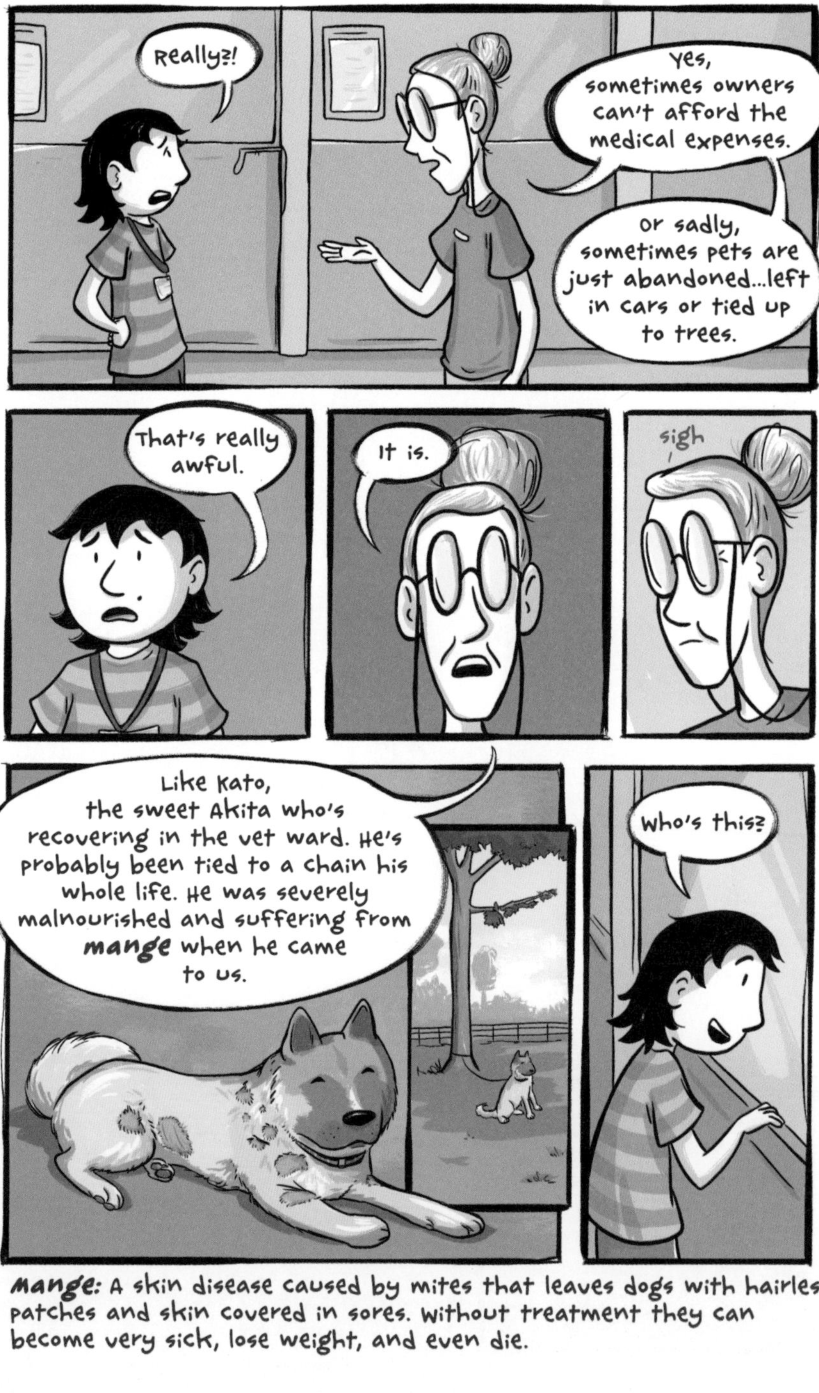
Really?!
Yes, sometimes owners can't afford the medical expenses.
Or sadly, sometimes pets are just abandoned...left in cars or tied up to trees.
That's really awful.
It is.
sigh
Like Kato, the sweet Akita who's recovering in the vet ward. He's probably been tied to a chain his whole life. He was severely malnourished and suffering from **mange** when he came to us.
Who's this?

Mange: A skin disease caused by mites that leaves dogs with hairless patches and skin covered in sores. Without treatment they can become very sick, lose weight, and even die.

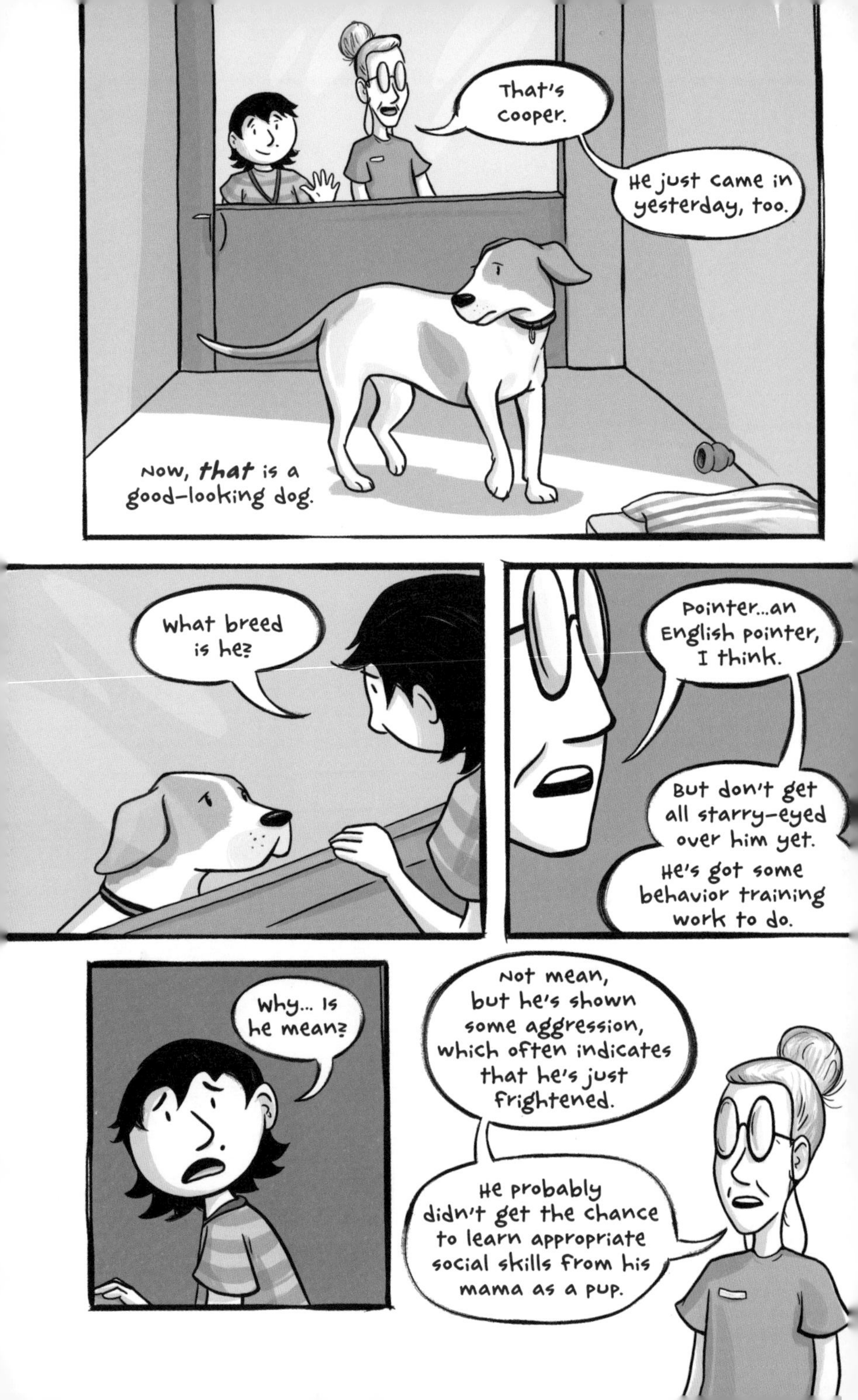
That's cooper.
He just came in yesterday, too.
Now, that is a good-looking dog.
What breed is he?
Pointer...an English pointer, I think.
But don't get all starry-eyed over him yet.
He's got some behavior training work to do.
Why... Is he mean?
Not mean, but he's shown some aggression, which often indicates that he's just frightened.
He probably didn't get the chance to learn appropriate social skills from his mama as a pup.

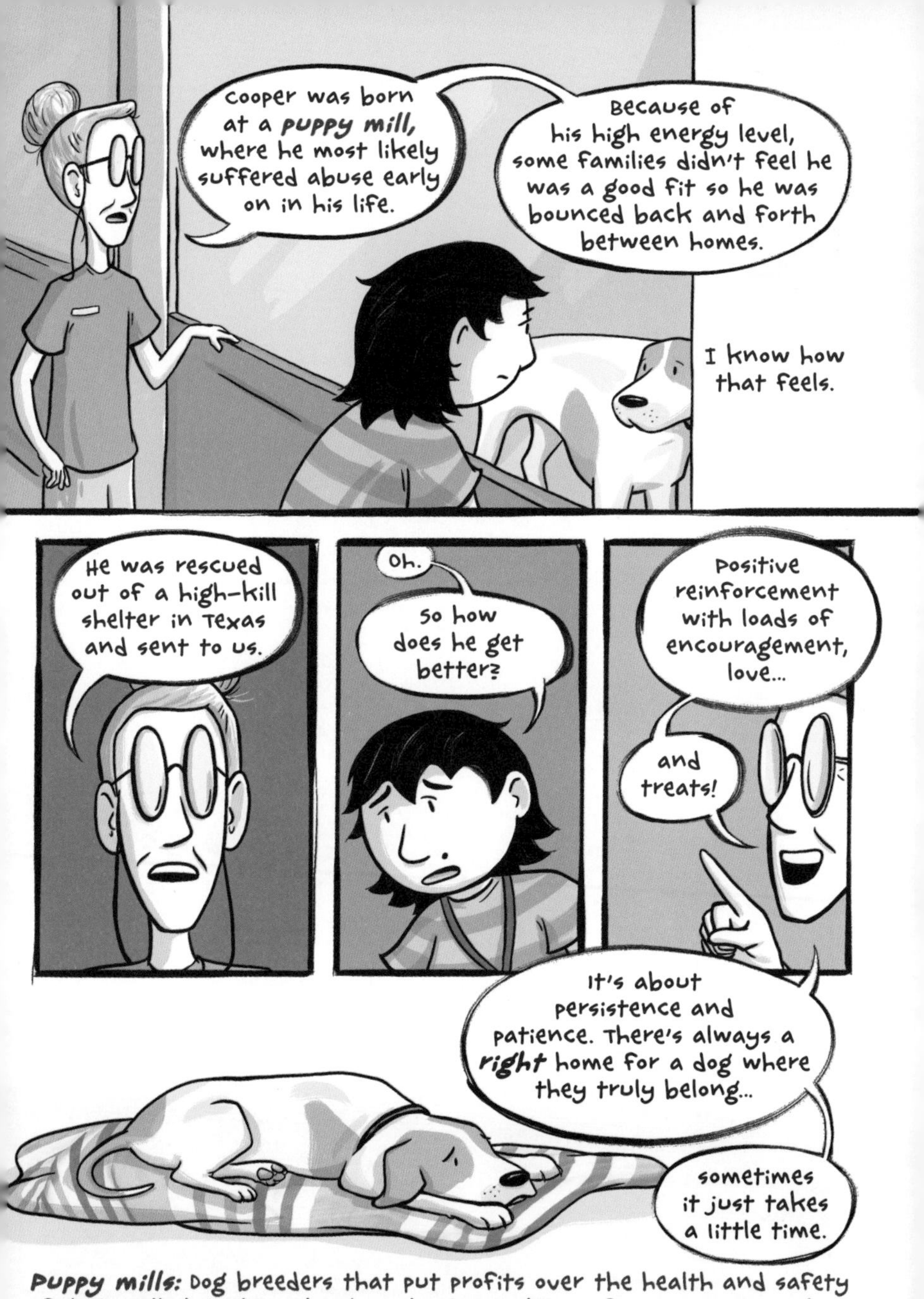
Cooper was born at a *puppy mill,* where he most likely suffered abuse early on in his life.
Because of his high energy level, some families didn't feel he was a good fit so he was bounced back and forth between homes.
I know how that feels.
He was rescued out of a high-kill shelter in Texas and sent to us.
Oh.
So how does he get better?
Positive reinforcement with loads of encouragement, love...
and treats!
It's about persistence and patience. There's always a *right* home for a dog where they truly belong...
sometimes it just takes a little time.

Puppy mills: Dog breeders that put profits over the health and safety of dogs. Mills breed purebreds in large numbers, often in very cruel conditions. Puppies are taken from their mothers too young (which can cause serious health or behavioral issues) and shipped to pet stores or online sellers. A responsible breeder will meet you in person and let you see where the puppy and its mother are housed.

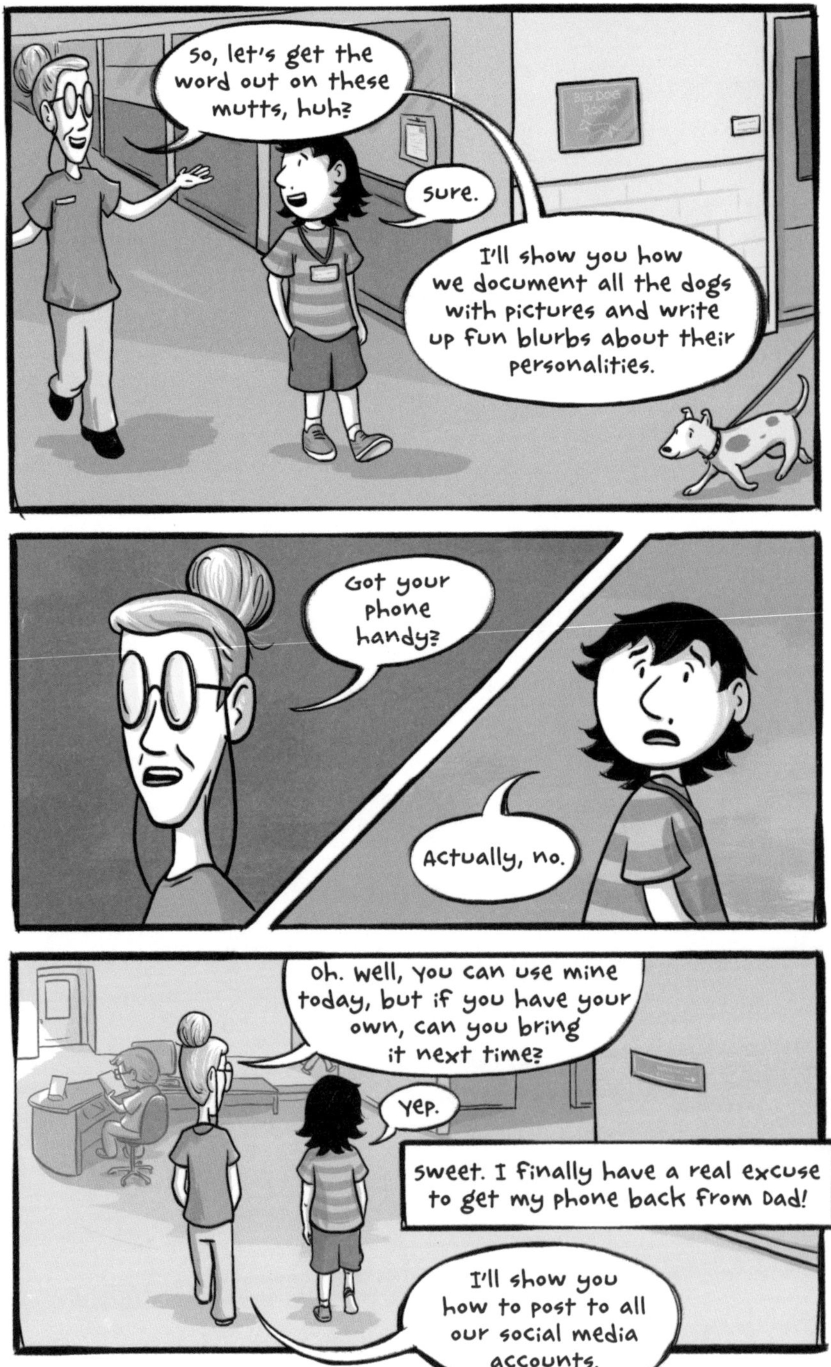
So, let's get the word out on these mutts, huh?
Sure.
I'll show you how we document all the dogs with pictures and write up fun blurbs about their personalities.
Got your phone handy?
Actually, no.
Oh. Well, you can use mine today, but if you have your own, can you bring it next time?
Yep.
Sweet. I finally have a real excuse to get my phone back from Dad!
I'll show you how to post to all our social media accounts.

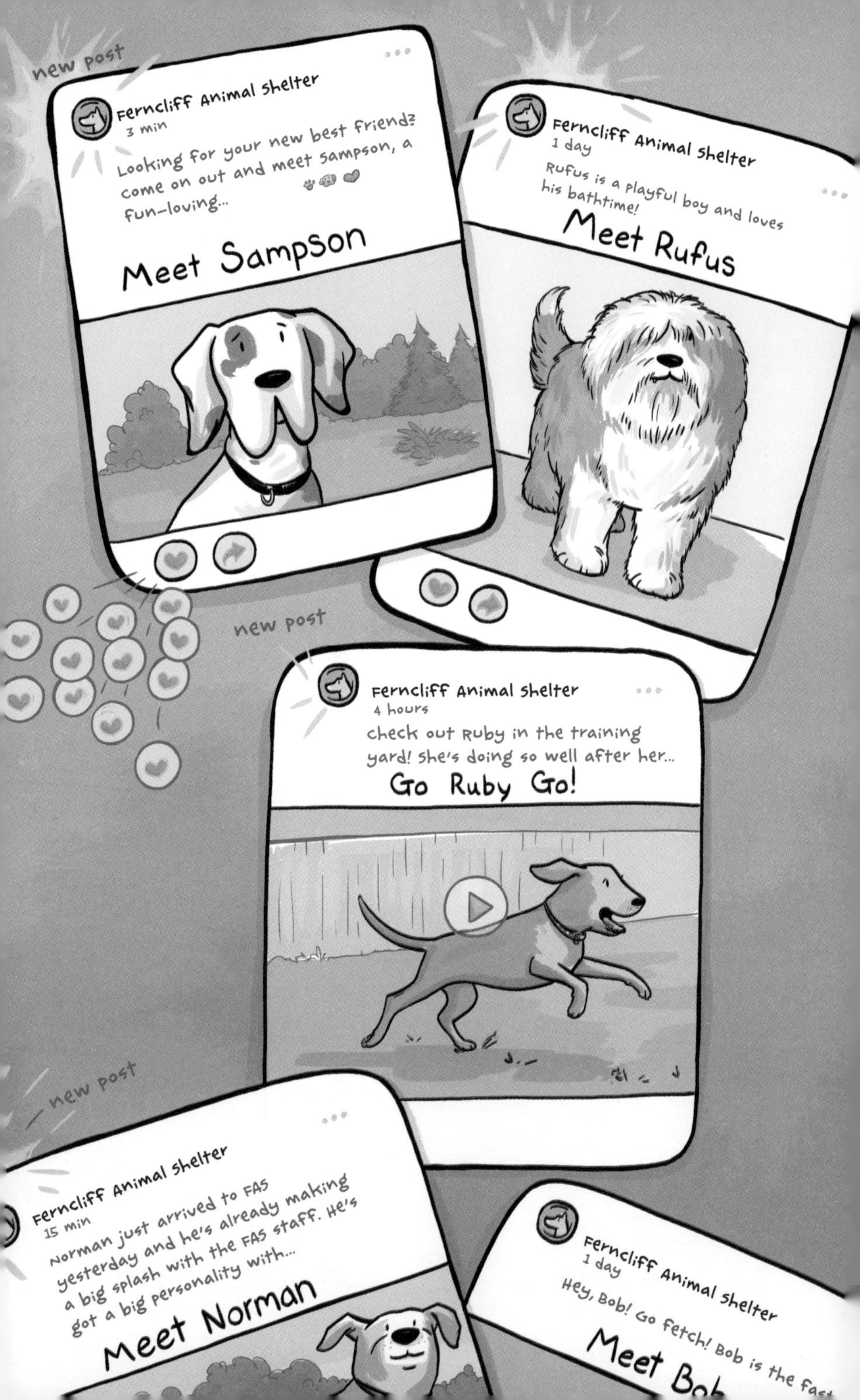

new post
Ferncliff Animal shelter
3 min
Looking for your new best friend? come on out and meet sampson, a fun-loving...
Meet Sampson
Ferncliff Animal shelter
1 day
Rufus is a playful boy and loves his bathtime!
Meet Rufus
new post
Ferncliff Animal shelter
4 hours
check out Ruby in the training yard! she's doing so well after her...
Go Ruby Go!
new post
Ferncliff Animal shelter
15 min
Norman just arrived to FAS yesterday and he's already making a big splash with the FAS staff. He's got a big personality with...
Meet Norman
Ferncliff Animal shelter
1 day
Hey, Bob! Go fetch! Bob is the fast
Meet Bob

Day 13 at shelter

The chores seem to be getting easier now, and I don't even notice the smells anymore.

Ash, here's a sticker for your badge.

Each time you've completed ten hours of walking, you'll get a new sticker. By the end of the summer, you'll probably have enough hours logged to become an advanced dog walker!

10 Hours

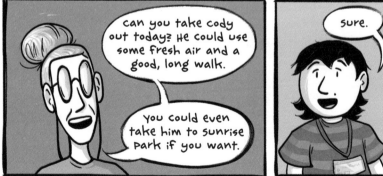

Can you take Cody out today? He could use some fresh air and a good, long walk.

Sure.

You could even take him to Sunrise Park if you want.

96

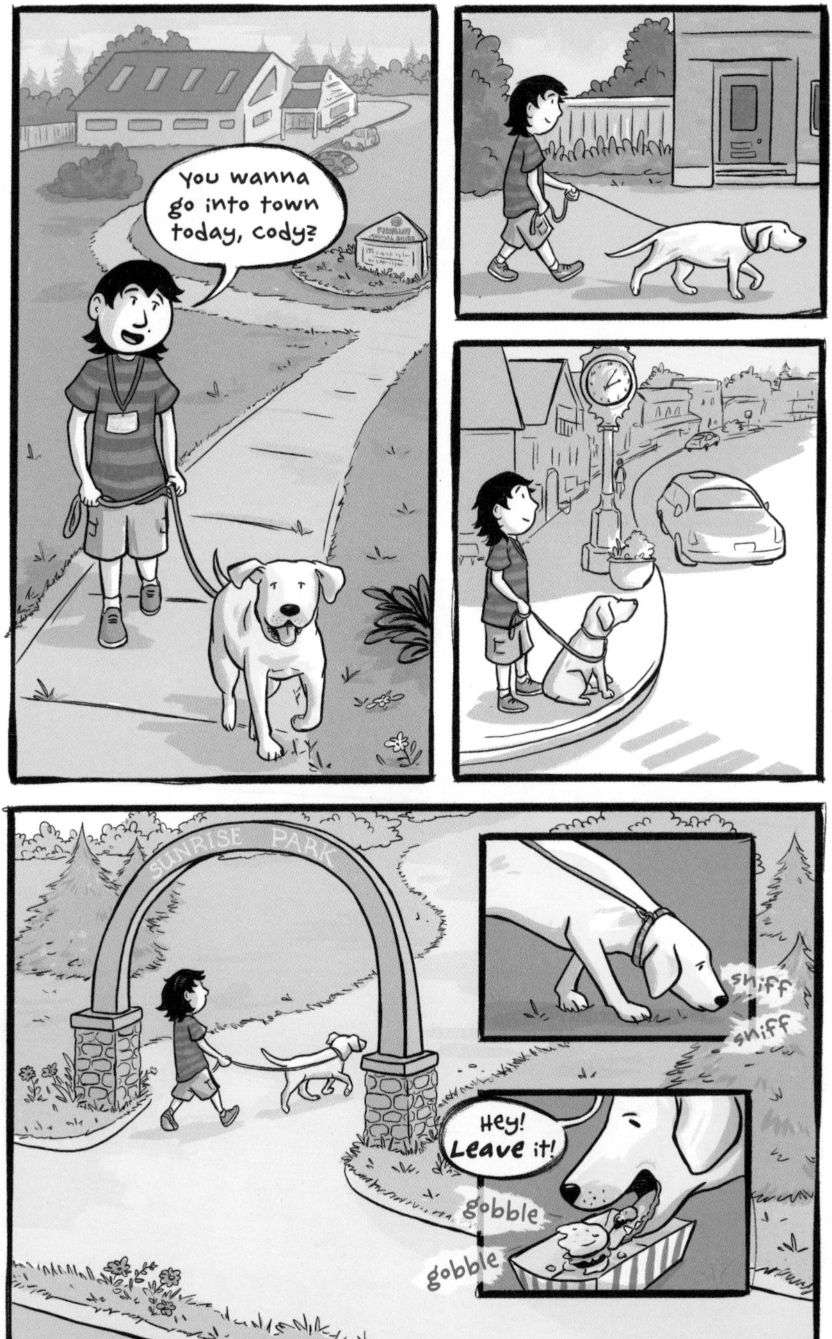
You wanna go into town today, Cody?
SUNRISE PARK
sniff
sniff
Hey! Leave it!
gobble
gobble

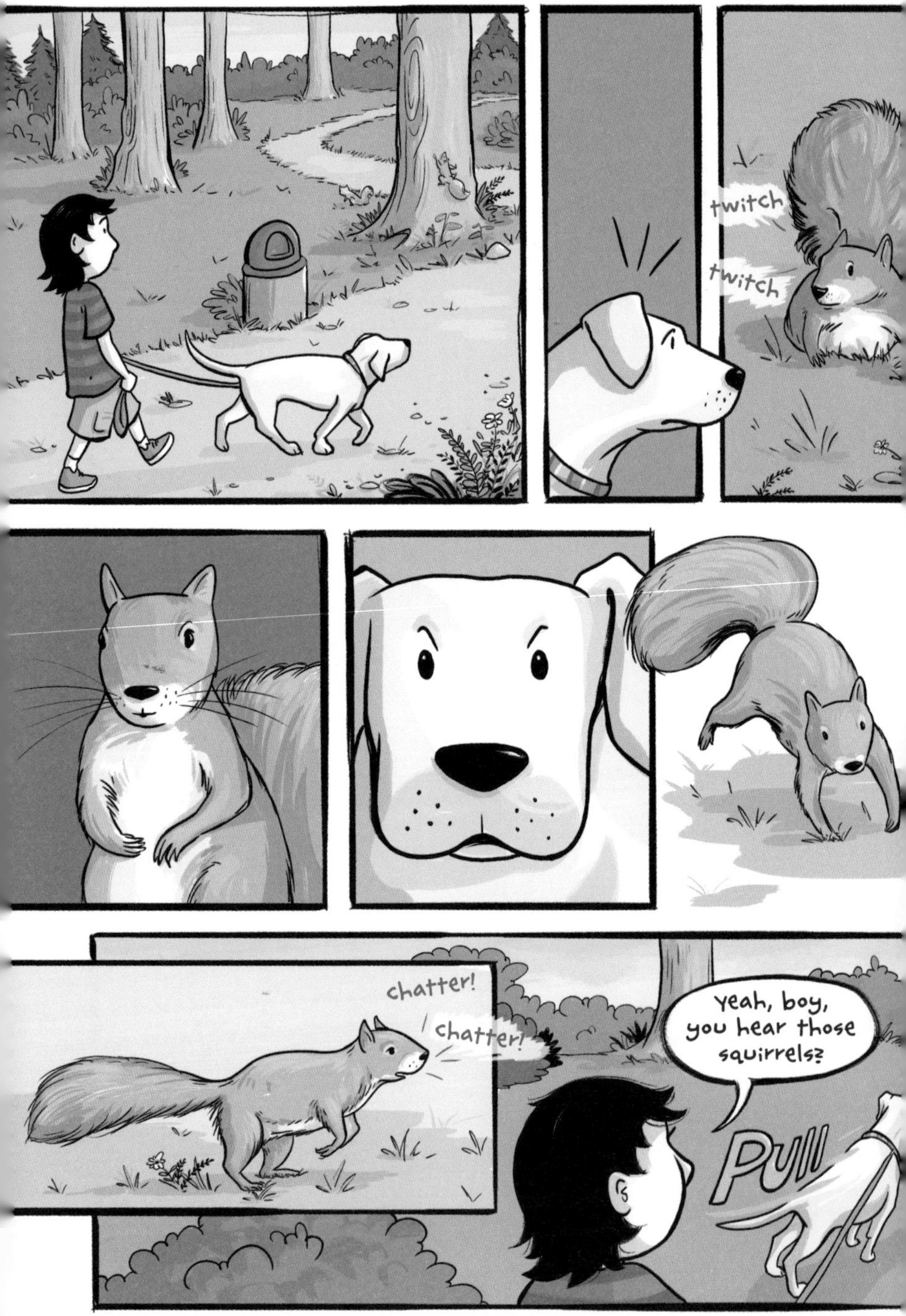
twitch
twitch
chatter!
chatter!
Yeah, boy, you hear those squirrels?
PULL

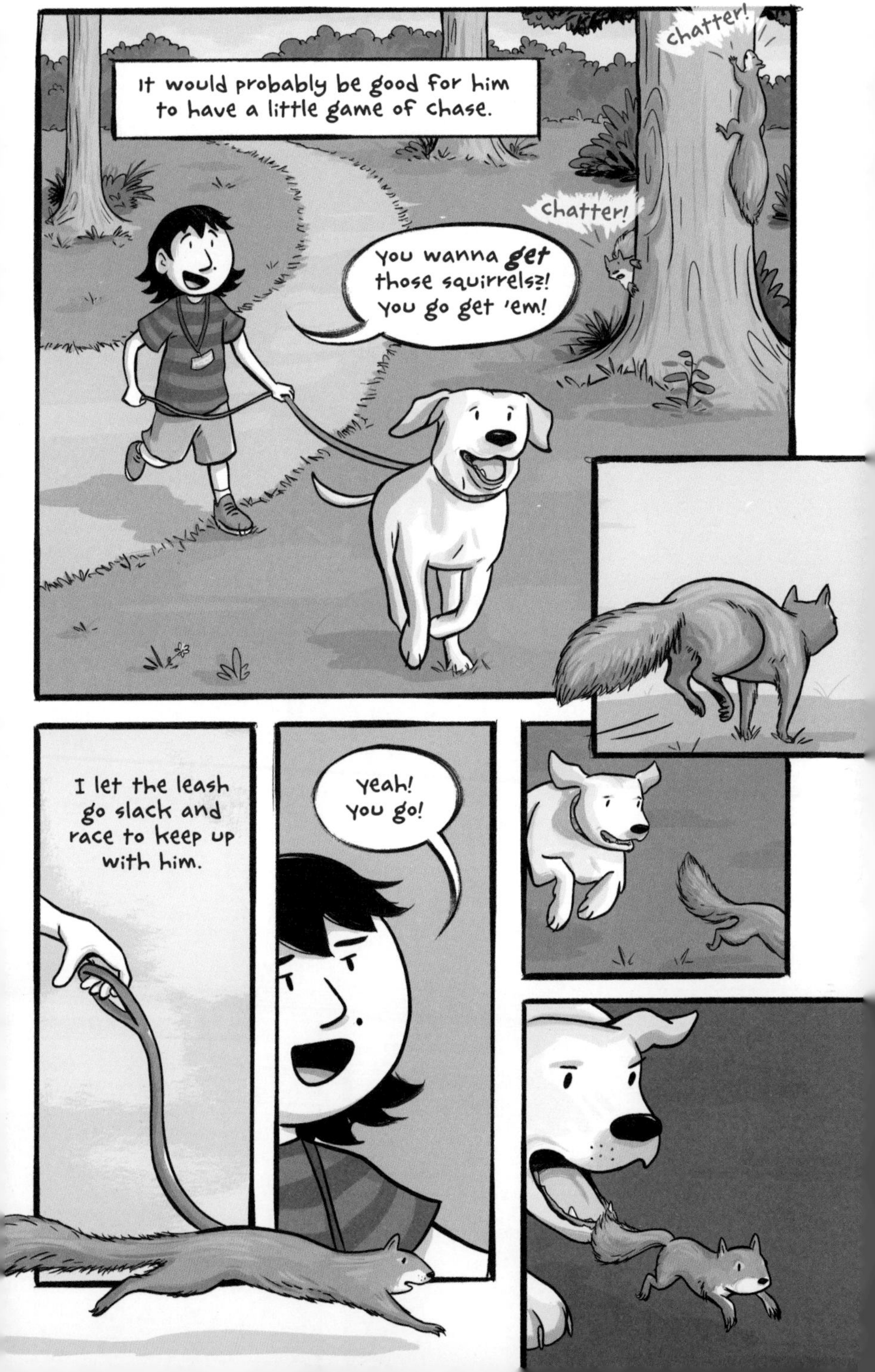
It would probably be good for him to have a little game of chase.
chatter!
chatter!
You wanna get those squirrels?! You go get 'em!
I let the leash go slack and race to keep up with him.
Yeah! You go!

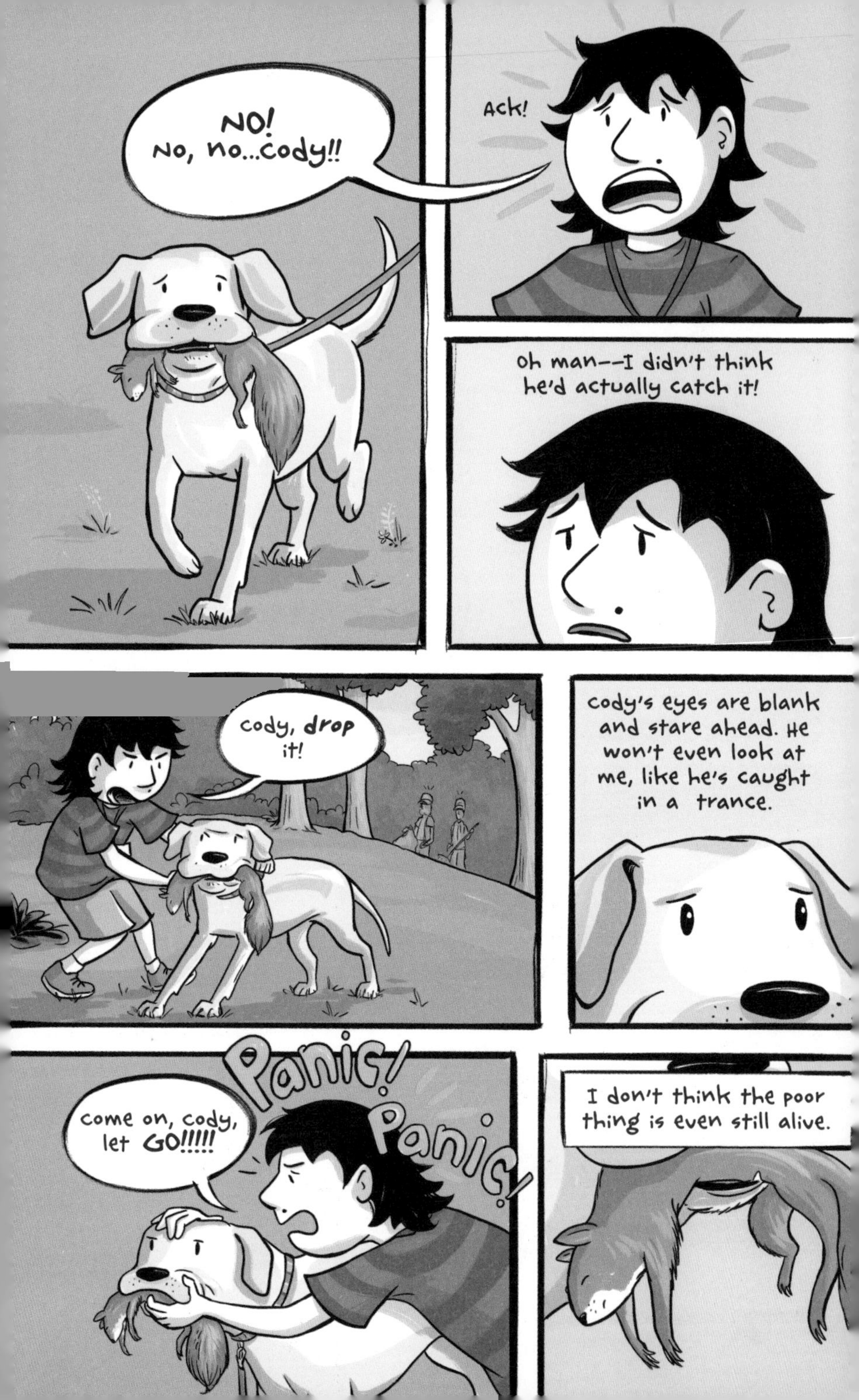

NO!
No, no...Cody!!
ACK!
Oh man--I didn't think he'd actually catch it!
Cody, drop it!
Cody's eyes are blank and stare ahead. He won't even look at me, like he's caught in a trance.
Come on, Cody, let GO!!!!!
Panic! Panic!
I don't think the poor thing is even still alive.

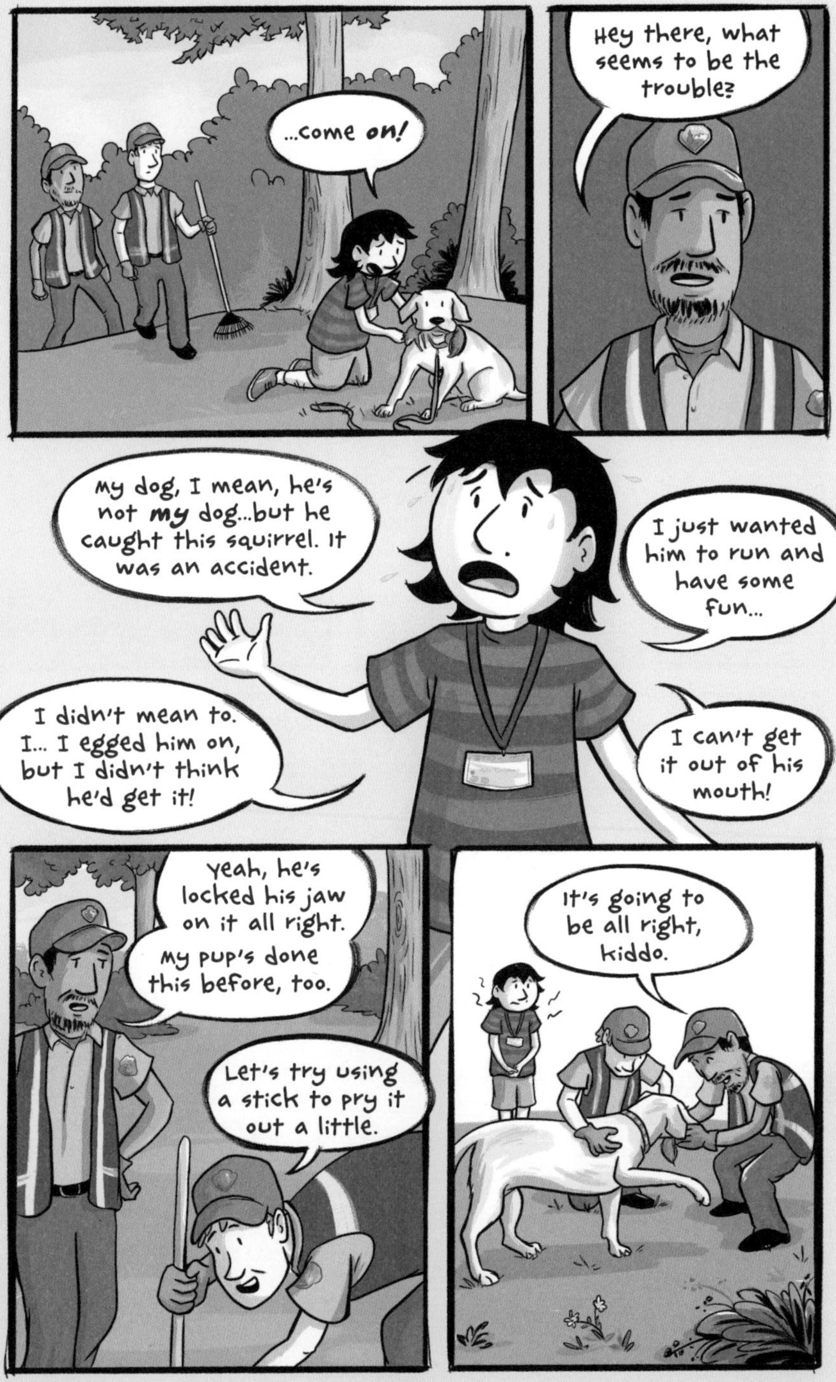

...come on!
Hey there, what seems to be the trouble?
My dog, I mean, he's not my dog...but he caught this squirrel. It was an accident.
I just wanted him to run and have some fun...
I didn't mean to. I... I egged him on, but I didn't think he'd get it!
I can't get it out of his mouth!
Yeah, he's locked his jaw on it all right.
My pup's done this before, too.
Let's try using a stick to pry it out a little.
It's going to be all right, kiddo.

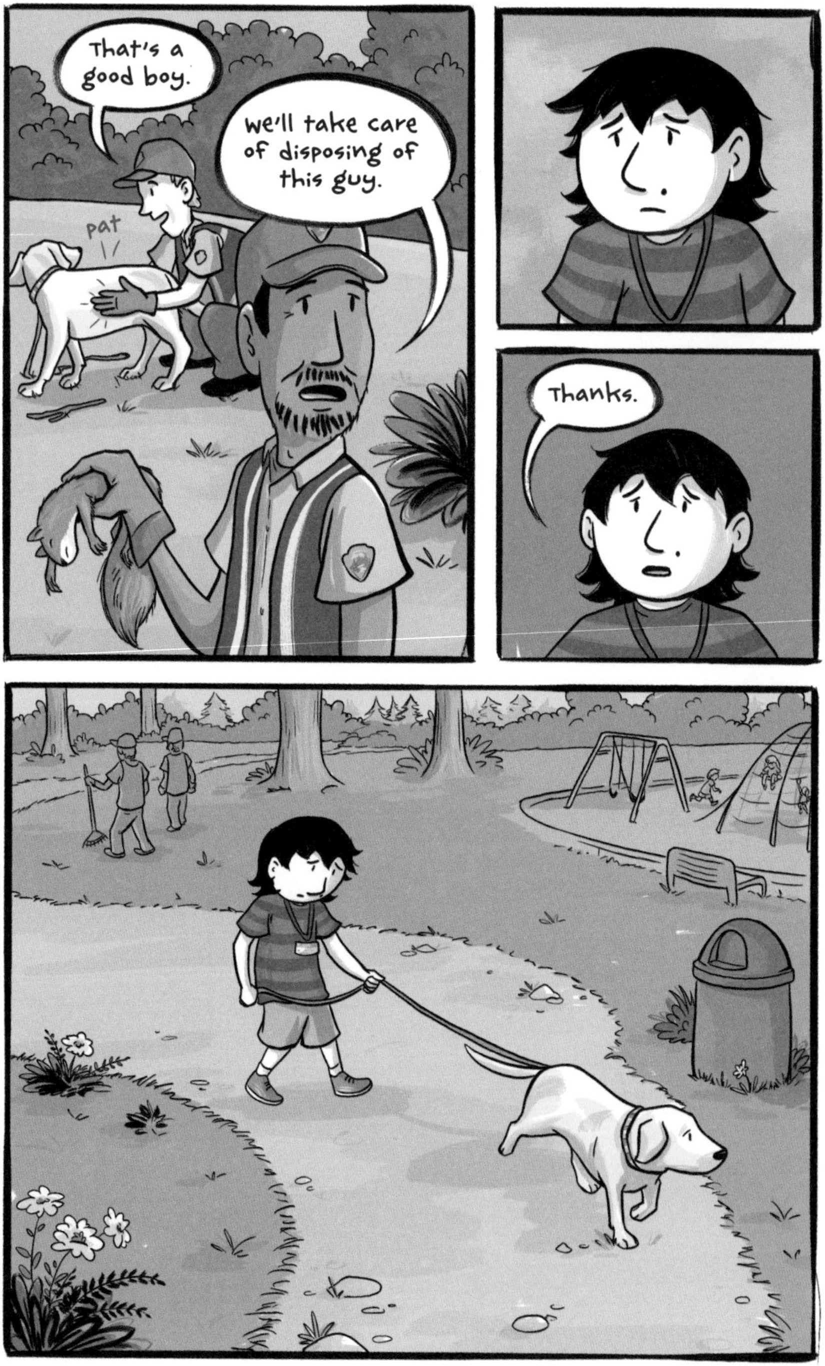
That's a good boy.
pat
We'll take care of disposing of this guy.
Thanks.

I can't get the image of that dead squirrel out of my head the whole way back to the shelter.

kick

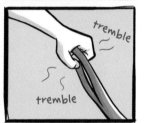

tremble

tremble

Why didn't it *run* faster?!

I feel sick to my stomach.

WELCO
OPEN

I gotta get out of here.

Hey, Ash...

grunt

I blow by Darren...

...and hurry by Jo before she can ask any questions.

Jo, I'm going to head home early today. I'm not feeling good.

Oh. Is everything--

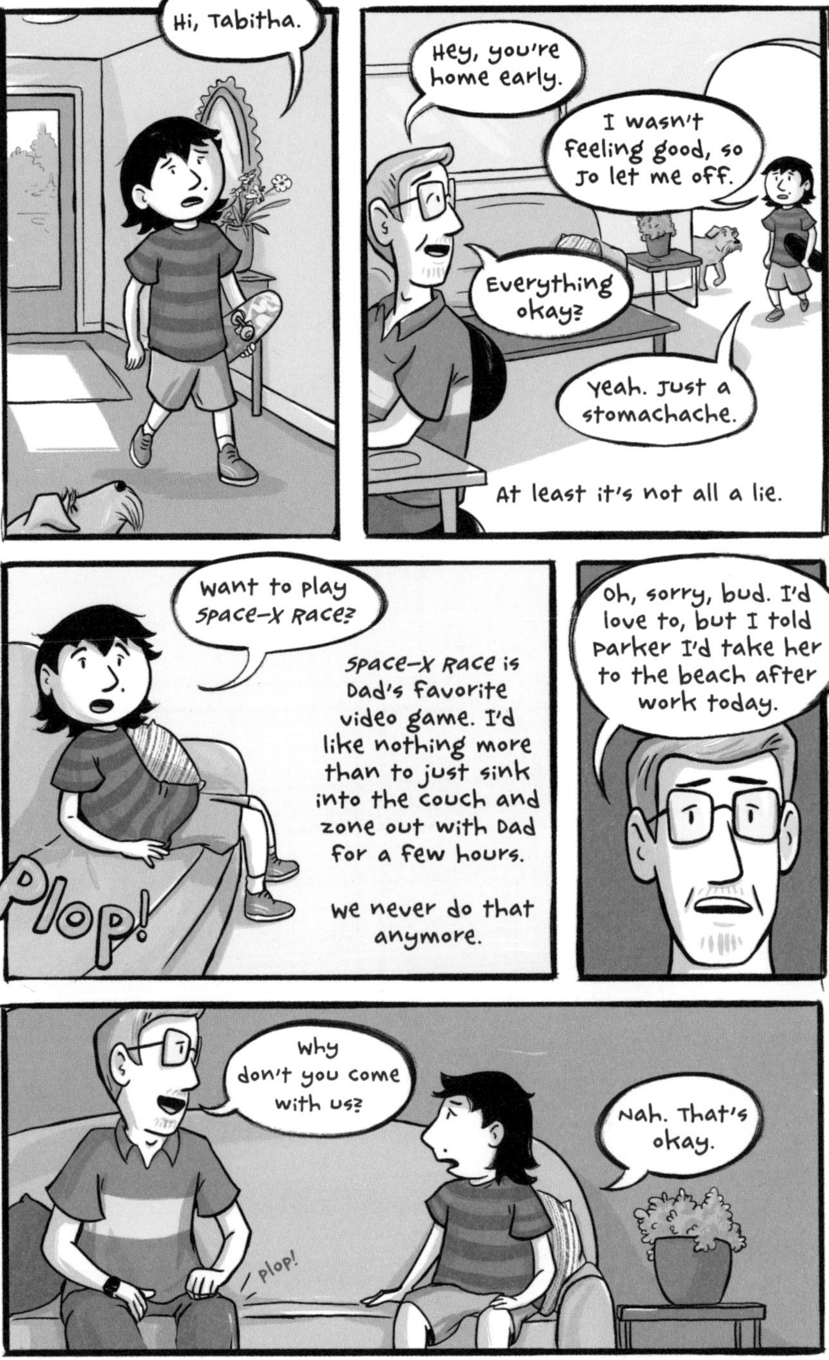
Hi, Tabitha.
Hey, you're home early.
I wasn't feeling good, so Jo let me off.
Everything okay?
Yeah. Just a stomachache.
At least it's not all a lie.
Want to play Space-X Race?
Space-X Race is Dad's favorite video game. I'd like nothing more than to just sink into the couch and zone out with Dad for a few hours.
We never do that anymore.
PLOP!
Oh, sorry, bud. I'd love to, but I told Parker I'd take her to the beach after work today.
Why don't you come with us?
Nah. That's okay.
plop!

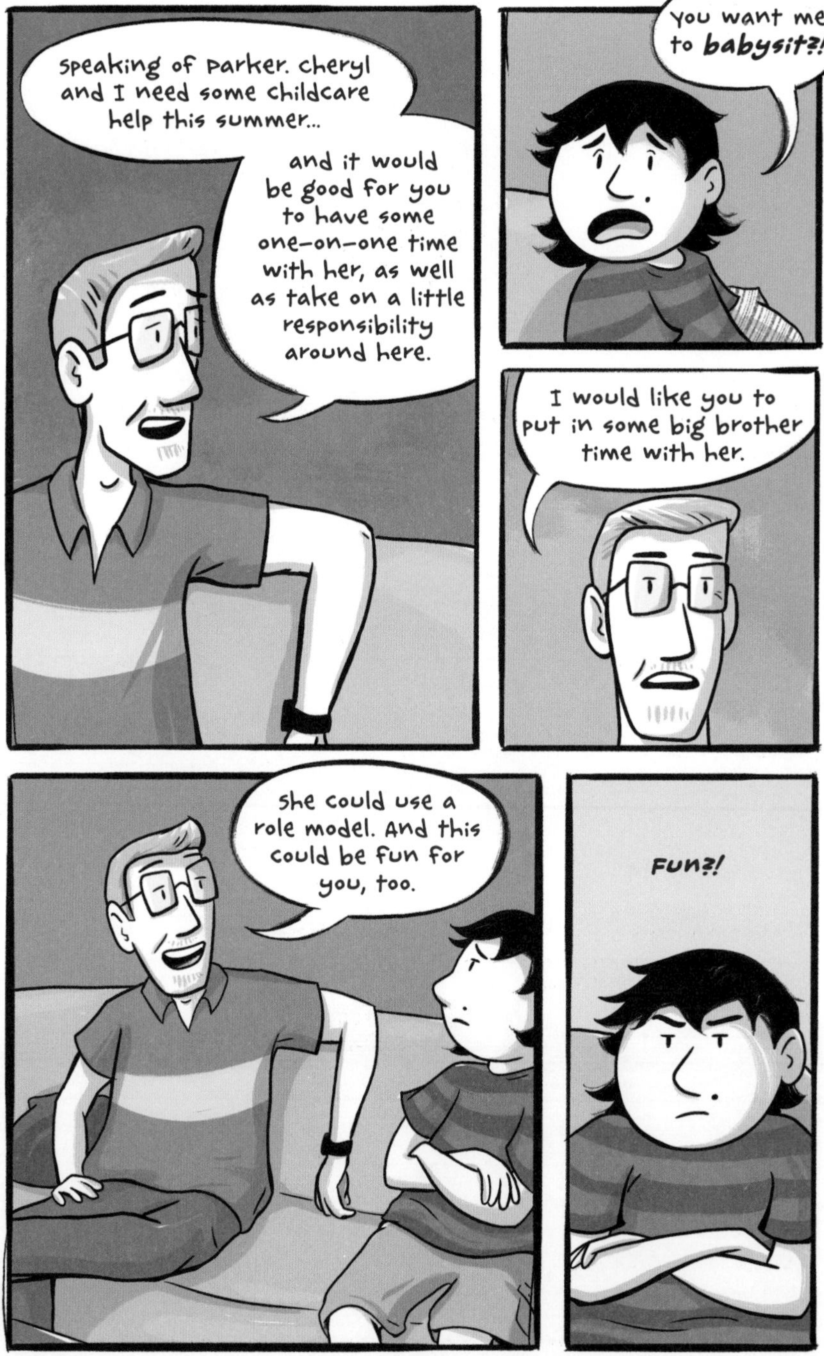
Speaking of Parker. Cheryl and I need some childcare help this summer...
and it would be good for you to have some one-on-one time with her, as well as take on a little responsibility around here.
You want me to *babysit?!*
I would like you to put in some big brother time with her.
She could use a role model. And this could be fun for you, too.
FUN?!

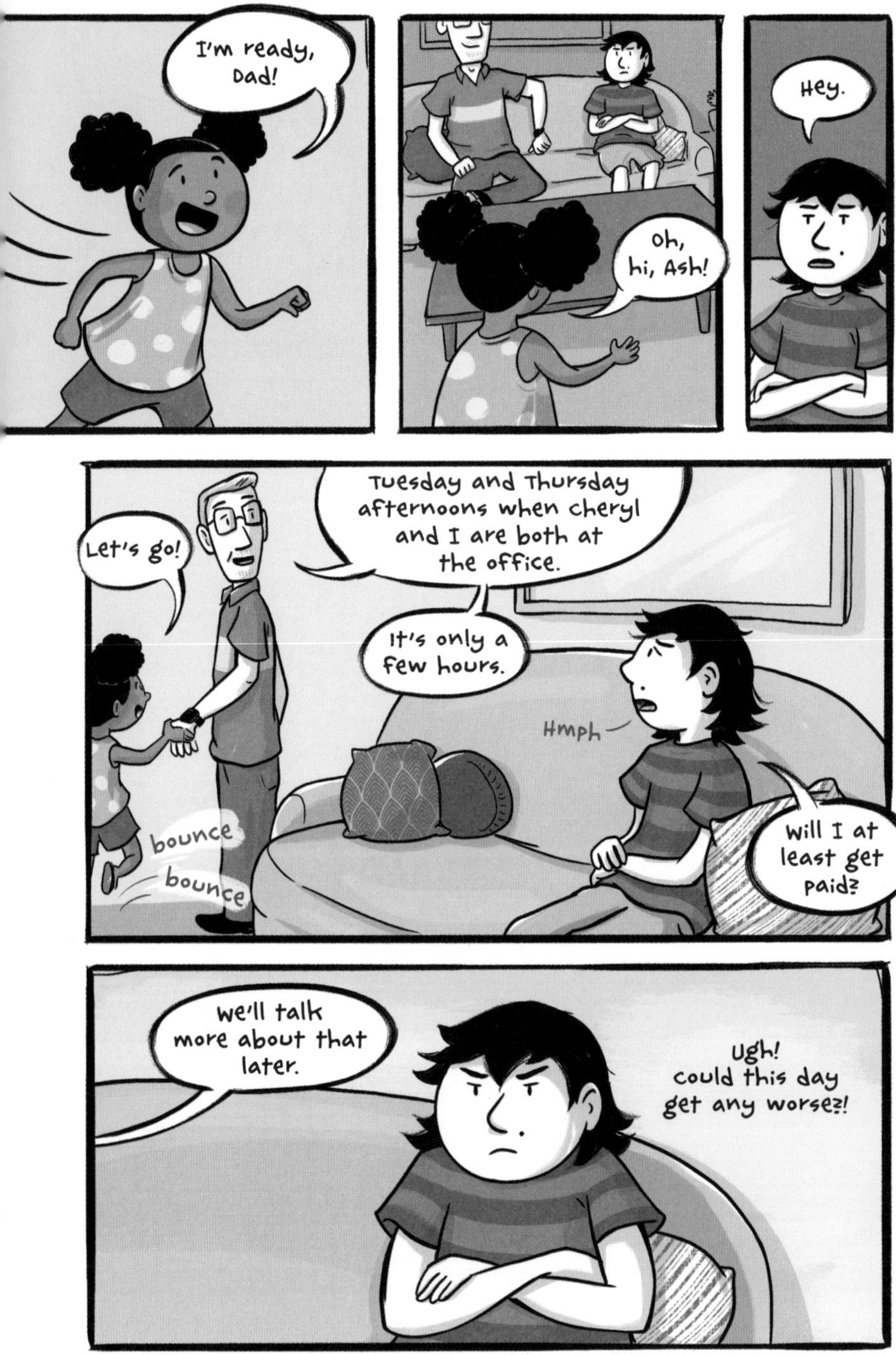
I'm ready, Dad!
Oh, hi, Ash!
Hey.
Let's go!
Tuesday and Thursday afternoons when Cheryl and I are both at the office.
It's only a few hours.
Hmph
Will I at least get paid?
bounce
bounce
We'll talk more about that later.
Ugh! Could this day get any worse?!

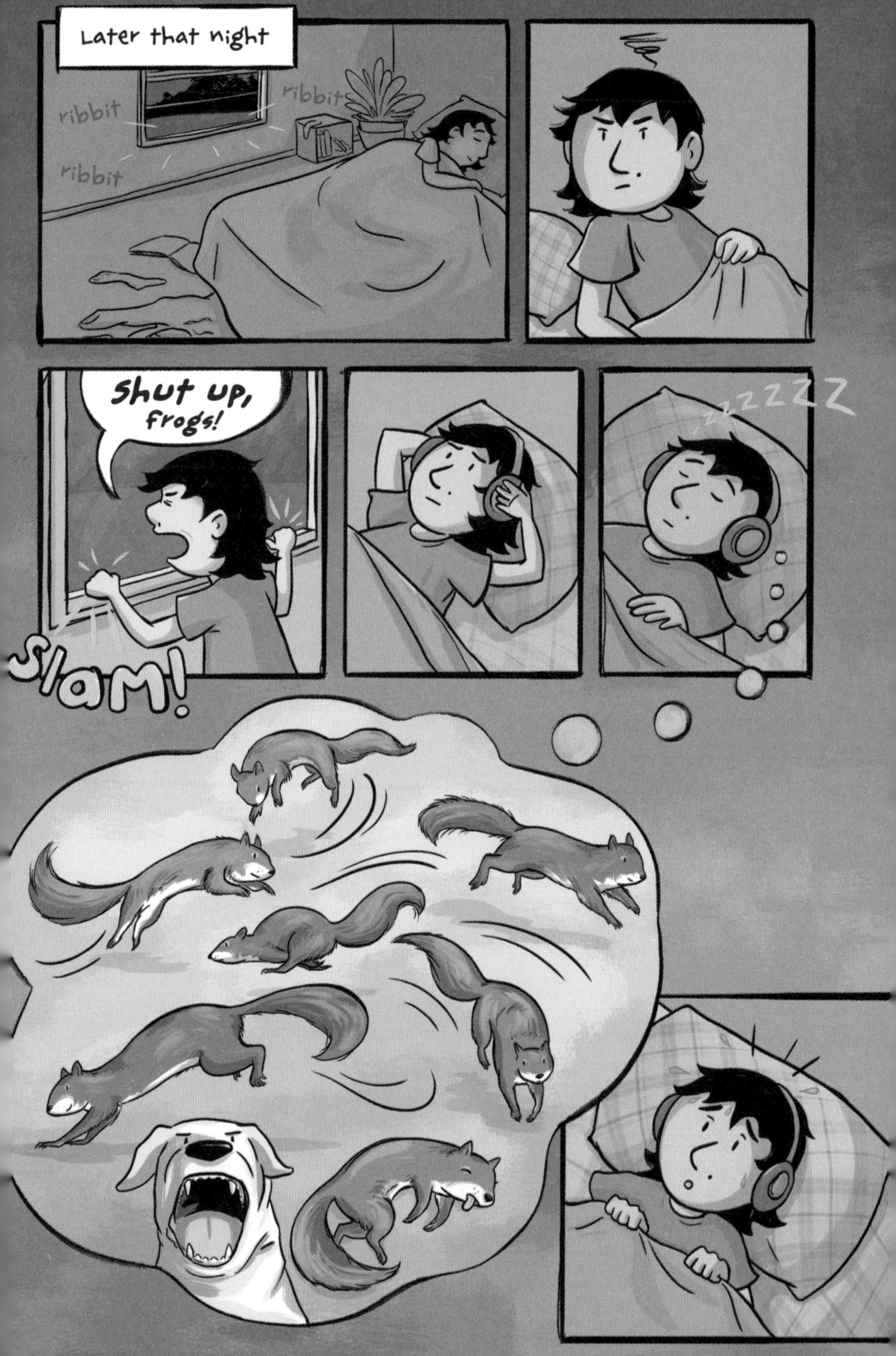
Later that night
ribbit
ribbit
ribbit
Shut up, frogs!
SLAM!
ZZZZZZ

CHAPTER 5

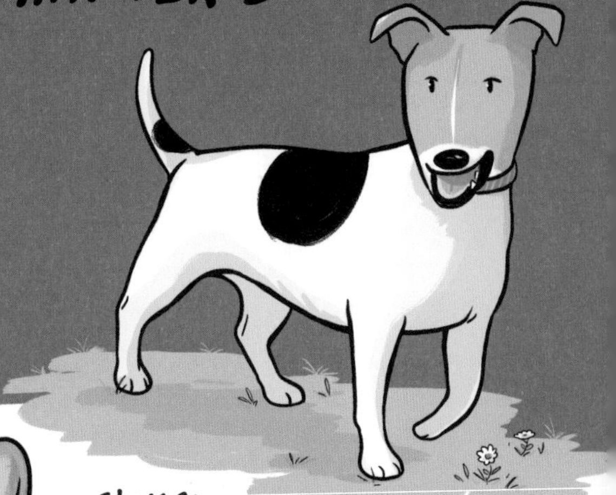

• Stoney •

A scrappy Jack Russell terrier whose favorite game is batting his jingle ball under the couch and then whining until it's fetched for him. Russells are energetic with ***big*** personalities. They're charming and affectionate, but they can be a handful to train and manage.

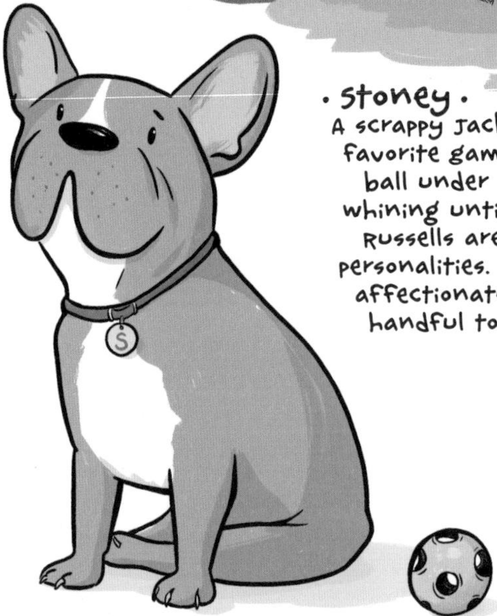

• Spatula •

A French bulldog who loves to sleep completely buried under the covers of her owner's bed. Considered to be one of the best companion dogs, Frenchies are small and muscular in build. They love to play but also enjoy spending their days relaxing on the sofa.

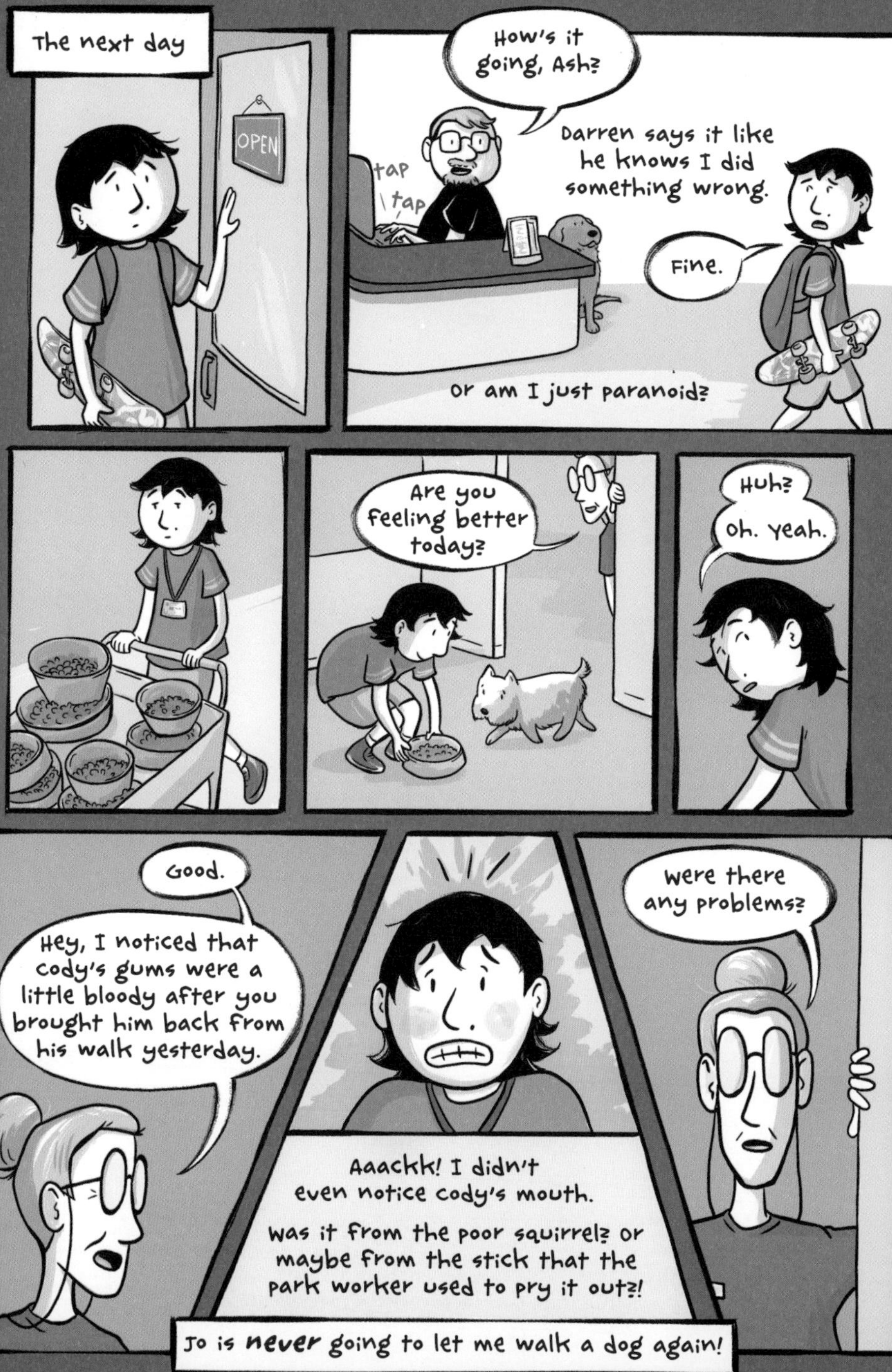
The next day
OPEN
How's it going, Ash?
tap
tap
Darren says it like he knows I did something wrong.
Fine.
Or am I just paranoid?
Are you feeling better today?
Huh?
Oh. Yeah.
Good.
Hey, I noticed that Cody's gums were a little bloody after you brought him back from his walk yesterday.
Were there any problems?
Aaackk! I didn't even notice Cody's mouth.
Was it from the poor squirrel? Or maybe from the stick that the park worker used to pry it out?!
Jo is never going to let me walk a dog again!

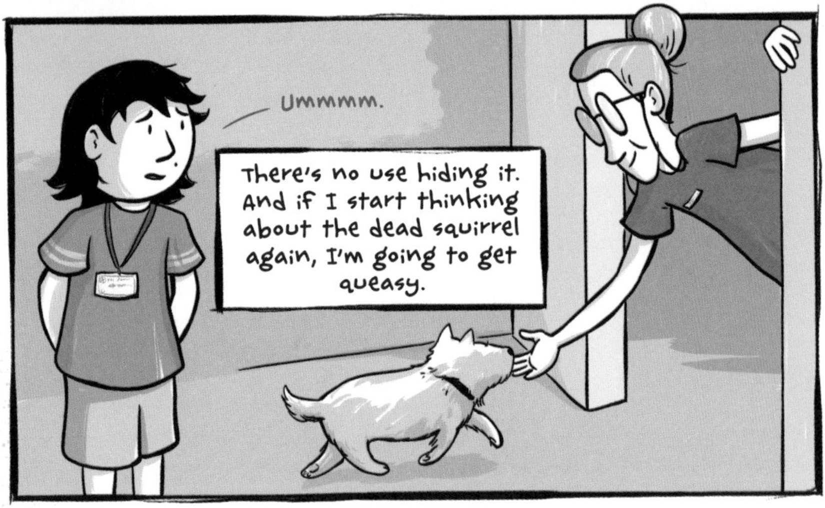
Ummmm.
There's no use hiding it. And if I start thinking about the dead squirrel again, I'm going to get queasy.

My voice uncontrollably jumps a few octaves higher and I'm a blubbering idiot as I spill out my confession...trying to make Jo understand.

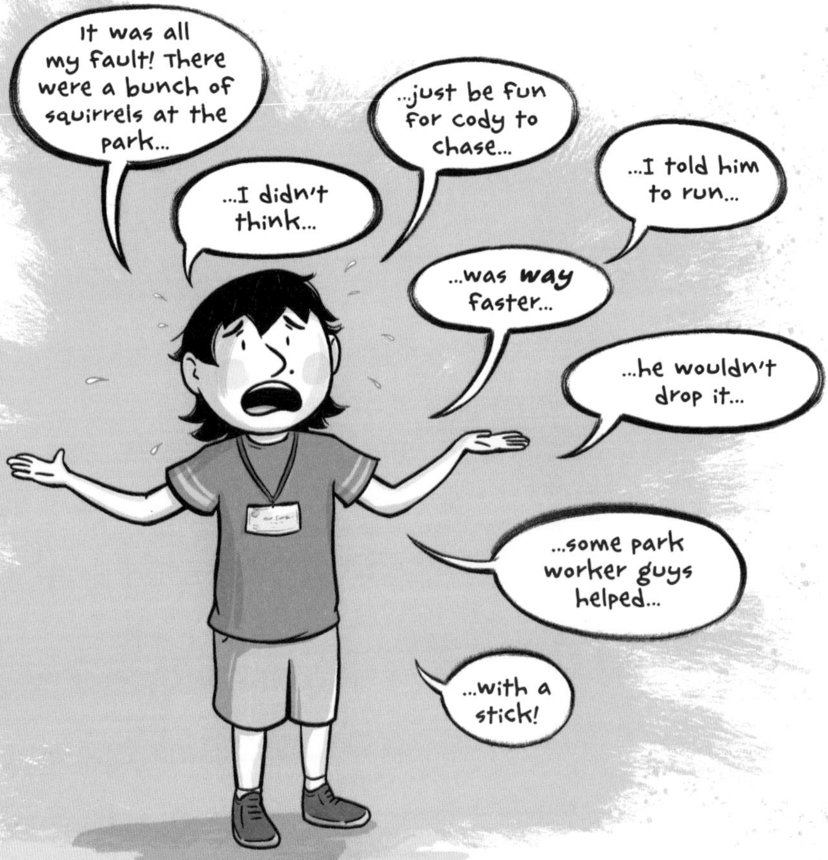
It was all my fault! There were a bunch of squirrels at the park...
...I didn't think...
...just be fun for Cody to chase...
...I told him to run...
...was way faster...
...he wouldn't drop it...
...some park worker guys helped...
...with a stick!

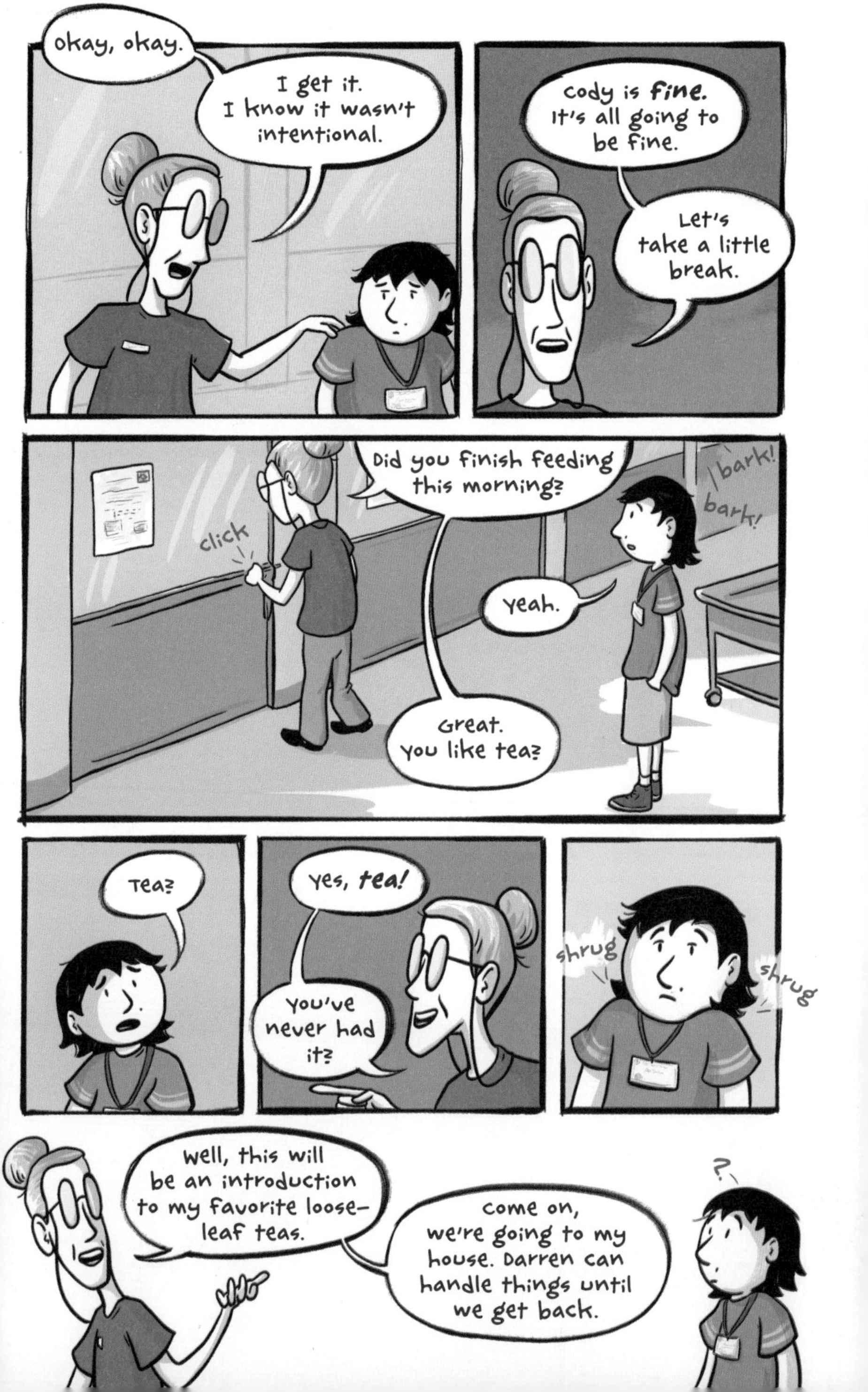
okay, okay.
I get it. I know it wasn't intentional.
cody is fine. It's all going to be fine.
Let's take a little break.
Did you finish feeding this morning?
click
bark!
bark!
Yeah.
Great. You like tea?
Tea?
Yes, tea!
You've never had it?
shrug
shrug
Well, this will be an introduction to my favorite loose-leaf teas.
come on, we're going to my house. Darren can handle things until we get back.
?

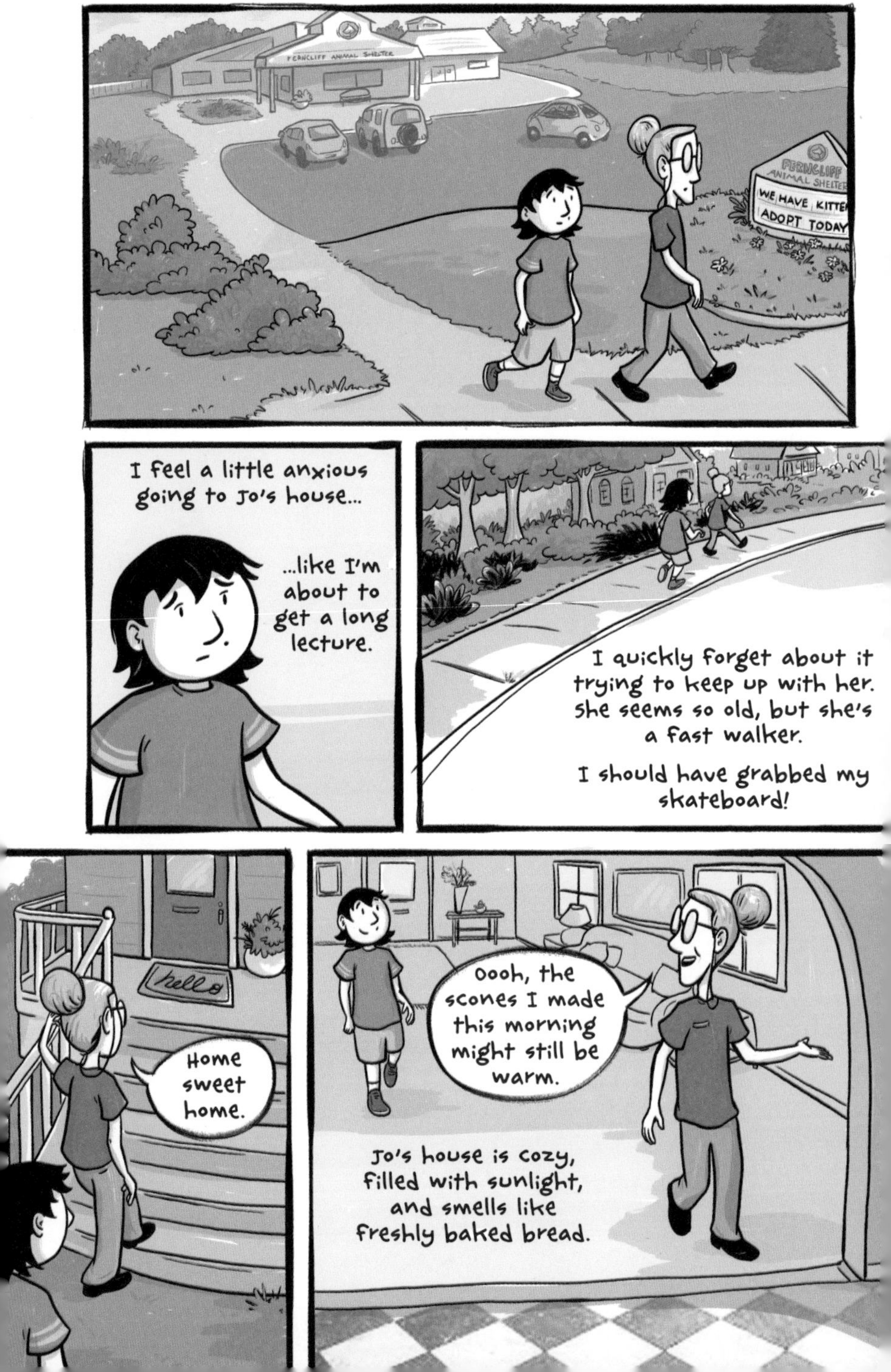
FERNCLIFF ANIMAL SHELTER
FERNCLIFF ANIMAL SHELTER
WE HAVE KITTE
ADOPT TODAY
I feel a little anxious going to Jo's house...
...like I'm about to get a long lecture.
I quickly forget about it trying to keep up with her. She seems so old, but she's a fast walker.
I should have grabbed my skateboard!
hello
Home sweet home.
Oooh, the scones I made this morning might still be warm.
Jo's house is cozy, filled with sunlight, and smells like freshly baked bread.

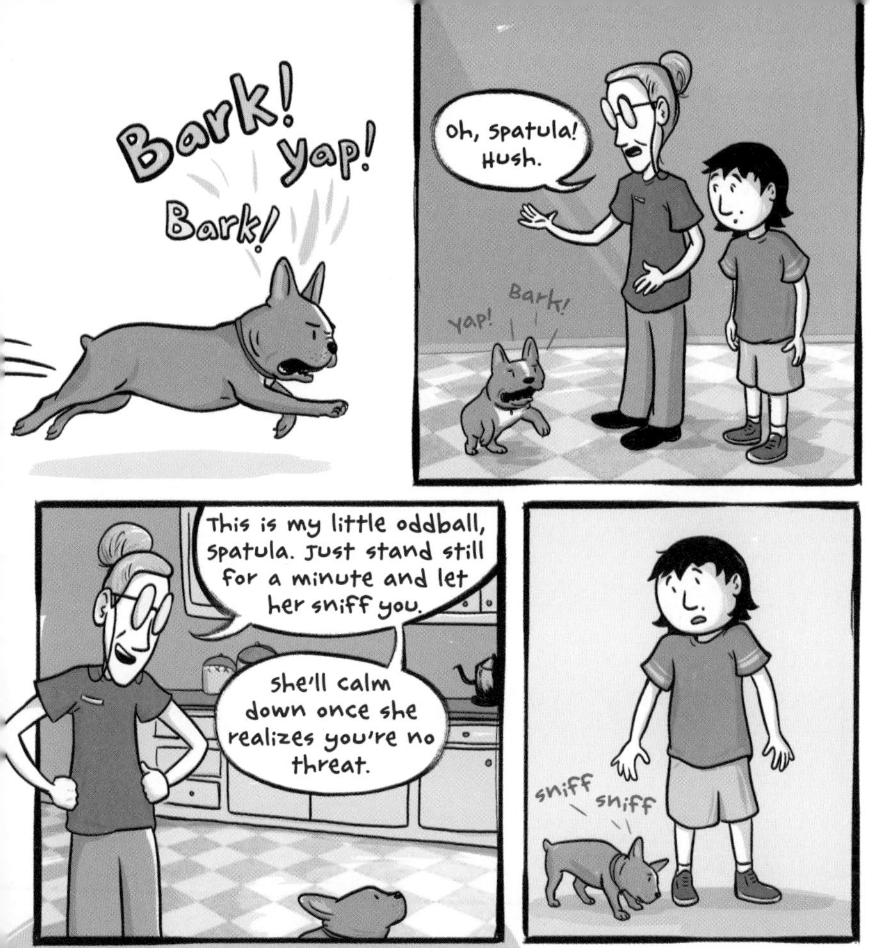
Bark!
Yap!
Bark!
Oh, Spatula! Hush.
Yap!
Bark!
This is my little oddball, Spatula. Just stand still for a minute and let her sniff you.
She'll calm down once she realizes you're no threat.
sniff
sniff

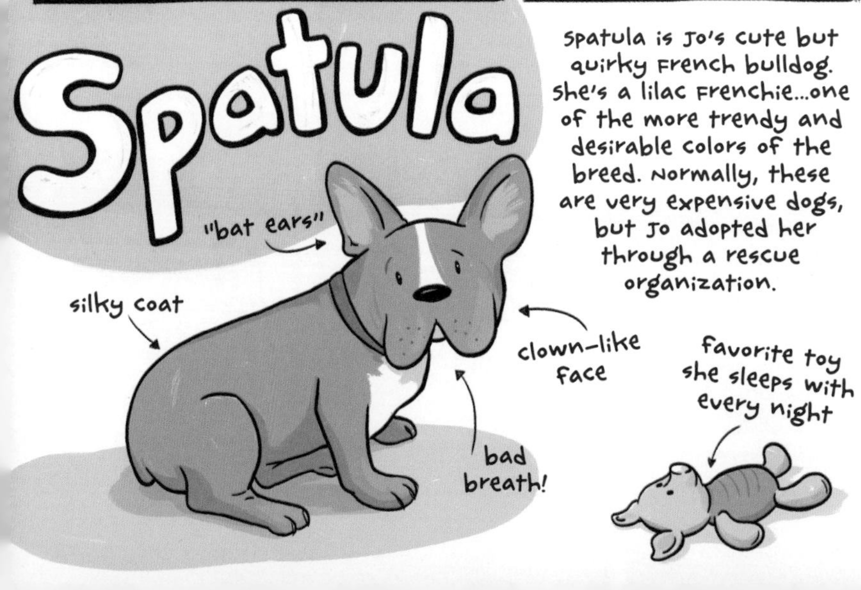
Spatula
Spatula is Jo's cute but quirky French bulldog. She's a lilac Frenchie...one of the more trendy and desirable colors of the breed. Normally, these are very expensive dogs, but Jo adopted her through a rescue organization.
"bat ears"
silky coat
clown-like face
bad breath!
favorite toy she sleeps with every night

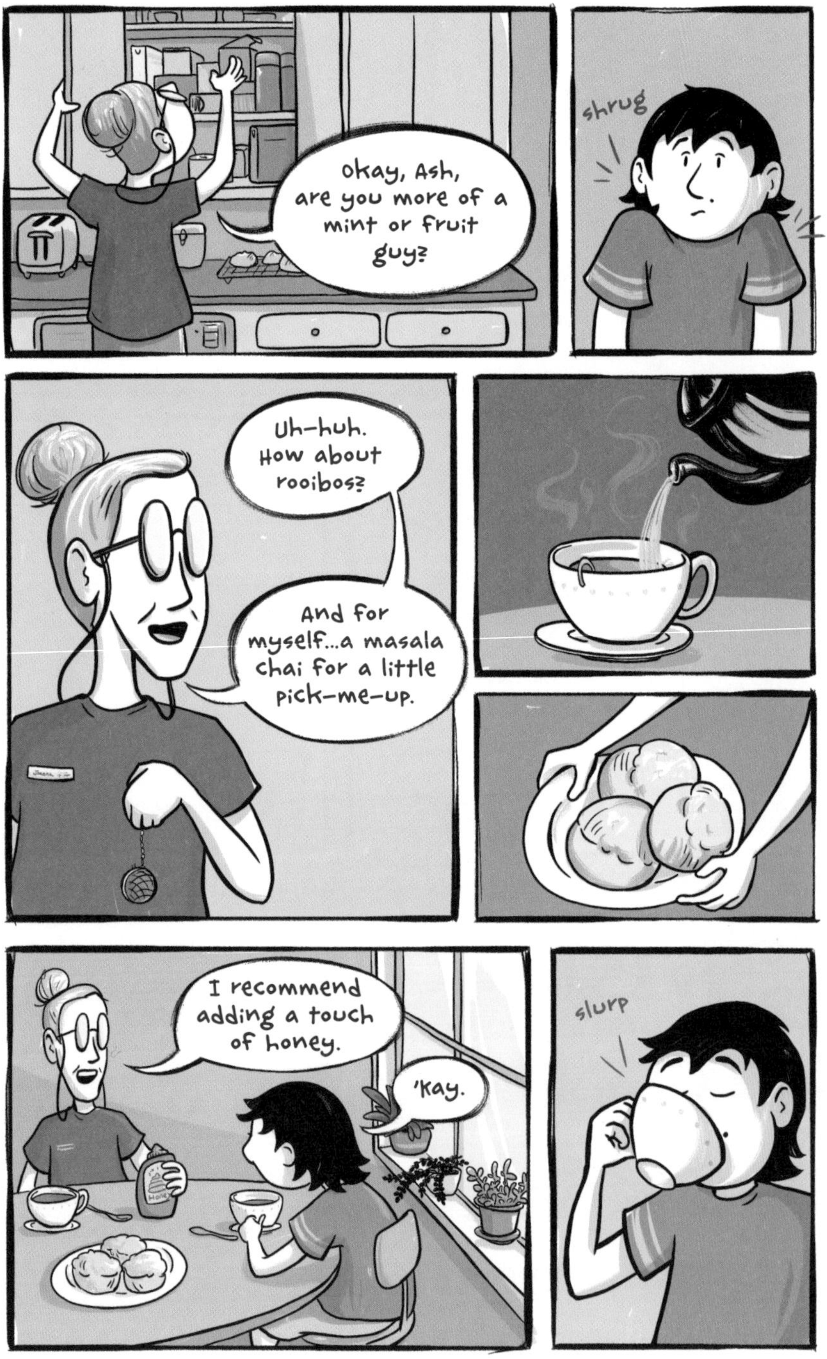
Okay, Ash, are you more of a mint or fruit guy?
shrug
Uh-huh. How about rooibos?
And for myself...a masala chai for a little pick-me-up.
I recommend adding a touch of honey.
'Kay.
slurp

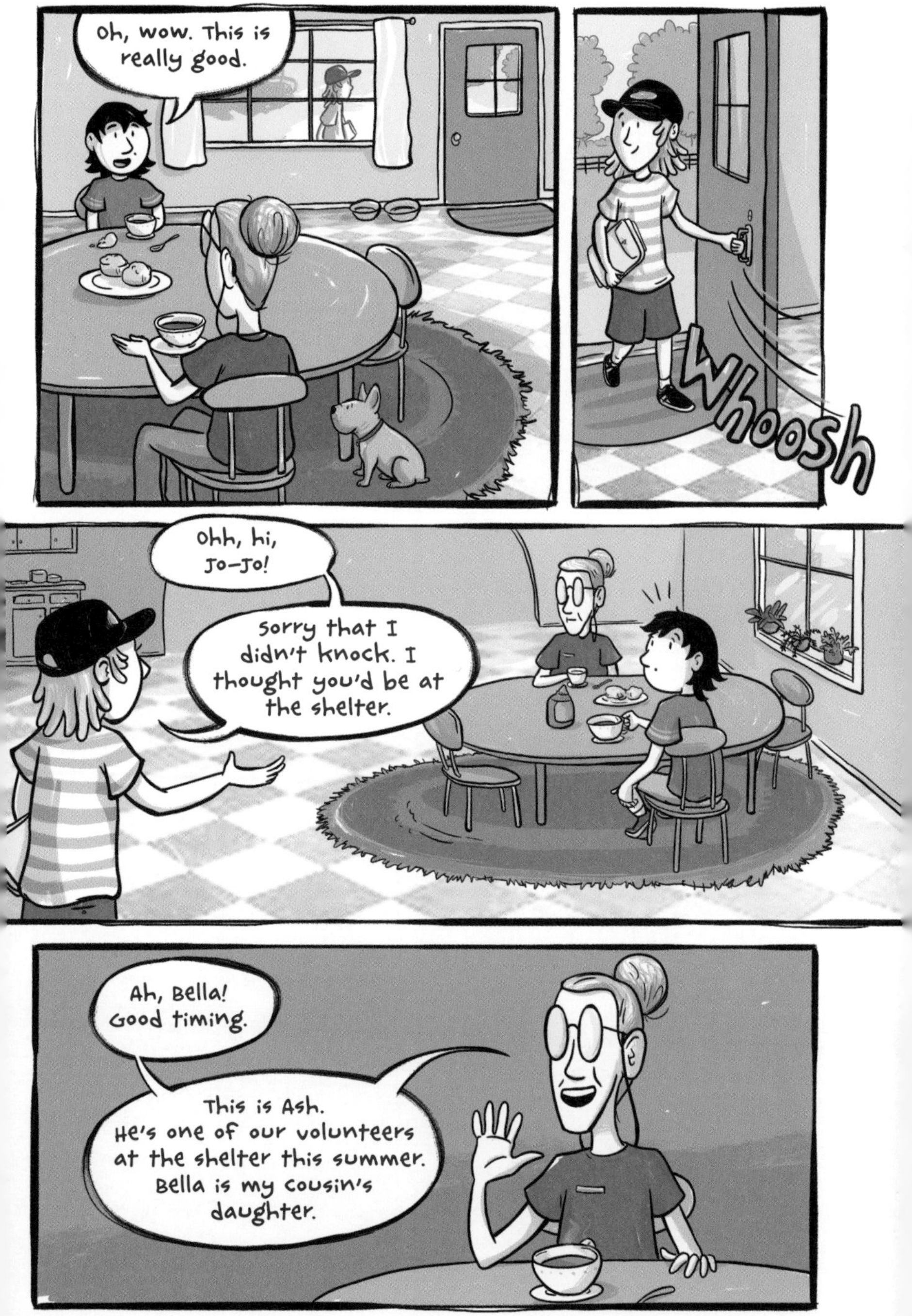
Oh, wow. This is really good.
Whoosh
Ohh, hi, Jo-Jo!
Sorry that I didn't knock. I thought you'd be at the shelter.
Ah, Bella! Good timing.
This is Ash. He's one of our volunteers at the shelter this summer. Bella is my cousin's daughter.

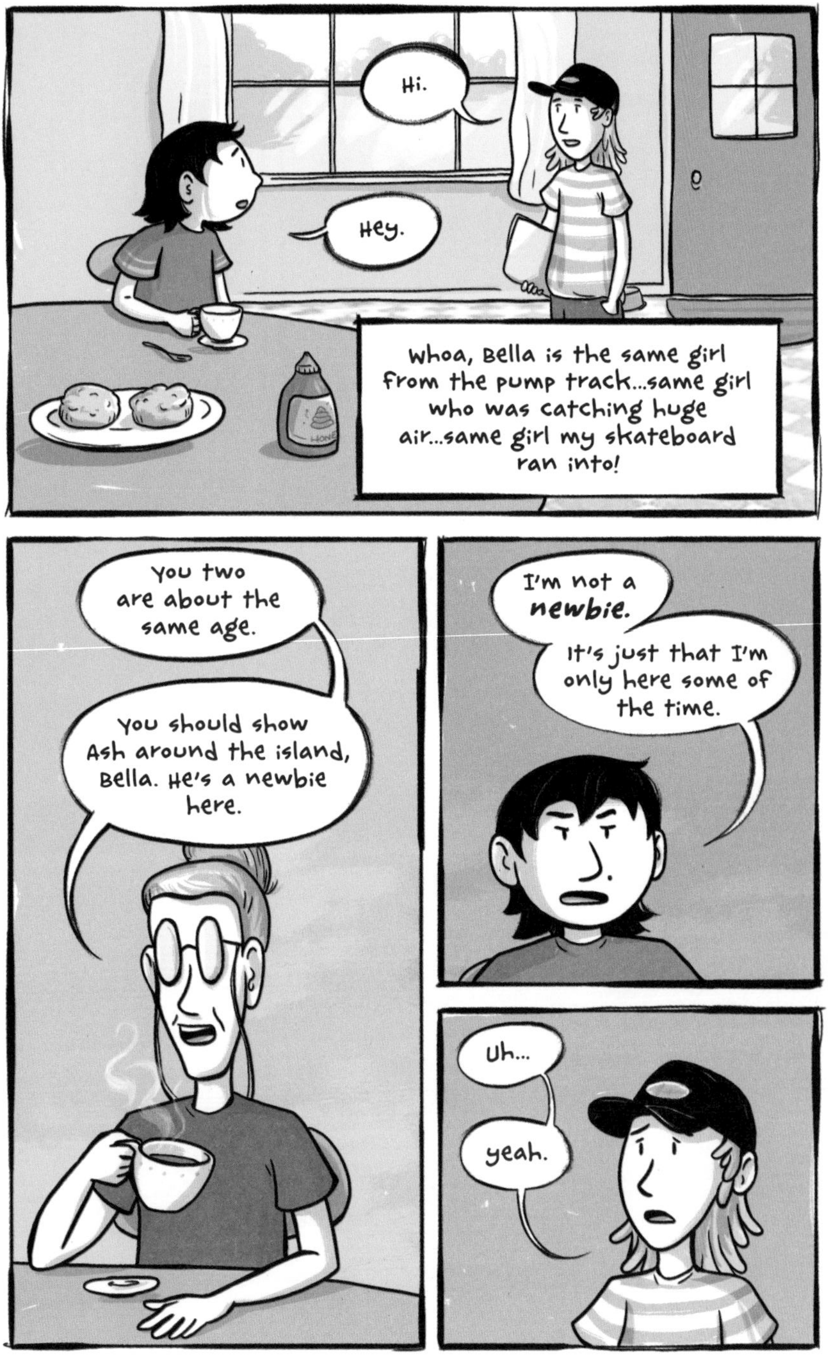
Hi.
Hey.
Whoa, Bella is the same girl from the pump track...same girl who was catching huge air...same girl my skateboard ran into!
You two are about the same age.
You should show Ash around the island, Bella. He's a newbie here.
I'm not a **newbie.**
It's just that I'm only here some of the time.
Uh...
yeah.

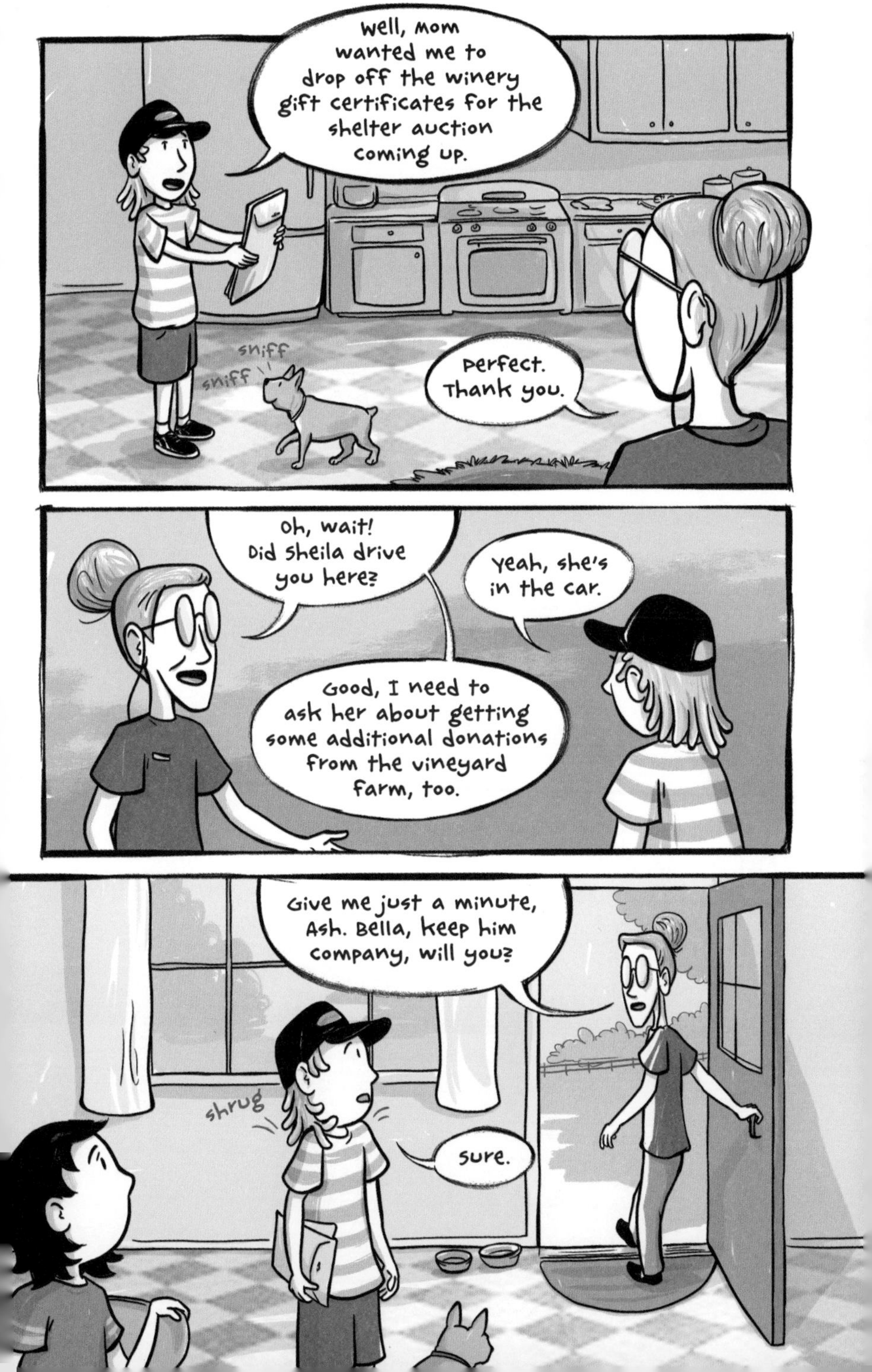

Well, mom wanted me to drop off the winery gift certificates for the shelter auction coming up.
sniff
sniff
Perfect. Thank you.
Oh, wait! Did Sheila drive you here?
Yeah, she's in the car.
Good, I need to ask her about getting some additional donations from the vineyard farm, too.
Give me just a minute, Ash. Bella, keep him company, will you?
shrug
Sure.

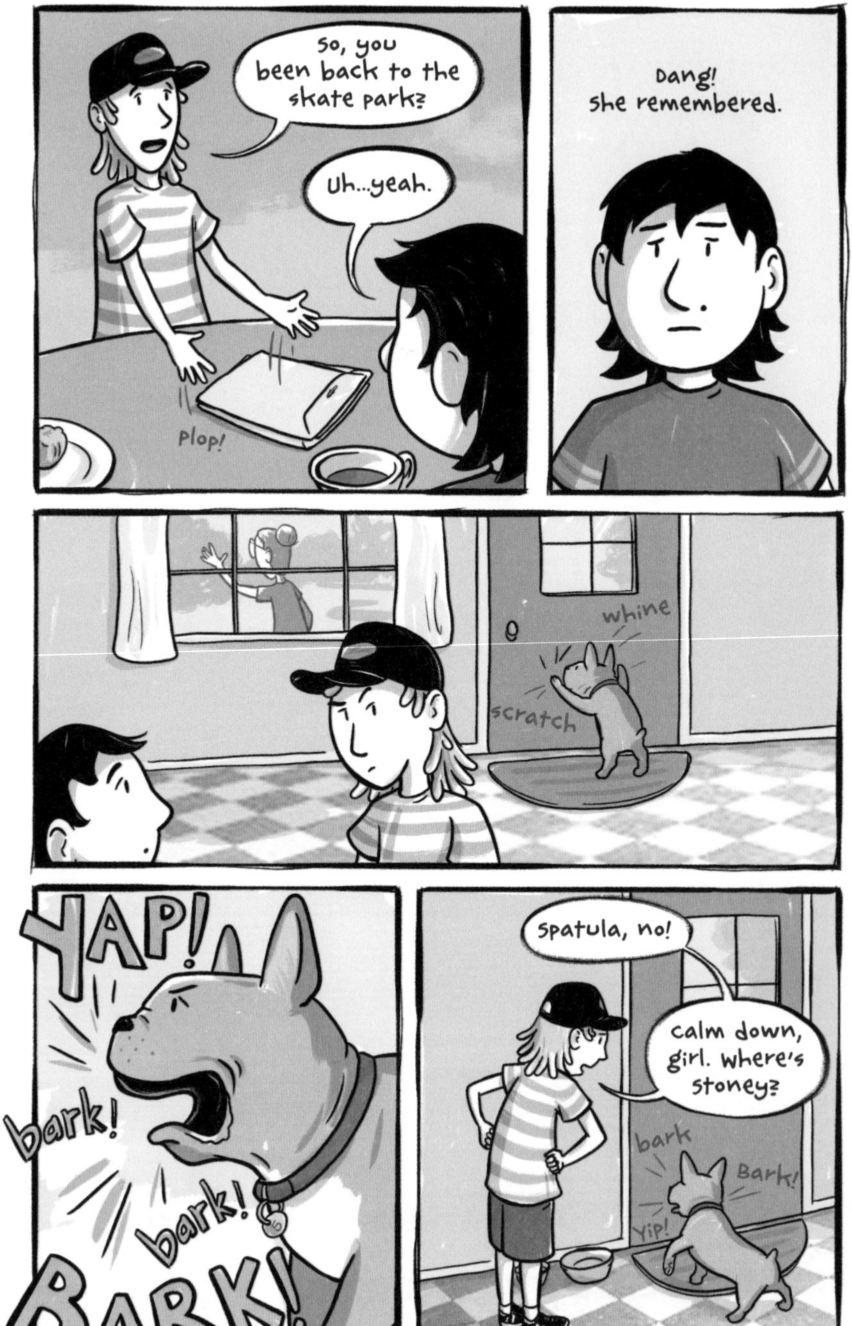
So, you been back to the skate park?
Uh...yeah.
Plop!
Dang! She remembered.
whine
scratch
YAP!
bark!
bark!
BARK!
Spatula, no!
Calm down, girl. Where's Stoney?
bark
Bark!
Yip!

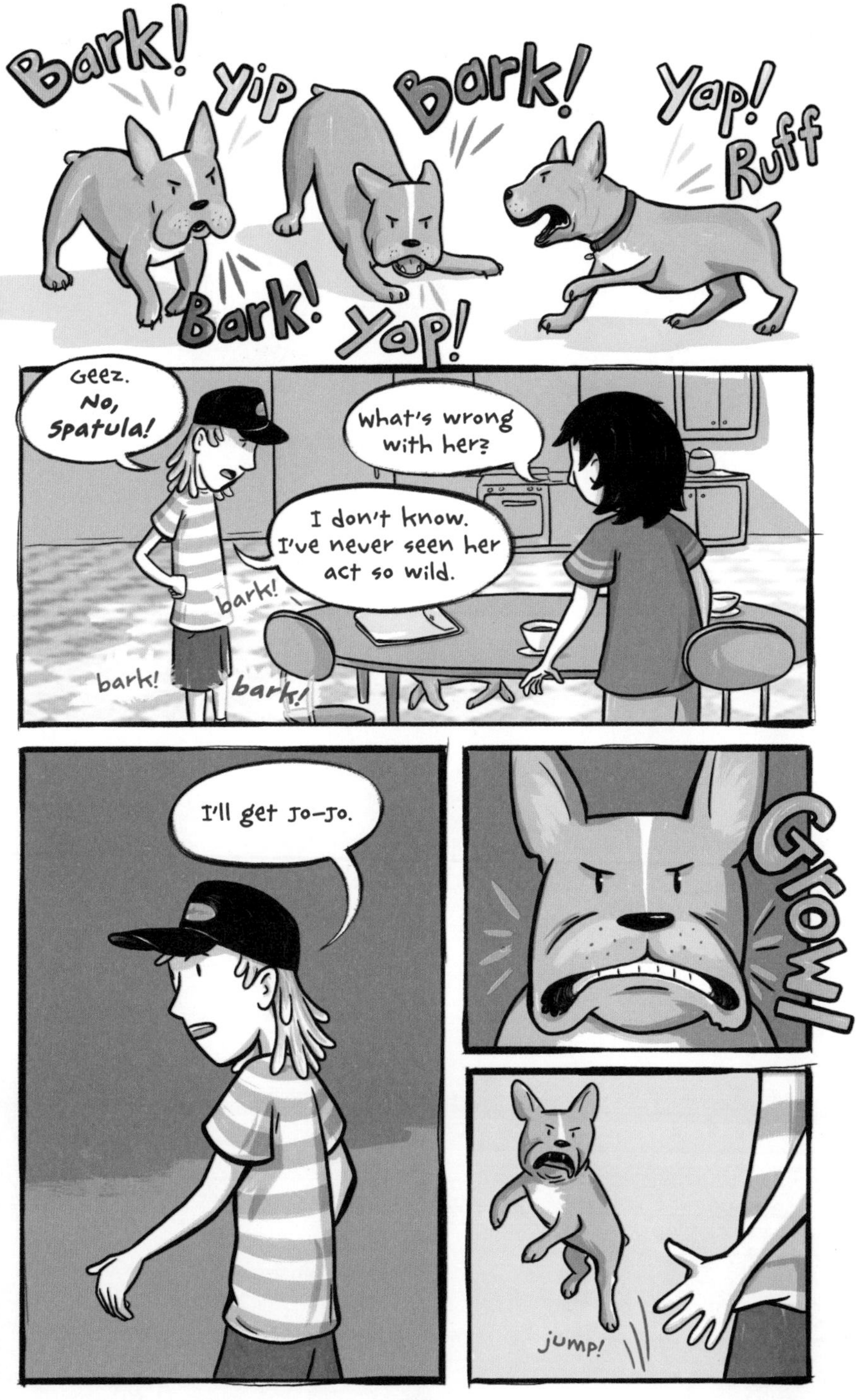
Bark!
Yip
Bark!
Yap!
Ruff
Bark!
Yap!
Geez.
No,
Spatula!
What's wrong
with her?
I don't know.
I've never seen her
act so wild.
bark!
bark!
bark!
I'll get Jo-Jo.
GROWL
jump!

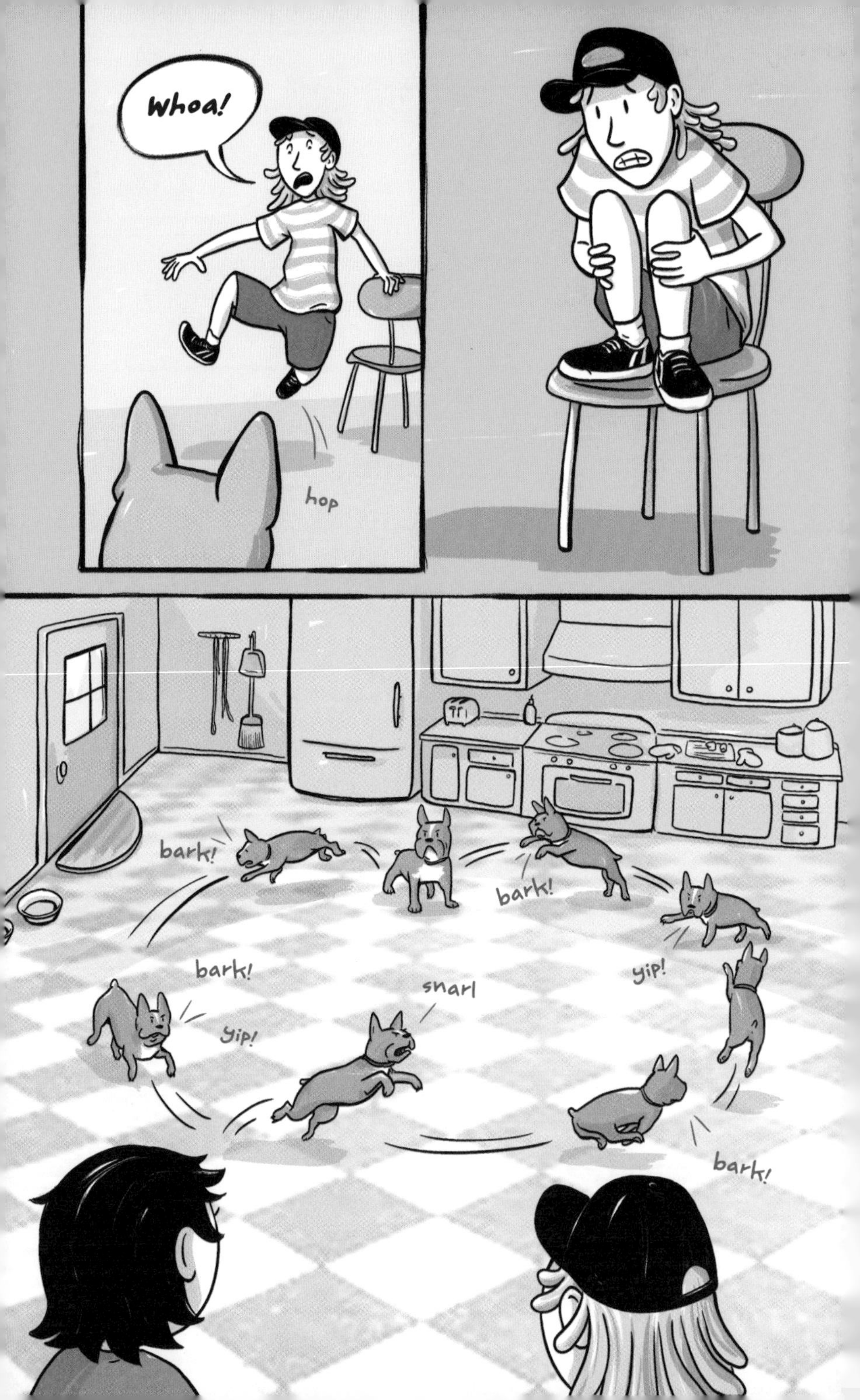
Whoa!
hop
bark!
bark!
bark!
snarl
yip!
yip!
bark!

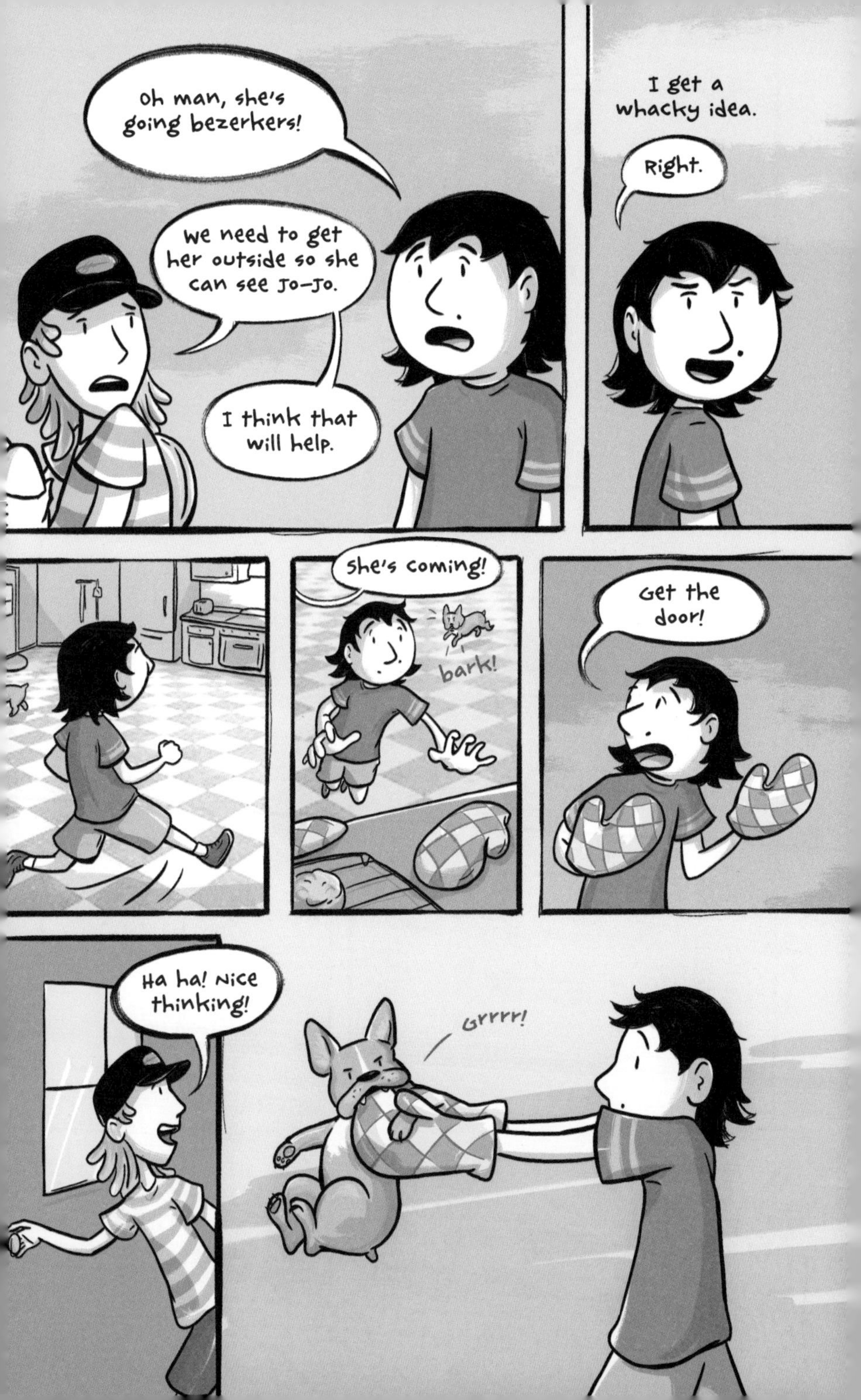
Oh man, she's going bezerkers!
We need to get her outside so she can see Jo-Jo.
I think that will help.
I get a whacky idea.
Right.
She's coming!
bark!
Get the door!
Ha ha! Nice thinking!
Grrrr!

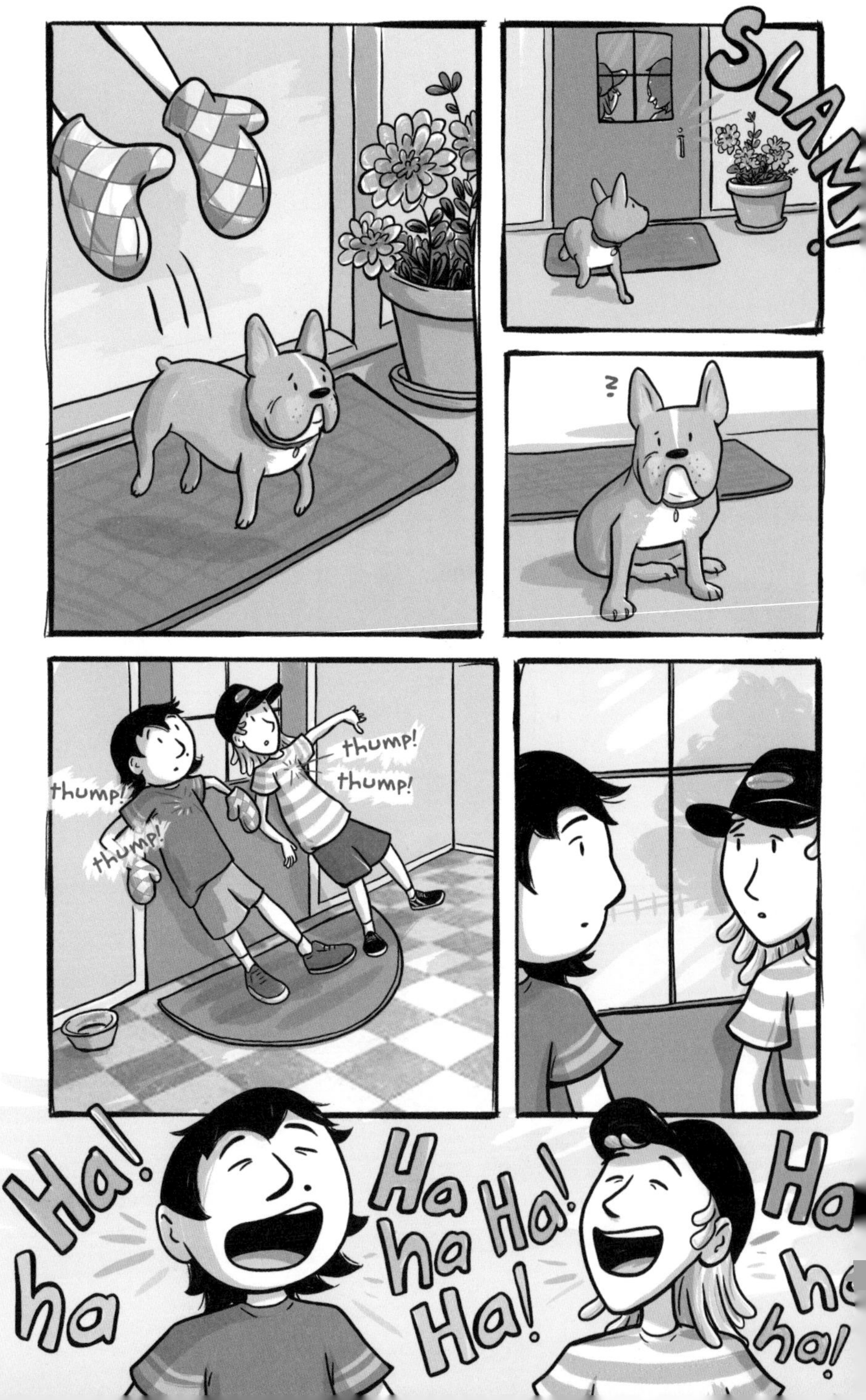
SLAM!
z
thump!
thump!
thump!
thump!
Ha!
ha
Ha
ha
Ha!
Ha!
Ha
ha
ha!

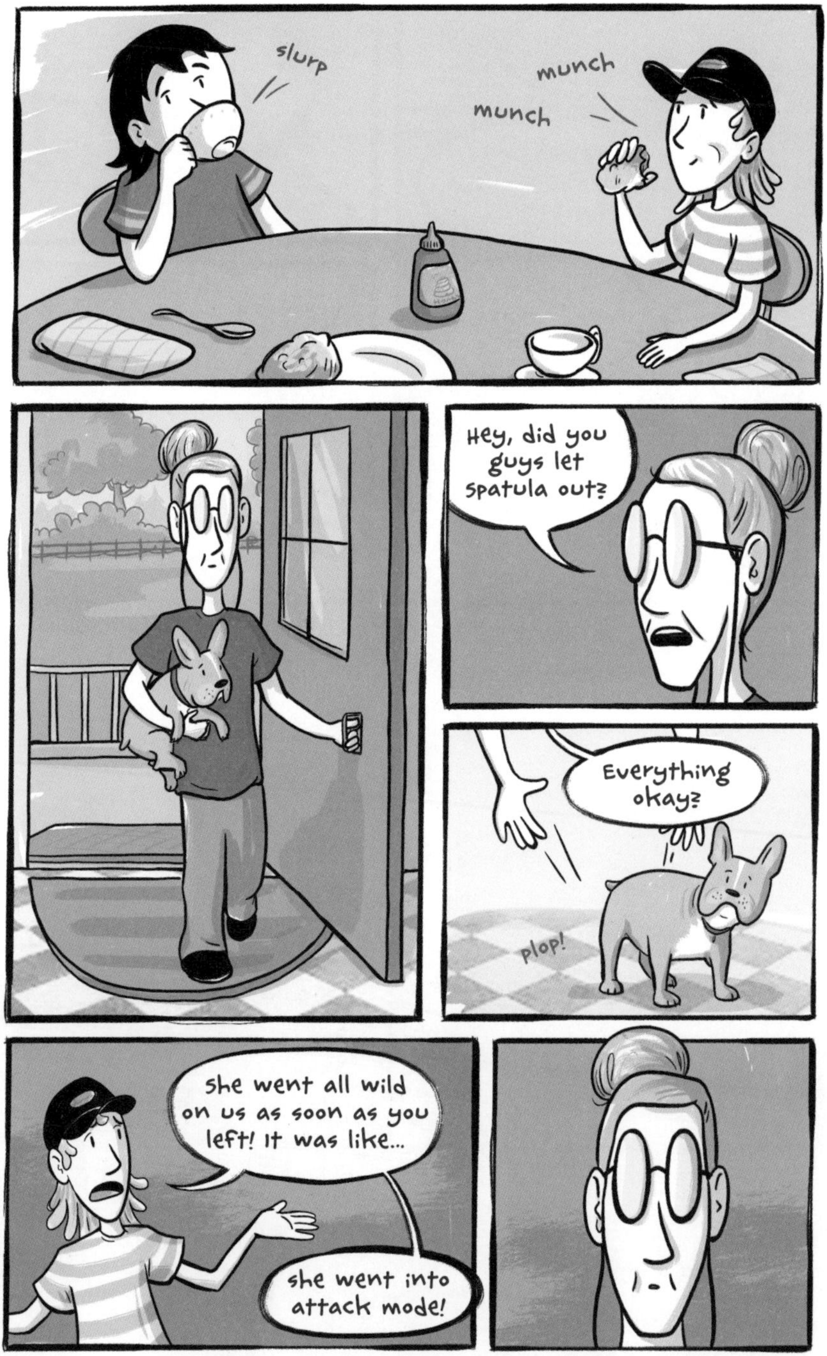
slurp
munch
munch
Hey, did you guys let spatula out?
Everything okay?
plop!
she went all wild on us as soon as you left! It was like...
she went into attack mode!

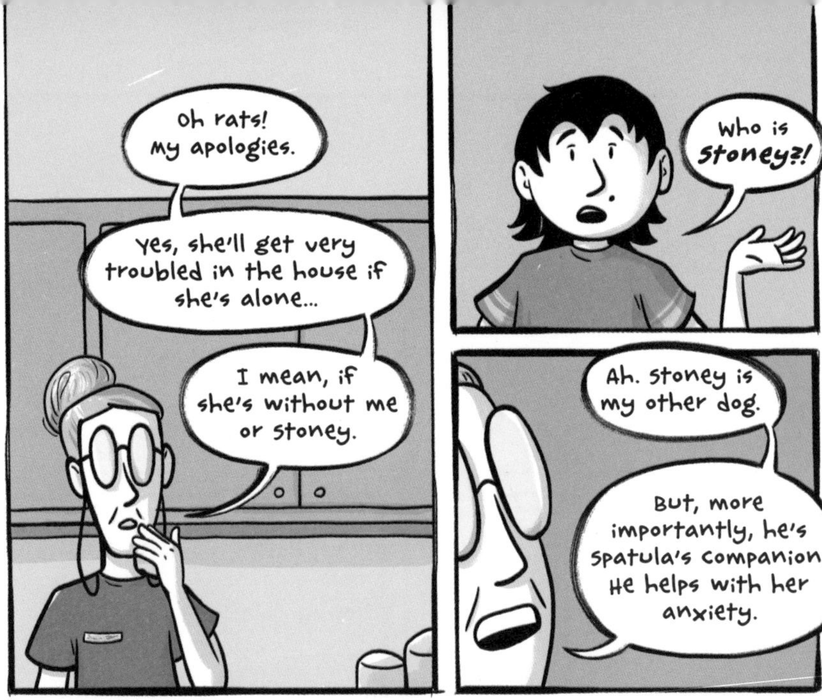
Oh rats! My apologies.
Yes, she'll get very troubled in the house if she's alone...
I mean, if she's without me or Stoney.
Who is Stoney?!
Ah. Stoney is my other dog.
But, more importantly, he's Spatula's companion. He helps with her anxiety.

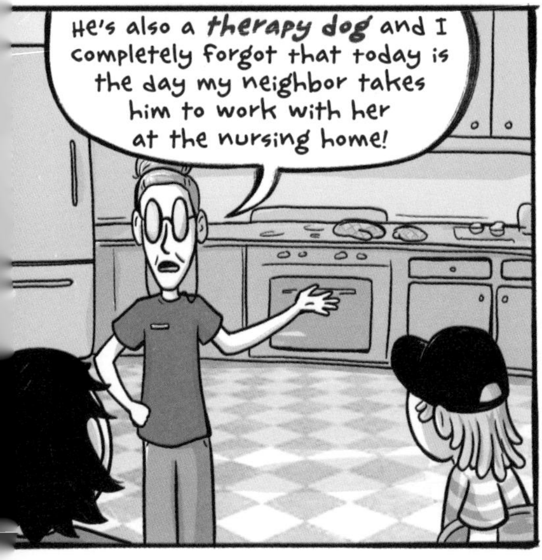
He's also a therapy dog and I completely forgot that today is the day my neighbor takes him to work with her at the nursing home!

Stoney is Jo's Russell, who in his younger years was a spunky ball of energy, tearing through the house--chasing cats and rodents with glee, and regularly digging holes in the yard.

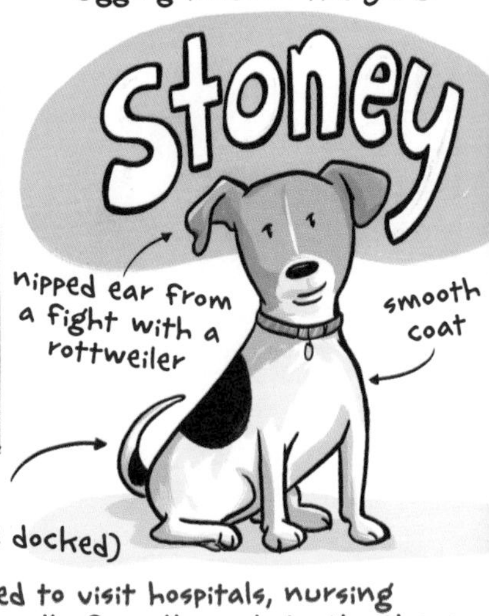
Stoney
nipped ear from a fight with a rottweiler
smooth coat
long tail (often Russells are docked)

Therapy dogs: Dogs that are trained to visit hospitals, nursing homes, and other care facilities. Typically friendly and gentle, these animals can bring happiness and promote good mental health to those unable to care for their own pets.

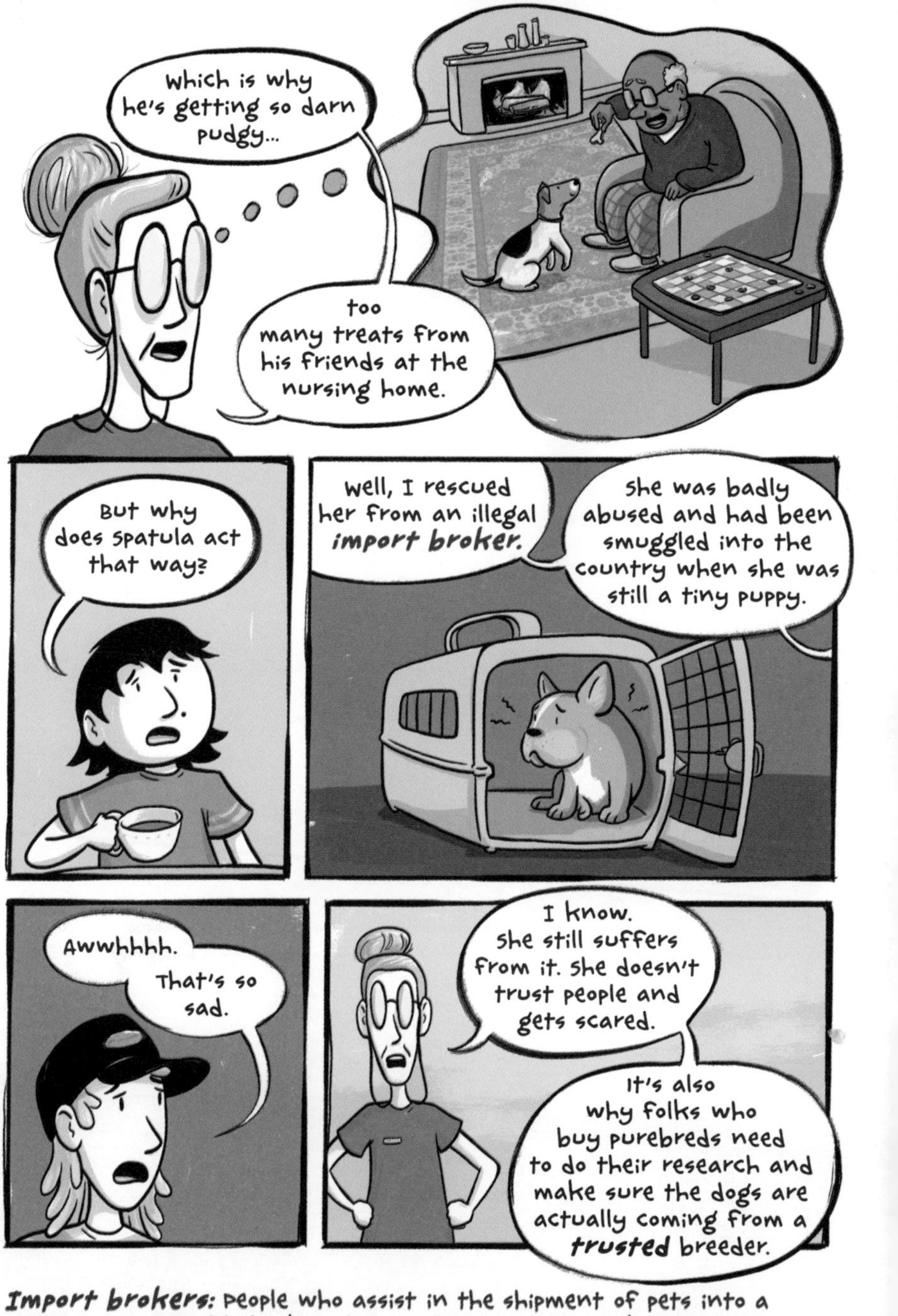
Which is why he's getting so darn pudgy...
too many treats from his friends at the nursing home.
But why does Spatula act that way?
Well, I rescued her from an illegal *import broker.*
She was badly abused and had been smuggled into the country when she was still a tiny puppy.
Awwhhhh.
That's so sad.
I know. She still suffers from it. She doesn't trust people and gets scared.
It's also why folks who buy purebreds need to do their research and make sure the dogs are actually coming from a *trusted* breeder.

Import brokers: People who assist in the shipment of pets into a country. Disreputable brokers buy underage and/or sick puppies from mills or irresponsible breeders, then resell them to pet stores or research facilities, or they pose as breeders and sell litters online. The profit made is often at the expense of the puppy's health and well-being.

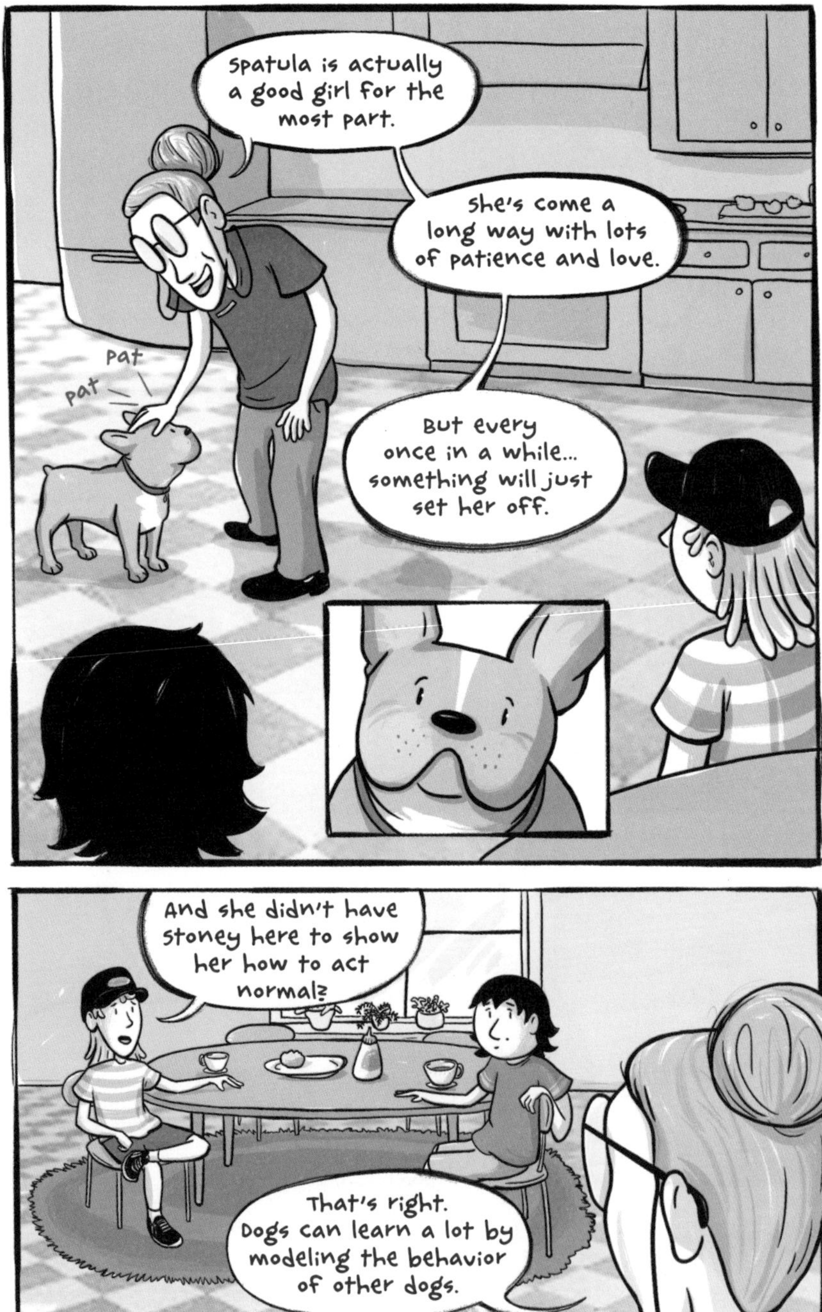
Spatula is actually a good girl for the most part.
She's come a long way with lots of patience and love.
pat
pat
But every once in a while... something will just set her off.
And she didn't have Stoney here to show her how to act normal?
That's right. Dogs can learn a lot by modeling the behavior of other dogs.

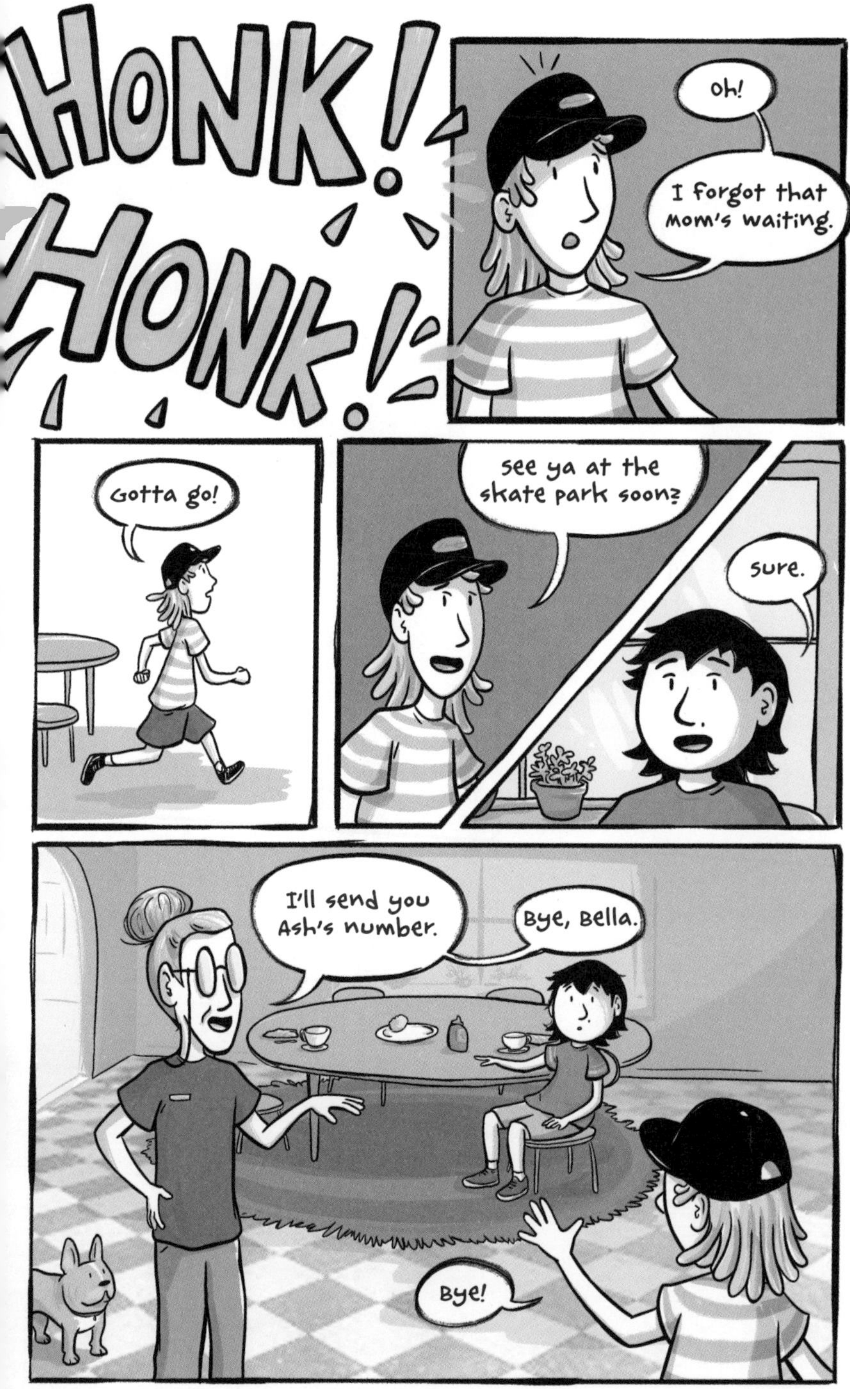
HONK! HONK!
Oh!
I forgot that mom's waiting.
Gotta go!
See ya at the skate park soon?
Sure.
I'll send you Ash's number.
Bye, Bella.
Bye!

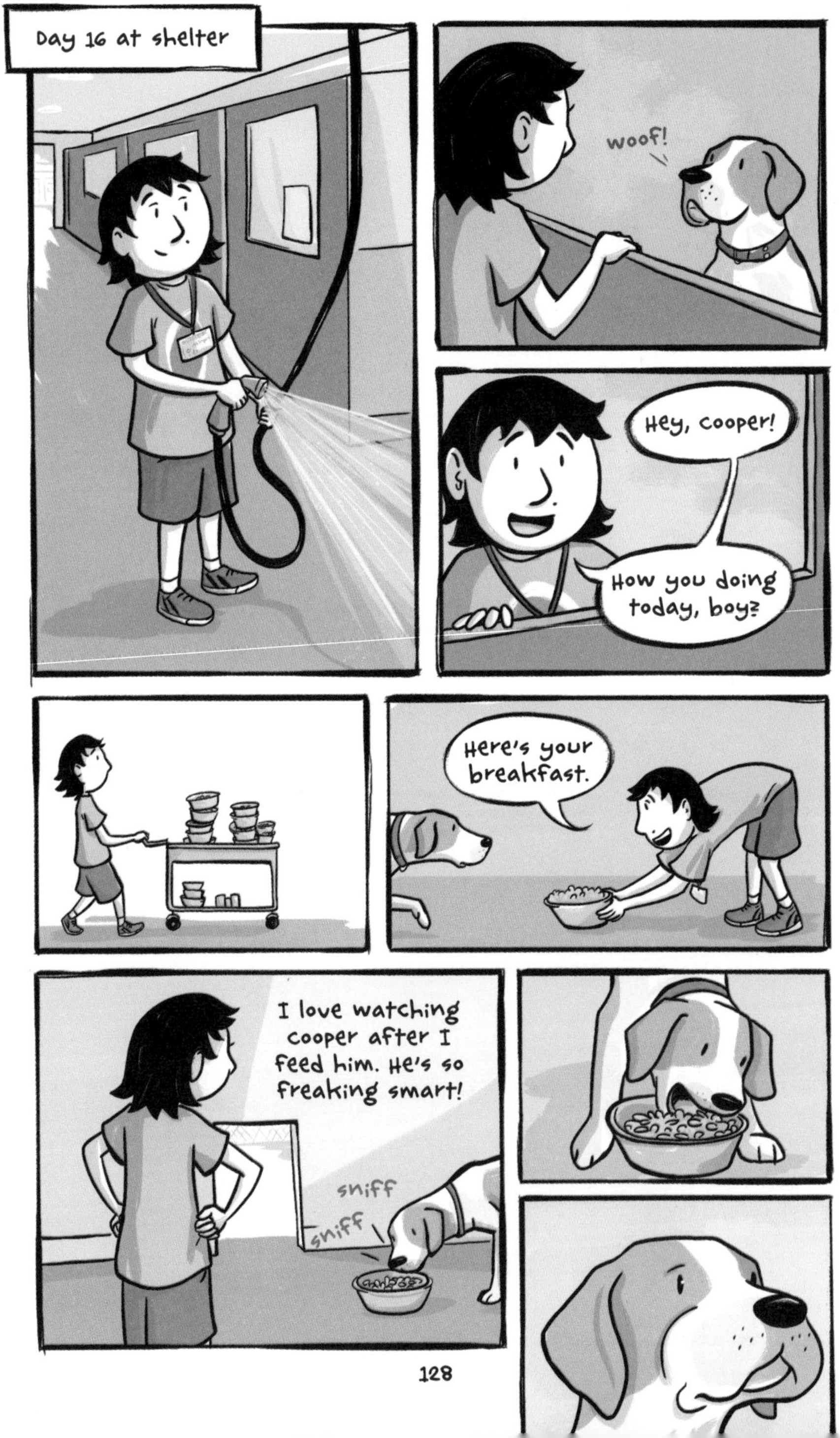
Day 16 at shelter
woof!
Hey, cooper!
How you doing today, boy?
Here's your breakfast.
I love watching cooper after I feed him. He's so freaking smart!
sniff
sniff

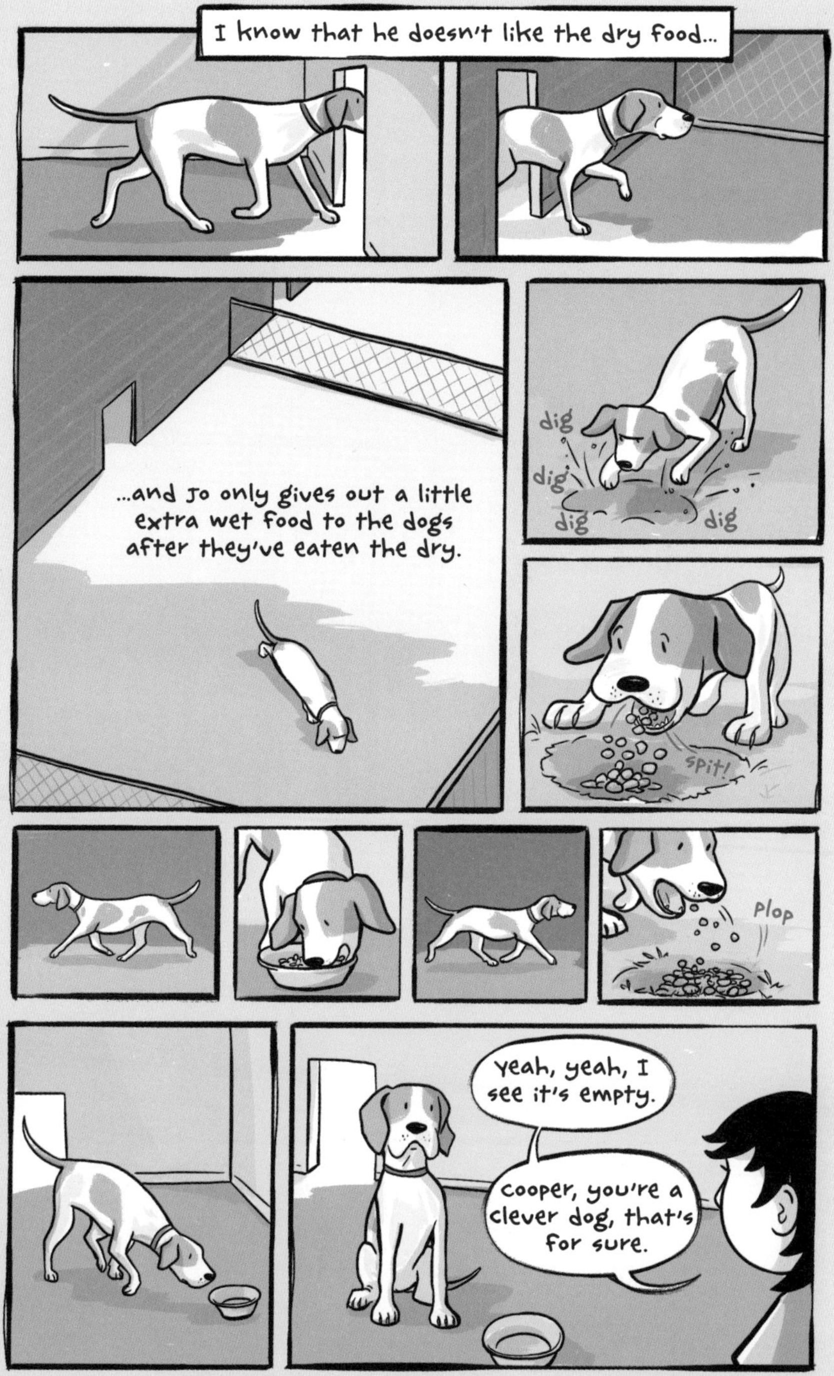
I know that he doesn't like the dry food...
...and Jo only gives out a little extra wet food to the dogs after they've eaten the dry.
dig
dig
dig
dig
spit!
Plop
Yeah, yeah, I see it's empty.
Cooper, you're a clever dog, that's for sure.

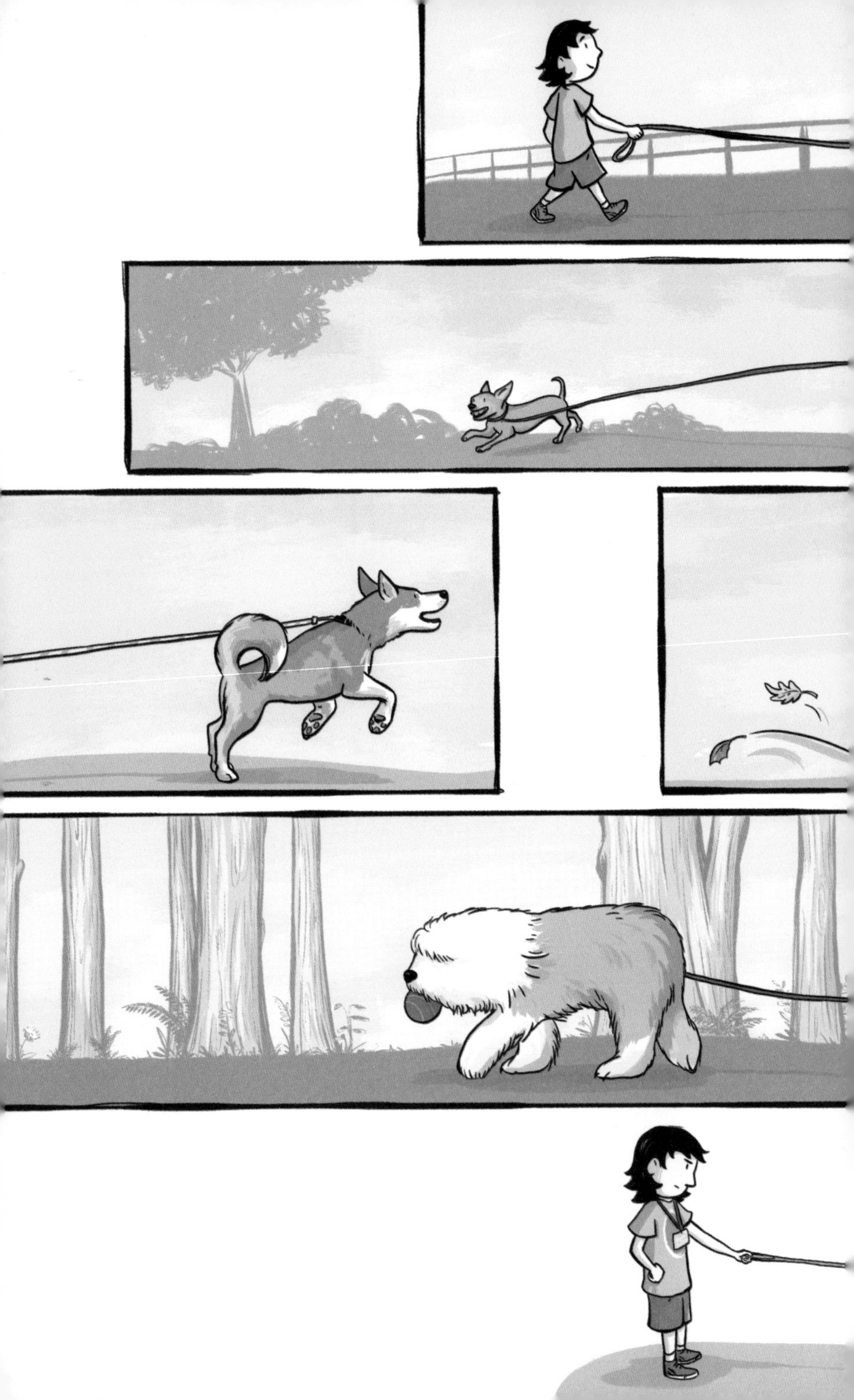

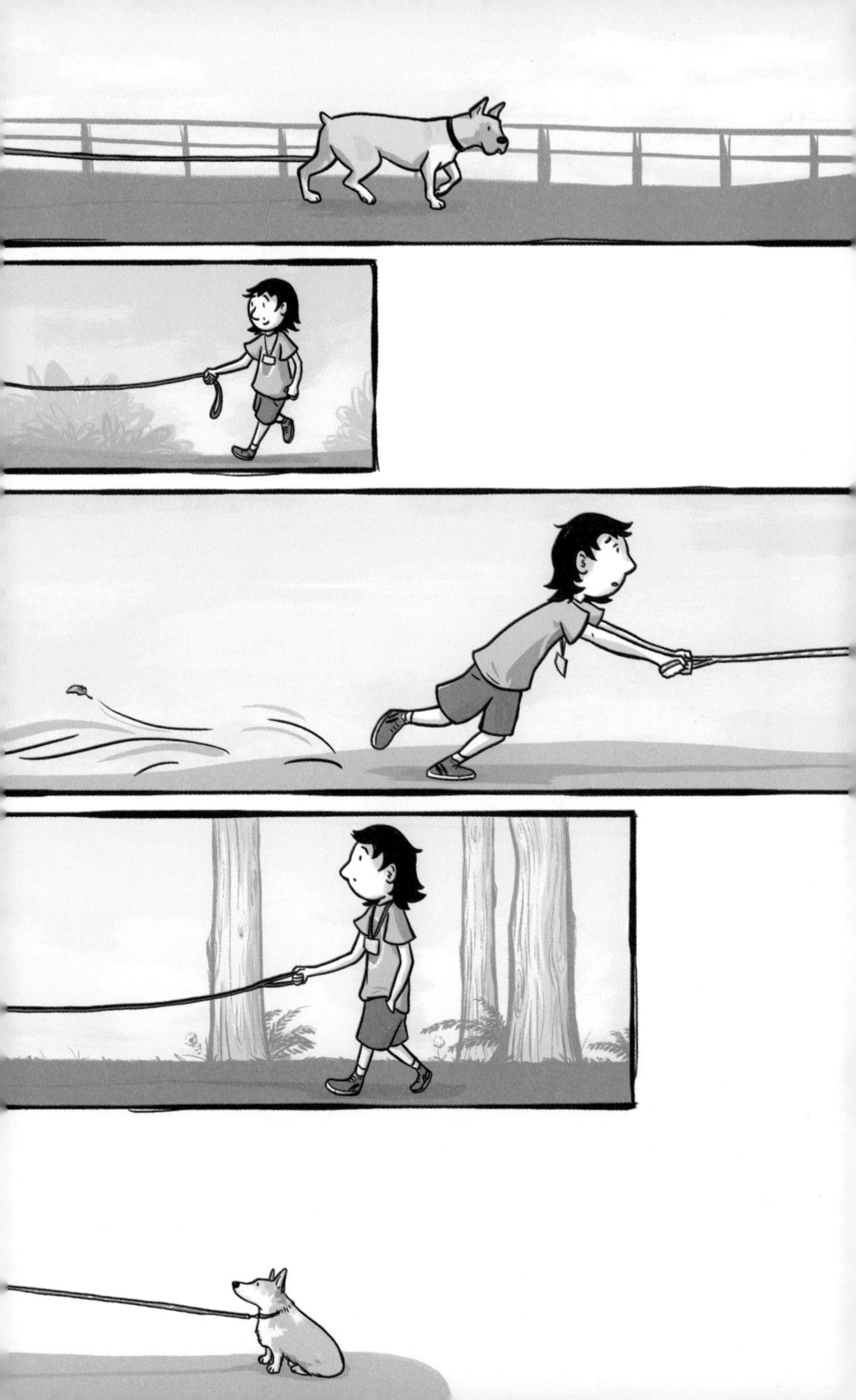

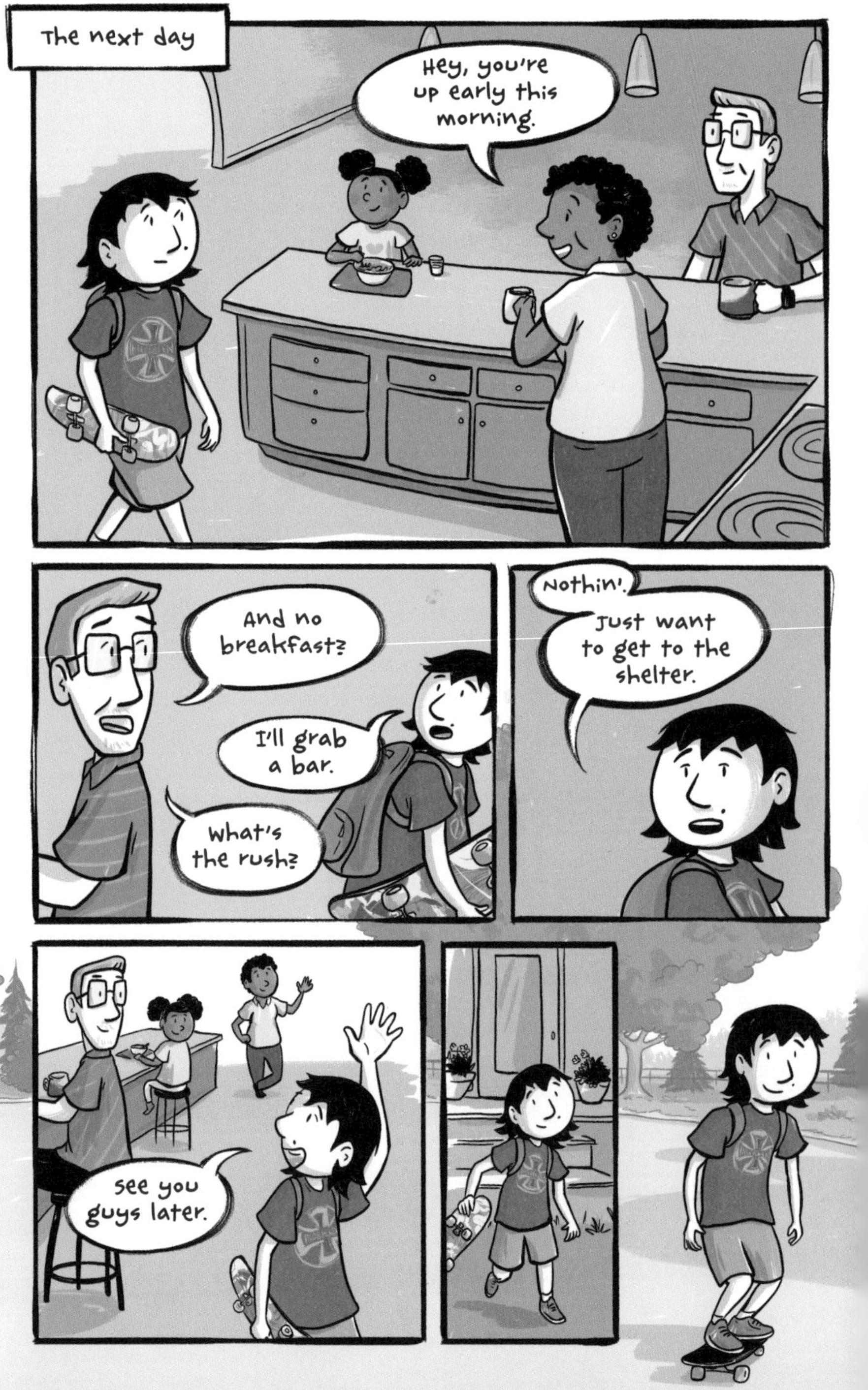
The next day
Hey, you're up early this morning.
And no breakfast?
I'll grab a bar.
What's the rush?
Nothin'.
Just want to get to the shelter.
See you guys later.

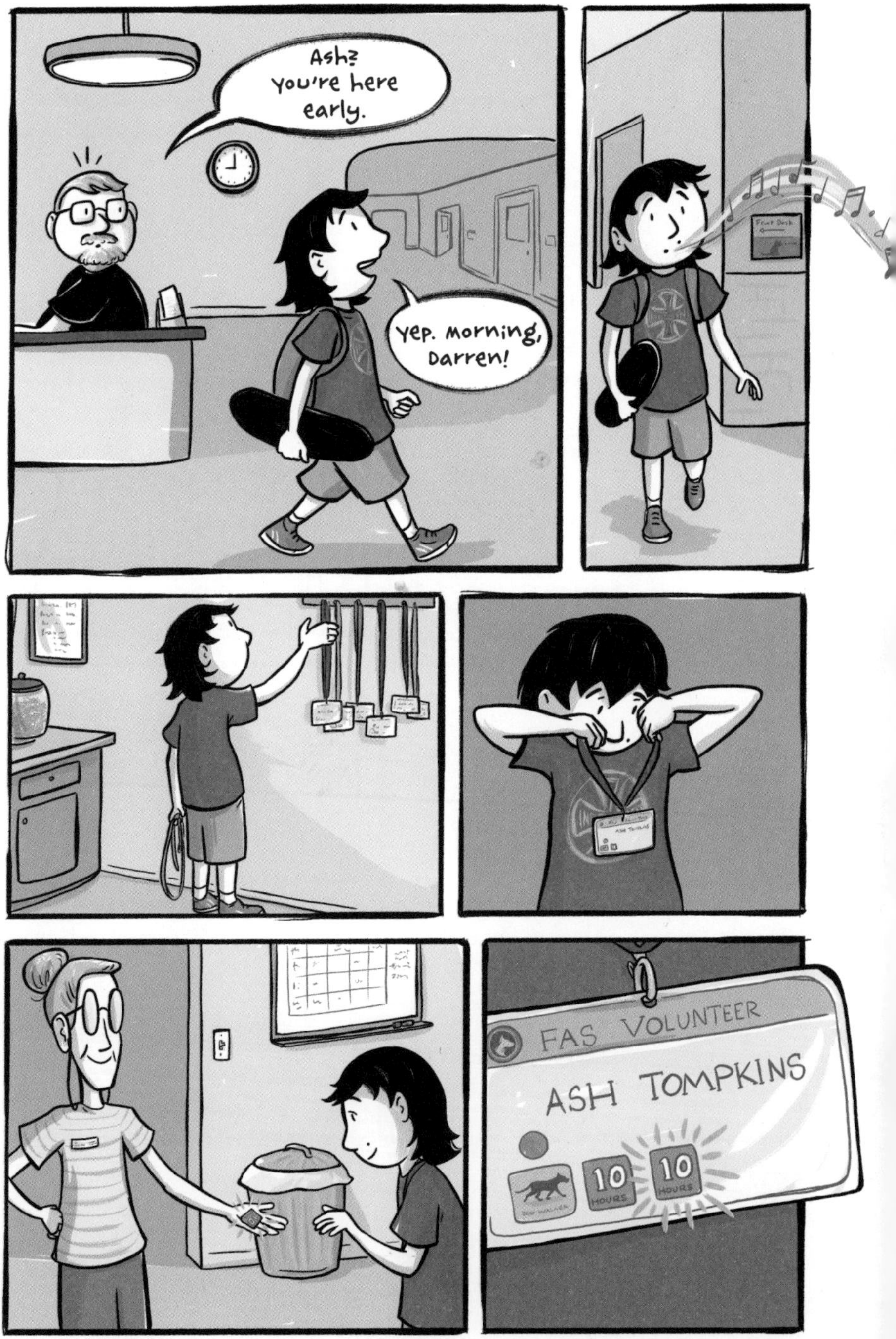
Ash? You're here early.
Yep. Morning, Darren!
FAS VOLUNTEER
ASH TOMPKINS
10 HOURS
10 HOURS

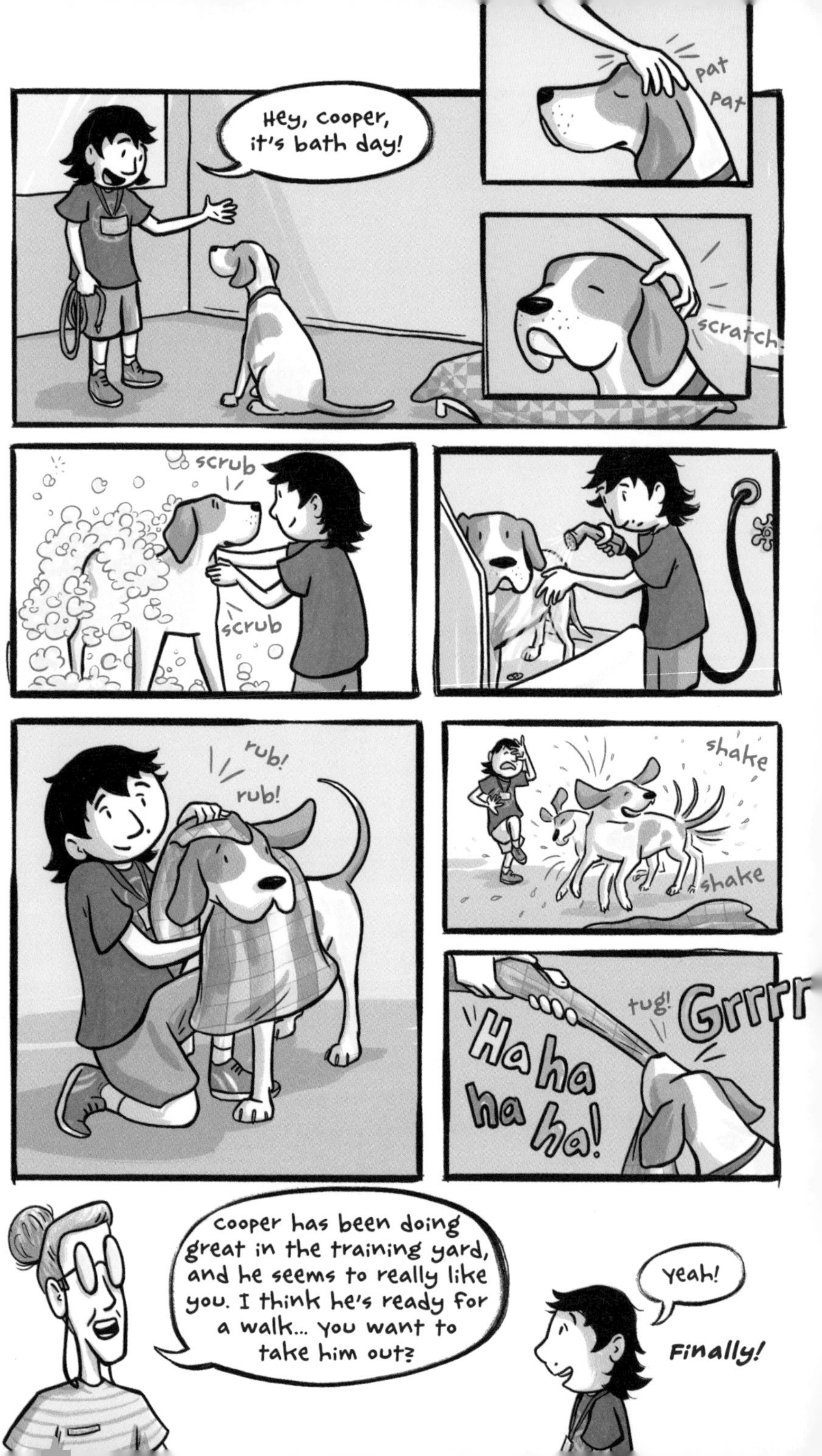
Hey, Cooper, it's bath day!
pat
pat
scratch
scrub
scrub
rub!
rub!
shake
shake
tug!
Grrrr
Ha ha ha ha!
Cooper has been doing great in the training yard, and he seems to really like you. I think he's ready for a walk… you want to take him out?
Yeah!
Finally!

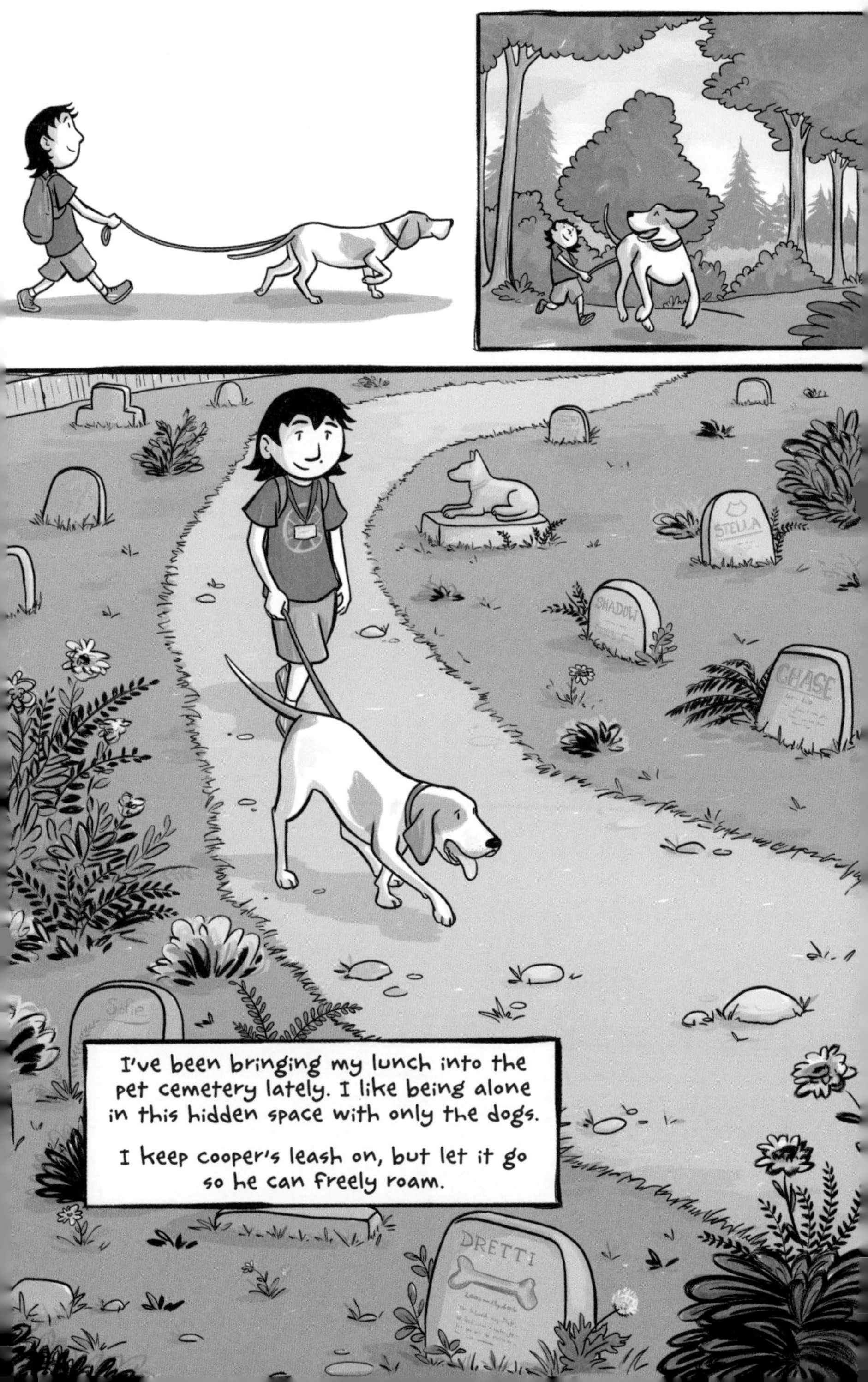
STELLA
SHADOW
CHASE
I've been bringing my lunch into the pet cemetery lately. I like being alone in this hidden space with only the dogs.
I keep cooper's leash on, but let it go so he can freely roam.
DRETTI

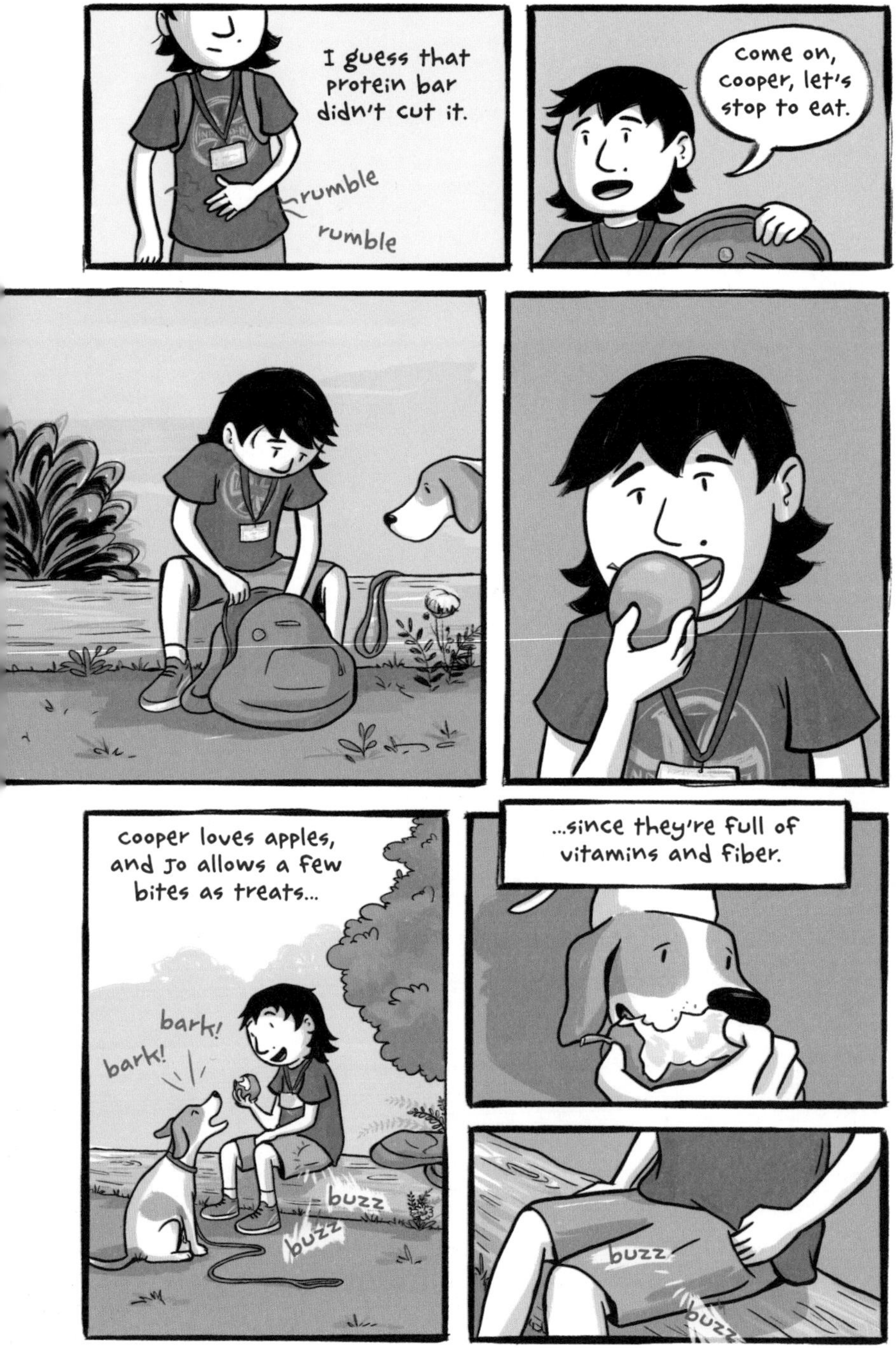
I guess that protein bar didn't cut it.
rumble
rumble
come on, cooper, let's stop to eat.
cooper loves apples, and Jo allows a few bites as treats...
bark!
bark!
buzz
buzz
...since they're full of vitamins and fiber.
buzz
buzz

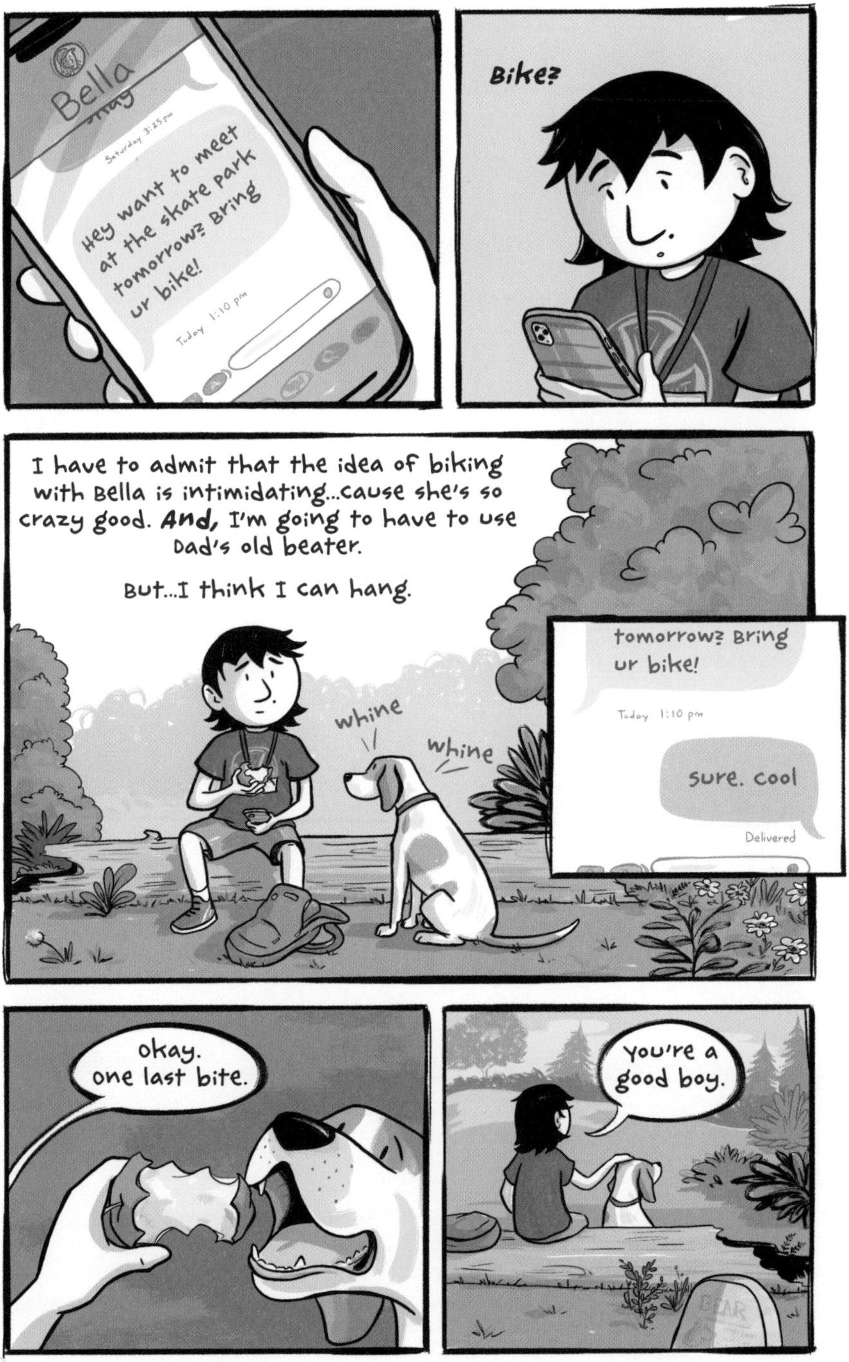
Bella
Saturday 3:25 pm
Hey want to meet at the skate park tomorrow? Bring ur bike!
Today 1:10 pm
Bike?
I have to admit that the idea of biking with Bella is intimidating...cause she's so crazy good. **And,** I'm going to have to use Dad's old beater.
But...I think I can hang.
whine
whine
tomorrow? Bring ur bike!
Today 1:10 pm
sure. cool
Delivered
okay. one last bite.
you're a good boy.

CHAPTER 6

howl!

• Bogie •

A fiercely smart and cunning Siberian husky mix who howls at
marching bands, or whenever he hears the national anthem. Huskies
were originally bred as sled dogs and are a sight to behold––
beautiful, powerful, and athletic. Although they can be difficult and
are not recommended for first-time dog owners, huskies make
wonderful family companions when properly trained and cared for.

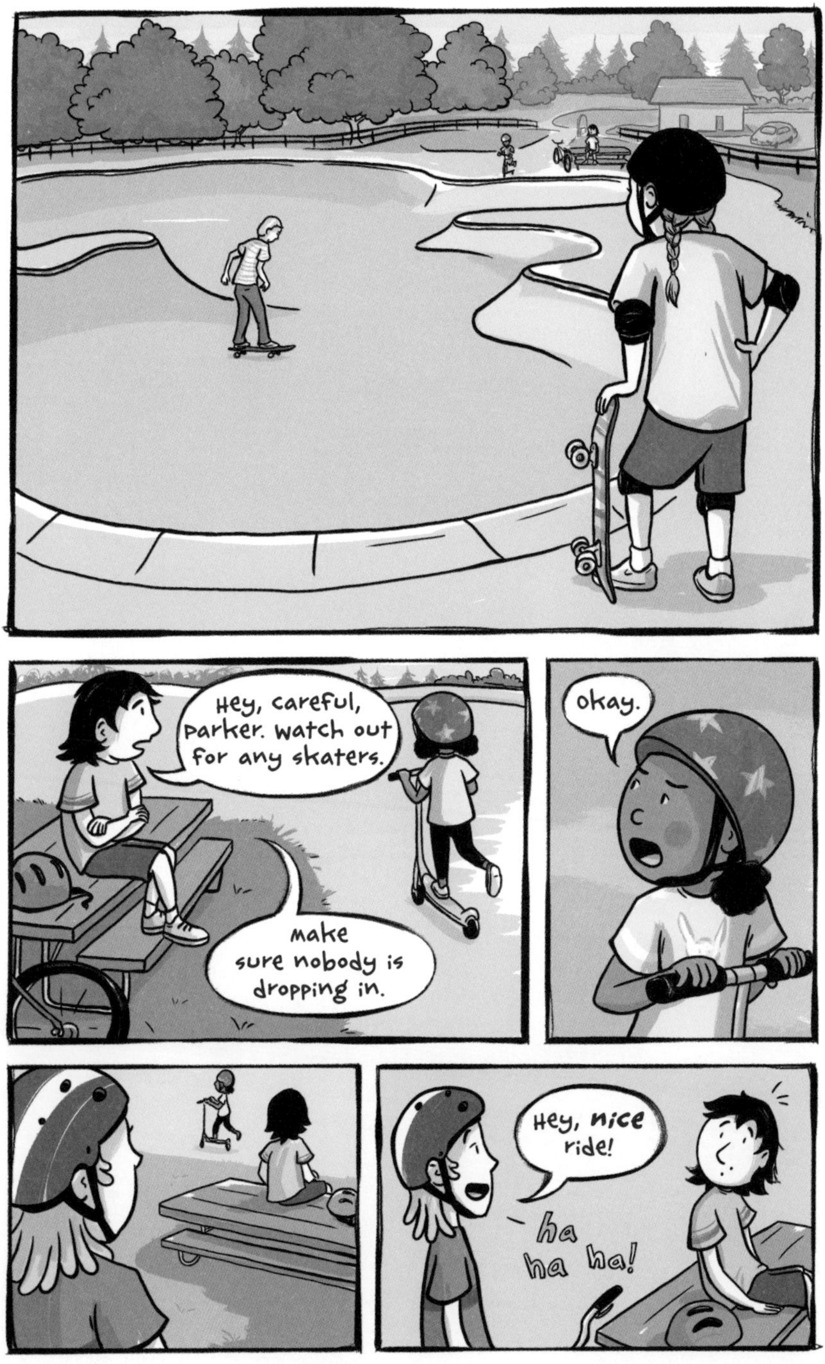
Hey, careful, Parker. Watch out for any skaters.
make sure nobody is dropping in.
okay.
Hey, nice ride!
ha ha ha!

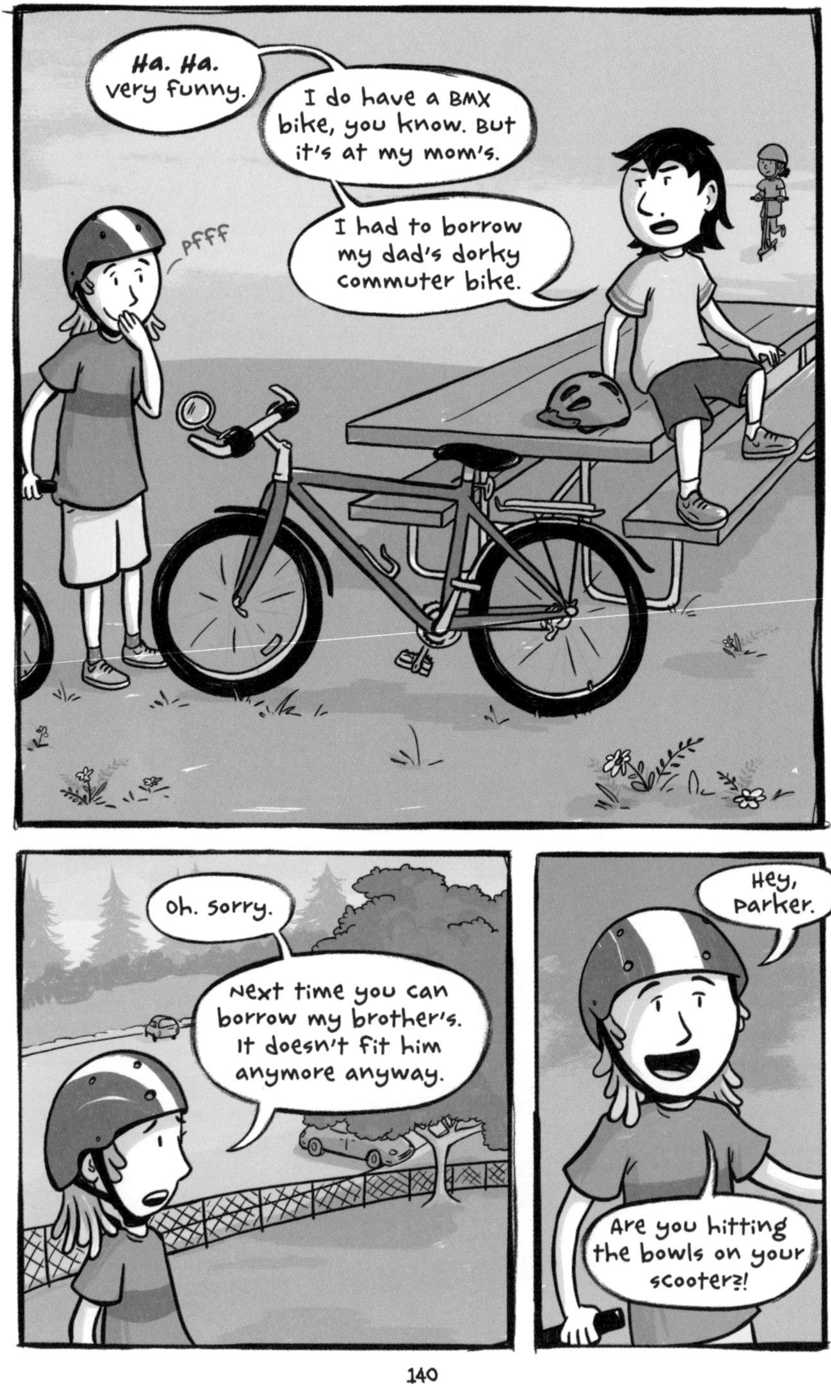
Ha. Ha.
very funny.
I do have a BMX bike, you know. But it's at my mom's.
pfff
I had to borrow my dad's dorky commuter bike.
Oh. sorry.
Next time you can borrow my brother's. It doesn't fit him anymore anyway.
Hey, Parker.
Are you hitting the bowls on your scooter?!

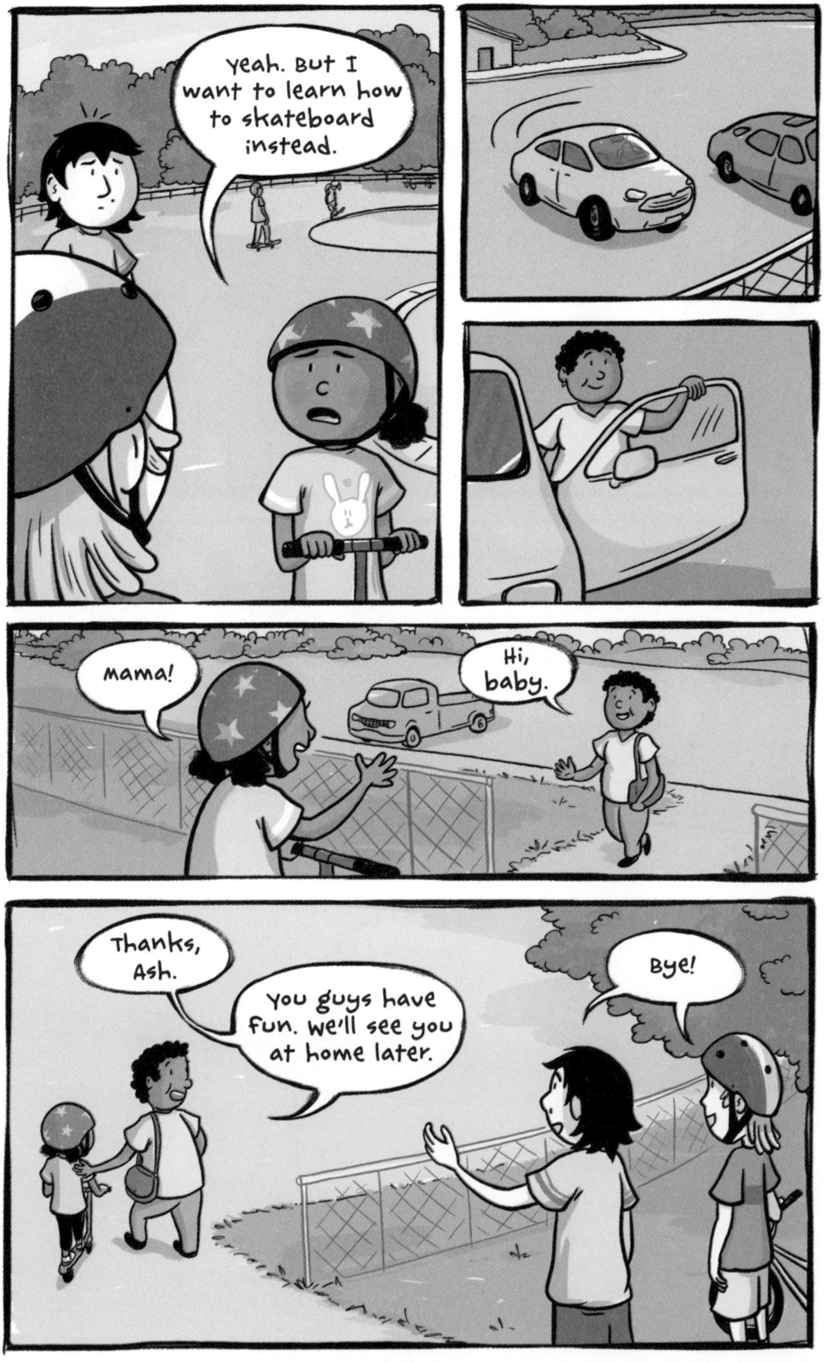
Yeah. But I want to learn how to skateboard instead.
Mama!
Hi, baby.
Thanks, Ash.
You guys have fun. We'll see you at home later.
Bye!

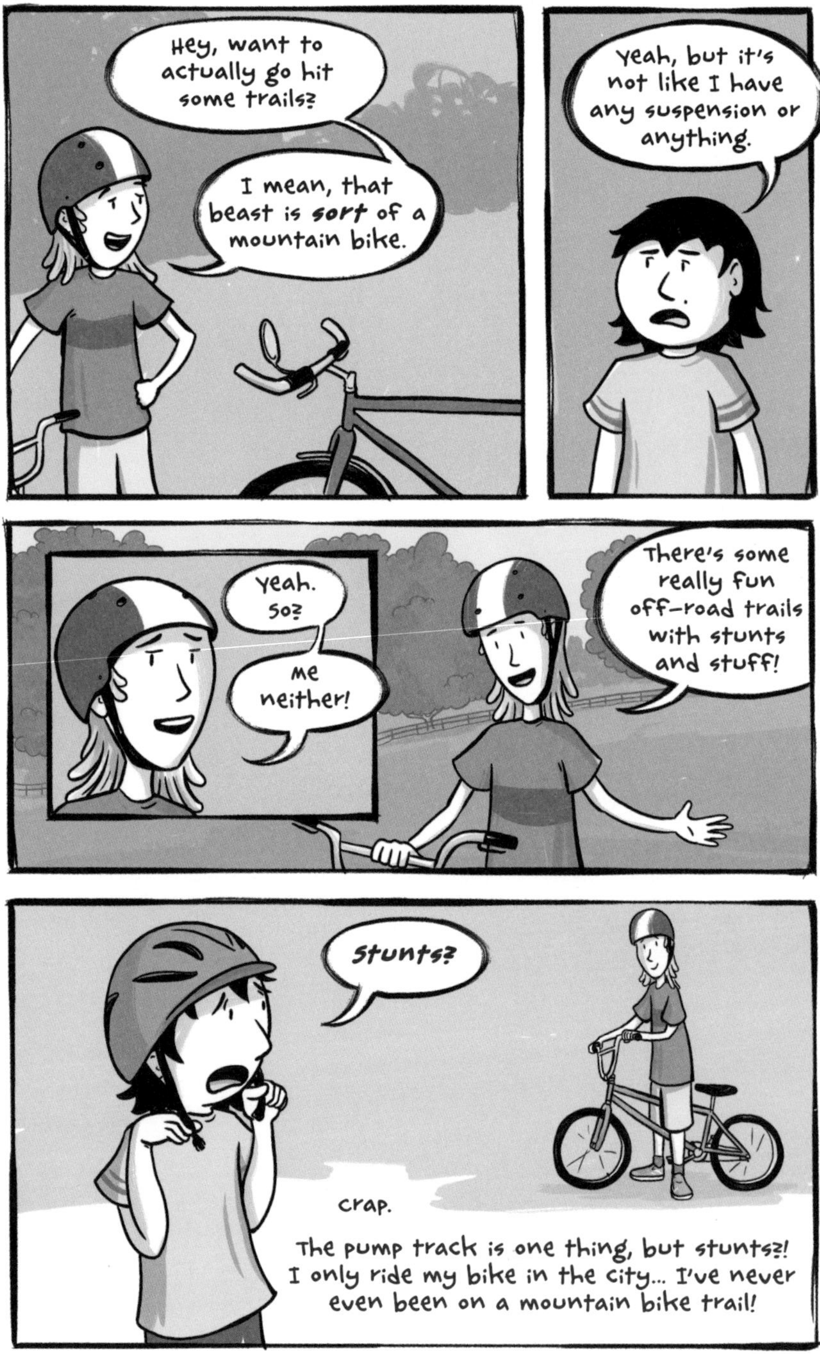

Hey, want to actually go hit some trails?
I mean, that beast is *sort* of a mountain bike.
Yeah, but it's not like I have any suspension or anything.
There's some really fun off-road trails with stunts and stuff!
Yeah. So?
Me neither!
Stunts?
crap.
The pump track is one thing, but stunts?! I only ride my bike in the city... I've never even been on a mountain bike trail!

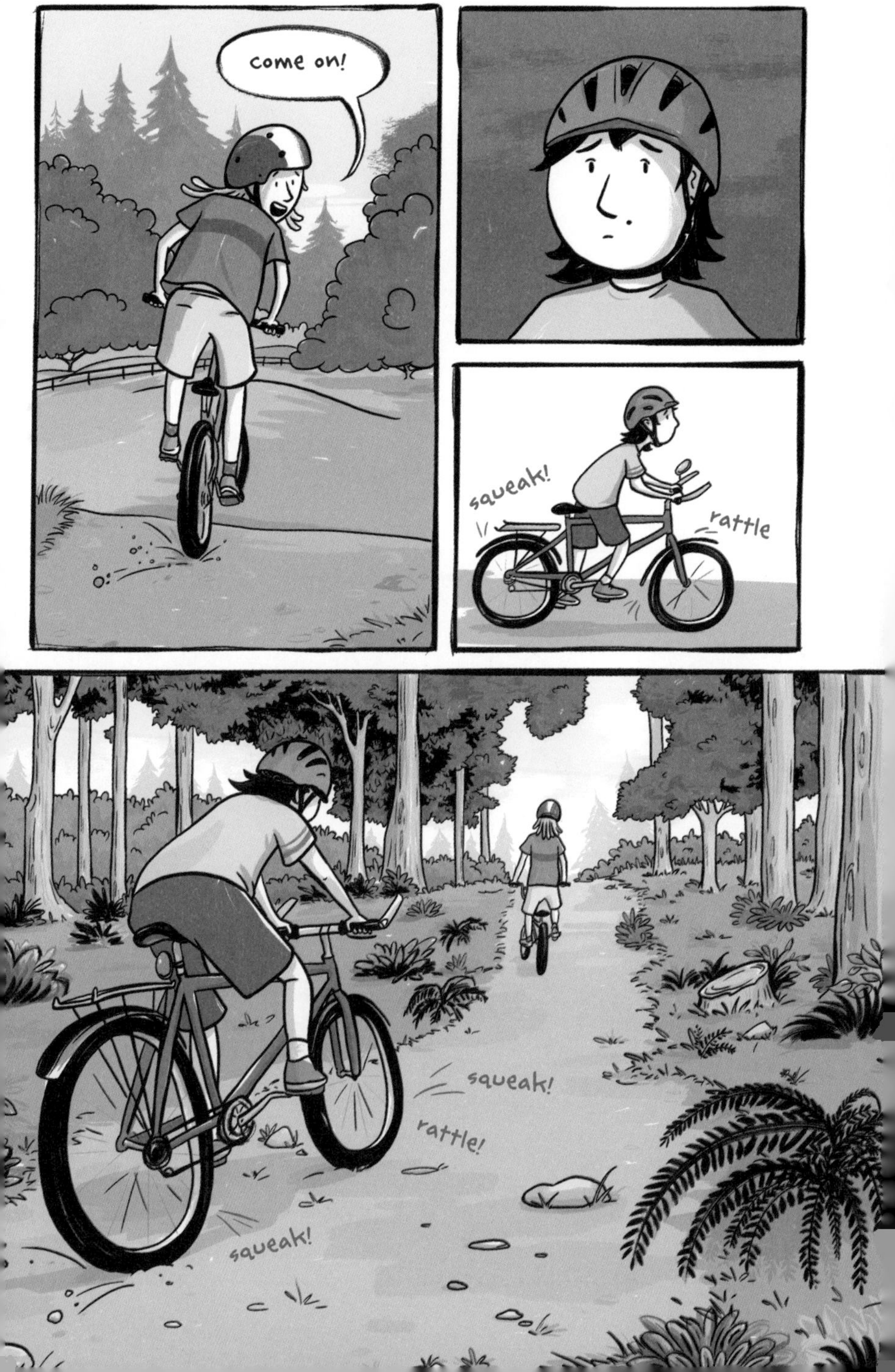
come on!
squeak!
rattle
squeak!
rattle!
squeak!

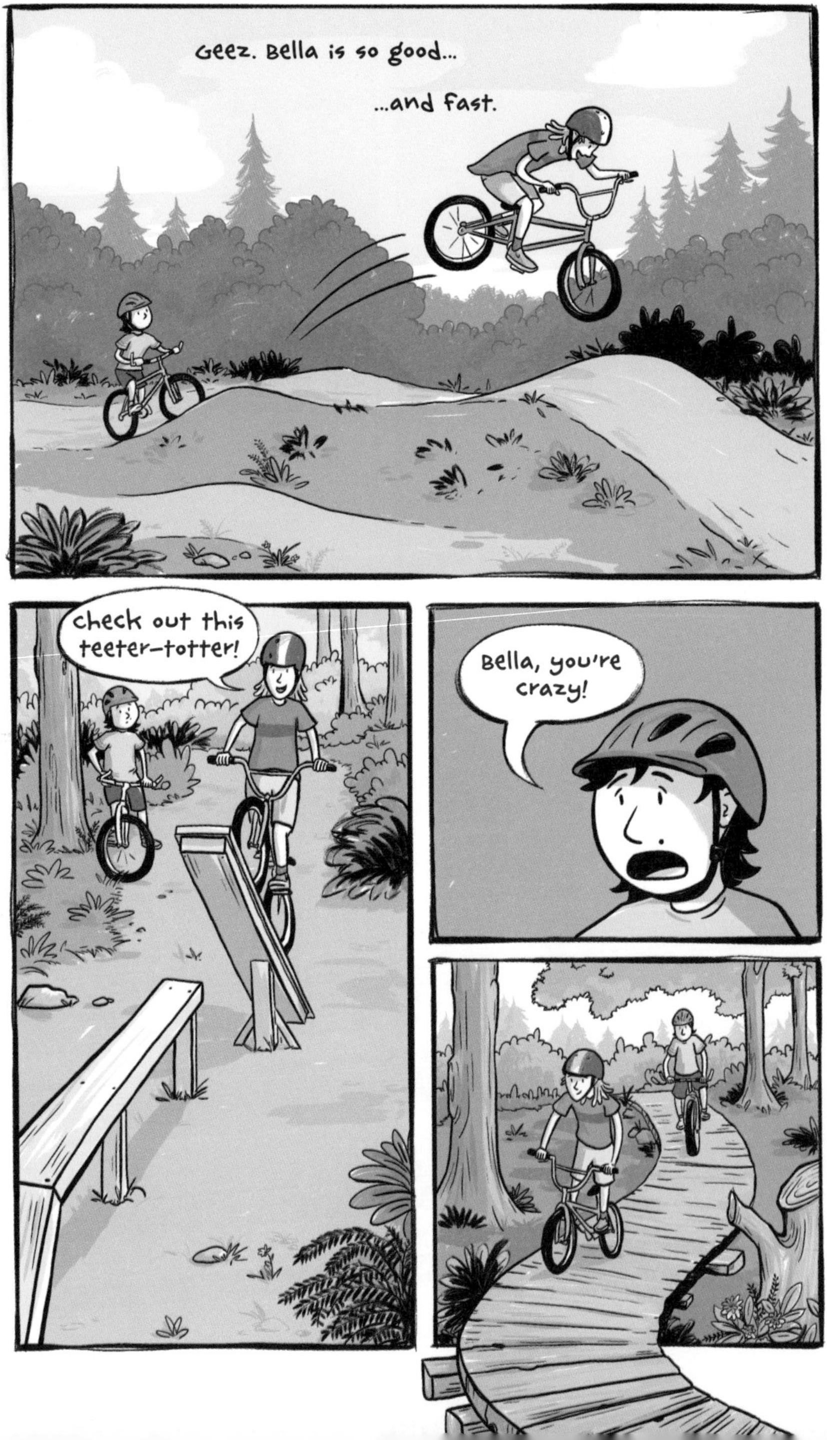
Geez. Bella is so good...
...and fast.
Check out this teeter-totter!
Bella, you're crazy!

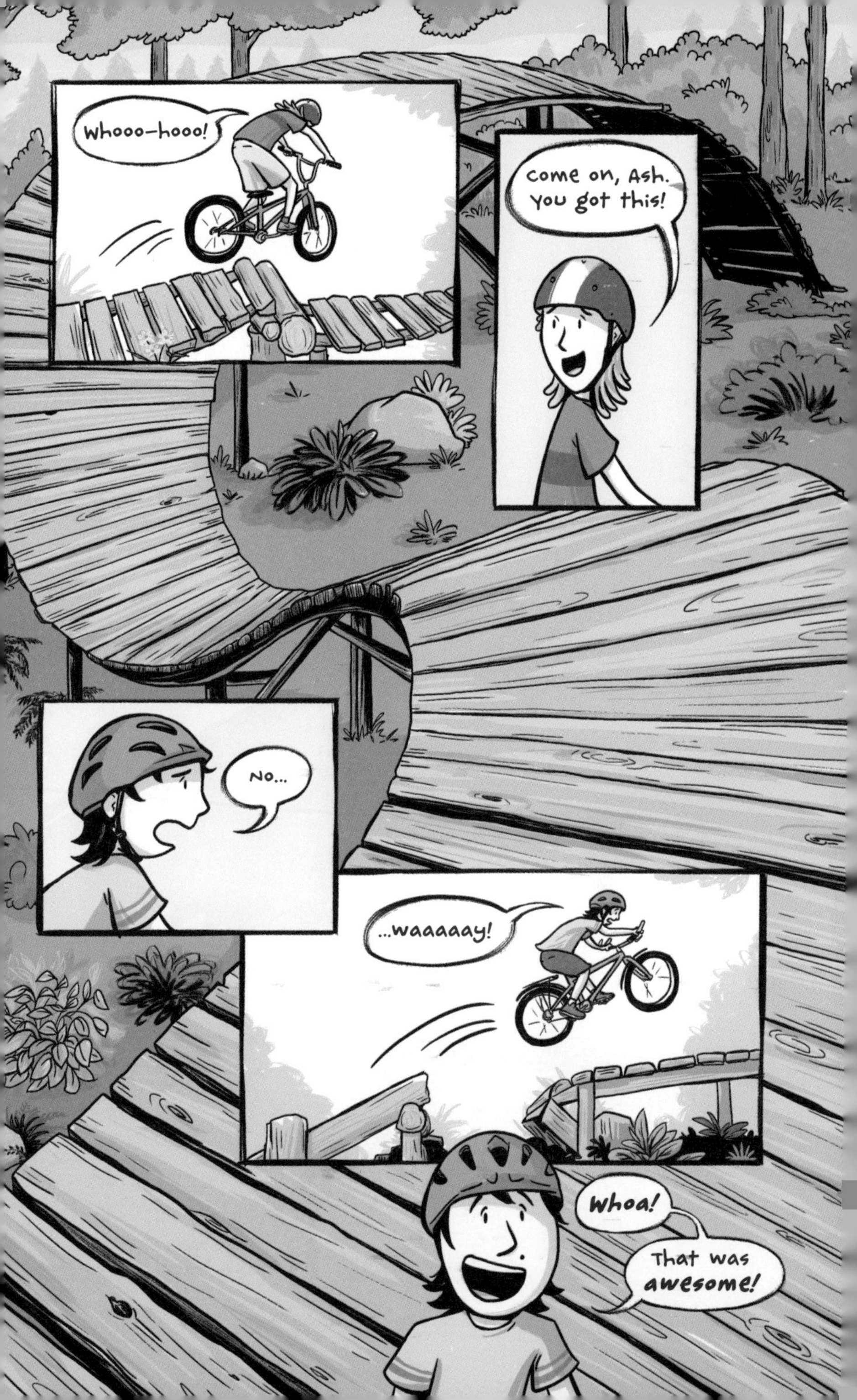

Whooo-hooo!
Come on, Ash. You got this!
No...
...waaaaay!
Whoa!
That was awesome!

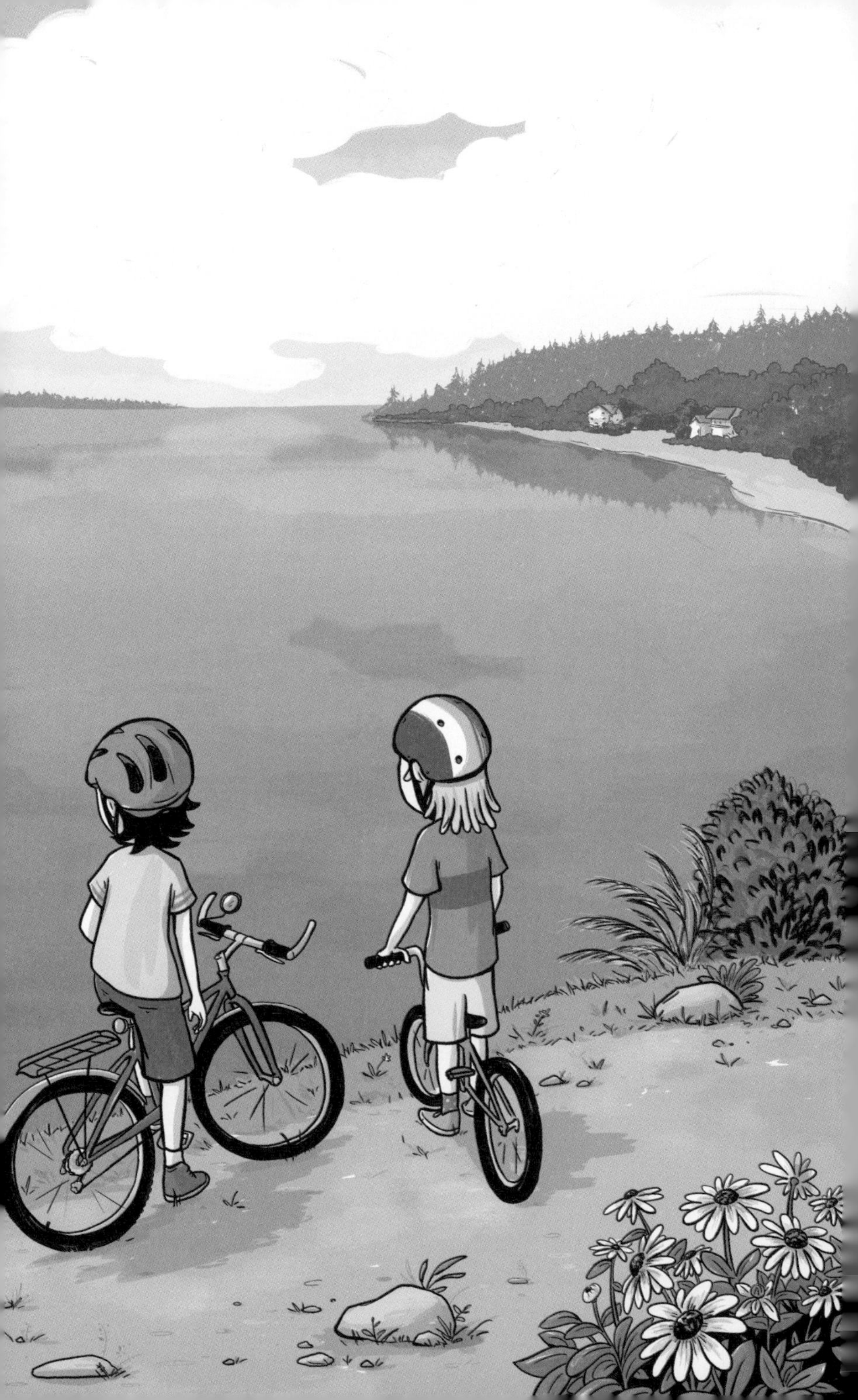

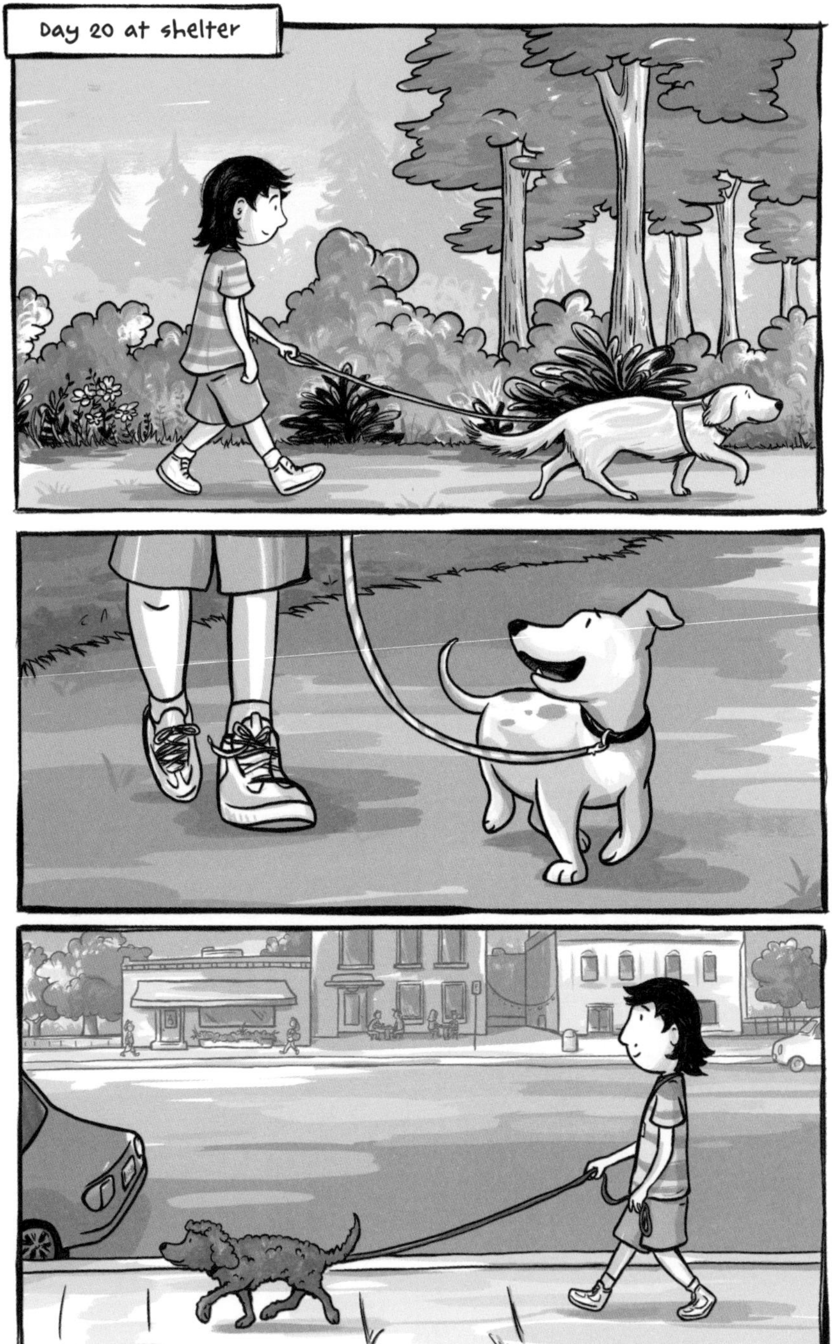
Day 20 at shelter

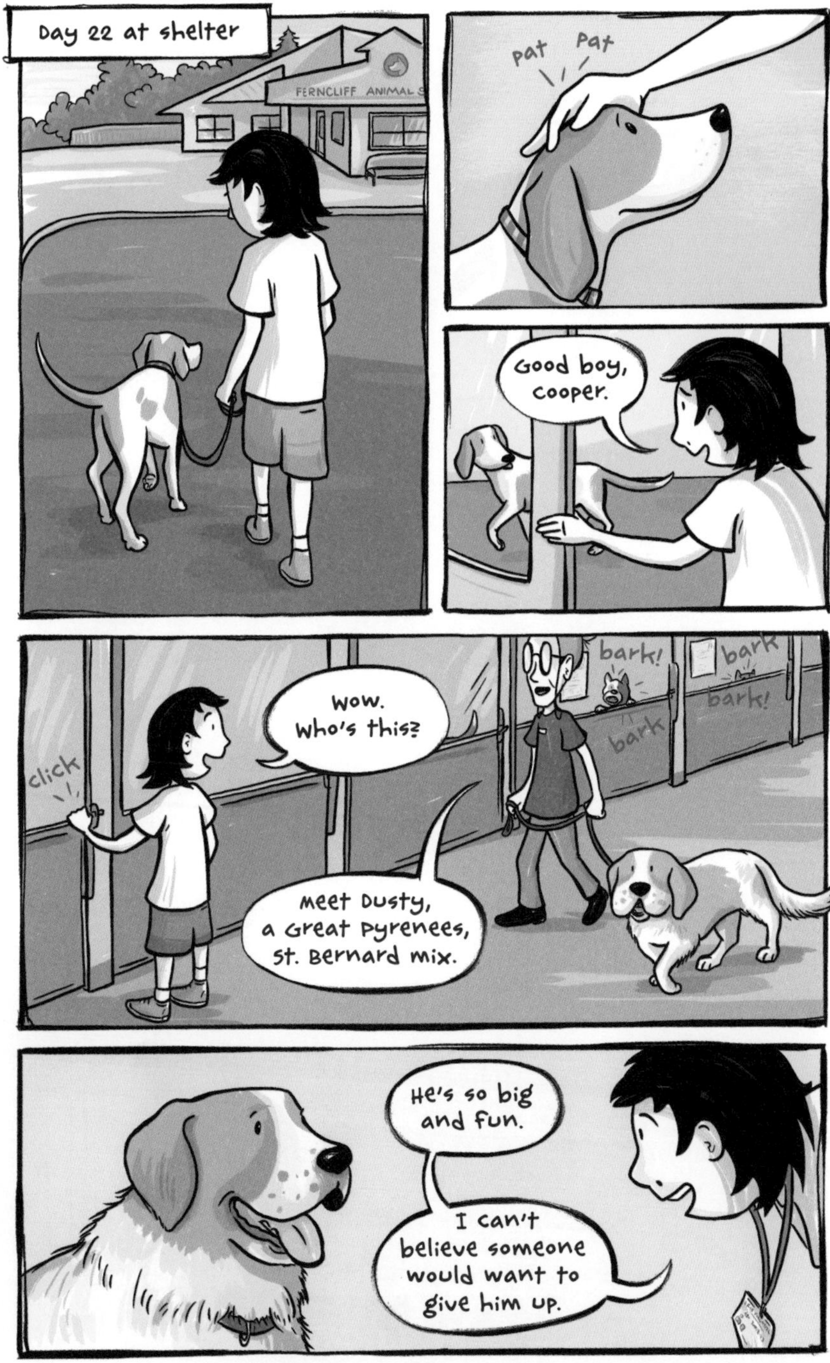

Day 22 at shelter
FERNCLIFF ANIMAL S
pat Pat
Good boy, Cooper.
click
Wow. Who's this?
bark!
bark
bark!
bark
Meet Dusty, a Great Pyrenees, St. Bernard mix.
He's so big and fun.
I can't believe someone would want to give him up.

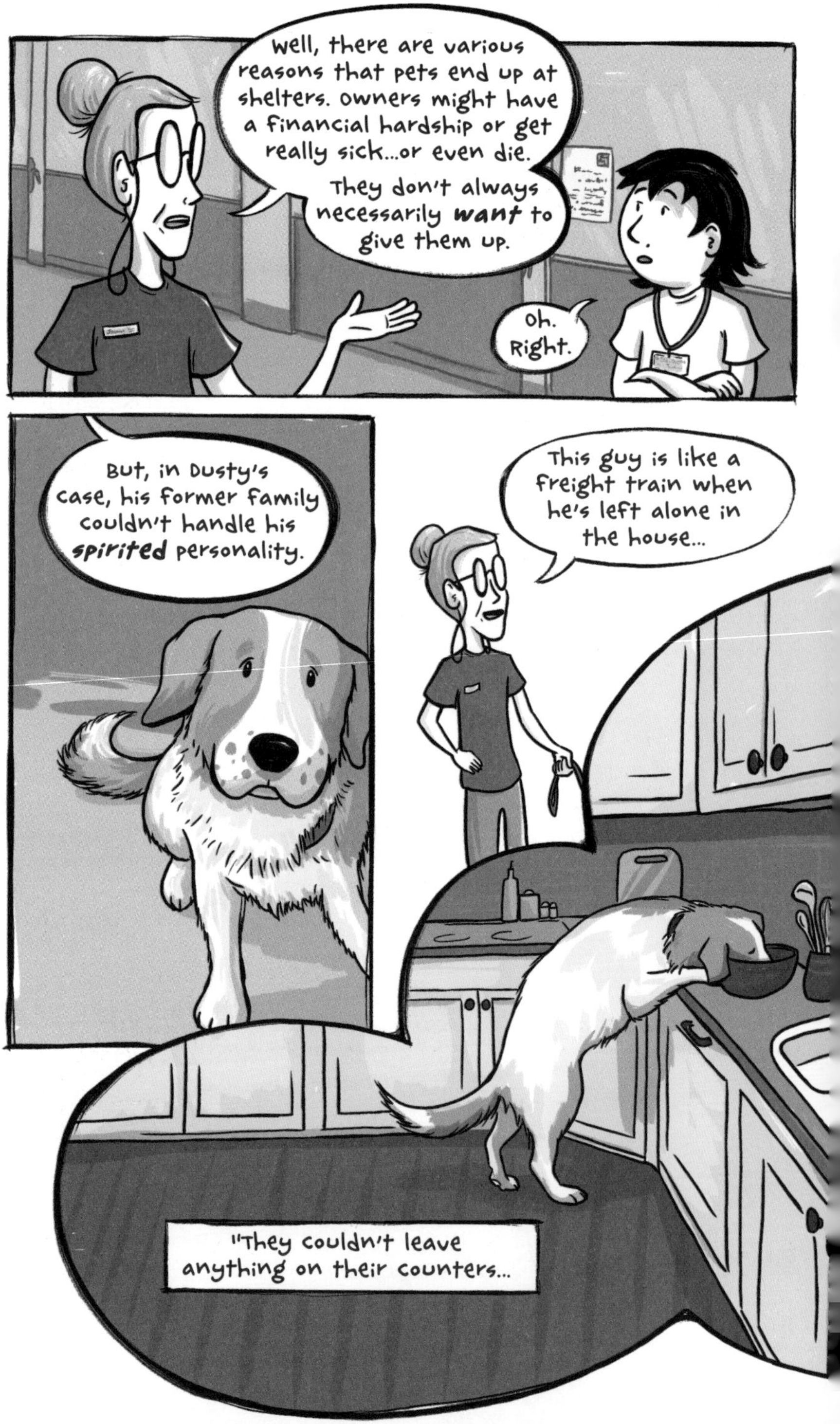
Well, there are various reasons that pets end up at shelters. Owners might have a financial hardship or get really sick...or even die.
They don't always necessarily **want** to give them up.
Oh. Right.
But, in Dusty's case, his former family couldn't handle his **spirited** personality.
This guy is like a freight train when he's left alone in the house...
"They couldn't leave anything on their counters...

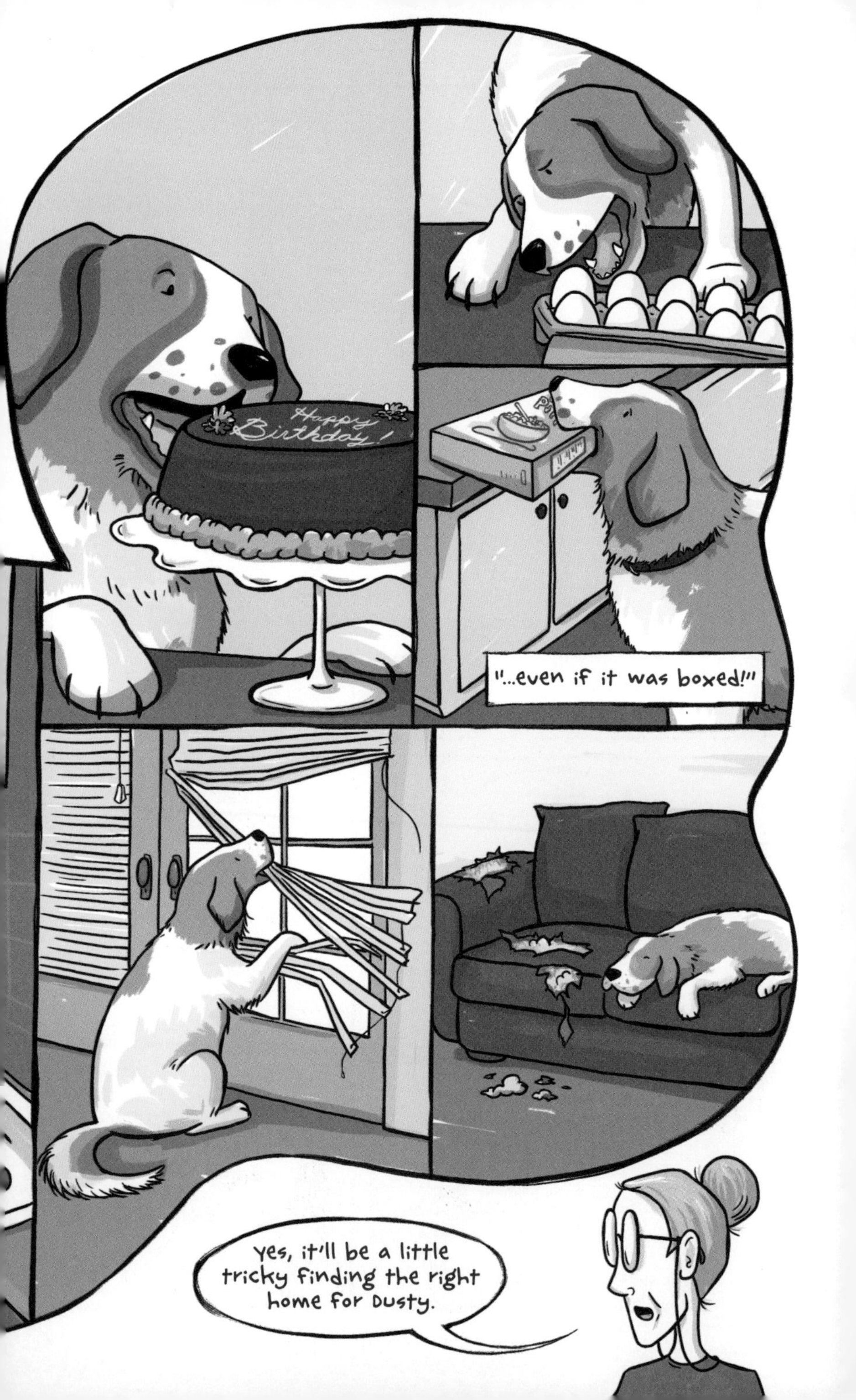
Happy Birthday!
"...even if it was boxed!"
Yes, it'll be a little tricky finding the right home for Dusty.

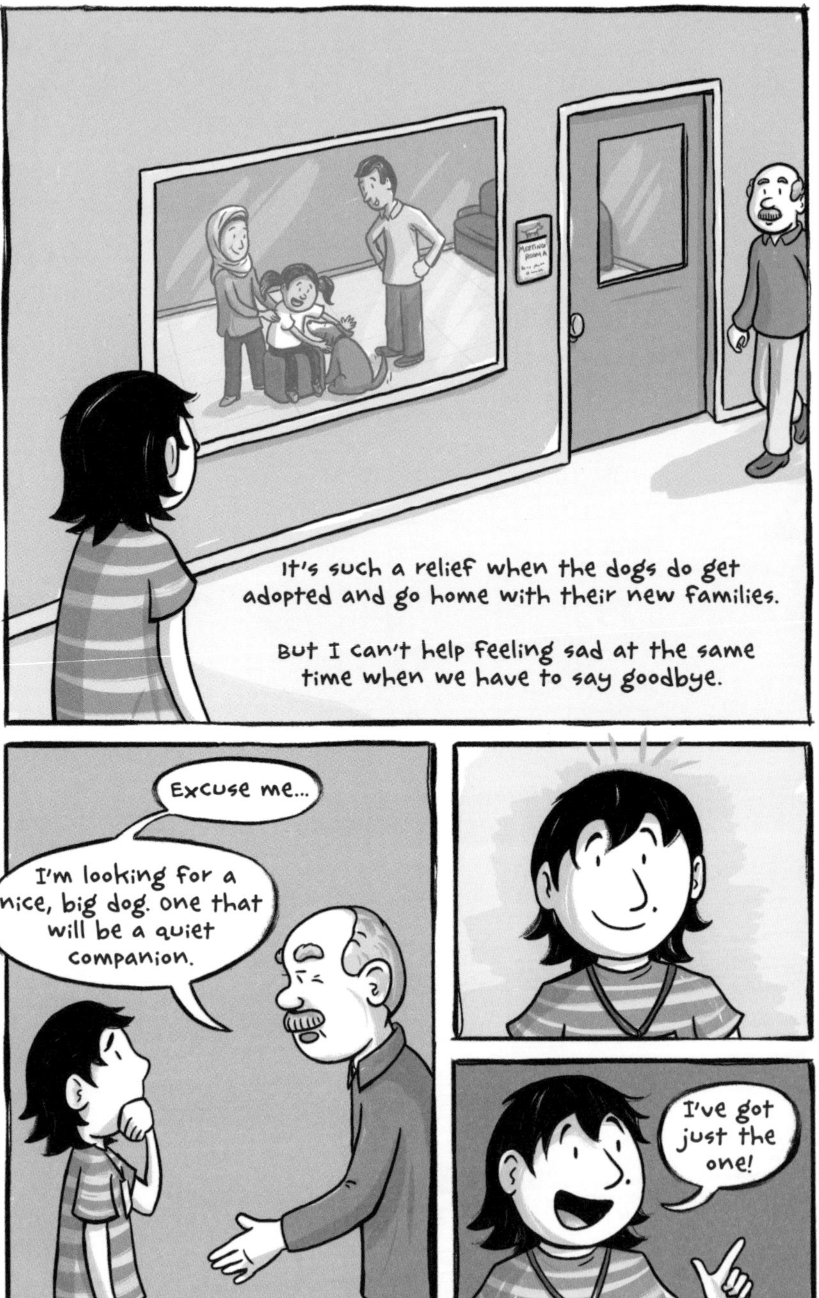
It's such a relief when the dogs do get adopted and go home with their new families.
But I can't help feeling sad at the same time when we have to say goodbye.
Excuse me...
I'm looking for a nice, big dog. One that will be a quiet companion.
I've got just the one!

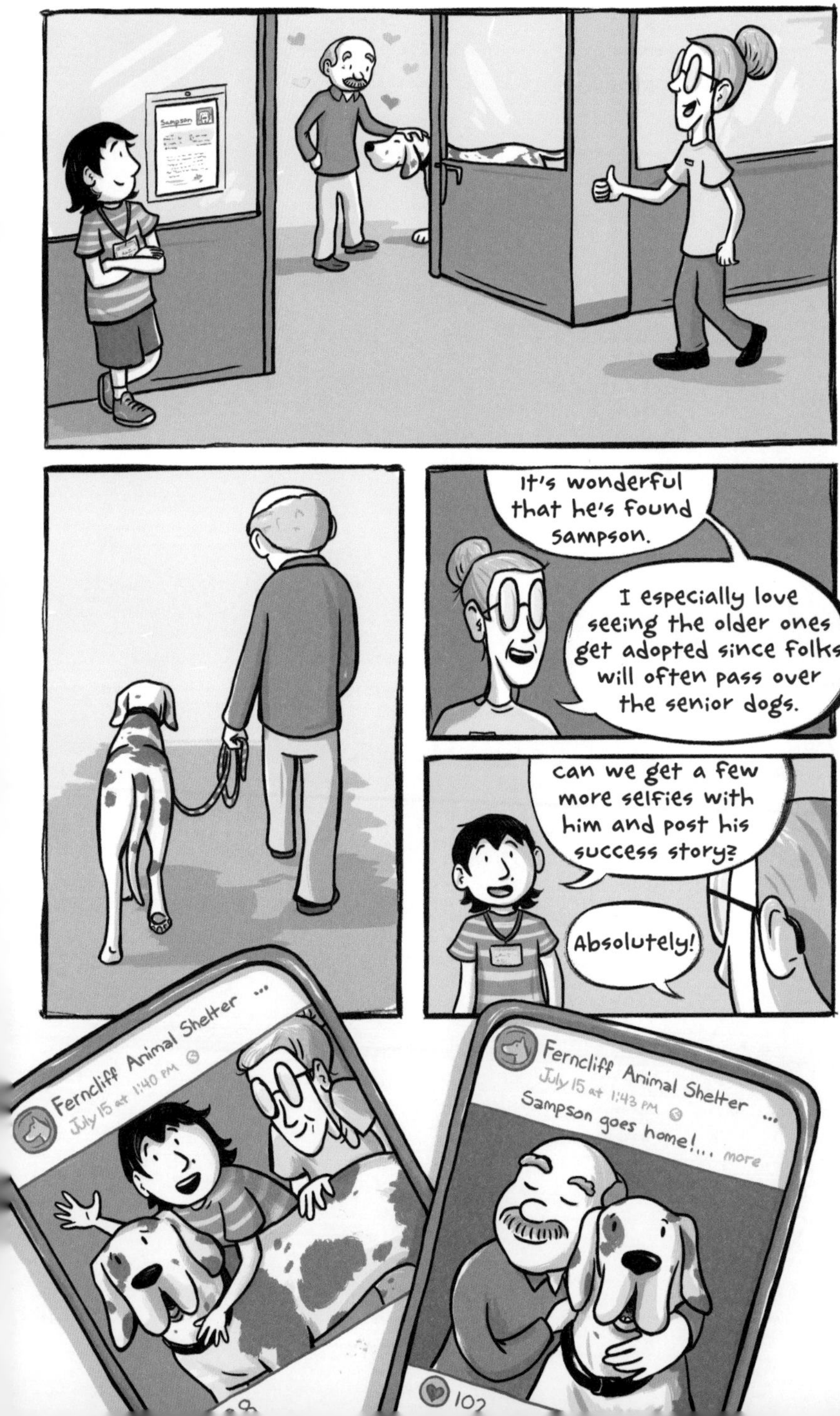
Sampson
It's wonderful that he's found Sampson.
I especially love seeing the older ones get adopted since folks will often pass over the senior dogs.
can we get a few more selfies with him and post his success story?
Absolutely!
Ferncliff Animal Shelter ...
July 15 at 1:40 PM
Ferncliff Animal Shelter ...
July 15 at 1:43 PM
Sampson goes home!... more
102

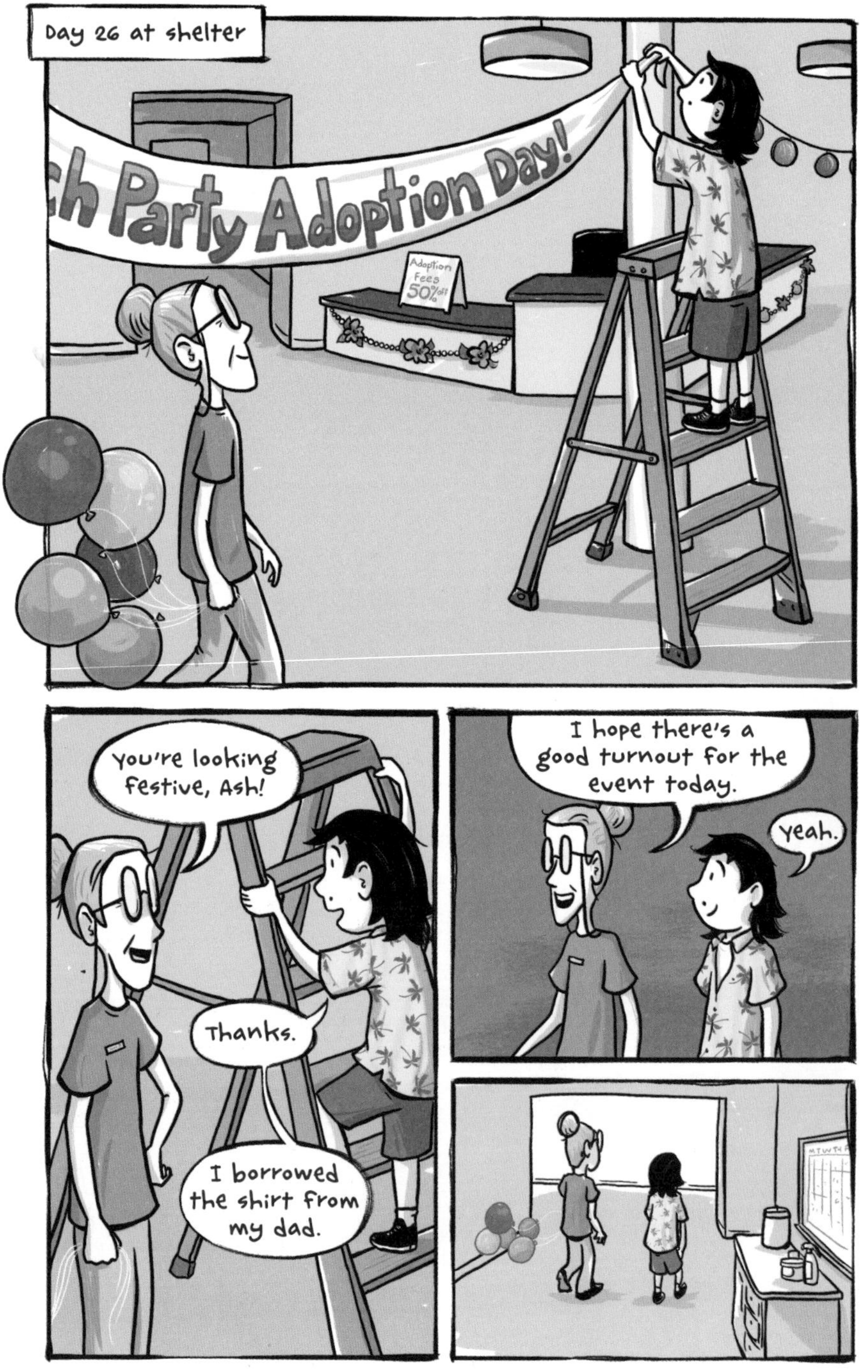
Day 26 at shelter
ch Party Adoption Day!
Adoption Fees 50% off
You're looking festive, Ash!
Thanks.
I borrowed the shirt from my dad.
I hope there's a good turnout for the event today.
Yeah.

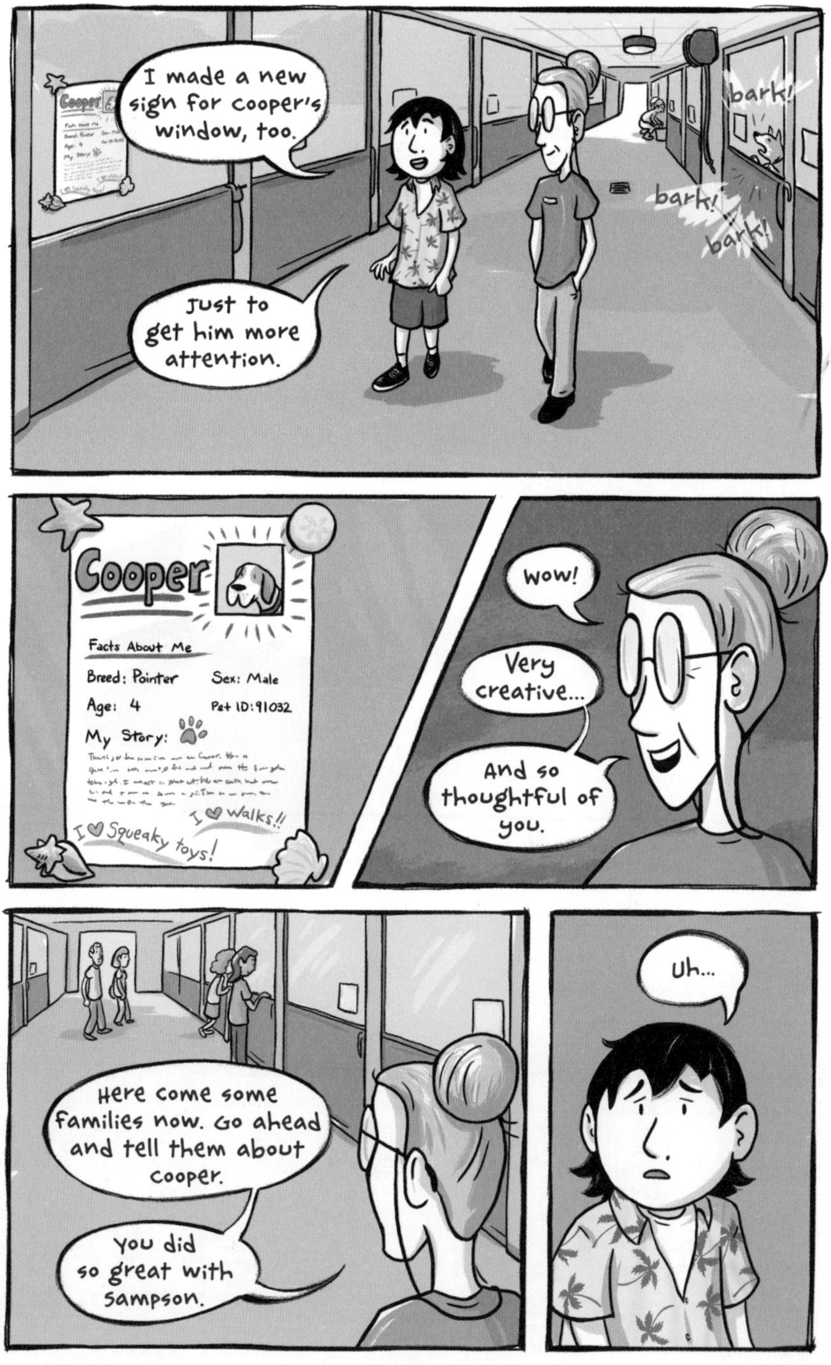
I made a new sign for cooper's window, too.
bark!
bark!
bark!
Just to get him more attention.
Cooper
Facts About Me
Breed: Pointer
Sex: Male
Age: 4
Pet ID: 91032
My Story:
I ♥ Walks!!
I ♥ Squeaky toys!
Wow!
Very creative...
And so thoughtful of you.
Here come some families now. Go ahead and tell them about cooper.
You did so great with sampson.
Uh...

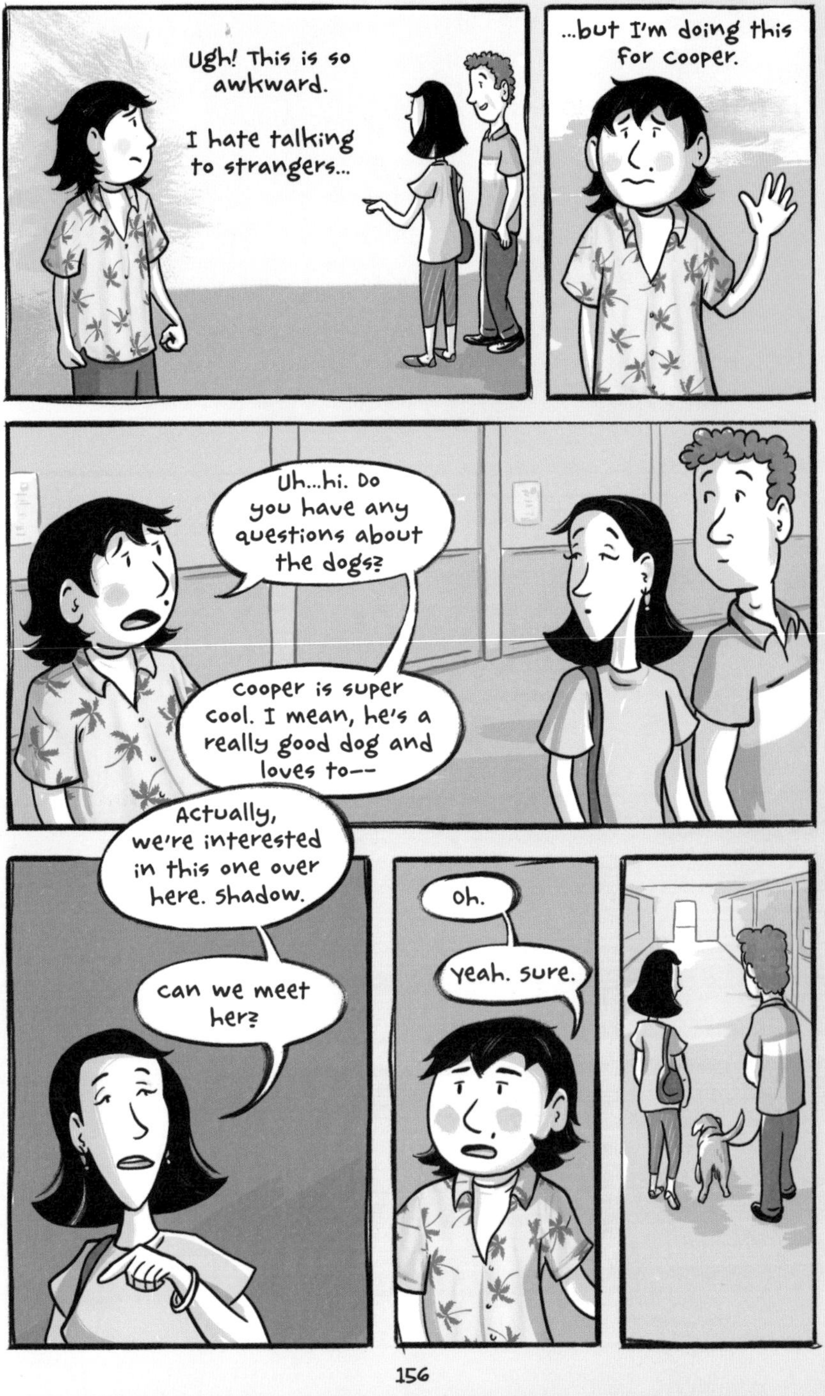
Ugh! This is so awkward.
I hate talking to strangers...
...but I'm doing this for cooper.
Uh...hi. Do you have any questions about the dogs?
cooper is super cool. I mean, he's a really good dog and loves to--
Actually, we're interested in this one over here. shadow.
can we meet her?
Oh.
Yeah. sure.

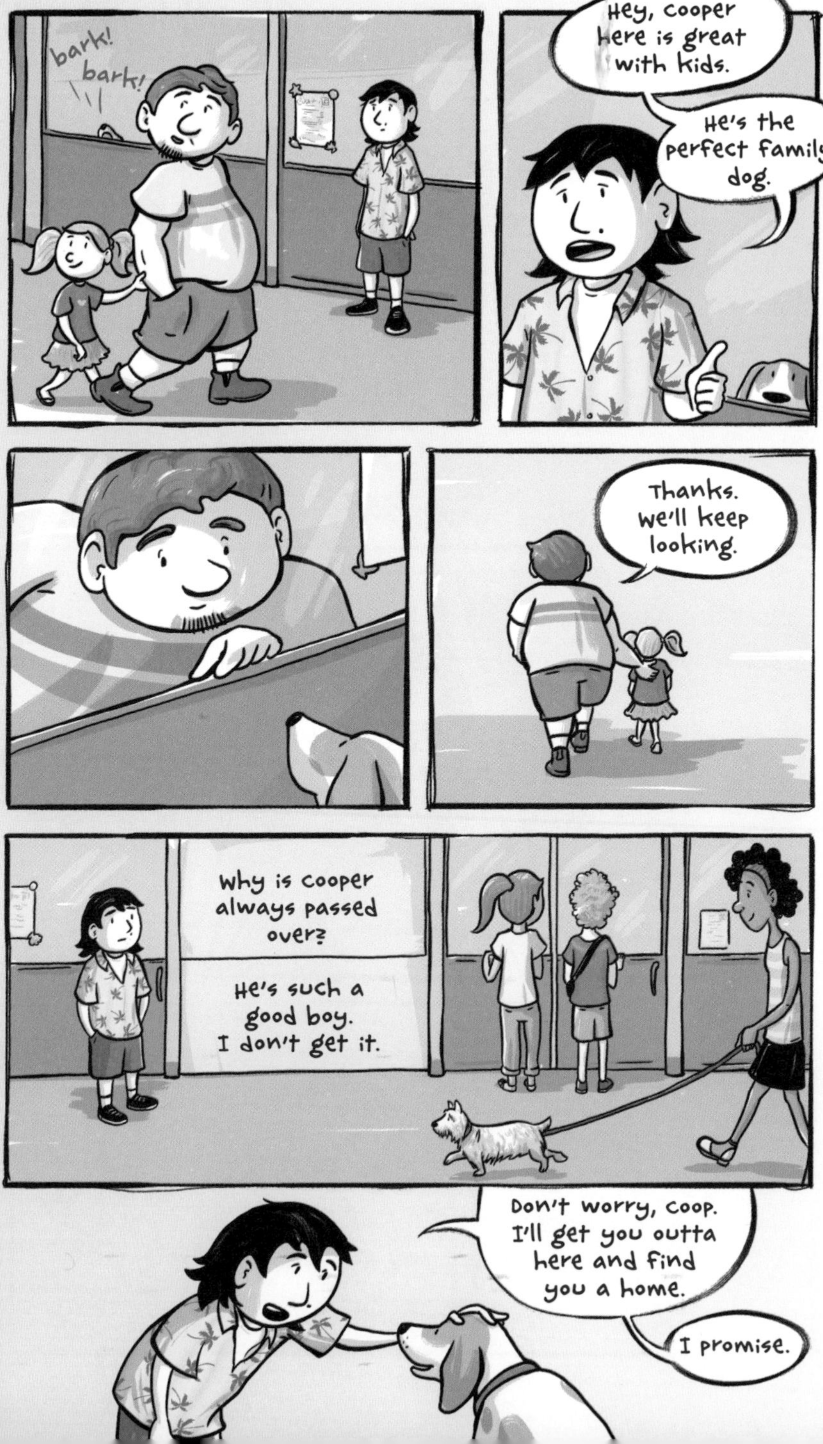
bark! bark!
Hey, cooper here is great with kids.
He's the perfect family dog.
Thanks. We'll keep looking.
Why is cooper always passed over?
He's such a good boy. I don't get it.
Don't worry, coop. I'll get you outta here and find you a home.
I promise.

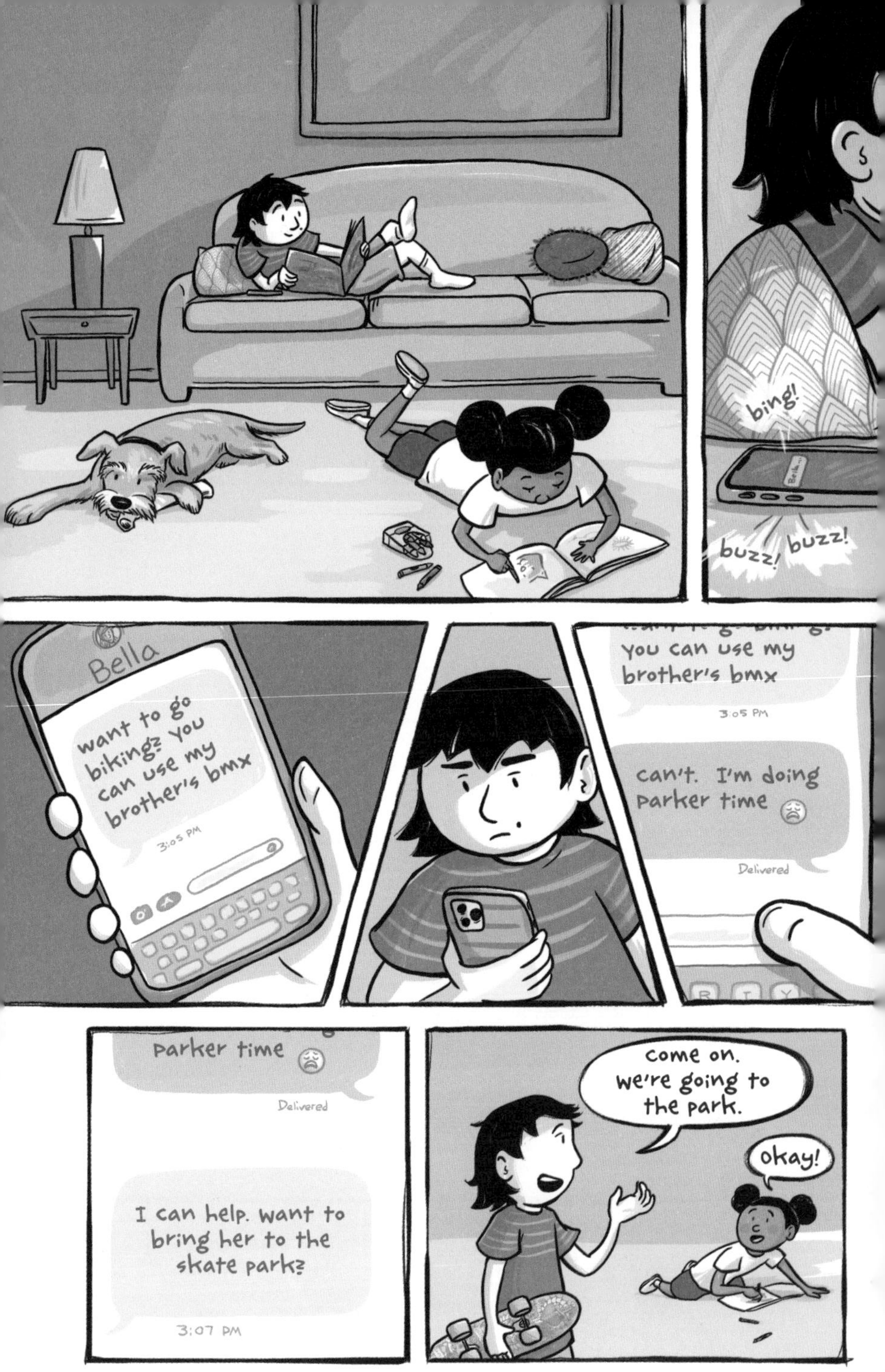
bing!
Bella...
buzz!
buzz!
Bella
want to go biking? you can use my brother's bmx
3:05 PM
you can use my brother's bmx
3:05 PM
can't. I'm doing parker time
Delivered
parker time
Delivered
I can help. want to bring her to the skate park?
3:07 PM
come on. we're going to the park.
okay!

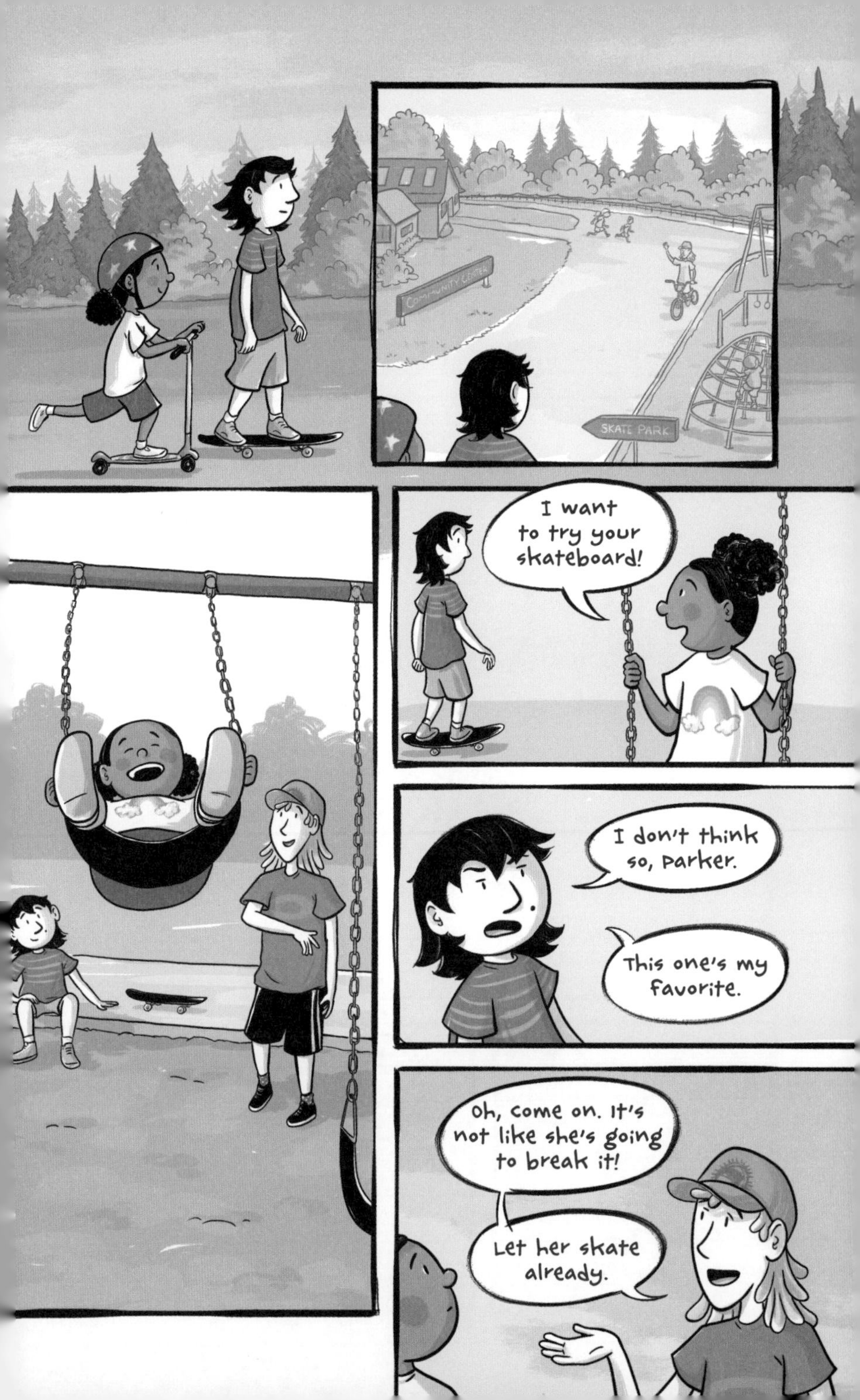
COMMUNITY CENTER
SKATE PARK
I want to try your skateboard!
I don't think so, Parker.
This one's my favorite.
Oh, come on. It's not like she's going to break it!
Let her skate already.

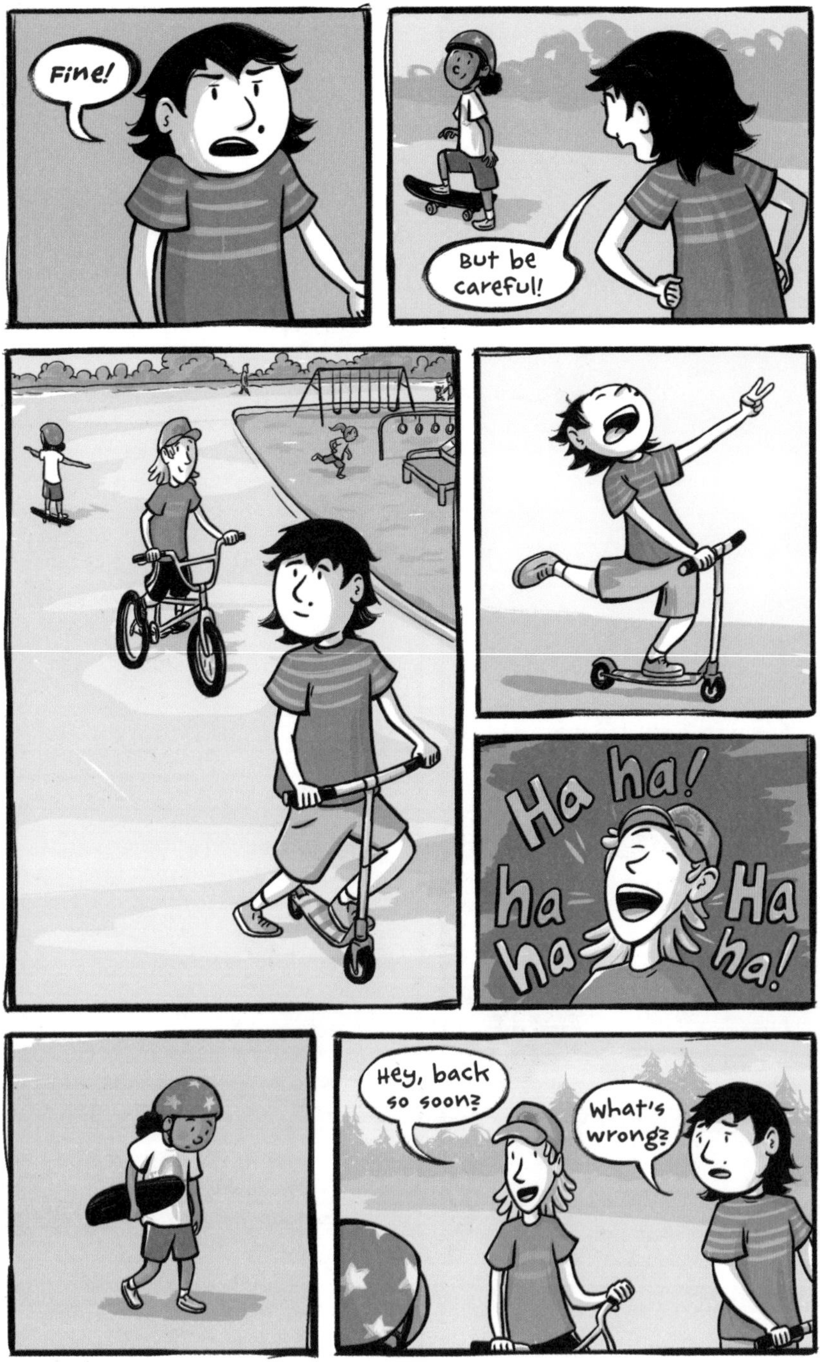
Fine!
But be careful!
Ha ha!
ha ha
Ha ha!
Hey, back so soon?
What's wrong?

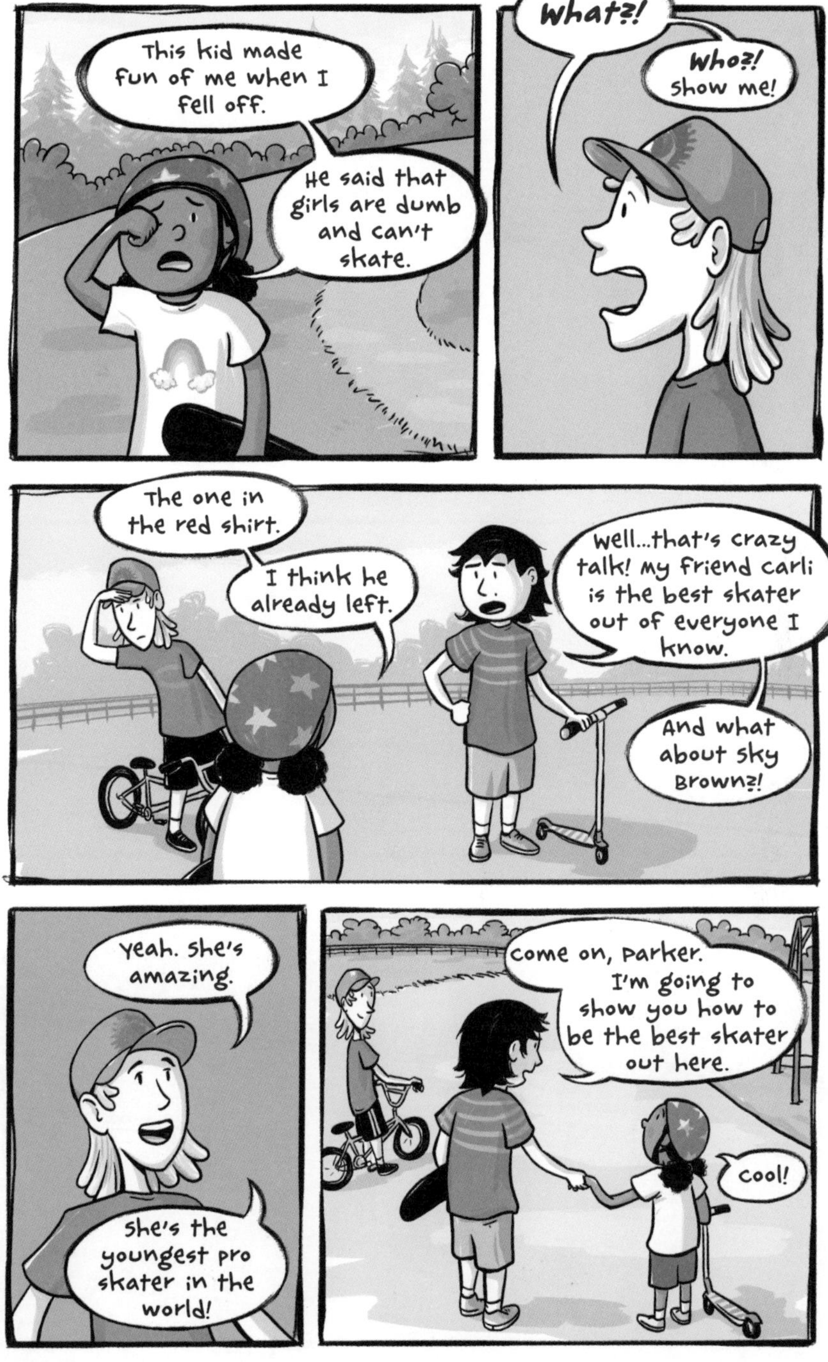
This kid made fun of me when I fell off.
He said that girls are dumb and can't skate.
What?!
Who?! Show me!
The one in the red shirt.
I think he already left.
Well...that's crazy talk! My friend Carli is the best skater out of everyone I know.
And what about Sky Brown?!
Yeah. She's amazing.
She's the youngest pro skater in the world!
Come on, Parker. I'm going to show you how to be the best skater out here.
Cool!

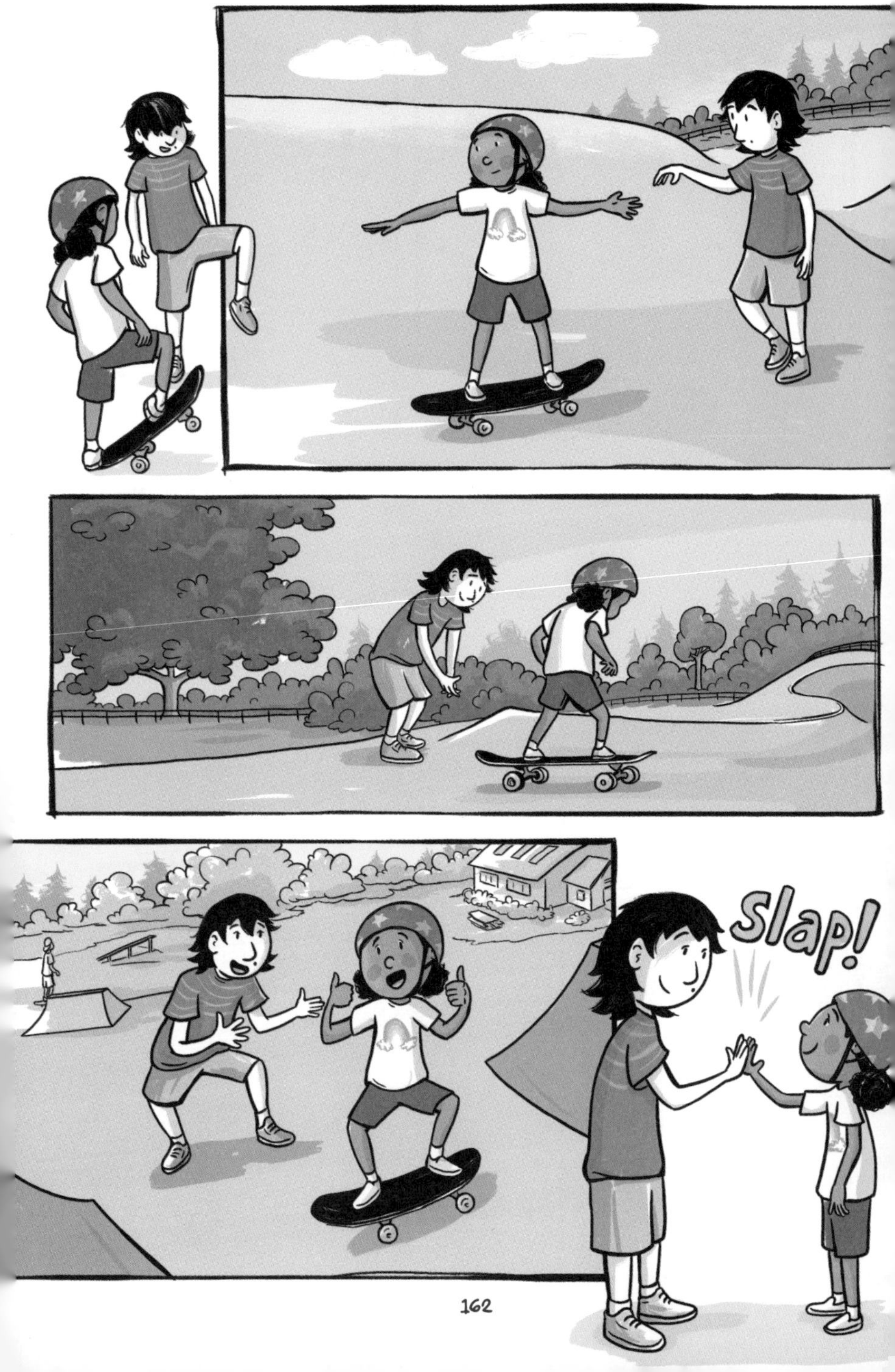
Slap!

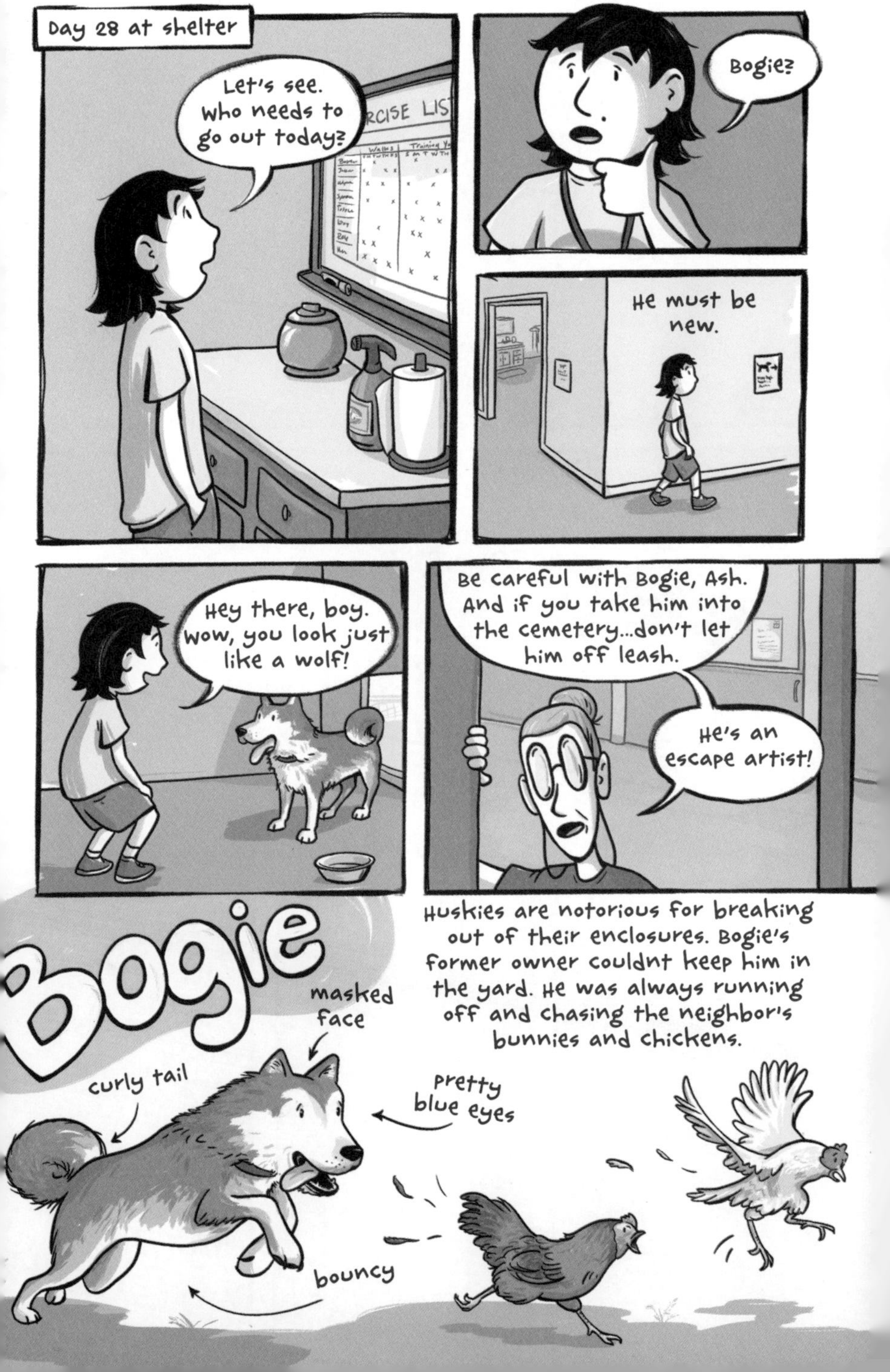
Day 28 at shelter
Let's see. Who needs to go out today?
RCISE LIST
Bogie?
He must be new.
Hey there, boy. Wow, you look just like a wolf!
Be careful with Bogie, Ash. And if you take him into the cemetery...don't let him off leash.
He's an escape artist!
Bogie
Huskies are notorious for breaking out of their enclosures. Bogie's former owner couldnt keep him in the yard. He was always running off and chasing the neighbor's bunnies and chickens.
masked face
curly tail
pretty blue eyes
bouncy

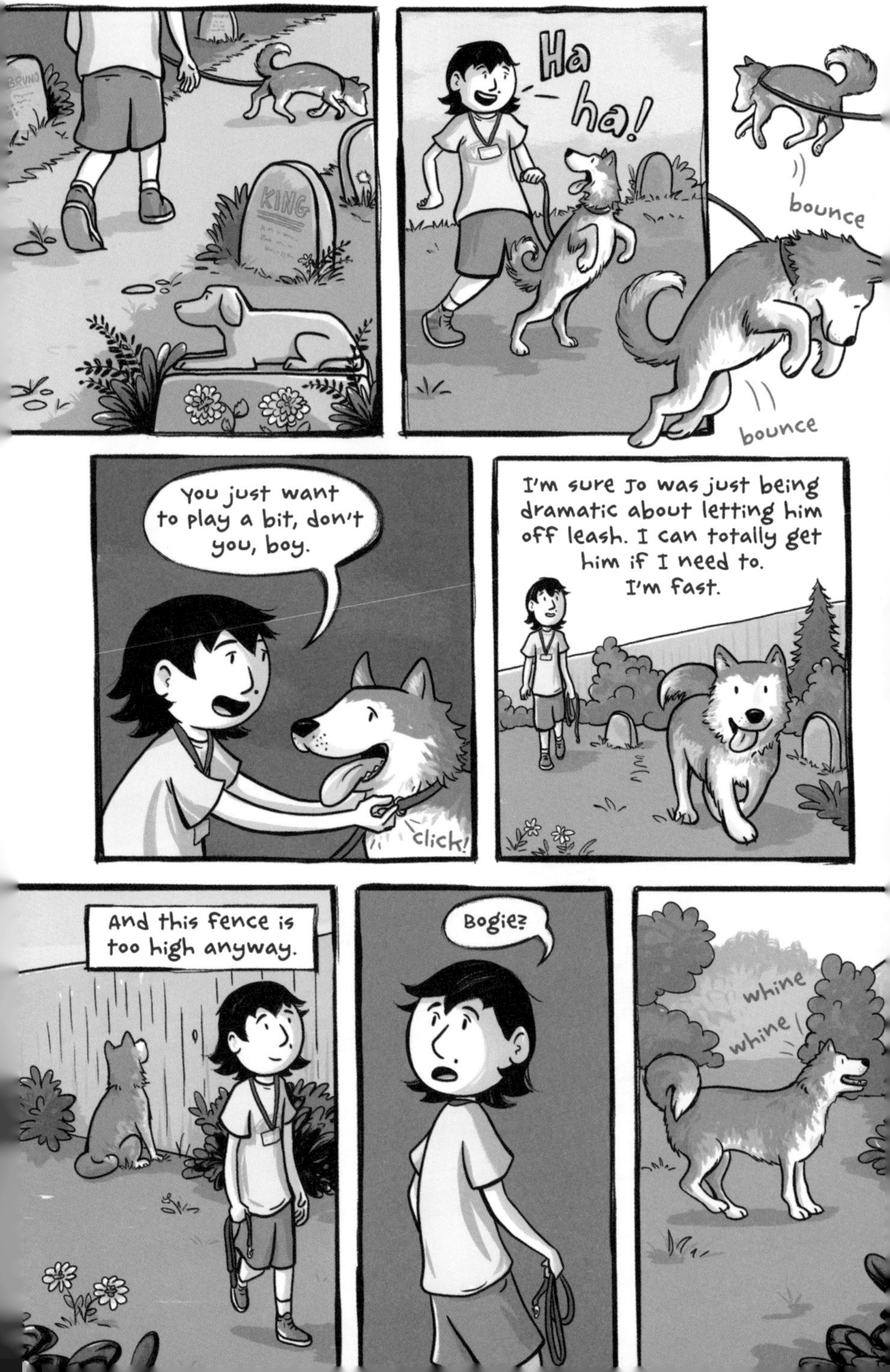
BRUNO
KING
Ha ha!
bounce
bounce
You just want to play a bit, don't you, boy.
click!
I'm sure Jo was just being dramatic about letting him off leash. I can totally get him if I need to. I'm fast.
And this fence is too high anyway.
Bogie?
whine
whine

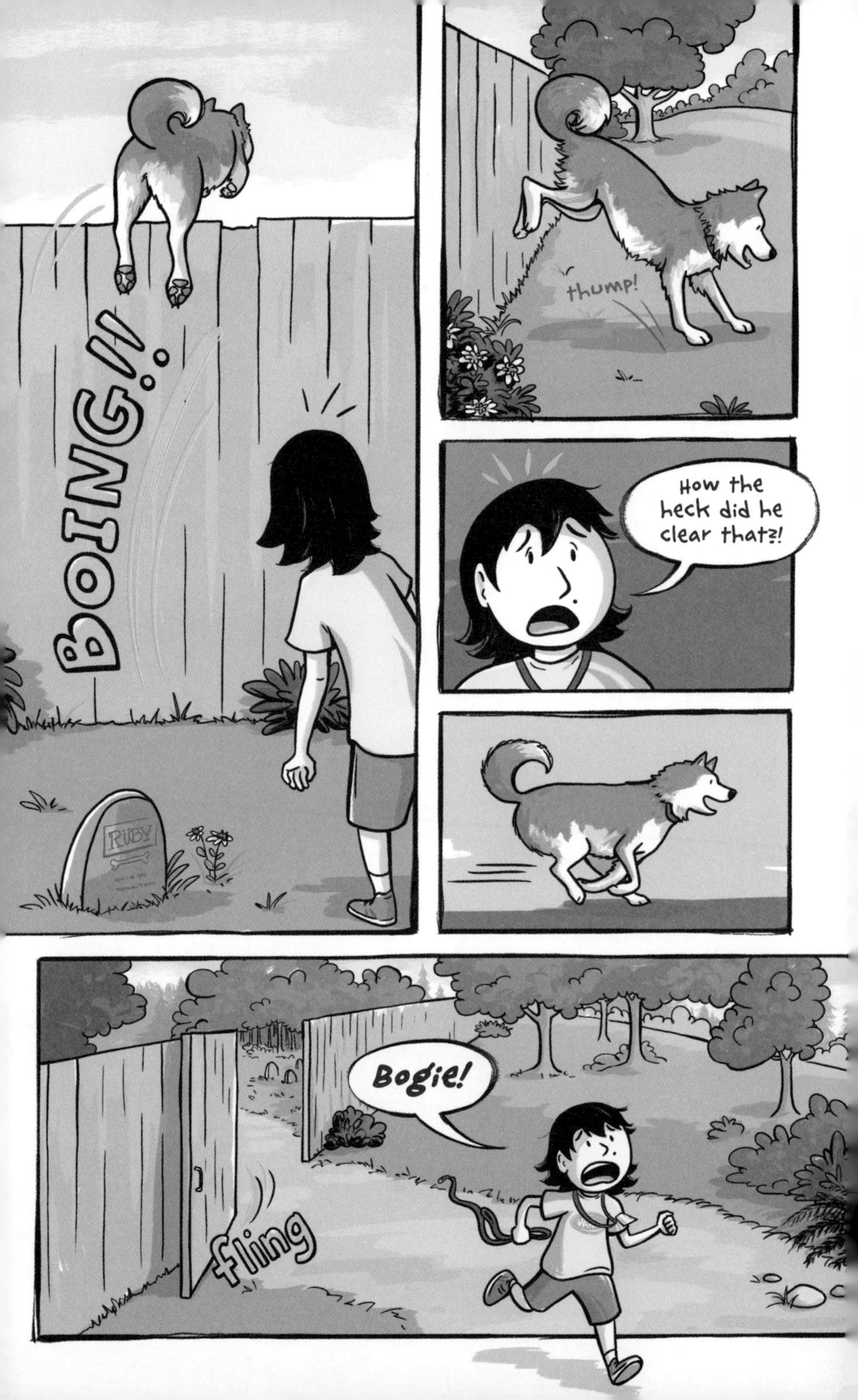
BOING!!
thump!
How the heck did he clear that?!
RUBY
fling
Bogie!

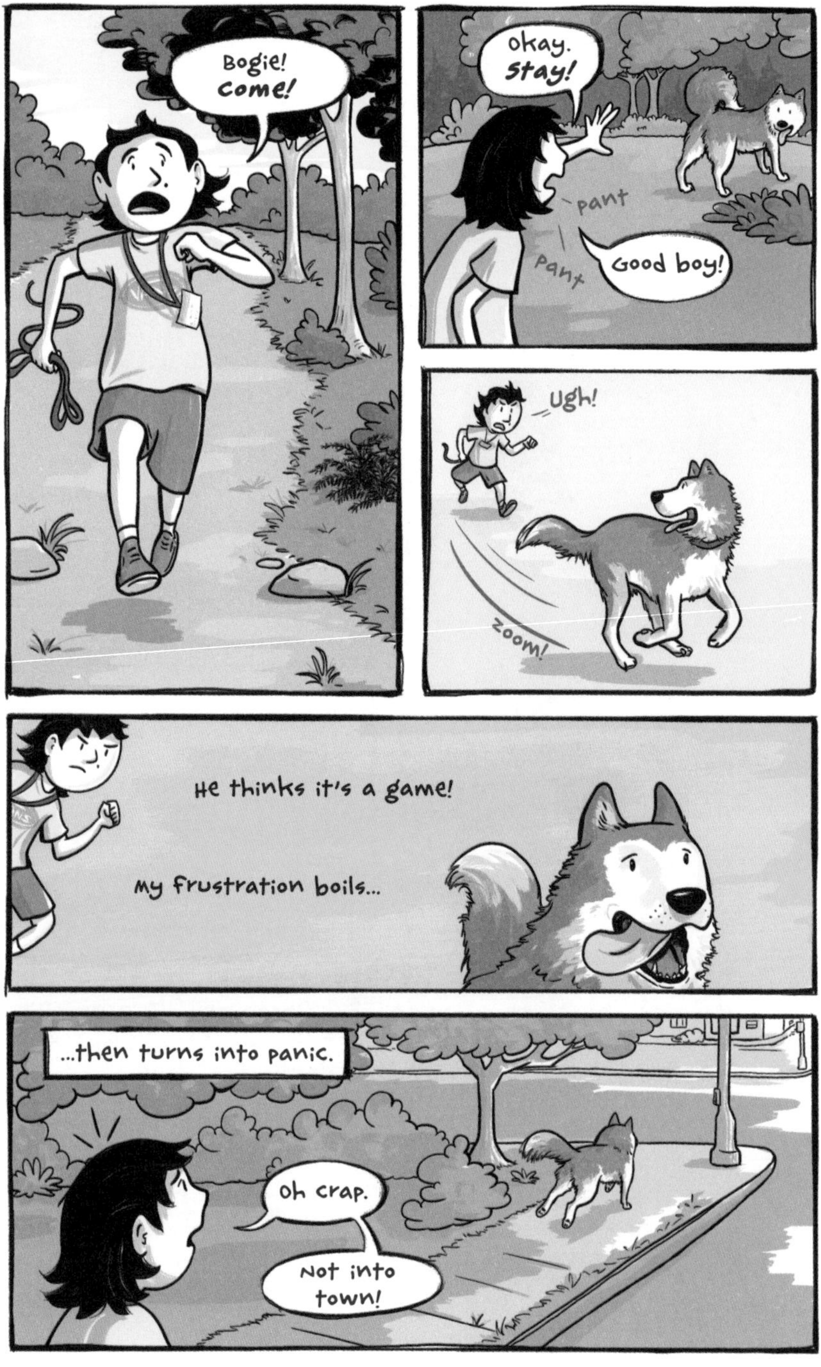
Bogie! Come!
Okay. Stay!
pant
pant
Good boy!
Ugh!
zoom!
He thinks it's a game!
My frustration boils...
...then turns into panic.
Oh crap.
Not into town!

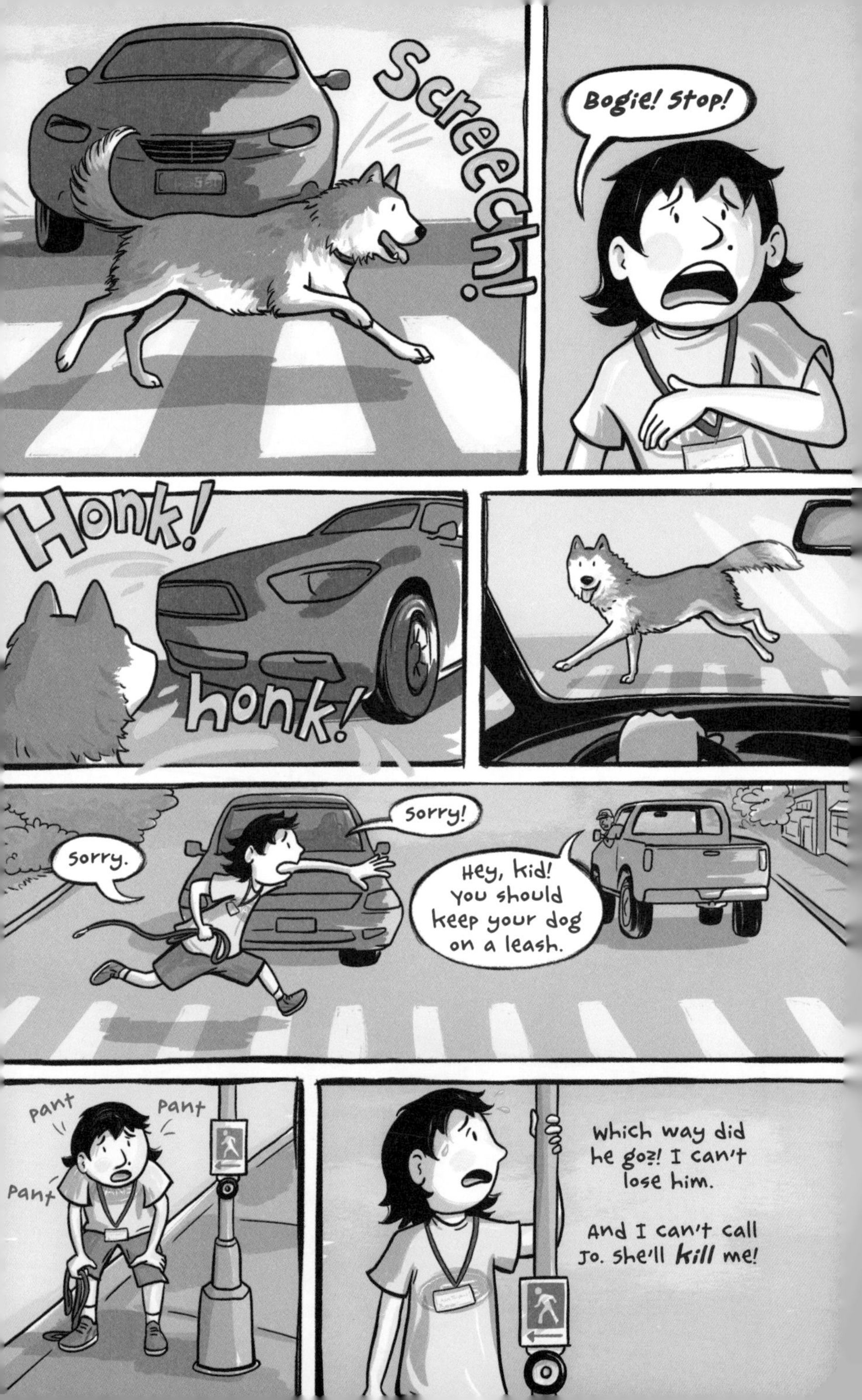
Screech!
Bogie! Stop!
Honk!
honk!
Sorry!
Sorry.
Hey, kid! You should keep your dog on a leash.
pant
pant
pant
Which way did he go?! I can't lose him.
And I can't call Jo. She'll *kill* me!

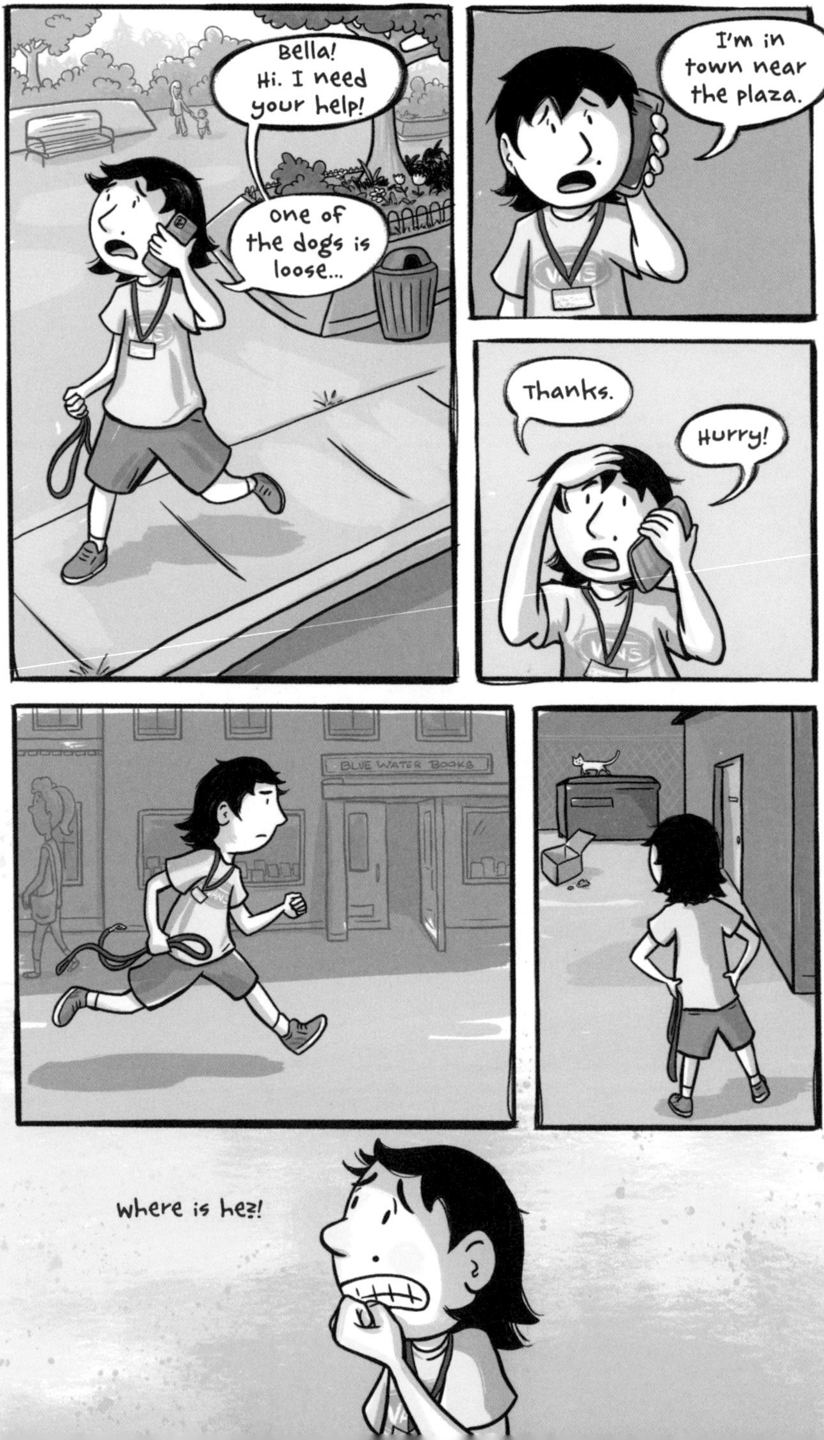
Bella!
Hi. I need your help!
one of the dogs is loose...
I'm in town near the plaza.
Thanks.
Hurry!
BLUE WATER BOOKS
Where is he?!

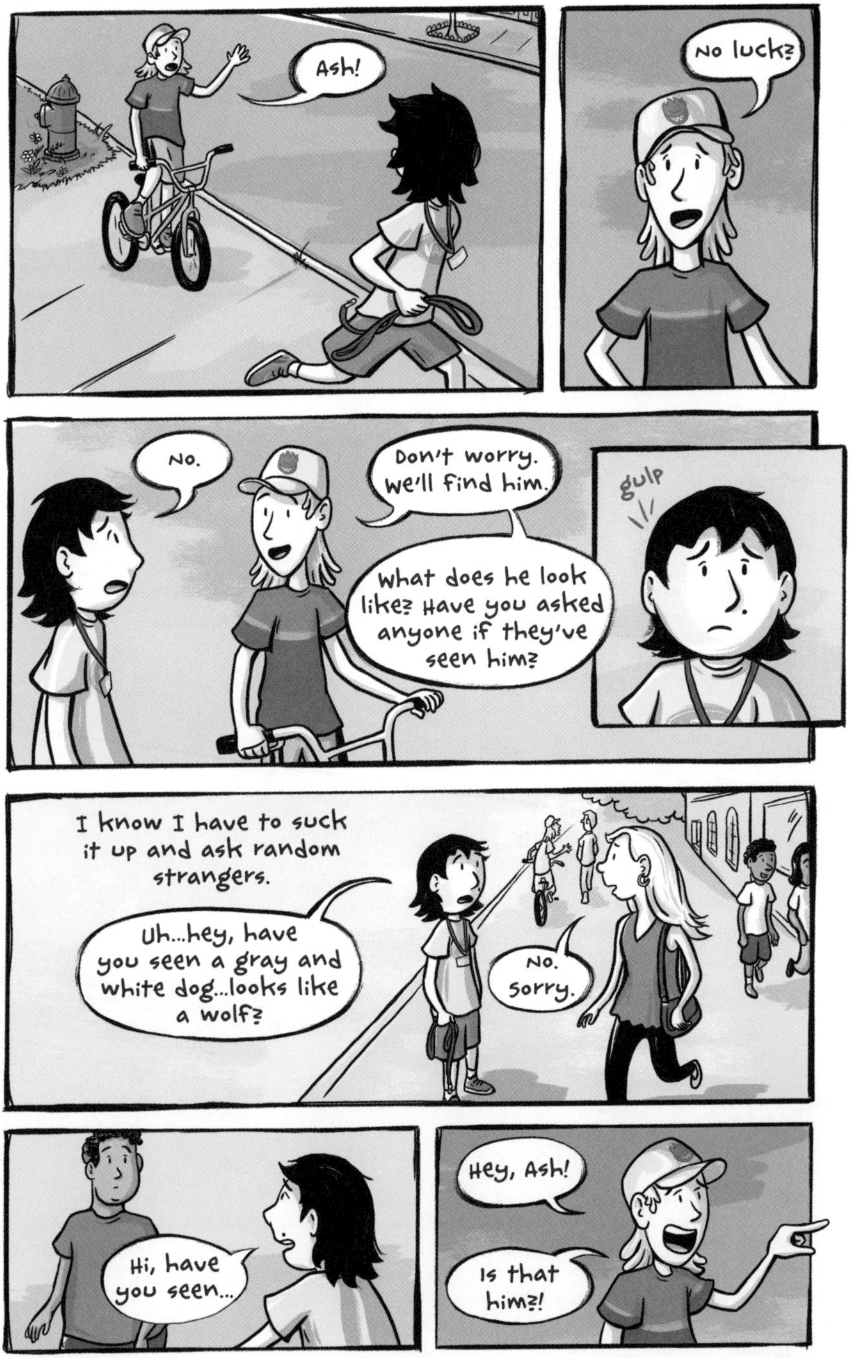
Ash!
No luck?
No.
Don't worry. We'll find him.
What does he look like? Have you asked anyone if they've seen him?
gulp
I know I have to suck it up and ask random strangers.
Uh...hey, have you seen a gray and white dog...looks like a wolf?
No. Sorry.
Hi, have you seen...
Hey, Ash!
Is that him?!

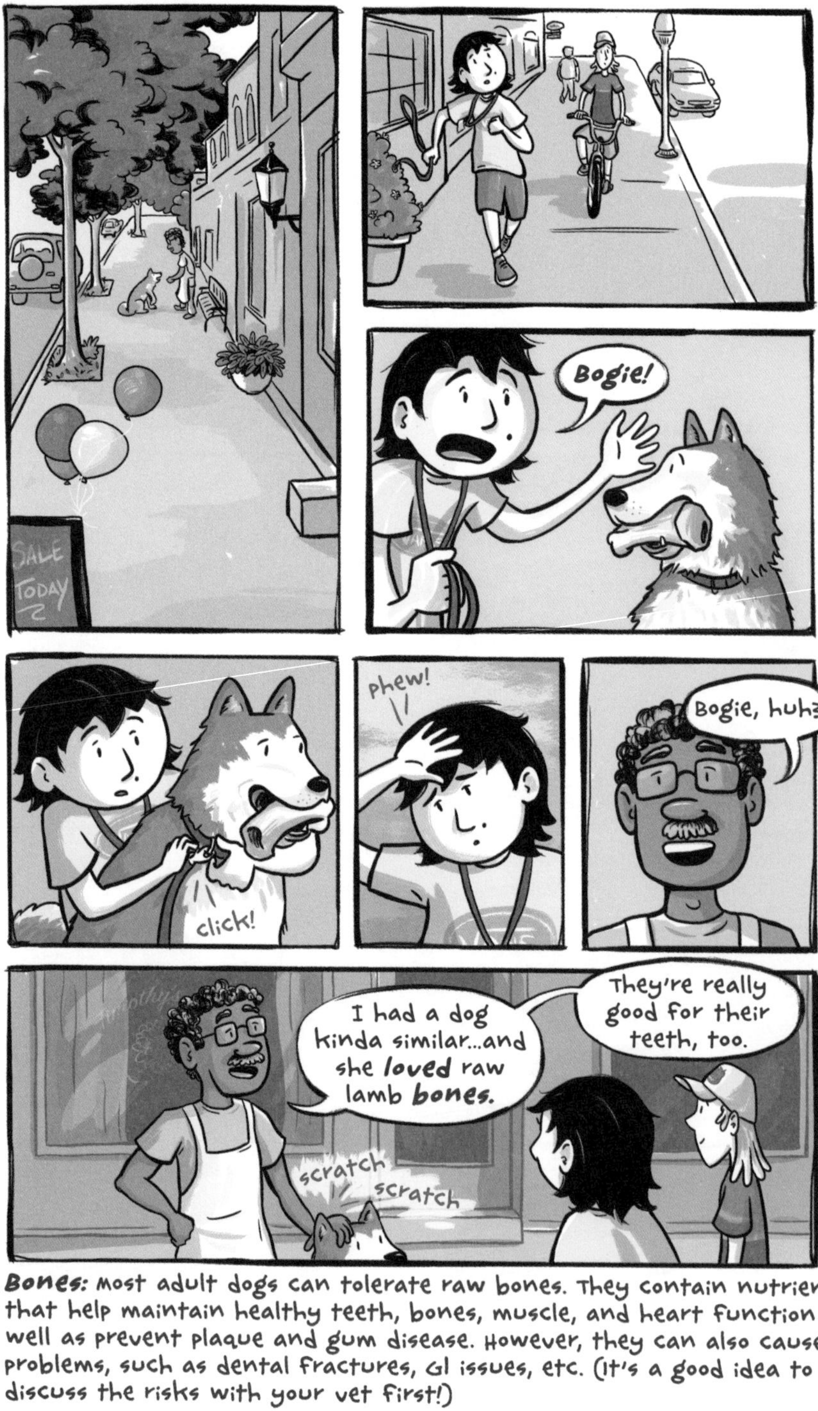
SALE
TODAY
Bogie!
click!
phew!
Bogie, huh?
I had a dog kinda similar...and she *loved* raw lamb **bones.**
They're really good for their teeth, too.
scratch
scratch

Bones: Most adult dogs can tolerate raw bones. They contain nutrients that help maintain healthy teeth, bones, muscle, and heart function as well as prevent plaque and gum disease. However, they can also cause problems, such as dental fractures, GI issues, etc. (It's a good idea to discuss the risks with your vet first!)

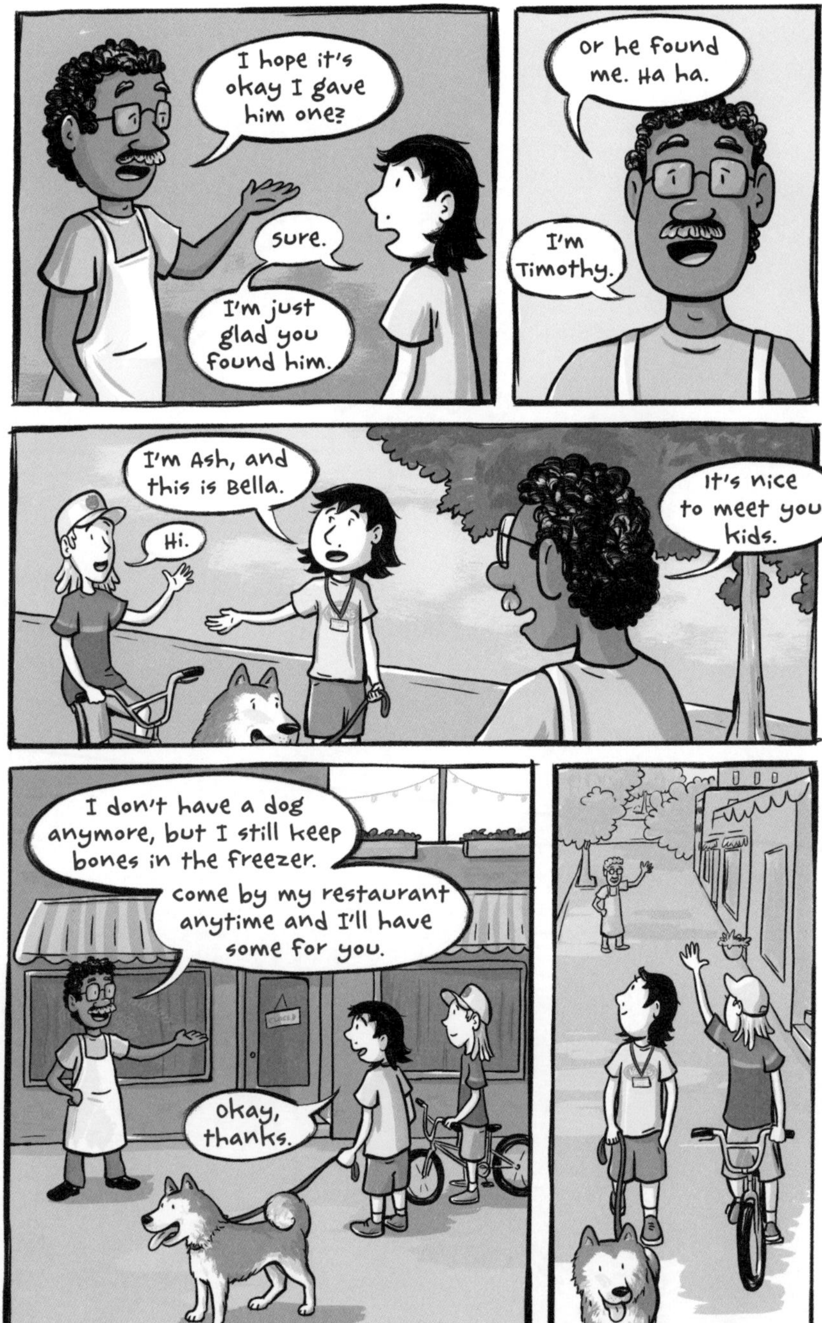
I hope it's okay I gave him one?
Sure.
I'm just glad you found him.
Or he found me. Ha ha.
I'm Timothy.
I'm Ash, and this is Bella.
Hi.
It's nice to meet you kids.
I don't have a dog anymore, but I still keep bones in the freezer.
Come by my restaurant anytime and I'll have some for you.
Okay, thanks.

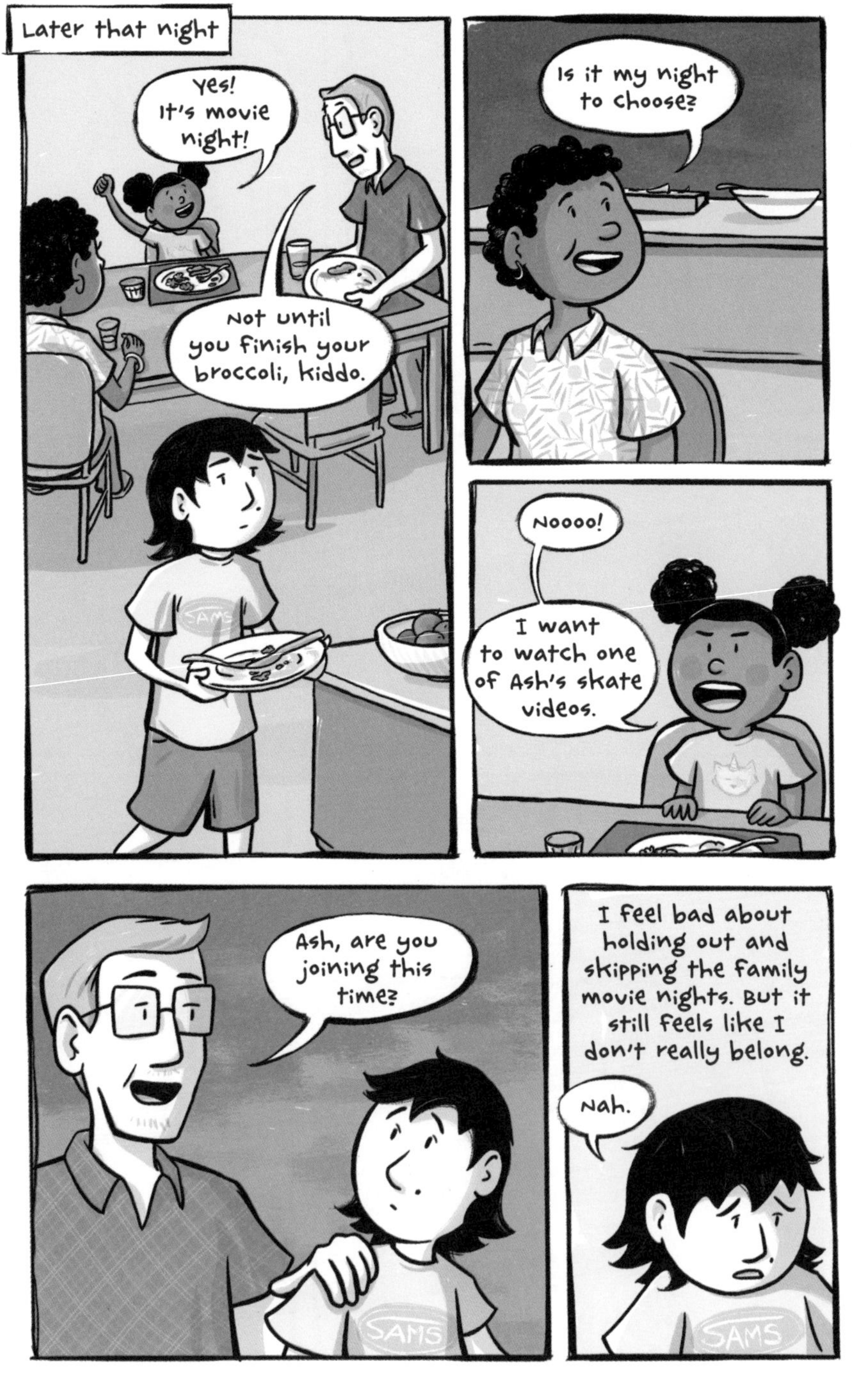
Later that night
Yes! It's movie night!
Not until you finish your broccoli, kiddo.
Is it my night to choose?
Noooo!
I want to watch one of Ash's skate videos.
Ash, are you joining this time?
I feel bad about holding out and skipping the family movie nights. But it still feels like I don't really belong.
Nah.

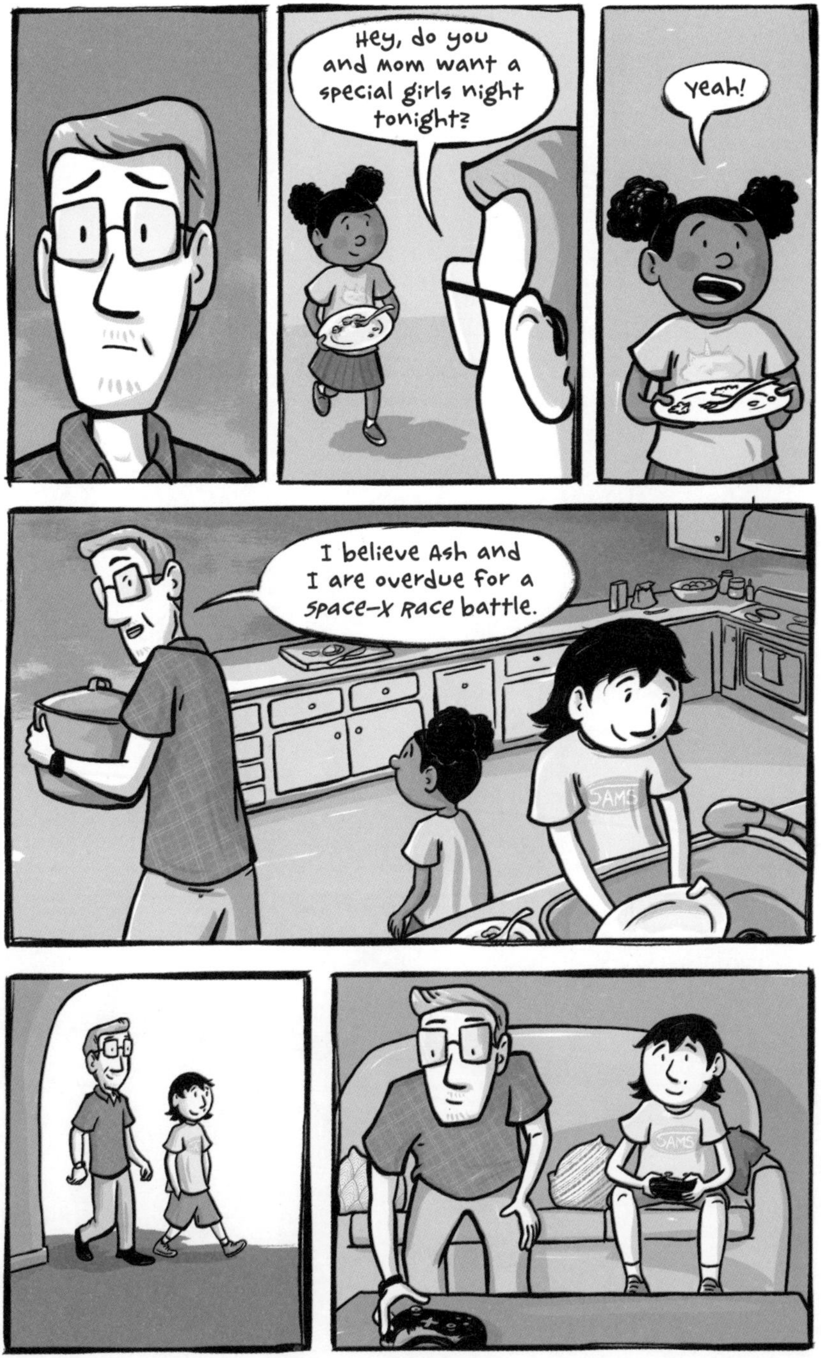
Hey, do you and mom want a special girls night tonight?
Yeah!
I believe Ash and I are overdue for a Space-X Race battle.
SAMS
SAMS
SAMS

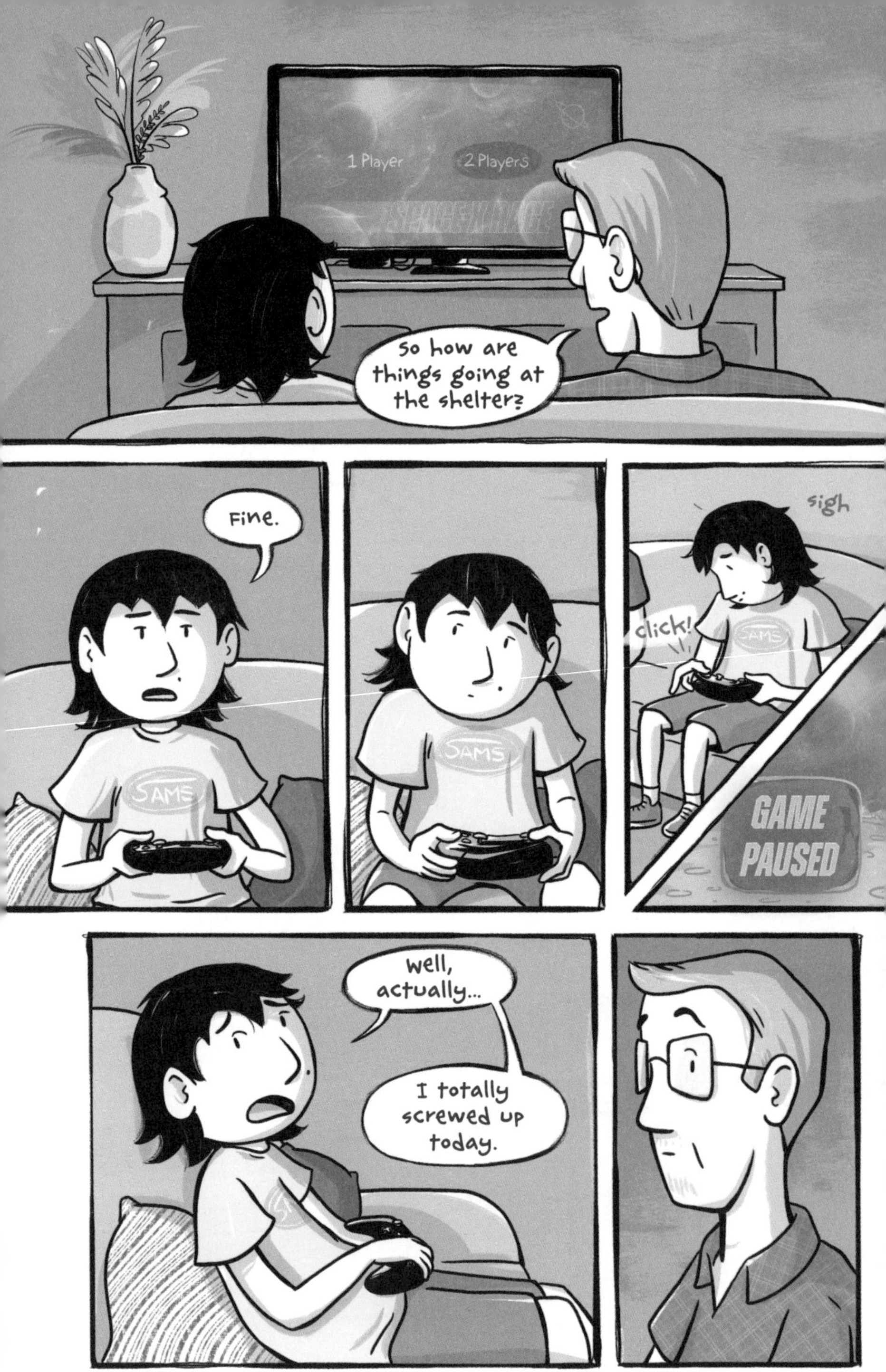
1 Player
2 Players
So how are things going at the shelter?
Fine.
sigh
click!
GAME PAUSED
Well, actually...
I totally screwed up today.

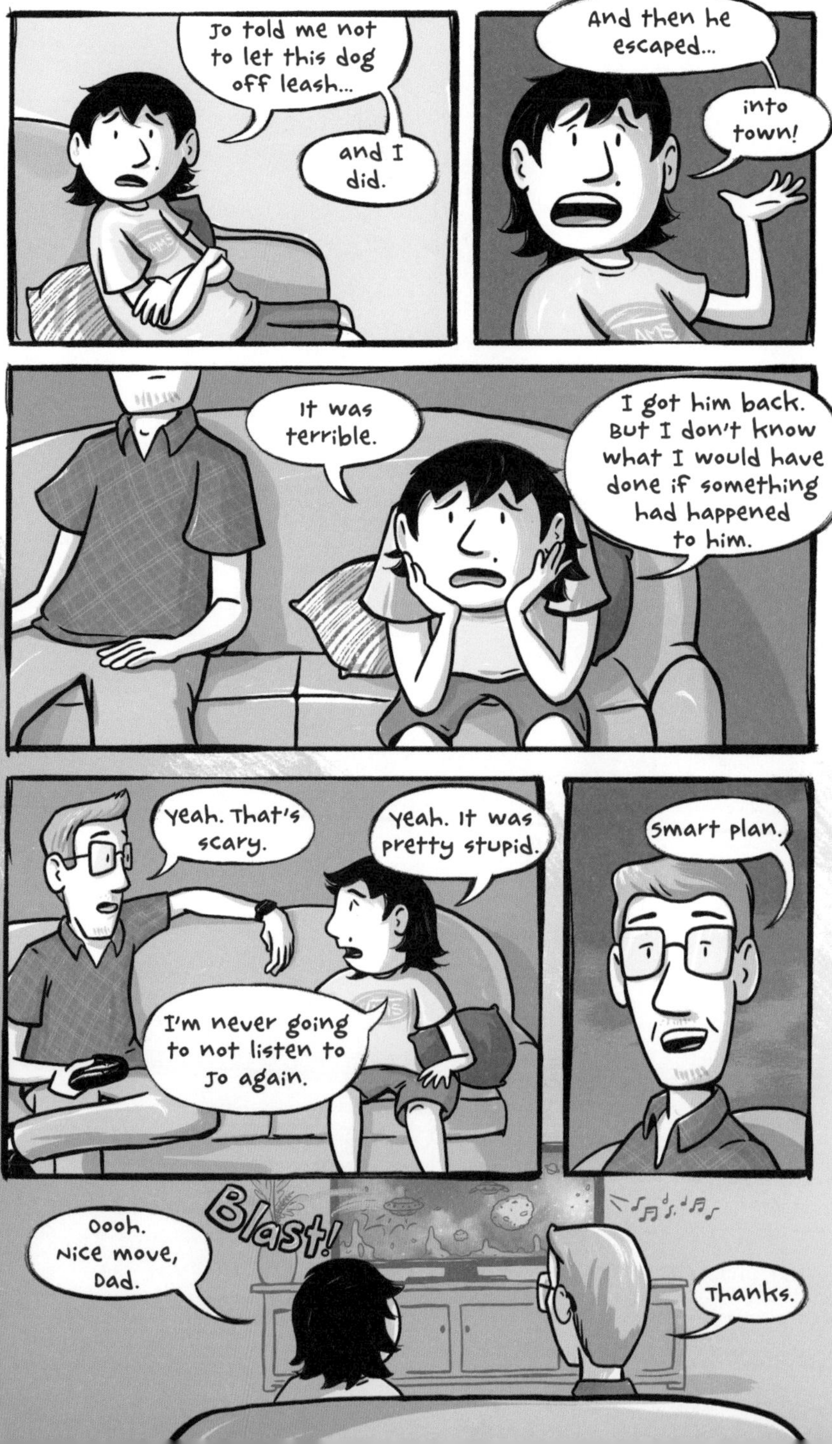

Jo told me not to let this dog off leash...
and I did.
And then he escaped...
into town!
It was terrible.
I got him back. But I don't know what I would have done if something had happened to him.
Yeah. That's scary.
Yeah. It was pretty stupid.
I'm never going to not listen to Jo again.
Smart plan.
Blast!
Oooh. Nice move, Dad.
Thanks.

CHAPTER 7

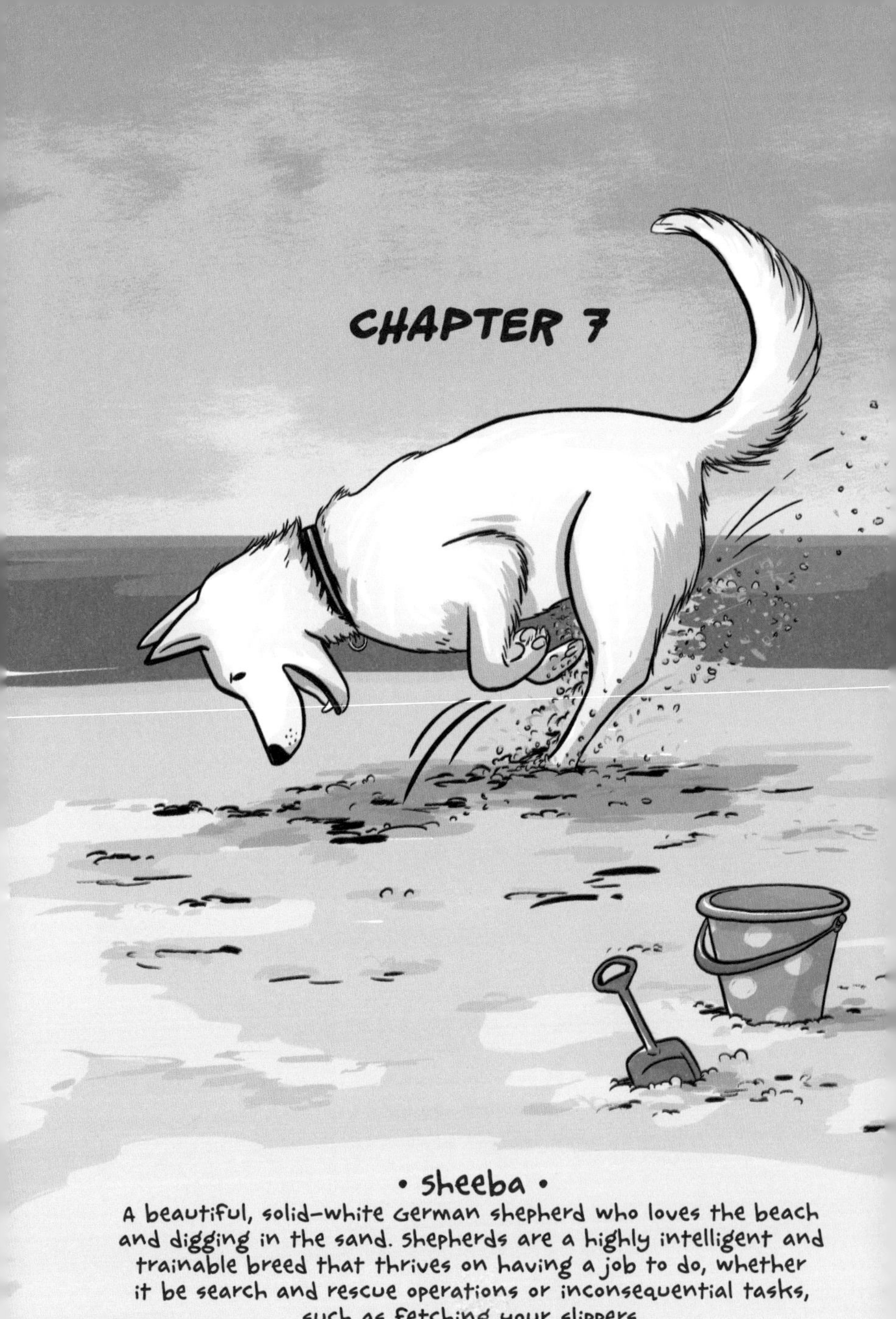

• sheeba •

A beautiful, solid-white German shepherd who loves the beach and digging in the sand. Shepherds are a highly intelligent and trainable breed that thrives on having a job to do, whether it be search and rescue operations or inconsequential tasks, such as fetching your slippers.

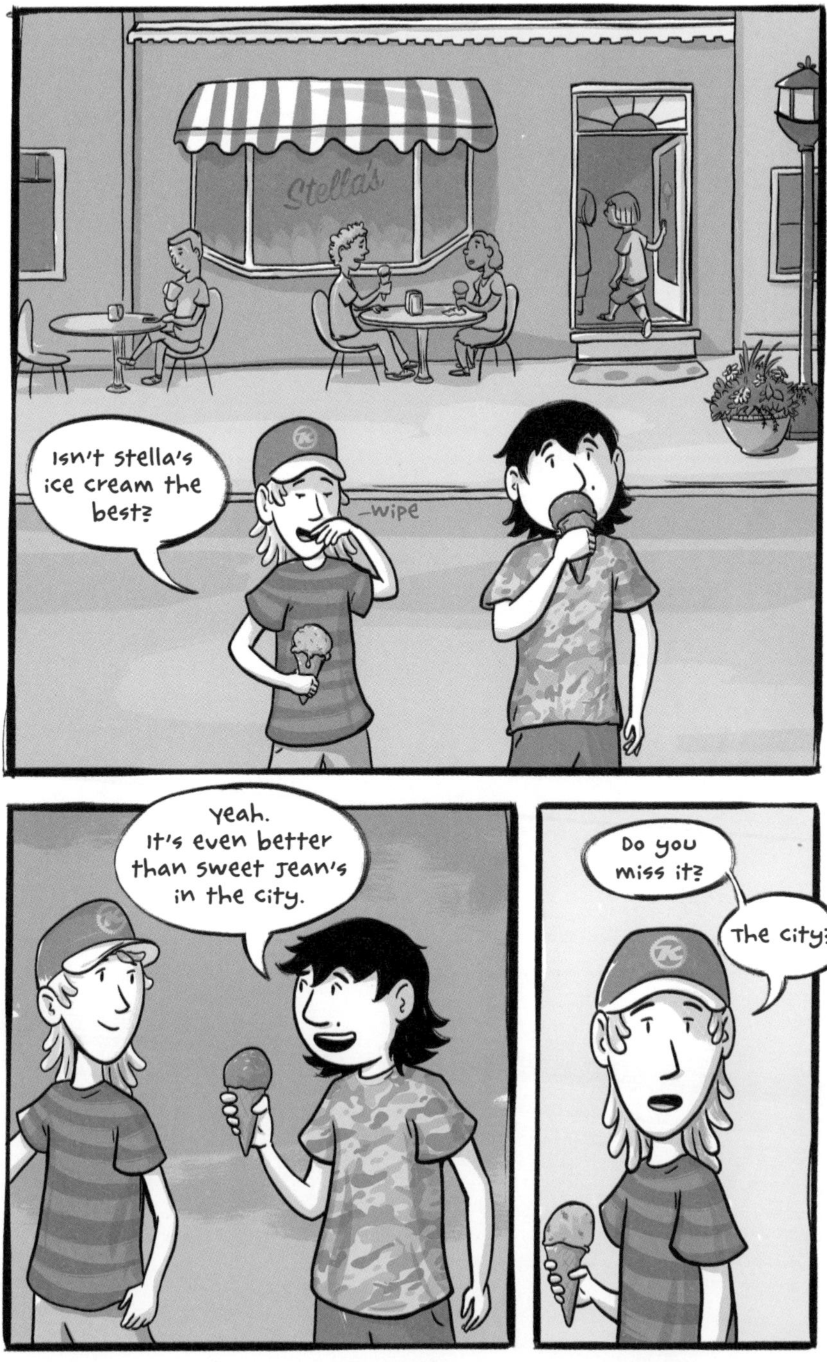
Stella's
Isn't Stella's ice cream the best?
wipe
Yeah. It's even better than Sweet Jean's in the city.
Do you miss it?
The city?

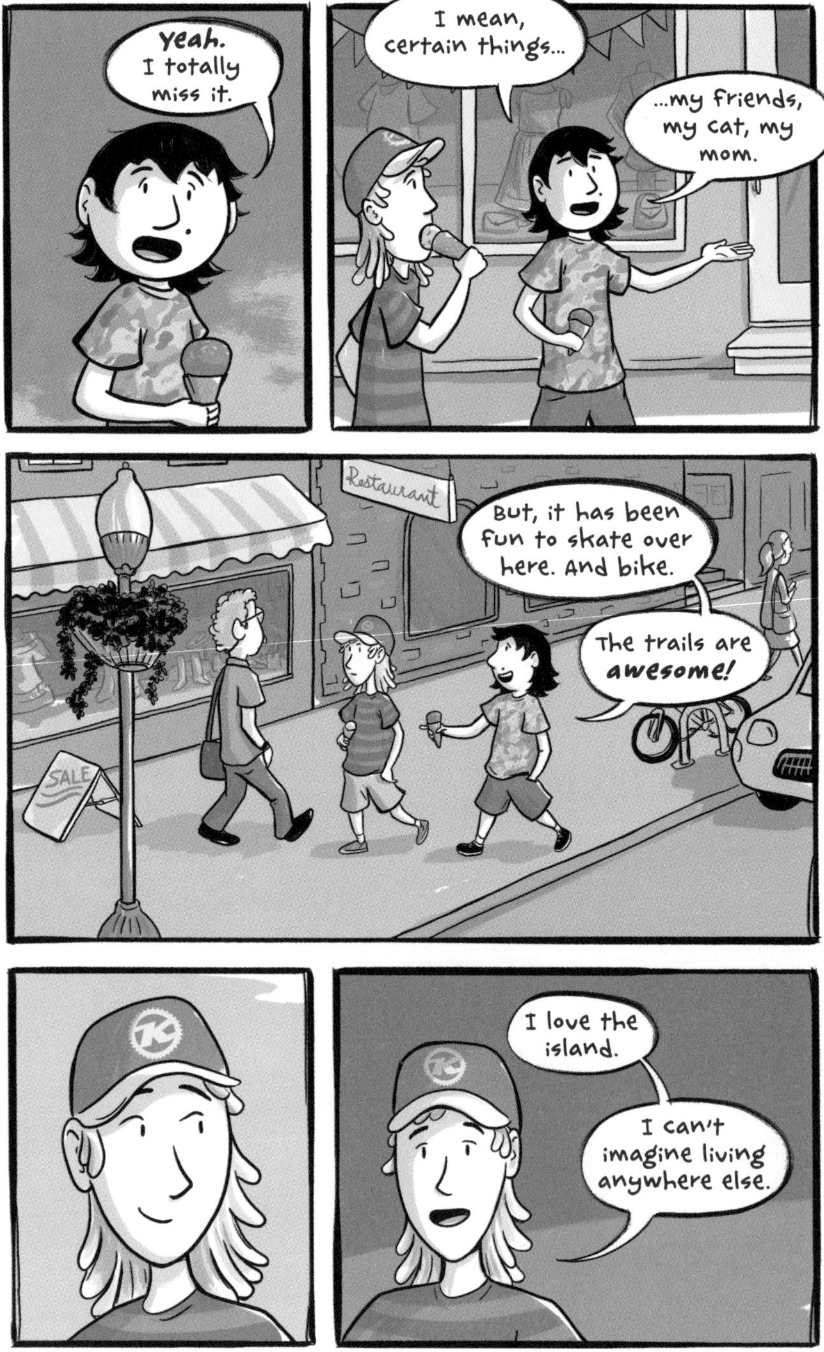
Yeah. I totally miss it.
I mean, certain things...
...my friends, my cat, my mom.
Restaurant
SALE
But, it has been fun to skate over here. And bike.
The trails are awesome!
I love the island.
I can't imagine living anywhere else.

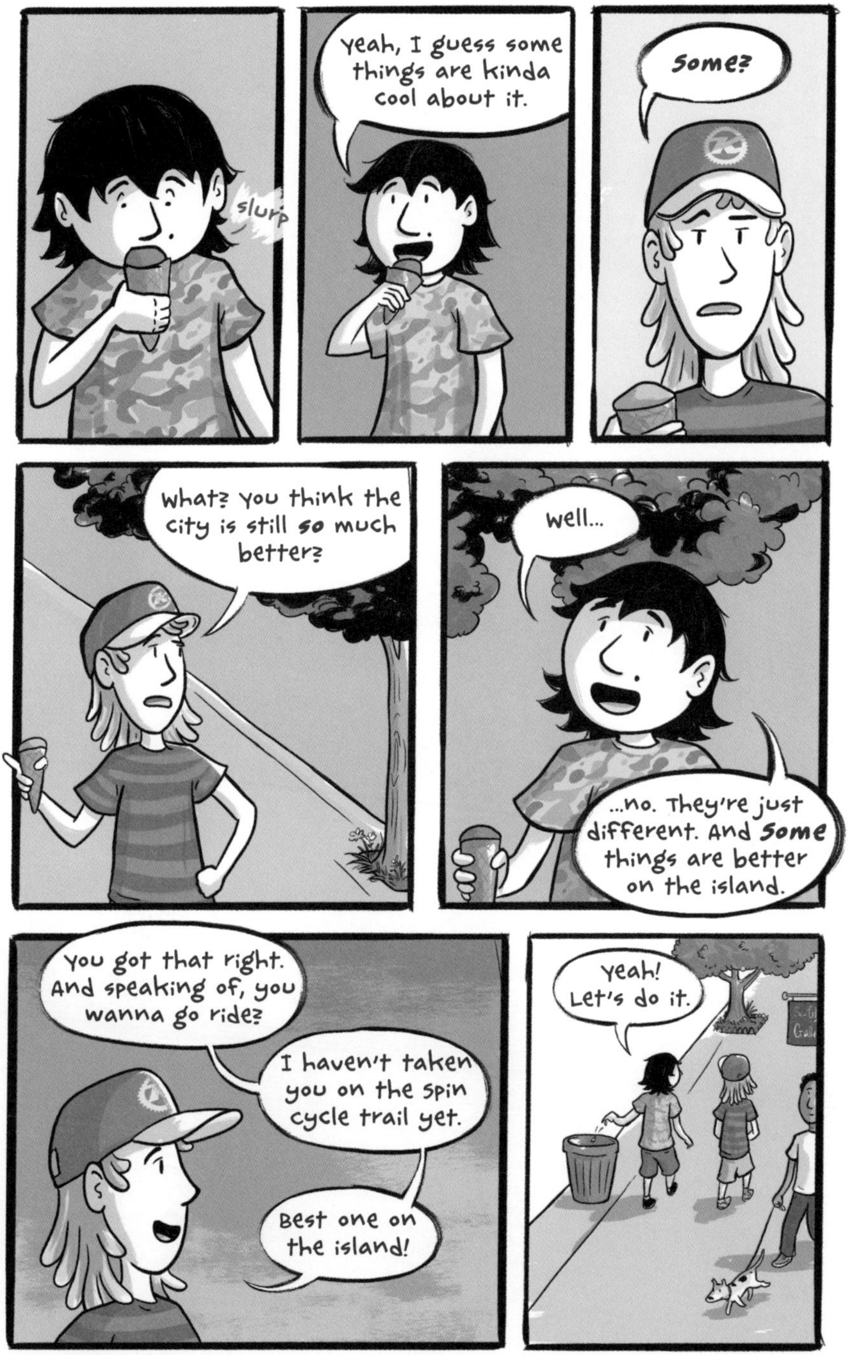
slurp
Yeah, I guess some things are kinda cool about it.
Some?
What? You think the city is still so much better?
Well...
...no. They're just different. And some things are better on the island.
You got that right. And speaking of, you wanna go ride?
I haven't taken you on the spin cycle trail yet.
Best one on the island!
Yeah! Let's do it.

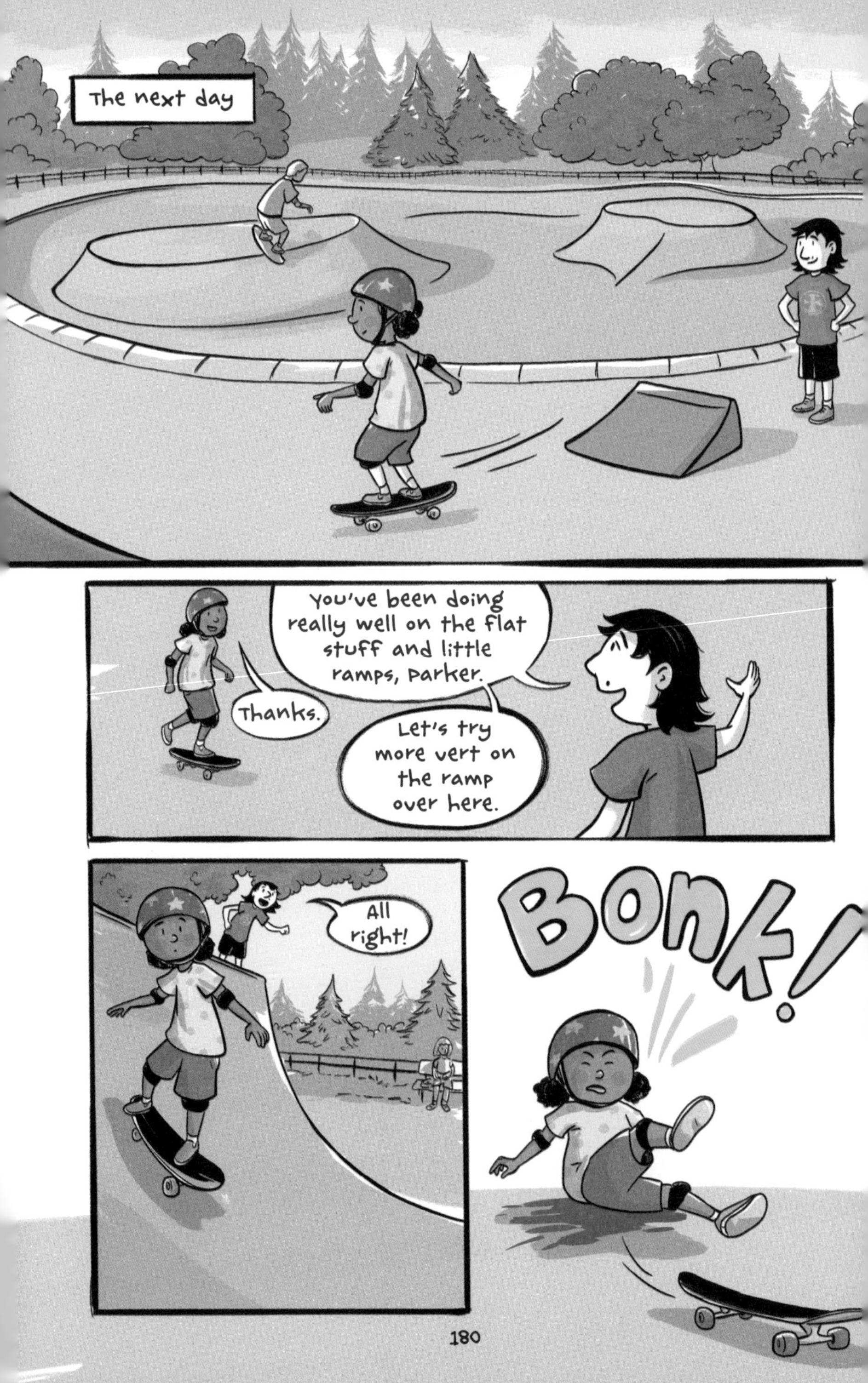
The next day
You've been doing really well on the flat stuff and little ramps, Parker.
Thanks.
Let's try more vert on the ramp over here.
All right!
BONK!

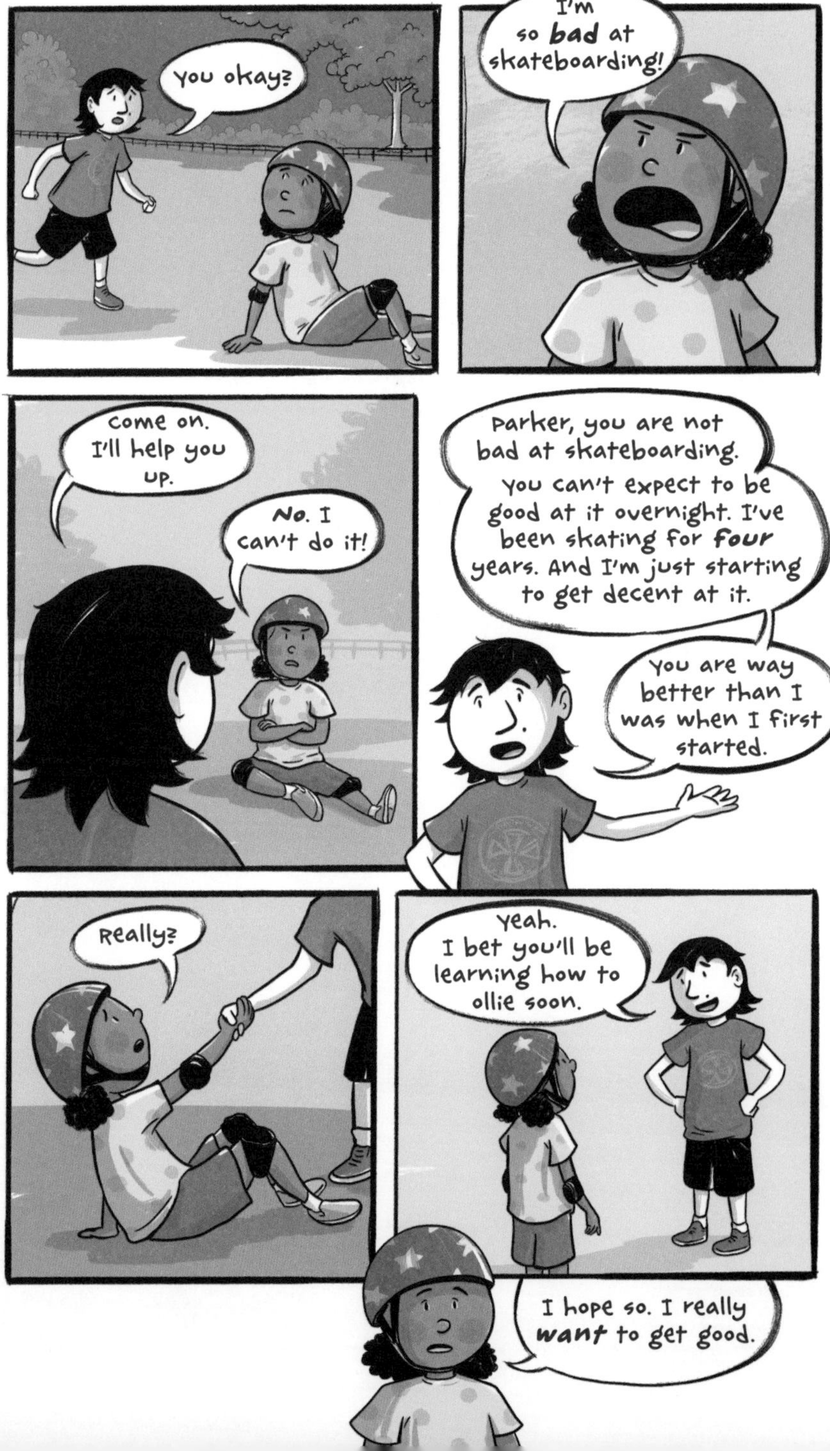
You okay?
I'm so bad at skateboarding!
Come on. I'll help you up.
No. I can't do it!
Parker, you are not bad at skateboarding.
You can't expect to be good at it overnight. I've been skating for four years. And I'm just starting to get decent at it.
You are way better than I was when I first started.
Really?
Yeah. I bet you'll be learning how to ollie soon.
I hope so. I really want to get good.

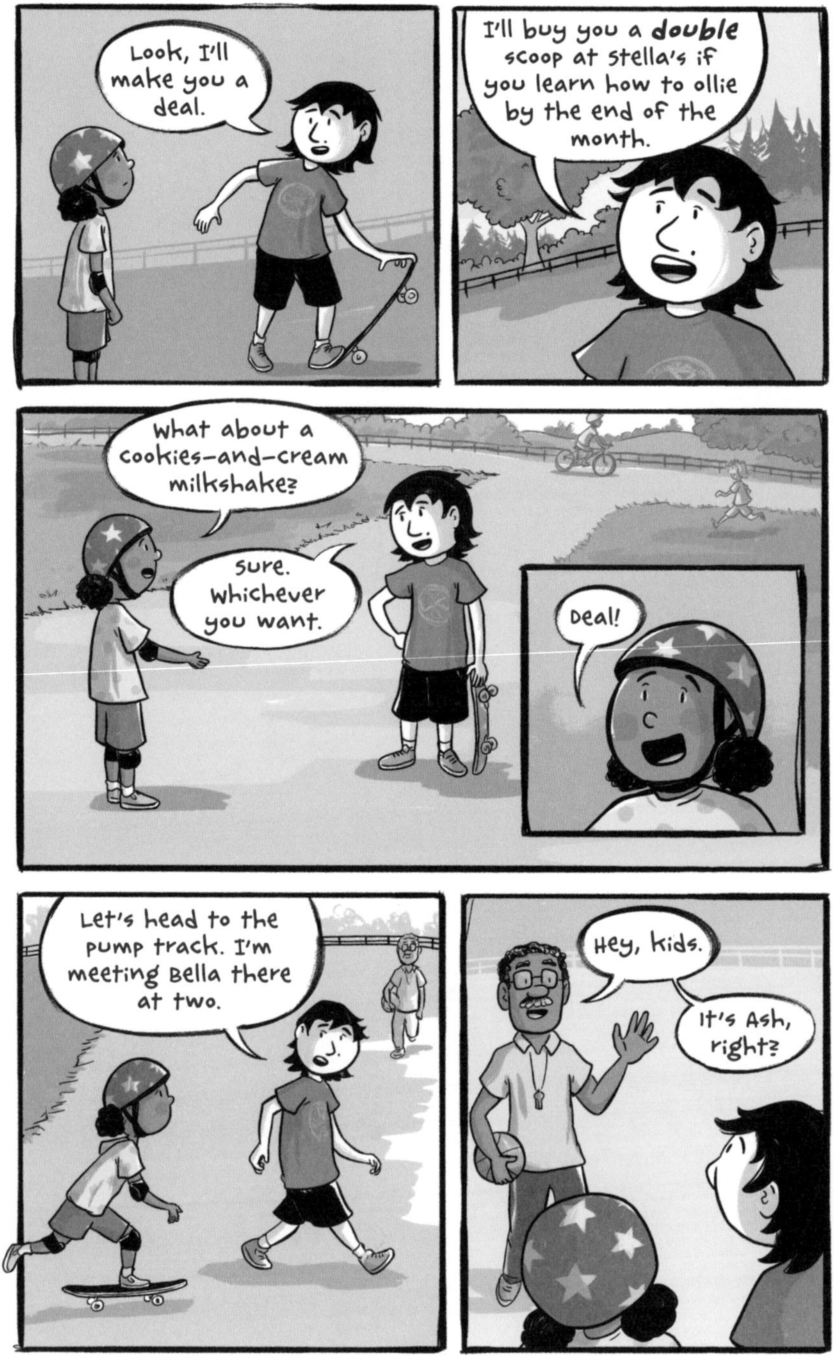
Look, I'll make you a deal.
I'll buy you a **double** scoop at Stella's if you learn how to ollie by the end of the month.
What about a cookies-and-cream milkshake?
Sure. Whichever you want.
Deal!
Let's head to the pump track. I'm meeting Bella there at two.
Hey, kids.
It's Ash, right?

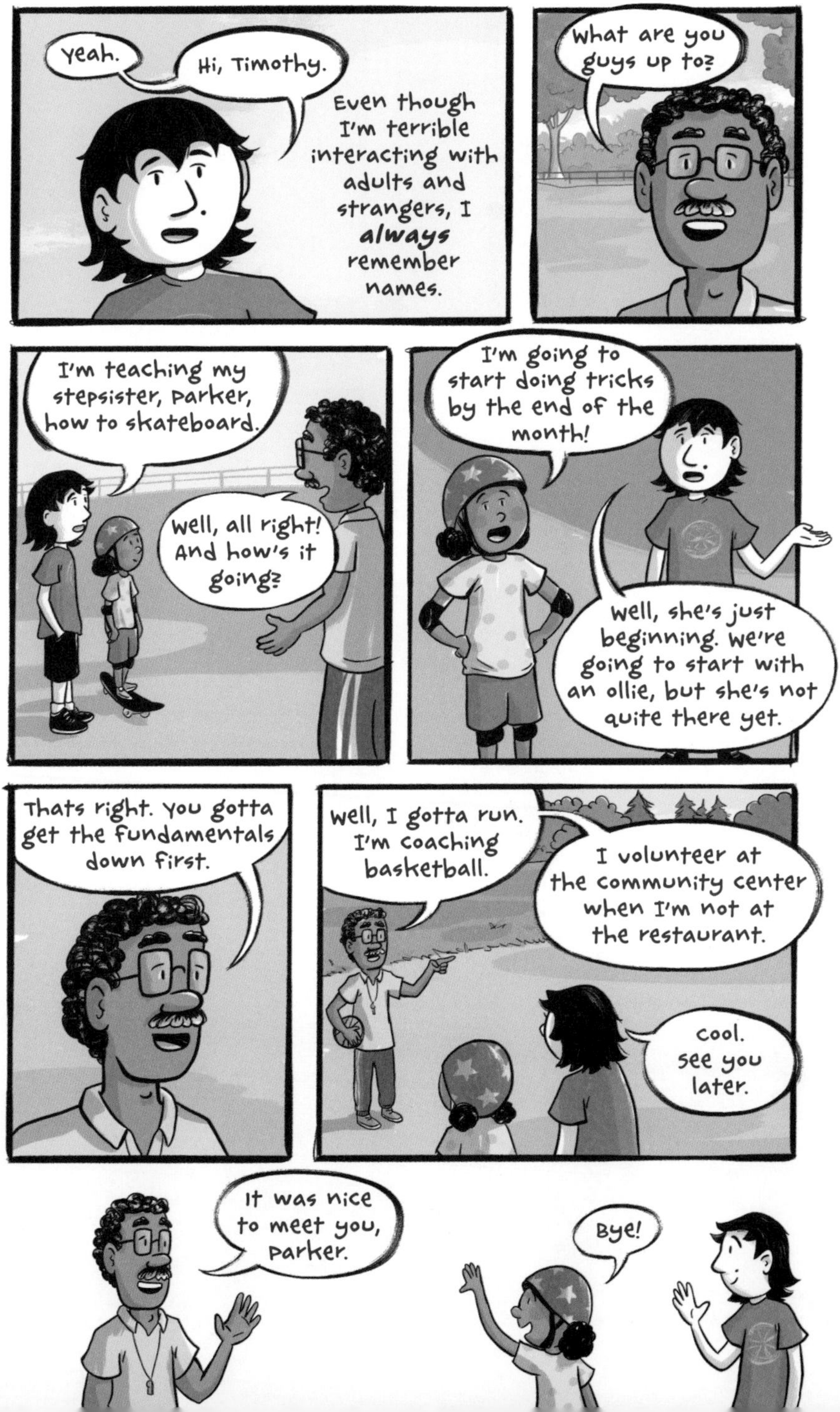
Yeah.
Hi, Timothy.
Even though I'm terrible interacting with adults and strangers, I *always* remember names.
What are you guys up to?
I'm teaching my stepsister, Parker, how to skateboard.
Well, all right! And how's it going?
I'm going to start doing tricks by the end of the month!
Well, she's just beginning. We're going to start with an ollie, but she's not quite there yet.
Thats right. You gotta get the fundamentals down first.
Well, I gotta run. I'm coaching basketball.
I volunteer at the community center when I'm not at the restaurant.
Cool. See you later.
It was nice to meet you, Parker.
Bye!

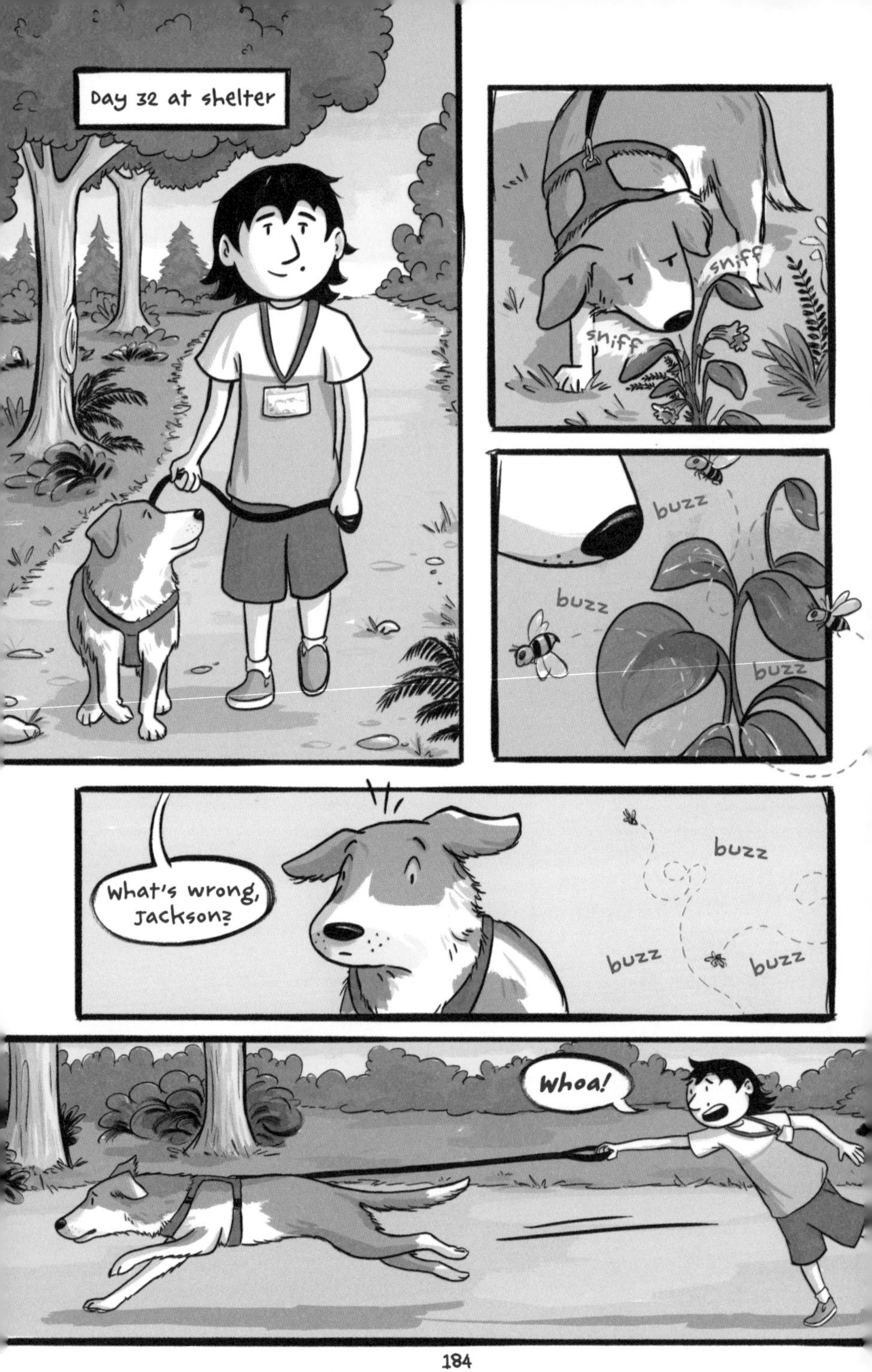
Day 32 at shelter
sniff
sniff
buzz
buzz
buzz
What's wrong, Jackson?
buzz
buzz
buzz
Whoa!

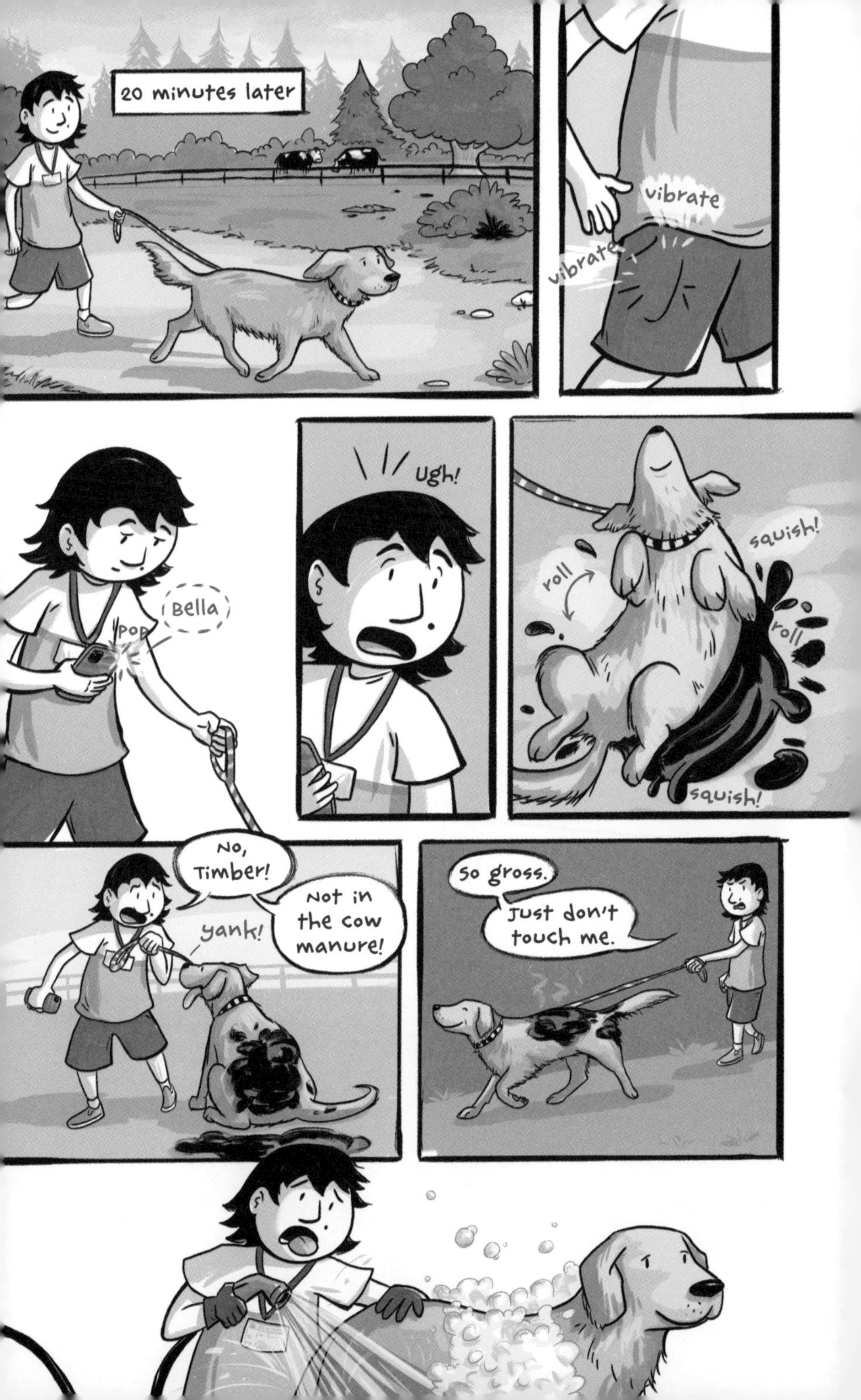

20 minutes later
vibrate
vibrate
Bella
pop
Ugh!
roll
squish!
roll
squish!
No, Timber!
yank!
Not in the cow manure!
So gross.
Just don't touch me.

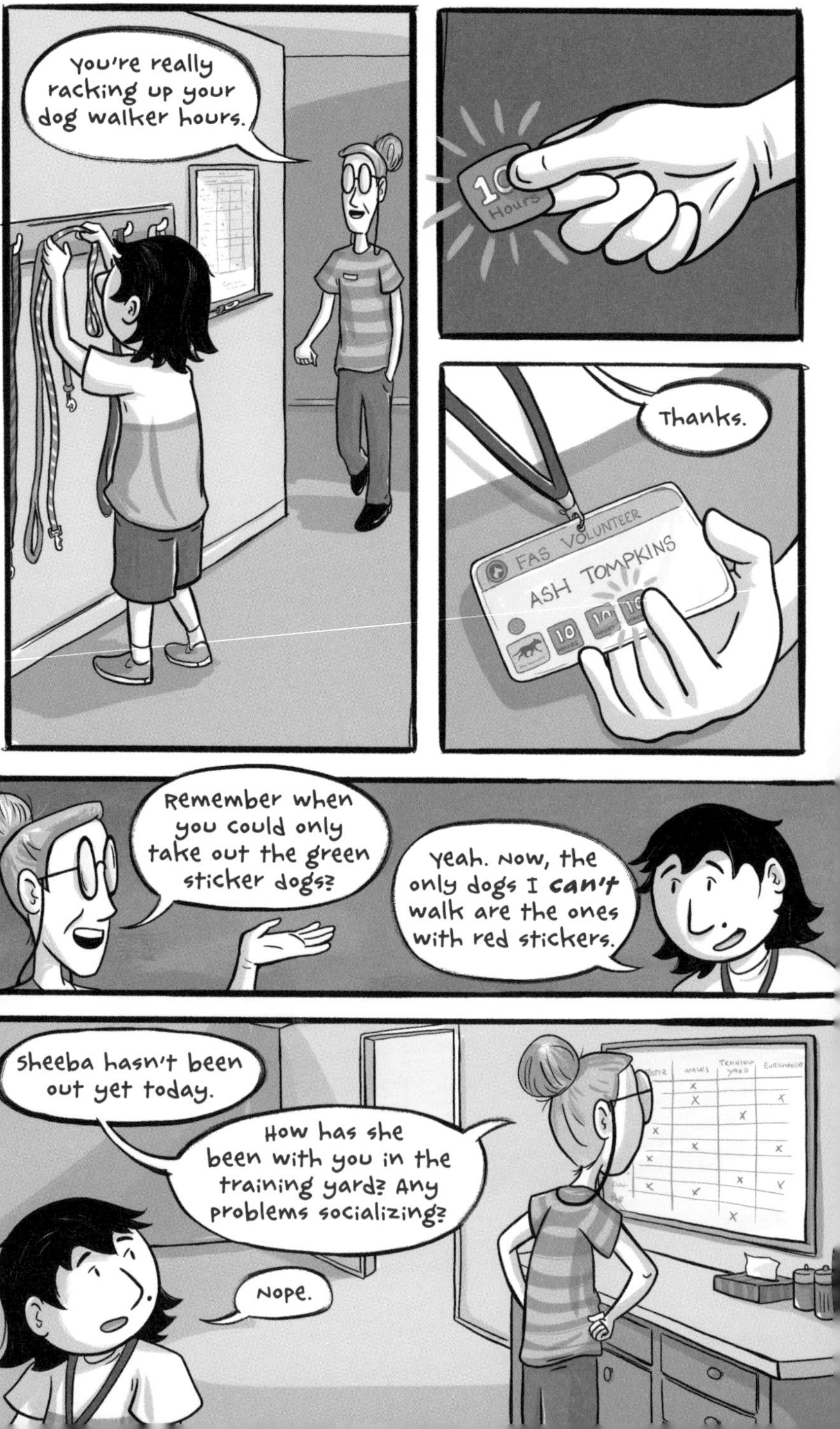
You're really racking up your dog walker hours.
10 Hours
Thanks.
FAS VOLUNTEER
ASH TOMPKINS
10
Remember when you could only take out the green sticker dogs?
Yeah. Now, the only dogs I **can't** walk are the ones with red stickers.
Sheeba hasn't been out yet today.
How has she been with you in the training yard? Any problems socializing?
Nope.

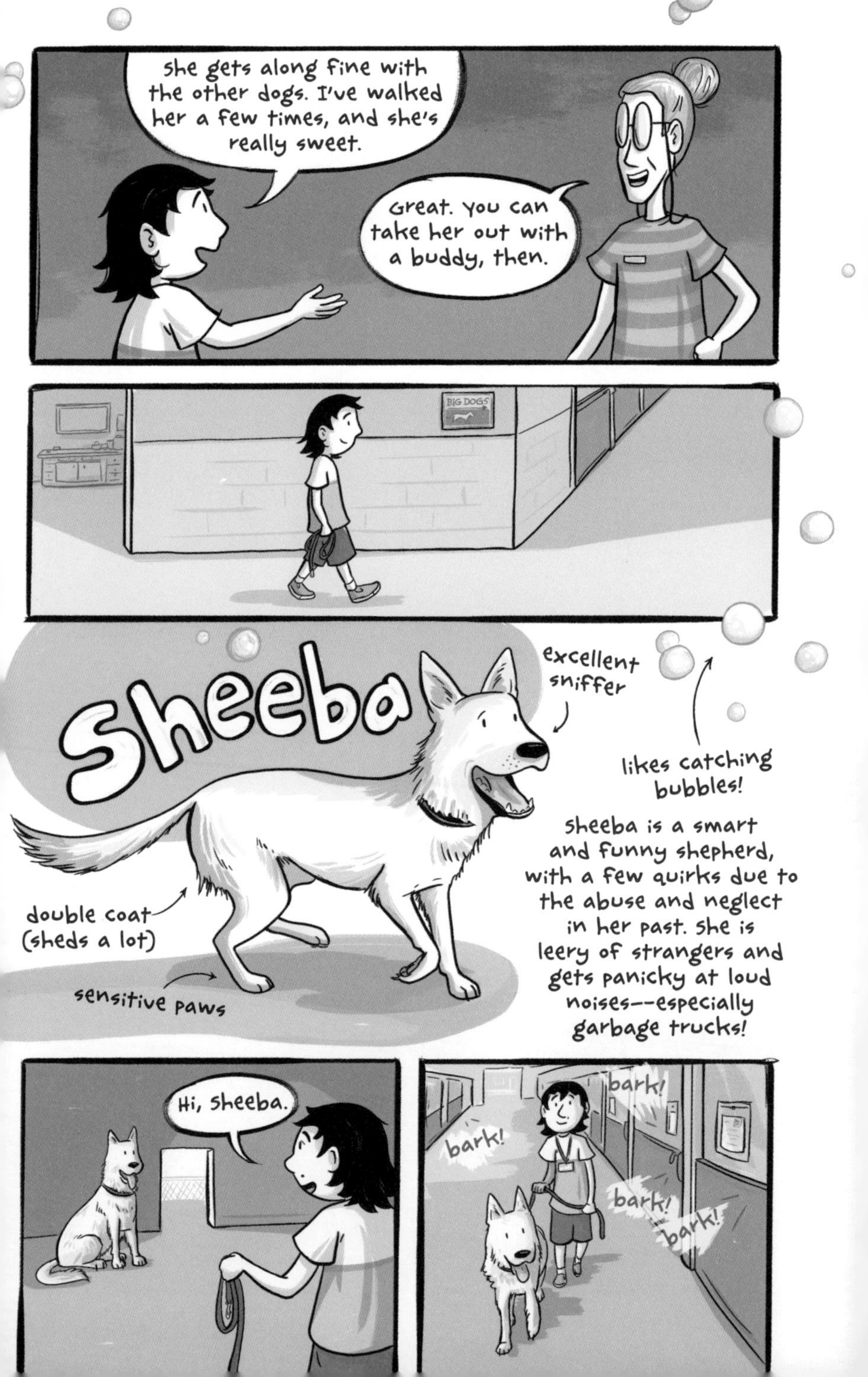
She gets along fine with the other dogs. I've walked her a few times, and she's really sweet.
Great. You can take her out with a buddy, then.
BIG DOGS
Sheeba
excellent sniffer
likes catching bubbles!
Sheeba is a smart and funny shepherd, with a few quirks due to the abuse and neglect in her past. She is leery of strangers and gets panicky at loud noises––especially garbage trucks!
double coat (sheds a lot)
sensitive paws
Hi, Sheeba.
bark!
bark!
bark!
bark!

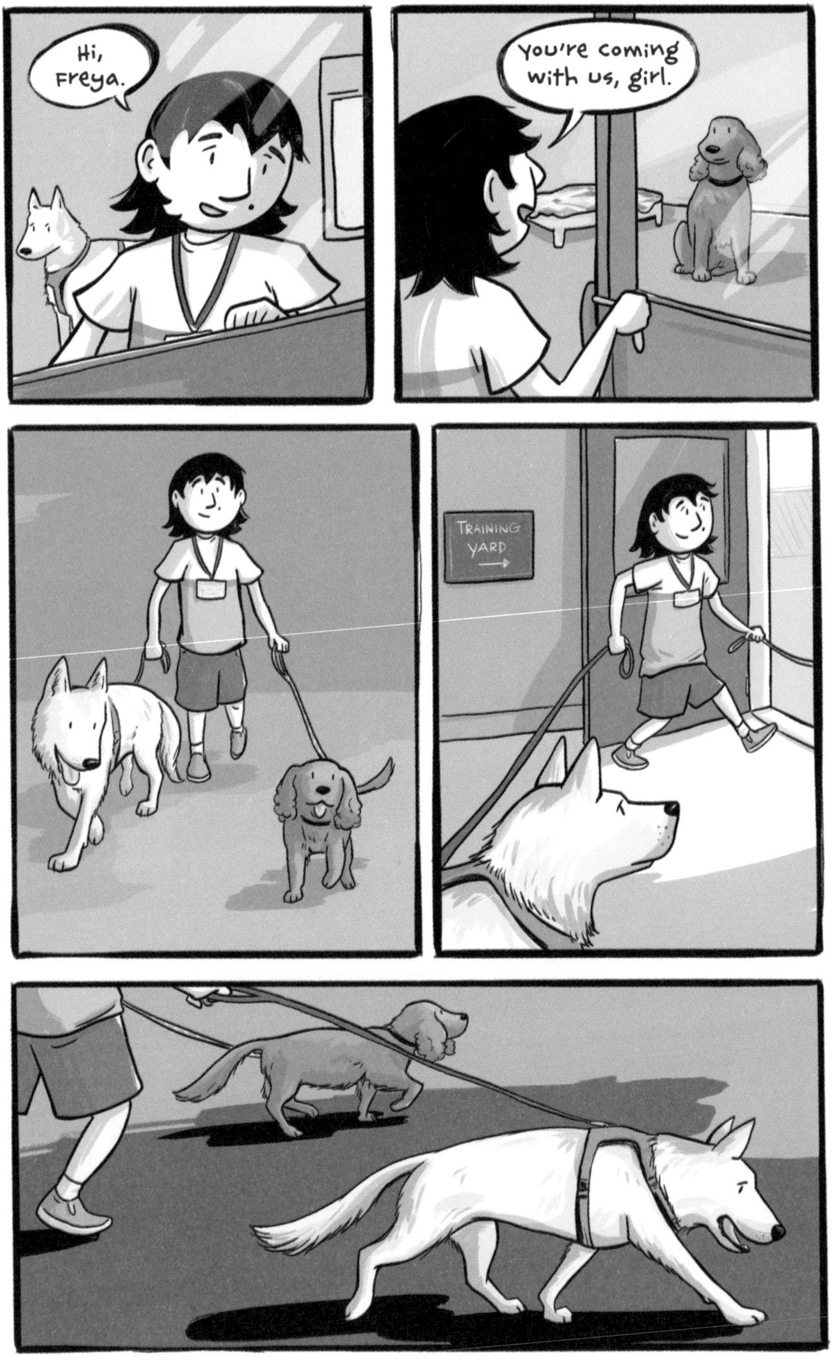
Hi, Freya.
You're coming with us, girl.
TRAINING YARD

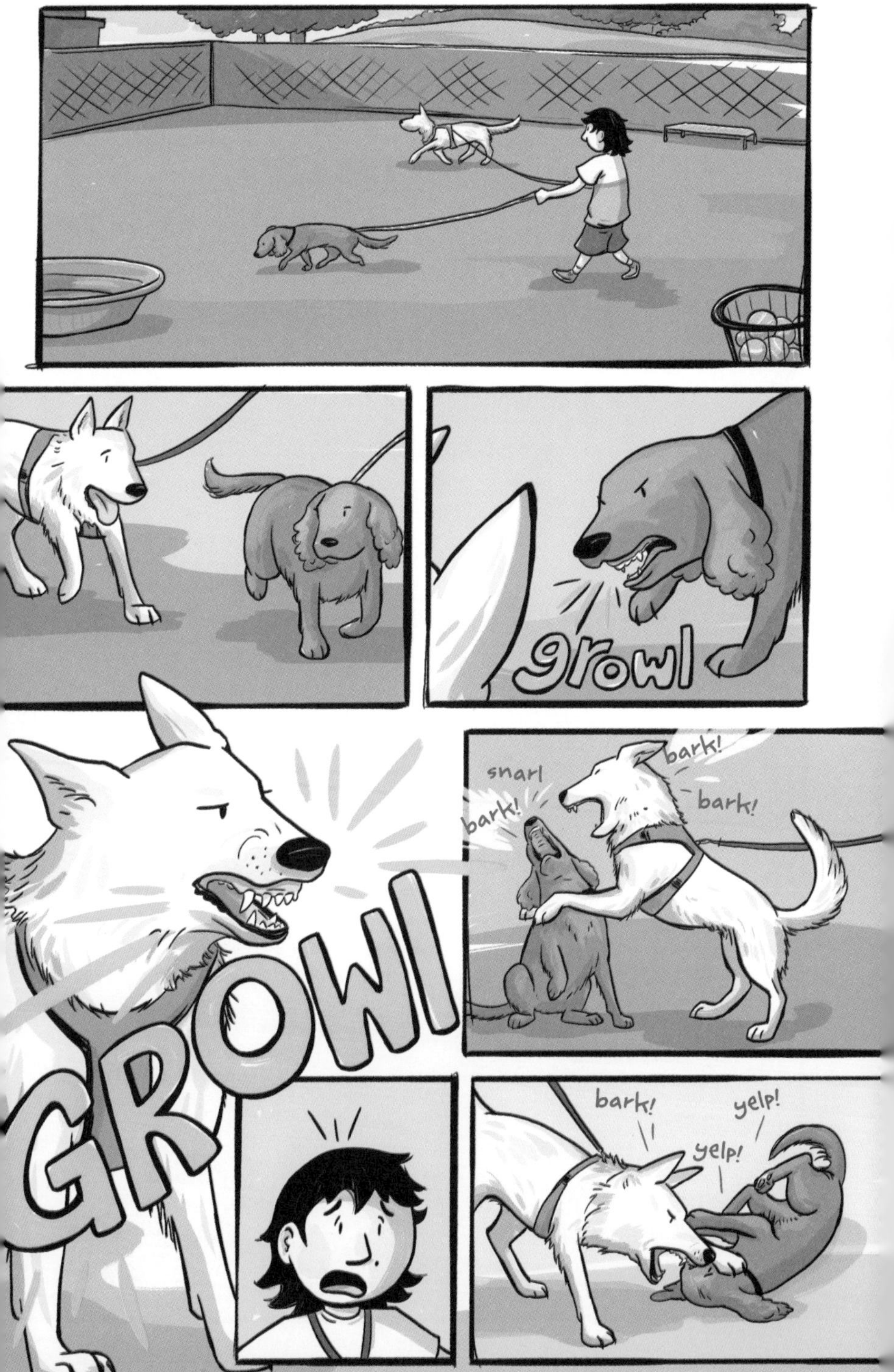
growl
GROWL
snarl
bark!
bark!
bark!
bark!
yelp!
yelp!

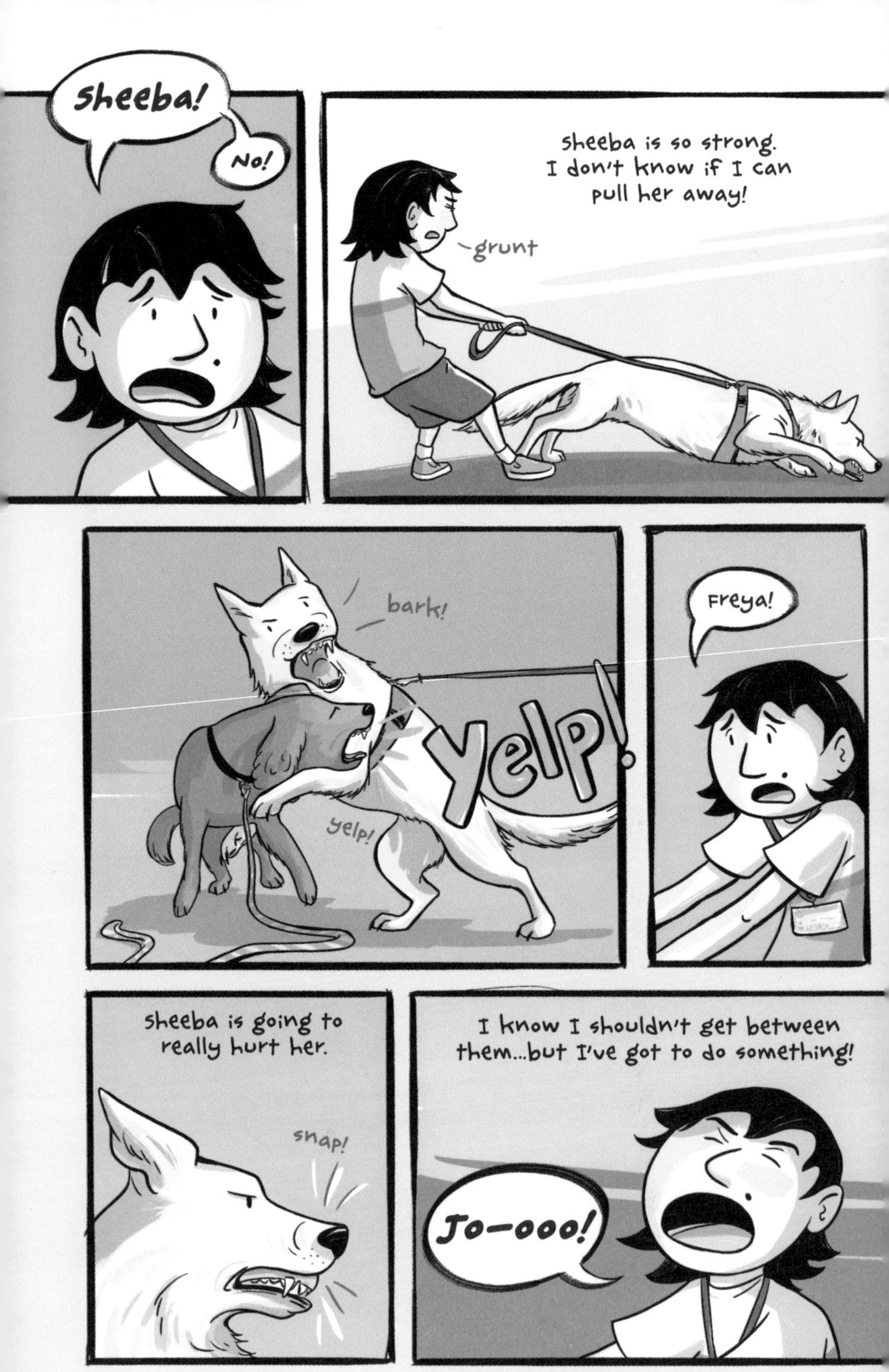
Sheeba!
No!
Sheeba is so strong. I don't know if I can pull her away!
-grunt
bark!
Yelp!
yelp!
Freya!
Sheeba is going to really hurt her.
snap!
I know I shouldn't get between them...but I've got to do something!
Jo-ooo!

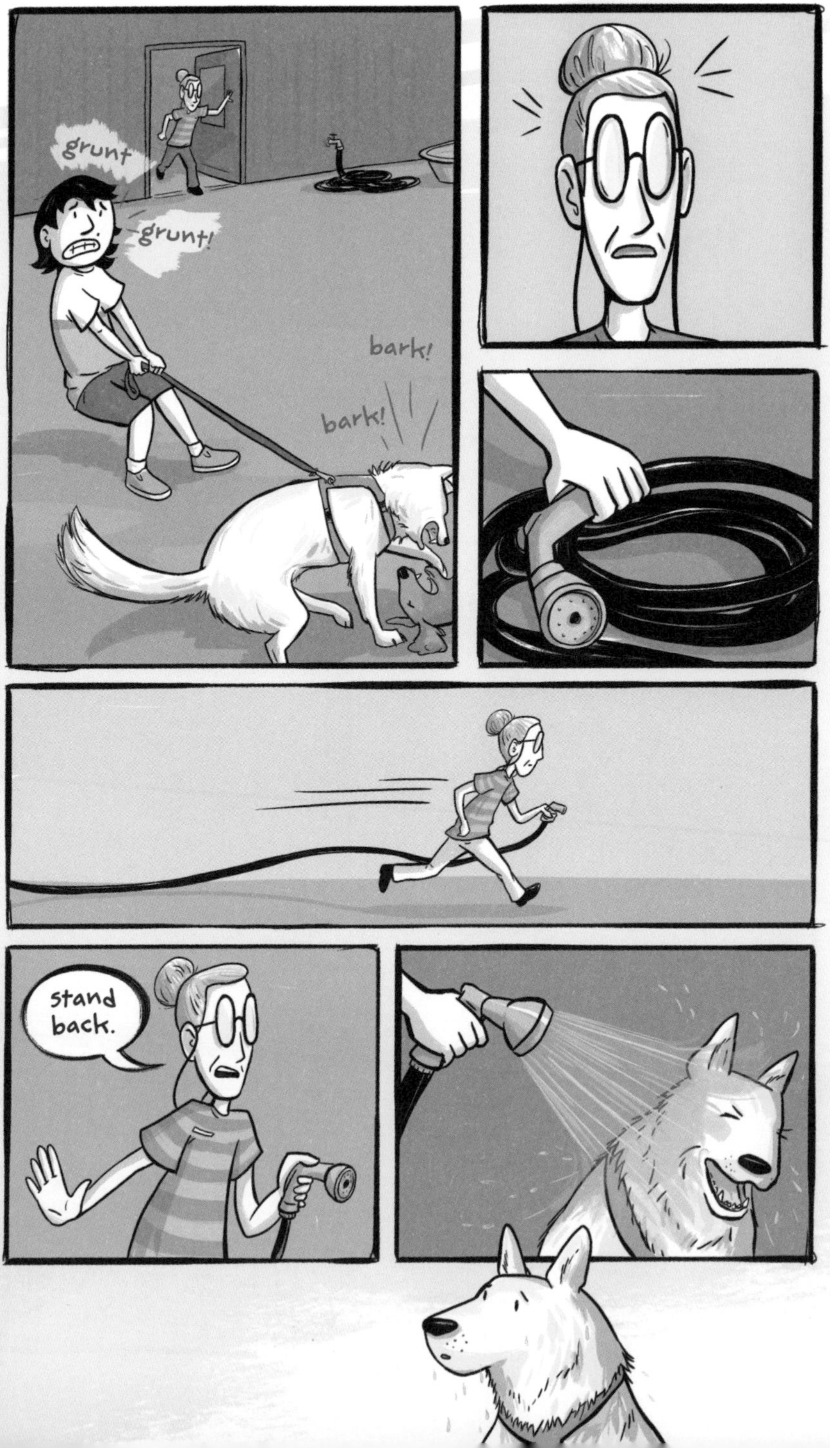
grunt
grunt!
bark!
bark!
stand back.

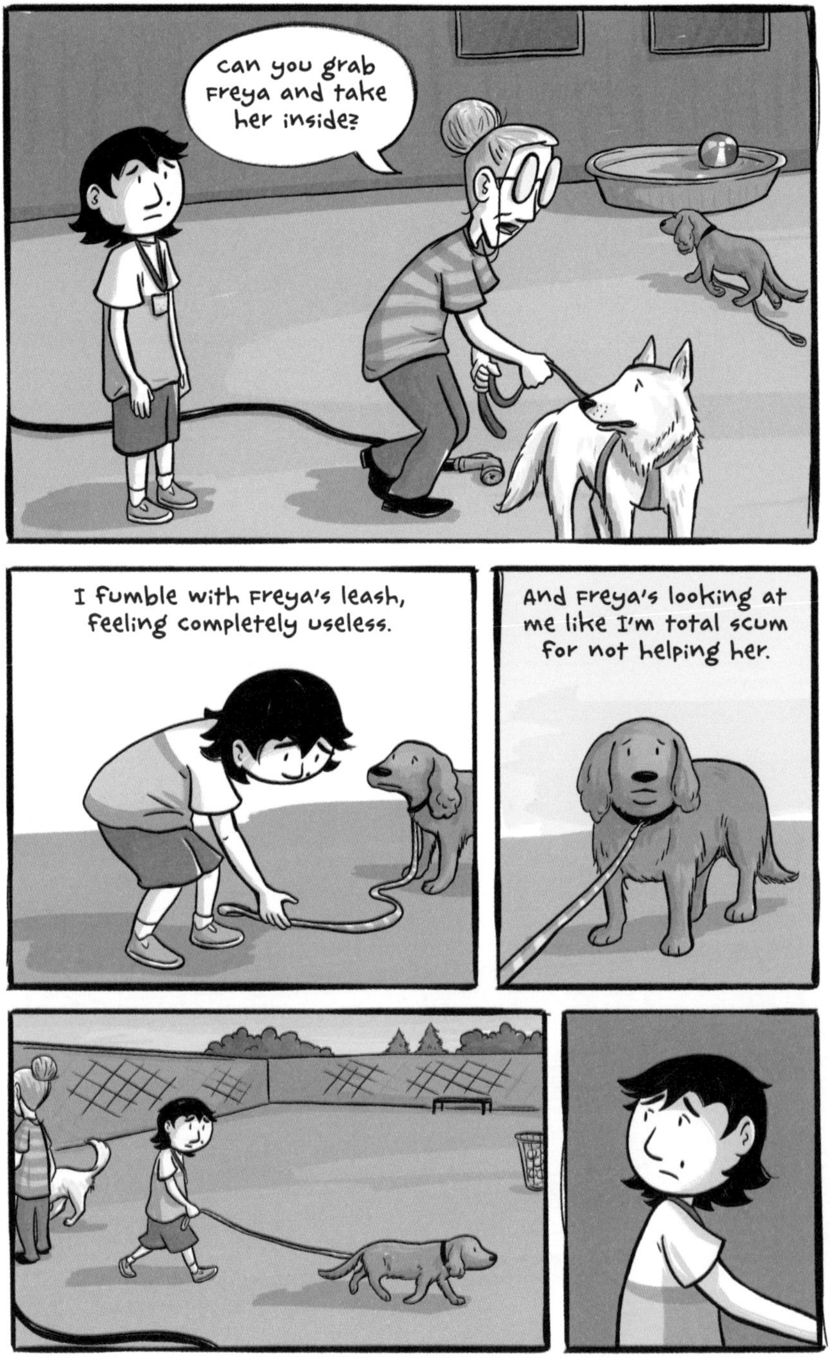
Can you grab Freya and take her inside?
I fumble with Freya's leash, feeling completely useless.
And Freya's looking at me like I'm total scum for not helping her.

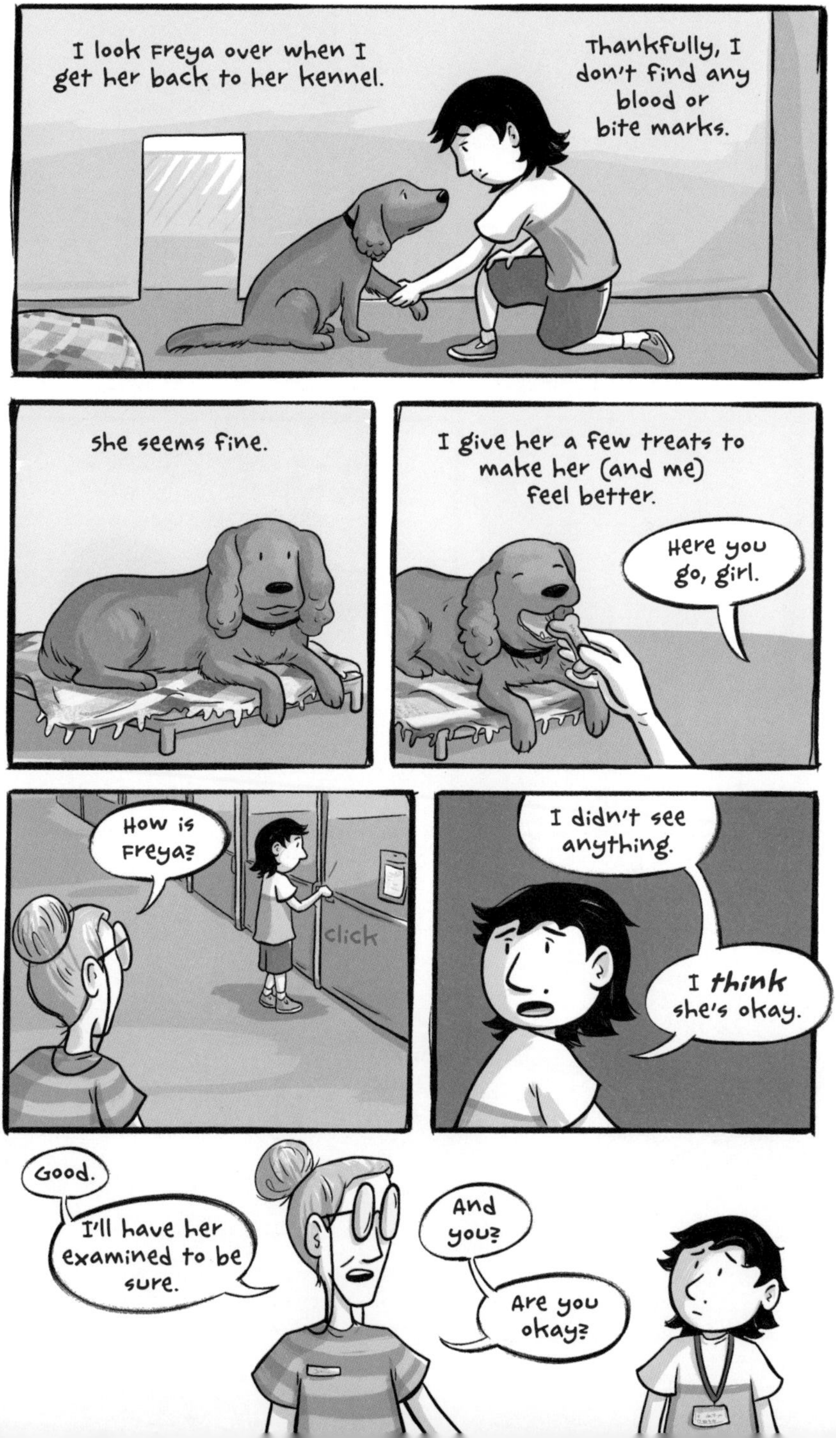
I look Freya over when I get her back to her kennel.
Thankfully, I don't find any blood or bite marks.
She seems fine.
I give her a few treats to make her (and me) feel better.
Here you go, girl.
How is Freya?
click
I didn't see anything.
I *think* she's okay.
Good.
I'll have her examined to be sure.
And you?
Are you okay?

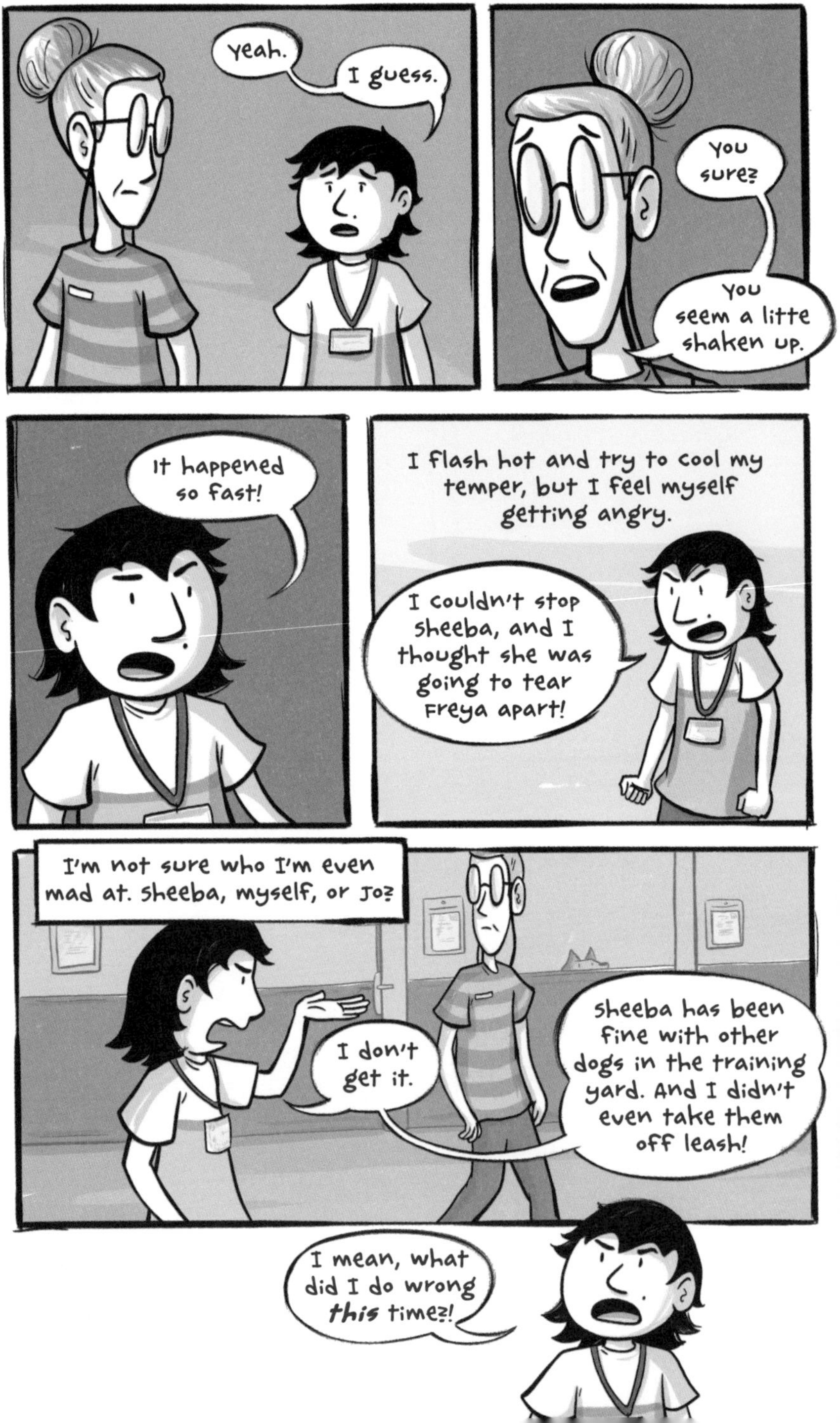
Yeah.
I guess.
You sure?
You seem a litte shaken up.
It happened so fast!
I flash hot and try to cool my temper, but I feel myself getting angry.
I couldn't stop Sheeba, and I thought she was going to tear Freya apart!
I'm not sure who I'm even mad at. Sheeba, myself, or Jo?
I don't get it.
Sheeba has been fine with other dogs in the training yard. And I didn't even take them off leash!
I mean, what did I do wrong *this* time?!

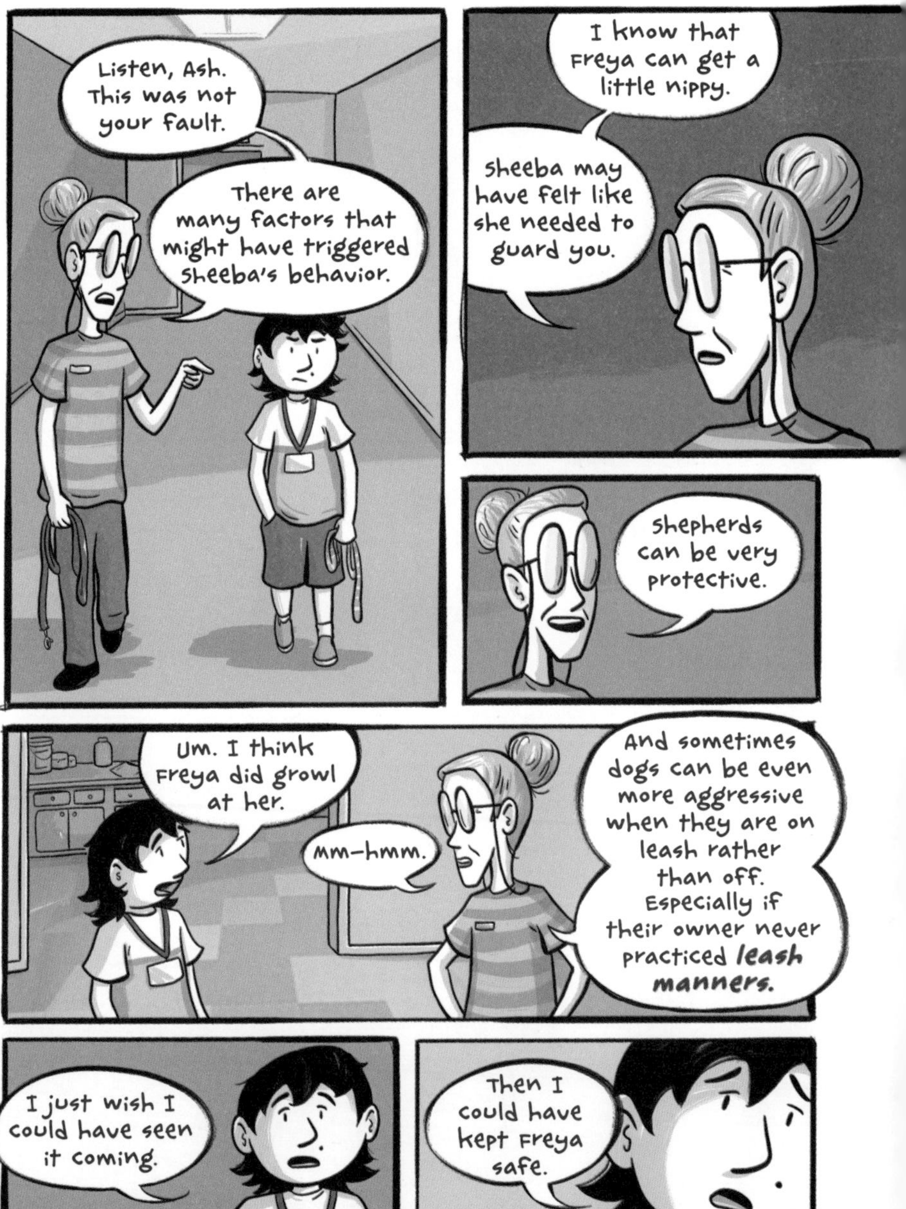
Listen, Ash. This was not your fault.
There are many factors that might have triggered Sheeba's behavior.
I know that Freya can get a little nippy.
Sheeba may have felt like she needed to guard you.
Shepherds can be very protective.
Um. I think Freya did growl at her.
Mm-hmm.
And sometimes dogs can be even more aggressive when they are on leash rather than off. Especially if their owner never practiced **leash manners.**
I just wish I could have seen it coming.
Then I could have kept Freya safe.

Leash manners: Training that teaches dogs not to pull on the leash when they see other dogs. Often, dogs can sense how their owners are feeling. If they're tense or angry, the dog can associate these emotions with being on leash and that might cause them to act out.

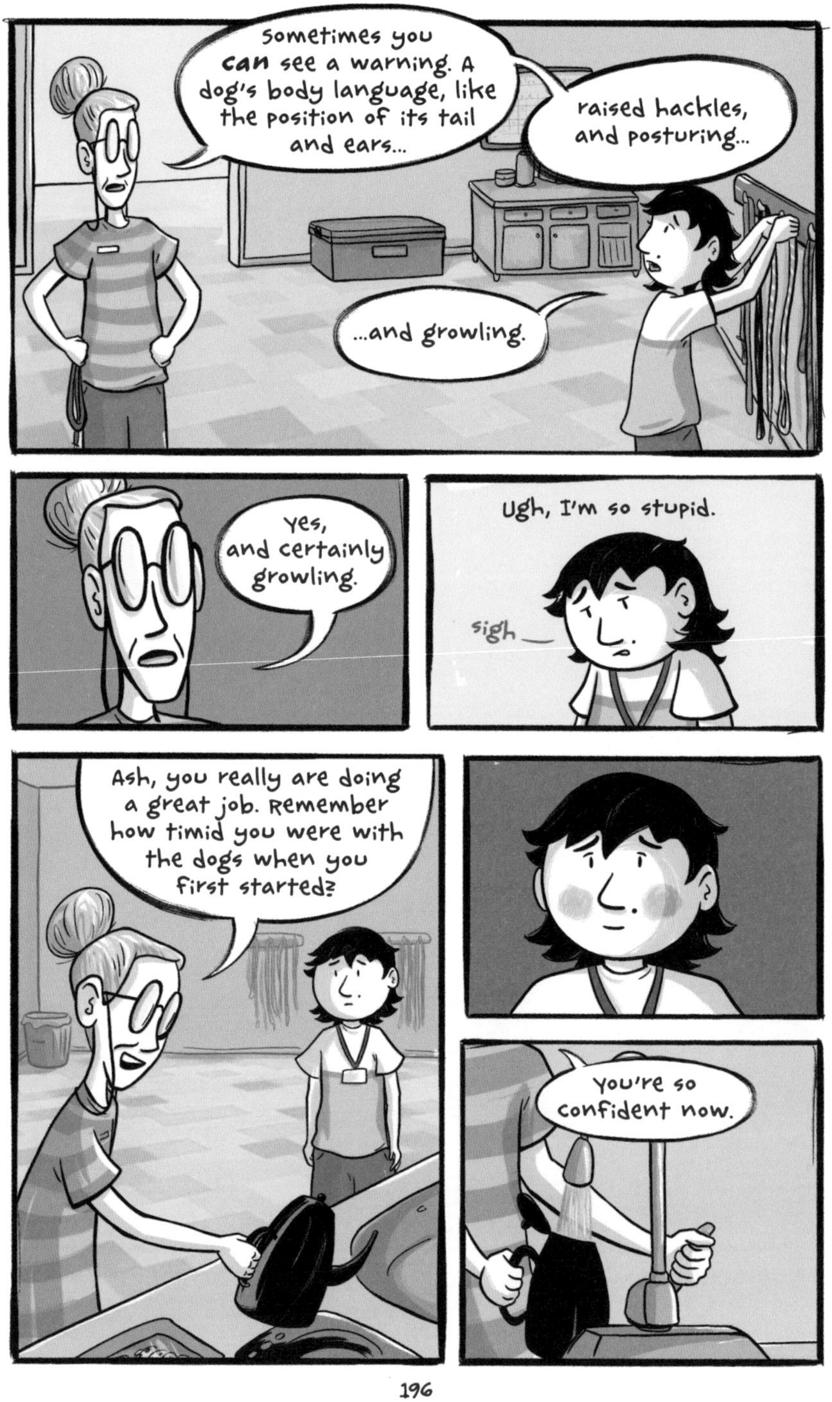
Sometimes you **can** see a warning. A dog's body language, like the position of its tail and ears...
raised hackles, and posturing...
...and growling.
Yes, and certainly growling.
Ugh, I'm so stupid.
sigh
Ash, you really are doing a great job. Remember how timid you were with the dogs when you first started?
You're so confident now.

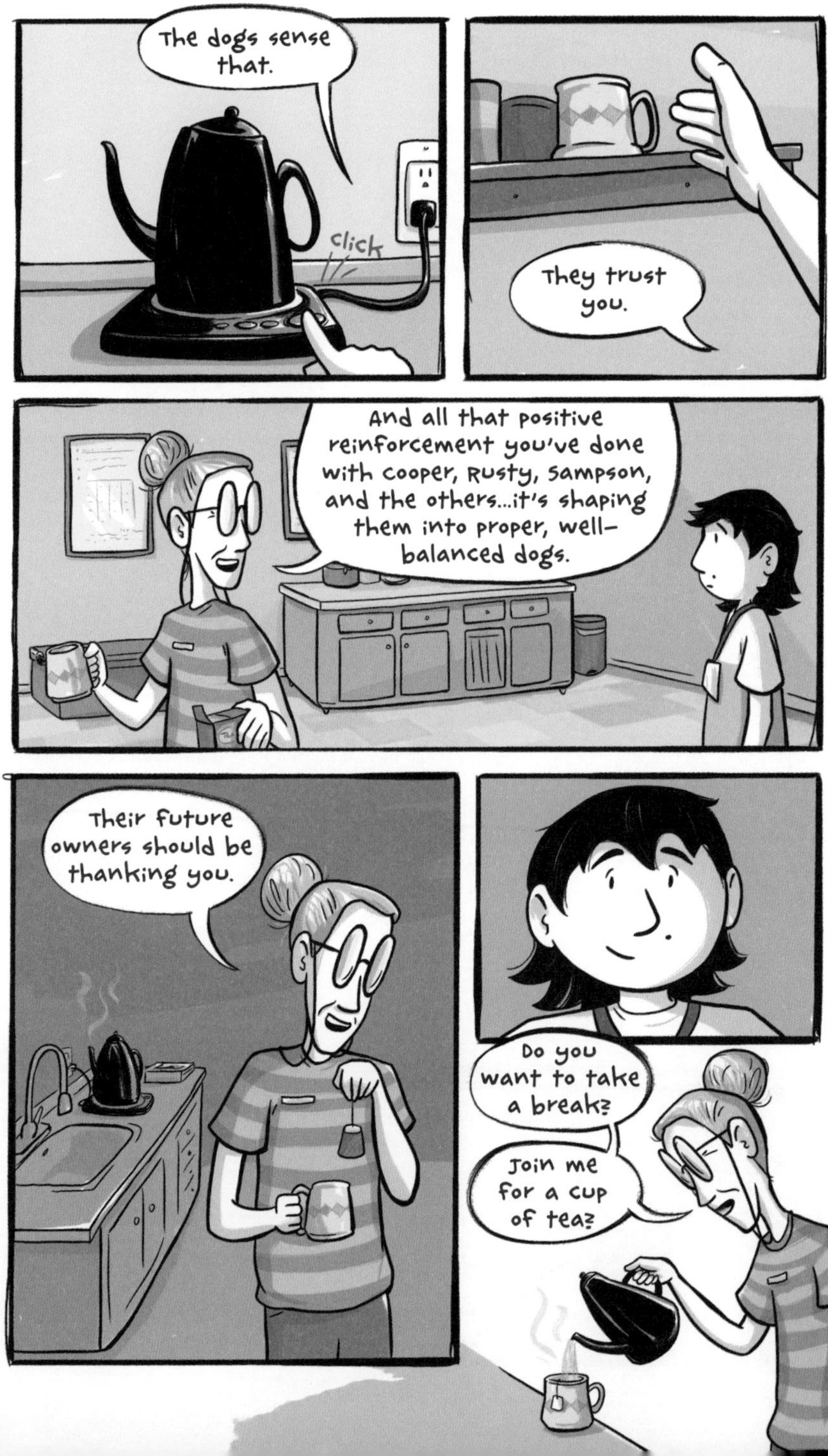
The dogs sense that.
click
They trust you.
And all that positive reinforcement you've done with cooper, Rusty, Sampson, and the others...it's shaping them into proper, well-balanced dogs.
Their future owners should be thanking you.
Do you want to take a break?
Join me for a cup of tea?

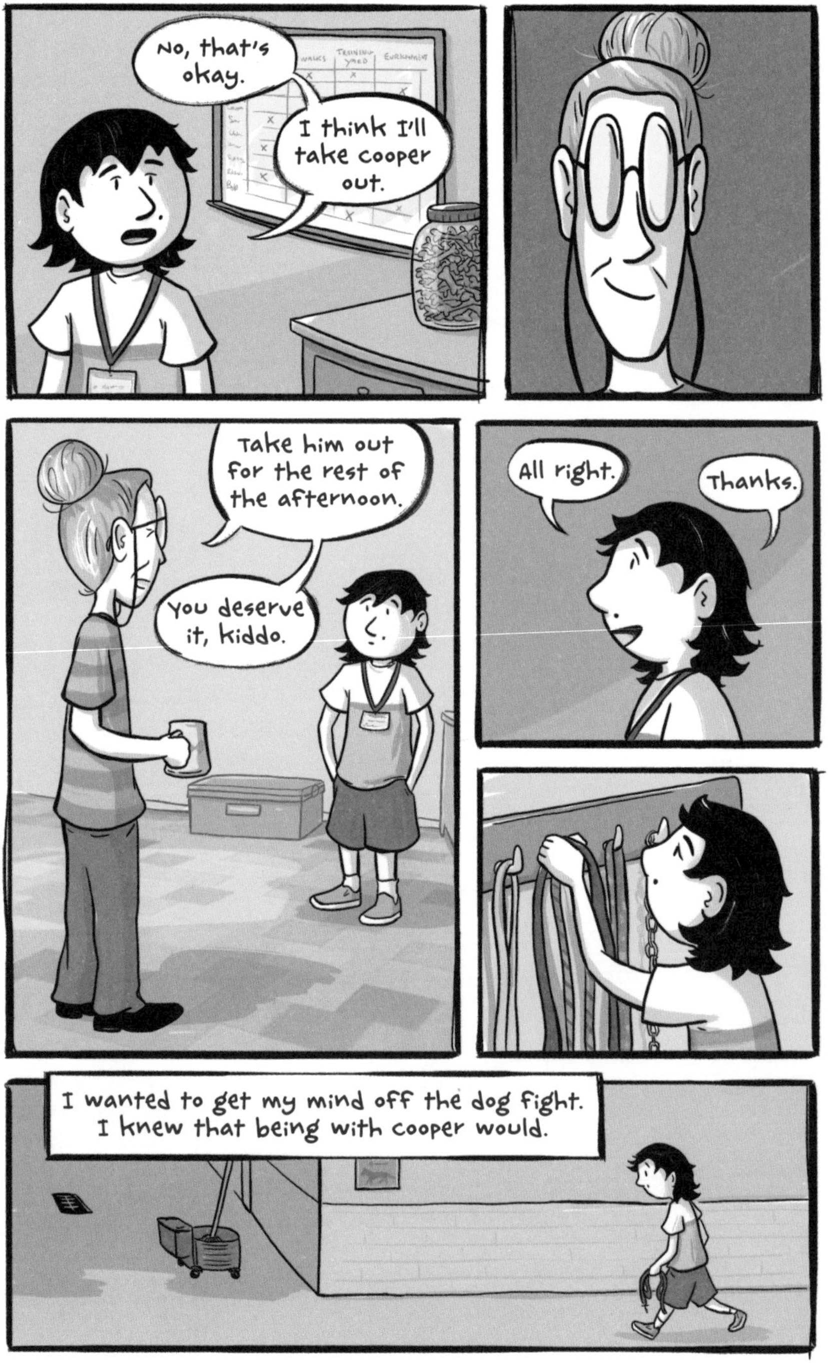
No, that's okay.
I think I'll take cooper out.
Take him out for the rest of the afternoon.
You deserve it, kiddo.
All right.
Thanks.
I wanted to get my mind off the dog fight. I knew that being with cooper would.

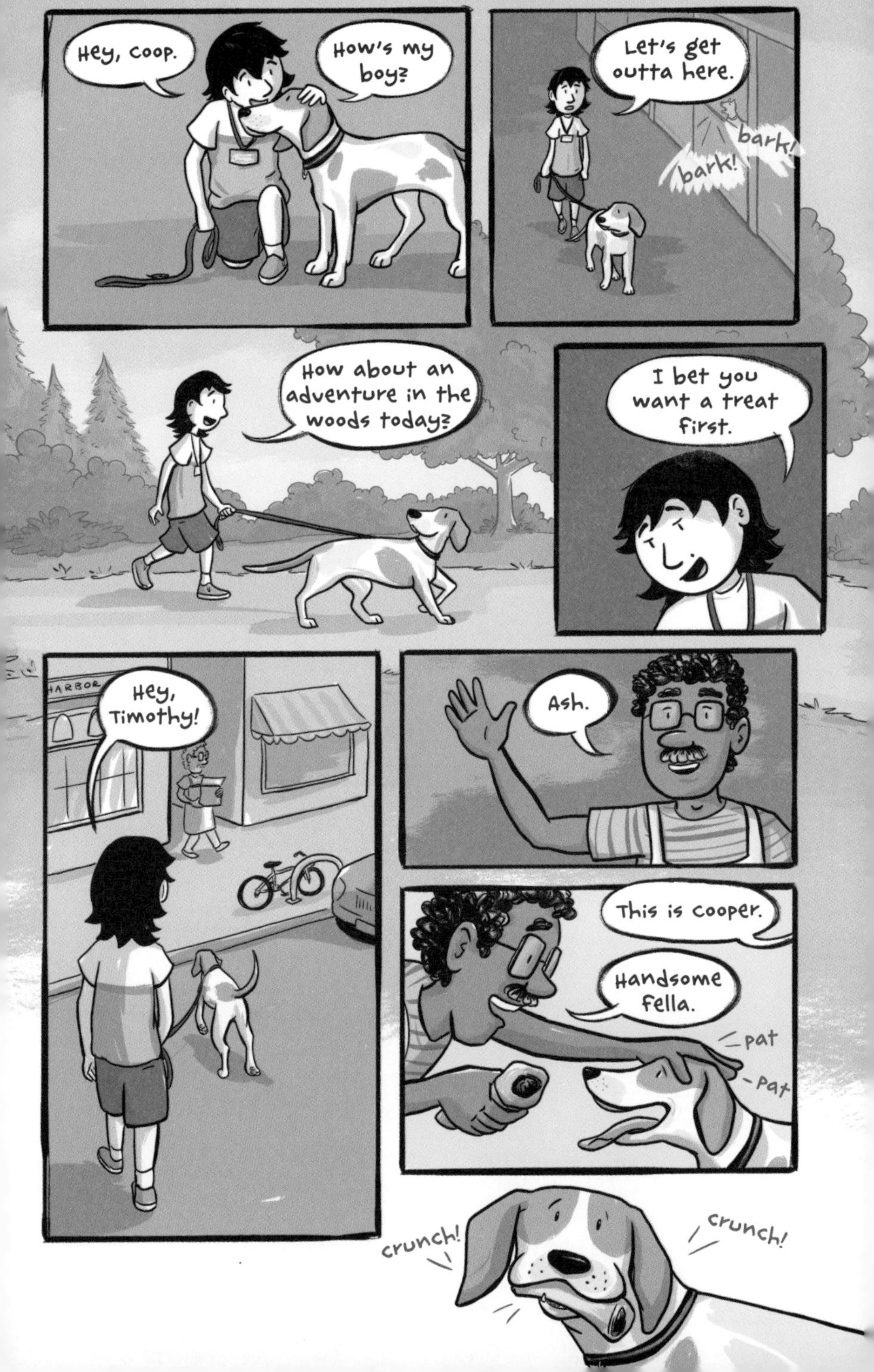
Hey, Coop.
How's my boy?
Let's get outta here.
bark!
bark!
How about an adventure in the woods today?
I bet you want a treat first.
Hey, Timothy!
HARBOR
Ash.
This is Cooper.
Handsome fella.
pat
pat
crunch!
crunch!

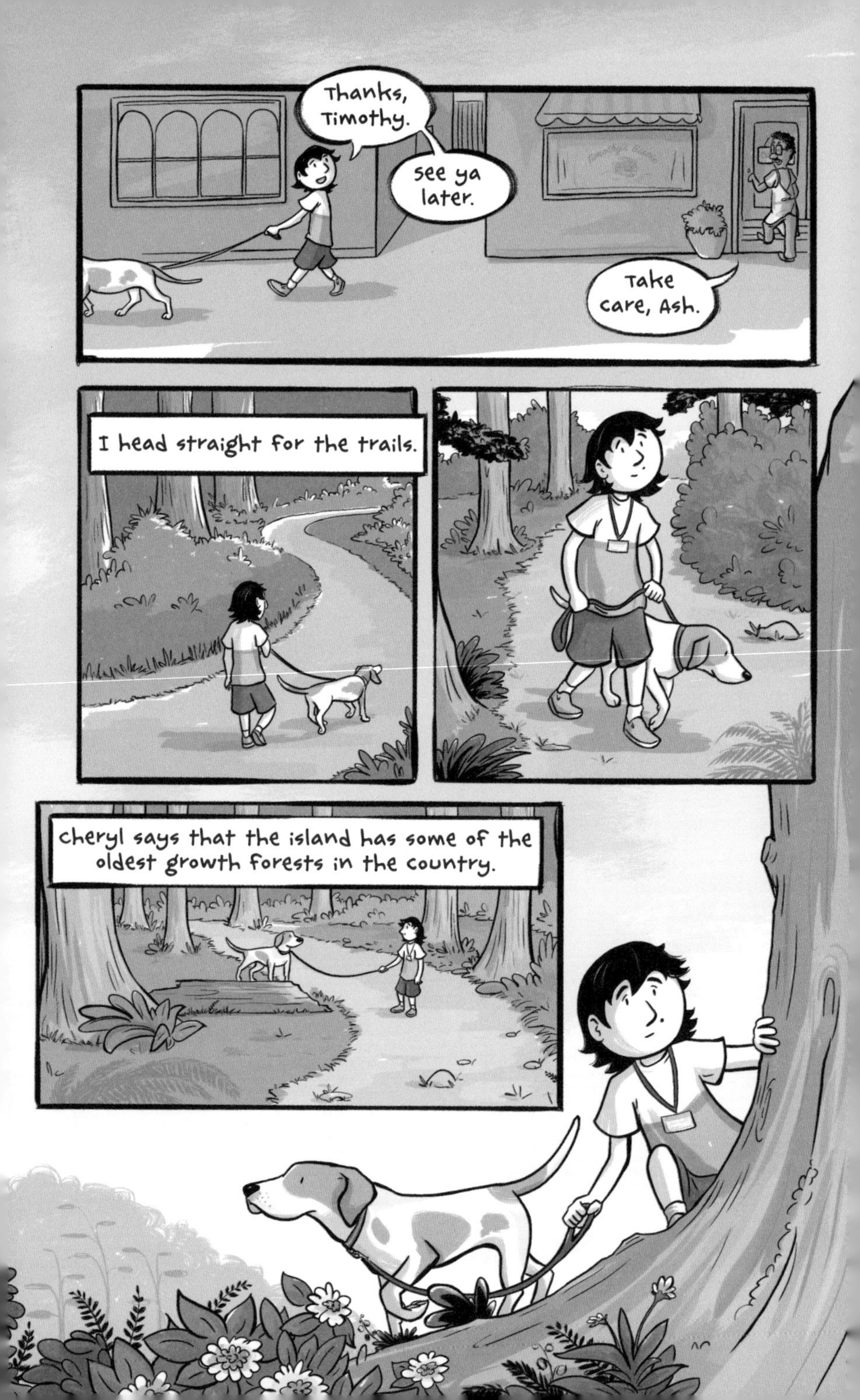
Thanks, Timothy.
See ya later.
Take care, Ash.
I head straight for the trails.
Cheryl says that the island has some of the oldest growth forests in the country.

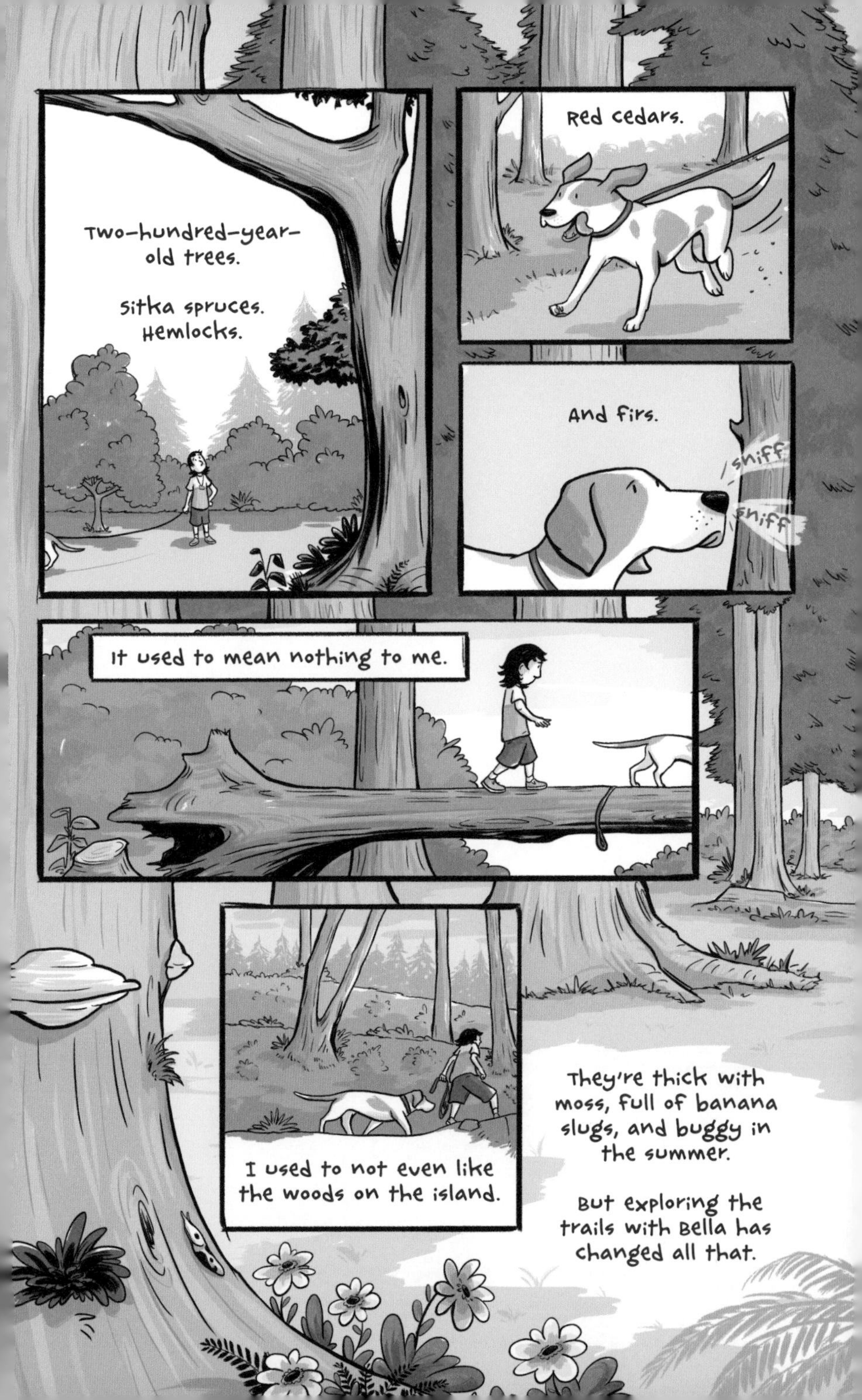
Two-hundred-year-old trees.
Sitka spruces. Hemlocks.
Red cedars.
And firs.
sniff
sniff
It used to mean nothing to me.
I used to not even like the woods on the island.
They're thick with moss, full of banana slugs, and buggy in the summer.
But exploring the trails with Bella has changed all that.

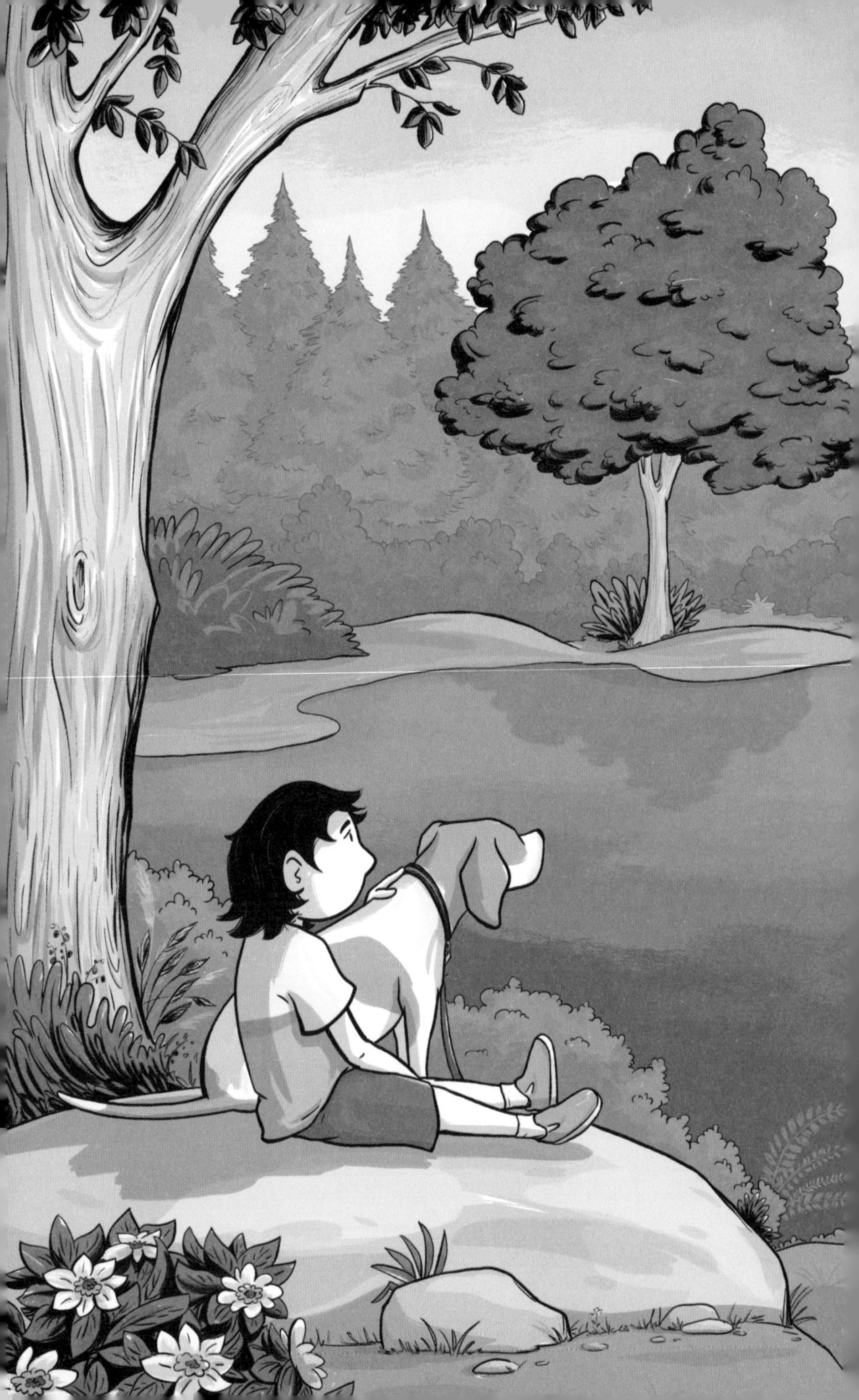

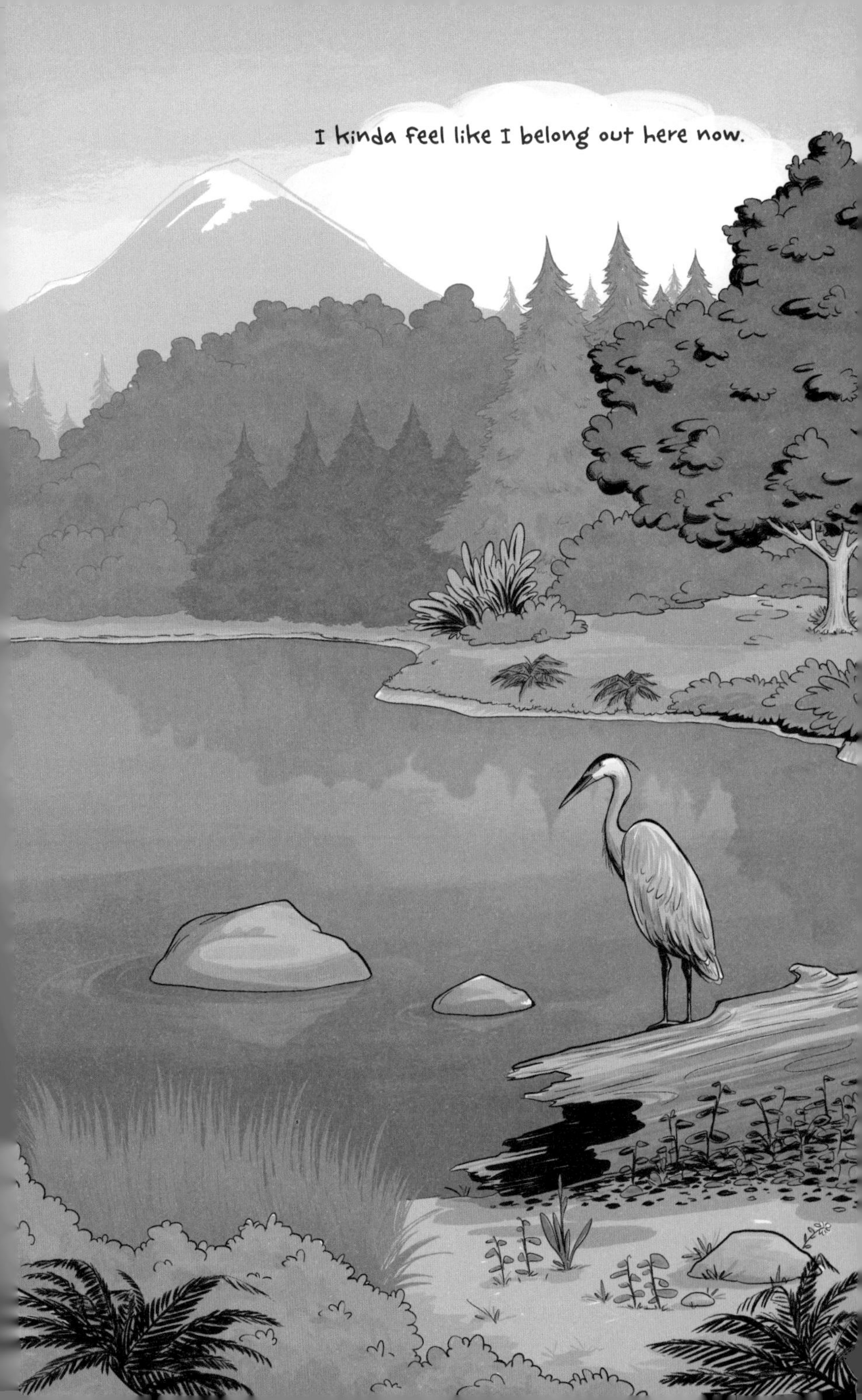
I kinda feel like I belong out here now.

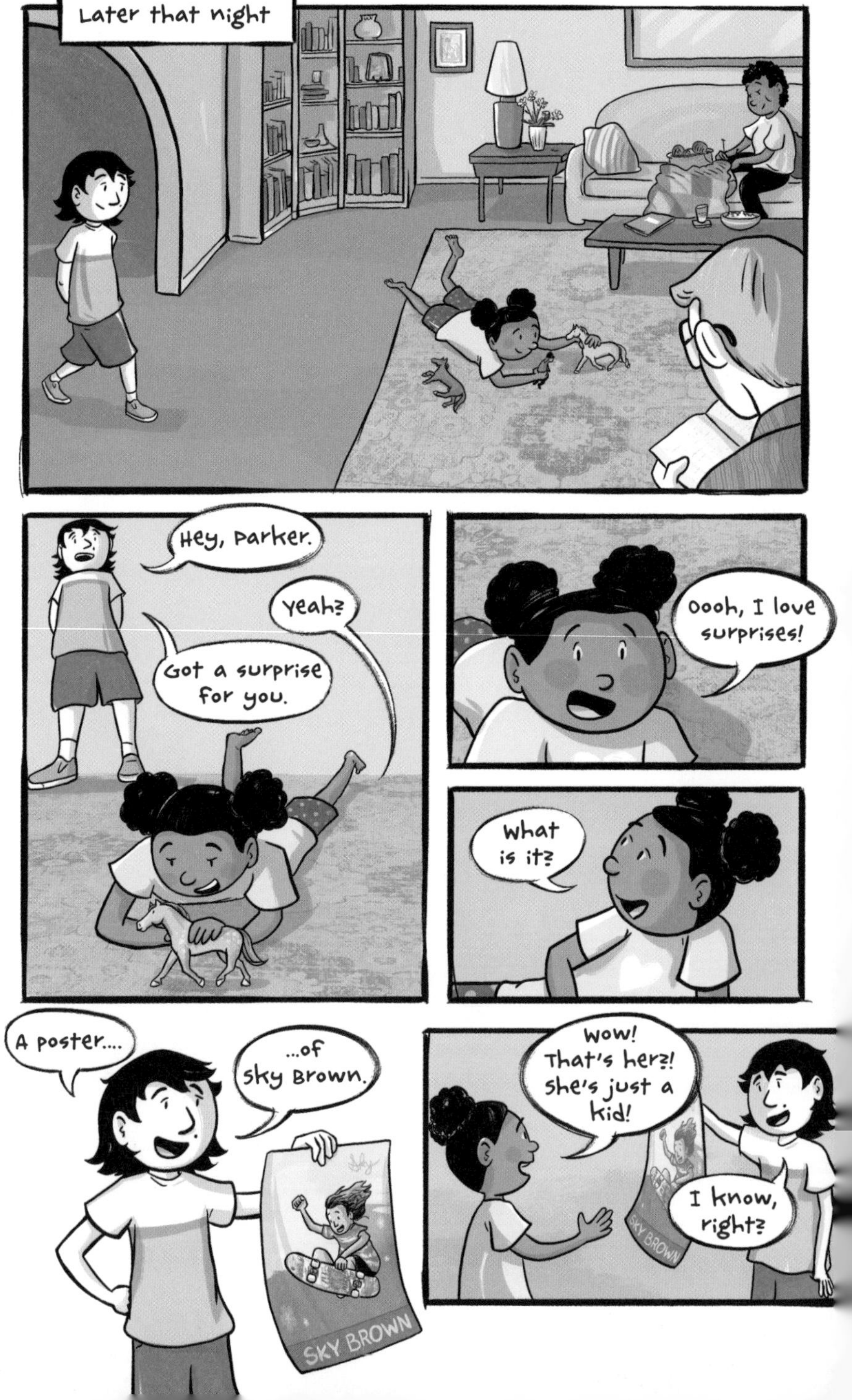
Later that night
Hey, Parker.
Yeah?
Got a surprise for you.
Oooh, I love surprises!
What is it?
A poster....
...of Sky Brown.
SKY BROWN
Wow! That's her?! She's just a kid!
I know, right?
SKY BROWN

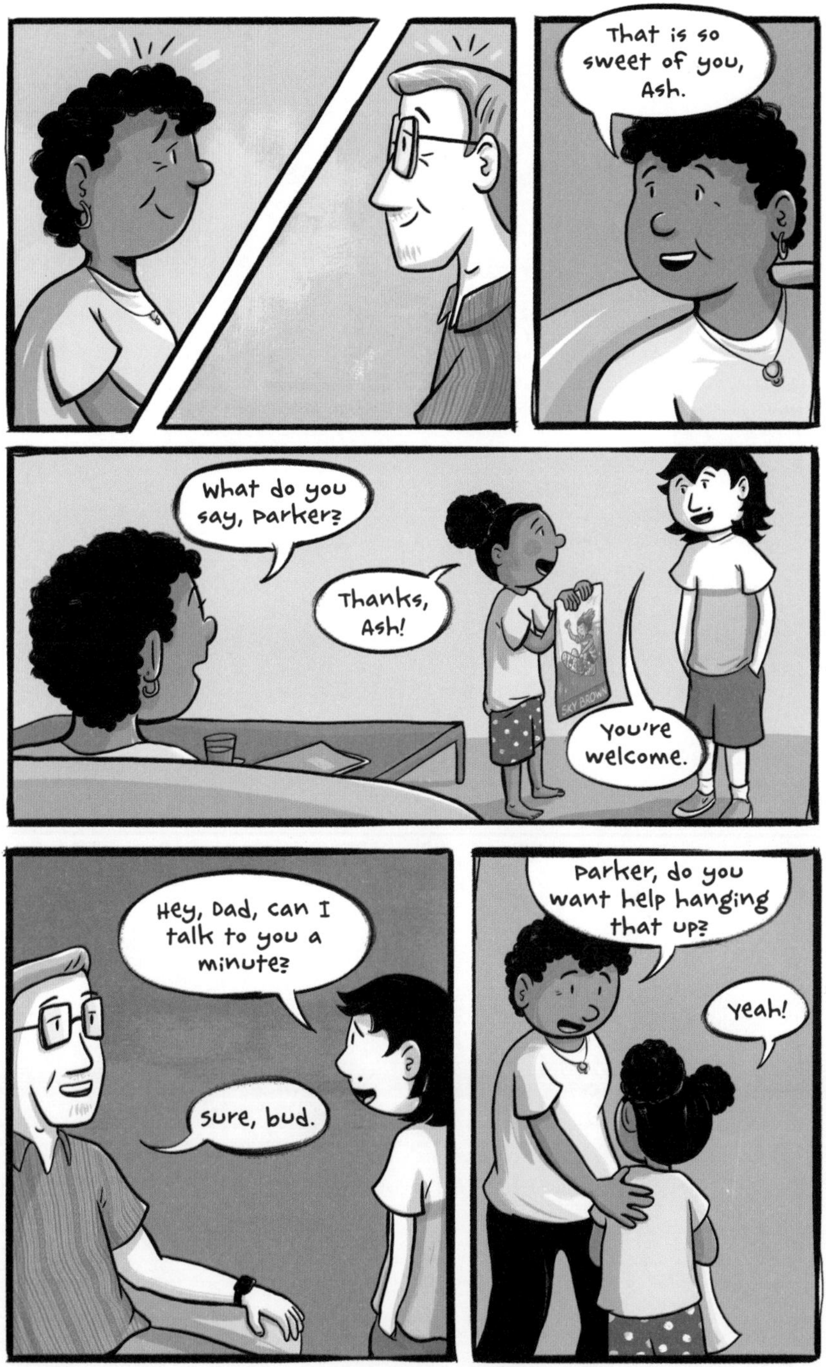
That is so sweet of you, Ash.
What do you say, Parker?
Thanks, Ash!
SKY BROWN
You're welcome.
Hey, Dad, can I talk to you a minute?
Sure, bud.
Parker, do you want help hanging that up?
Yeah!

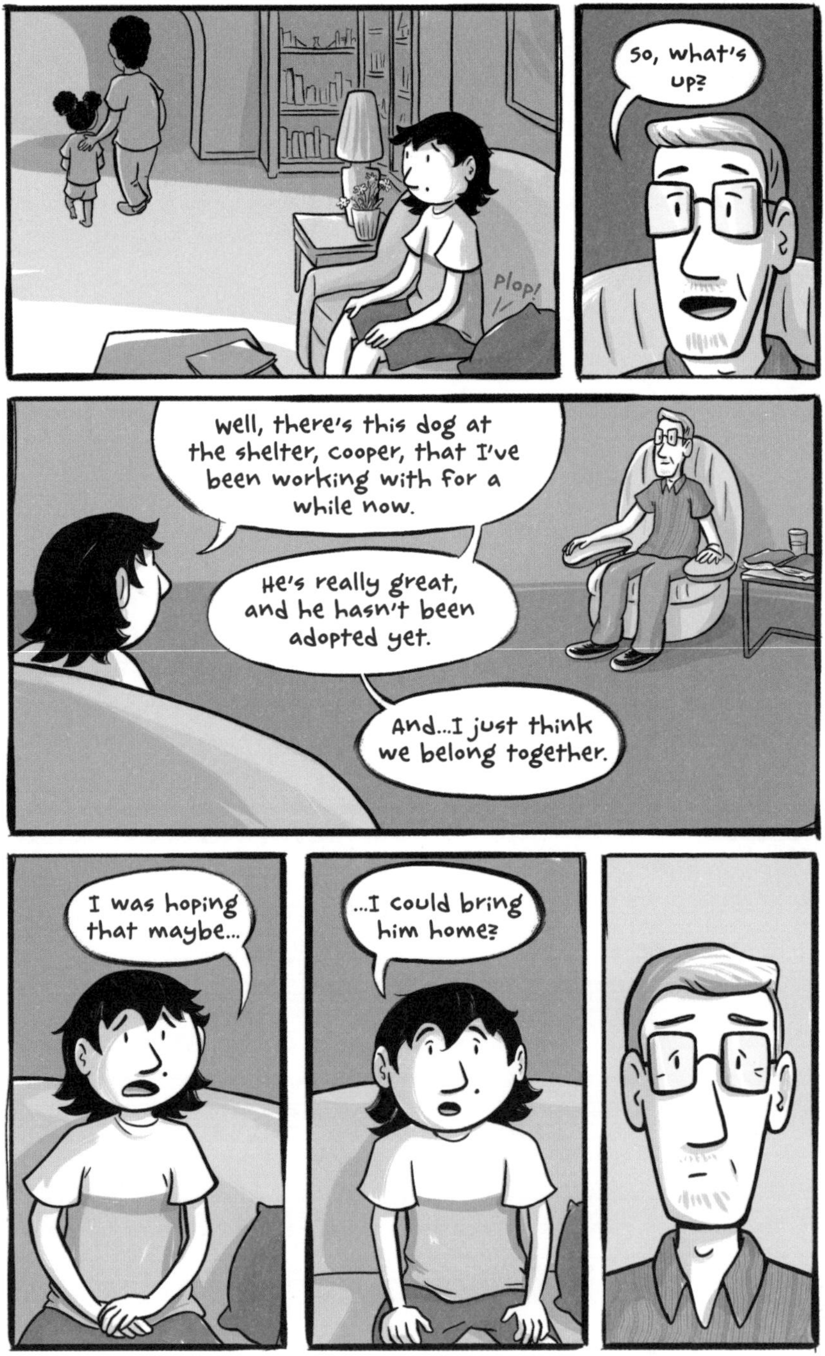
Plop!
So, what's up?
Well, there's this dog at the shelter, Cooper, that I've been working with for a while now.
He's really great, and he hasn't been adopted yet.
And...I just think we belong together.
I was hoping that maybe...
...I could bring him home?

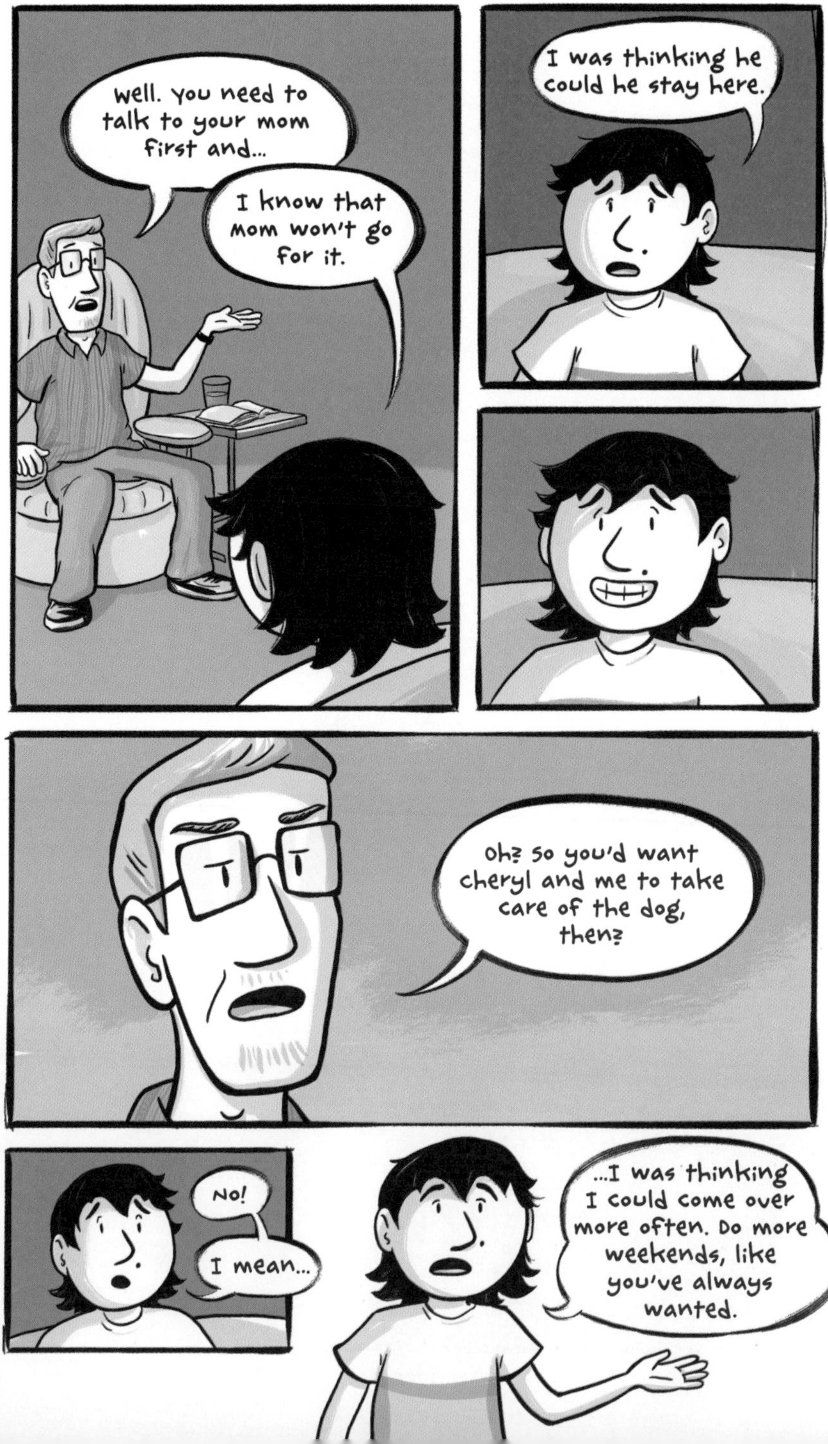
well. you need to talk to your mom first and...
I know that mom won't go for it.
I was thinking he could he stay here.
Oh? So you'd want cheryl and me to take care of the dog, then?
No!
I mean...
...I was thinking I could come over more often. Do more weekends, like you've always wanted.

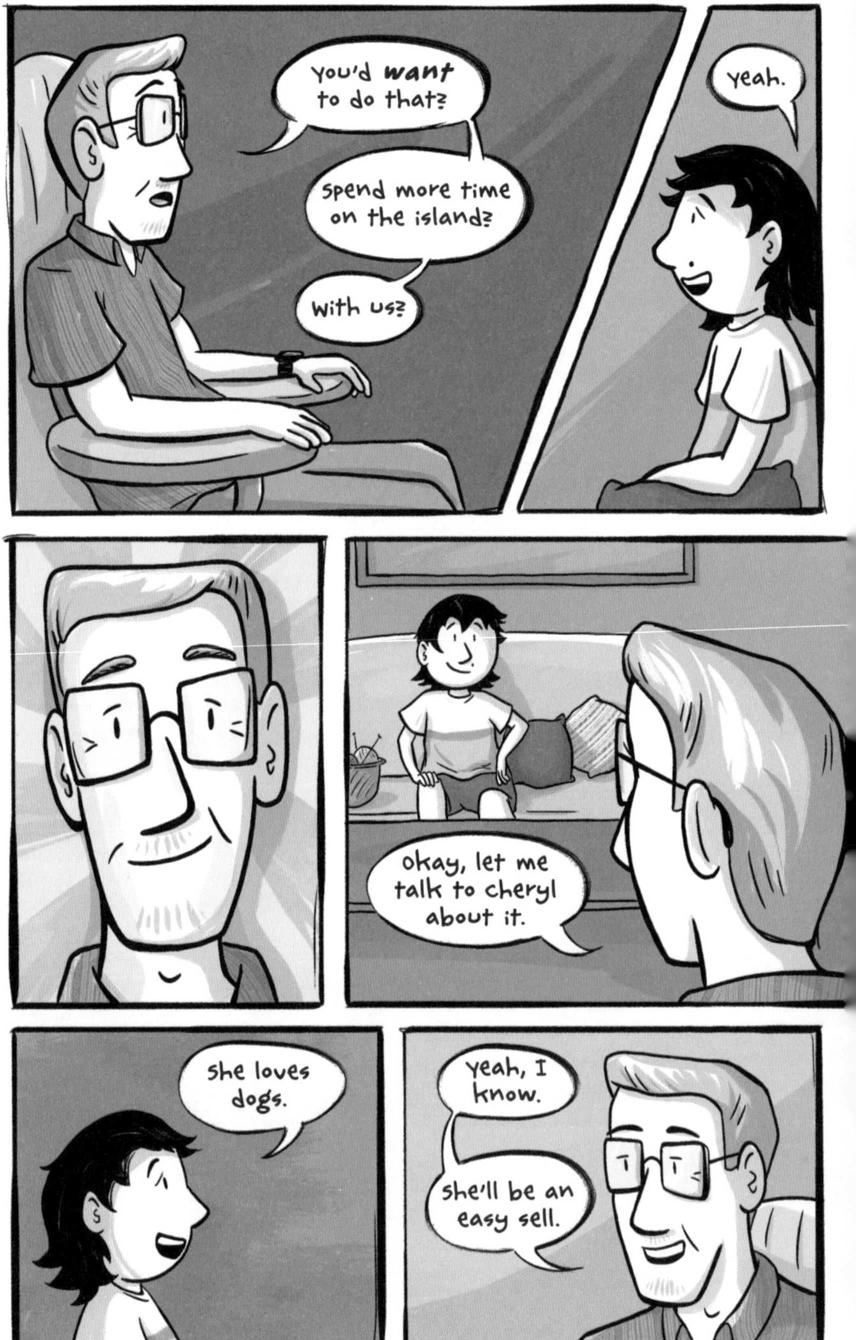
you'd **want** to do that?
spend more time on the island?
with us?
yeah.
okay, let me talk to cheryl about it.
she loves dogs.
yeah, I know.
she'll be an easy sell.

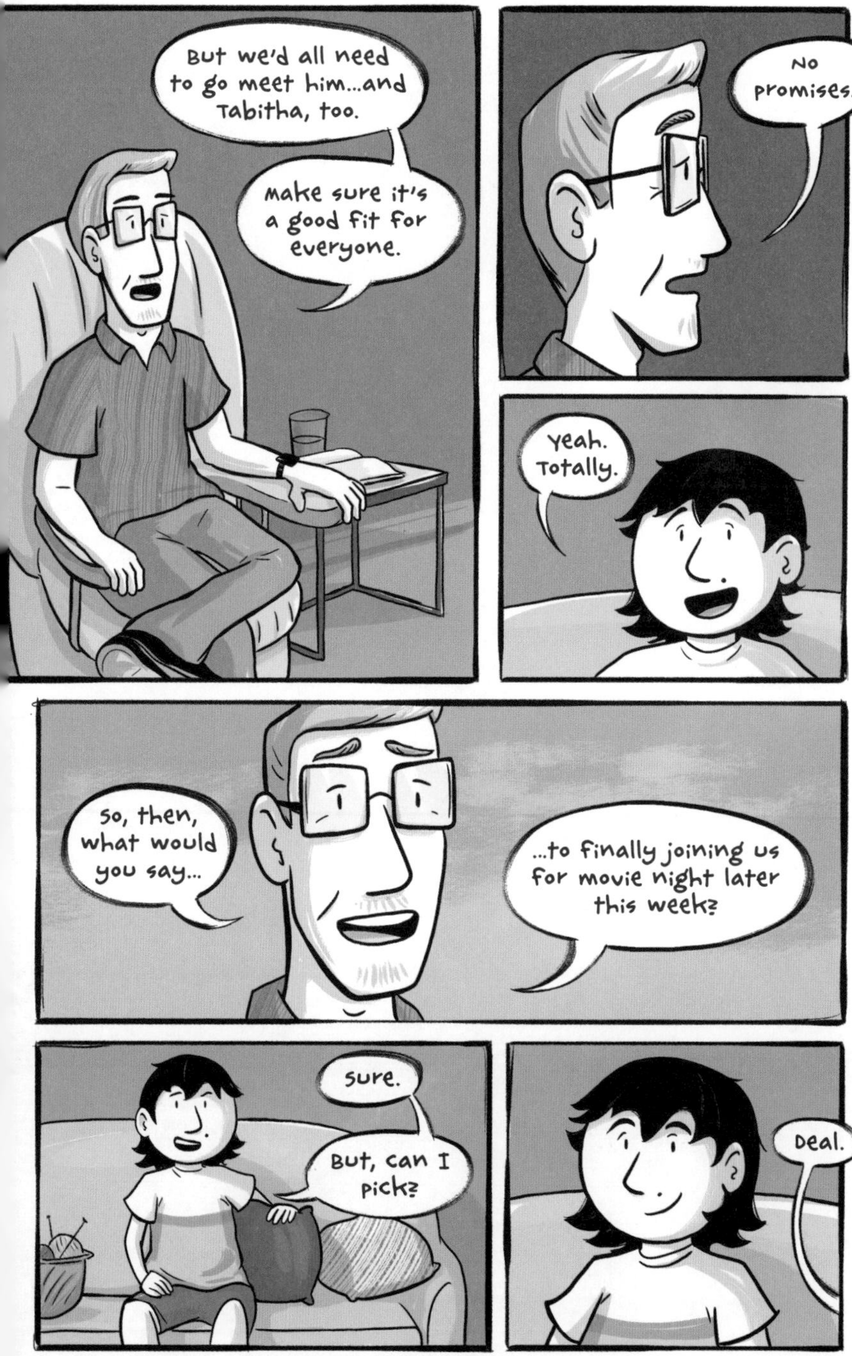
But we'd all need to go meet him...and Tabitha, too.
Make sure it's a good fit for everyone.
No promises.
Yeah. Totally.
So, then, what would you say...
...to finally joining us for movie night later this week?
Sure.
But, can I pick?
Deal.

CHAPTER 8

• Cooper •

A clever, fun-loving pointer that likes giving sloppy kisses. Pointers are high-energy sporting dogs with bold personalities, and as their name suggests, they point with their nose while on the hunt.

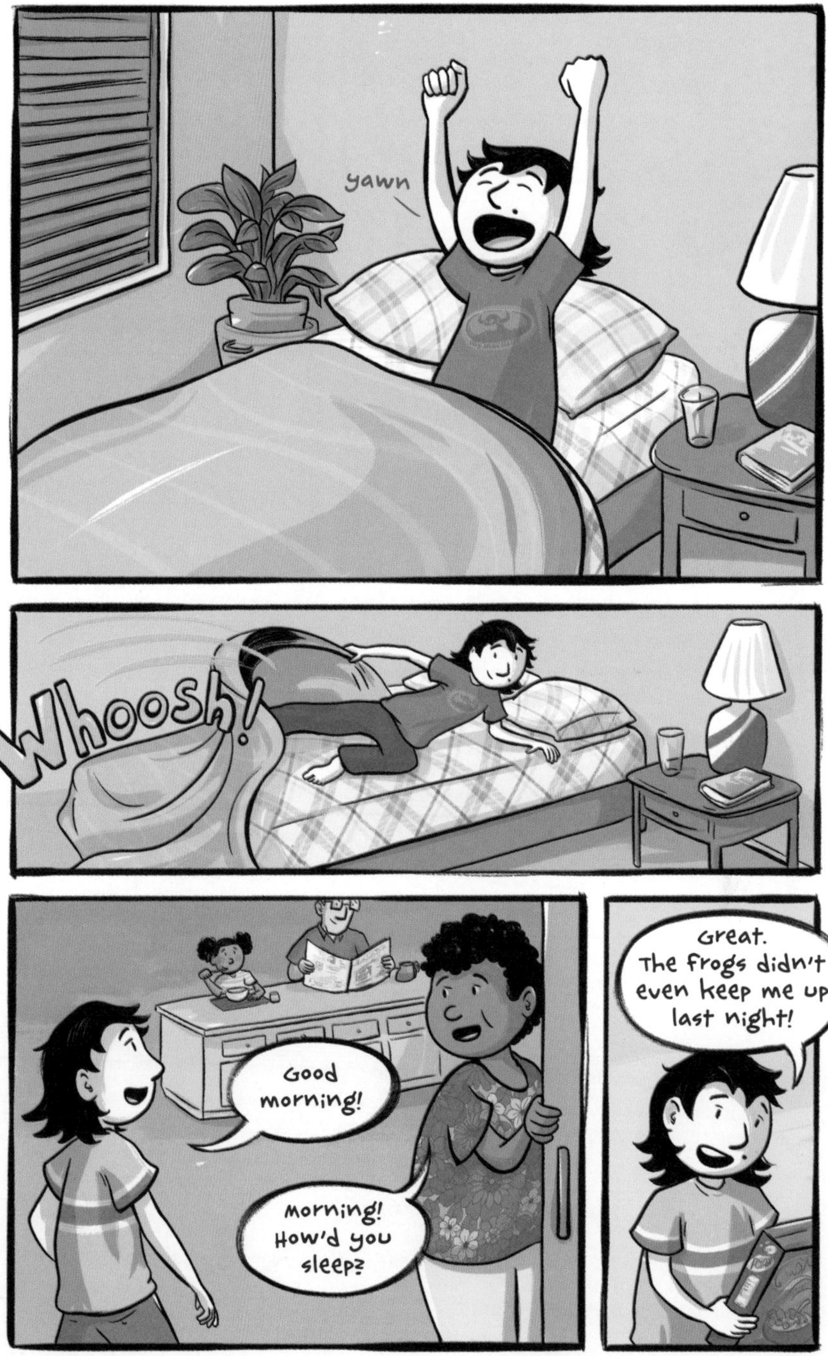
yawn
Whoosh!
Good morning!
Morning! How'd you sleep?
Great. The frogs didn't even keep me up last night!

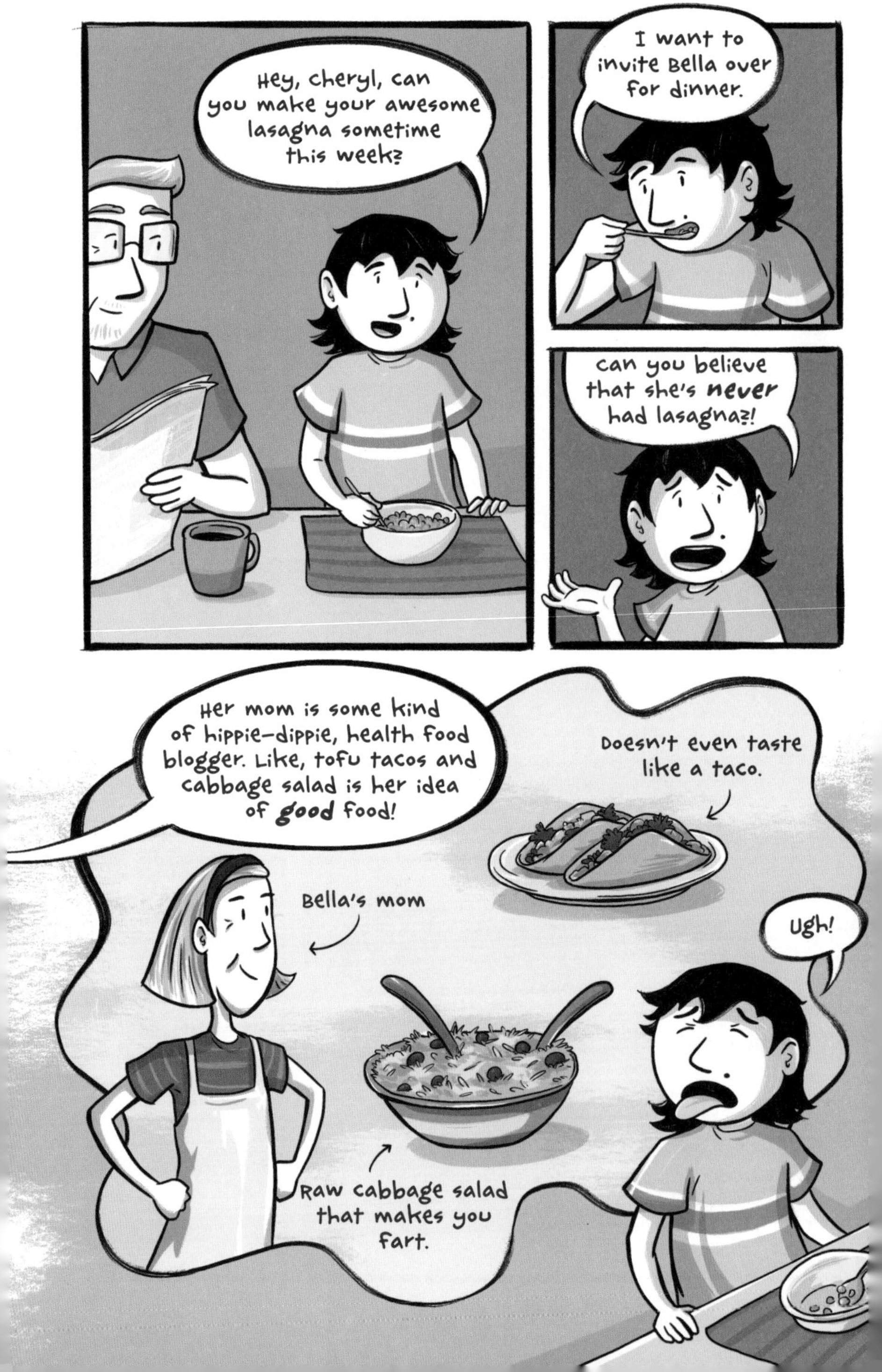
Hey, Cheryl, can you make your awesome lasagna sometime this week?
I want to invite Bella over for dinner.
Can you believe that she's **never** had lasagna?!
Her mom is some kind of hippie-dippie, health food blogger. Like, tofu tacos and cabbage salad is her idea of ***good*** food!
Doesn't even taste like a taco.
Bella's mom
Ugh!
Raw cabbage salad that makes you fart.

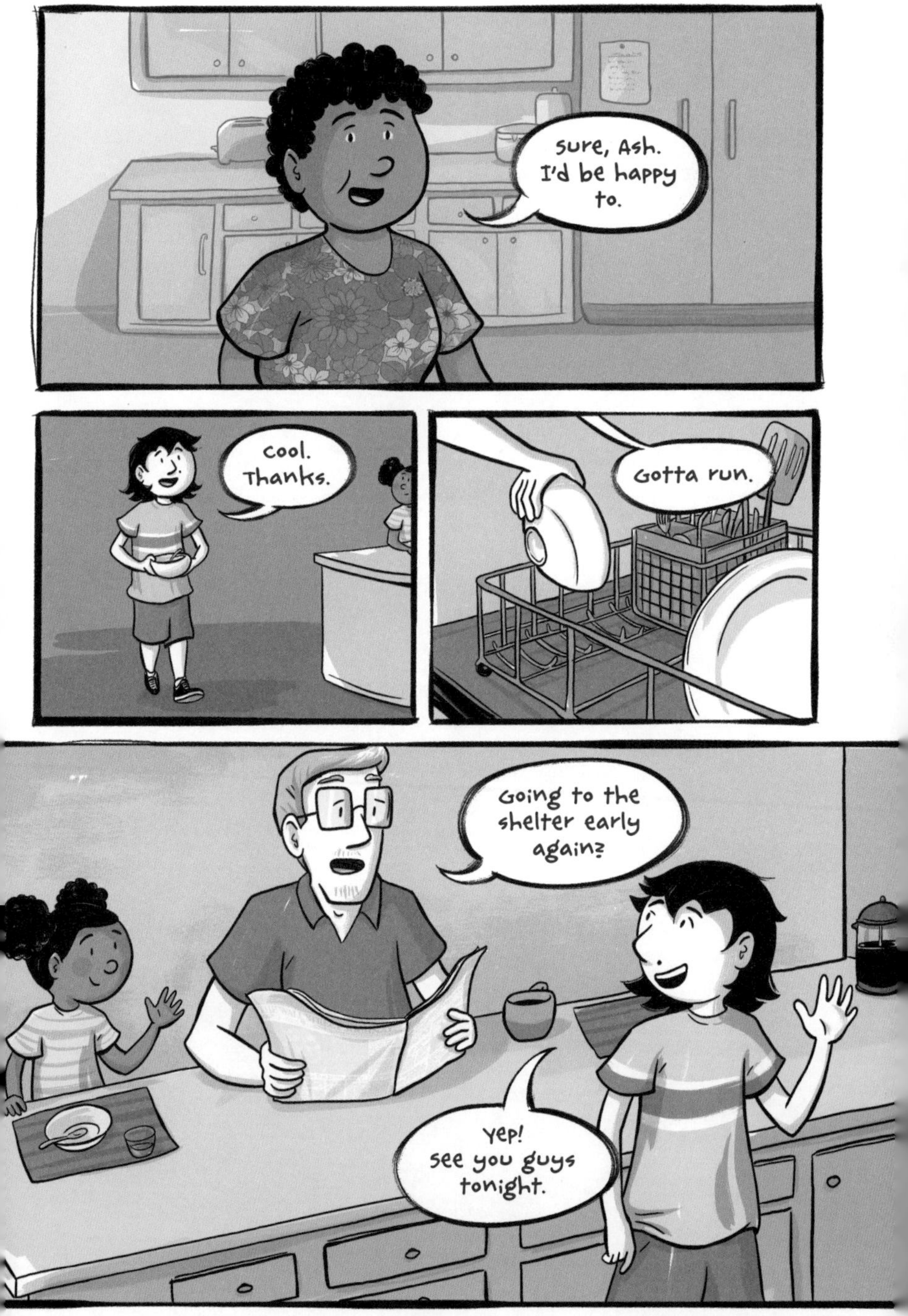
Sure, Ash. I'd be happy to.
Cool. Thanks.
Gotta run.
Going to the shelter early again?
Yep! See you guys tonight.

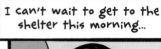

I can't wait to get to the shelter this morning...

...and tell Jo about adopting cooper!

Slam!

I have butterflies in my stomach just thinking about it.

I mean, I know it's not for certain, but it feels like it's going to happen. It feels right.

COOPER

upturned nose

slobbery tennis ball

long, flappy ears

tail that points!

OPEN

The fastest, smartest, and most loyal dog at the shelter. cooper is **the best** dog ever.

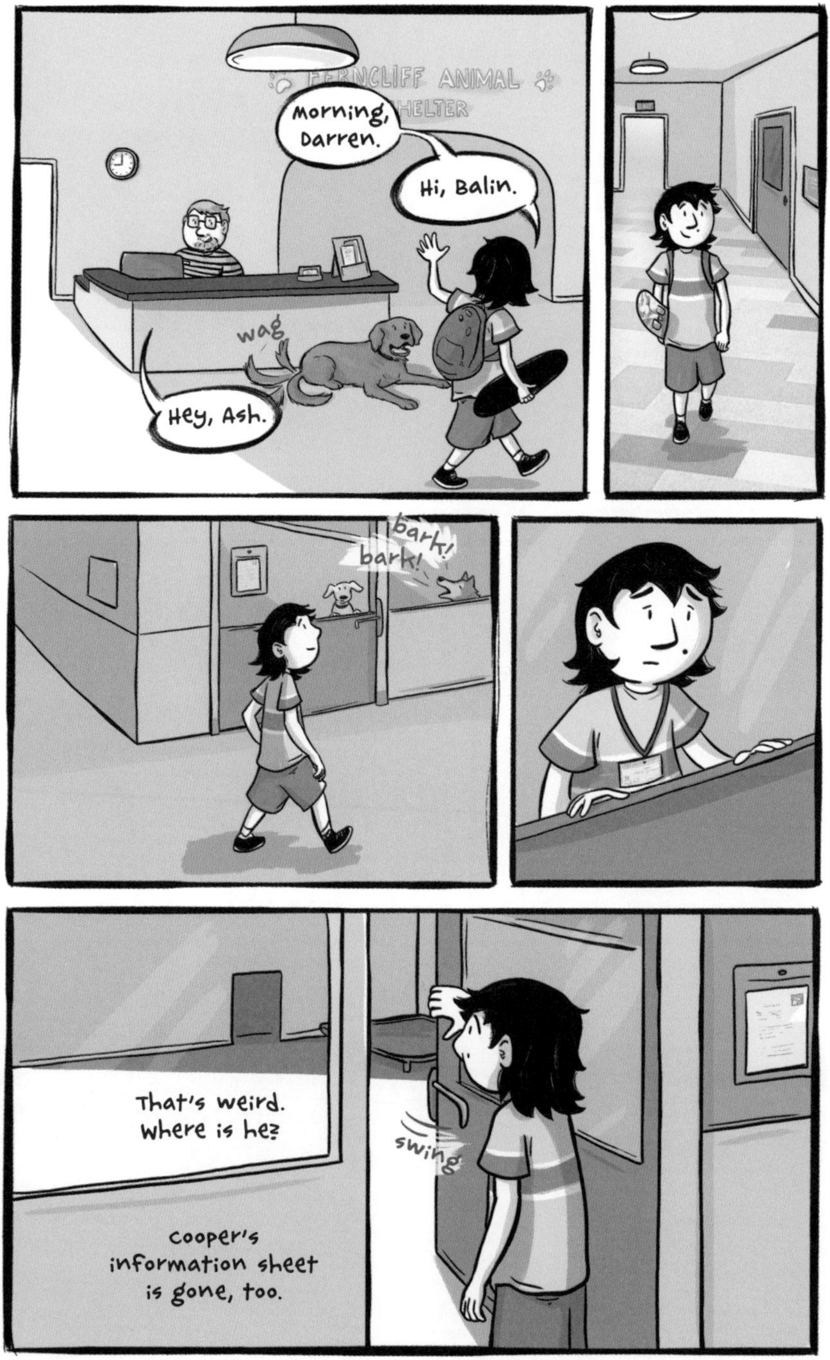
FERNCLIFF ANIMAL SHELTER
Morning, Darren.
Hi, Balin.
wag
Hey, Ash.
bark!
bark!
That's weird. Where is he?
swing
Cooper's information sheet is gone, too.

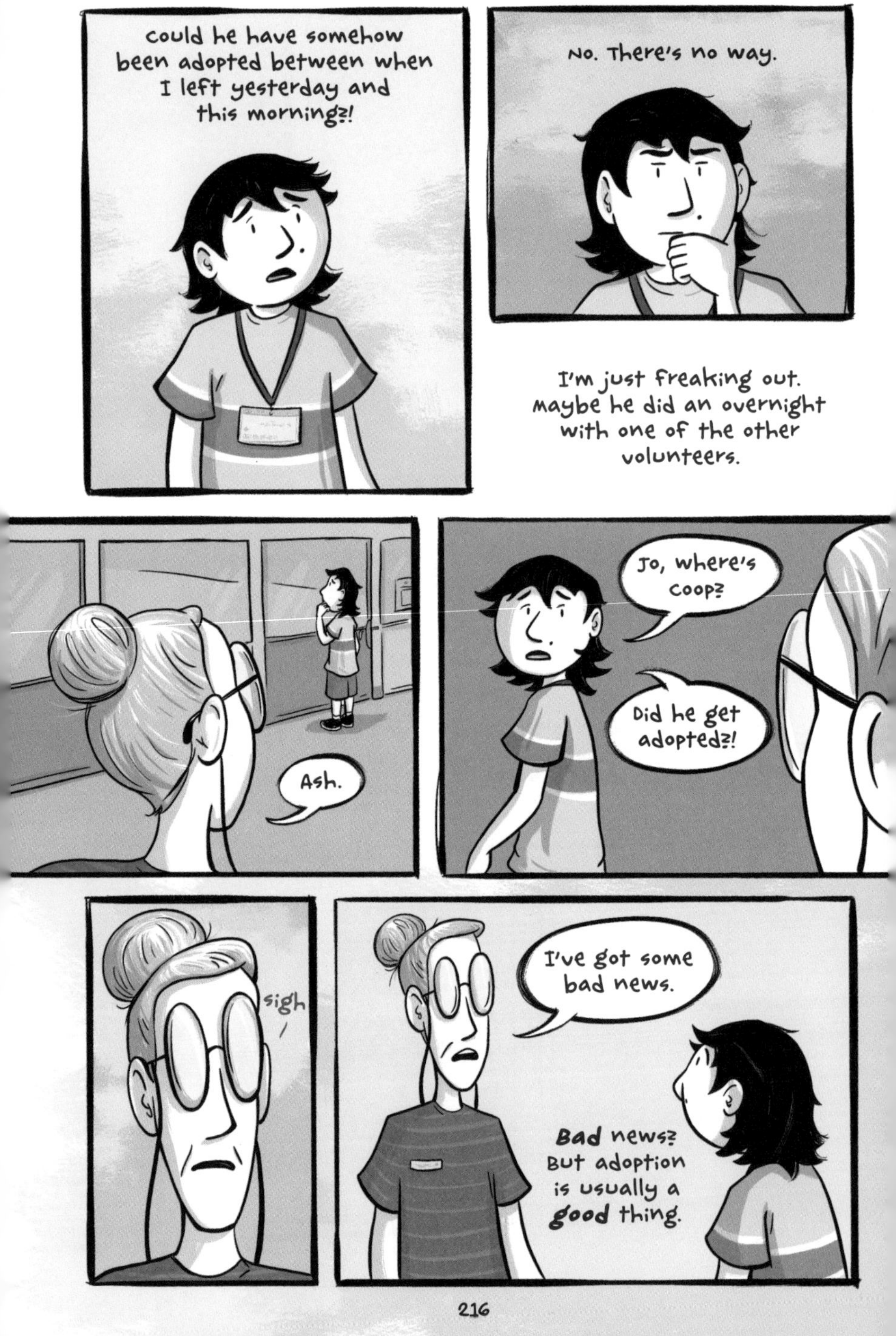
Could he have somehow been adopted between when I left yesterday and this morning?!
No. There's no way.
I'm just freaking out. Maybe he did an overnight with one of the other volunteers.
Ash.
Jo, where's Coop?
Did he get adopted?!
sigh
I've got some bad news.
Bad news? But adoption is usually a **good** thing.

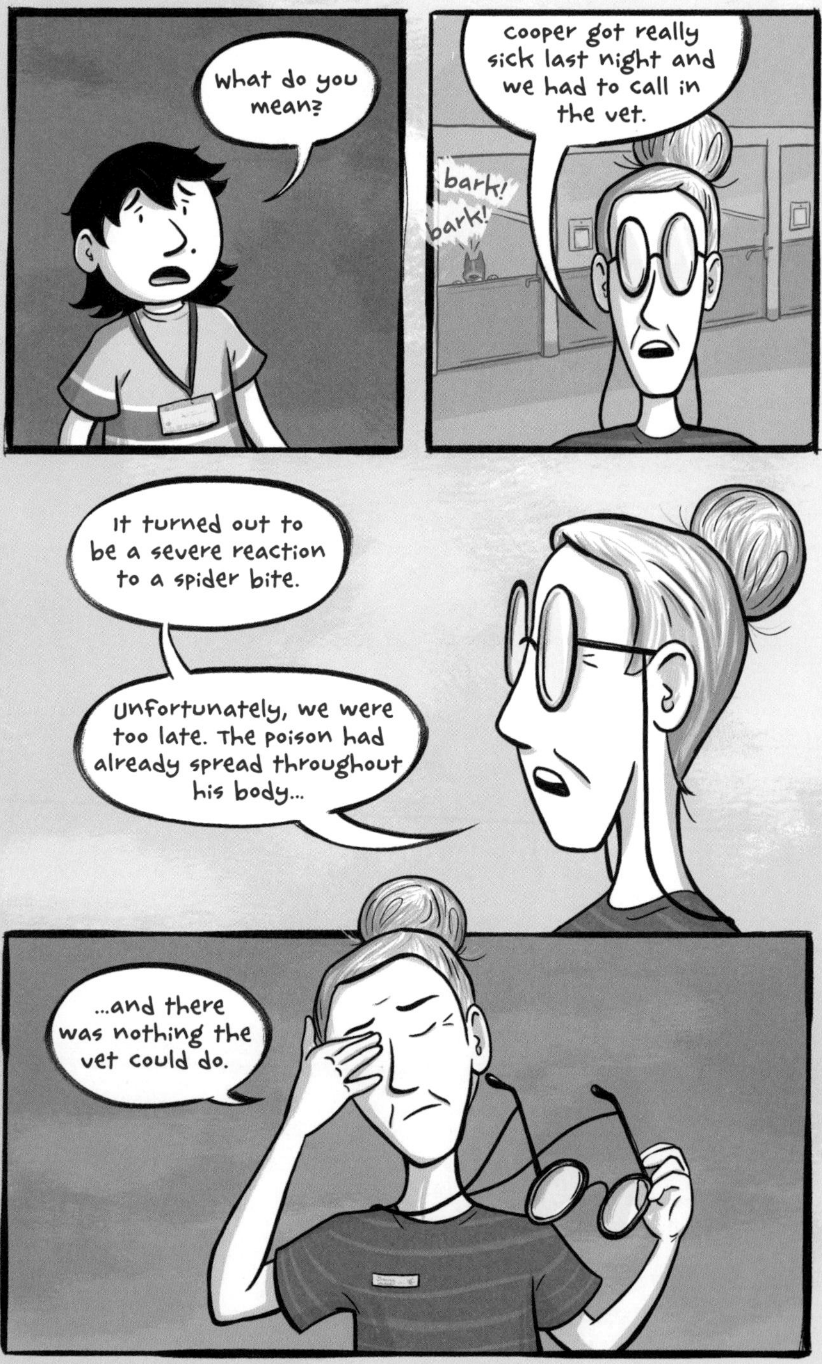
What do you mean?
Cooper got really sick last night and we had to call in the vet.
bark!
bark!
It turned out to be a severe reaction to a spider bite.
Unfortunately, we were too late. The poison had already spread throughout his body...
...and there was nothing the vet could do.

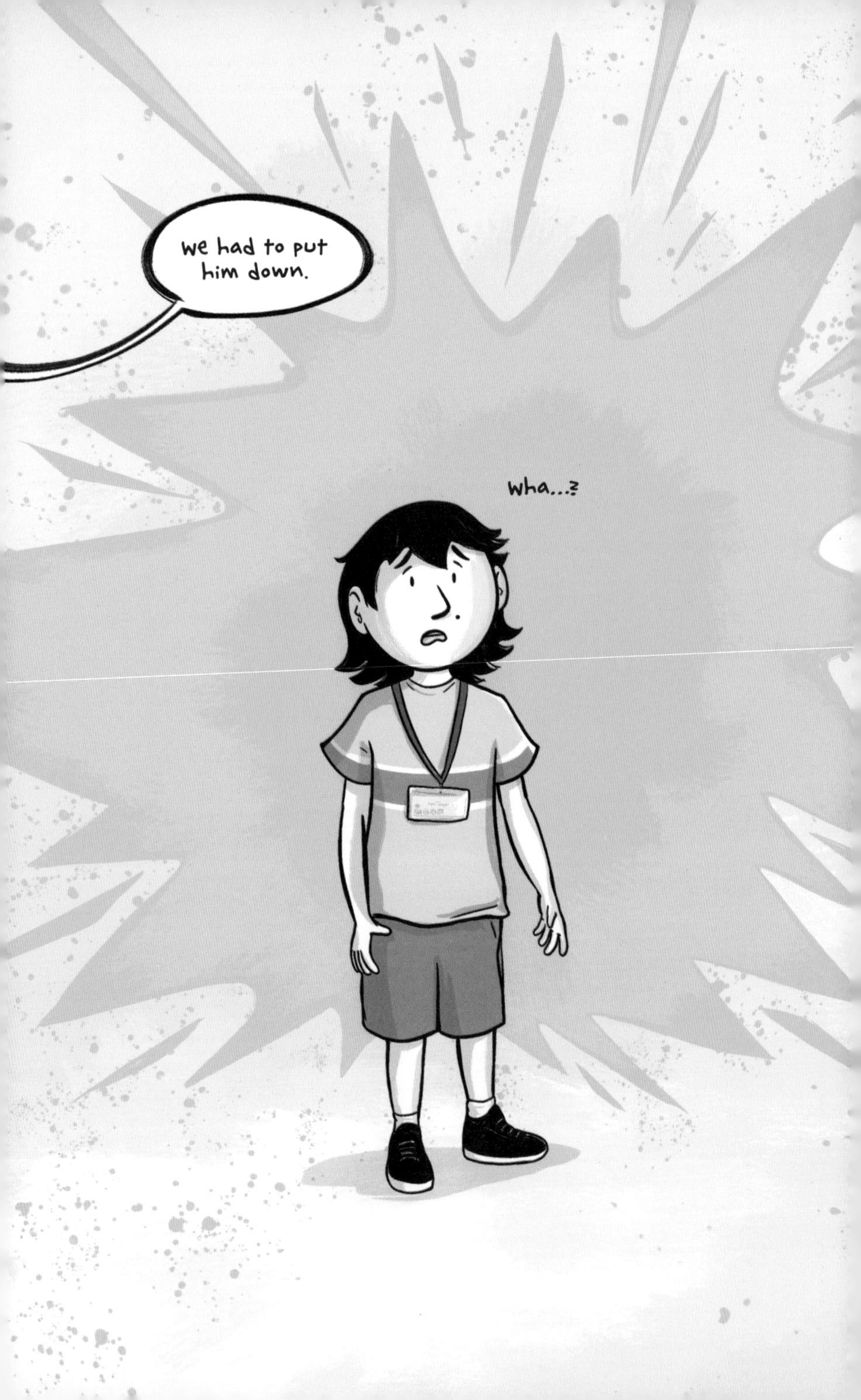
we had to put him down.
wha...?

NO. I can't believe...

...a spider?

What kind?!

Not entirely sure.

It could have been a *hobo*, but due to the severity, it was most likely a *black widow*.

My head spins trying to absorb the shock of Cooper...just being gone.

Because of a what?! A dumb little spider?

I didn't even know we had black widows on the island!

slide

I'm sorry, Ash. I know you'd really grown attached to him.

Although fatal bites are uncommon, there are a few venomous spiders such as the *hobo, black widow,* and the *brown recluse* that can be quite dangerous and toxic to pets.

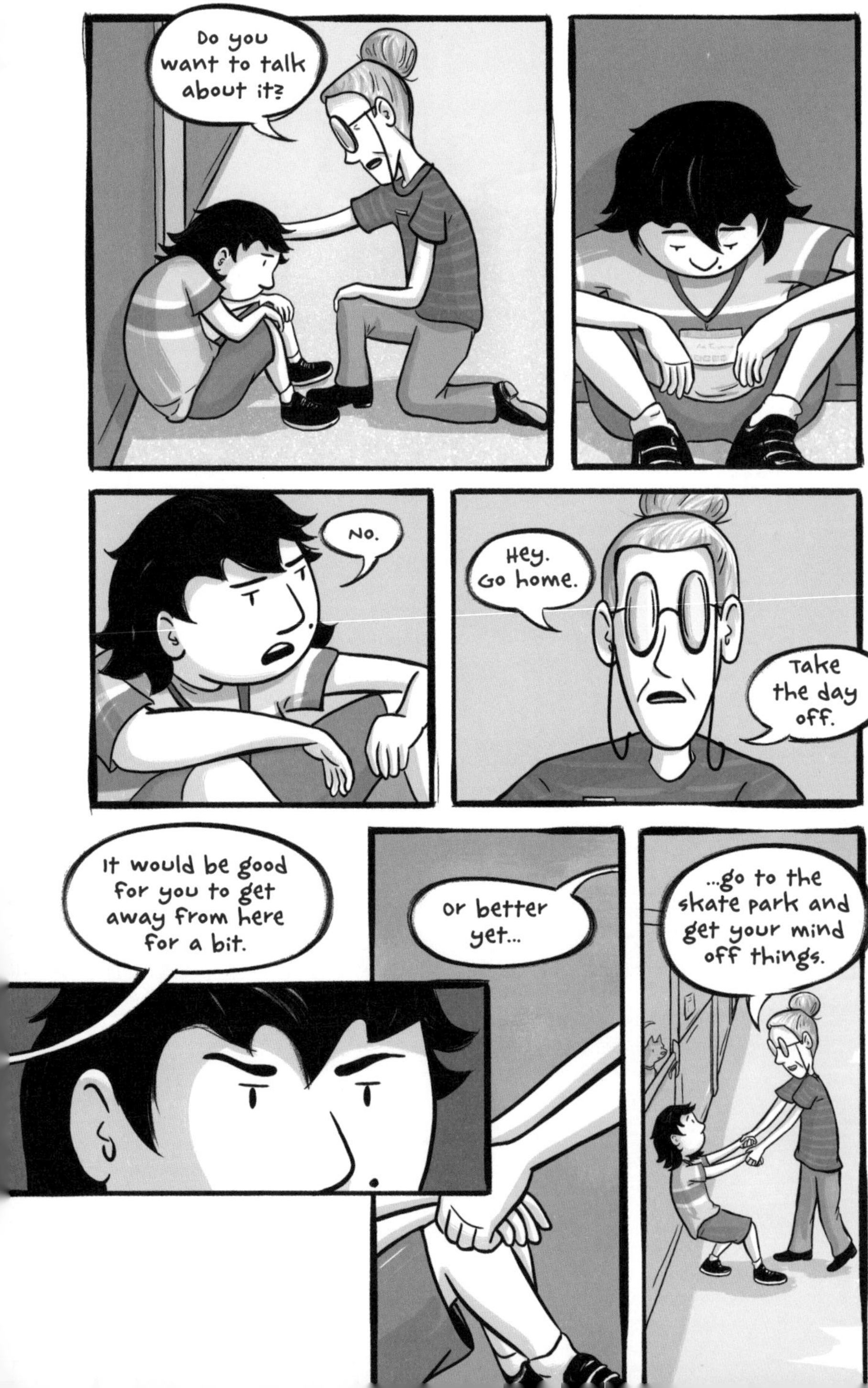
Do you want to talk about it?
No.
Hey. Go home.
Take the day off.
It would be good for you to get away from here for a bit.
Or better yet...
...go to the skate park and get your mind off things.

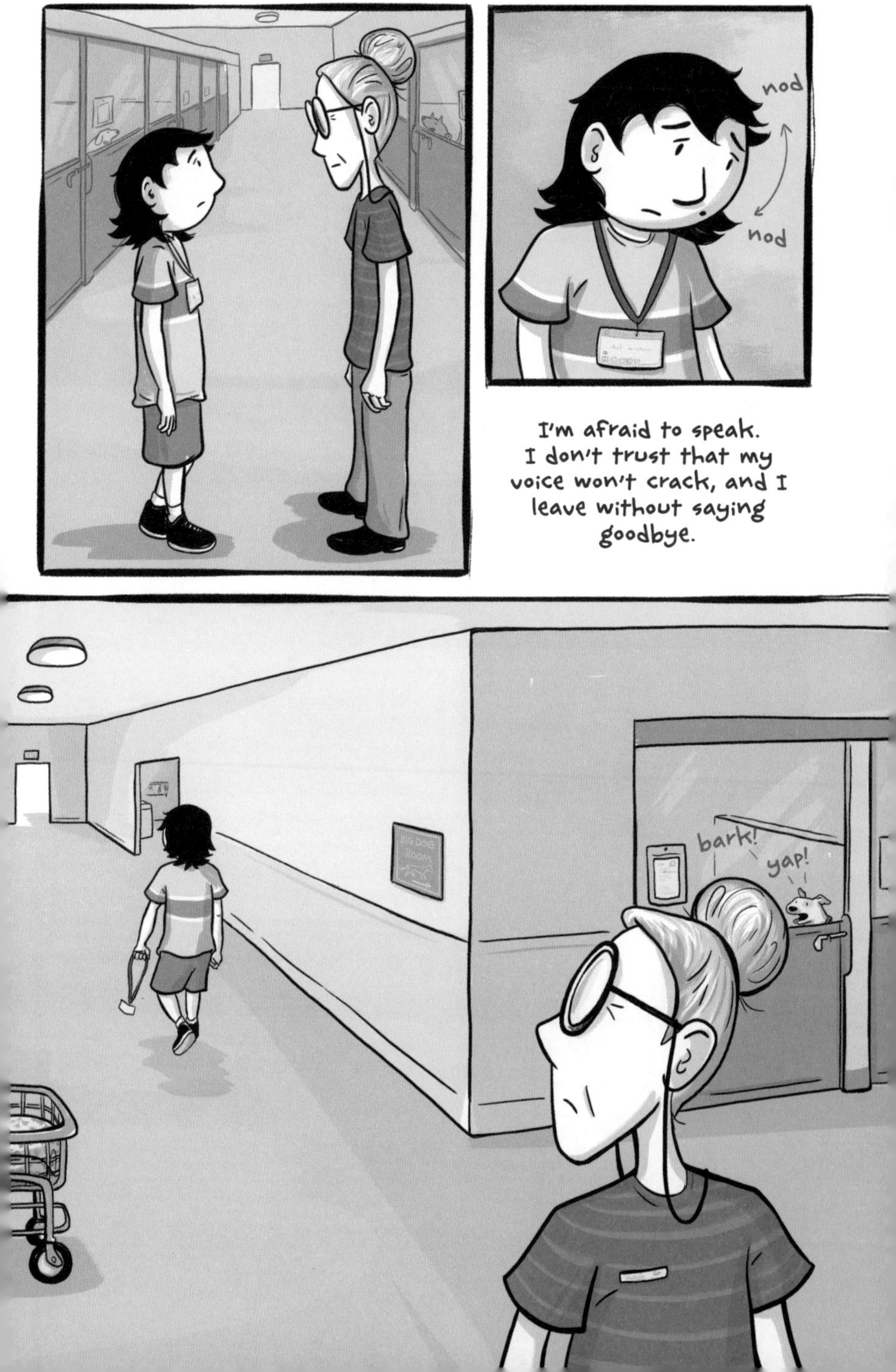
nod
nod
I'm afraid to speak. I don't trust that my voice won't crack, and I leave without saying goodbye.
bark!
yap!

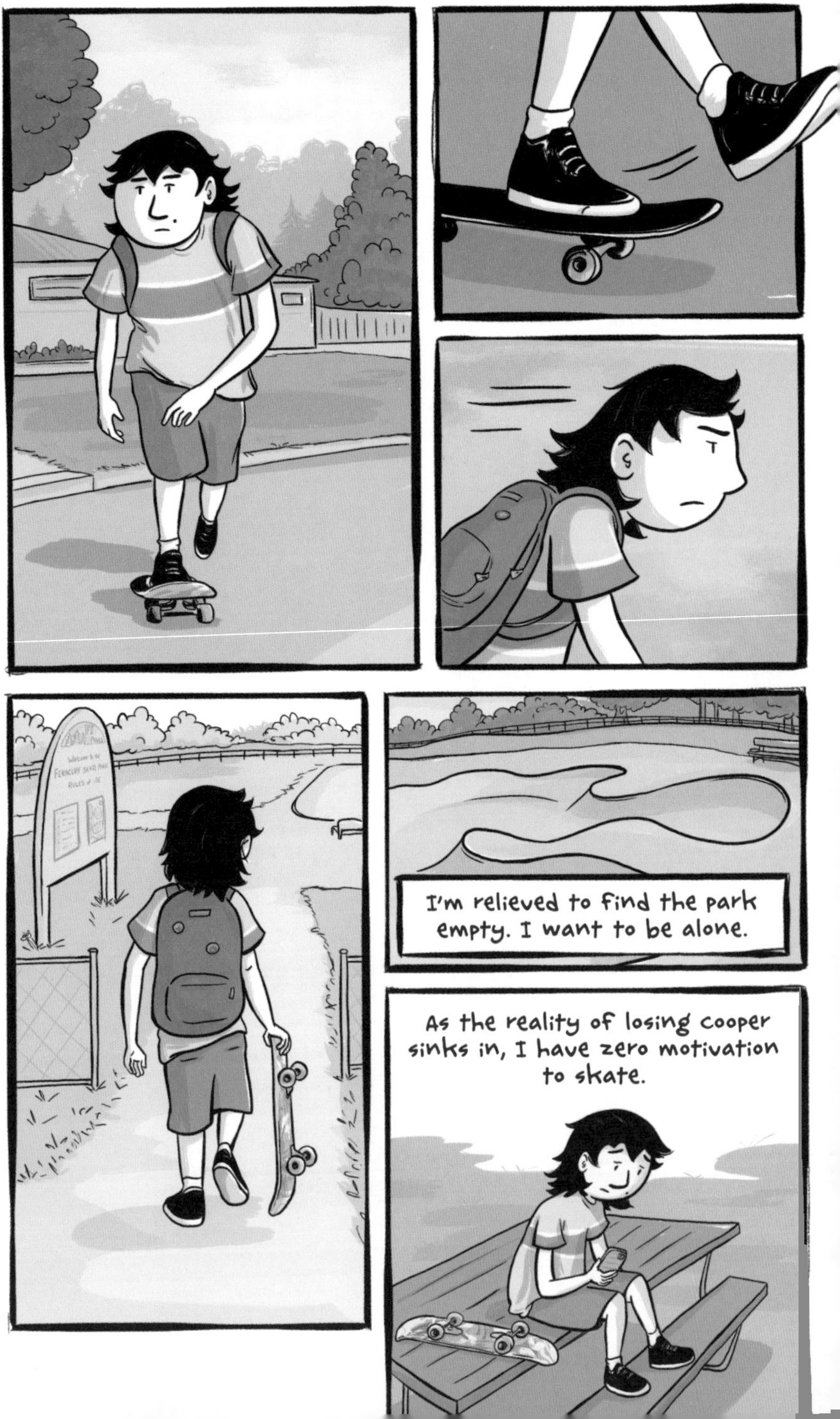
I'm relieved to find the park empty. I want to be alone.
As the reality of losing cooper sinks in, I have zero motivation to skate.

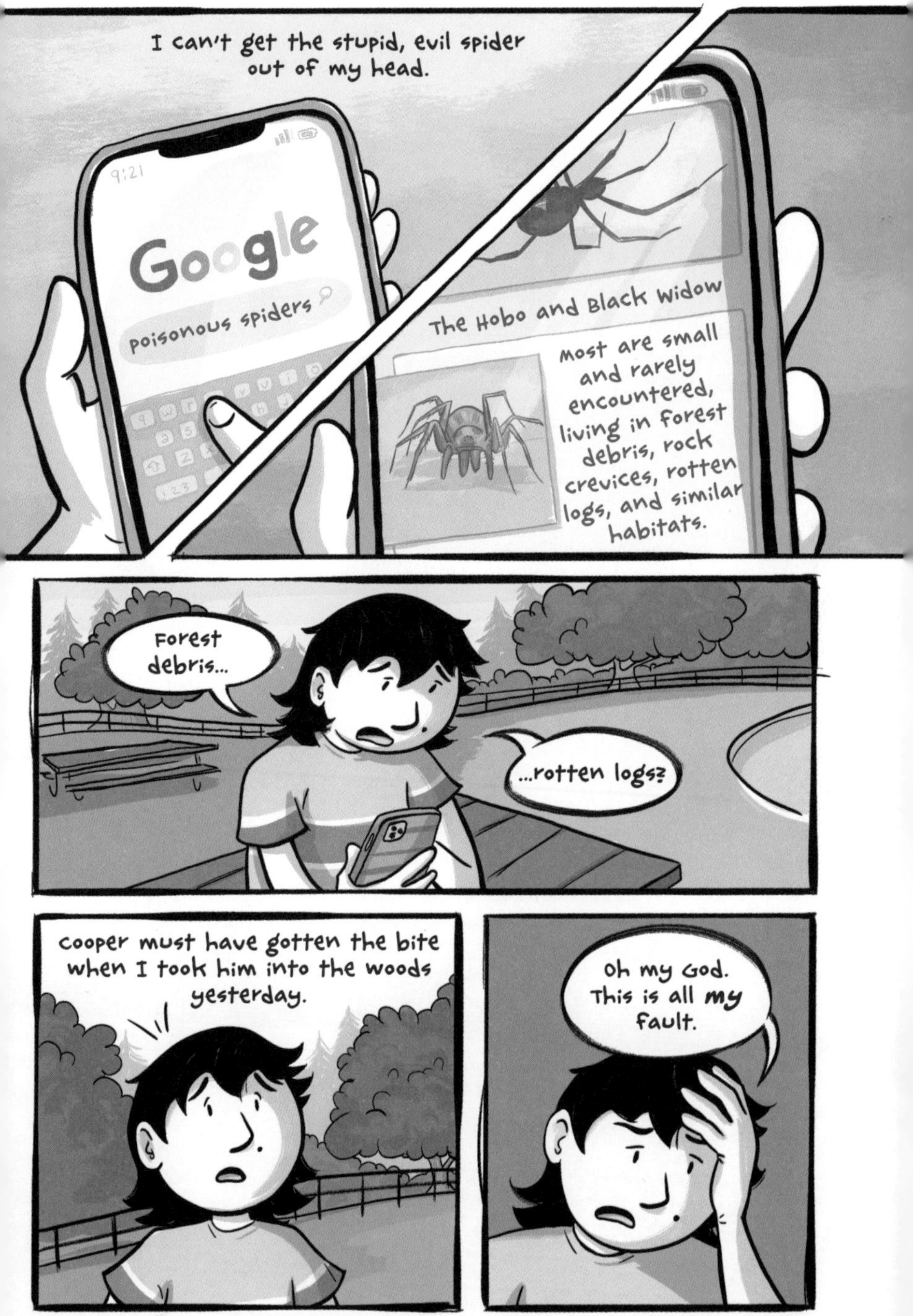
I can't get the stupid, evil spider out of my head.
Google
poisonous spiders
The Hobo and Black Widow
most are small and rarely encountered, living in forest debris, rock crevices, rotten logs, and similar habitats.
Forest debris...
...rotten logs?
Cooper must have gotten the bite when I took him into the woods yesterday.
Oh my God. This is all my fault.

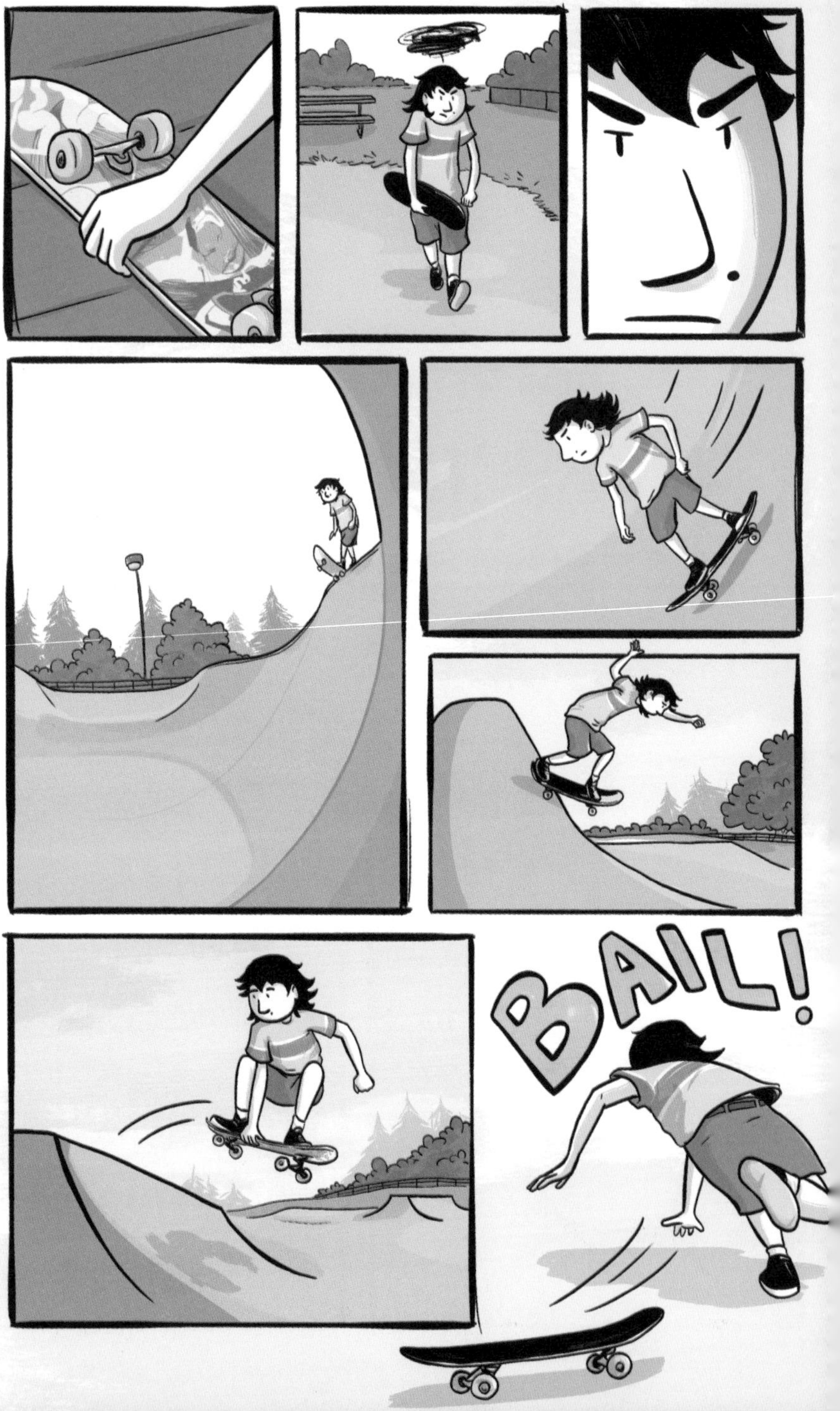
BAIL!

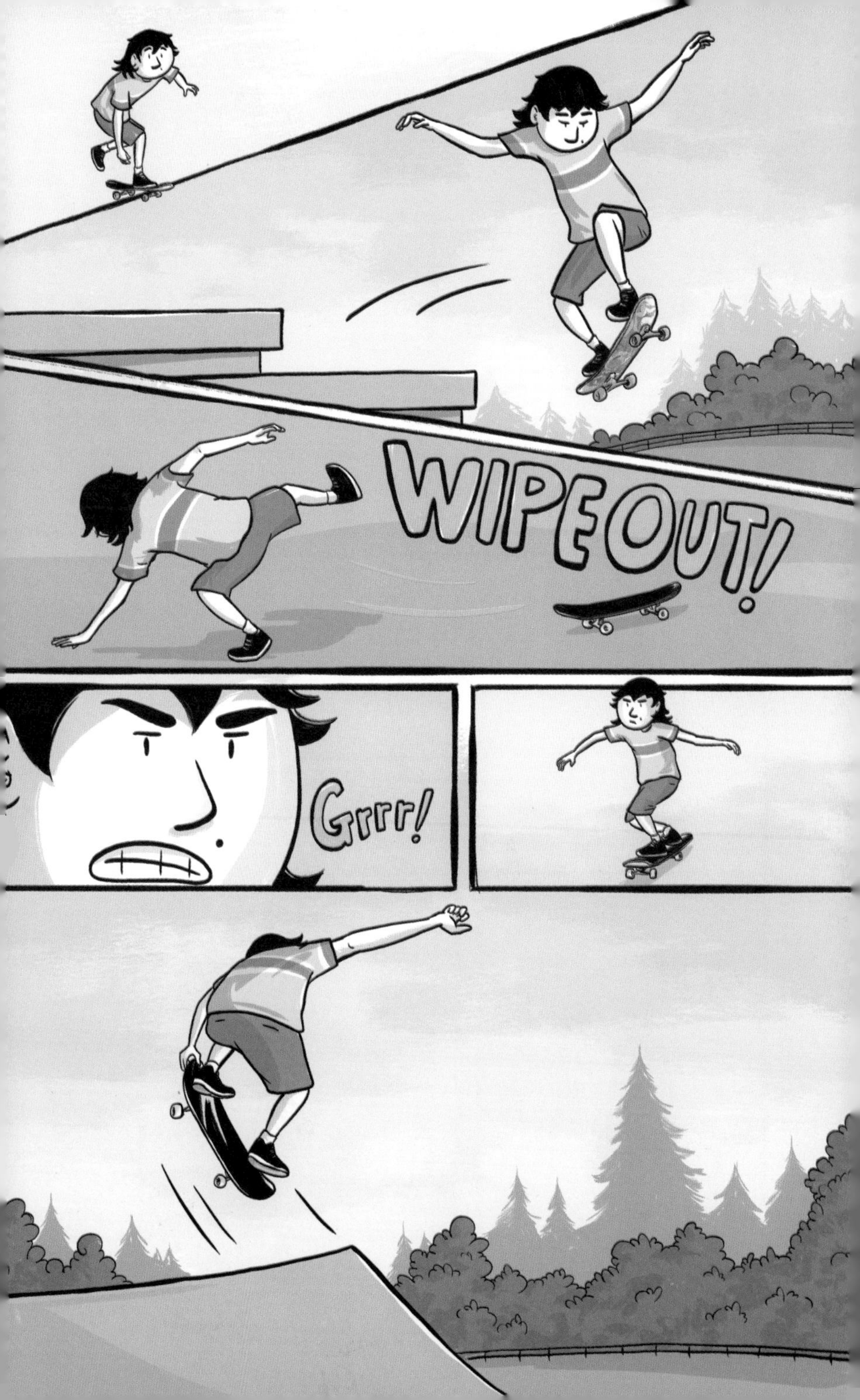
WIPEOUT!
Grrr!

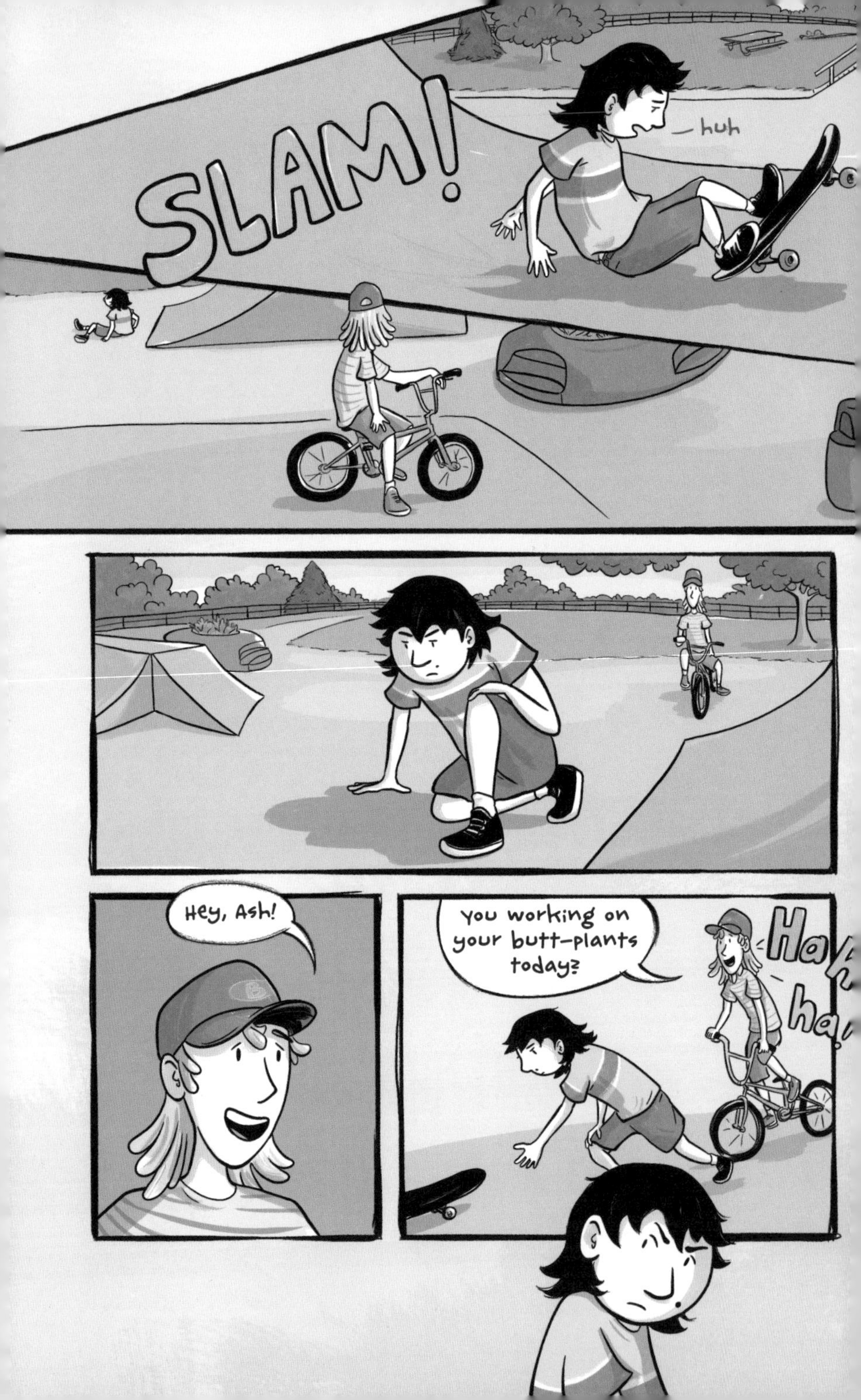
SLAM!
huh
Hey, Ash!
You working on your butt-plants today?
Ha
ha

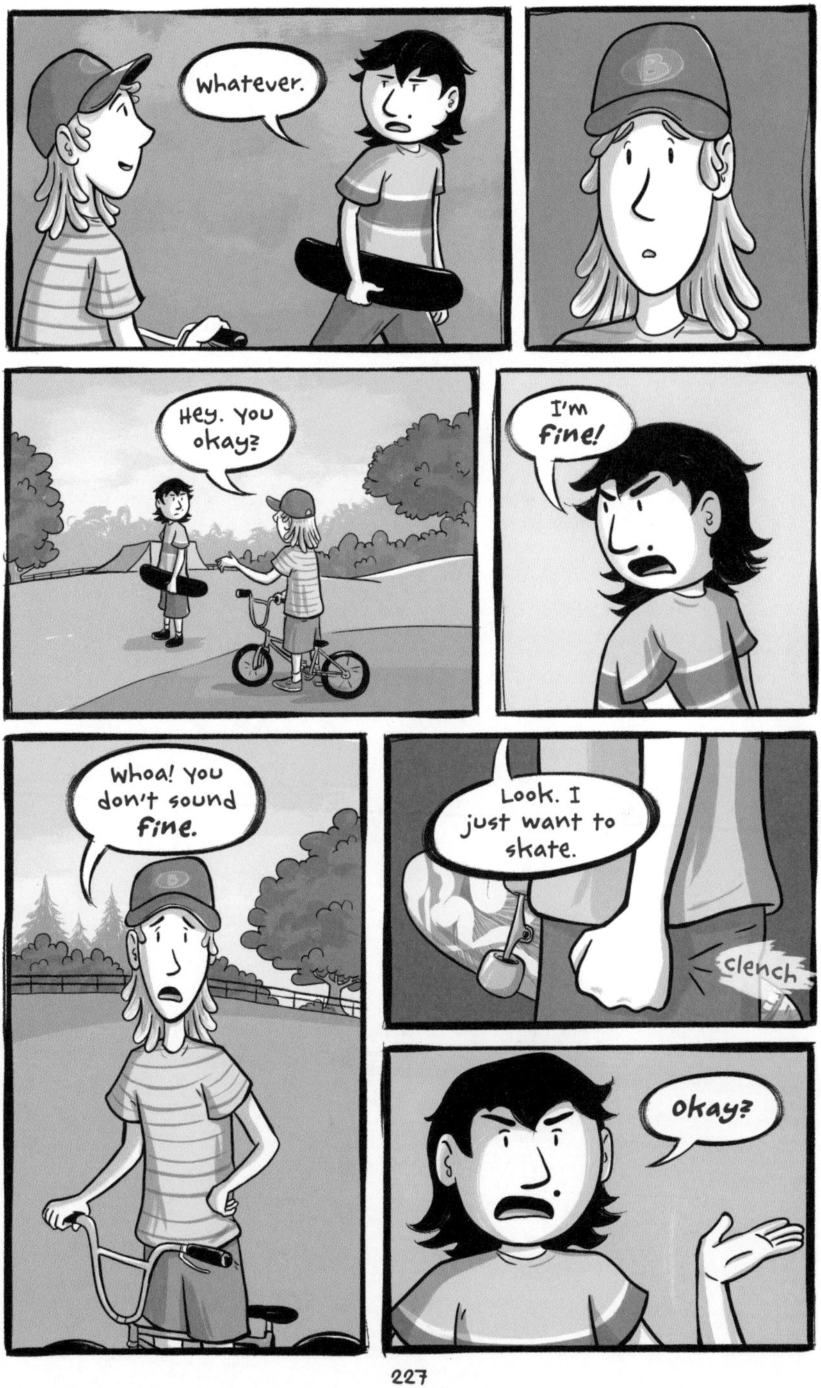
Whatever.
Hey. You okay?
I'm fine!
Whoa! You don't sound fine.
Look. I just want to skate.
clench
Okay?

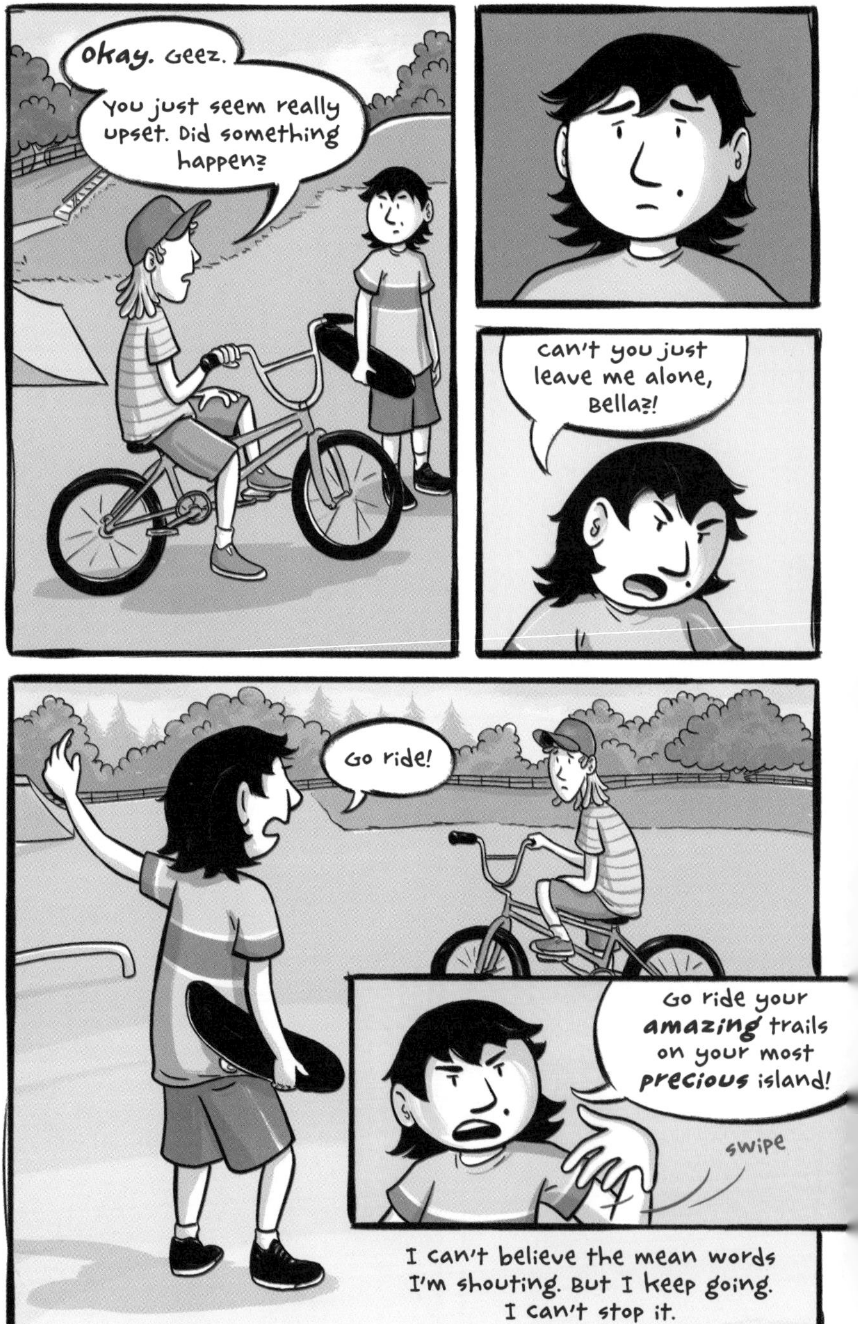
Okay. Geez.
You just seem really upset. Did something happen?
Can't you just leave me alone, Bella?!
Go ride!
Go ride your amazing trails on your most precious island!
swipe
I can't believe the mean words I'm shouting. But I keep going. I can't stop it.

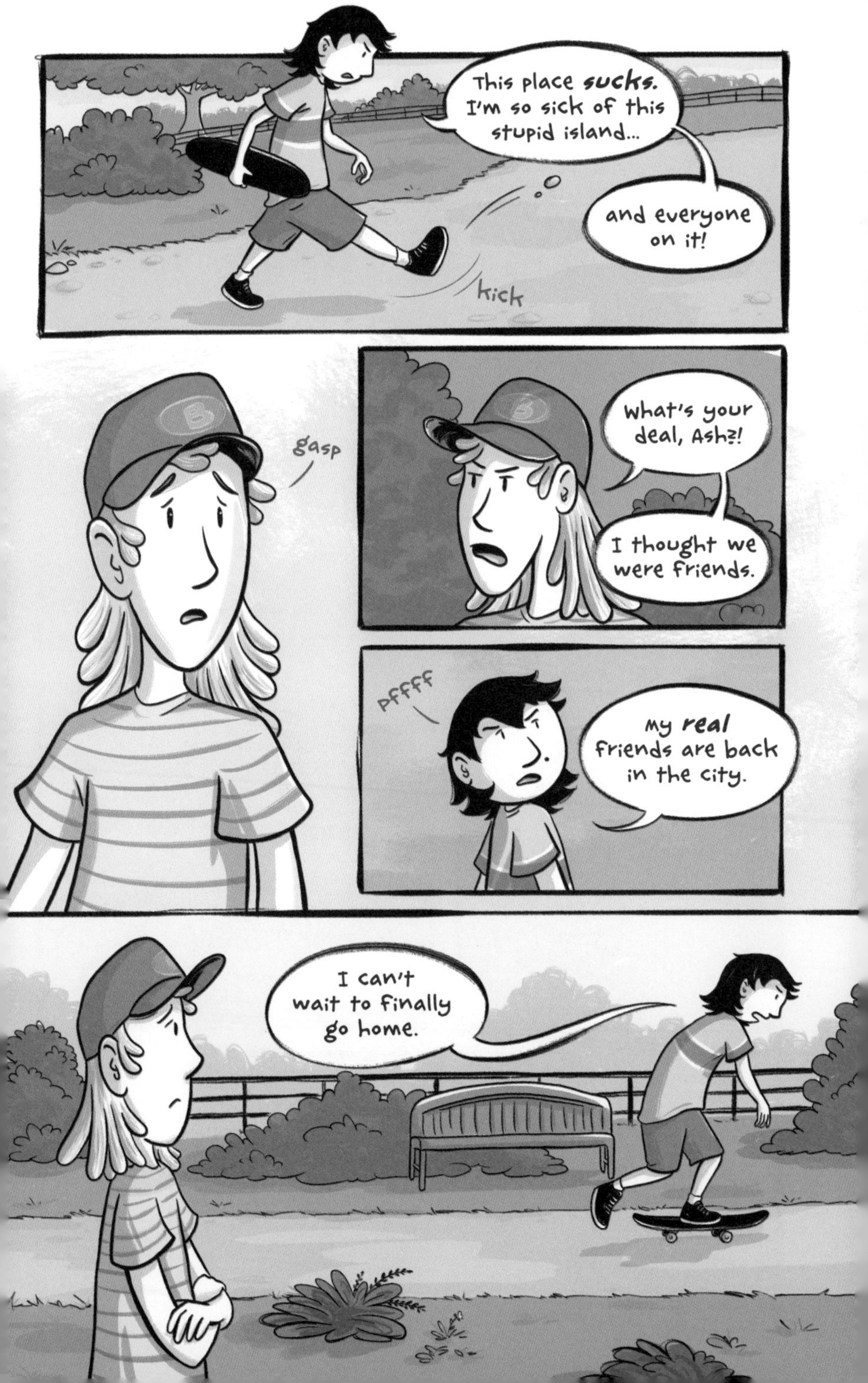
This place **sucks.** I'm so sick of this stupid island...
and everyone on it!
kick
gasp
What's your deal, Ash?!
I thought we were friends.
pffff
My **real** friends are back in the city.
I can't wait to finally go home.

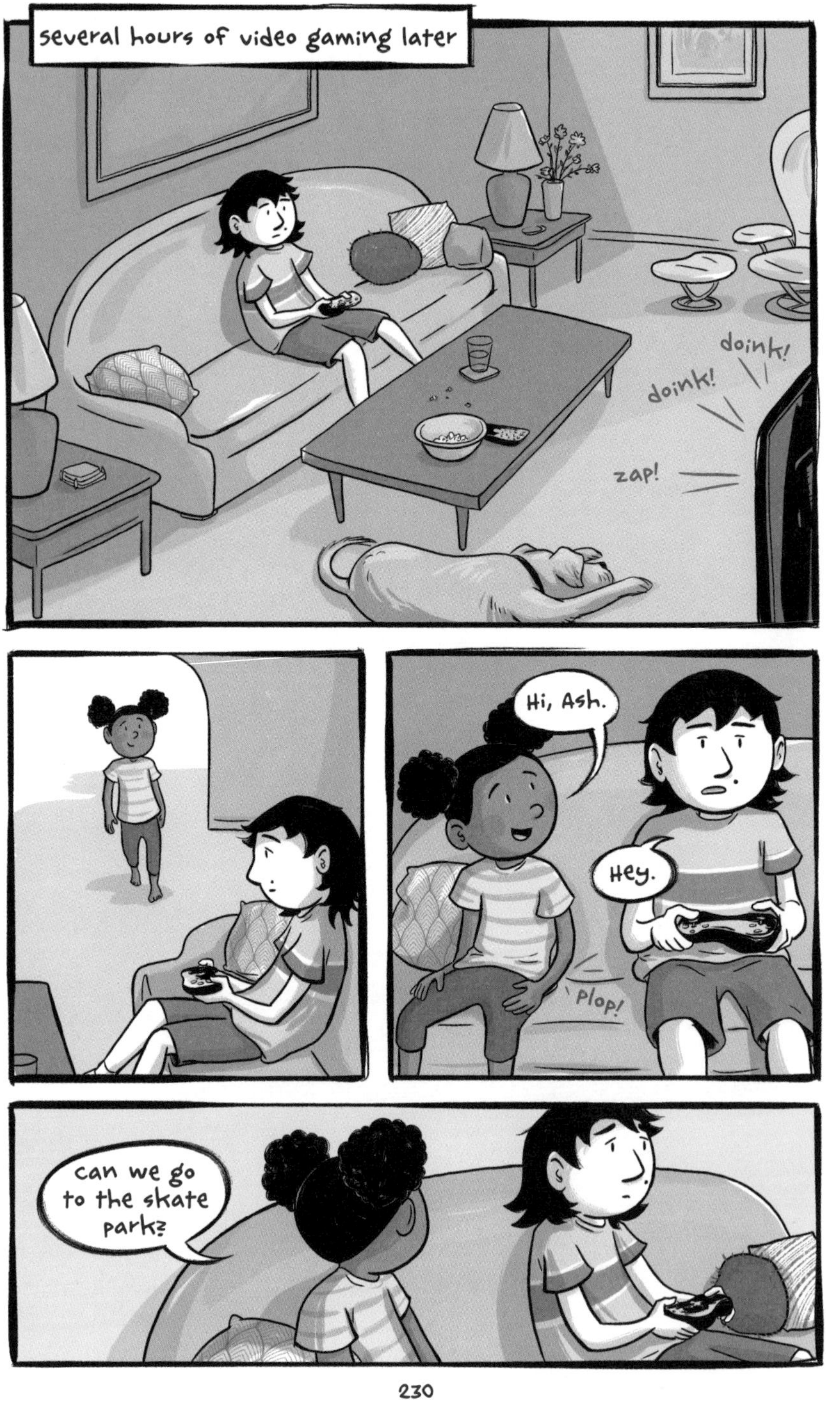
several hours of video gaming later
doink!
doink!
zap!
Hi, Ash.
Hey.
Plop!
can we go to the skate park?

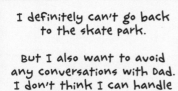

I definitely can't go back to the skate park.

But I also want to avoid any conversations with Dad. I don't think I can handle it if he brings up Cooper.

Let's just work on some stuff here.

You can try the ramps that Dad built for us.

Okay.

I'm going to go grab my board!

'Kay. Just let me finish this game.

sigh

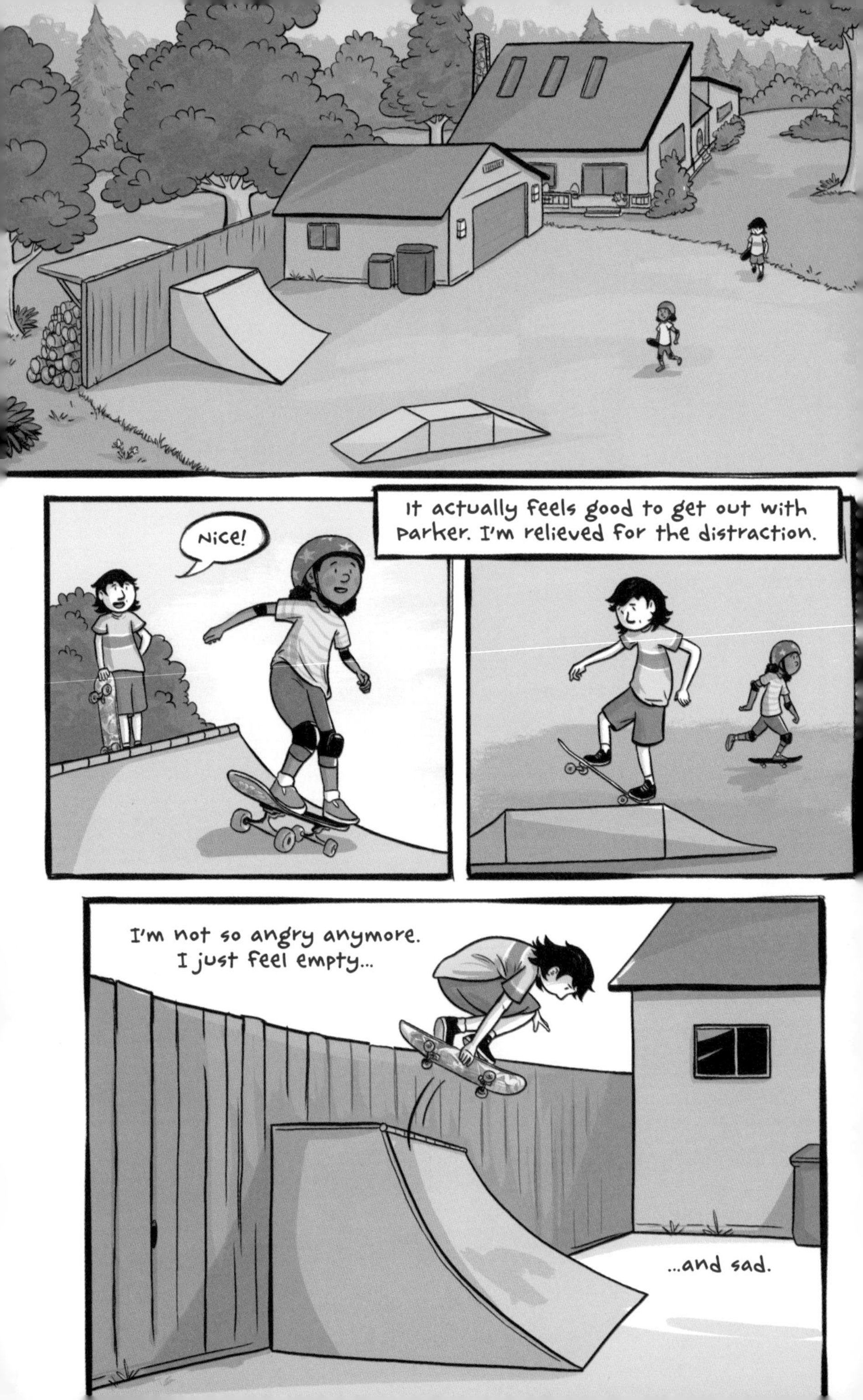
It actually feels good to get out with Parker. I'm relieved for the distraction.
Nice!
I'm not so angry anymore. I just feel empty...
...and sad.

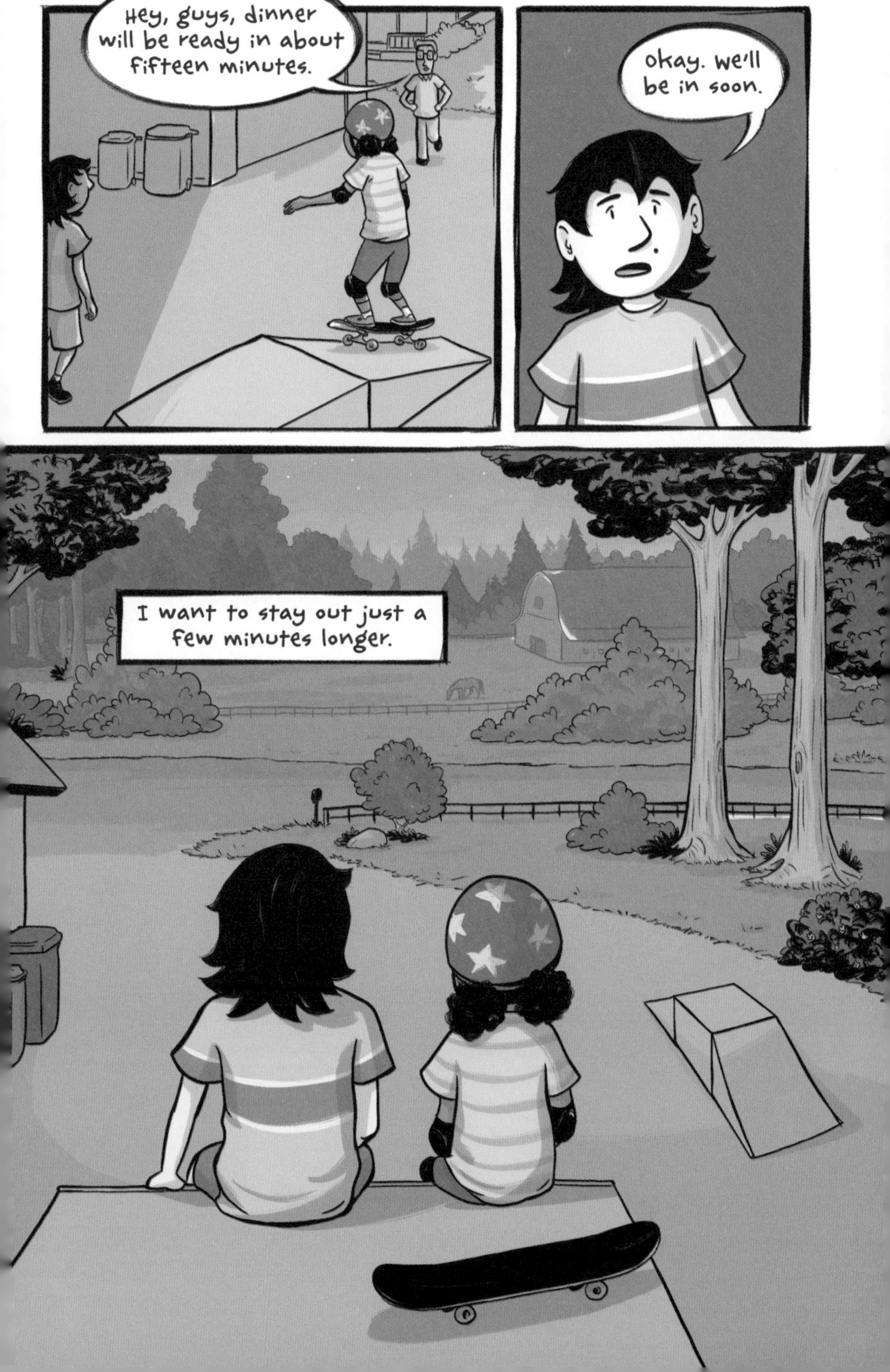
Hey, guys, dinner will be ready in about fifteen minutes.
Okay. We'll be in soon.
I want to stay out just a few minutes longer.

CHAPTER 9

• ROXY •

A sweet pit bull known for her vicious lick attacks and under-the-blanket cuddles. Despite their negative reputation as being dangerous, pitties are loving dogs and sometimes nicknamed the "Nanny Dog" due to their particular affection toward children and inclination to protect them.

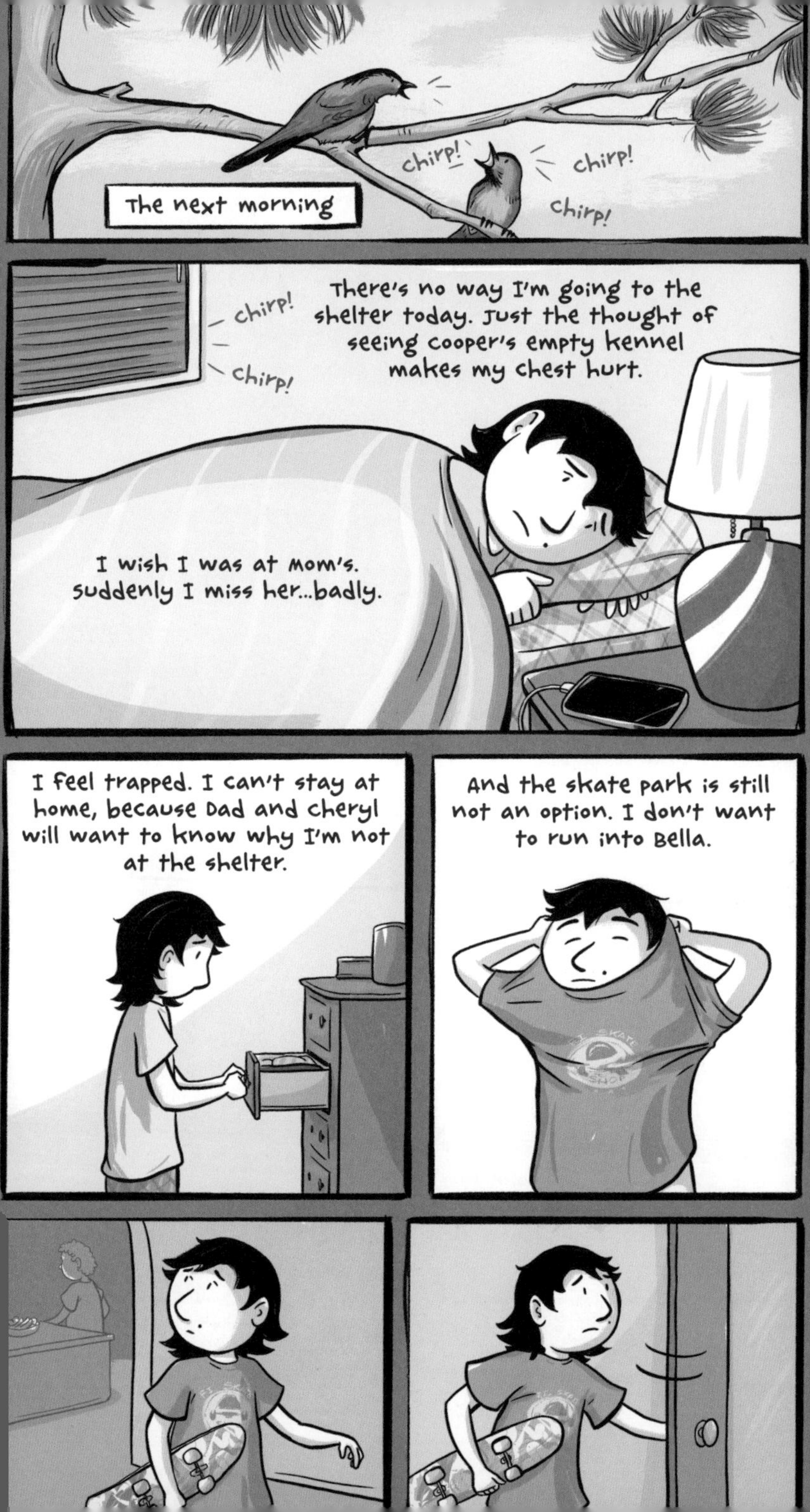
The next morning
chirp!
chirp!
chirp!
chirp!
chirp!
There's no way I'm going to the shelter today. Just the thought of seeing Cooper's empty kennel makes my chest hurt.
I wish I was at Mom's. Suddenly I miss her...badly.
I feel trapped. I can't stay at home, because Dad and Cheryl will want to know why I'm not at the shelter.
And the skate park is still not an option. I don't want to run into Bella.

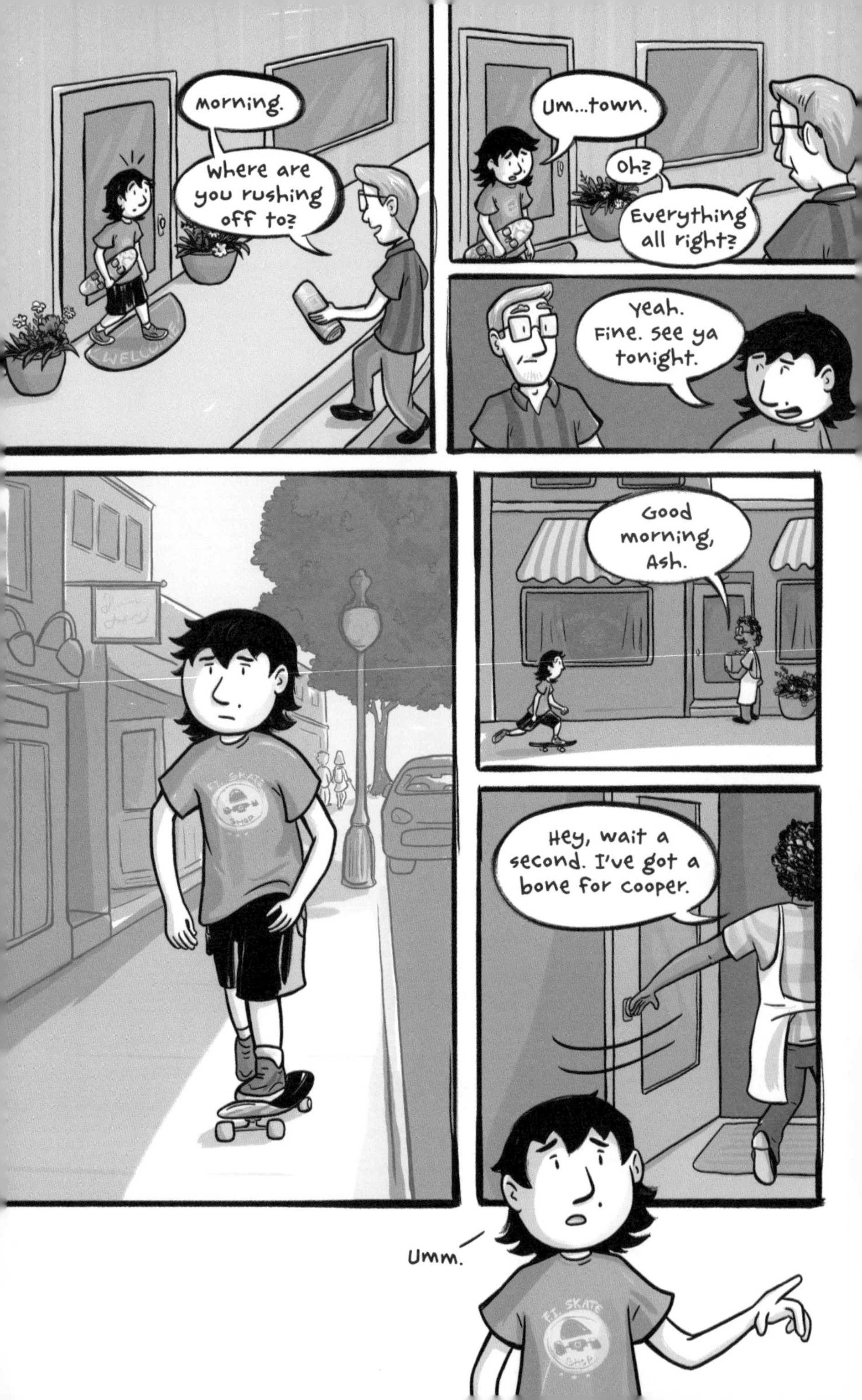
Morning.
Where are you rushing off to?
Um...town.
Oh?
Everything all right?
Yeah. Fine. See ya tonight.
Good morning, Ash.
Hey, wait a second. I've got a bone for Cooper.
Umm.

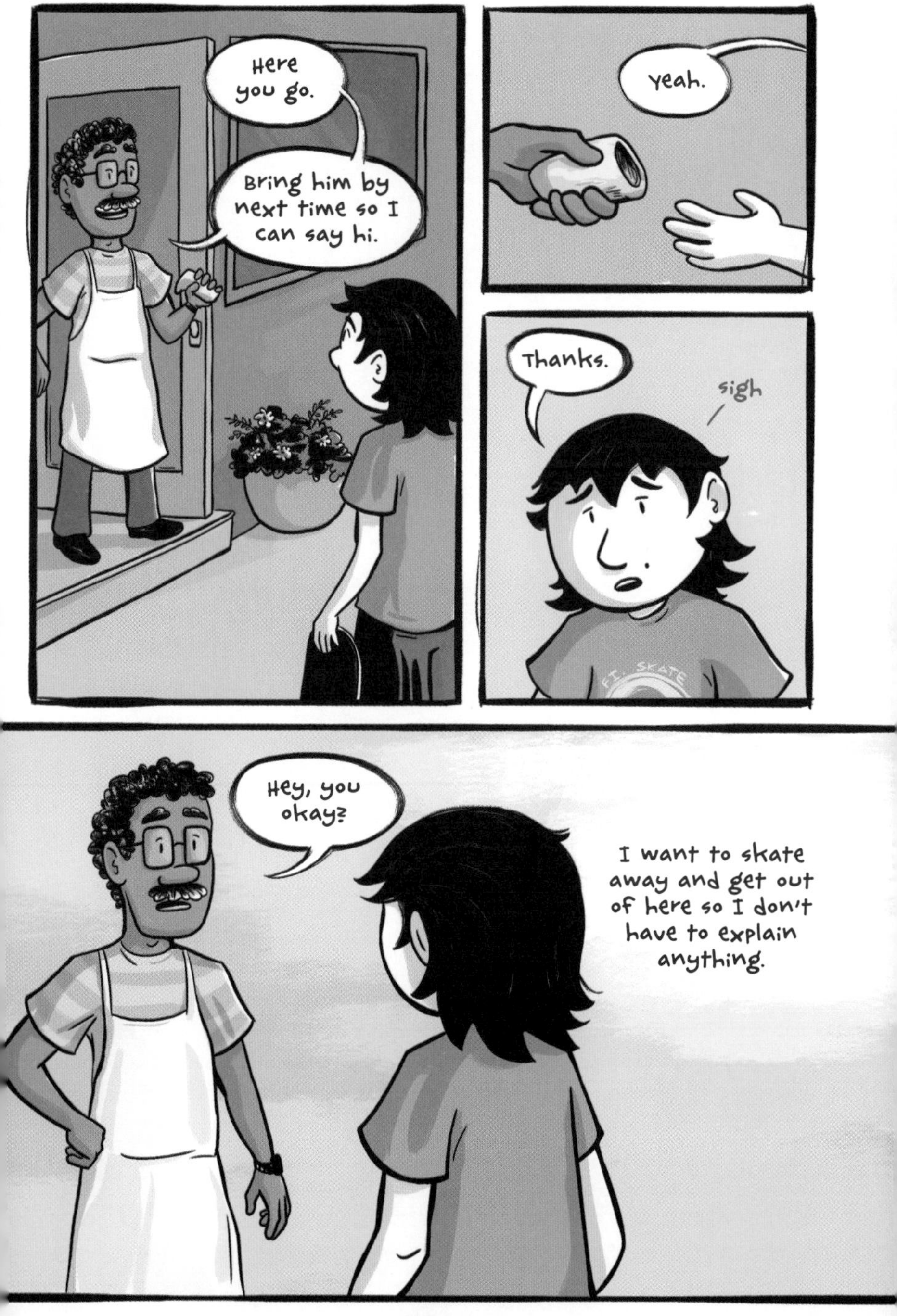
Here you go.
Bring him by next time so I can say hi.
Yeah.
Thanks.
sigh
Hey, you okay?
I want to skate away and get out of here so I don't have to explain anything.
F.T. SKATE

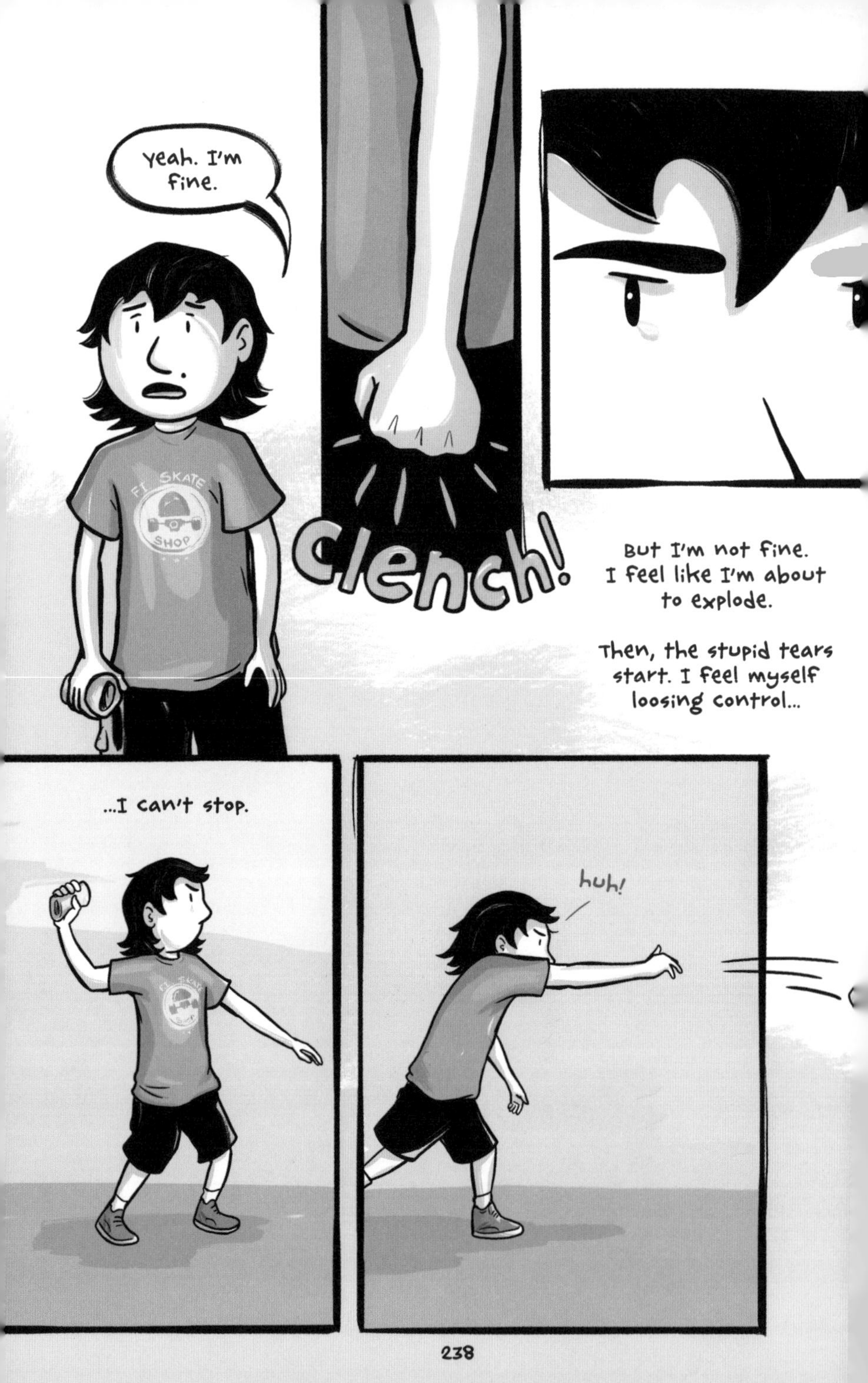
Yeah. I'm fine.
CLENCH!
But I'm not fine. I feel like I'm about to explode.
Then, the stupid tears start. I feel myself loosing control...
...I can't stop.
huh!

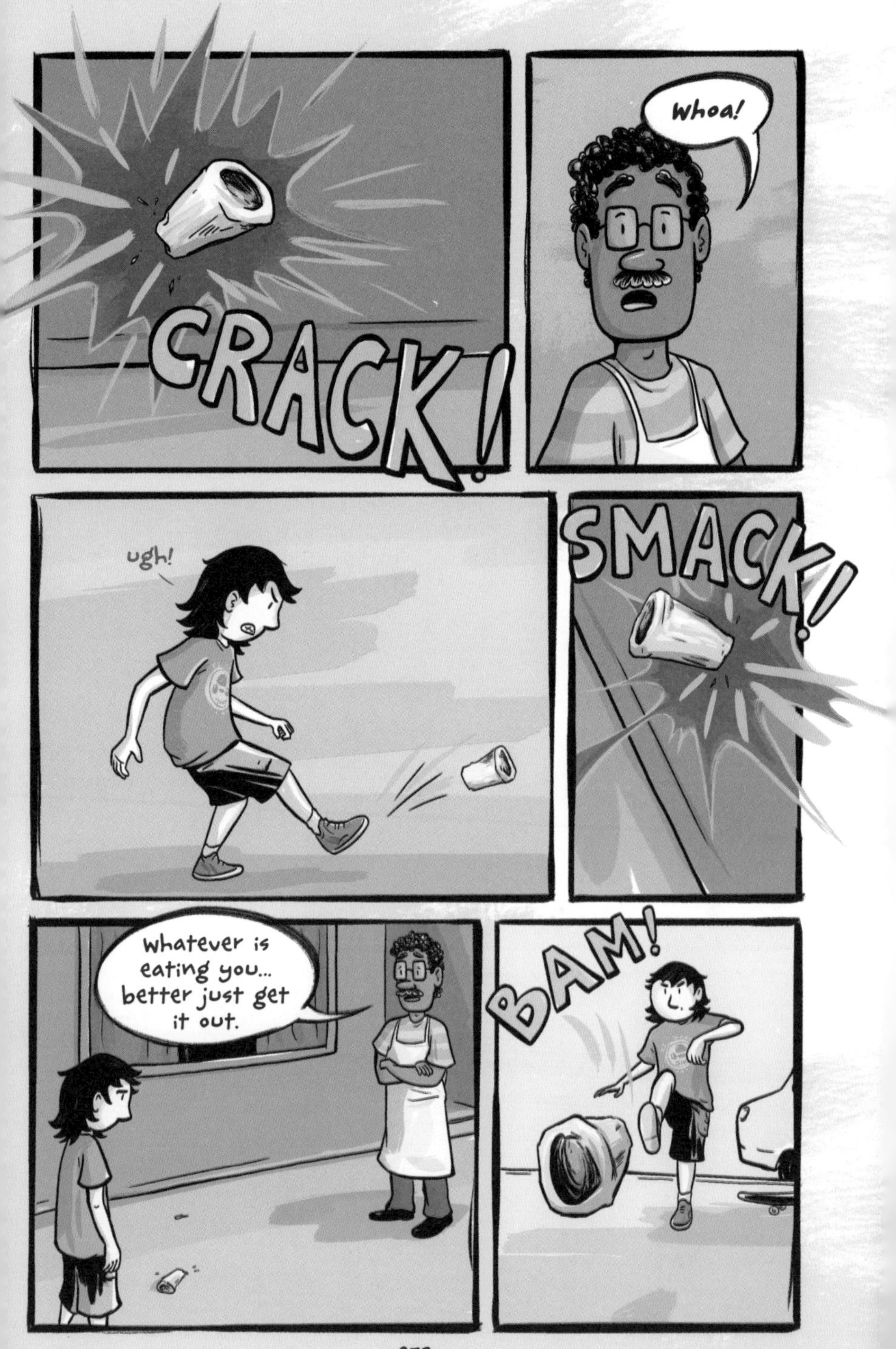
CRACK!
Whoa!
ugh!
SMACK!
Whatever is eating you... better just get it out.
BAM!

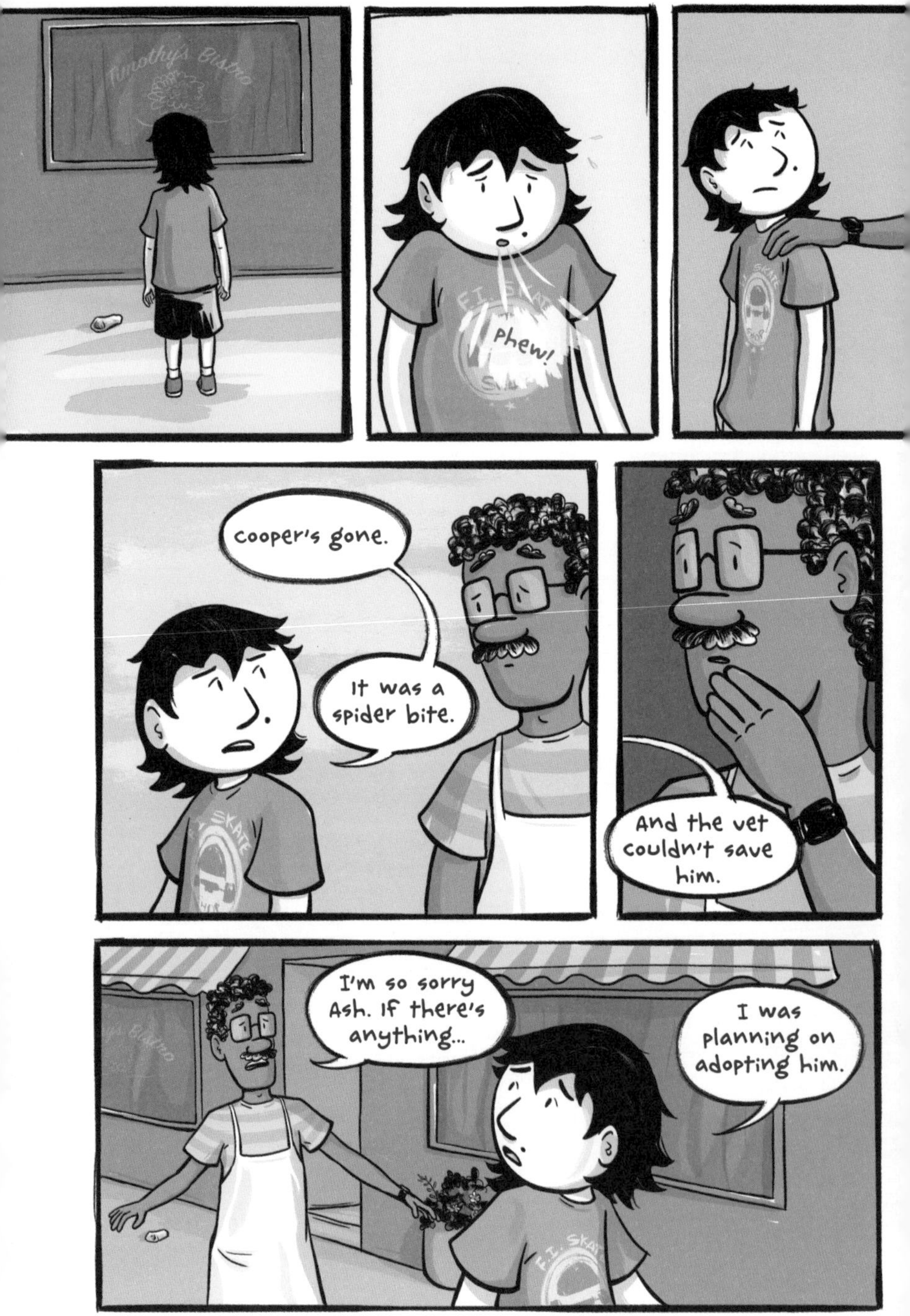
Timothy's Bistro
Phew!
cooper's gone.
It was a spider bite.
And the vet couldn't save him.
I'm so sorry Ash. If there's anything...
I was planning on adopting him.

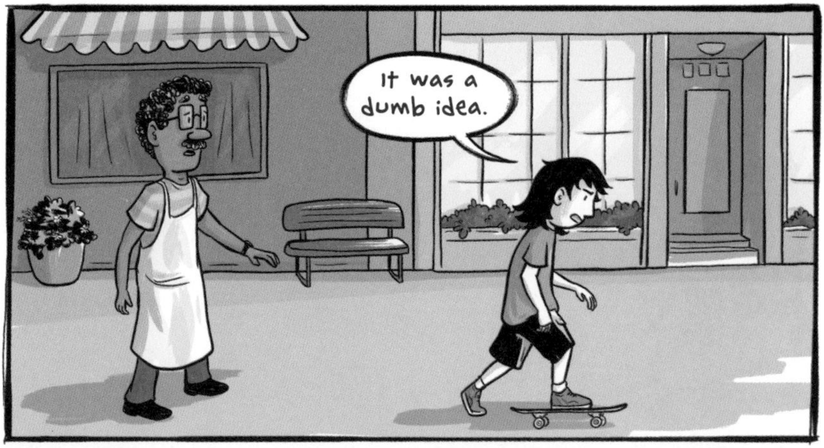
It was a dumb idea.

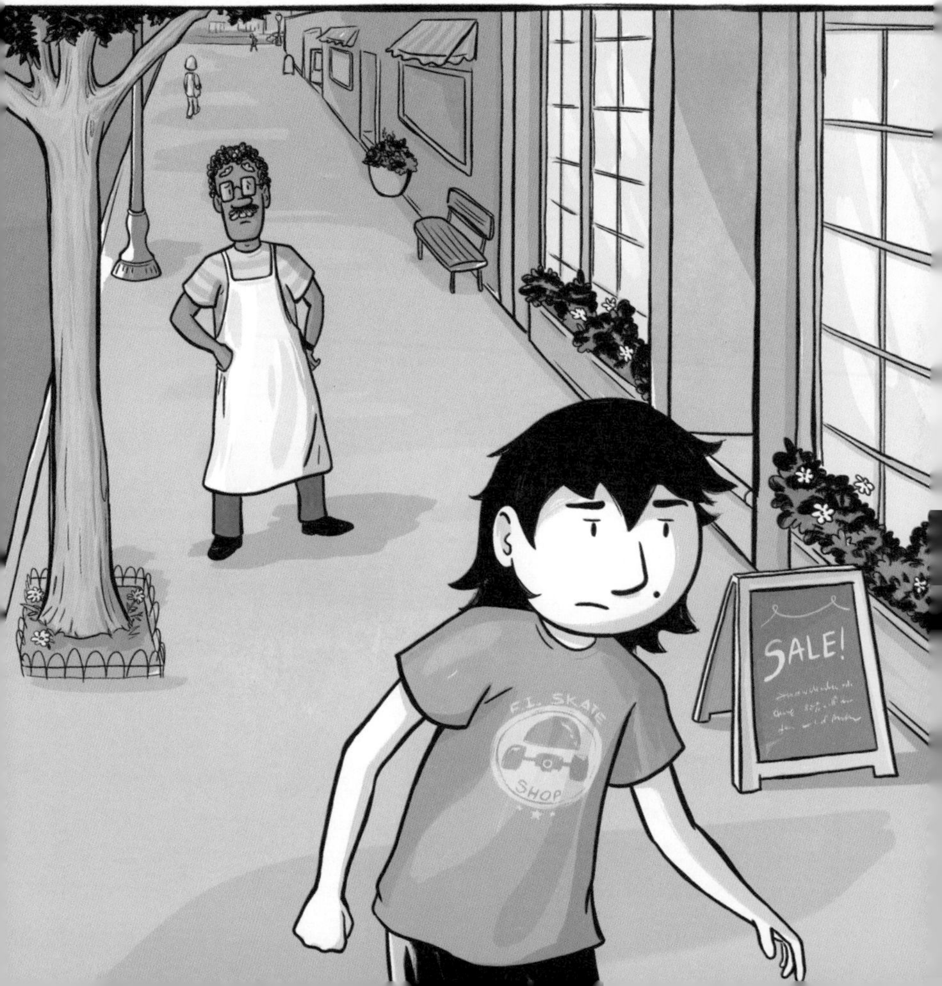
SALE!
F.I. SKATE
SHOP

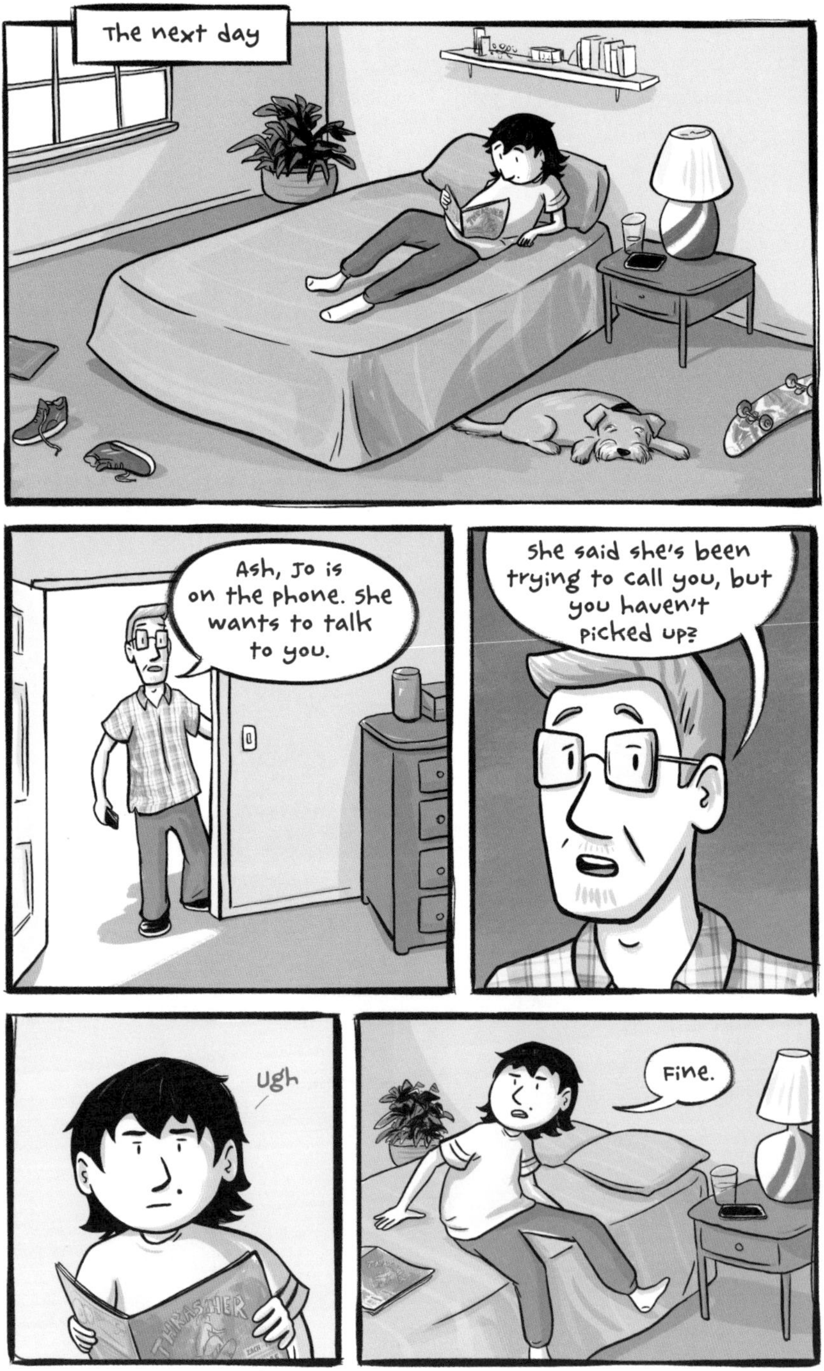
The next day
Ash, Jo is on the phone. She wants to talk to you.
She said she's been trying to call you, but you haven't picked up?
Ugh
THRASHER
Fine.

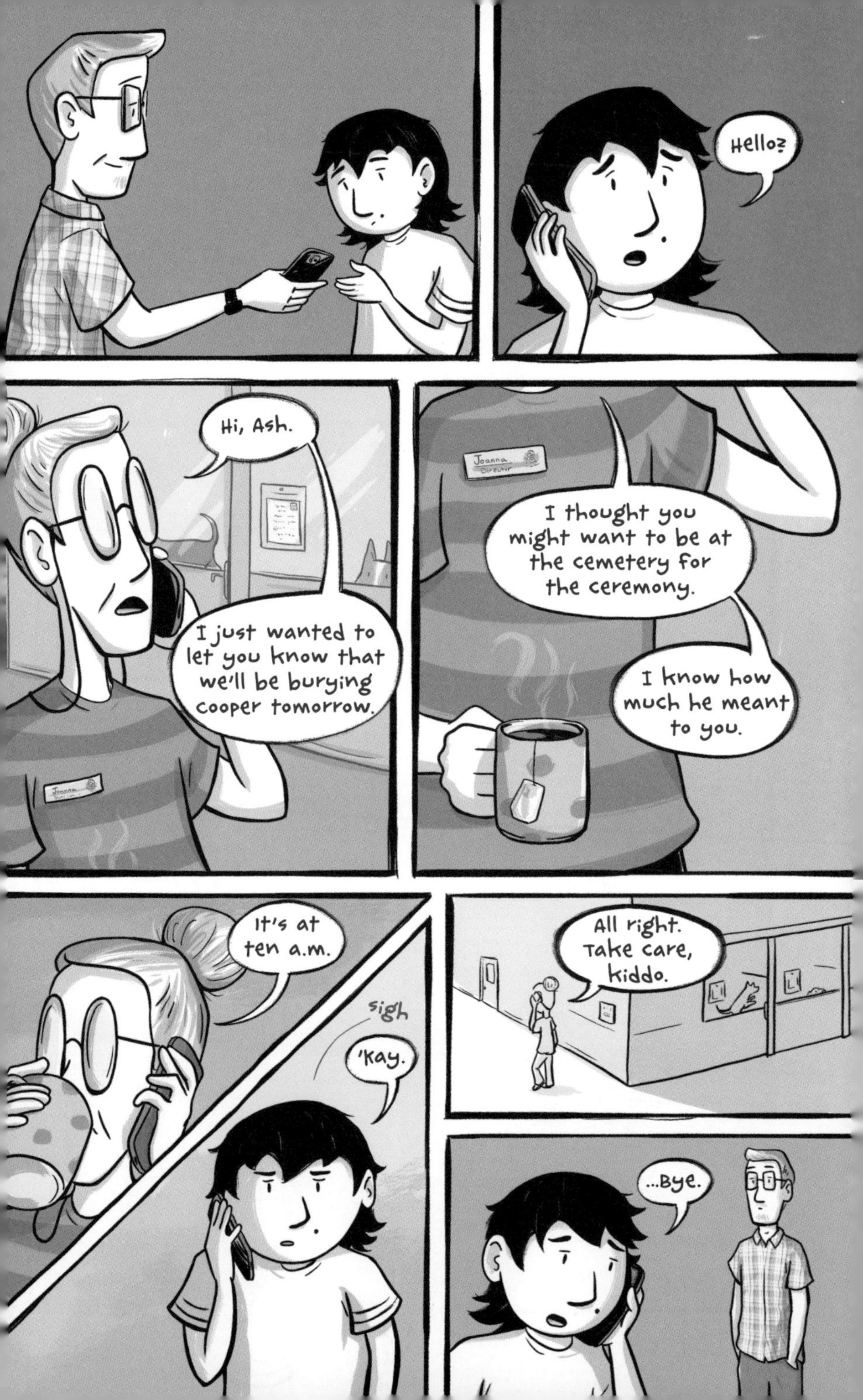
Hello?
Hi, Ash.
I just wanted to let you know that we'll be burying cooper tomorrow.
Joanna
Director
I thought you might want to be at the cemetery for the ceremony.
I know how much he meant to you.
It's at ten a.m.
sigh
'Kay.
All right. Take care, kiddo.
...Bye.

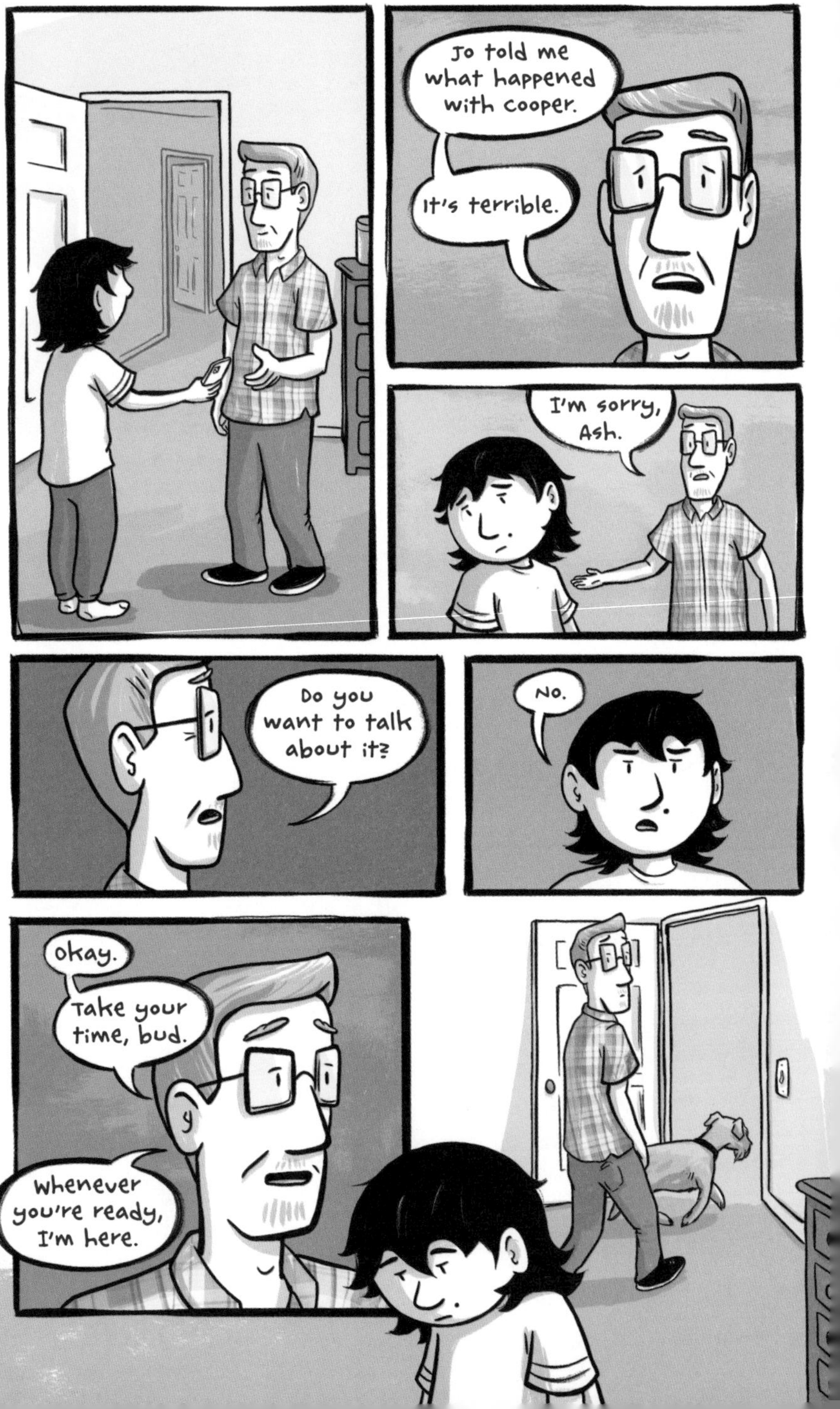
Jo told me what happened with cooper.
It's terrible.
I'm sorry, Ash.
Do you want to talk about it?
No.
okay.
Take your time, bud.
Whenever you're ready, I'm here.

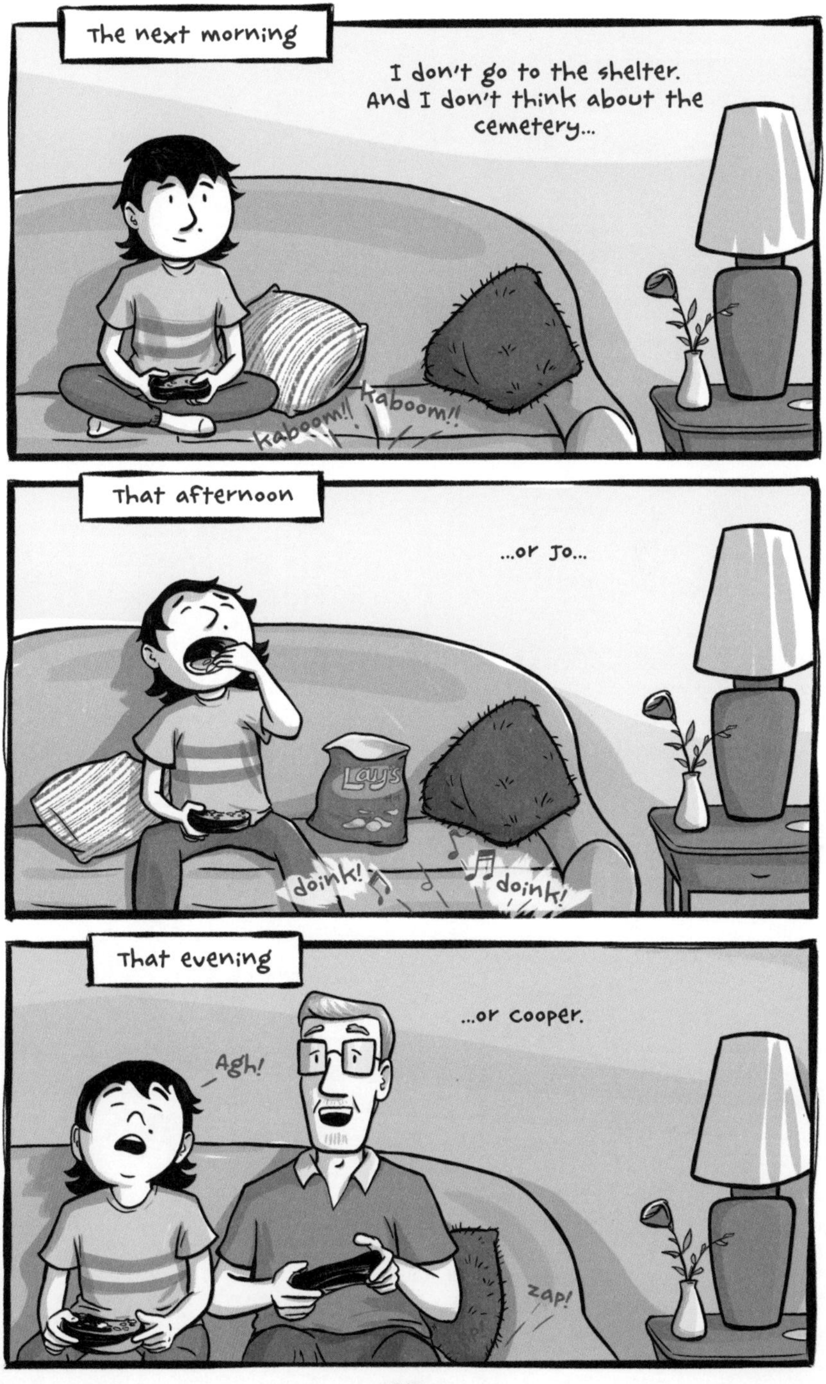
The next morning
I don't go to the shelter. And I don't think about the cemetery...
kaboom!!
kaboom!!
That afternoon
...or Jo...
Lay's
doink!
doink!
That evening
...or cooper.
Agh!
zap!

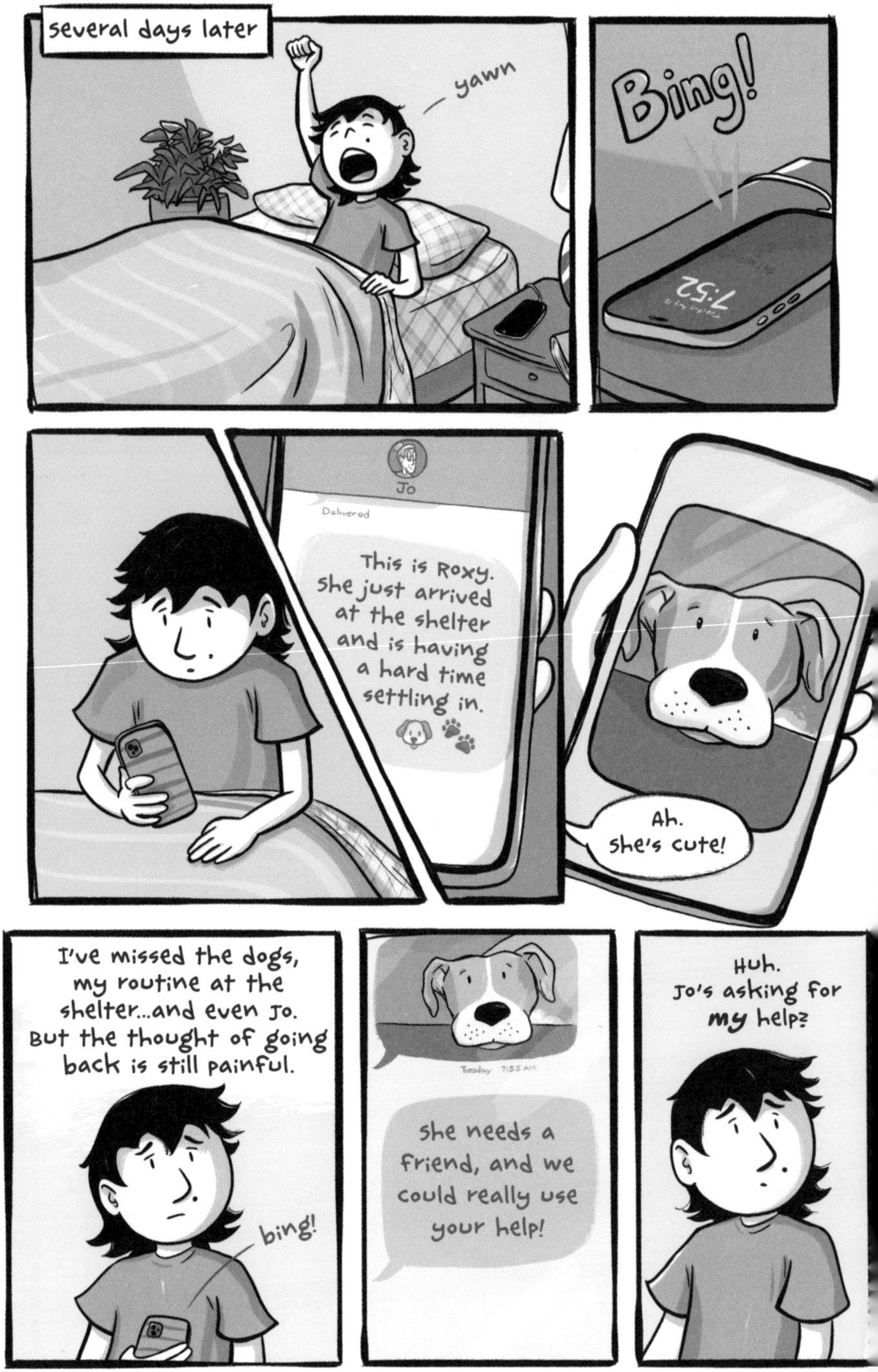
several days later
yawn
Bing!
7:52
Jo
Delivered
This is Roxy. She just arrived at the shelter and is having a hard time settling in.
Ah. She's cute!
I've missed the dogs, my routine at the shelter...and even Jo. But the thought of going back is still painful.
bing!
Tuesday 7:55 AM
She needs a friend, and we could really use your help!
Huh. Jo's asking for **my** help?

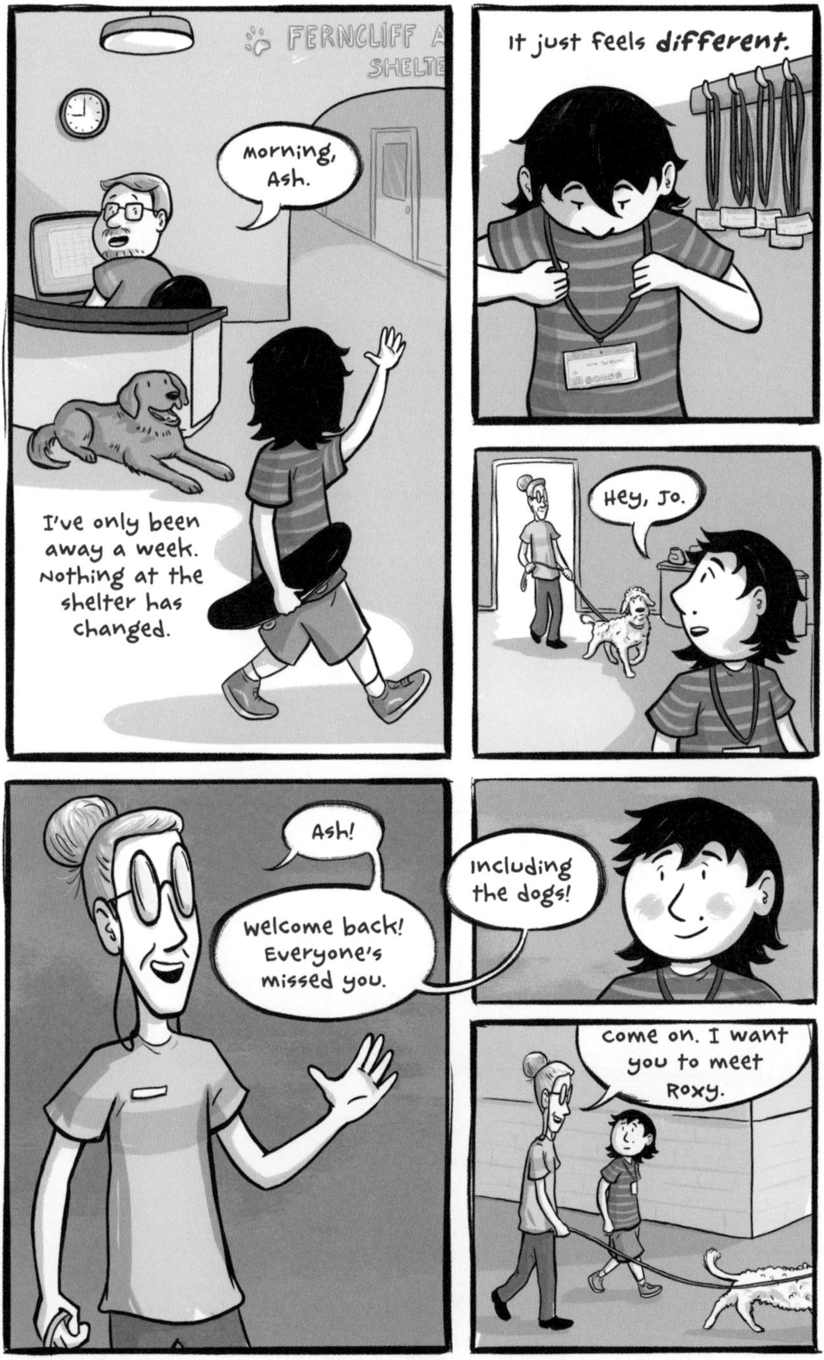
FERNCLIFF A
SHELTE
Morning, Ash.
I've only been away a week. Nothing at the shelter has changed.
It just feels different.
Hey, Jo.
Ash!
Welcome back! Everyone's missed you.
Including the dogs!
Come on. I want you to meet Roxy.

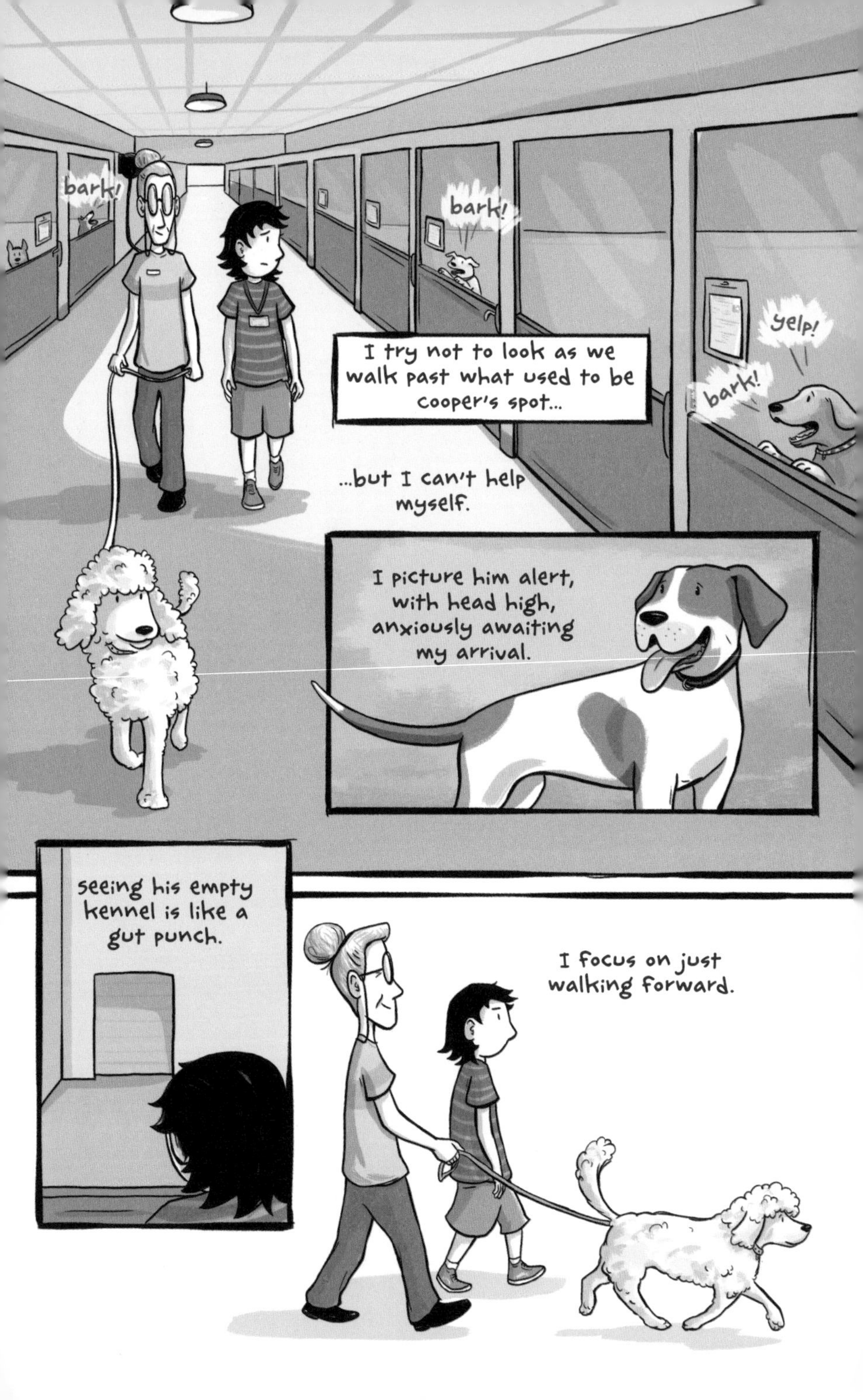
bark!
bark!
yelp!
bark!
I try not to look as we walk past what used to be cooper's spot...
...but I can't help myself.
I picture him alert, with head high, anxiously awaiting my arrival.
seeing his empty kennel is like a gut punch.
I focus on just walking forward.

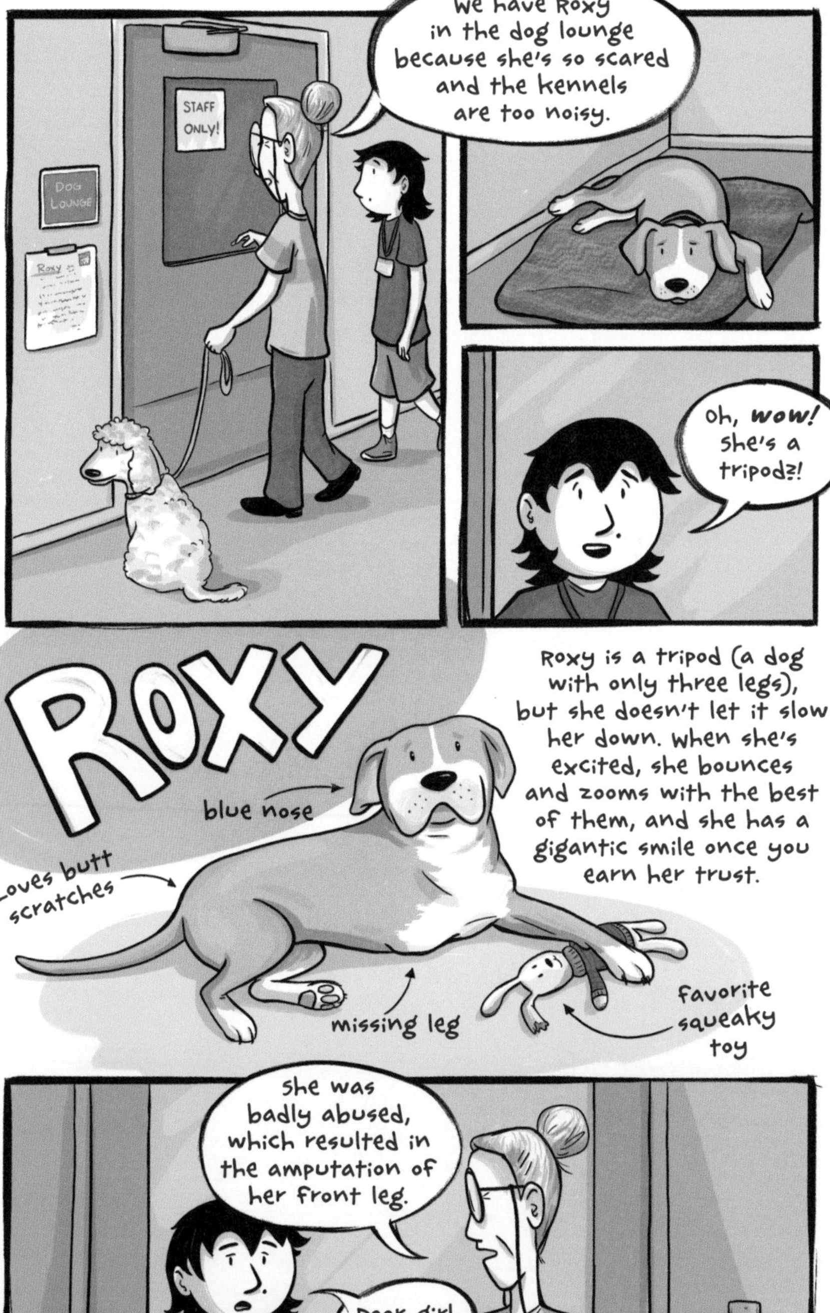
We have Roxy in the dog lounge because she's so scared and the kennels are too noisy.
STAFF ONLY!
DOG LOUNGE
Roxy
Oh, wow! She's a tripod?!
ROXY
Roxy is a tripod (a dog with only three legs), but she doesn't let it slow her down. When she's excited, she bounces and zooms with the best of them, and she has a gigantic smile once you earn her trust.
blue nose
Loves butt scratches
missing leg
favorite squeaky toy
She was badly abused, which resulted in the amputation of her front leg.
Poor girl.

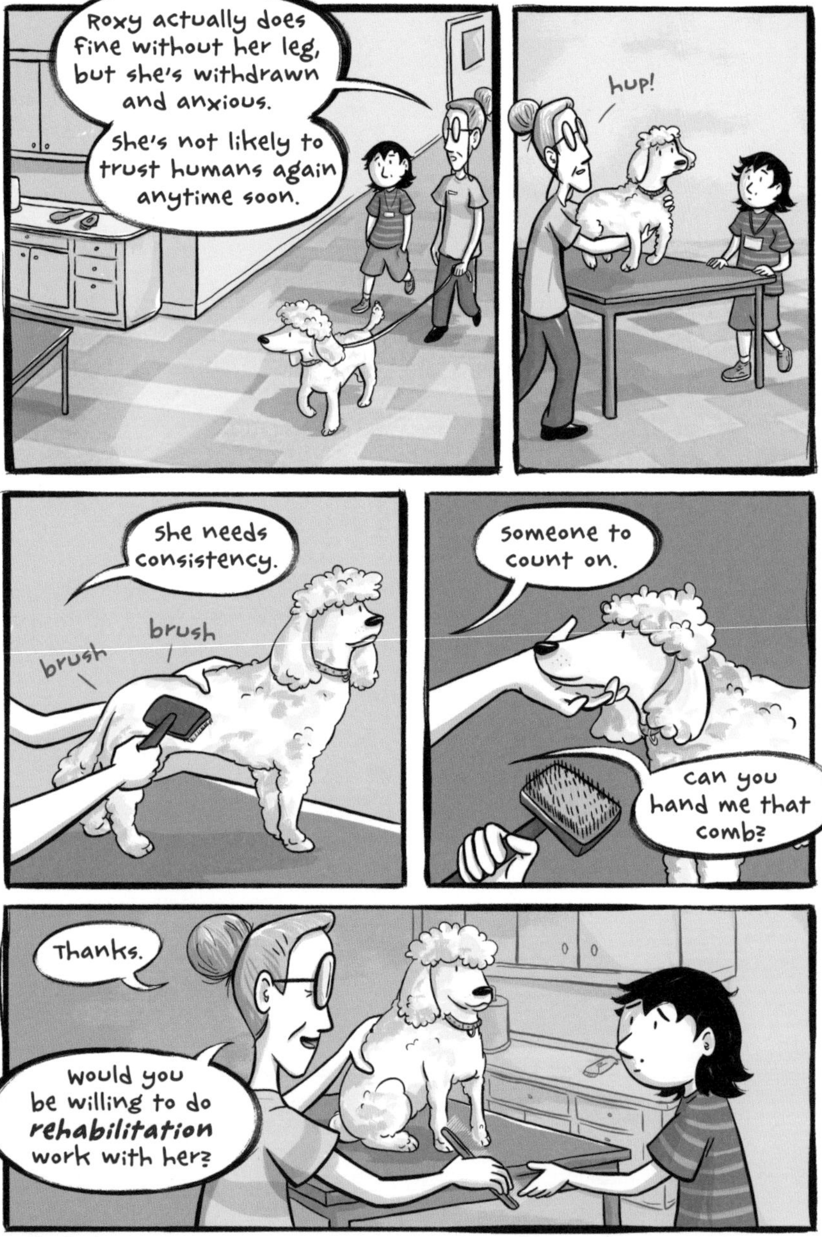
Roxy actually does fine without her leg, but she's withdrawn and anxious.
She's not likely to trust humans again anytime soon.
hup!
She needs consistency.
brush
brush
Someone to count on.
Can you hand me that comb?
Thanks.
Would you be willing to do rehabilitation work with her?

Rehabilitation: Training techniques that restore healthy behavior and readjust dogs after suffering from abuse. This process can take weeks or months depending upon the severity of each dog's behavioral problems and how well they respond to treatment.

me?!

yeah. you.

Uhmm

I think of all the screwups I've already had with dogs this summer. cody, Bogie, sheeba...cooper.

I can't bear another one!

I'm asking you to do this because I saw the amazing work you did with cooper.

He was a different dog when he first came to the shelter.

The devotion of daily care and love that you gave him shaped him into the good boy that everyone now misses.

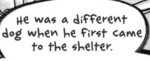

Your love changed that dog.

And you can do it again.

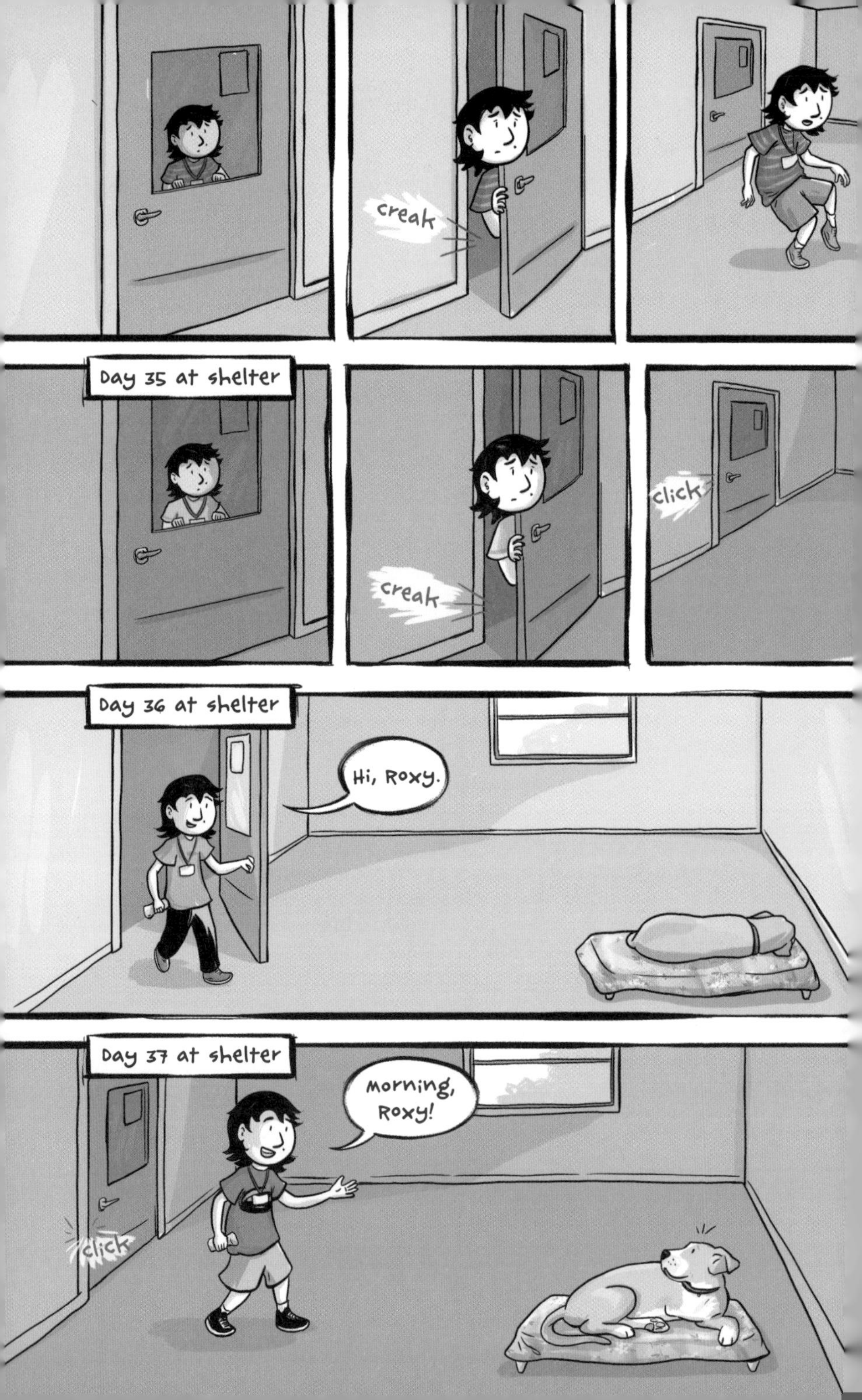
creak
Day 35 at shelter
creak
click
Day 36 at shelter
Hi, Roxy.
Day 37 at shelter
Morning, Roxy!
click

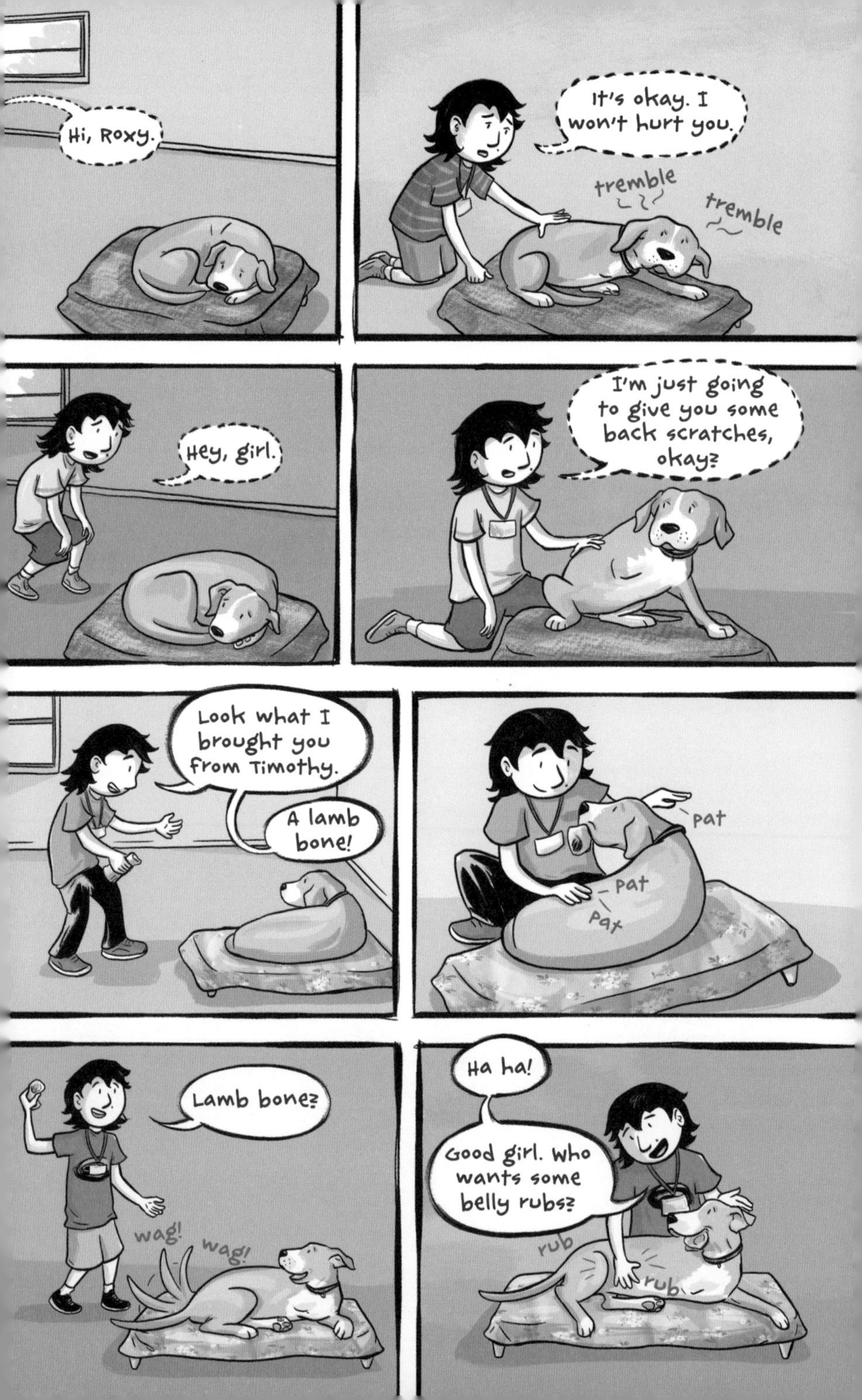
Hi, Roxy.
It's okay. I won't hurt you.
tremble
tremble
Hey, girl.
I'm just going to give you some back scratches, okay?
Look what I brought you from Timothy.
A lamb bone!
pat
pat
pat
Lamb bone?
wag!
wag!
Ha ha!
Good girl. Who wants some belly rubs?
rub
rub

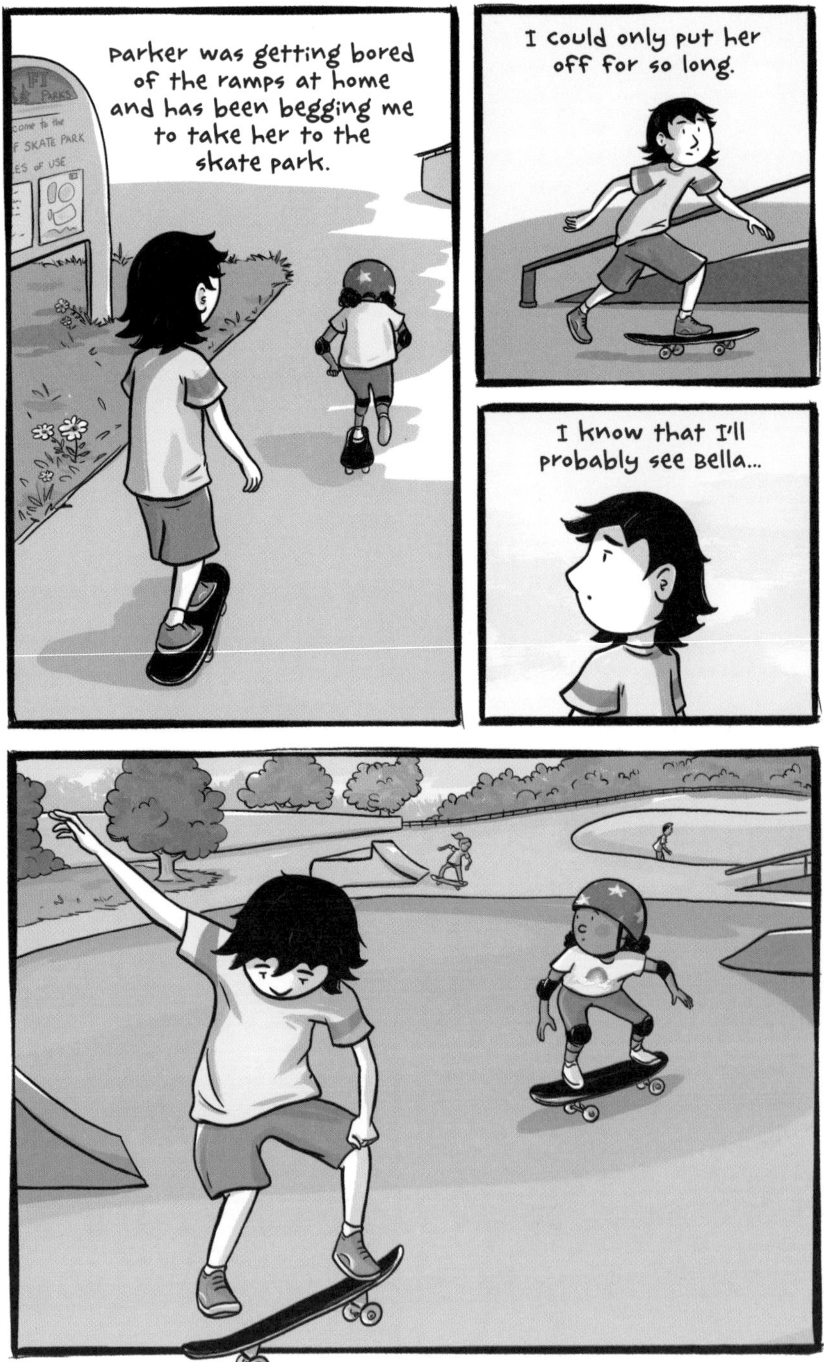
Parker was getting bored of the ramps at home and has been begging me to take her to the skate park.
I could only put her off for so long.
I know that I'll probably see Bella...

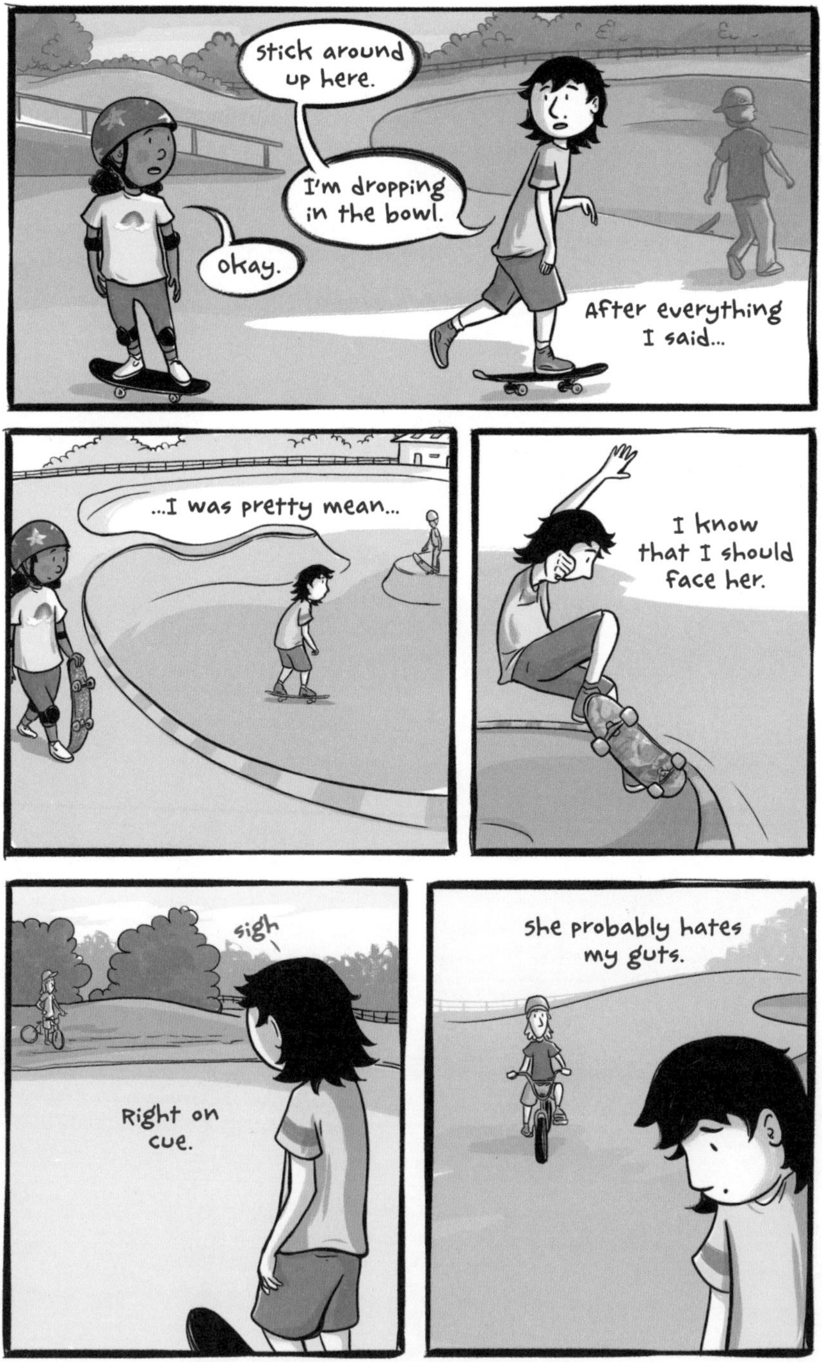
Stick around
up here.
I'm dropping
in the bowl.
Okay.
After everything
I said...
...I was pretty mean...
I know
that I should
face her.
sigh
Right on
cue.
She probably hates
my guts.

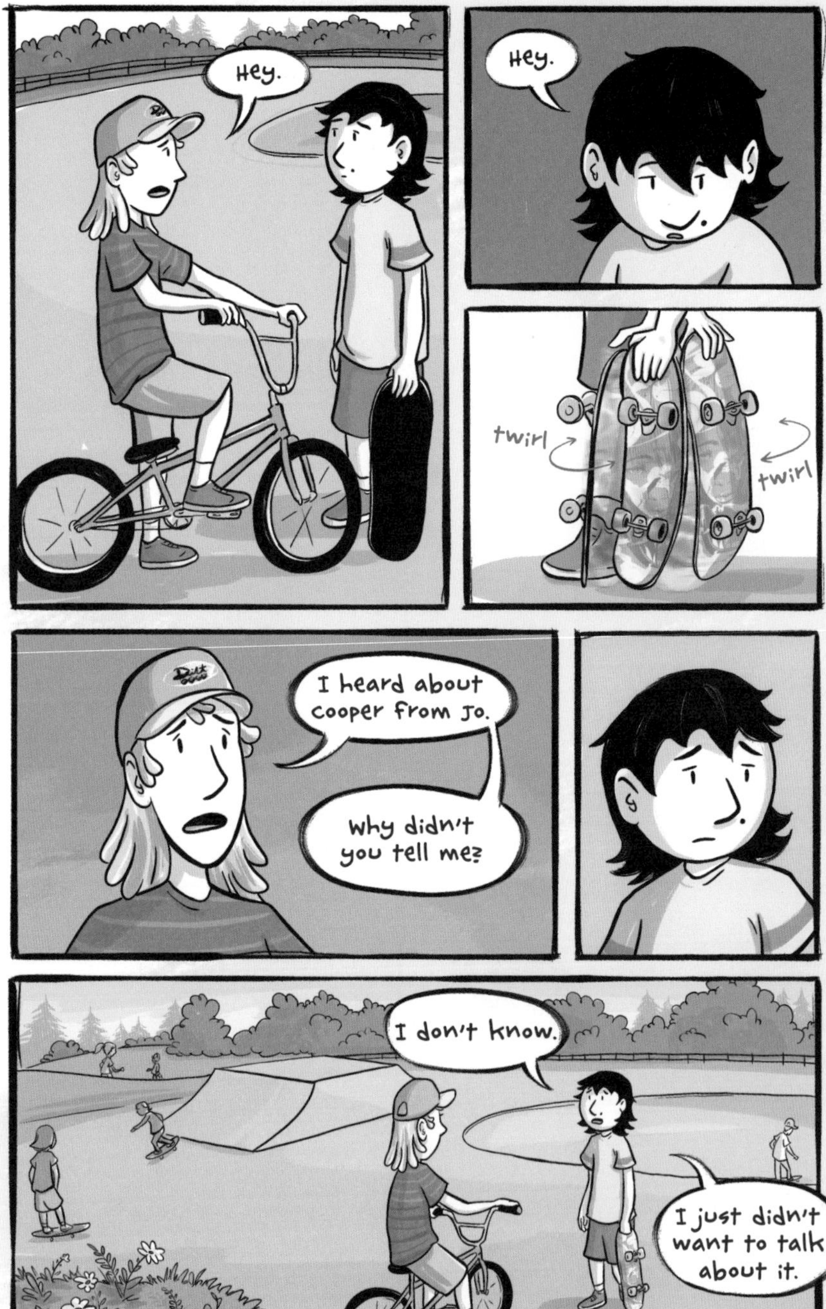
Hey.
Hey.
twirl
twirl
I heard about cooper from Jo.
Why didn't you tell me?
I don't know.
I just didn't want to talk about it.

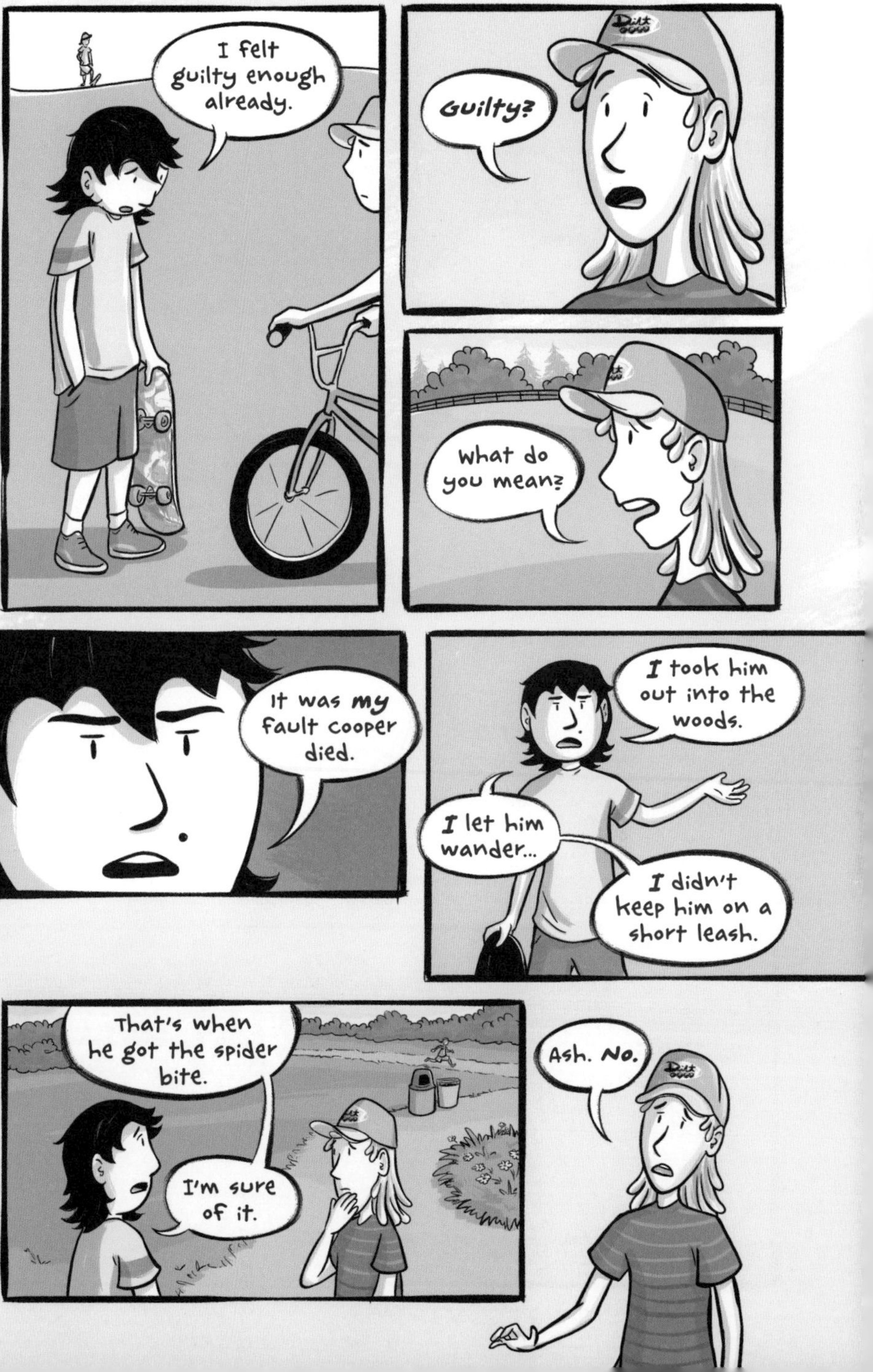
I felt guilty enough already.
Guilty?
What do you mean?
It was my fault cooper died.
I took him out into the woods.
I let him wander...
I didn't keep him on a short leash.
That's when he got the spider bite.
I'm sure of it.
Ash. No.

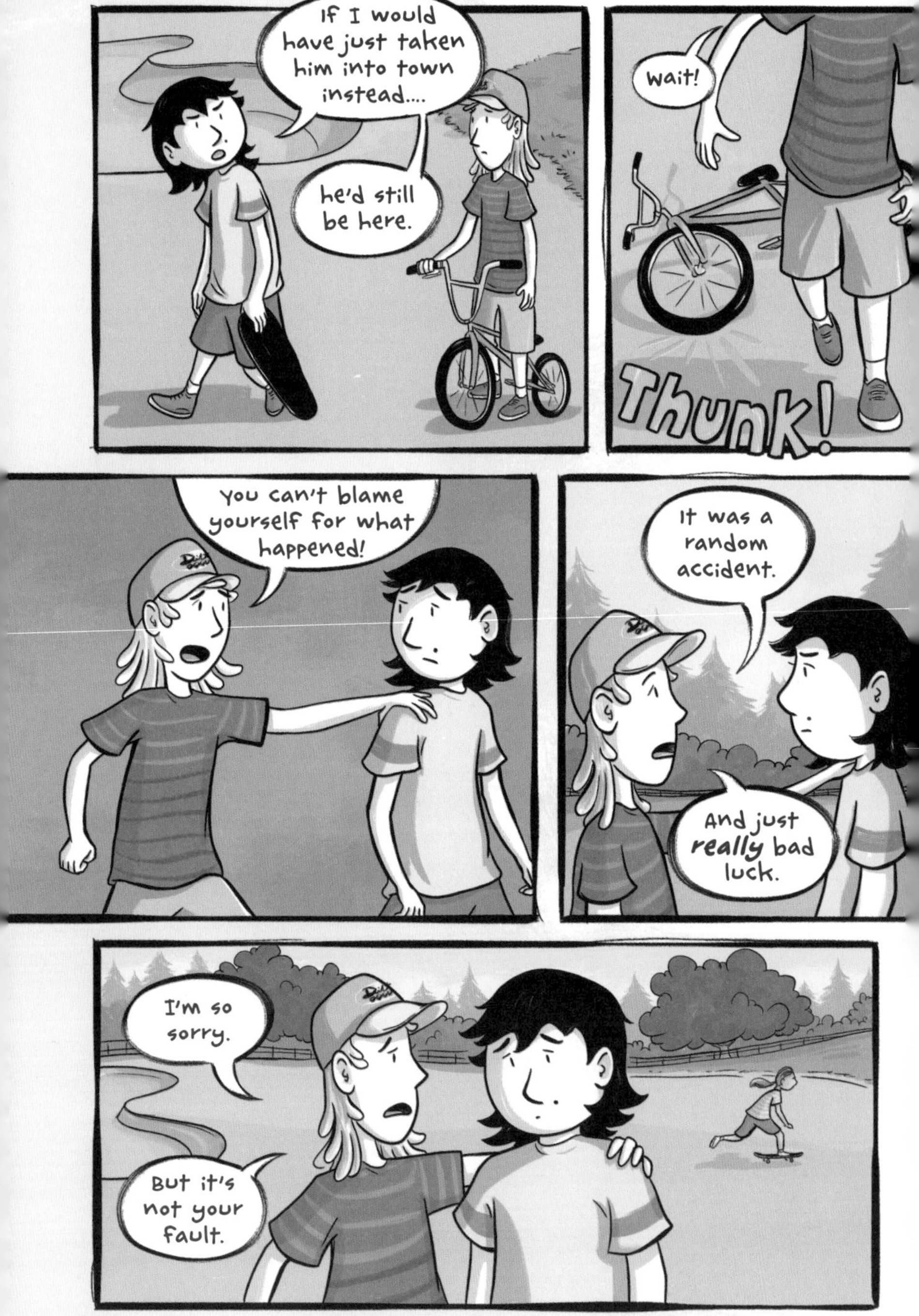
If I would have just taken him into town instead....
he'd still be here.
Wait!
THUNK!
You can't blame yourself for what happened!
It was a random accident.
And just *really* bad luck.
I'm so sorry.
But it's not your fault.

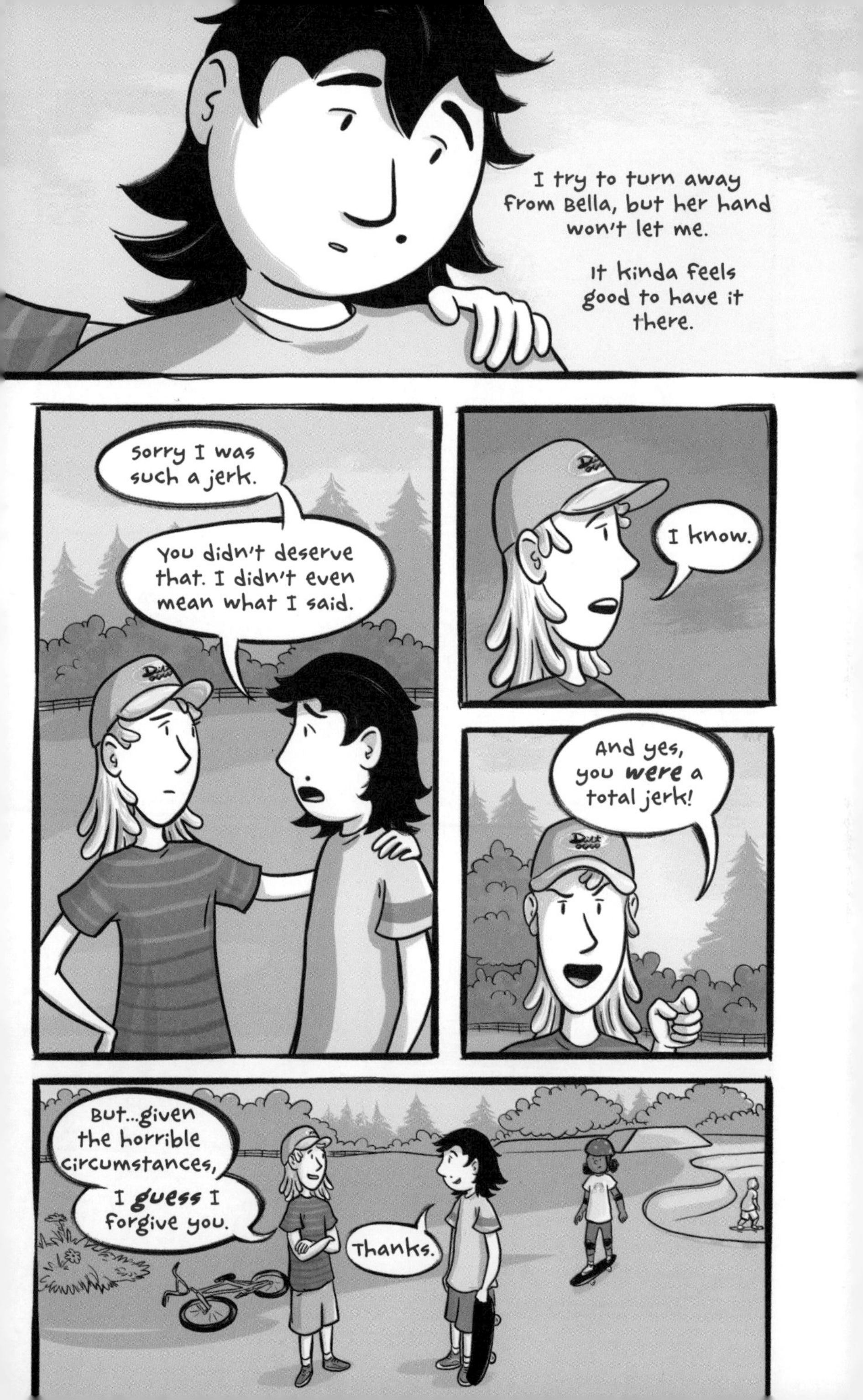
I try to turn away from Bella, but her hand won't let me.
It kinda feels good to have it there.
Sorry I was such a jerk.
You didn't deserve that. I didn't even mean what I said.
I know.
And yes, you **were** a total jerk!
But...given the horrible circumstances,
I **guess** I forgive you.
Thanks.

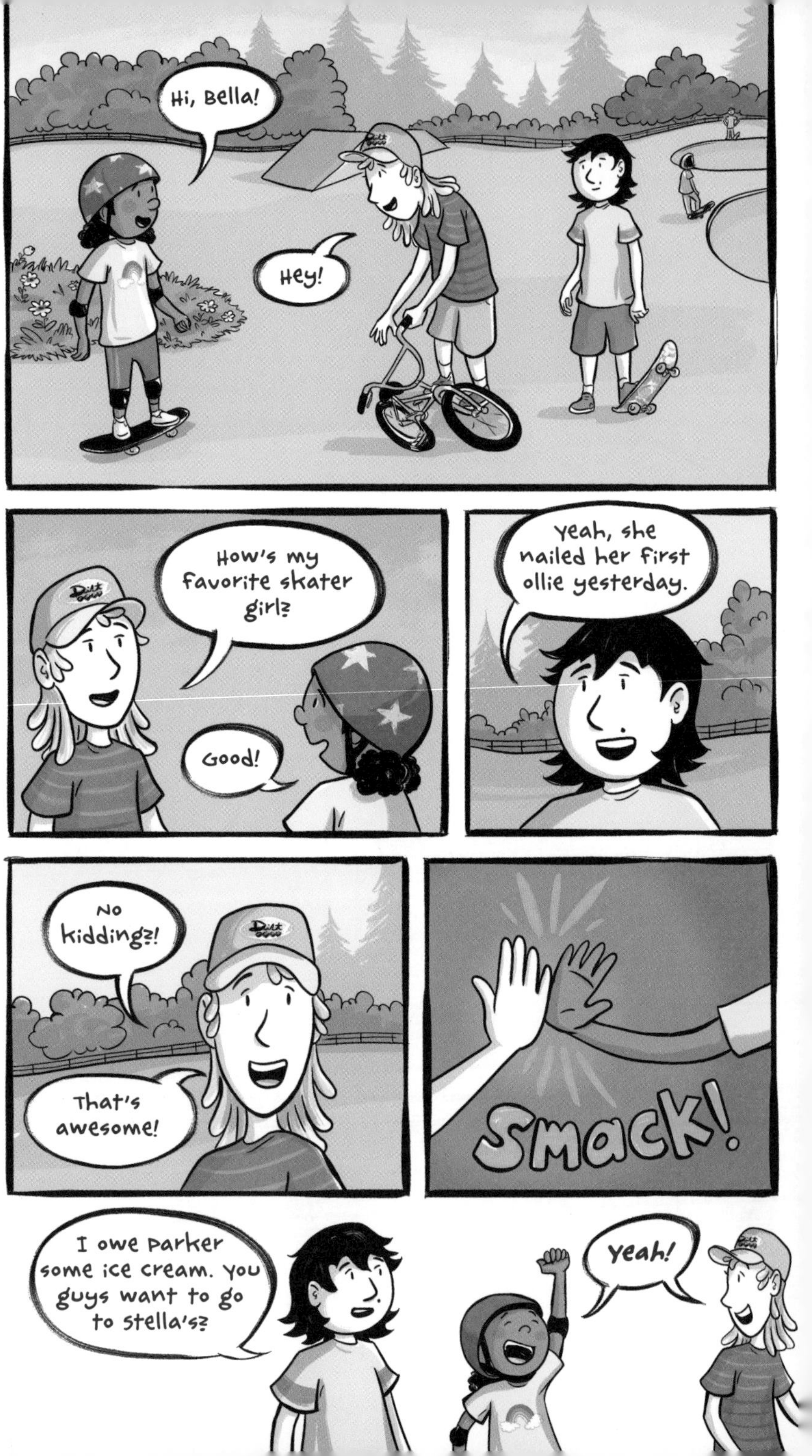
Hi, Bella!
Hey!
How's my favorite skater girl?
Good!
Yeah, she nailed her first ollie yesterday.
No kidding?!
That's awesome!
SMACK!
I owe Parker some ice cream. You guys want to go to Stella's?
Yeah!

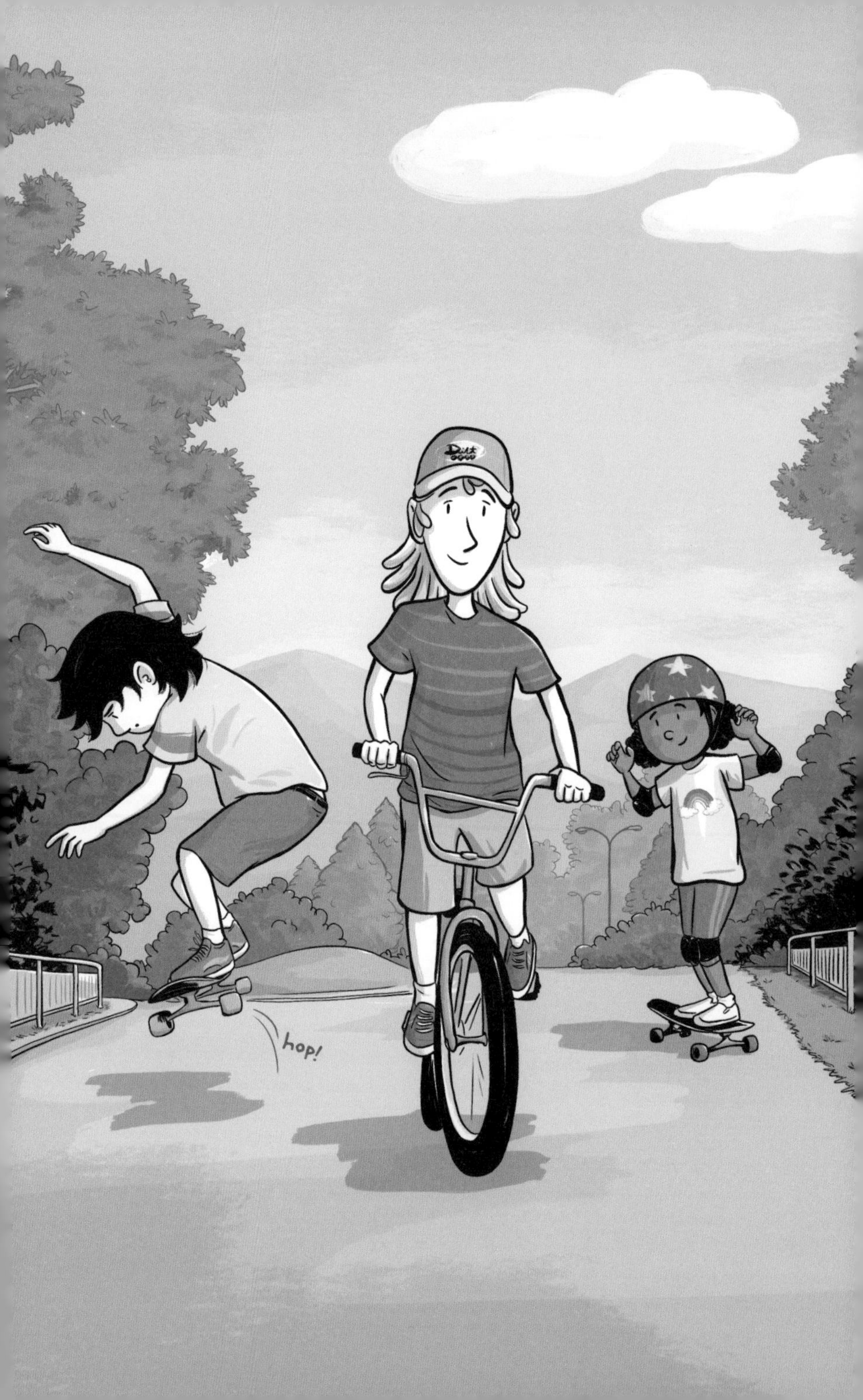
hop!

CHAPTER 10

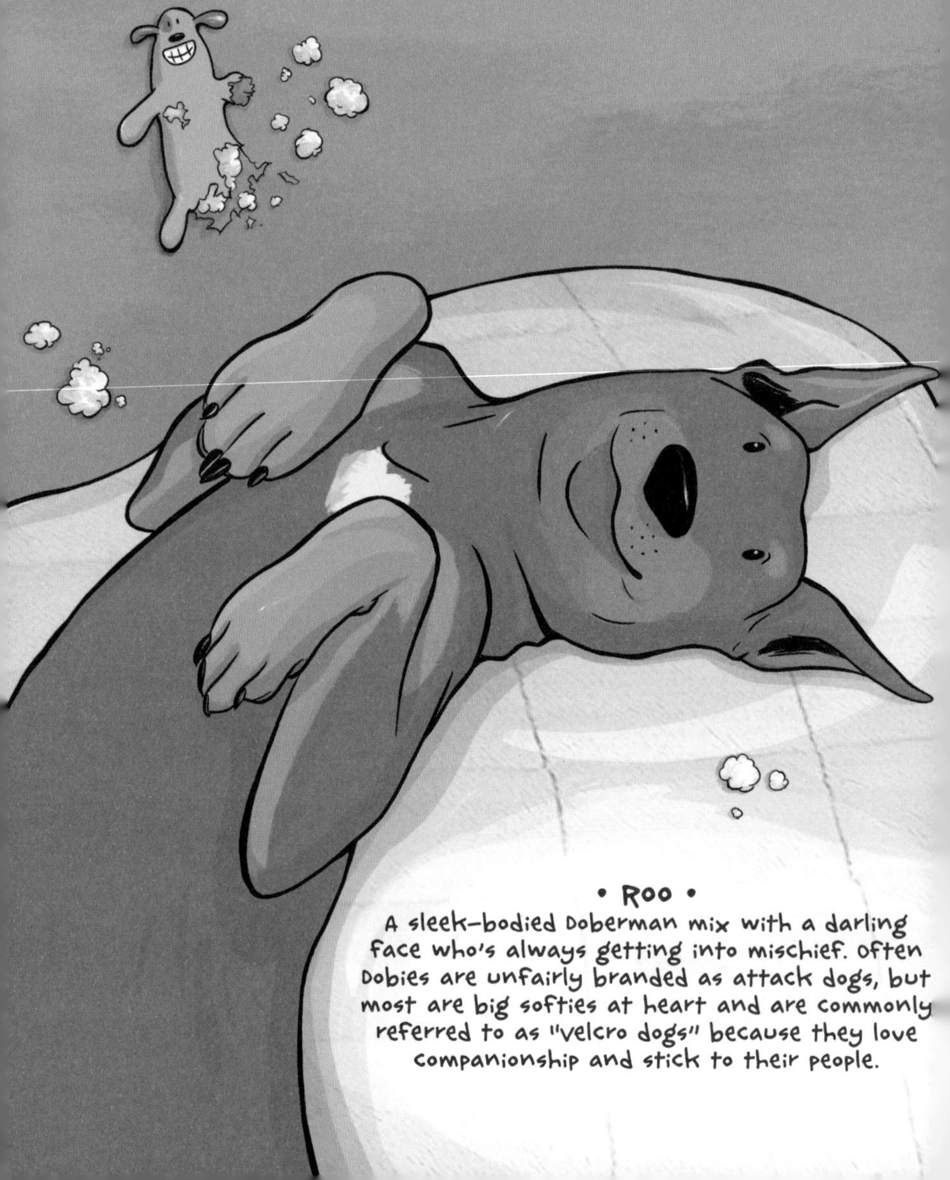

• ROO •

A sleek-bodied Doberman mix with a darling face who's always getting into mischief. Often Dobies are unfairly branded as attack dogs, but most are big softies at heart and are commonly referred to as "velcro dogs" because they love companionship and stick to their people.

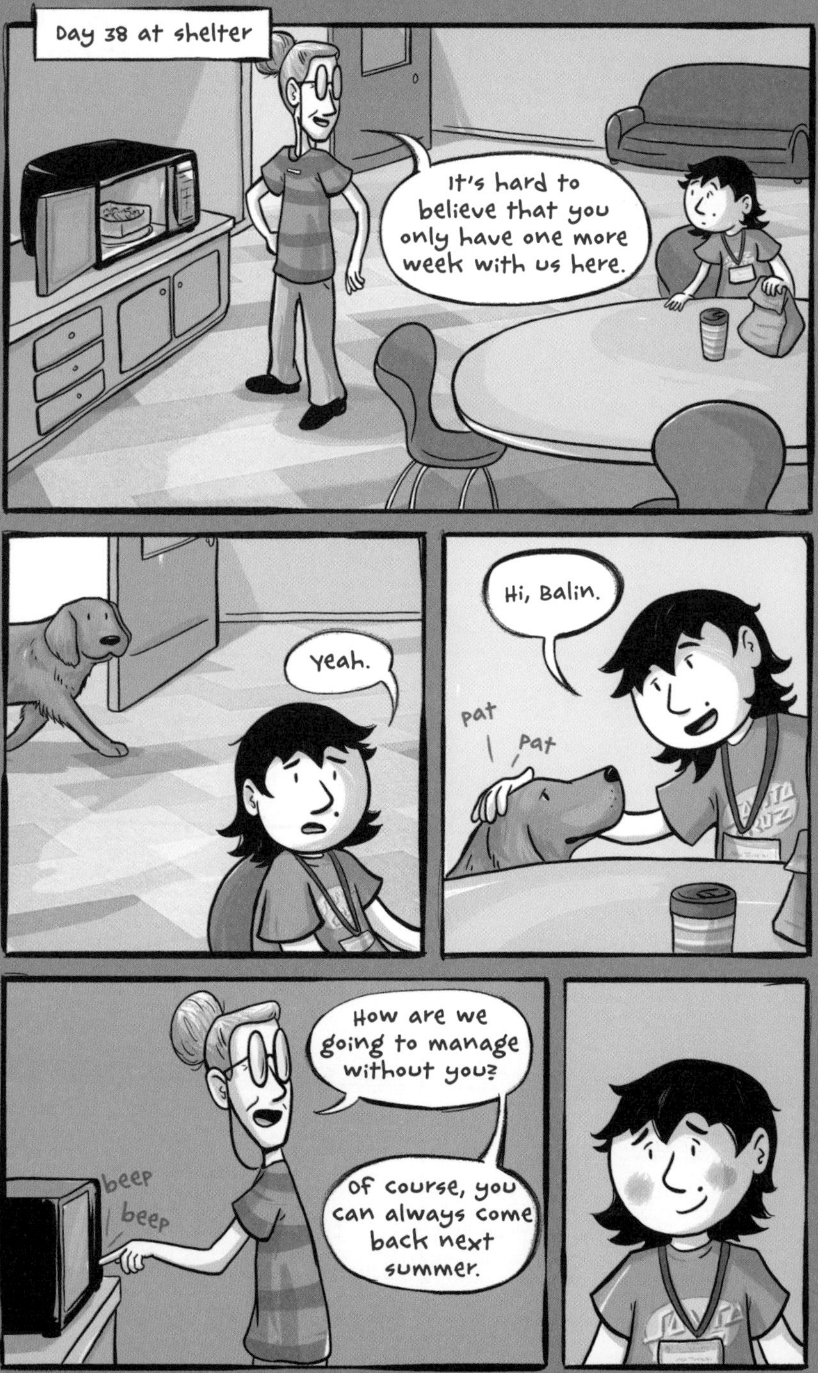
Day 38 at shelter
It's hard to believe that you only have one more week with us here.
Yeah.
Hi, Balin.
pat
pat
How are we going to manage without you?
beep
beep
Of course, you can always come back next summer.

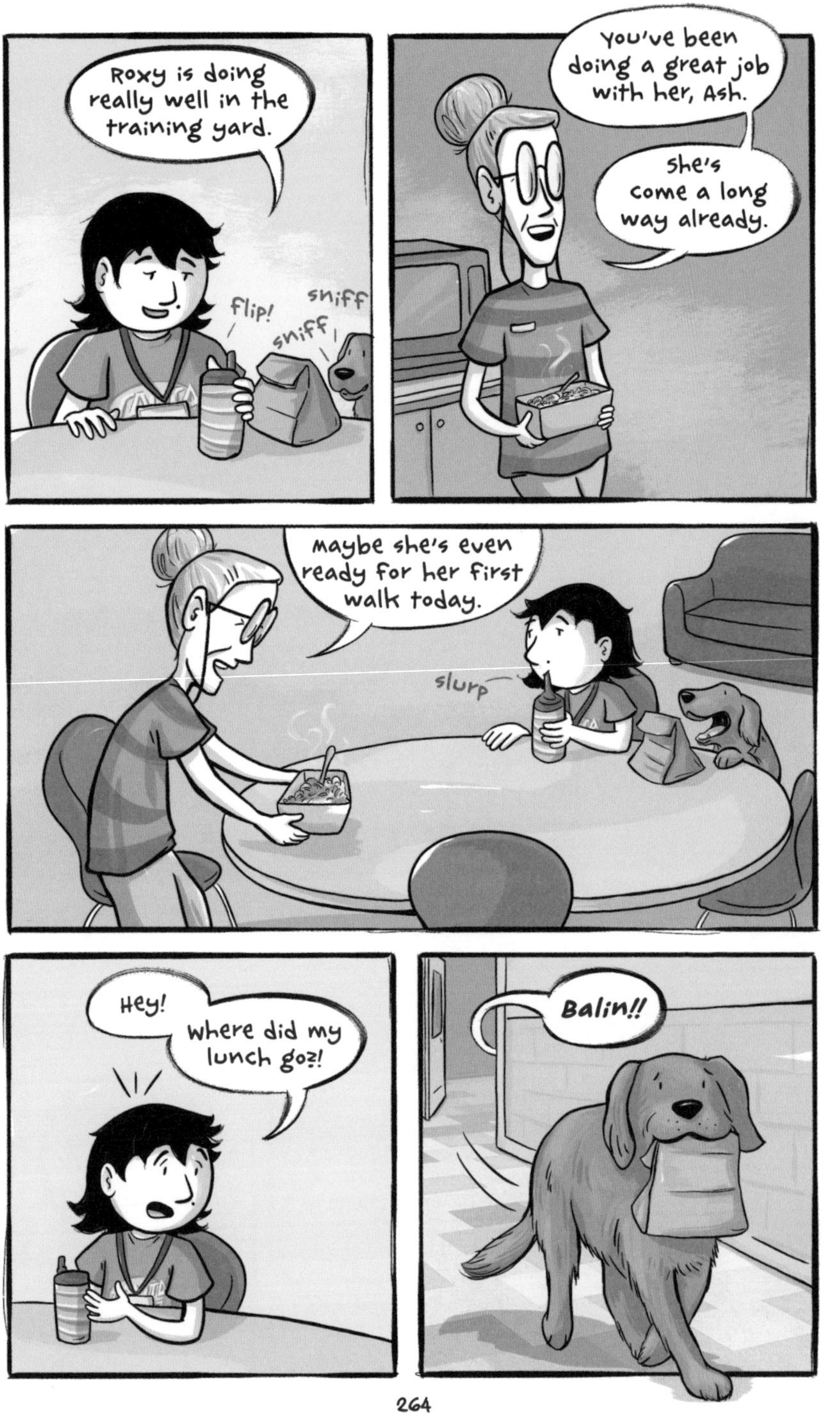
Roxy is doing really well in the training yard.
flip!
sniff
sniff
You've been doing a great job with her, Ash.
She's come a long way already.
Maybe she's even ready for her first walk today.
slurp
Hey!
Where did my lunch go?!
Balin!!

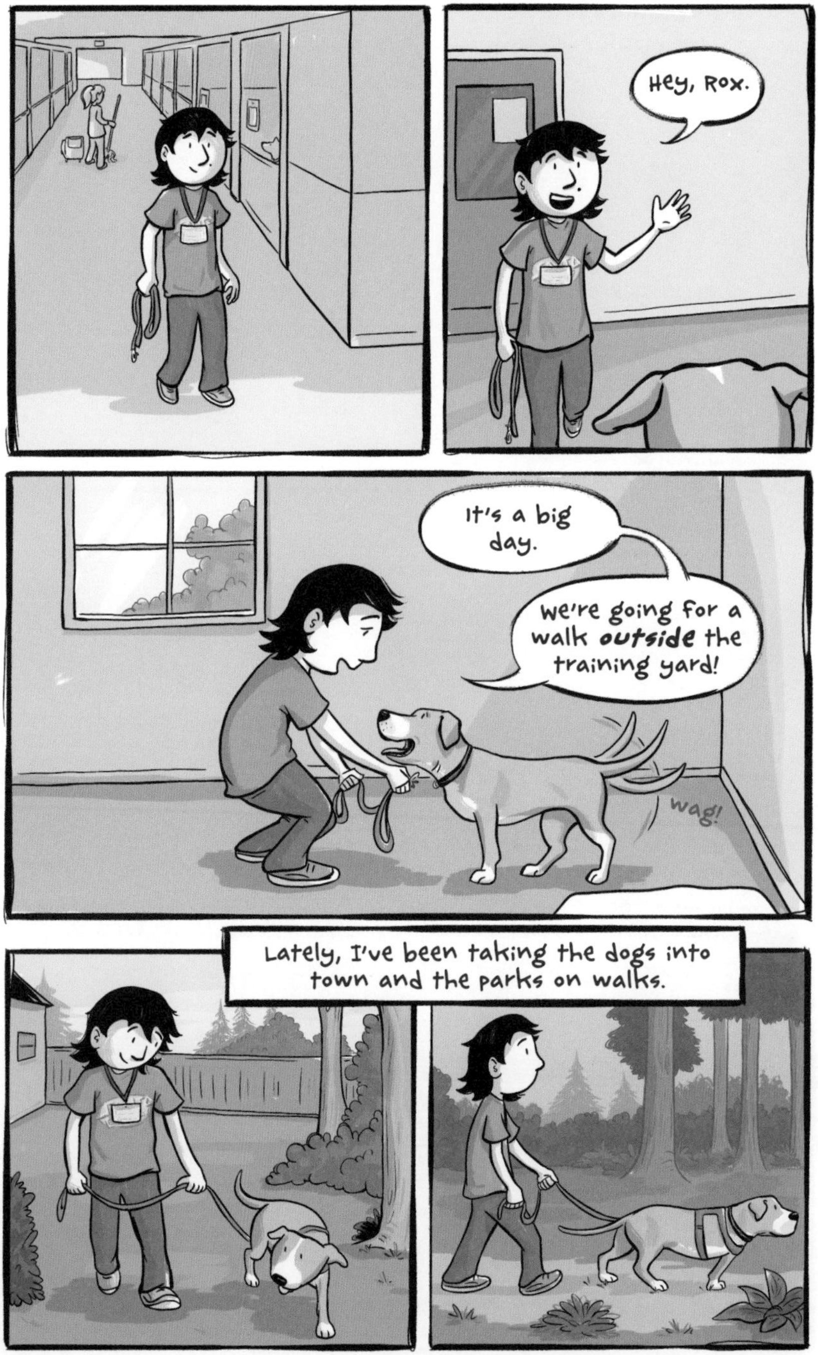
Hey, Rox.
It's a big day.
We're going for a walk outside the training yard!
wag!
Lately, I've been taking the dogs into town and the parks on walks.

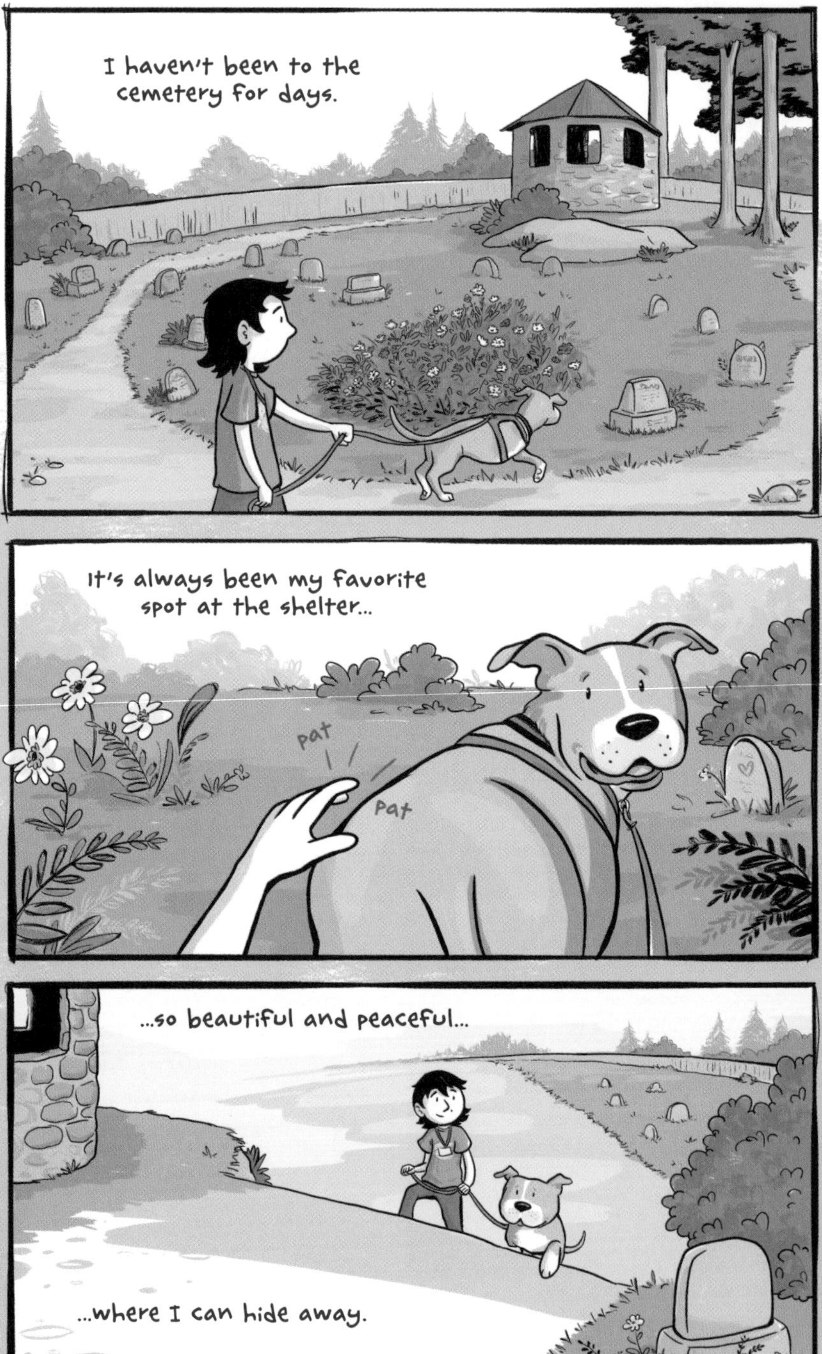
I haven't been to the cemetery for days.
It's always been my favorite spot at the shelter...
pat
pat
...so beautiful and peaceful...
...where I can hide away.

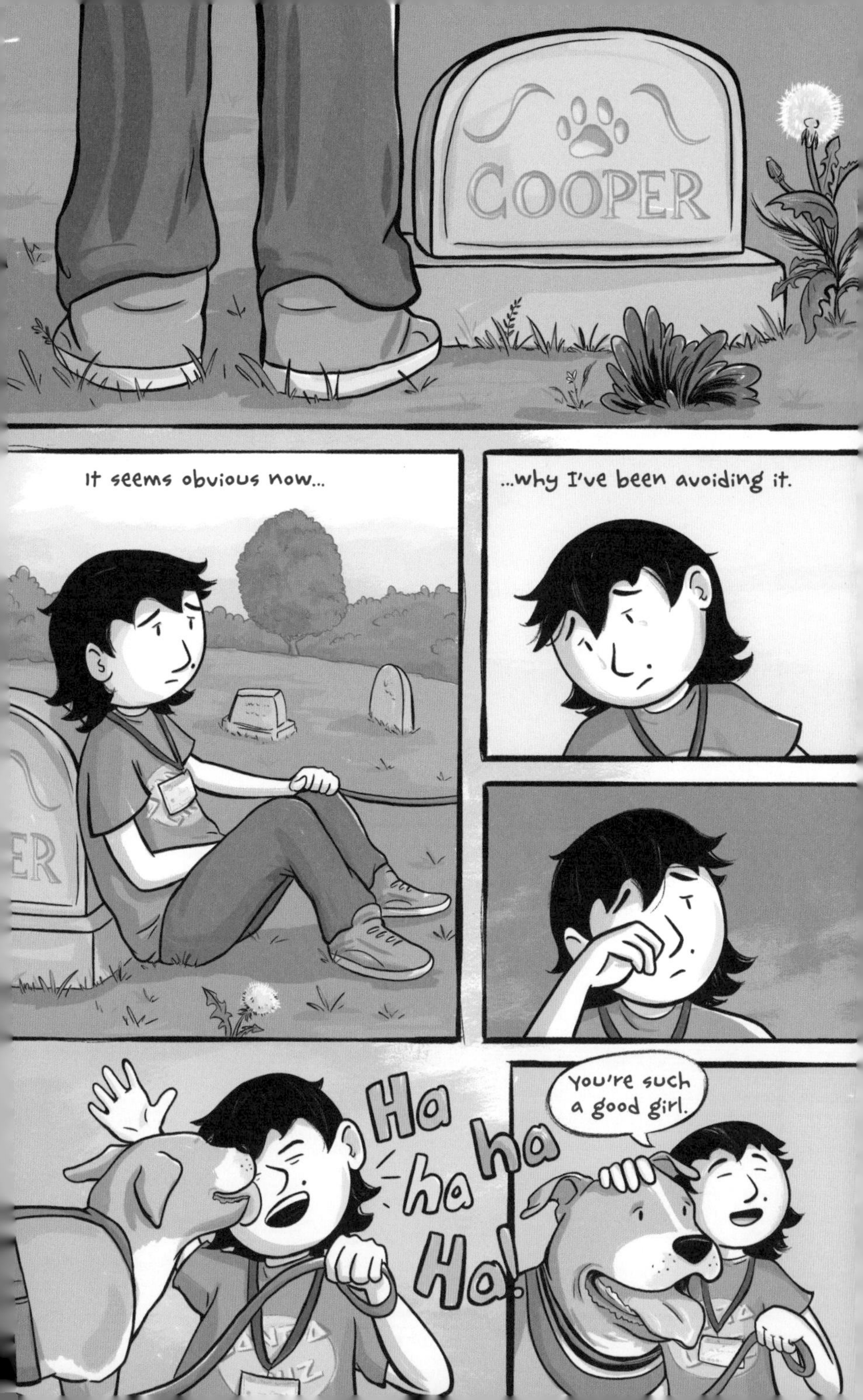
COOPER
It seems obvious now...
...why I've been avoiding it.
Ha
ha
ha
Ha!
You're such a good girl.

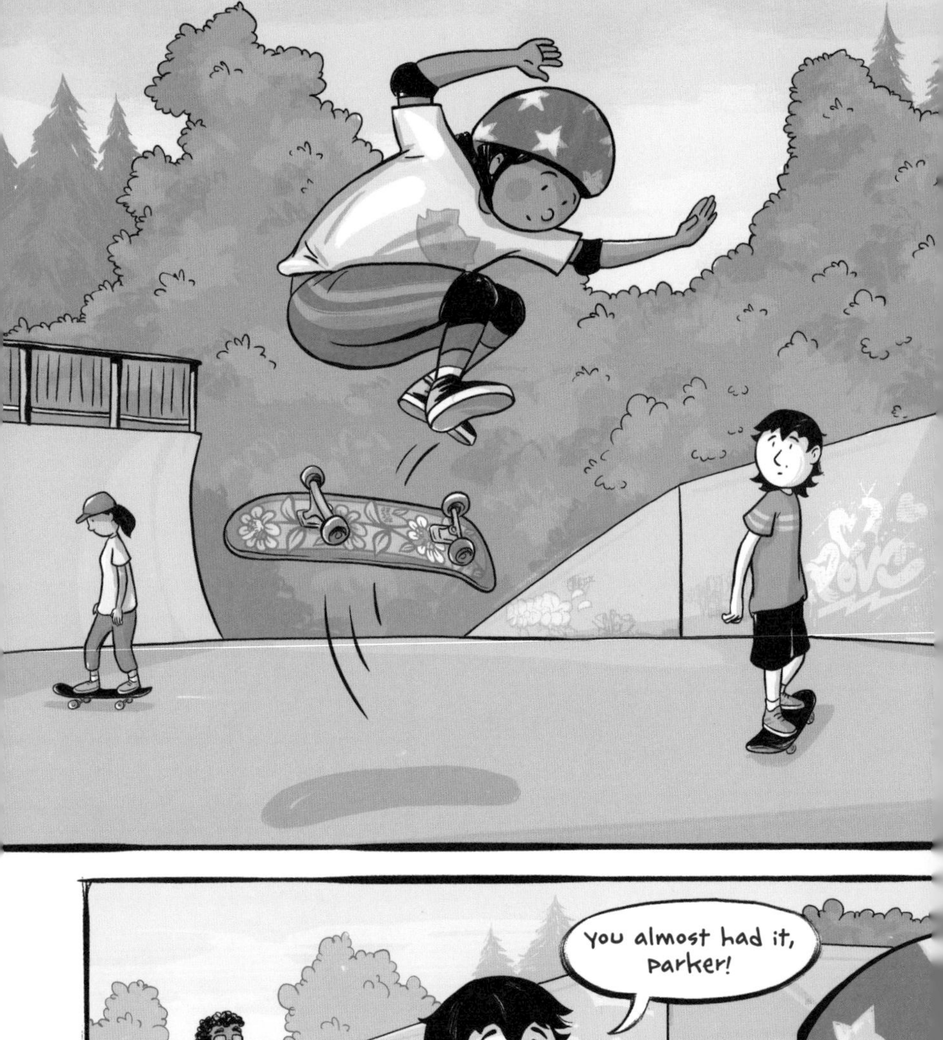

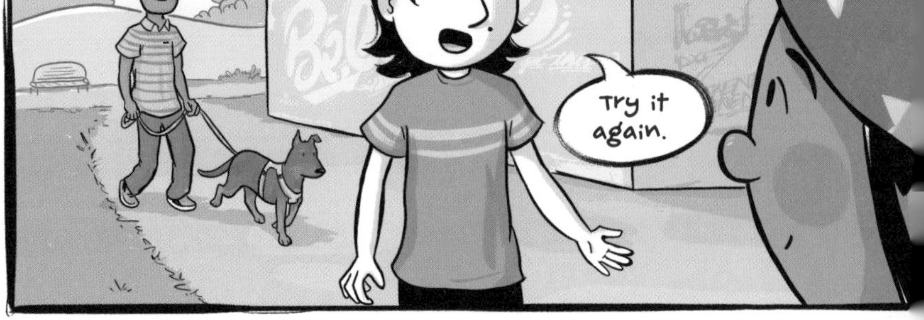
You almost had it, Parker!
Try it again.

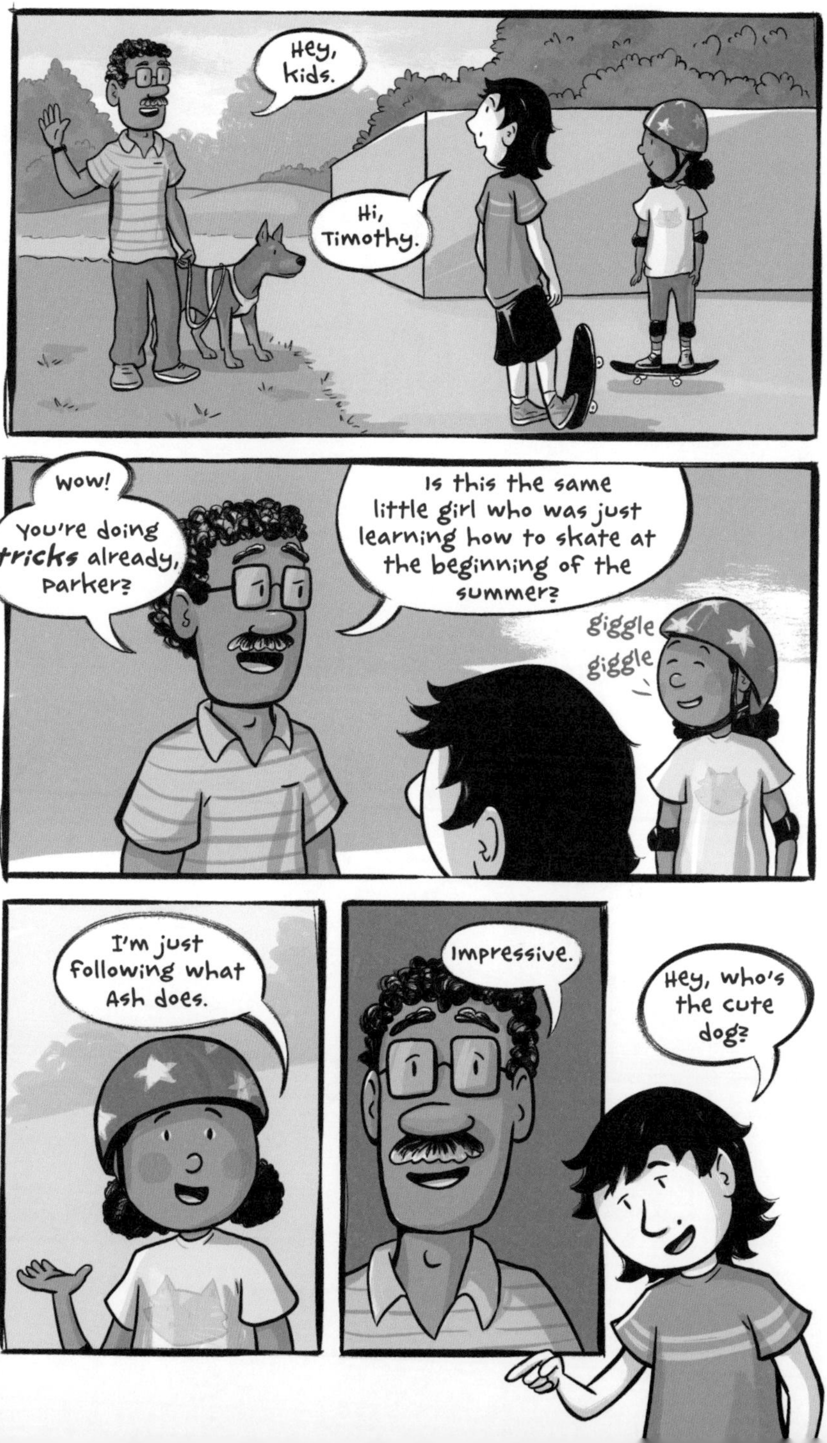

Hey, kids.
Hi, Timothy.
Wow!
You're doing tricks already, Parker?
Is this the same little girl who was just learning how to skate at the beginning of the summer?
giggle giggle
I'm just following what Ash does.
Impressive.
Hey, who's the cute dog?

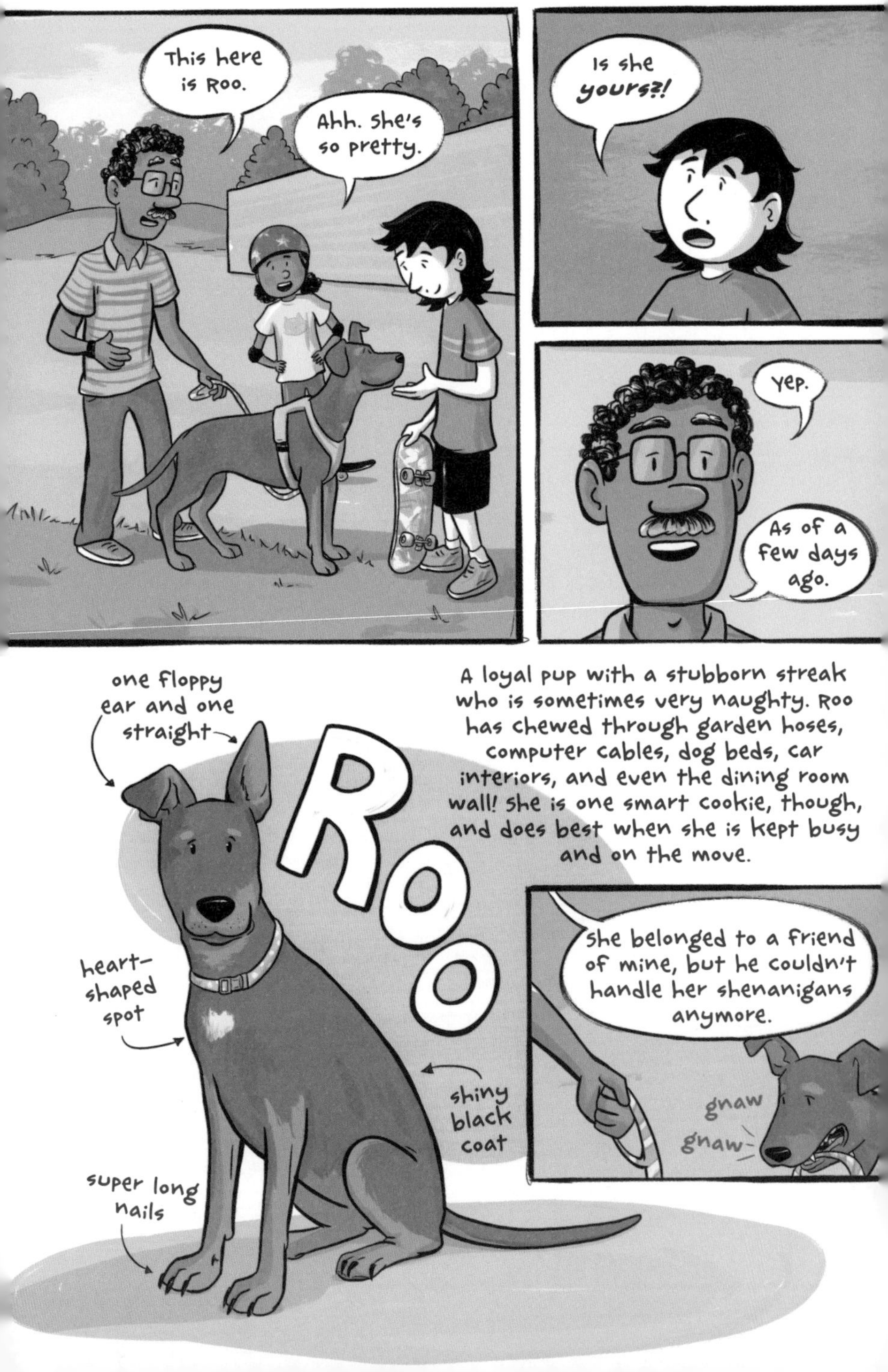
This here is Roo.
Ahh. She's so pretty.
Is she *yours?!*
Yep.
As of a few days ago.
ROO
one floppy ear and one straight
heart-shaped spot
shiny black coat
super long nails
A loyal pup with a stubborn streak who is sometimes very naughty. Roo has chewed through garden hoses, computer cables, dog beds, car interiors, and even the dining room wall! She is one smart cookie, though, and does best when she is kept busy and on the move.
She belonged to a friend of mine, but he couldn't handle her shenanigans anymore.
gnaw
gnaw

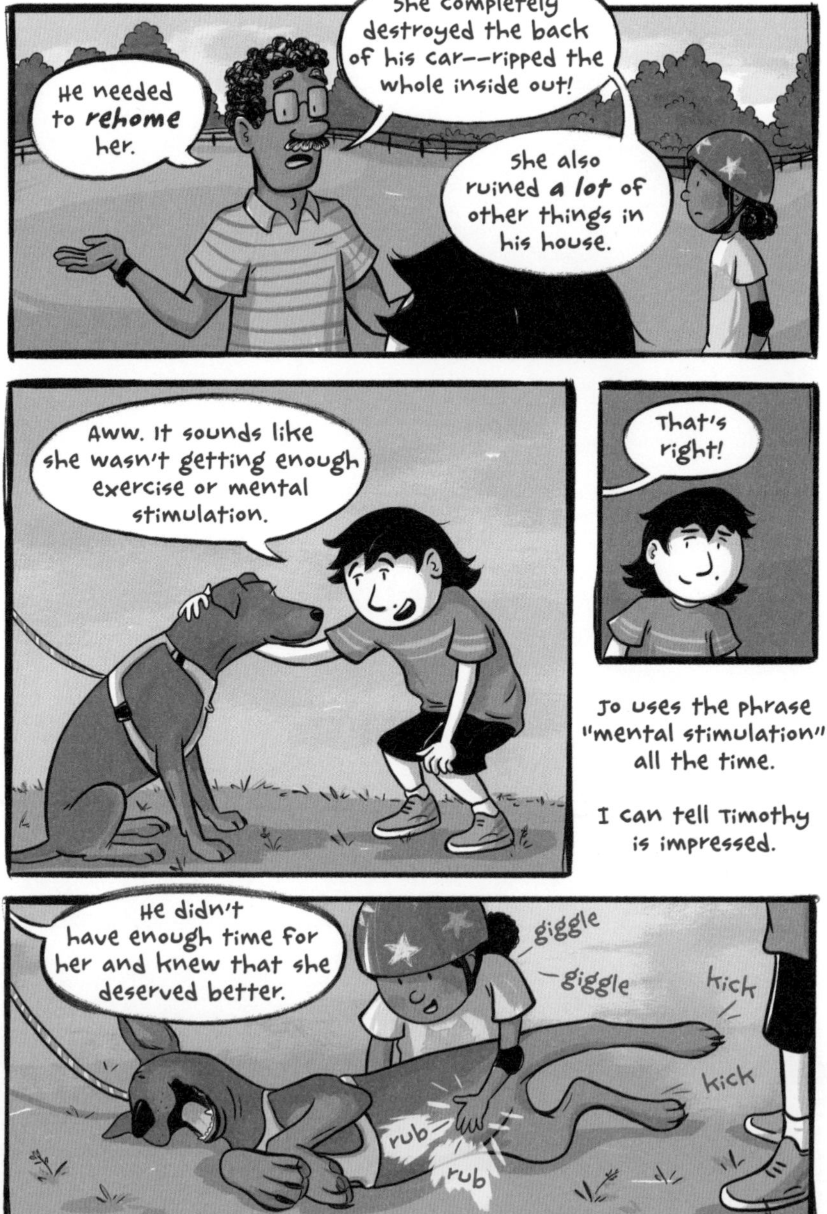
He needed to rehome her.
She completely destroyed the back of his car--ripped the whole inside out!
She also ruined a lot of other things in his house.
Aww. It sounds like she wasn't getting enough exercise or mental stimulation.
That's right!
Jo uses the phrase "mental stimulation" all the time.
I can tell Timothy is impressed.
He didn't have enough time for her and knew that she deserved better.
giggle
giggle
kick
kick
rub
rub

Rehoming: Sometimes owners can no longer care for or need to give up their pets. Rather than taking them to a shelter, many adoption organizations offer options where owners can search for a home better suited for their pet.

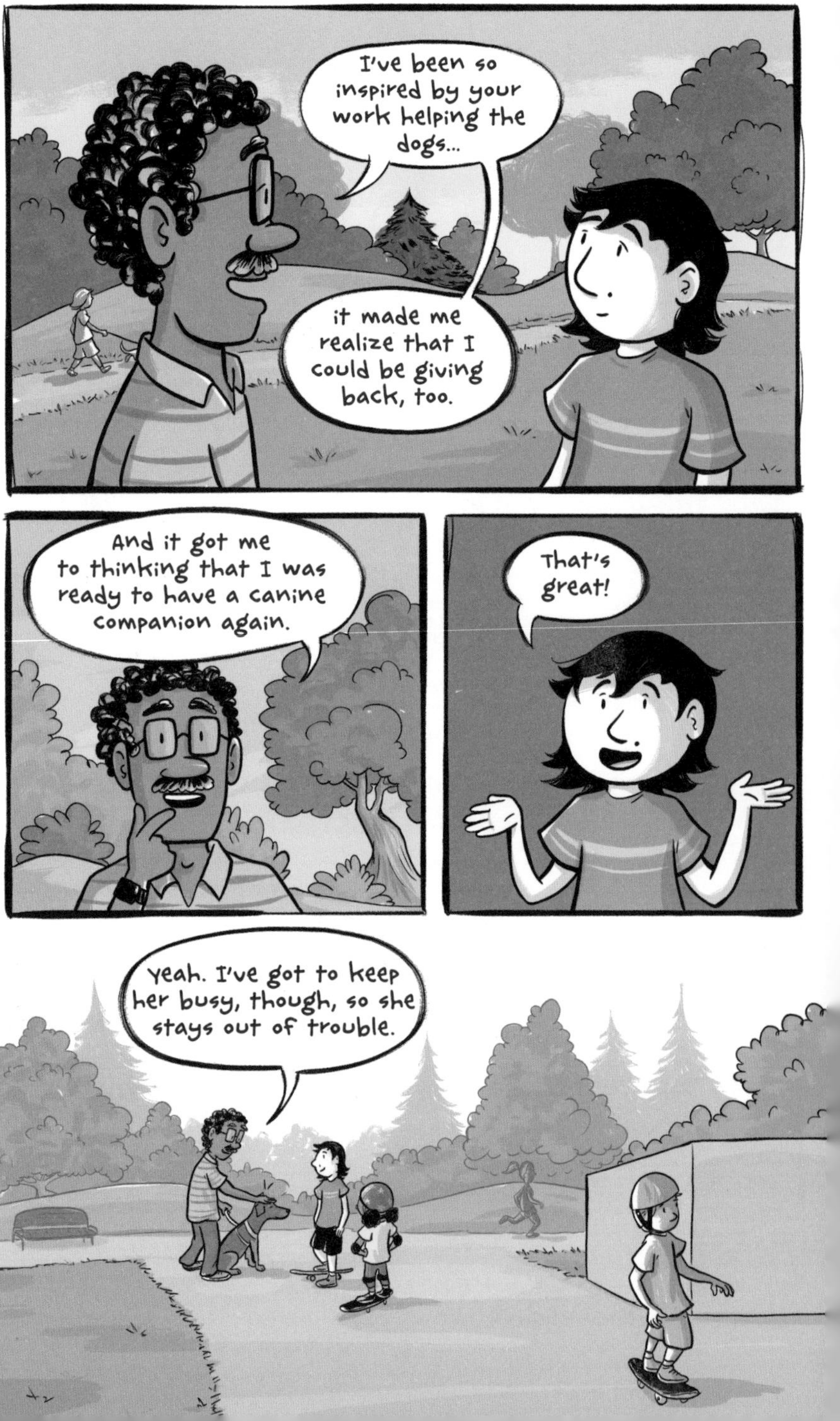
I've been so inspired by your work helping the dogs...
it made me realize that I could be giving back, too.
And it got me to thinking that I was ready to have a canine companion again.
That's great!
Yeah. I've got to keep her busy, though, so she stays out of trouble.

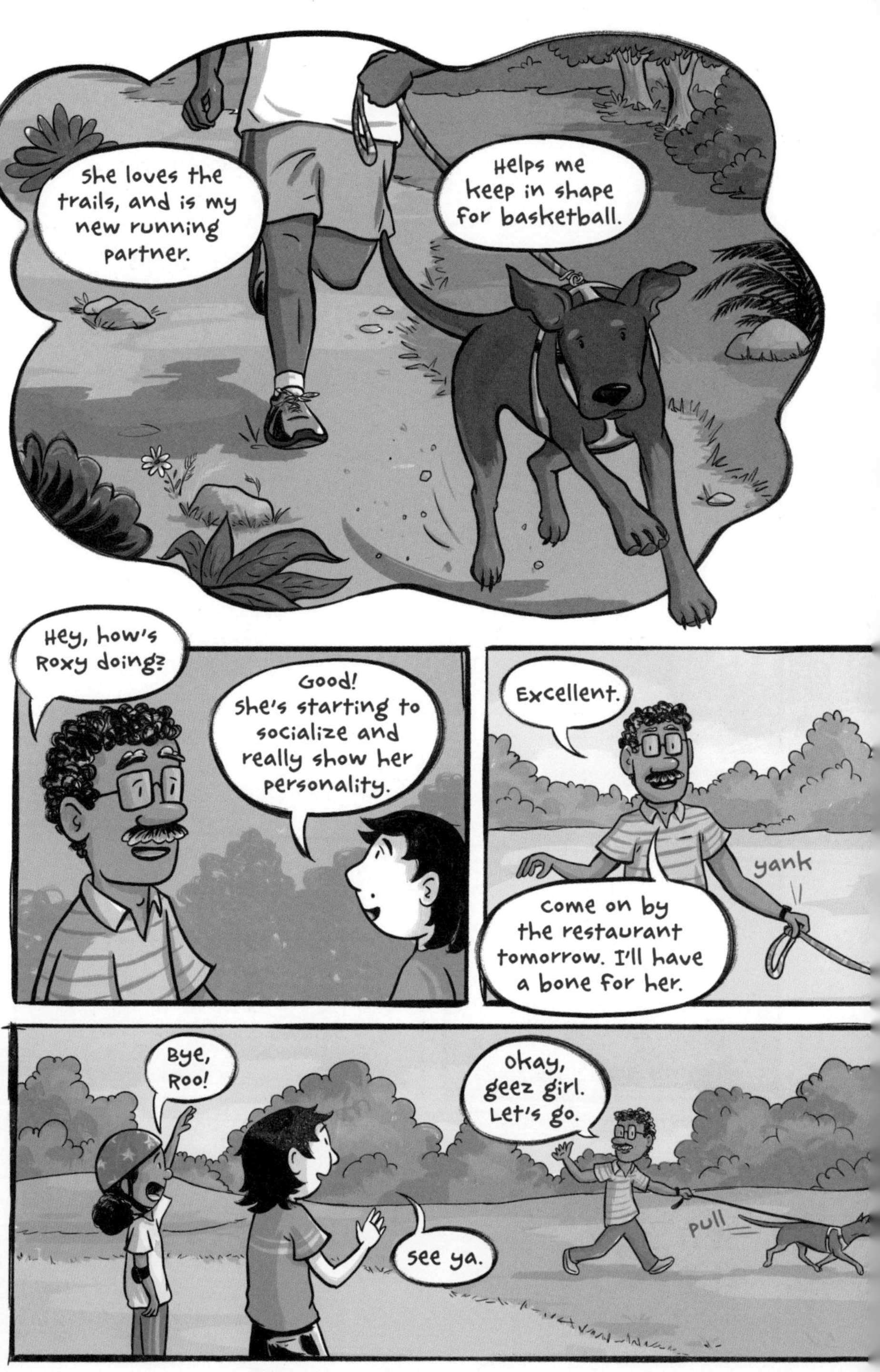
She loves the trails, and is my new running partner.
Helps me keep in shape for basketball.
Hey, how's Roxy doing?
Good! She's starting to socialize and really show her personality.
Excellent.
Come on by the restaurant tomorrow. I'll have a bone for her.
yank
Bye, Roo!
Okay, geez girl. Let's go.
See ya.
pull

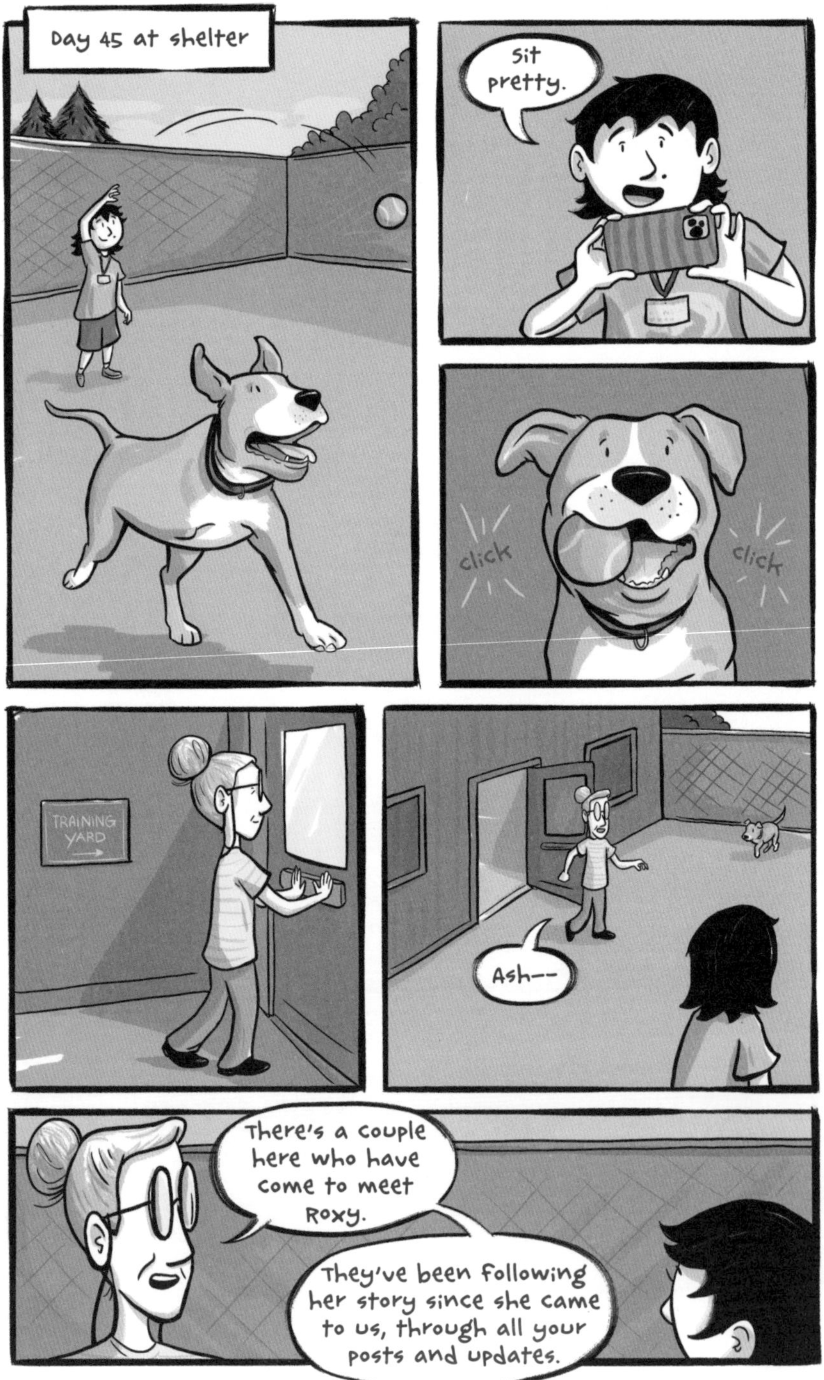
Day 45 at shelter
Sit pretty.
click
click
TRAINING YARD
Ash--
There's a couple here who have come to meet Roxy.
They've been following her story since she came to us, through all your posts and updates.

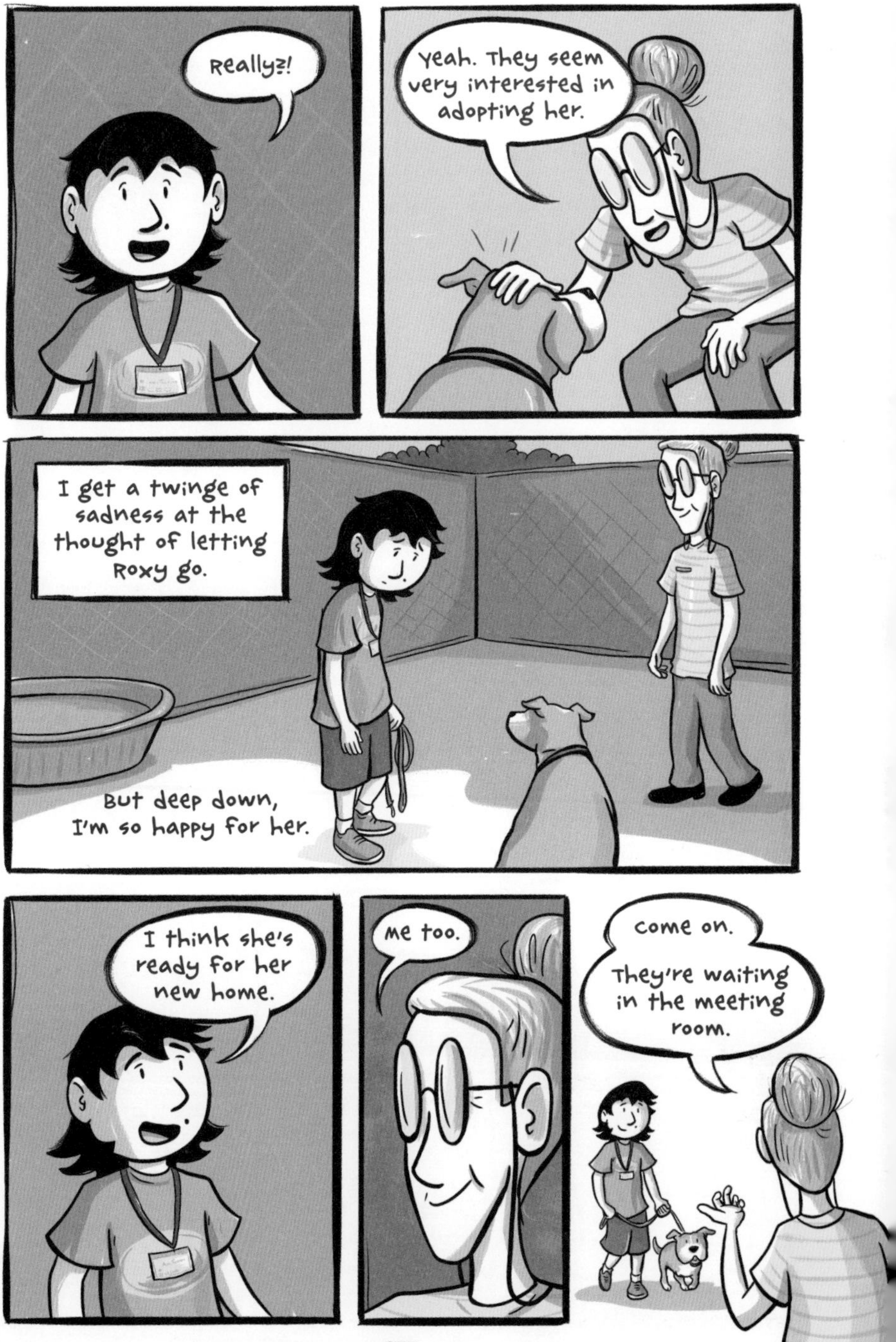
Really?!
Yeah. They seem very interested in adopting her.
I get a twinge of sadness at the thought of letting Roxy go.
But deep down, I'm so happy for her.
I think she's ready for her new home.
Me too.
Come on.
They're waiting in the meeting room.

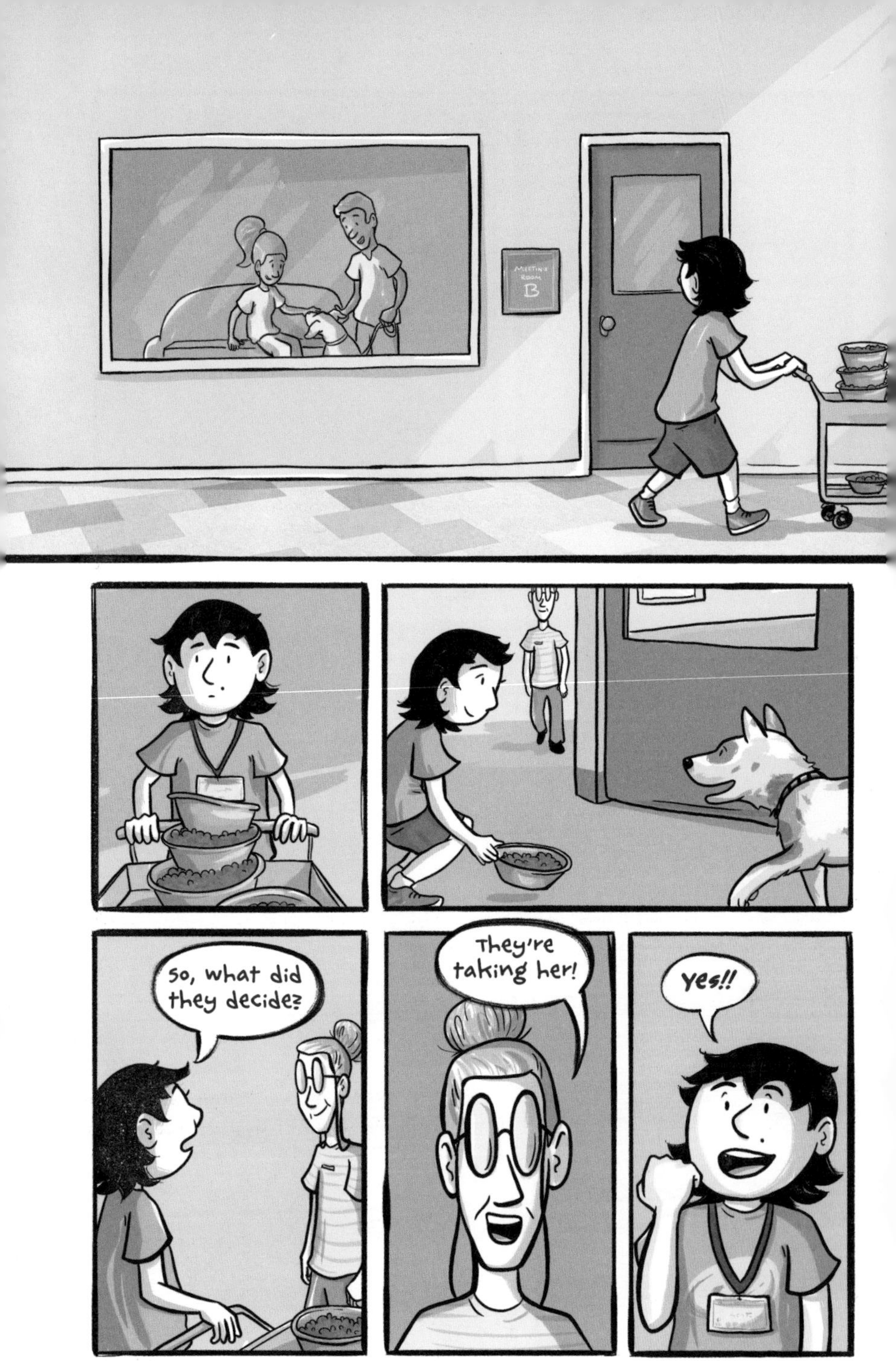
MEETING ROOM B
So, what did they decide?
They're taking her!
Yes!!

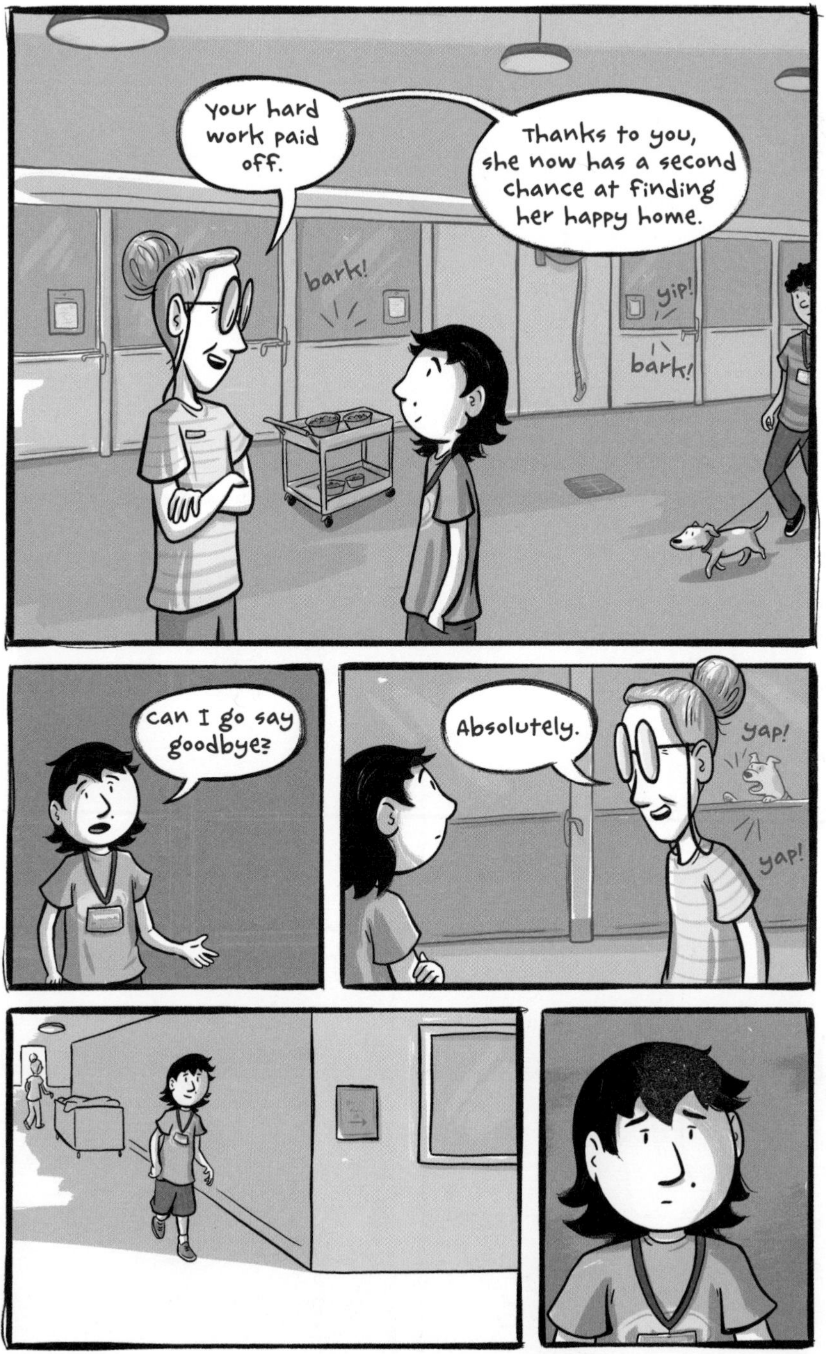
Your hard work paid off.
Thanks to you, she now has a second chance at finding her happy home.
bark!
yip!
bark!
Can I go say goodbye?
Absolutely.
yap!
yap!

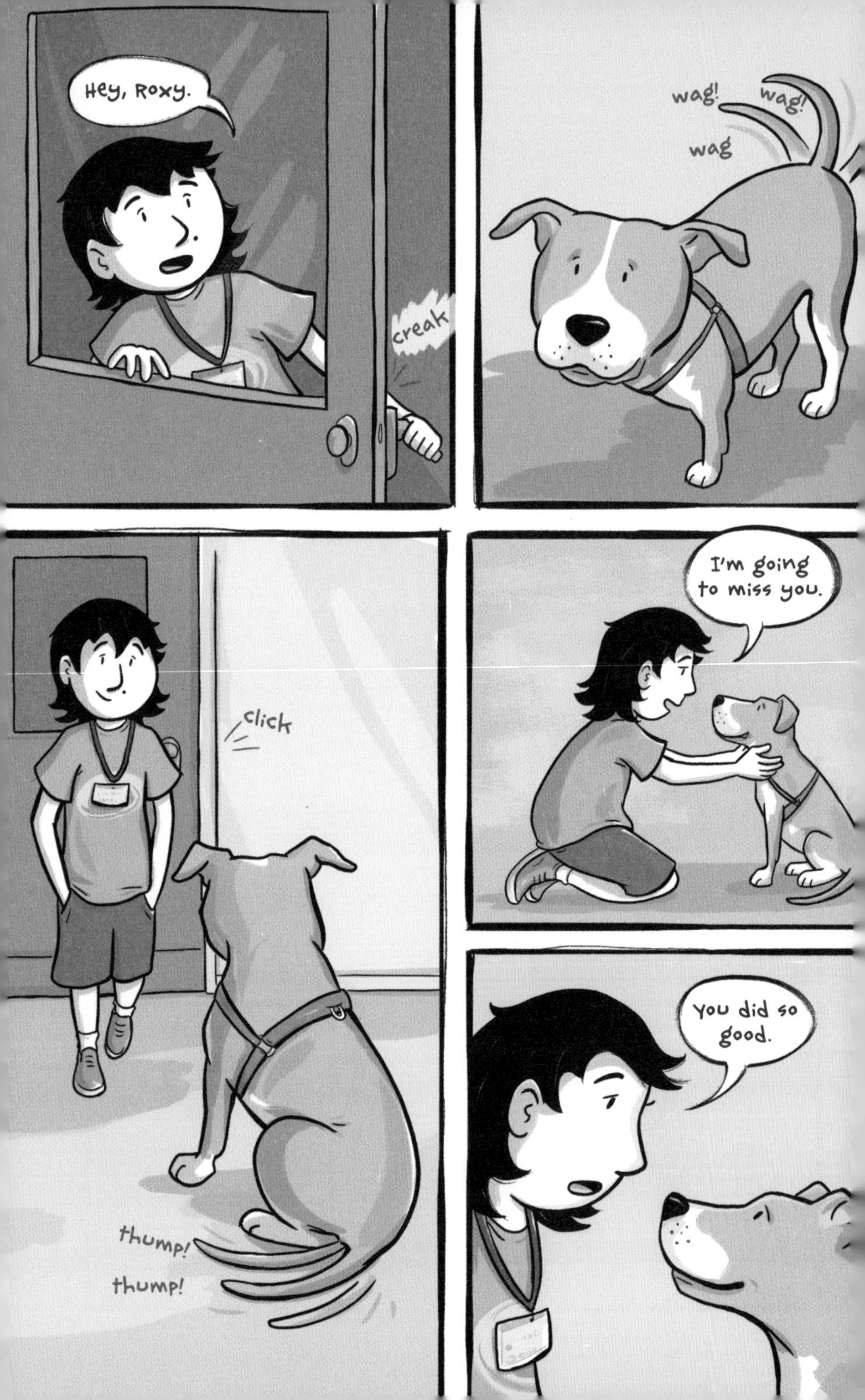
Hey, Roxy.
creak
wag!
wag!
wag
click
thump!
thump!
I'm going to miss you.
You did so good.

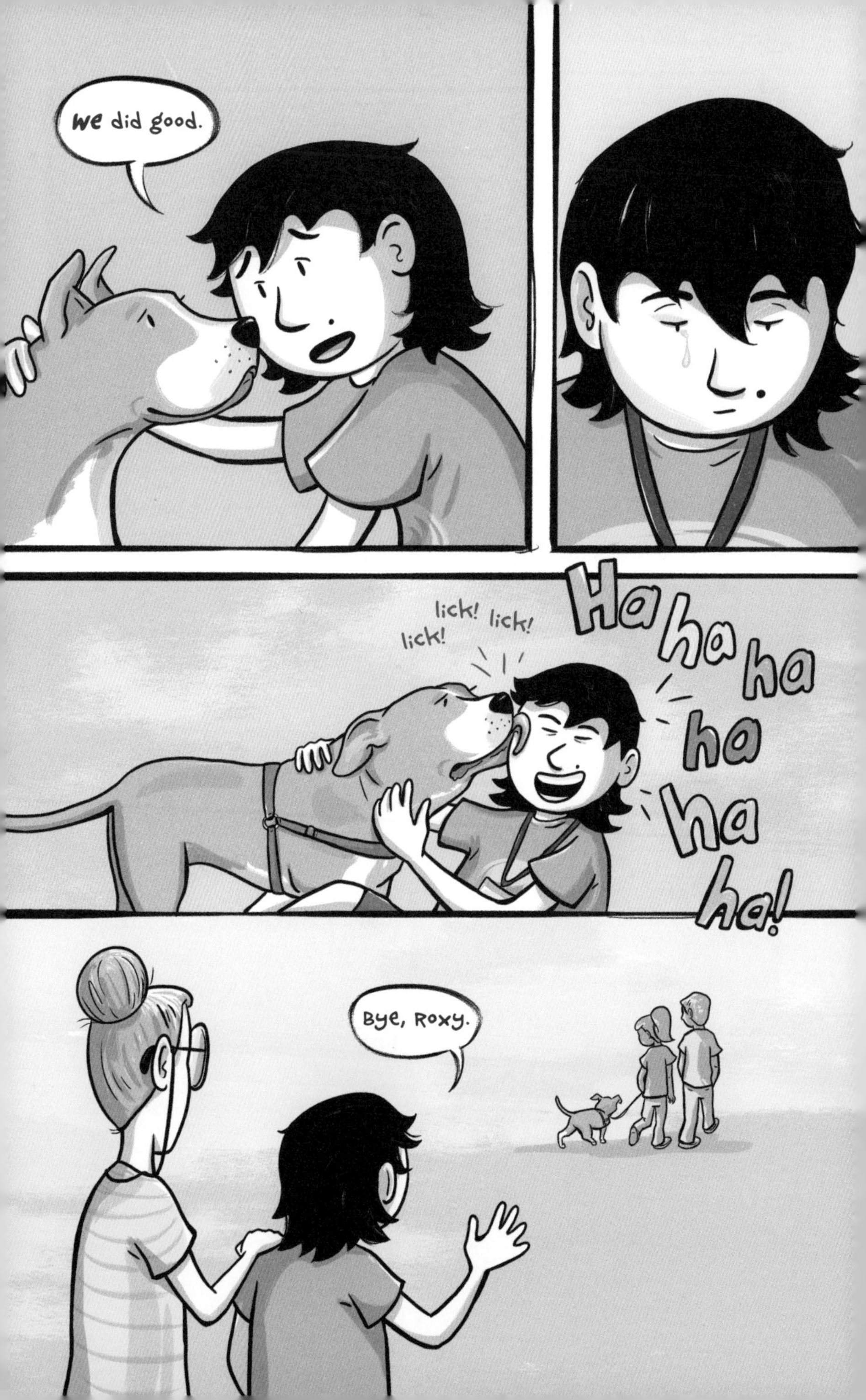

we did good.
lick! lick!
lick!
Ha ha ha ha ha ha!
Bye, Roxy.

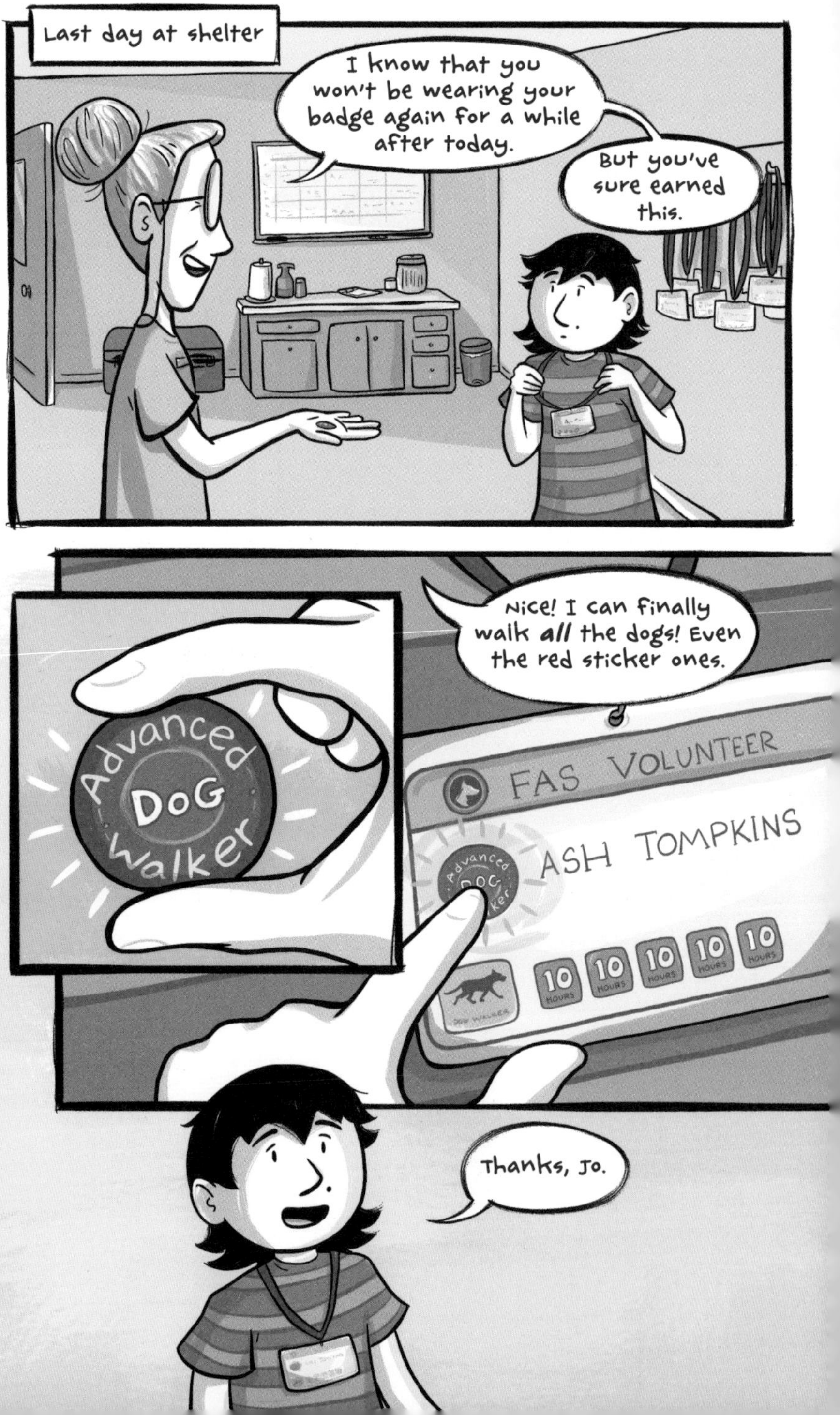
Last day at shelter
I know that you won't be wearing your badge again for a while after today.
But you've sure earned this.
Advanced DoG Walker
Nice! I can finally walk *all* the dogs! Even the red sticker ones.
FAS VOLUNTEER
ASH TOMPKINS
10 HOURS
10 HOURS
10 HOURS
10 HOURS
10 HOURS
Thanks, Jo.

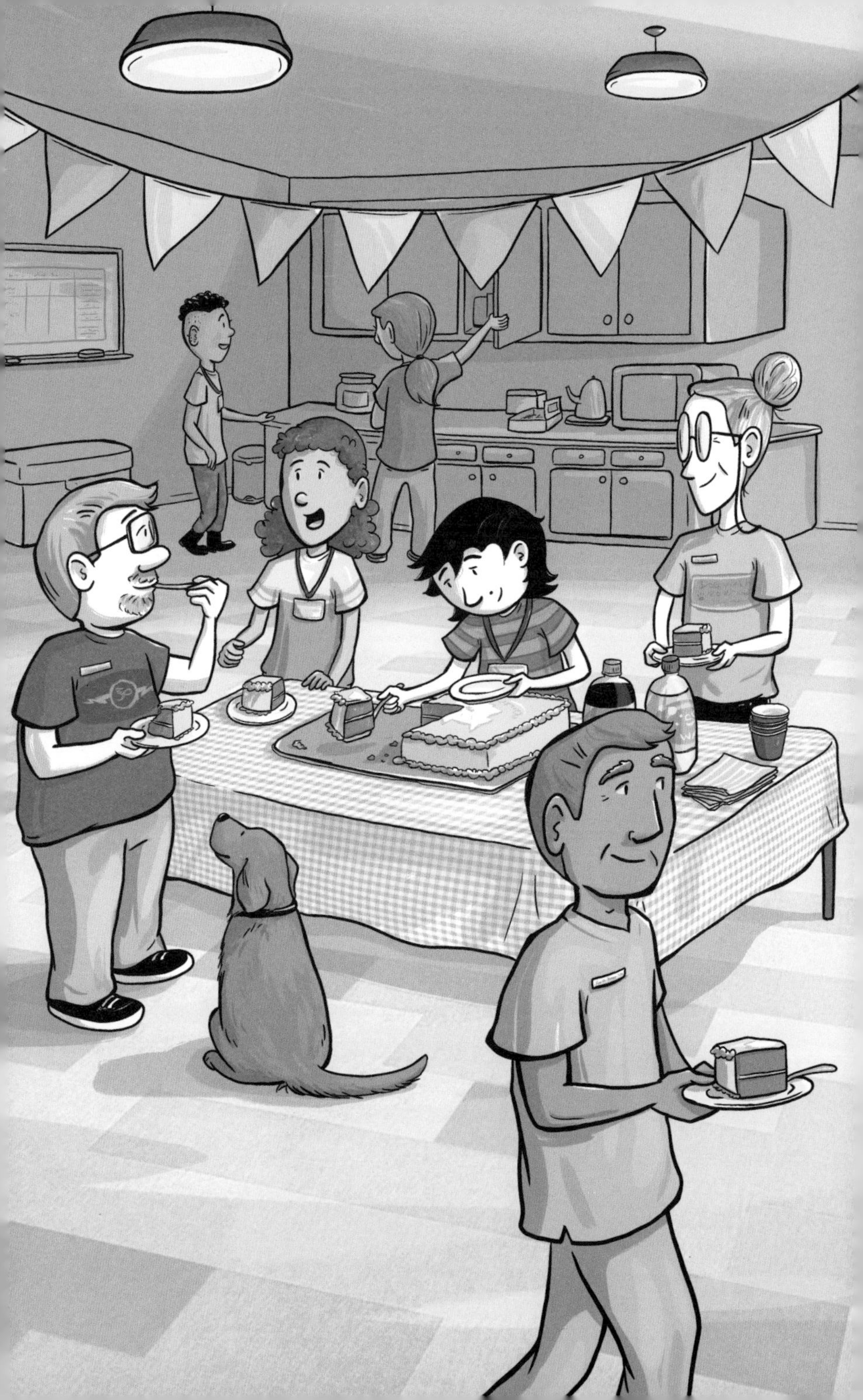

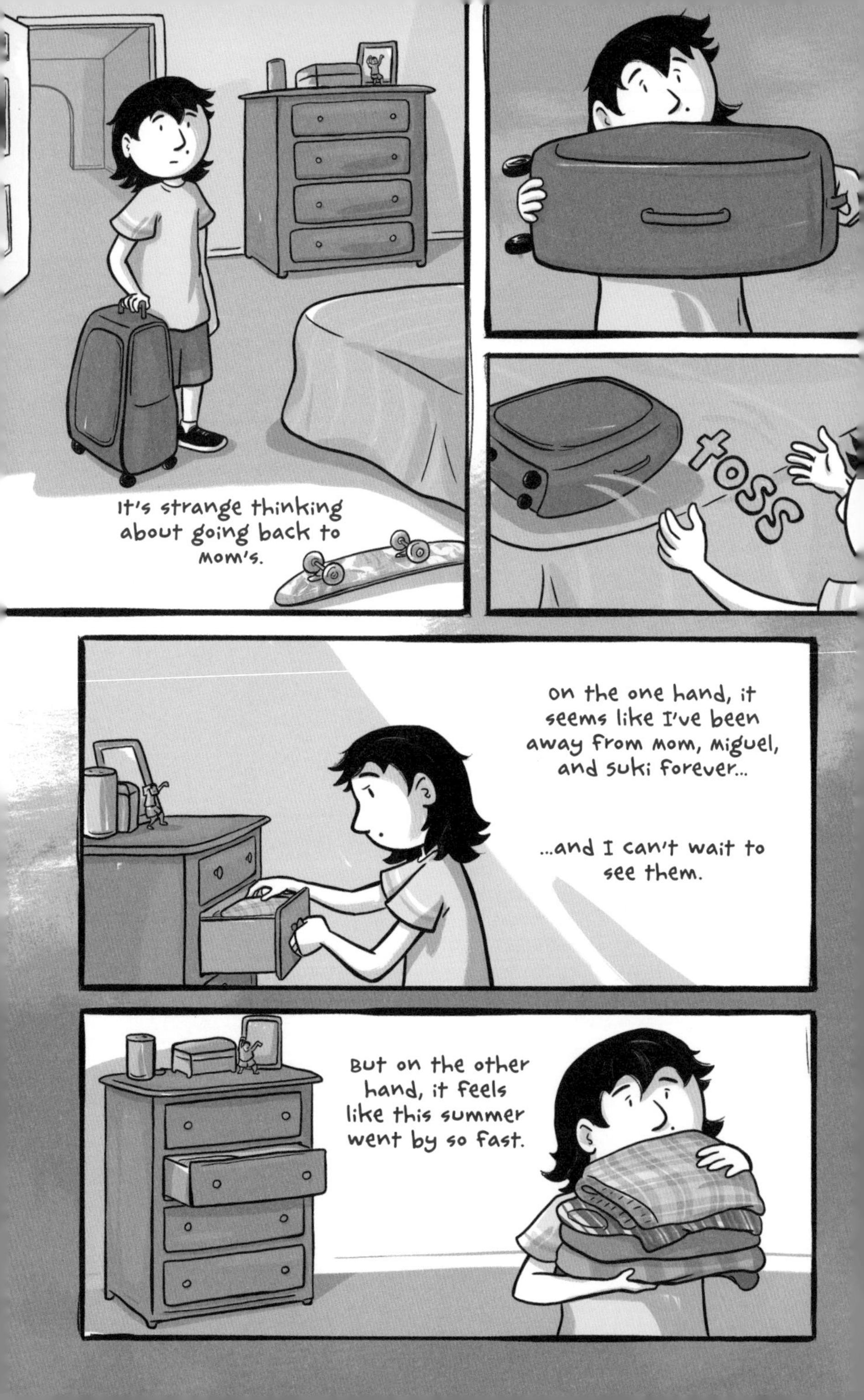
It's strange thinking about going back to mom's.
TOSS
on the one hand, it seems like I've been away from mom, miguel, and suki forever...
...and I can't wait to see them.
But on the other hand, it feels like this summer went by so fast.

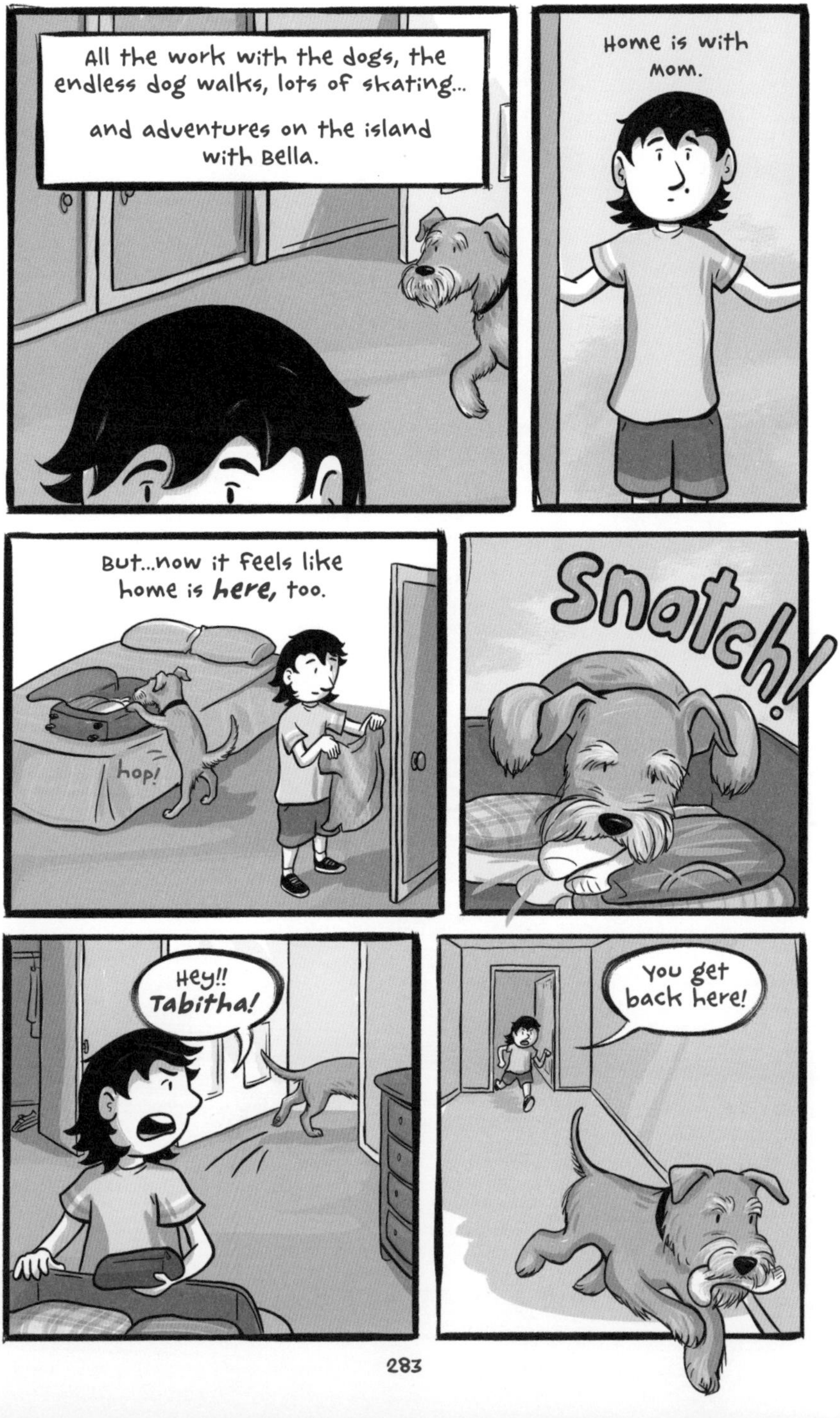
All the work with the dogs, the endless dog walks, lots of skating...
and adventures on the island with Bella.
Home is with Mom.
But...now it feels like home is *here,* too.
hop!
Snatch!
Hey!! Tabitha!
You get back here!

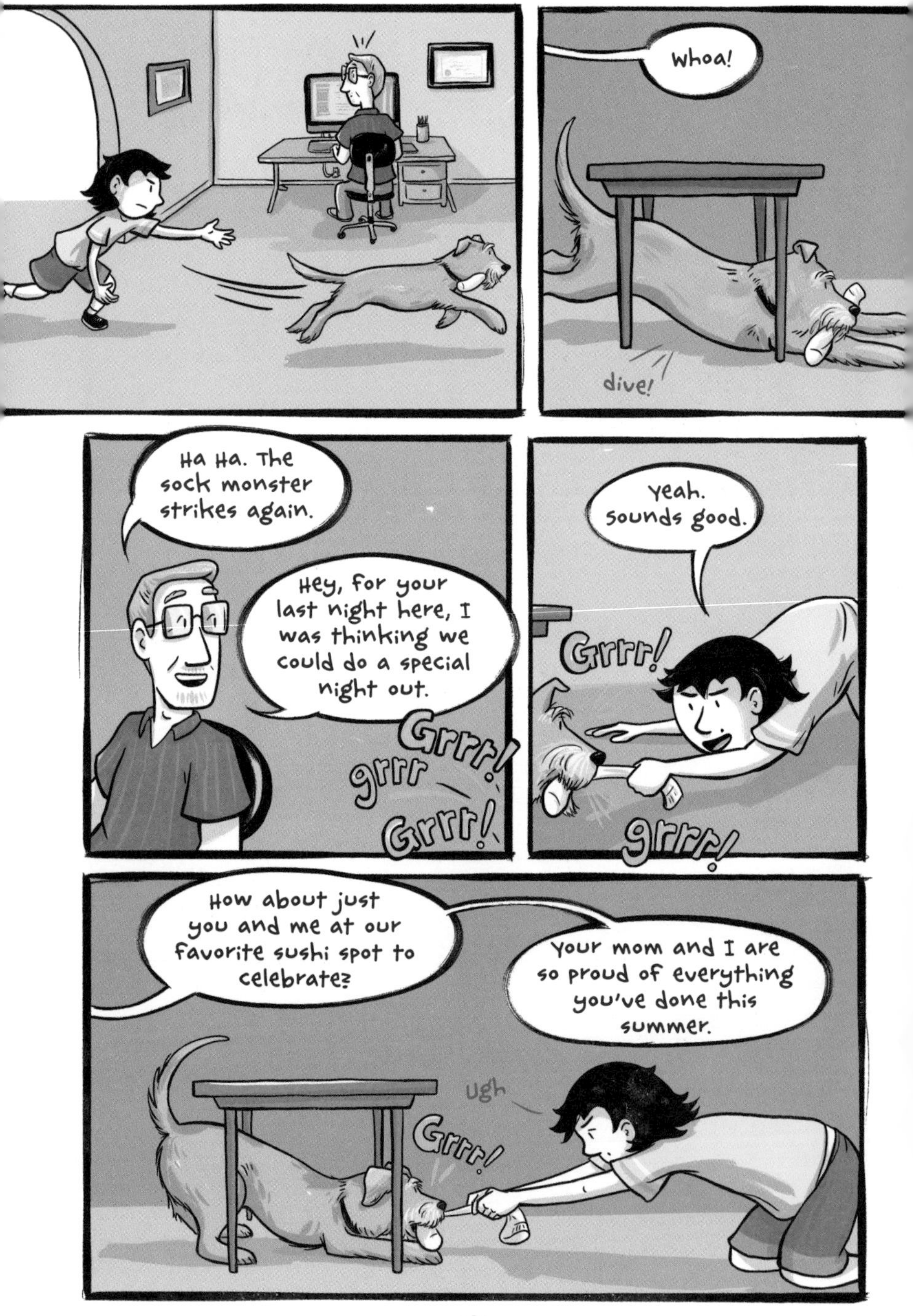
Whoa!
dive!
Ha Ha. The sock monster strikes again.
Hey, for your last night here, I was thinking we could do a special night out.
Grrr!
grrr
Grrr!
Yeah. Sounds good.
Grrr!
grrr!
How about just you and me at our favorite sushi spot to celebrate?
Your mom and I are so proud of everything you've done this summer.
Ugh
Grrr!

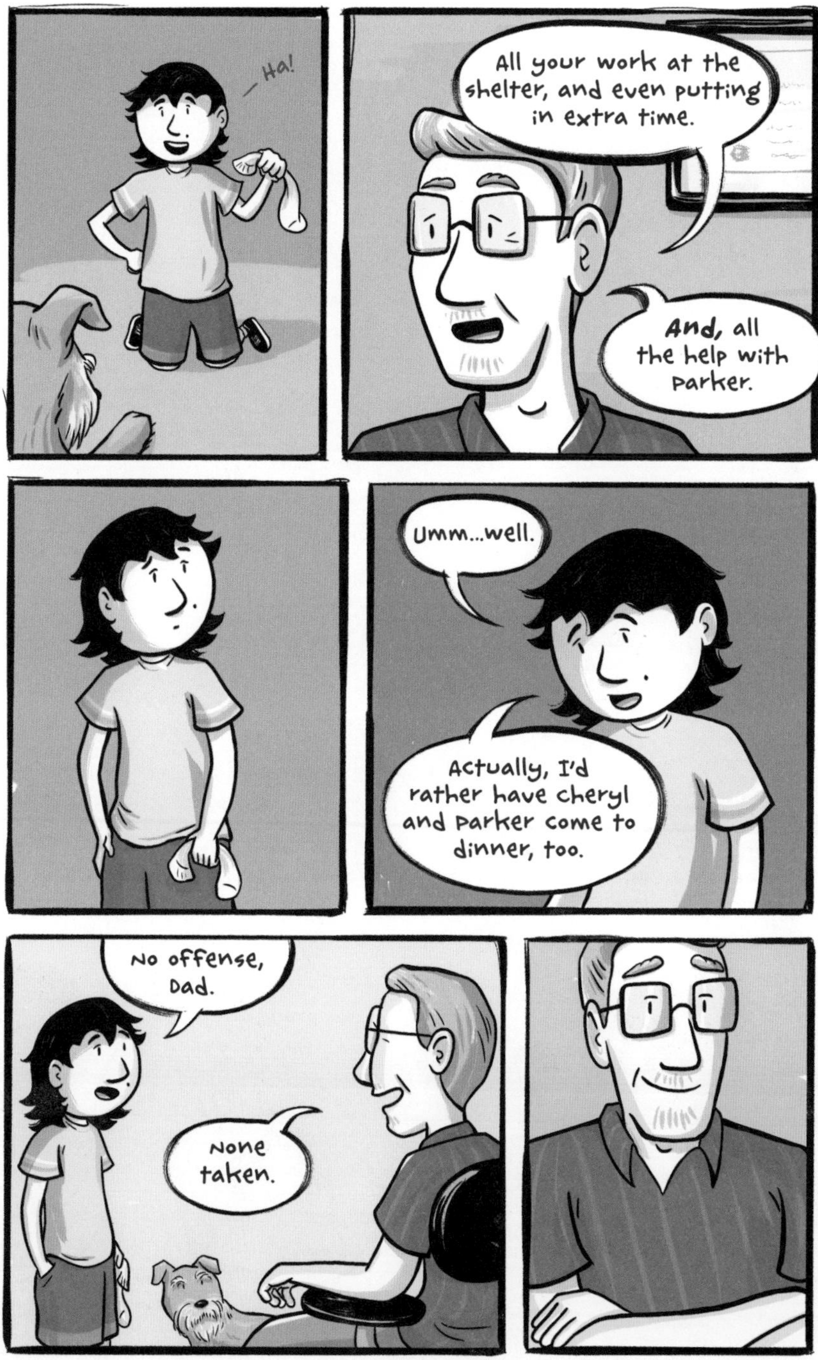
Ha!
All your work at the shelter, and even putting in extra time.
And, all the help with Parker.
Umm...well.
Actually, I'd rather have Cheryl and Parker come to dinner, too.
No offense, Dad.
None taken.

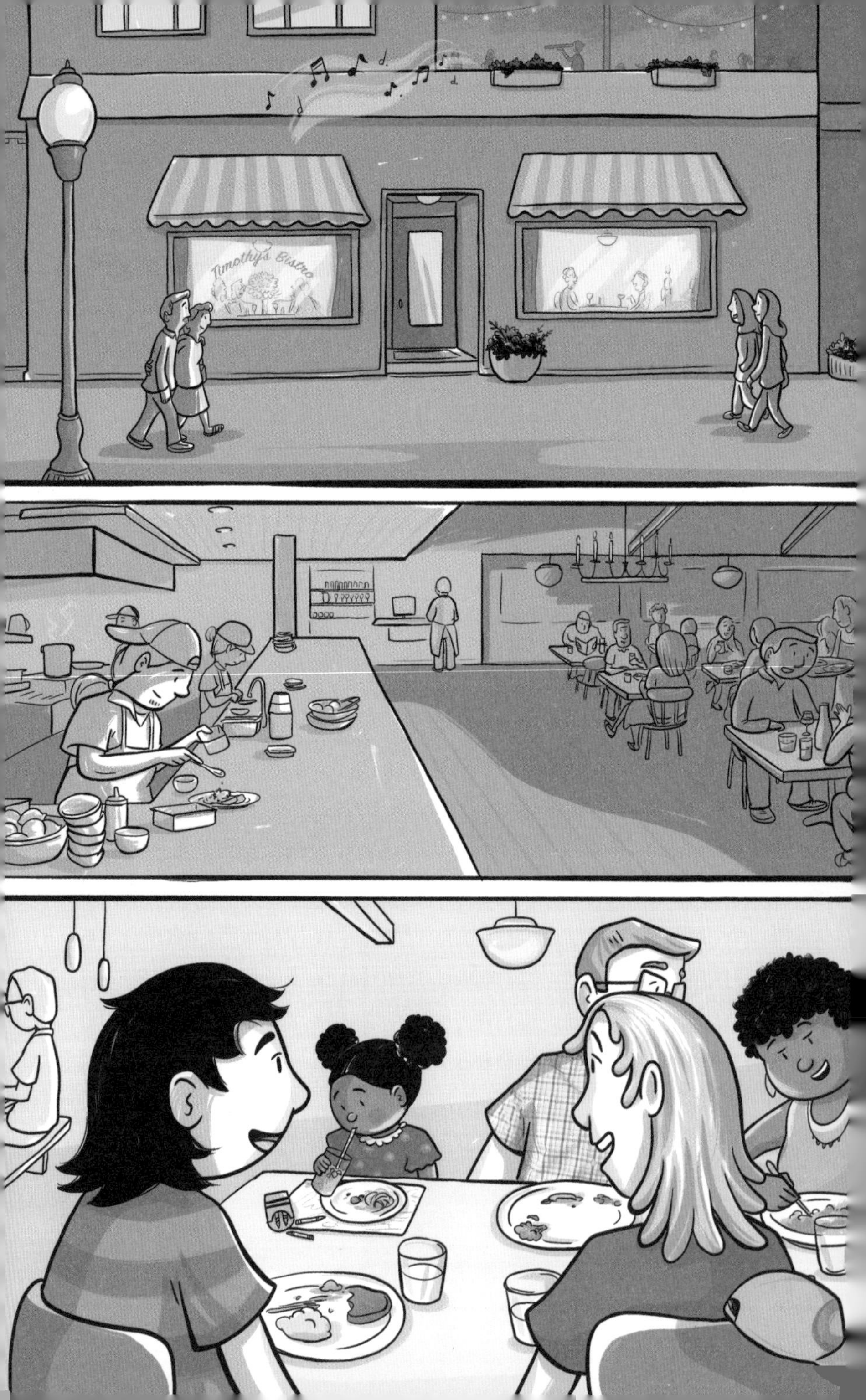
Timothy's Bistro

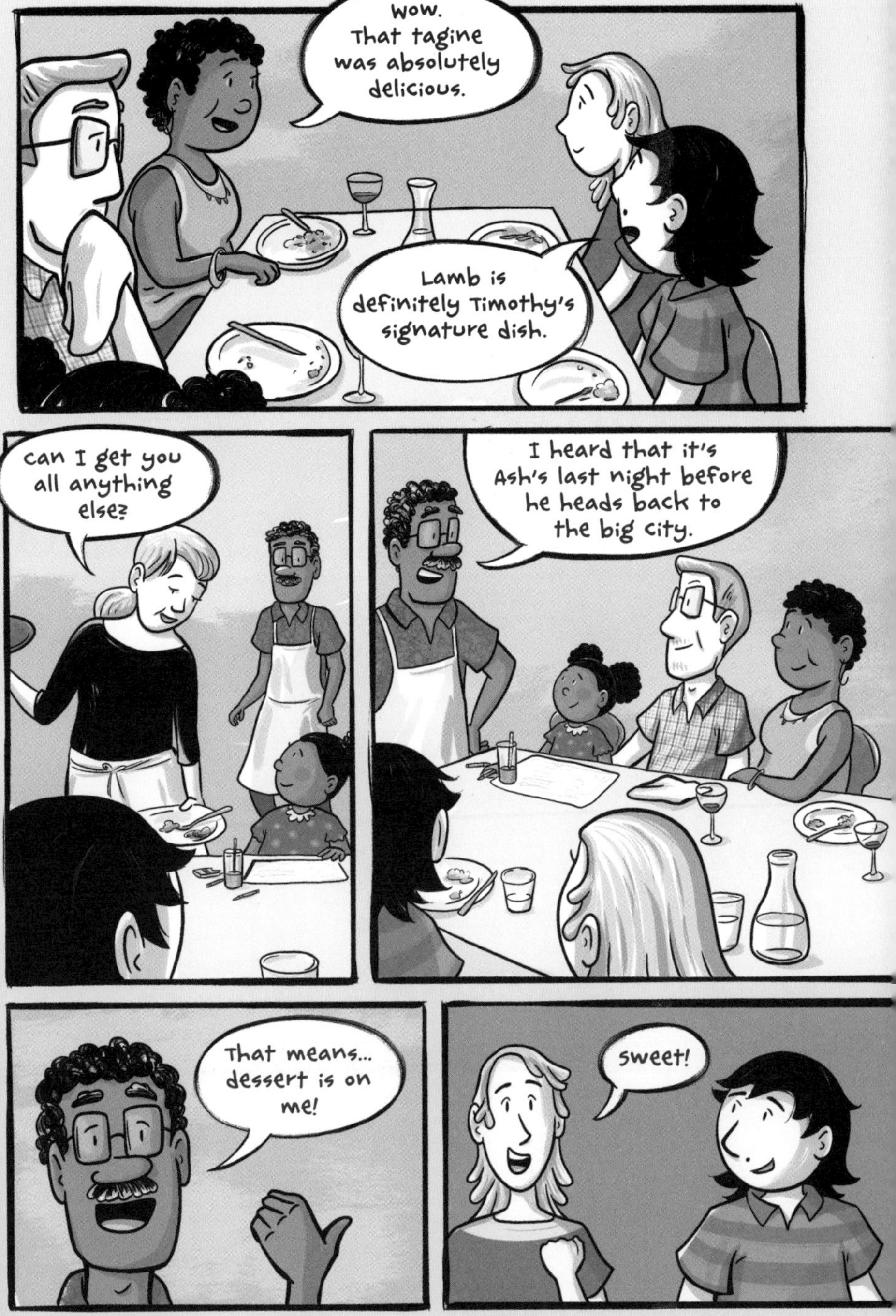
Wow.
That tagine
was absolutely
delicious.
Lamb is
definitely Timothy's
signature dish.
Can I get you
all anything
else?
I heard that it's
Ash's last night before
he heads back to
the big city.
That means...
dessert is on
me!
Sweet!

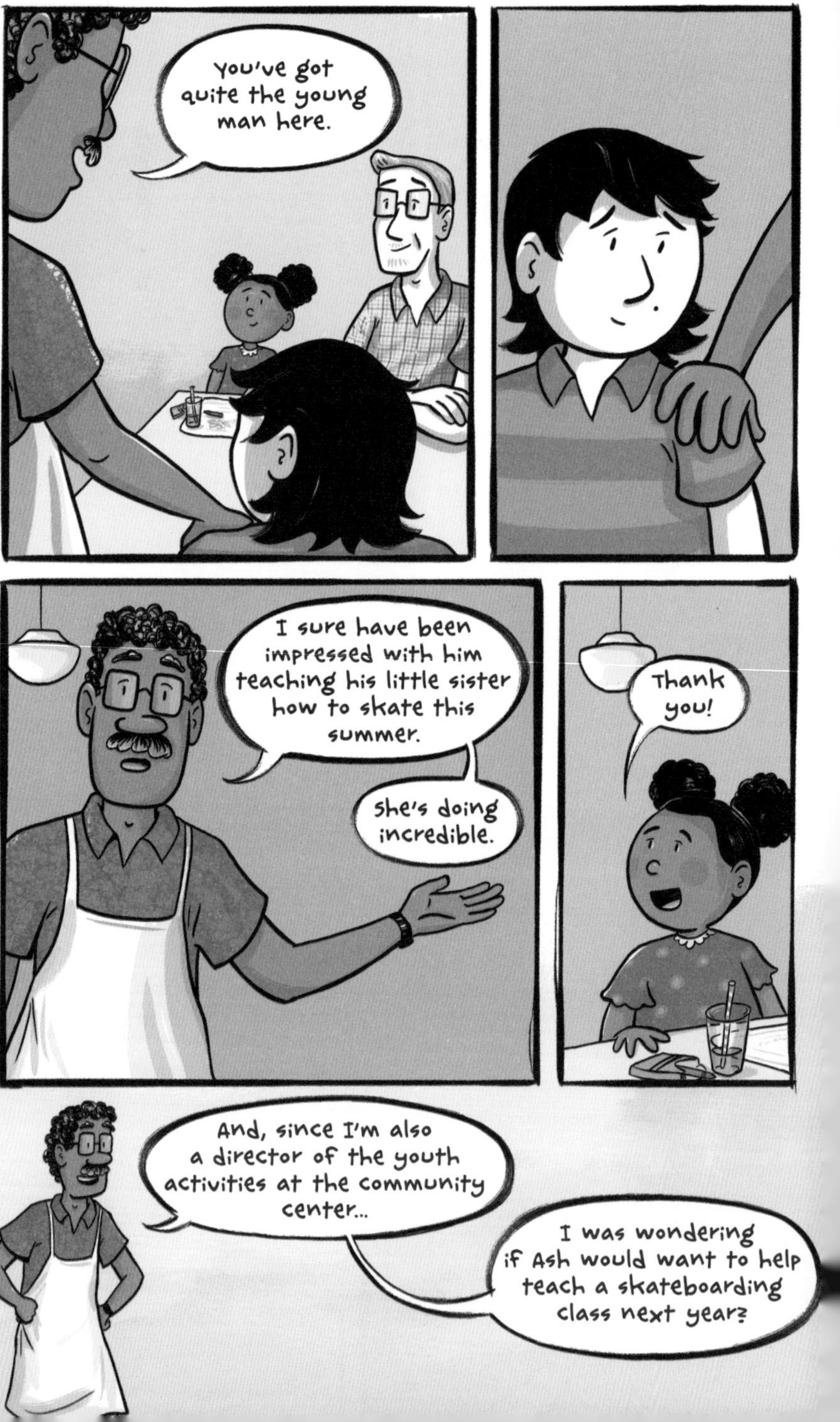

You've got quite the young man here.
I sure have been impressed with him teaching his little sister how to skate this summer.
She's doing incredible.
Thank you!
And, since I'm also a director of the youth activities at the community center...
I was wondering if Ash would want to help teach a skateboarding class next year?

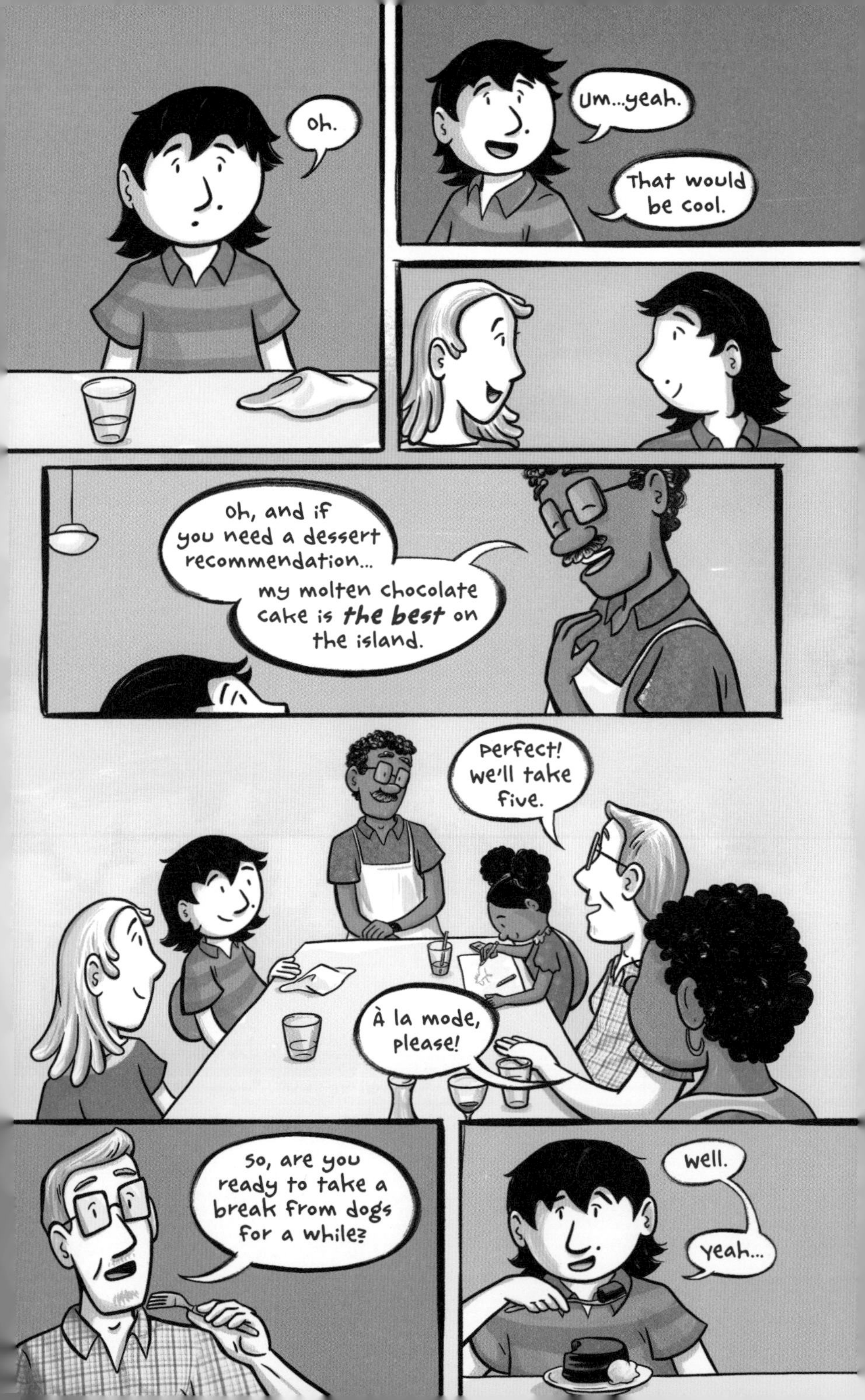
Oh.
Um...yeah.
That would be cool.
Oh, and if you need a dessert recommendation...
my molten chocolate cake is ***the best*** on the island.
Perfect! We'll take five.
À la mode, please!
So, are you ready to take a break from dogs for a while?
Well.
Yeah...

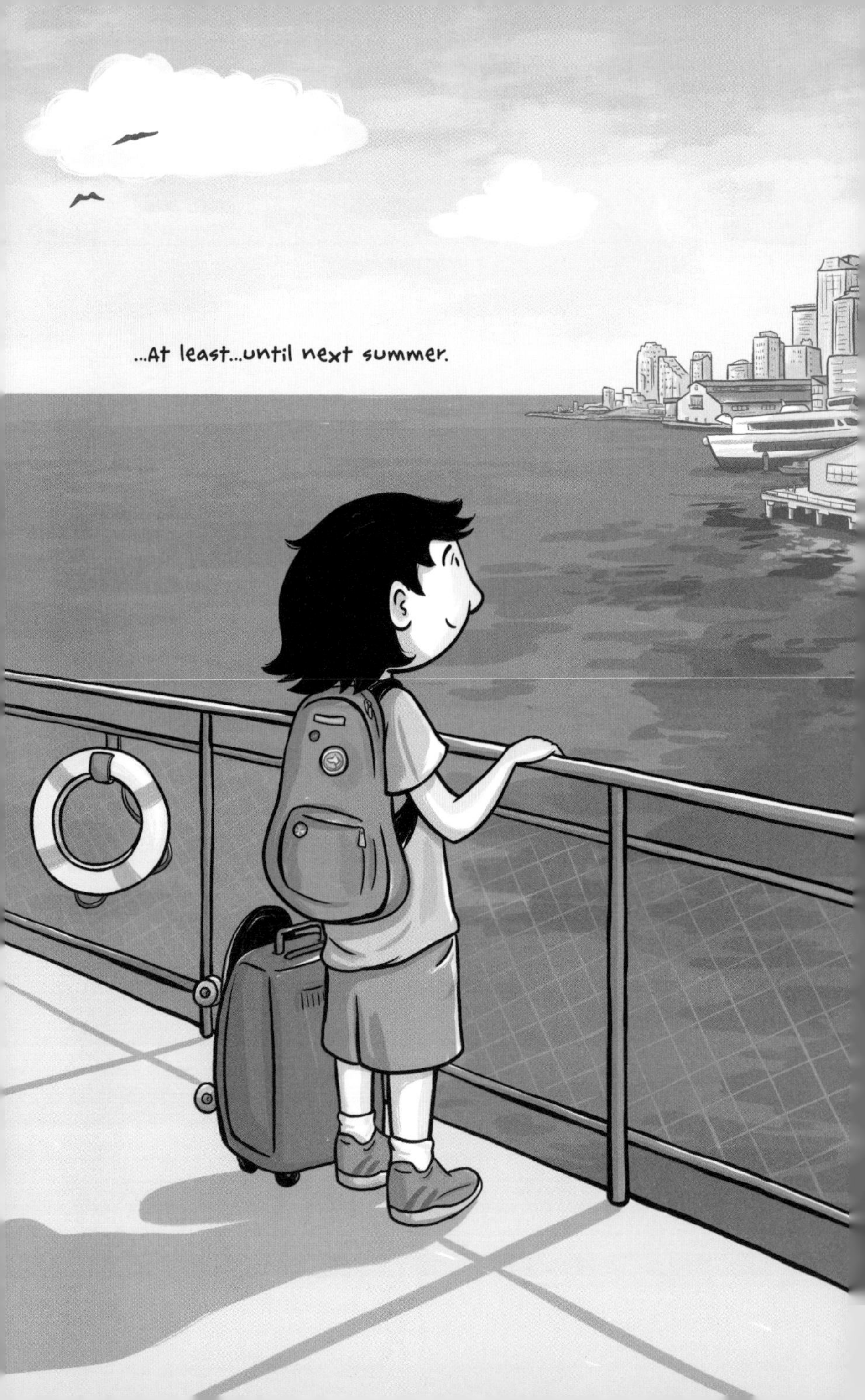
...At least...until next summer.

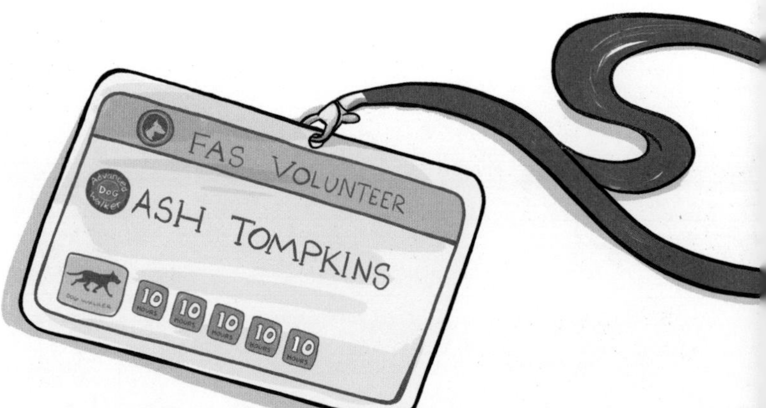
FAS VOLUNTEER
Advanced DoG Walker
ASH TOMPKINS

How To Help

Most animal shelters and rescue organizations rely on the generous support of their communities. If you are a compassionate animal lover and want to help, there are many ways to get involved!

Volunteer—Many shelters have youth volunteer opportunities, and some even offer after-school programs, workshops, and summer camps. Contact your local shelter to find out more.

Organize a donation drive—Work together as a family, or with friends or a local club or others in your neighborhood to organize a donation drive for the necessary supplies that shelters require to operate, such as pet food, bedding, toys, and cat litter.

Fundraisers—You can also help raise money for homeless pets by holding bake sales, yard sales, and craft sales; participating in walk-a-thons; and much more! Use your imagination to come up with great fundraising ideas.

DIY treats—Make healthy pet treats at home and bring them by the shelter to share with the adoptable animals and spread some love.

try these!

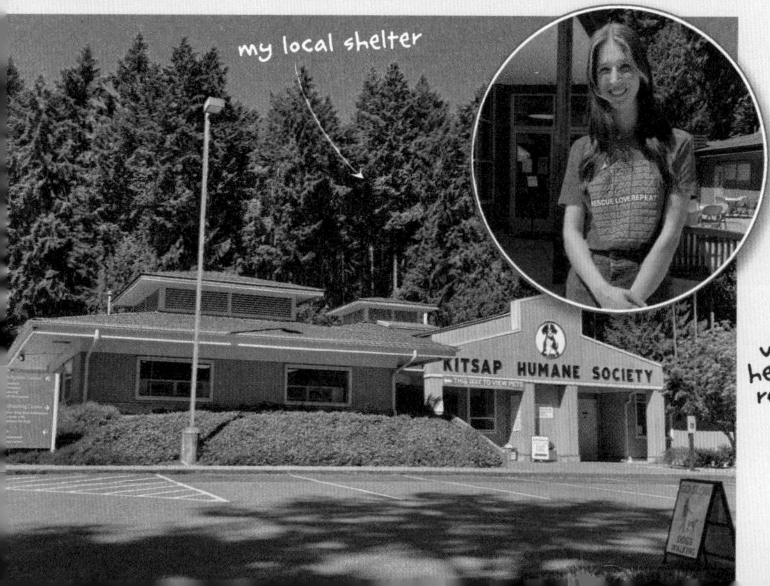
my local shelter
KITSAP HUMANE SOCIETY
THIS WAY TO VIEW PETS
RESCUE LOVE REPEAT

This is victoria, who helped with my research here!

me and Sparrow, my Doberman/shephard rescue from Texas

Photo credit: Francis Dillon & Belle Spruance

Pumpkin-Carrot Dog Treats

¾ cup canned pumpkin puree
(be sure it only has pumpkin in it, not canned pumpkin pie puree)
1 egg, slightly beaten
¼ cup shredded carrots
1 cup whole wheat flour

- Preheat oven to 350°F.
- Stir pumpkin, egg, carrots, and flour in a large bowl until combined.
- Roll the batter into small balls and place on an ungreased baking sheet.
- Bake for 30–35 minutes.

Author's Note

When I was in high school, we were required to complete a semester of community service work. I loved the idea of working with animals and immediately chose do my volunteer hours at my local shelter, the Humane Society of Utah. Two of my school buddies, Chris and Brian, joined me for the adventure.

It was 1991, and at that time, things were pretty bleak for animals in Utah. This was before most animal protection laws were passed and many people weren't educated to spay and neuter their pets. So unfortunately, the Utah shelter was very different from the one in this book. The facility was dark, smelly, and rundown with an air of despair...undoubtably from the large number of dogs and cats that were regularly euthanized. The bright light in an otherwise dismal space was our supervisor, Lillian. Lillian didn't ask us to organize or clean or feed the animals, or to do anything really, other than give the dogs what they desperately needed...love and attention.

My favorite spot at the shelter was the pet cemetery—there actually was one! It was enclosed with a chain-link fence, neglected and overgrown, but it was a happy place. We would take the dogs out for walks into the cemetery, sometimes two or three at time, and let them play and run free, and...just love them.

Although I have long forgotten their names, I still remember several of the dogs we worked with at the shelter. Unlike Ash, we were pretty lucky about avoiding mishaps with them. However, most of the dog stories in this book actually did happen. Many of these are my own experiences I've had with dogs over the years, and some are stories I borrowed from friends and family. I think that everyone has a really great dog story to tell, I just wish I could have fit them all in this book!

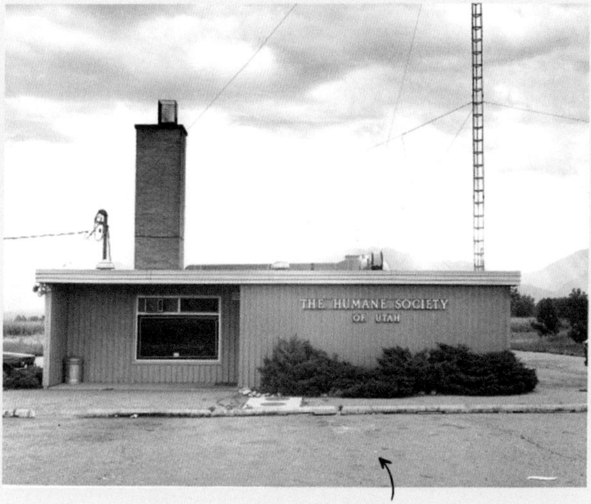
THE HUMANE SOCIETY
OF UTAH

The old shelter where I volunteered.

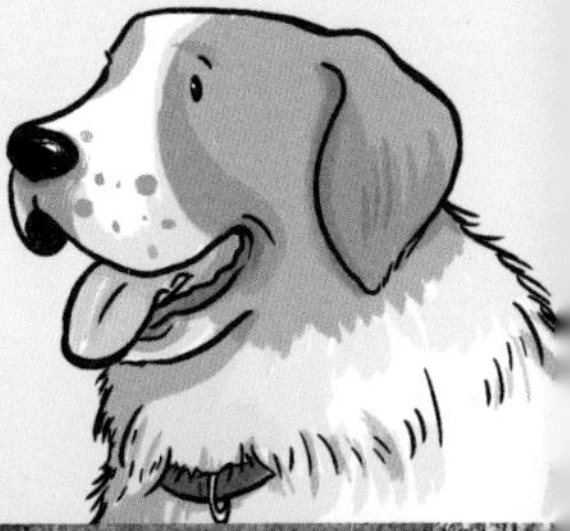

A bench at the current Humane Society of Utah facility, dedicated to my supervisor, Lillian.

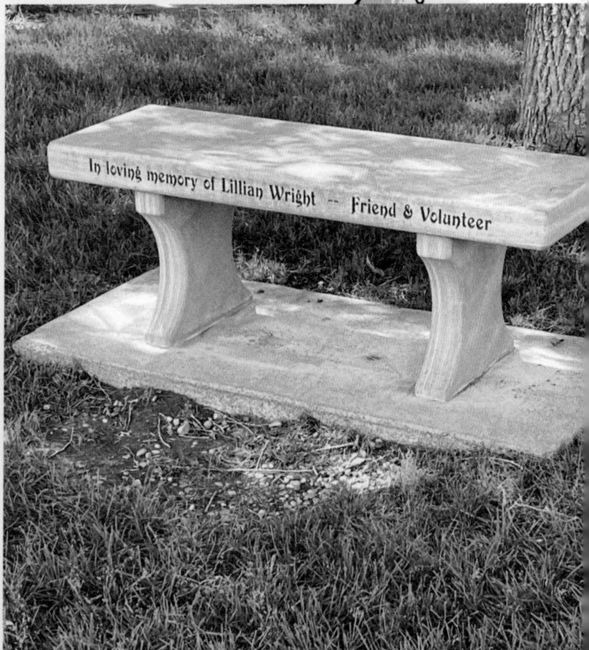
In loving memory of Lillian Wright -- Friend & Volunteer

Photos courtesy of the Humane Society of Utah

Cover Sketches

Here's a look at a few of the sketches that were done for the *Dog Trouble* cover. This is one of my favorite stages of the bookmaking process!

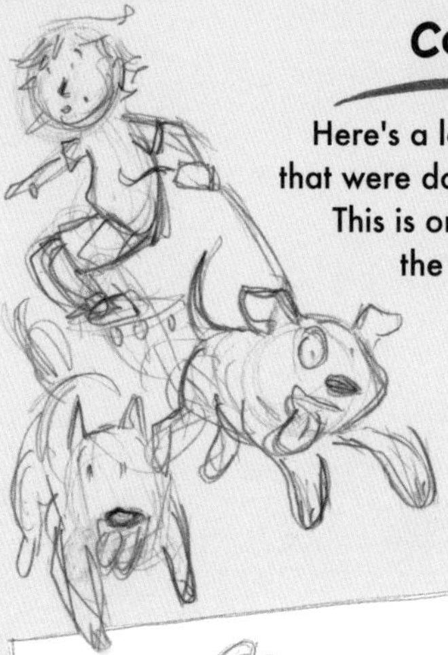

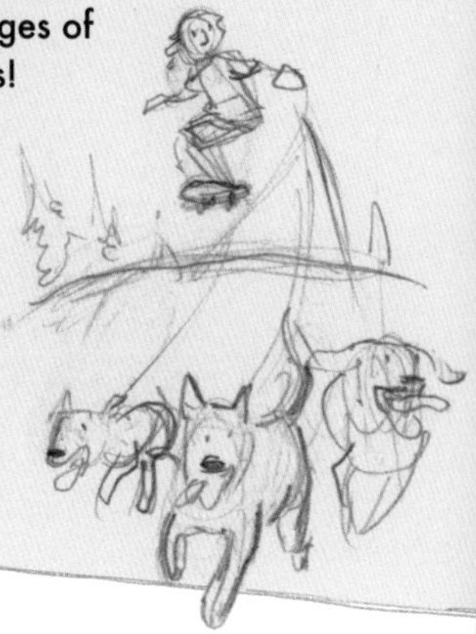

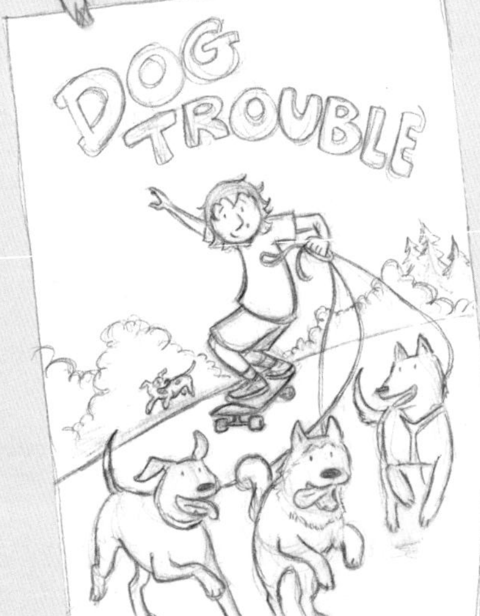
DOG TROUBLE

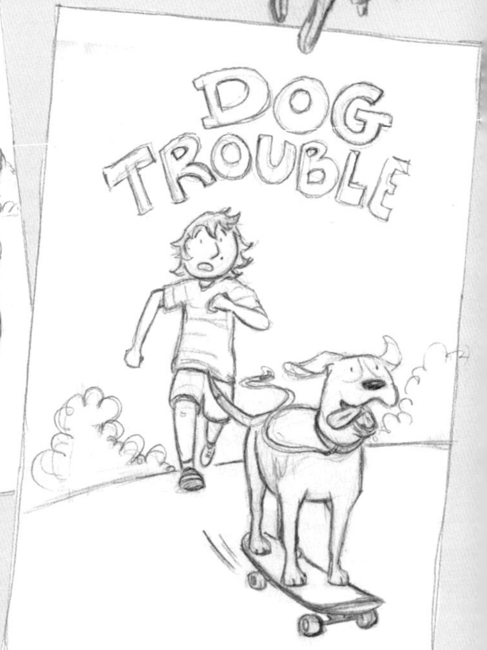
DOG TROUBLE

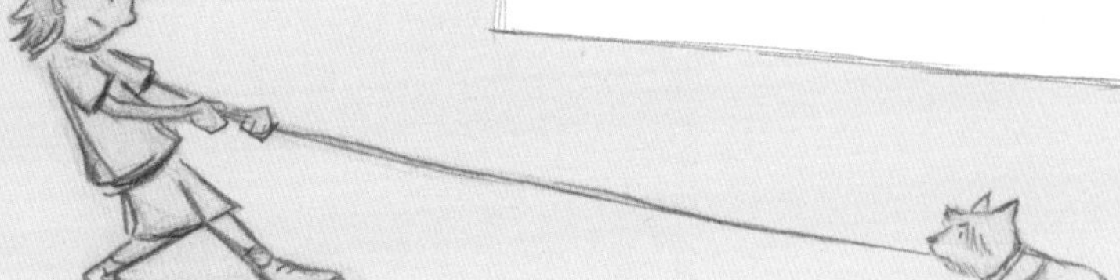

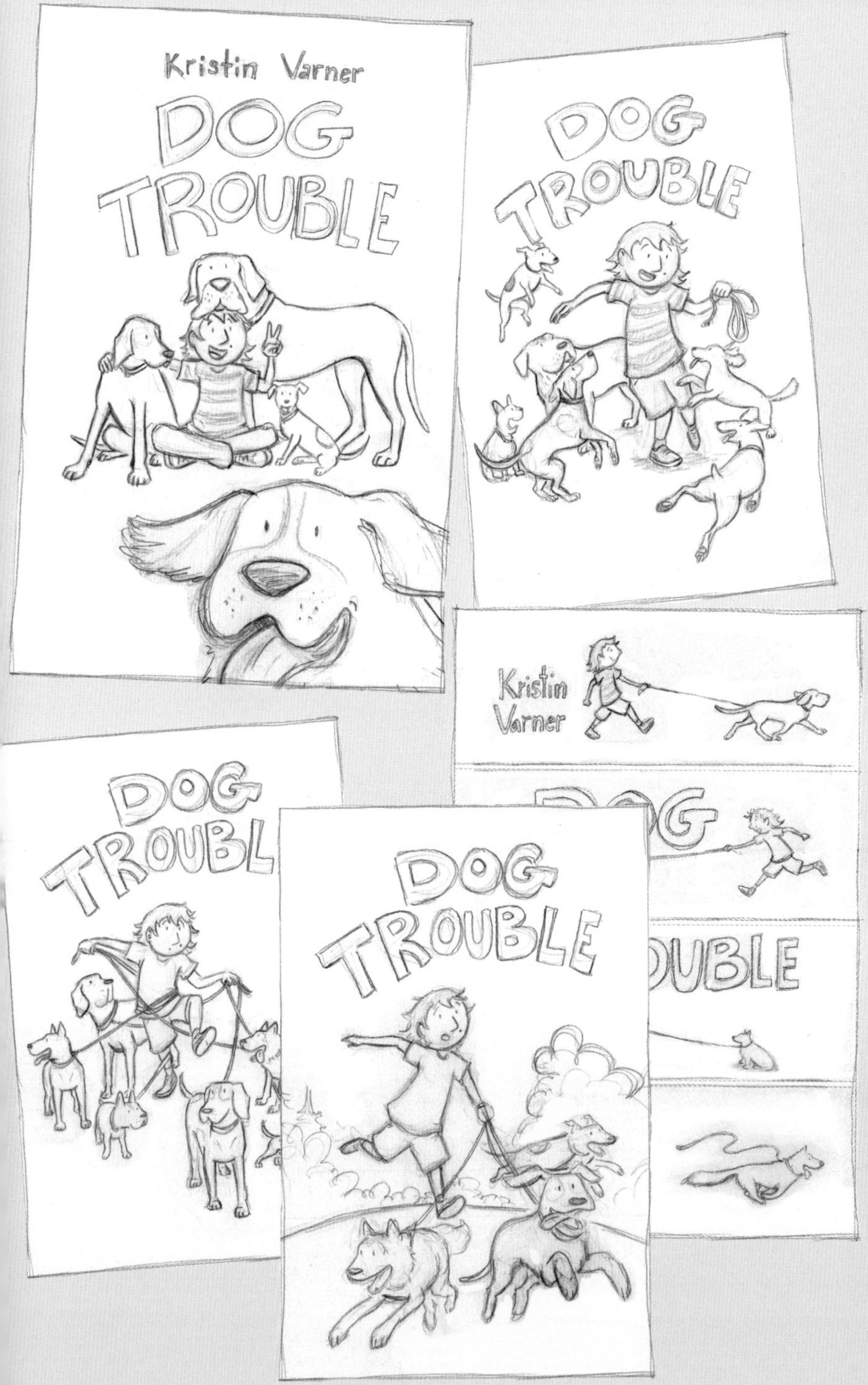
Kristin Varner
DOG
TROUBLE
DOG
TROUBLE
Kristin
Varner
OUBLE
DOG
TROUBL
DOG
TROUBLE

Acknowledgments

I am so appreciative to the many who have given me support and assistance in shaping *Dog Trouble* into a real book. My heartfelt thanks to...

My amazing and wise agent, Teresa Kietlinski.

My editors, Robyn Chapman and Michael Moccio, for your supreme insight and guidance and for nudging me to go deeper with this narrative. Michael, your diligence with comic lettering rules and design was relentless and fabulous! Thank you for having so much patience with me. My art director, Kirk Benshoff, and the entire team at First Second, it is such a pleasure to work with you all.

My friends and family who openly shared with me their favorite dog stories and allowed me to adapt them into the folds of this book. Linda, Ron, and Sharon Varner, the Stonich family, Ian Webster, Matthew Gray, Magan Payne, and Laura Cary. I hope that this book might, in some small way, honor the memories of your beloved pets.

Victoria Gingrey and the Kitsap Humane Society, who were beyond helpful in allowing me to tour the facility, take tons of photos, and get a peek at the "behind the scenes" operations at the shelter.

Dr. Catherine Parks at Catnip Veterinary Care, for providing feedback on definitions and for fact-checking the book.

Lillian Wright, longtime volunteer and friend of the Humane Society of Utah (HSU) and my supervisor at the old shelter...where the inspiration for this story began. Also, to Pauline Edwards, Guinnevere Shuster, Craig Cook, and Carlene at HSU for helping me uncover Lillian's lost identity.

My amazing little family. Michael you are a rock—absolutely unflappable while enduring the long game with me! And Francis, your no-nonsense opinions and advice are priceless. I am so lucky to be your mom.

Lastly, to all the dogs I have been fortunate enough to have known throughout my life, whose names and personalities I have borrowed for this story. Thank you, dogs, for showing us the true meaning of unconditional love.

STEP INTO SOMEONE ELSE'S STORY...

These great graphic novels have it all!

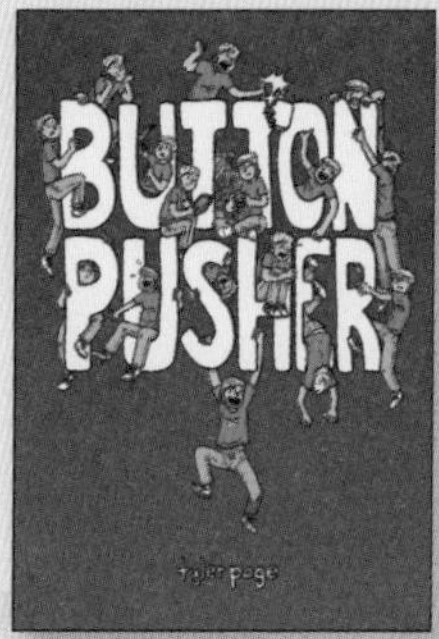
BUTTON PUSHER
tyler page

BUTTON PUSHER

BY TYLER PAGE

Tyler's brain is different. He doesn't want to cause trouble, but sometimes it's hard for him to focus.

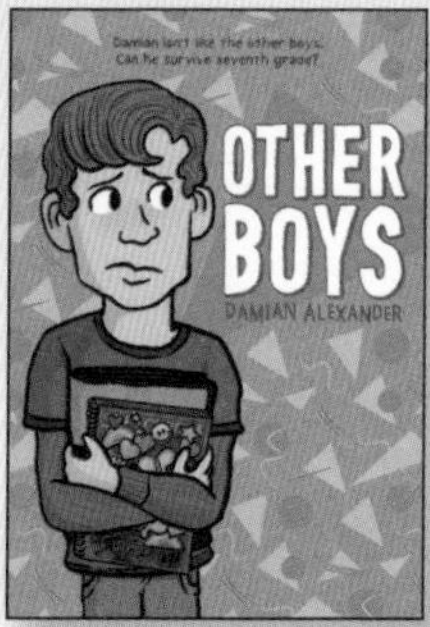
OTHER BOYS
DAMIAN ALEXANDER

OTHER BOYS

BY DAMIAN ALEXANDER

Damian is the new kid at school, and he has a foolproof plan to avoid the bullies: he's going to stop talking.

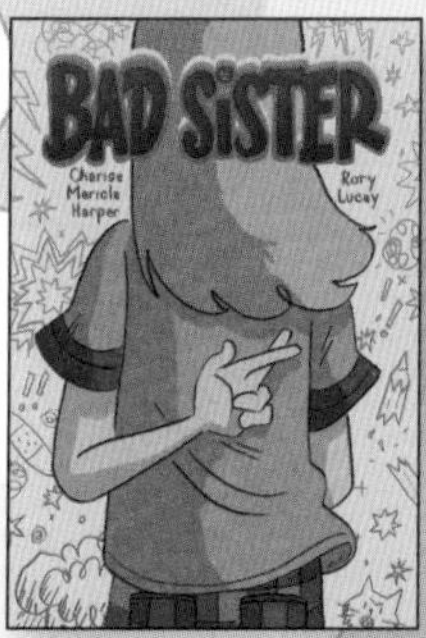
BAD SISTER
Charise Mericle Harper
Rory Lucey

BAD SISTER

BY CHARISE MERICLE HARPER & RORY LUCEY

Being the older sibling means having power, but recently Charise has realized she might have been taking this privilege too far.

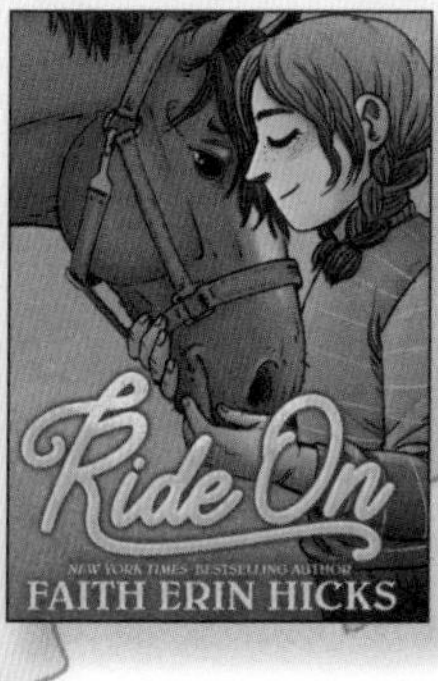
Ride On
NEW YORK TIMES-BESTSELLING AUTHOR
FAITH ERIN HICKS

RIDE ON

BY FAITH ERIN HICKS

Despite being burnt out by the high-pressure world of riding competitions, Victoria slowly finds her way back to her love of horses.

© 2024 Jenny Jimenez

Kristin Varner grew up in the Rocky Mountains of Utah, where she fell in love with animals at a young age. Kristin received her degree in illustration from Rhode Island School of Design and has created art for children's books, games, apparel, and toys. *Dog Trouble* is her second graphic novel, following her debut title with First Second books, *Horse Trouble*. She lives on a wooded island near Seattle, Washington with her husband, daughter, and one smelly, adorable mutt.